OXFORD WORl

AN ENQUIRY (
POLITICA:

T0069556

WILLIAM GODWIN was born in 1756 in Wisbech, Cambridgeshire, one of only six of thirteen siblings to survive into adulthood. He declared a vocation to follow in his father's footsteps as a dissenting minister and was educated with that objective from the age of 11. He practised his vocation for four years but found his convictions changing and he moved to London in 1783 to pursue a career as a writer. In the summer of 1791, following the onset of the French Revolution and the surge of public debate in Britain about France and reform at home, he wrote *An Enquiry Concerning Political Justice* (1793), a review of recent political philosophy that developed a powerful and systematic case for the progress of the human mind and the elimination of government. It established his reputation as a writer and philosopher, which he consolidated the following year with his best novel, *Things As They Are; or, The Adventures of Caleb Williams*. He became a central figure for literary and political circles and was closely associated with many who pressed for reform of the legislature and protested against the war with France. In 1797 he married the feminist writer Mary Wollstonecraft, who died after giving birth to a daughter (later Mary Shelley) a few months later. His reputation was tarnished by his candid memoir of Wollstonecraft, and at the end of the decade he was under fierce attack from the loyalist presses and former friends. He remarried in 1801 and founded a children's bookshop and publisher with his wife, Mary Jane Clairmont. For twenty years he struggled to make the bookshop work, while also writing occasional novels and historical and literary studies. He was eventually declared bankrupt in 1825, which released him for a late surge of creativity. He was awarded a sinecure in 1833 by the Whig government and he died in March 1836.

MARK PHILP is Professor of History and Politics at the University of Warwick. He is the General Editor of the *Collected Novels and Memoirs of William Godwin*, 8 volumes (1992), and *Political and Philosophical Writings of William Godwin*, 7 volumes (1993), and co-editor of *The Diary of William Godwin* (Oxford Digital Library, 2010), <http://godwindiary.bodleian.ox.ac.uk>.

OXFORD WORLD'S CLASSICS

For over 100 years Oxford World's Classics have brought readers closer to the world's great literature. Now with over 700 titles — from the 4,000-year-old myths of Mesopotamia to the twentieth century's greatest novels — the series makes available lesser-known as well as celebrated writing.

The pocket-sized hardbacks of the early years contained introductions by Virginia Woolf, T. S. Eliot, Graham Greene, and other literary figures which enriched the experience of reading. Today the series is recognized for its fine scholarship and reliability in texts that span world literature, drama and poetry, religion, philosophy, and politics. Each edition includes perceptive commentary and essential background information to meet the changing needs of readers.

OXFORD WORLD'S CLASSICS

WILLIAM GODWIN

An Enquiry Concerning Political Justice

Edited with an Introduction and Notes by
MARK PHILP

OXFORD
UNIVERSITY PRESS

OXFORD

UNIVERSITY PRESS

Great Clarendon Street, Oxford OX2 6DP
United Kingdom

Oxford University Press is a department of the University of Oxford.
It furthers the University's objective of excellence in research, scholarship,
and education by publishing worldwide. Oxford is a registered trade mark of
Oxford University Press in the UK and in certain other countries

Editorial material © Mark Philp 2013

First published as an Oxford World's Classics paperback 2013

9

British Library Cataloguing in Publication Data

Data available

ISBN 978–0–19–964262–5

Printed in Great Britain by
Clays Ltd, Elcograf S.p.A.

ACKNOWLEDGEMENTS

I AM grateful to Ruth Turvey for her indispensable assistance in preparing the text, Judith Luna and OUP for taking on this edition, Richard Fisher at Cambridge for releasing me to take the more proselytizing route offered by Oxford World's Classics, and Laurien Berkeley and Bruno Currie for editorial and classical wisdom respectively. I also owe thanks for their help in the final stages of production to Jenni Crosskey and Peter Gibbs at the Press and to Mira Wolf-Bauwns who made the first assault on the index.

My thanks are also due to David O'Shaughnessy, Vickie Myers, James Grande, and Kathryn Barush, fellow labourers on the Godwin Diary project, <http://godwindiary.bodleian.ox.ac.uk>; to Jon Mee at Warwick University, Edward Pope in Oxford, and Bruce Barker-Benfield at the Bodleian Library; to Pamela Clemit, the editor of Godwin's letters; and to the playwright Helen Edmundson, director Polly Teale, and the cast of Shared Experience, for bringing Godwin and his family to life for a new generation in *Mary Shelley*.

M.P.

CONTENTS

INTRODUCTION

In July 1789, at the beginning of the French Revolution, Charles James Fox, the leader of the Whig opposition in Parliament, wrote to his friend Richard Fitzpatrick, who was setting out to France: 'It is not impossible but I may go too. How much the greatest Event it is that ever happened in the World! & how much the best.'[1] Fox was far from alone in his enthusiasm. Many welcomed the French Revolution as the dawning of a new age, promising an end to the traditional enmity between Britain and France. William Godwin's *An Enquiry Concerning Political Justice and its Influence on General Virtue and Happiness* (1793) epitomized the philosophical optimism in Britain in response to events in France and gave it its most distinctive and original voice.

The enthusiasm for France's Revolution, which followed hard on the heels of the American Revolution, quickly led to expectations in Britain that domestic reforms might counter the power of the Crown and ensure a proper representation of the people. Over the following three years these hopes met increasing opposition, both from William Pitt's government and from a group of parliamentary Whigs who were concerned at the popular tenor of demands for change. The most outspoken of this group, Edmund Burke, set out his position in his *Reflections on the Revolution in France* (1790) and spawned a huge pamphlet controversy on France and reform in Britain. This evolved into a process of mobilization and counter-mobilization of reform and loyalist associations. Opinions became more polarized, the government became more cautious, and more stringent measures were introduced against sedition, which prompted accusations of tyranny and of a conspiracy against English liberties, and then further state action in response. Following the declaration of war with France in January 1793, reformers were portrayed as subversives and French sympathizers. They, in turn, ratcheted up their rhetoric to enlist those disaffected by brutal recruitment practices, food shortages, and the heavy taxation needed to fund the war. The government became increasingly intransigent, responding with a combination of repressive legislation, prosecutions, and the suspension of habeas corpus that was described by contemporaries as Pitt's 'Reign of Terror'.[2] Over a period of eight

---

[1] L. G. Mitchell, *Charles James Fox* (Oxford, 1992), 111.

[2] J. A. Hone, *For the Cause of Truth: Radicalism in London, 1796–1821* (Oxford, 1982), chs. 2–3; Albert Goodwin, *The Friends of Liberty* (London, 1979), ch. 12.

years Britain experienced an intense political controversy that pushed
to the limits the government's ability to retain order (in Ireland there
was rebellion and a French landing in 1798).

As befits such moments, it was also an era of extraordinary intellectual ferment and creativity; as Wordsworth later put it, '*Bliss* was it in
that dawn to be alive, | But to be young was very heaven!'[3] Evidence of
this creativity encompasses both those who fought for the old order,
such as Burke in his *Reflections*, and those who fought for something
new. Godwin's *Political Justice*, Burke's *Reflections*, Thomas Paine's
Rights of Man (1791–2), Mary Wollstonecraft's *Vindication of the Rights
of Woman* (1792), and James Mackintosh's *Vindiciae Gallicae* are only a
fractional part of a stream of pamphlets, novels, plays, poems, and
ephemera that explored the political issues of the day, many of which
deservedly remain widely read today.

Political Justice was the most philosophically rigorous and, simultaneously, one of the most visionary works of this tumultuous decade. It
was published in February 1793, shortly after the execution of Louis
XVI and the outbreak of war with France's regicide republic. The book
criticized and synthesized a wide range of eighteenth-century philosophy, and constructed a case for what we would now call philosophical
anarchism, combining this with a set of arguments for the perfectibility
of mankind and predicting the triumph of mind over body and the elimination of illness and ageing. Despite the increasingly strained political
atmosphere, Godwin and his work were warmly received by the capital's literary and philosophical circles and beyond, and for much of the
rest of the decade he enjoyed an enviable reputation. His book became a
central part of the literary landscape of the decade and had a profound
influence on what we now think of as Romanticism, with Coleridge,
Southey, Wordsworth, Hazlitt, and a host of Britain's most widely read
novelists, dramatists, essayists, and literary men and women reading
and reacting to this seminal work. Moreover, even if some of the ideas
in *Political Justice* are now more often associated with Jeremy Bentham
and John Stuart Mill than with Godwin, many of the questions he raises
remain of central importance to modern ethics and political philosophy.

Godwin's Central Argument

Godwin's first substantive philosophical argument appears at the
beginning of the second book of *Political Justice* with the biblical

---

[3] William Wordsworth, *Prelude*, X. 692–3.

precept 'that we should love our neighbour as ourselves'. He suggests that, while the precept possesses 'considerable merit as a popular principle', it lacks philosophical accuracy. People, he argues, are differentially meritorious, both because their faculties are developed to greater or lesser degrees and, more importantly, because they do not make an equal contribution to the general good of mankind. Godwin uses as an example François Fénelon (1651–1715), archbishop of Cambray. Fénelon was the author of *Les Aventures de Télémaque* (1699), a major work of French political philosophy in the early modern period, which recounts the moral and political education of Odysseus' son Telemachus at the hands of Mentor (the goddess Athena, Odysseus' protector, in disguise). Godwin asks his readers to compare Fénelon with a common chambermaid. If both were trapped in a burning room at the point at which Fénelon conceived his work, and we could rescue only one of them, should we not prefer the person who will make the greatest future contribution to mankind? On what other grounds could we make the decision and with what other conclusion? What if the chambermaid was my wife, or mother, or my benefactor? 'This would not alter the truth of the proposition.' The life of Fénelon would still be more valuable 'and justice, pure, unadulterated justice' demands that we prefer that which is most valuable (p. 53).

Godwin's defence of the claim that it is our duty to save Fénelon is an example of a demand for first-order impartiality.[4] That is, our decisions should be guided in all matters by judgments about which acts will produce the greatest value or happiness in society, in which our own needs and preferences have no more weight than any other person's. If first-order impartiality asks us to weigh our own interests and concerns in the balance with all others, second-order impartiality recognizes the legitimacy of personal and private preferences and concerns and asks only that the rules under which we live together are such that they can form the basis for the free and fair agreement of those affected. We are not strangers to second-order impartiality, since the idea underlies many of our institutions and practices; but first-order impartiality seems like a very burdensome morality.

Godwin's commitment to first-order impartiality has been widely criticized, both in his lifetime and subsequently. One thought is that it is simply over-demanding: someone who acts in this way can give little significance to his or her own projects and commitments. Yet it is a powerful principle. If I have money that I plan to spend on an

---

[4] Brian Barry, *Justice as Impartiality* (Oxford, 1995), chs. 1 and 9.

expensive meal and I meet someone whose life I could save by giving them some of the money instead, should I not do that? Of course, there are issues about the boundaries between necessity and superfluity, questions of levels of urgency, and problems in mapping between collective responsibilities and individual responsibilities (if we all did a moderate amount we could cure global poverty, but do I have a responsibility to pick up the slack when others do not do their share?[5]). Despite these difficulties, for many people the principle retains some core intuitive appeal.

The principle of first-order impartiality was central to Godwin's position as it developed in *Political Justice*. It was also a crucial component in his distancing himself from a great deal of the reformist literature that attacked Burke. Although Godwin believed in the 'propriety of applying one unalterable rule of justice to every case that may arise' (p. 65), he insisted that merits and virtues are not equally distributed, and that these inequalities must be recognized in the way we respond to others. In contrast to an equality of natural rights, he argued that justice could not simply be a matter of equal treatment: it had to be understood as appropriately responding to the individual qualities of, and differences between, people. Godwin rejected rights claims because they imply the existence of a liberty or a sphere of discretion in which we are free to choose. His innovation was to believe that this freedom is always conditioned by our responsibilities or duties. The prior question is always one of duty. As a first-order impartialist I have to ask of myself, at every moment, what duty demands: what I ought to do, with my talents and resources, in this situation, here and now, recognizing these needs and problems. For Godwin, there is no situation in which I do not have responsibilities to my fellow human beings, and 'I have no right to omit what my duty prescribes' (p. 68).

This dismissal of the idea of the rights of man in favour of an endorsement of a duty of first-order impartiality did not mean that Godwin thought it unimportant to protect individuals from interference by others. Indeed, his criticism of the idea of rights as liberties ends up doing rather little practical work. If Paine celebrated individual rights as rights not to be interfered with by government, Godwin similarly endorsed that conclusion, but derived it instead from the claim that it is the individual who must judge in what his or her

---

[5] See Zofia Stemplowska, 'Doing More Than One's Share', Oct. 2011, <http://ethicsinsociety.stanford.edu/working-papers/Stemplowska-papers>.

duty consists. In his chapter 'Of the Exercise of Private Judgment', Godwin brought to bear a central aspect of his inheritance from his background in religious dissent—the right of conscience in matters of religious belief—and he extended it to encompass all aspects of moral and political life. 'The universal exercise of private judgment is a doctrine so unspeakably beautiful, that the true politician will certainly resolve to interfere with it as sparingly and in as few instances as possible' (p. 77). Having set out the principle, Godwin then applied it as consistently as possible across his whole field of enquiry: promises and contracts, government, resistance, law, punishment, property, and marriage. In doing so, he turned away from his original intention, to show the importance of political institutions to virtue, and he came to see them as an increasingly dispensable constraint on the development of individual character and the improvement of society. Godwin pronounced that the sole and proper end of justice is utility, but he conceived of utility as being, as John Stuart Mill later phrased it, 'grounded in the permanent interests of man as a progressive being'. Indeed, Godwin would also have shared Mill's endorsement of Wilhelm von Humboldt's belief in 'the absolute and essential importance of human development' as encapsulating the content of utility, with that development being conceived entirely in intellectual terms, tied to the progress of mind and truth.[6]

Political Justice was originally conceived as a critical compendium of, and reflection on, recent developments in moral and political philosophy. But by the time that Godwin had concluded Book II, he had found his distinctive path, and the principles of private judgment, utility, and first-order impartiality combined to provide the foundation for one of the most powerful works of moral and political philosophy of his age. There was work still to be done: Godwin needed to show why it is reasonable to expect agreement on principles, since continuing disagreement renders the nature and direction of progress contentious and therefore something that must be subject to authoritative regulation (which usurps private judgment). He had to demonstrate that people are capable of appreciating the truth and of being motivated by it, so that our understanding comes to dominate and direct our passions and interests, allowing us to treat ourselves and others with the same impartial regard. He had to make a case for thinking that the development of intellect and virtue is infinitely progressive, so that we can expect ever greater areas of political and social life to

[6] John Stuart Mill, *On Liberty and Other Essays*, ed. John Gray (Oxford, 1991), 15, 2.

be managed on the basis of consensus rather than authority. And he needed to say more about his conception of individual virtue and its connection with utility and to work out in detail the implications of his view for our expectations of future societies. This, in broad outline, is what he devoted the remaining six books of *Political Justice* to doing.

Individual Judgment and Human Perfectibility

Godwin was 35 when he began his major work. He had been brought up in a dissenting family and from an early age he had aspired to become a minister. As an 11-year-old he was sent to lodge with and be educated by the Revd Samuel Newton of Norwich, a strict Calvinist with quick recourse to the rod, to which Godwin took strong exception. He lasted four years before withdrawing for six months and then returning briefly to be dismissed as adequately educated at the age of 15. He subsequently attended Hoxton Dissenting Academy, completing his studies with success after five years in 1778.

Throughout his education Godwin subscribed to a very exclusive, hyper-Calvinist, doctrine of the elect (damning ninety-nine out of each of the hundred souls Calvin believed saved), derived from the work of the theologian Robert Sandeman and known as Sandemanianism. When he was released into the world to preach, this doctrine failed him. One of his parishioners in Stowmarket, Suffolk, lent him several key works of the French Enlightenment—Holbach, Helvétius, and Rousseau—and his theology dwindled towards deism, while in politics he turned to support the Whig opposition.[7] After failing to recover his vocation, he quit the ministry, took up residence in London, and sought to make a living with his pen. In 1783 his former tutor at Hoxton, Andrew Kippis, rescued him from the penury of his first years in London by inviting him to contribute the 'British and Foreign History' section of the *New Annual Register* (a historical, literary, and bibliographical review of the year established to compete with the more conservative *Annual Register*). The work kept him in close touch with events in British and overseas politics, and he became acquainted with a number of leading Whig politicians, including Richard Sheridan, the playwright and party manager, for whom he served briefly as editor to the Whig periodical the *Political Herald*. He also followed closely

---

[7] See Godwin's Preface to *Political Justice* and his account in his 'Autobiographical Fragments', in *Collected Novels and Memoirs of William Godwin*, i, ed. Mark Philp (London, 1992), 44.

the growing crisis in the French state from 1787, the onset of the French Revolution, and the developing British reaction to it, most notably, Burke's excoriating attack on French principles in his *Reflections*, published in November 1790. Within a year or so over two hundred pamphlets had appeared attacking or defending Burke and France.[8] At the same time, events in France became more unstable, culminating in Louis XVI's flight to Varennes in June 1791, his return to Paris in ignominy, and the beginning of the republican movement in France.

Also in June 1791 Godwin approached George Robinson, the publisher of the *New Annual Register*, proposing that Robinson support him financially while he undertook a work on political principles. Gambling on his confidence in Godwin's abilities, Robinson agreed on a generous contract for the work, and in September 1791 Godwin began his labours. The significance he attributed to his task is reflected in the way that his diary became, from that date, a much more detailed and exacting record of his reading, writing, and conversations.[9] Robinson required Godwin to submit his material as it was written, so that it could be typeset (and to allow him to monitor progress in his investment). In his *Autobiography* Godwin describes his initial purpose as trying to respond to the imperfections and errors of Montesquieu's *De l'esprit des lois* (1748), but it is clear that his own ideas developed quickly.[10] The introductory first book critiques Montesquieu's view that climate, national character, and luxury are the determining forces in politics, with Godwin emphasizing instead the importance of political institutions in shaping nations. But in the concluding chapter he resolved upon the question that subsequently drove his thinking in the rest of the work and reversed his position on the positive role of government: whether the human understanding can be made the recipient of truth. If it can, then progress becomes possible entirely through the development of mind, and Godwin's distinctive path was opened.

In the process of writing *Political Justice* Godwin drew on a range of sources, traditions, and influences, coming to appreciate elements

---

[8] See Gayle Trusdel Pendleton, 'Towards a Bibliography of the *Reflections* and *Rights of Man* Controversy', *Bulletin of Research in the Humanities*, 85 (1982), 65–103; Gregory Claeys, 'The French Revolution and British Political Thought', *History of Political Thought*, 11/1 (1990), 59–80.

[9] *The Diary of William Godwin*, ed. Victoria Myers, David O'Shaughnessy, and Mark Philp (Oxford, 2010), <http://godwindiary.bodleian.ox.ac.uk>.

[10] Godwin, 'Autobiographical Fragments', 49.

on which he had initially placed little weight but that gradually assumed a more central role. This was principally the case with the endorsement and expansion of the doctrine of private judgment. Here he seems to have drawn on his education as a Dissenter and on discussions with key figures in the world of rational dissent who campaigned at the end of the 1780s, and again in 1790, for the repeal of the Test and Corporation Acts, which prevented avowed Dissenters from holding certain public offices.[11] The pamphlet literature of the movement consistently emphasized the sanctity of private judgment as a means to true belief. Nonetheless, the move from the sanctity of individual conscience in religious matters to advocating private judgment as a basic principle for matters of politics was a dramatic one. For many Dissenters, conscience was understood as a private matter, and therefore as one in which the state had no legitimate interest; but to say that the individual's judgment should be sacrosanct in all areas of social and moral life threatened political authority, no less than the principle of conscience threatened church authority.

In making this move, Godwin drew upon a conviction of the discoverability, communicability, and progressive character of truth: 'Truth is in reality single and uniform' (p. 102). In its secular domain this truth is grounded in the uniform nature of humanity, and corresponding to that humanity there must be better and worse forms of government and arrangements of society. Godwin combined an Enlightenment confidence in people's ability to gain a rational understanding of the world, and to order it so as to secure the best possible outcomes for its inhabitants, with a more theological conviction in moral truth that at times seems to have been much influenced by Platonism, perhaps through the work of the dissenting minister and moral philosopher Richard Price.[12] But it was his conviction that the human mind is able to grasp the truths of our nature and to act on those truths that turned Godwin's Enlightenment rationalism into a powerful story of human perfectibility. That conviction was supported by appeal to his reading of the doctrine of necessity, derived in part from David Hartley and Joseph Priestley in England but buttressed too by his reading of Helvétius and Holbach.[13] Godwin developed this

---

[11] G. M. Ditchfield, 'The Parliamentary Struggle over the Repeal of the Test and Corporation Acts, 1787–90', *English Historical Review*, 89/352 (1974), 551–77.

[12] Richard Price, *A Review of the Principal Questions in Morals*, 3rd edn (1787).

[13] David Hartley, *Observations on Man, his Frame, his Duty, and his Expectations* (1749); Joseph Priestley, *The Doctrine of Philosophical Necessity Illustrated, being an Appendix to the Disquisitions Relating to Matter and Spirit* (1777); Jean-Baptiste de

doctrine by arguing that the association of ideas is also a matter of necessity, and that, as we gain clear and distinct ideas and combine these in propositions, we are moved by those ideas to act. Seeing some-one in want and being in a position to relieve their want will, in so far as we have formed the appropriate judgments and deductions, move us to act to assist them. Although Godwin refers to David Hume rela-tively frequently in *Political Justice*, he fundamentally rejected Hume's comment that "'Tis not contrary to reason to prefer the destruction of the whole world to the scratching of my finger.'[14] Far from separat-ing the spheres of ideas and motives, the understanding and the pas-sions, Godwin treated sensations merely as raw forms of idea, and thereby made possible a view in which the understanding could come to master and direct the passions and the organs of sensation. Rejecting nominalism, in which we call what we want 'good', Godwin argued that what we come through the understanding to appreciate as good, we are both moved and enabled to bring about.

The five concluding chapters to Book IV, to which he attached a note for readers who might be 'indisposed to abstruse speculations' (p. 154) suggesting that these chapters are unnecessary for an under-standing of the rest of the work, are, in fact, the place where Godwin develops his thinking on these issues in detail. It is here that he assesses and rejects 'the doctrine of self love', or the idea that we are only ever motivated to act by a concern to promote our own interests. And it is here that he further elaborates the idea that 'man becomes a moral being' only in so far as he is directed by the exercise of mind, that 'the true perfection of mind consists in disinterestedness', and that the highest form of happiness involves the cultivation of mind and virtue (pp. 186 and 194). In these commitments Godwin stands alongside Socrates in Plato's *Republic*: for both, justice is less a distributive principle and more a state of mind and character, involving the self-mastery of the individual under the direction of reason, guided by a knowledge of the good. It is this perfection of mind that Godwin sees as the goal of all rational action and as the true content of utility.

The full practical implications of this doctrine are developed at length in the final four books of *Political Justice*, but we have already been given several indications of its impact on ordinary conduct. The idea of an original social contract is rejected as violating the duty

Mirabaud [Baron d'Holbach], *Système de la nature* (1770); Claude-Adrien Helvétius, *De l'esprit* (1758).

[14] David Hume, *A Treatise of Human Nature* (Oxford, 1978), II. iii. 3, p. 416.

to judge each situation as it occurs; promises and future commitments likewise interfere with our duty to judge how best to act at these points of time; indeed, all political authority is a usurpation of individual judgment, and can be defended only in so far as it is supported by common deliberation: 'Private judgment and public deliberation are not themselves the standard of moral right and wrong; they are only the means of discovering right and wrong, and of comparing particular propositions with the standard of eternal truth' (p. 94). Of course, we have to judge when we should challenge authority and when we should submit as to an unavoidable necessity. And, for Godwin, there were few occasions on which martyrdom would be called for, since 'The true instruments for changing the opinions of men are argument and persuasion' (p. 112) and it was by the slow dissemination of truth, through public discussion and the stimulation of private judgment, that authority would gradually be rendered redundant. Godwin was not a hot-headed enthusiast for revolution: he saw the dangers of barbarity and appreciated the fragility of civilization. The virtuous man will seek to inform, rather than inflame, the public. Nonetheless, he believed that the revolutions of America and France involved something close to 'a general concert of all orders and descriptions of men' (p. 113). Indeed, had they been delayed somewhat, the majority in favour would have been so extensive that not one drop of blood would have been shed.

Godwin was clear that the political process is one in which people's passions are often excited, and in which implicit deference to others too frequently corrupts judgment. Although he believed passionately in the importance of candid discussion and conversation, and was an active member of the debating society the Philomaths, he was an active critic of the political associations developed by reformers and loyalists to promote their causes.[15] He saw them as encouraging partisanship, intolerance, and faction. He believed that the promotion of the best interests of humanity depends upon the freedom of social communication. Private discussion and conversation will promote the end, but it will cease to do so whenever judgment becomes constrained by fears that our compatriots will disclaim us (pp. 114–21). If we understand things rightly, we are bound by a duty to truth and to the development of the understanding, to speak our minds and to do so with complete candour. To censor our tongues for fear of the

---

[15] David O'Shaughnessy, 'Caleb Williams and the Philomaths: Recalibrating Political Justice for the Nineteenth Century', *Nineteenth-Century Literature*, 66/4 (2012), 423–48.

consequences is effectively to censor our thoughts, to attach to them fears and concerns that are extrinsic to them and distort their true character and value. For Godwin, that was too high a price to pay.

Godwin's conception of the virtuous person drew heavily on a set of Stoic traditions and models, among which Joseph Addison's tragedy about the last days of the Stoic Cato the Younger was a central source.[16] The core legacy of the Stoics, for him, was their sense of autarky, or self-direction, their indifference to bodily pains and impulses, and their commitment to intellectual life and to the pursuit of truth. Although Cato was a traditional republican hero because of his defence of his country, this aspect of the classical legacy played rather little role in Godwin's thinking. What mattered to him was that Cato transcended his sufferings and his personal interests and was wholly committed to doing what he believed was right. If Godwin began *Political Justice* with a sense of the potentially transformative impact of political institutions on individuals that owed something to the languages of republicanism and civic humanism, as he developed his case he reversed the order of priority, so that individual integrity and self-development, based around the pursuit and communication of truth, replaced the traditional republican motives of honour, fame, and commitment to one's country.

Godwin was rightly recognized as making a central contribution to political and moral theory by those seeking reform in Britain, with many of whom he was intimately linked. But he was not a partisan or a polemicist: he sought dispassionately to assess the value of propositions and general ideas and claims; he engaged critically with the political writings of those arguing for reform and those defending the status quo; and while his own judgment led him to support and expect reform, he retained a profound respect for the work of Edmund Burke, the man most associated with reaction against France. In contrast to the Enlightenment rationalism of someone such as Thomas Paine, Godwin appreciated the importance of history, tradition, and even prejudice in explaining how social orders cohered and evolved. While he, like Paine, saw history as progressive, and as a process of emancipation from political and religious imposture, he had a deeper appreciation than Paine of the political sociology of the aristocratic societies of Europe, and a stronger sense that the process was a gradual one and that precipitate violence and chaos could undo the benefits of civilization and its accompanying intellectual developments. He contrived to

---

[16] Joseph Addison, *Cato: A Tragedy* (1713).

xx   *Introduction*

bring together the ideas of both Burke and Paine largely by seeing the progress of truth as embedded in people's social relations and the political and social systems they inhabited. Even if we are ultimately to transcend those systems, they provide necessary preconditions for the development of the arts and the sciences, for the spread of education and the advancement of mind. We cease to be dependent on their authority, but many of their achievements are critical to the creation of a social and intellectual climate within which people engage in the disinterested pursuit of truth. If this line of thought was most evident in *Political Justice* in the material on resistance and the improvement of mind, it was also a central theme that he repeatedly revisited in his six mature novels, from *Things As They Are; or, The Adventures of Caleb Williams* (1794) to *Deloraine* (1833). The failures of the aristocratic society that he delineates, and the tragic consequences that flow from those whose lives and convictions are entirely shaped by that society, do not detract from Godwin's own sense that they contain many of the building blocks that the human mind needs in order to progress beyond them.

One way of reading Godwin is against the downward spiral described in books 8 and 9 of Plato's *Republic*. Here a perfect order under the direction of the guardian class becomes successively corrupted as tiny flaws in one generation become magnified in each subsequent generation. *Political Justice* reverses the process: human reason allows each generation to reflect upon and reform the flaws of the previous generation, in an ever ascending process towards a fuller and deeper understanding of the nature of the good. In that task Godwin brought to bear his extensive reading in French and Scottish Enlightenment literature, and his subtle, if unconventional, engagement with Burke. He utilized Burke's sense of the fragility of social order and his rejection of the idea that there are natural rights or principles of natural law that provide absolute standards against which to measure any political or social order. In contrast to the natural rights thinking of Paine, Godwin developed a conception of the development of 'mind' that was rooted in socio-historical processes. The good of rational self-mastery and self-development was an objective good; but its realization required an evolving interaction between the intellect and the institutions and practices of society and government. As mind conquered the passions and the appetites, so too it would absorb into itself fields of activity in which power and authority once held sway. The individual's emancipation from nature would be simultaneously a process of emancipation from political and social control.

Accordingly, Godwin turned to explore government, its surveillance of opinion, and the institutions of the law and punishment in three of the last four books of *Political Justice*. Much as in the opening books, his growing confidence in his vision led him to press his case still further. He finds little positive to say about any form of government, save that in which individual opinion is given maximum liberty, and in which areas requiring authoritative jurisdiction are rooted in consensual decisions based on extensive deliberation. He rejects absolutely the right of government to control opinion. And he sees law as an increasingly redundant procrustean constraint, insensitive to the details of issues and cases, and imposing a single pattern that overrides and distorts people's judgment. His philosophical anarchism — for this is what his doctrine had become — envisaged an era, at not too great a distance, in which the orbit of government will have shrunk to a bare and diminishing residual.

Godwin is at his most speculative in the final book of *Political Justice*. Property will cease to be a matter of monopoly and an occasion for exploitation. Since luxury, which is simply a pandering to appetites and passions, will disappear, there will be adequate resources for all with minimal labour. No man will withhold from another what is necessary to his needs. A dramatically more egalitarian order will ensue. When Godwin considers the objections to this hypothesis from the suggestion that population would expand unchecked, reintroducing want (an argument Malthus made more forcibly against Godwin a few years later in his *Essay on Population*, 1798[17]), he develops some of his most controversial arguments. He proposes 'as matter of probable conjecture' that, as mental faculties gain increasing control over our physical wants and subsequently our physiological process, we will learn to retard ageing and decay (pp. 458–9). He rejects marriage as the 'most odious of all monopolies', envisaging a world in which men and women will value each other for their virtues and wisdom rather than their appearance, and in which people will associate with each other freely, unconstrained by vows (pp. 447–8). If this sounds

---

[17] Godwin regarded Malthus' *Essay* as the most searching criticism advanced against his perspective, and he met and talked to Malthus at length. He also responded to his work in his *Thoughts Occasioned by the Perusal of Dr. Parr's Spital Sermon* (1800); in a subsequent letter to the *Monthly Magazine*, 10 Nov. 1801; and, when Malthus ignored Godwin's comments and expanded subsequent editions of his *Essay* (1803, 1817), with his monumental *Of Population: An Enquiry Concerning the Power of Increase in the Numbers of Mankind, being an Answer to Mr. Malthus's Essay on that Subject* (1820). Godwin believed that Malthus ignored the prospects for moral restraint, which, once acknowledged, supported limits on population and undermined Malthus' own case.

too much like free love, he also thought that the 'grosser' aspects of attraction between the sexes, just as with other areas of physiological imperfection (such as the need for sleep), would lose their sway as mind advanced, and that, as life is prolonged, the production of further generations will decline, leaving a steady state of population.

Reception and Revision

Godwin's *Political Justice* brought him immediate renown, perhaps above all as a philosopher who had raised issues of contemporary political debate to a more elevated sphere. Hazlitt's account of Godwin's reputation, written nearly thirty years later, captures some of the reaction:

> he blazed as a sun in the firmament of reputation; no one was more talked of, more looked up to, more sought after, and wherever liberty, truth, justice was the theme, his name was not far off. . . . No work in our time gave such a blow to the philosophical mind of the country. . . . Tom Paine was considered for the time as Tom Fool to him, Paley an old woman, Edmund Burke a flashy sophist. Truth, moral truth, it was supposed, had here taken up its abode; and these were the oracles of thought.[18]

There were criticisms of the work, although these were few and relatively slow to come. Many reviews published long extracts and comments across a number of issues, with the more conservative reviews generally starting positively, and then reacting negatively as the thrust of Godwin's argument became clear. The loyalist *British Critic*, for example, denounced the work as a *reductio ad absurdum* of French Enlightenment principles, mixed with the influence of 'some English writers of equal extravagance'.[19]

Political Justice was published in mid-February 1793. It was not a propitious time. The execution of Louis at the end of January precipitated war with Britain, adding further fuel to the upsurge of loyalist activities against British advocates of reform. Indeed, what had begun as a pamphlet dispute centred on Burke's *Reflections* had spiralled into an increasingly ill-tempered and practical struggle for ascendancy between loyalists and reformers. The government had become alarmed at the resurgence of the Society for Constitutional Information and the emergence of the artisan-based London Corresponding Society at the end of 1792, both of which spread

---

[18] William Hazlitt, 'William Godwin', in *Spirit of the Age* (1825).
[19] *British Critic and Quarterly Theological Review*, 1 (1793), 317.

reformist literature and drew into political debate and discussion men (and sometimes women) from the middling and artisanal classes who were largely excluded from parliamentary representation. The parallels with the sansculottes of Paris were not lost on the government. At the same time, those advocating reform found increasing reason for believing that the government was orchestrating a campaign to attack the basic rights and liberties of the people. Prosecutions for seditious speech were brought against reformers for comments made in coffee-houses (a traditionally private sphere), or for words uttered when under the influence.[20] In May 1792 a royal proclamation against seditious writings was issued, aimed partly, but certainly not exclusively, at Paine and those circulating his work. In that summer loyal addresses were solicited in the counties and sent to the Crown. In November, Paine was tried *in absentia* for the publication of *Rights of Man: Part the Second* (1792) and was outlawed. In December the loyalist Association for the Preservation of Liberty and Property Against Republicans and Levellers was founded, with tacit government support.

On 25 May 1793 Godwin noted in his diary, 'Prosecution of P.J. (*Political Justice*) debated this week'. Although there is no corroboration to show that the Privy Council discussed it, the matter of the book could well have been regarded as being just as incendiary as Paine's. On the other hand, the Attorney-General had defended his prosecution of Paine on the grounds that 'with an industry incredible, it [Paine's *Rights of Man*] was either totally or partially thrust into the hands of all persons in this country, of subjects of every description . . . to the ignorant, to the credulous, to the desperate'.[21] That claim could not be made about Godwin's work: the two substantial quarto volumes sold for £1 16s. as against the cheap editions of *Rights of Man*, which could be had for sixpence. Nonetheless, an Irish octavo edition was quickly produced, and the work was extensively excerpted in periodicals and popular literature in ways that ensured that Godwin's readership was not confined to the elite.

Following publication of *Political Justice*, Godwin was taken up by society: indeed, between 1791 and 1794 the number of people he saw each year quadrupled.[22] Nonetheless, he maintained the rhythms established while writing *Political Justice*. He would read and write

---

[20] John Barrell, *The Spirit of Despotism* (Oxford, 2006), ch. 2.

[21] Mark Philp, *Godwin's 'Political Justice'* (London, 1986), 66.

[22] See 'Statistics: People by Year', Godwin's Diary, <http://godwindiary.bodleian.ox.ac.uk/stats/people.html>.

in the morning, receive or visit friends and dine in the afternoon, and attend the theatre or have supper with friends in the evening. But in addition he was now called on and written to by all and sundry, and was sought by and introduced to a far wider circle of acquaintance, developing friendships with a range of artists, sculptors, historians, antiquarians, classical scholars, politicians, scientists, medical men, poets, and novelists. This wide and eclectic mix of acquaintance was something he worked hard to retain throughout his life, sharing an interest in their intellectual concerns but also being attracted to variety of character as a source of insight into human frailties and possibilities. He dined regularly with the reprobate money broker John King, but when King asked him to appear for him as a character witness in a court case, Godwin refused point blank: 'Remember, I can dine at a man's table, without being prepared to be the partisan of his measures and proceedings.'[23] Although his social life blossomed, he sustained his writing: letters to newspapers (signed Mucius, after the legendary Roman hero Gaius Mucius Scaevola); an essay against the war; and in April 1793 he began work on what was to be his most famous novel, *Things As They Are; or, The Adventures of Caleb Williams*. He completed the work in May the following year, and its success consolidated his reputation as one of the country's leading writers. Almost immediately he commenced work revising *Political Justice*.

A number of Godwin's critics and commentators have accused him of having 'bent before the blast', of turning conservative and cautious in the light of political repression.[24] That charge is difficult to support since he was certainly aware of the changing atmosphere in 1792, at the same time that he was writing the most radical concluding parts of *Political Justice*. He also remained closely in touch with developments as the tensions between reformers and the government continued to increase after the declaration of war. In Scotland, in September 1793, four reformers, Thomas Muir, William Skirving, Maurice Margarot, and Thomas Fyshe Palmer, were accused of sedition and sentenced to terms of between seven and fourteen years' transportation to the penal colony in Botany Bay. And after a 'British Convention' was held in Edinburgh at the end of that year, Judge Braxfield handed out draconian sentences at the subsequent trials in March 1794. Godwin visited

---

[23] Pamela Clemit and Jenny McAuley, 'Sociability in the Diary: The Case of John King', *Bodleian Library Record*, 24/1 (2011), 51–6.

[24] George Woodcock, 'Introduction', in *W. Godwin: Selections from 'Political Justice'*, [ed. George Woodcock] (London, 1943), 4; H. N. Brailsford, *Shelley, Godwin and their Circle*, 2nd edn (Oxford, 1951), 68.

Muir and Palmer in the Woolwich prison hulks, where they were awaiting transfer to the transports to Australia, and he called regularly on his friend Joseph Gerrald, another victim of Braxfield's zeal, who was incarcerated in Newgate awaiting transportation, where he also met a number of other reformers. Rather than inducing caution, these experiences bore fruit in the prison scenes of *Caleb Williams*,[25] in which he denounced the injustices of the British legal and penal system. Even as he was completing the novel, further storm clouds were gathering. He set down his pen on 10 May 1794. The following day he walked across London to Wimbledon to visit the leading radical John Horne Tooke for one of his traditional open-house Sunday dinners. William Sharp, John Thelwall, Henry Richter, and Jeremiah Joyce were among those present.[26] Within days all had been arrested and interrogated by a special parliamentary committee of secrecy, and were languishing in the Tower or Newgate. Others present, though not Godwin, were sought for interrogation by the government. Habeas Corpus was suspended and the list of those incarcerated grew. In October, Lord Chief Justice Eyre issued a charge to the grand jury, which accused twelve of the reformers of treason, including Godwin's close friends Thomas Holcroft, the dramatist, Thelwall, and Horne Tooke.

When the charge was issued, Godwin was in Worcestershire visiting friends. He immediately returned to London and undertook an analysis of Eyre's case. *Cursory Strictures on the Charge Delivered . . . to the Grand Jury* was published anonymously. It was a forensic demolition of the case of constructive treason assembled by Eyre and the Attorney-General. It aroused widespread public interest and helped galvanize the legal talents defending the men. At the end of 1794, after the unsuccessful trials of Thomas Hardy (founder and general secretary of the London Corresponding Society), Horne Tooke, and Thelwall, the prosecutions were abandoned and the remaining prisoners released. Godwin proudly recorded that, at another dinner in the May after the acquittal of his friends, Horne Tooke asked him whether he had written the pamphlet. When Godwin acknowledged that he had, Horne Tooke seized and kissed his hand, saying he could do nothing less by the hand that had given existence to that production.[27]

[25] e.g. *Things As They Are; or, The Adventures of Caleb Williams* (1794), vol. ii, chs. xi–xiv.
[26] See John Barrell, *Imagining the King's Death* (Oxford, 2000); John Barrell, '11 May 1794', *Bodleian Library Record*, 24/1 (Apr. 2011), 19–24.
[27] Godwin, 'Autobiographical Fragments', 50–1.

Although the revisions to *Political Justice* certainly do not seem to be the result of prudence in the face of government repression, they were extensive. Moreover, not content with these, he revised the text still further in the first seven months of 1797 for a third edition, and had a further fit of corrections (no longer extant) in the autumn of 1832 in anticipation of a fourth edition. The revisions systematically eradicate the early references to the positive role of political institution, they moderate some of the more Platonic language of truth, they introduce greater empiricism in Godwin's account of the nature of human knowledge, and they weaken some of the more speculative claims made in the final book. The essayist Thomas De Quincey later announced that 'The second edition, as regards principles, is not a recast, but absolutely a travesty of the first: nay, it is all but a palinode.'[28] That judgment is too harsh, and the suggestion of increasing conservatism (or fearfulness) similarly misses the mark; but it is clear that Godwin's work was the fruit of considerable further thought and discussion, and that, as his social circles expanded, he was brought into contact with a range of new ideas and challenges to his position. In a note in his papers written in 1800, Godwin reported that his *Political Justice* was blemished by three principal errors: '1. Stoicism, or an inattention to the principle, that pleasure and pain are the only bases upon which morality can rest. 2. Sandemanianism, or an inattention to the principle, that feeling, not judgment, is the source of human actions. 3. The unqualified condemnation of the private affections.' He also noted with some insight 'how strongly these errors are connected with the Calvinist system, which had been deeply wrought into my mind in early life, as to enable these errors long to survive the general system of religious opinions of which they formed a part'.[29] He also recorded that he thought that he had rooted out the Stoicism in his revisions to the first edition, while his changed assessment of the place of feeling and private affections, which he ascribed to the perusal of Hume's *Treatise of Human Nature*, was only incompletely integrated in the final chapters of each volume in the second edition. It is a perceptive analysis, and yet Godwin persisted in the belief that it was possible to remedy such errors and leave the principles intact, when it is plausible to think that a great deal falls apart if we remove his Stoicism and his relative indifference to worldly and bodily things, his emphasis on intellect

---

[28] Thomas De Quincey, 'William Godwin', in *Biographical and Historical Essays* (Boston, 1887), 337.

[29] Godwin, 'The Principal Revolutions of Opinion', in *Collected Novels and Memoirs of William Godwin*, i. 53–4.

over passion, the motivational power of truth, and the centrality of impartiality in judgment. Moreover, as a result of these changes, *Political Justice* becomes a rather different book—one that no longer offers the same powerful and visionary account of the progressive perfectibility of mankind that astonished and inspired the literary world at the beginning of 1793 and that so perfectly expressed that moment of intellectual aspiration sparked by the revolutions of America and France.

Godwin's Later Years

John Thelwall, the poet, radical, and popular lecturer, whom Godwin candidly criticized for his willingness to stir up the passions of his audiences in his even-handed critique of government oppression and radical populism in his 1795 pamphlet *Considerations on Lord Grenville's and Mr Pitt's Bills*, responded to the criticism by accusing Godwin and his 'visionary peculiarities of mind' of both recommending 'the most extensive plan of freedom and innovation ever discussed by any writer in the English language' and coupling this with a conviction that it was necessary 'to reprobate every measure from which even the most moderate reform can rationally be expected'.[30] This is a plausible attack, although it ignores Godwin's sense of the interconnection between opinion and government and the importance of avoiding precipitate action that might derail the gradual emancipation of mankind through intellectual progress. It also ignores one major area in which Godwin's practice did answer to his philosophical speculation, and in which his experiences probably did lead him to reconsider elements of his doctrine, especially concerning the role of private affections and marriage.

Godwin was a somewhat stiff and formal man, candid to the point of bluntness, and yet easily hurt by the comments of others. In the 1780s and early 1790s he lived a relatively secluded life. The list of acquaintances he drew up around the year 1803, and in which he identified the years in which he met certain people, was a resolutely masculine one, until Helen Maria Williams appeared in 1787. And she remained a solitary exception until 1791. However, his circles of female acquaintance grew dramatically after the publication of his book. He became friendly with Elizabeth Inchbald, the playwright and novelist; Maria Reveley, the wife of his acquaintance Henry Reveley;

---

[30] John Thelwall, *The Tribune*, ii/2 (London, 1796).

Amelia Alderson, the daughter of a Norfolk friend; Mary Hays, the novelist who wrote him such long and detailed letters that Godwin insisted on responding in person to save time; Mary Robinson, who had previously been mistress to the prince of Wales; and many others. In contact with admiring women, and subject to some unorthodox approaches, Godwin discarded his usual drab 'ministerial' dress and became caught up in a certain amount of flirtation and teasing. It was not his natural métier. Then, in January 1796, Mary Hays invited him to take tea with her and her new friend Mary Wollstonecraft, who had returned from Paris in 1795. The pair had met occasionally earlier in the decade, most famously when they dined together with Thomas Paine at Joseph Johnson's publishing house in November 1791. That occasion had not gone well. Godwin had not read her work and was curious to hear Paine: 'Paine, in his general habits, is no great talker; and, though he threw in occasionally some shrewd and striking remarks, conversation lay principally between me and Mary. I, of consequence, heard her, very frequently when I wished to hear Paine.'[31] Their reacquaintance was more positive and they were soon meeting on a regular basis. Wollstonecraft was known in London as Mrs Imlay, after the father of her child Fanny, whom most people assumed she had married in Paris. But Wollstonecraft had long entertained rather unorthodox views about relationships, and her relationship with Imlay was extramarital; it was also over, a fact that occasioned such despair that she twice tried to kill herself in 1795.

In August 1796 Godwin and Wollstonecraft became lovers, staying late into the evenings at each other's lodgings, always wary of the prying eyes of Wollstonecraft's landlady. Their notes and letters to each other are both charming and moving: it is clear how vulnerable Wollstonecraft felt, and how ill-prepared Godwin was for such an intense physical and emotional relationship. Within four months Wollstonecraft was pregnant, and in March 1797 the couple married, with some philosophical embarrassment, although they maintained their own circles of acquaintance and Godwin even took a room near to their now shared lodgings so as to preserve an independent place of work. Several friends promptly cut Wollstonecraft from their acquaintance since the marriage revealed her relationship to Imlay to be illicit, but most accepted the couple. The six or so months they spent prior to the birth of their child, and jointly caring for Mary's daughter

---

[31] Godwin, *Memoirs of the Author of 'A Vindication of the Rights of Woman'*, in *Collected Novels and Memoirs of William Godwin*, i. 112–13.

Fanny, were largely happy ones, and probably contributed to Godwin's revaluation of his austerity towards the private affections and to the emotions and feelings. When Wollstonecraft died ten days after the birth of their daughter Mary (later Mary Shelley), Godwin was bereft and he threw himself into publishing her works, including much personal correspondence, and commemorating her in his candid *Memoirs of the Author of 'A Vindication of the Rights of Woman'* (1798).

With the publication of the *Memoirs*, Godwin exposed himself to the full backlash against the radical intellectual culture of the 1790s. The poet Robert Southey accused him of a 'want of all feeling in stripping his dead wife naked' and putting her on display,[32] and anti-radical pub- lications had a field-day in lampooning Godwin and denouncing Wollstonecraft as a common whore. At a time when popular politics was taking a more bitter, dangerous, and, in Ireland, more insurrec- tionary form, Godwin had offered himself up as a target for the spleen of the anti-Jacobin and loyalist press.

While Godwin's volume of essays, *The Enquirer* (1797), and the third edition of *Political Justice* (1798) both suggest Wollstonecraft's influence in concession to emotions and feeling, his second major novel, *St Leon* (1799), in which a man sacrifices an idyllic family life to gain knowledge of eternal life, only to find himself an outcast to every form of human society, is unequivocal testimony to her impact. In his *Thoughts Occasioned by the Perusal of Dr Parr's Spital Sermon* (1801) he made still further philosophical concessions to the importance of private affections and the emotions. But, while he sought to answer his critics in measured philosophical tones on those issues on which he felt he had a case to answer, the political and cultural climate of candid discussion and argument had fundamentally changed. He found him- self denounced by an increasingly virulent loyalist press, and former friends and allies turned against him. He was not an outcast. His circle of acquaintances remained extensive, although many of his closest friends from the early 1790s were now absent. He remarried in 1801, but this rather added to his burdens since his new wife, Mary Jane Clairmont, brought two more children to the family and they had a son together in 1803. Moreover, their relationship was not altogether happy, which led other old friends to steer clear of them. The family also faced mounting debts, which they sought unsuccessfully to meet by establishing a children's publisher and bookshop, but Godwin's reputation and fortunes never recovered.

---

[32] Mitzi Myers, 'Godwin's *Memoirs* of Wollstonecraft: The Shaping of Self and Subject', *Studies in Romanticism*, 20/3 (1981), 302.

Nonetheless, his work endured. It brought him the attention of the social reformer and utopian philosopher Robert Owen, people came to see him from across Europe and America, and he sustained a succession of young acolytes whom he tried to groom in the principles of *Political Justice*. The most famous of these was Percy Bysshe Shelley, who helped bring Godwinian ideas to a younger generation, and who purported to be acting out of respect for them when he ran off to France with Godwin's daughter Mary and her stepsister Jane in 1814, leaving behind his pregnant wife and young daughter. Neither Mary nor Shelley found Godwin's subsequent rejection of them easy to bear, and the resulting tensions in Godwin's household probably exacerbated Fanny Imlay's despair, resulting in her suicide in October 1816. Nor were these wounds wholly healed when Godwin welcomed Shelley and Mary back into his circles on their marriage, after Shelley's first wife took her own life in December of that year. Mary Shelley's novel *Frankenstein* (1818) is in part a reflection on this traumatic period for the family, and on Godwin and Shelley's commitment to truth, and was in dialogue with Godwin's *Political Justice* and *St Leon*. All three texts raise questions about the power and importance of family and personal ties and reflect on the uneven progress of truth, the responsibilities of those who are more advanced, and the potential of ignorance to thwart the progressive development of mankind if new ideas are not introduced with care.

The studious and reflecting only can be expected to see deeply into future events. To conceive an order of society totally different from that which is now before our eyes, and to judge of the advantages that would accrue from its institution, are the prerogatives only of a few favoured minds . . . they cannot yet for some time be expected to be understood by the multitude. (p. 115)

This concern with the communication of truth, which was central to Godwin's *Political Justice*, returned over and over again in his later work, revisited in the light of his changing experience. *The Enquirer* (1797) adopts a more tentative approach than Godwin's earlier fierce didacticism, and treats private judgment as something that he aims to stimulate as widely as possible, by furnishing materials for reflection rather than seeking directly to instruct it. And Godwin's forays into the theatre, while partly motivated by the hope of making substantial amounts of money, also gave a central role to the communication of ideas: '[Drama] does that, which sermons were intended to do: it forms the link between the literary class of mankind & the uninstructed, the bridge by which the latter may pass over into the domain of the former.'[33] Godwin's turn to writing and publishing books for children was equally driven by an interest in instruction and the improvement of mind, both to generate the intellectual elite and to ensure that ordinary people would also develop their capacities for judgment. But his slightly restless experimentation with different forms and audiences seems to echo the anxiety expressed early in *Political Justice* that literature could not alone be 'adequate to all the purposes of human improvement' (p. 22).

Godwin was himself aware of the extent to which his own thinking was a product of the times and circumstances in which he lived, and that it was profoundly shaped by those with whom he conversed at length and in depth. He named in particular the influence of Joseph Fawcett (dissenting minister and poet), with whom he was a student at Hoxton; Thomas Holcroft (the novelist and dramatist), who was a powerful influence while he was writing *Political Justice* and whom Godwin credited with his conversion to atheism in the 1790s; George Dyson, a young and somewhat volatile follower of Godwin, who led him to revise his thinking on the principles of pleasure and pain after the first edition; and the poet Samuel Taylor Coleridge, who induced Godwin to doubt his atheism at the turn of the century. In his *Thoughts Occasioned by the Perusal of Dr Parr's Spital Sermon*, Godwin, in reflective mode, noted that 'The human intellect is a sort of barometer, directed by the variations that surround it.'[34]

The central theme of Godwin's life's work was his sense of the extent to which people's thoughts are rooted in their context, that it is only a few who are able to break free of the merely conventional, and that it is then a challenge to know how best to communicate their insights in a way that can produce a gradual, non-violent progress in the public mind. It was born of his distinctive intellectual background and his passion for the examination of ideas. But it needed the heady days of the 1790s for him to see in private judgment and the pursuit of the public good a pair of principles that would enable the dramatic progress of mankind, ushering a new kind of social world in which political authority was increasingly discarded in favour of individual moral judgment and public discussion. Despite his marginalization

---

[33] Bodleian Library, MS Abinger Dep. C.21, fo. 57, repr. in *The Letters of William Godwin*, i: *1778–1797*, ed. Pamela Clemit (Oxford, 2011), 66 n. 1; David O'Shaughnessy, *William Godwin and the Theatre* (London, 2010), p. x.

[34] *Political and Philosophical Writings of William Godwin*, ii, ed. Mark Philp (London, 1993), 170. See also the '1796 list' in which Godwin tries to identify his seminal influences: <http://godwindiary.bodleian.ox.ac.uk/diary/1796list.html>.

and his victimization by the increasingly ascendant loyalist culture, he never lost that faith, although he did recurrently reflect on the best way of communicating such truths.

Godwin's developing domestic relationships, and the intense conversational world in which he lived, led him to revise details and features of his position, often substantially, and often in ways that leave the reader unclear about how far the new synthesis really holds together. The introduction of a strong Humean train of scepticism in the third edition of *Political Justice*, for example, leaves one uncertain whether Godwin, in spite of his protestations to the contrary, still has grounds for thinking that there is a truth to be communicated. If it cannot be, then the thought that there can be convergence of ideas breaks down and the entire programme collapses. Also, Godwin became more consistently utilitarian, but, while his characterization of the content of utility remained primarily intellectual in form, he now identified the pleasures of benevolence as a key component. That move compromised his earlier resistance to self-love and his commitment to first-order impartiality, since the pleasure of performing our duty becomes part of the motive for our actions. It remains unclear whether Godwin thinks this compromises the impartial assessment of our duty, but the alloyed motivation suggests that it does.

Since Godwin's death at the age of 80 in 1836, interest in his work and life has grown steadily. He was a favourite author among early and later socialists—Engels described him as 'almost exclusively the property of the proletariat'—and he was an important influence on the anarchist tradition, partly through Kropotkin.[35] An exemplary first biography by Charles Kegan Paul appeared in 1876 and has been followed by several serious and weighty competitors. *An Enquiry Concerning Political Justice* has attracted a certain amount of philosophical analysis, partly because of the fruitfully unstable balance of ideas that mark his developing thought. His novels and plays have also drawn substantial recent critical attention, and while Romanticists have tended to retain the Lake Poets' ambivalence to Godwin and his work, he has increasingly been recognized as a literary figure both in his own right and as the linchpin of the most famous literary family of the period. A scholarly edition of his diary is available online and

[35] Friedrich Engels, *The Condition of the Working Class in England* (Oxford, 1993), 247; George Crowder, *Classical Anarchism: The Political Thought of Godwin, Proudhon, Bakunin, and Kropotkin* (Oxford, 1991).

the first meticulously edited volume of his letters has recently been published.[36]

Philosophers remain, for the most part, both sceptical about the force of claims for first-order impartiality and drawn to the principle. Peter Singer's *The Life You Can Save*[37] starts from a less demanding claim: not that we should do everything in our power to achieve the greatest possible good, but that we should not let people die when we are in a position to save their lives at relatively low cost to ourselves. This less demanding claim still seems too much for most people, who are reluctant to sacrifice their own interests in order to contribute more to eradicate malaria or Third World starvation. But the normative power of Godwin's principle in such cases is difficult to resist. Just as Singer rightly points out that we would treat with abhorrence the man who refused to save a drowning child when it was perfectly safe for him to do so, on the grounds that he would have got his suit wet, so too we can see that our own concerns should sometimes be set aside when there is a more pressing claim. How much more pressing is an important issue philosophically. It is not especially troubling practically, since it seems clear that the very great majority of people in the West are not prepared to sacrifice the relatively small amounts that would end the attrition suffered by populations in other parts of the world from curable illnesses, remediable malnutrition, and predictable disasters. We might treat this as a demonstration that Godwin was simply wildly over-ambitious in his expectations of people's capacity for selflessness and disinterested benevolence. But we might also think, as many of his contemporaries did, that he had a point: that we are over-invested in the personal pronoun 'mine', and that we wrong other people when we fail to provide them with support when they are in need. Writing at the height of public optimism about the future, arising from the collapse of French absolutism, Godwin and many of his friends believed that this heralded a new dawn. Many writers subsequently have had similar moments, although many of these have thought that a bit of violence might help speed the plough. In contrast, Godwin resolutely rejected force, appealed to private judgment, and sought to stimulate and educate it and to encourage people to think for themselves and to take responsibility for their lives, their actions, and their relations with their fellows; that is, to think for themselves and to ask themselves: What ought I to do? And, in weighing my own claims

[36] <http://godwindiary.bodleian.ox.ac.uk>; *Letters of William Godwin*, i: *1778–1797*.
[37] London, 2009.

in comparison to others at such and such a value, am I assessing them justly? This essentially Socratic question remains an important and enduring one, and it underlines the fact that, while *Political Justice* is a central text for literary studies, for Romanticism, and for our appreciation of the 1790s in Britain, it is so, in part, by having more than merely historical significance.

NOTE ON THE TEXT

THIS edition reproduces the first edition text, published in quarto by G. G. J. and J. Robinson, Paternoster Row, London, 1793. It amends the text in the light of the errata identified and appended to the Table of Contents of the original edition. This list is therefore omitted, as is the page directing a division of the work into two volumes at page 379 of the original edition (the end of Book IV). Cross-references in the titles of appendices have been silently omitted (as duplicating footnotes) but cross-references in footnotes retained. The chapter titles and Contents have been grouped together at the start of the book, rather than being divided as they were for the two-volume edition.

In the original edition, summary headings for each book preceded each volume, and were followed by a detailed Table of Contents for each volume. This detail was then repeated in the summary headings of each chapter, and these summary headings were inserted as side headings in the margin through each chapter. In the interests of space, a brief list of books and chapters is given at the beginning of the text, and the summary headings for chapters appear at the start of each chapter. Chapter divisions in the margins have been dispensed with, but book and chapter numbers appear in the running headlines.

Godwin's spelling remains uncorrected. It diverges from modern spellings in some respects. For example, 'anything', 'everyone', and 'forever' are invariably given as two words. Godwin prefers 'alledged' to 'alleged', 'cloake' (and sometimes 'cloke') to 'cloak', 'connexion' to 'connection', 'reflexion' to 'reflection', 'intrusted' to 'entrusted', 'inlisted' to 'enlisted', 'incumbrance' to 'encumbrance', 'shew' to 'show', and 'falshood' to 'falsehood'. Also 'recal' is used for 'recall', 'befal' for 'befall', in keeping with his practice in his diary, where he systematically misses off the second 'l' in names ending with a double 'l', as in Thelwall. His original spellings have been retained in all cases, even when there is a case for thinking this is a mistake. Double quotation marks have been reduced to single.

Godwin's footnotes have been preserved at the foot of pages. Explanatory notes are at the back of the book, signalled by asterisks in the text. Godwin's cross-references have been retained but adapted to the page numbers of this edition.

Editions of An Enquiry Concerning Political Justice

Godwin published three editions of his *Enquiry* in his lifetime, in 1793, 1796, and 1798. These dates indicate the dates given in the text. In fact, the second edition appeared at the end of 1795 and the third at the end of 1797. The revisions between the editions are extensive. Previous editions of the text have tended to use the third edition, and a facsimile of this edition with extensive scholarly apparatus in a separate volume was produced by F. E. L. Priestley for the University of Toronto Press in 1946. As general editor of the *Political and Philosophical Writings of William Godwin* (London, 1993) I reversed Priestley's practice and gave a clean copy of the first edition, together with a volume of variants in the second and third editions (and including material from the manuscript and a previously unidentified first draft). I did so because, while the first edition may not represent Godwin's final thoughts, it more perfectly captures the spirit of the time in which he was writing than later editions (see Introduction, p. xxii). Moreover, it is this edition that launched his reputation and generated his following in the 1790s. Finally, while it is possible to read subsequent editions in the light of a clean first edition text, it is very much more difficult to reconstruct the first edition text using the third edition as the starting point. For readers interested in the literature and politics of the 1790s, the first edition is the best place to start. For those interested in the continuing philosophical relevance of Godwin's thought, the first edition offers a less coherent but more interesting text, from which subsequent changes of view may be followed up relatively easily.

The changes Godwin made between the editions are manifold; few chapters are unaltered. The nature of the changes is discussed in the Introduction, pp. xxvi–xxvii, and the major alterations are as follows:

TITLE

1796 Changed from *An Enquiry Concerning Political Justice* to *Enquiry Concerning Political Justice*

PRELIMINARY MATTER

1796 Second Preface added

1798 Summary of Principles and Index inserted prior to Chapter I

BOOK I

1796 Chapter I rewritten

Chapter II: four paragraphs added to the introduction

Chapter V becomes Chapter III, retitled 'Spirit of Political Institutions'

Chapter III rewritten and replaced by new Chapter IV, similarly titled

Chapter IV deleted and replaced by new Chapter V, entitled 'The Voluntary Actions of Men Originate in their Opinions'

Chapter VI moved to the end of the book as Chapter VIII and additional paragraphs added

Chapter VII becomes Chapter VI

Chapter VIII becomes Chapter VII

1798 Additional paragraphs added to Chapter VI
These changes remove the opening attribution of positive influence to political institutions and set out his argument more systematically than in the first edition.

BOOK II

1796 Chapter I significantly rewritten

Chapter III, 'Of Duty', significantly rewritten; becomes Chapter IV, 'Of Personal Virtue and Duty'

Chapter IV becomes Chapter III

Chapter V, 'Rights of Man', significantly rewritten as 'Of Rights'

BOOK III

1796 Chapter III, 'Of Promises', rewritten

Chapter VI, 'Of Obedience', rewritten

Chapter VII, 'Of Forms of Government', significantly rewritten

BOOK IV

1796 Chapter I, 'Of Resistance', rewritten

Chapter II, 'Of Revolutions', Section I, 'Duties of a Citizen', and Section II, 'Mode of Effecting Revolutions', rewritten as Chapter II

Chapter II, Section III, 'Of Political Associations', rewritten as Chapter III

Chapter II, Section IV, 'Of the Species of Reform to Be Desired', omitted

Chapter III becomes Chapter IV

Chapter IV, Section I, 'Of Abstract of General Truth', rewritten as Chapter V, 'Of the Cultivation of Truth'

Chapter IV, Section II, 'Of Sincerity', rewritten as Chapter VI, to which a new appendix is added, entitled 'Illustrations of Sincerity'

Chapter IV, Appendix I, 'Of the Connexion between Understanding and Virtue', becomes an appendix to Chapter V

Chapter IV, Appendix II, 'Of the Mode of Excluding Visitors', becomes Appendix II to Chapter VI

Chapter IV, Appendix III, 'Subject of Sincerity Resumed', omitted

Chapter V becomes Chapter VII

Chapter VI becomes Chapter VIII

Chapter VII becomes Chapter IX

Chapter VIII, 'Of the Principle of Virtue', rewritten as Chapter X, 'Of Self-Love and Benevolence'

Chapter IX, 'Of the Tendency of Virtue', rewritten as Chapter XI, 'Of Good and Evil'

BOOK V

1796 Chapter XV: a number of paragraphs added

1798 Chapters VII, X, and XIV: additional paragraphs added

Chapter XI, 'Moral Effects of Aristocracy': six paragraphs added

Chapter XV: more paragraphs added

BOOK VI

1798 Chapters I, III, and IX: several paragraphs added

BOOK VII

Changes to this book are comparatively minor

BOOK VIII

1796 Chapter I is considerably extended

New Chapter II inserted, 'The Principles of Property'

Chapter II becomes Chapter III

New Chapter IV inserted, 'Objection to this System from the Frailty of the Human Mind'

Chapter III becomes Chapter VII but is rewritten as 'Objection to this System from the Benefits of Luxury'

Chapter IV becomes Chapter VI

Chapter V significantly rewritten as 'Objections to this System from the Question of Permanence'

Chapter VI becomes Chapter VIII

An appendix, 'Of Cooperation, Cohabitation and Marriage', is introduced, drawing on some earlier material (to which further changes are made in 1798)

Chapter VII becomes Chapter IX; paragraphs are added; an appendix is introduced, 'Of Health, and the Prolongation of Human Life', that uses amended earlier material

Chapter VIII becomes Chapter X with additional material

These changes are discussed at length in my *Godwin's 'Political Justice'* (London, 1986), but are also scrutinized in a range of the critical material identified in the Select Bibliography for this edition. The precise significance of these changes and their impact on the character of Godwin's philosophy remain matters of scholarly debate.

SELECT BIBLIOGRAPHY

Bibliographic Works

Graham, Kenneth W., *William Godwin Reviewed: A Reception History, 1783–1834* (New York, 2001).

Pollin, Burton R., *Godwin Criticism: A Synoptic Bibliography* (Toronto, 1967).

Godwin's Works

Collected Novels and Memoirs of William Godwin, ed. Mark Philp, Pamela Clemit, and Maurice Hindle, 8 vols. (London, 1992).

The Diary of William Godwin, ed. Victoria Myers, David O'Shaughnessy, and Mark Philp (Oxford, 2010), <http://godwindiary.bodleian.ox.ac.uk>.

Enquiry Concerning Political Justice, ed. F. E. L. Priestley, 3 vols. (Toronto, 1946).

The Letters of William Godwin, 1 vol. to date (Oxford, 2011–), i: *1778–1797*, ed. Pamela Clemit (Oxford, 2011).

The Plays of William Godwin, ed. David O'Shaughnessy (London, 2010).

Political and Philosophical Writings of William Godwin, ed. Mark Philp, Pamela Clemit, and Martin Fitzpatrick, 7 vols. (London, 1993).

Biographies

Kegan Paul, Charles, *William Godwin and his Contemporaries*, 2 vols. (London, 1876).

Locke, Don, *A Fantasy of Reason: The Lie and Thought of William Godwin* (London, 1980).

Marshall, Peter H., *William Godwin* (New Haven, 1984).

St Clair, William, *The Godwins and the Shelleys: The Biography of a Family* (London, 1989).

Analysis and Criticism

Barry, Brian, *Justice as Impartiality* (Oxford, 1995).

Butler, Marilyn, 'Godwin, Burke and Caleb Williams', *Essays in Criticism*, 32 (1982), 237–57.

Claeys, Gregory, *The French Revolution Debate in Britain: The Origins of Modern Politics* (London, 2007).

Clemit, Pamela, *The Godwinian Novel: The Rational Fictions of Godwin, Brockden Brown, Mary Shelley* (Oxford, 1993).

Clark, J. P., *The Philosophical Anarchism of William Godwin* (Princeton, 1977).

Fleischer, David, *William Godwin: A Study in Liberalism* (London, 1951).

Kelly, Gary, *The English Jacobin Novel, 1780–1805* (Oxford, 1976).

Kramnick, Isaac, 'On Anarchism and the Real World: William Godwin and Radical England', *American Political Science Review*, 66 (1972), 114–28.

Lamb, Robert, 'The Foundations of Godwinian Impartiality', *Utilitas*, 18 (2006), 134–53.

—— 'Was William Godwin a Utilitarian?', *Journal of the History of Ideas*, 70 (2009), 119–41.

Maniquis, Robert M., and Myers, Victoria (eds.), *Godwinian Moments: From Enlightenment to Romanticism* (Toronto, 2011).

Monro, D. H., *Godwin's Moral Philosophy: An Interpretation of William Godwin* (Oxford, 1953).

Morrow, John, 'Republicanism and Public Virtue: William Godwin's History of the Commonwealth of England', *Historical Journal*, 34 (1991), 645–64.

Myers, Mitzi, 'Godwin's *Memoirs* of Wollstonecraft: The Shaping of Self and Subject', *Studies in Romanticism*, 20 (1981), 299–316.

O'Shaughnessy, David, 'Caleb Williams and the Philomaths: Recalibrating Political Justice for the Nineteenth Century', *Nineteenth-Century Literature*, 66/4 (2012), 423–48.

—— *William Godwin and the Theatre* (London, 2010).

Philp, Mark, *Godwin's 'Political Justice'* (London, 1986).

Pollin, Bruton R., *Education and Enlightenment in the Works of William Godwin* (New York, 1962).

Singer, Peter, *The Life You Can Save* (London, 2009).

—— Cannold, L., and Kuhse, H., 'William Godwin and the Defence of Impartialist Ethics', *Utilitas*, 7 (1995), 67–86.

Tysdahl, B. J., *William Godwin as Novelist* (London, 1981).

Further Reading in Oxford World's Classics

Godwin, William, *Caleb Williams*, ed. Pamela Clemit (Oxford, 2009).

A CHRONOLOGY OF
WILLIAM GODWIN

1756   3 March: Born at Wisbech in Cambridgeshire, the seventh of thirteen children, son of a dissenting minister.

1767   Becomes a pupil of Samuel Newton in Norwich.

1772   Death of his father, John Godwin.

1773   Admitted to Hoxton Dissenting Academy, having been turned down by Homerton Academy for unorthodox, Sandemanian views.

1778–83   Graduates from Hoxton. Becomes minister at Ware in Hertfordshire, and subsequently holds positions with various dissenting congregations before abandoning the ministry and settling in London.

1783   Publishes a life of Chatham and several minor works, political, historical, literary, and religious.

1784   Publishes three short novels, *Damon and Delia*, *Italian Letters*, and *Imogen*. July: Is employed on the *New Annual Register* (until 1791).

1785   Employed by Richard Brinsley Sheridan on the Whig periodical *Political Herald* (acting as editor in 1786, until it collapses in December).

1786   Meets the playwright Thomas Holcroft, who becomes his closest friend.

1787   First of three motions for repeal of the Test and Corporation Acts moved by Henry Beaufoy in March 1787 and May 1789, and by Charles James Fox in March 1790, coupled with an active extra-parliamentary campaign.

1788   Begins the diary, which he keeps systematically until two months before his death.

1789   4 May: Estates General convened at Versailles. 14 July: Storming of the Bastille in Paris. 6 October: March on Versailles and the return of the royal family to Paris.

1790   January: Godwin commences his tragedy *St Dunstan*, completing it in December. 1 November: Edmund Burke's *Reflections on the Revolution in France* published, initiating 'the revolution controversy'. 29 November: Mary Wollstonecraft publishes her *Vindication of the Rights of Men*.

1791   February, March: Thomas Paine's *Rights of Man* published. 6 May: Edmund Burke publicly breaks his political and personal friendship with Charles James Fox over the latter's support for France.

June: Godwin agrees terms with G. G. J. Robinson, his publisher, for a work on 'Political Principles'. 20 June: Flight to Varennes by the French royal family, followed by their forced return to Paris. 10 July: 'Political Principles' contract signed. 14 July: Anti-Dissenter riots in Birmingham. 17 July: Massacre of the Champ de Mars, Paris. September: Godwin begins work on *An Enquiry Concerning Political Justice*. 13 September: French king accepts new Constitution.

1792   January: Wollstonecraft's *Vindication of the Rights of Woman* published. April: War between France and Austria and the German states. September: Massacres in Paris. 20 September: First major French victory at Valmy and inauguration of the French National Assembly. November: Attends the trial *in absentia* of Thomas Paine and attends his first dinner at John Horne Tooke's in Wimbledon. December: Trial of the French king, Louis Capet.

1793   14 January: Louis found guilty. 20 January: Death of Louis decreed. 21 January: Louis executed. 1 February: France declares war on Britain. 14 February: *An Enquiry Concerning Political Justice* published; February–March: Godwin writes four letters to the *Morning Chronicle* attacking the loyalist response to reformers. September: The Scottish radicals Thomas Muir and Thomas Fyshe Palmer sentenced to transportation for sedition. December: Godwin attends his first meeting of the debating club the Philomaths.

1794   March: Joseph Gerrald and other radicals from the British Convention of the Delegates of the People, Associated to Obtain Universal Suffrage and Annual Parliaments held in Edinburgh in December 1793 sentenced to transportation or sedition. 12 May: Arrest of Thomas Hardy, John Thelwall, John Horne Tooke, and others on suspicion of treason. 26 May: Godwin's *Things As They Are; or, The Adventures of Caleb Williams* published. October: Detained radicals charged with treason; Thomas Holcroft arrested; Godwin writes *Cursory Strictures*. 5 November–5 December: Hardy, Horne Tooke, and Thelwall acquitted. December 1794–October 1795: Godwin revises *Political Justice* for a second edition.

1795   November: Gagging Acts against treasonable practices and unlawful assemblies introduced, prompting Godwin's pamphlet *Considerations on Lord Grenville and Mr Pitt's Bills*.

1796   8 January: Meets Mary Wollstonecraft at Mary Hays's lodgings. 21 August: Godwin and Wollstonecraft become lovers.

1797   February: Publishes essays, *The Enquirer: Reflections on Education, Manners and Literature*. March: Godwin and Wollstonecraft marry. 30 August: Birth of Mary Godwin. 10 September: Death of Mary Wollstonecraft. December: Publishes the third edition of *Political Justice*, revised between March and July.

1798   January: *Memoirs of the Author of 'A Vindication of the Rights of Woman'* published. May: Irish rebellion.

1799   December: Godwin's novel *St Leon* published.

1800   June–August: Visits John Philpott Curran in Ireland. December: His play *Antonio* performed.

1801   May: Meets Mary Jane Clairmont. June: His *Reply to Parr* published. October: Truce between Britain and France. November: Godwin's application for a passport to visit France rejected. December: Marries Mary Jane Clairmont.

1802   Napoleon becomes consul for life.

1803   March: Birth of William Godwin junior. May: Resumption of war with France.

1804   Napoleon declared emperor.

1805   February: His novel *Fleetwood* published. June: The Godwins open a children's bookshop. He writes a series of books for schools under several pseudonyms over the next six years. October: Battle of Trafalgar.

1807   Bookshop moves to Skinner Street, Strand. December: His tragedy *Faulkener* performed.

1812   October: Meets Percy Bysshe Shelley in London.

1813   January: Meets the utopian philanthropist Robert Owen.

1814   April: Napoleon abdicates. July: Shelley absconds to France with Mary Shelley and Godwin's stepdaughter Jane Clairmont.

1815   March: Napoleon escapes from Elba. June: Battle of Waterloo.

1816   April: Journey to Scotland, meets Walter Scott. October: Fanny Godwin commits suicide. 7 December: Suicide of Shelley's wife, Harriet. 30 December: Shelley and Mary Godwin marry and Godwin visits them, acknowledging Mary for the first time since July 1814.

1817   December: His novel *Mandeville* published.

1819   March: Civil suit brought against him for non-payment of rent; the court case drags on until 1823. August: Peterloo massacre in Manchester.

1820   November: *Of Population* published, being a reply to Thomas Malthus' *Essay on Population*, first published in 1798 but substantially revised for a second edition in 1803, and republished in 1817 with further changes.

1822   July: Shelley drowns.

1824   February: Volume I of Godwin's *History of the Commonwealth* published, with subsequent volumes in 1826, 1827, and 1828.

1825   Declared bankrupt and leaves Skinner Street shop.

1830   March: His novel *Cloudesley* published.

1831   February: Publishes *Thoughts on Man, his Nature, Productions and Discoveries*, his first major philosophical work since *The Enquirer* (1798).

1832   Reform Act passed by Parliament and receives royal assent. September: Death of William Godwin junior from cholera. October: Drafts a prospectus for a new edition of *Political Justice*.

1833   February: His novel *Deloraine* published. April: After lobbying the prime minister Lord Melbourne, Godwin is offered the post of yeoman usher in the Exchequer, which provides lodgings in New Palace Yard and a stipend.

1834   June: *Lives of the Necromancers* published.

1836   26 March: Godwin makes the last entry in his diary. 7 April: William Godwin dies.

AN ENQUIRY CONCERNING
POLITICAL JUSTICE
AND ITS INFLUENCE ON
GENERAL VIRTUE AND HAPPINESS

PREFACE

FEW works of literature are held in greater estimation, than those which treat in a methodical and elementary way of the principles of science. But the human mind in every enlightened age is progressive; and the best elementary treatises after a certain time are reduced in their value by the operation of subsequent discoveries. Hence it has always been desired by candid enquirers, that preceding works of this kind should from time to time be superseded, and that other productions including the larger views that have since offered themselves, should be substituted in their place.

It would be strange if something of this kind were not desirable in politics, after the great change that has been produced in men's minds upon this subject, and the light that has been thrown upon it by the recent discussions of America and France. A sense of the value of such a work, if properly executed, was the motive which gave birth to these volumes. Of their execution the reader must judge.

Authors who have formed the design of superseding the works of their predecessors, will be found, if they were in any degree equal to the design, not merely to have collected the scattered information that had been produced upon the subject, but to have increased the science with the fruit of their own meditations. In the following work principles will occasionally be found, which it will not be just to reject without examination, merely because they are new. It was impossible perseveringly to reflect upon so prolific a science, and a science which may be said to be yet in its infancy, without being led into ways of thinking that were in some degree uncommon.

Another argument in favour of the utility of such a work was frequently in the author's mind, and therefore ought to be mentioned. He conceived politics to be the proper vehicle of a liberal morality. That description of ethics deserves to be held in slight estimation, which seeks only to regulate our conduct in articles of particular and personal concern, instead of exciting our attention to the general good of the species. It appeared sufficiently practicable to make of such a treatise, exclusively of its direct political use, an advantageous vehicle of moral improvement. He was accordingly desirous of producing a work, from the perusal of which no man should rise without being strengthened in habits of sincerity, fortitude and justice.

Having stated the considerations in which the work originated, it is proper to mention a few circumstances of the outline of its history. The sentiments it contains are by no means the suggestions of a sudden effervescence of fancy. Political enquiry had long held a foremost place in the writer's attention. It is now twelve years since he became satisfied, that monarchy was a species of government unavoidably corrupt. He owed this conviction to the political writings of Swift and to a perusal of the Latin historians.* Nearly at the same time he derived great additional instruction from reading the most considerable French writers upon the nature of man in the following order, *Système de la Nature*, Rousseau and Helvetius.* Long before he thought of the present work, he had familiarised to his mind the arguments it contains on justice, gratitude, rights of man, promises, oaths and the omnipotence of truth. Political complexity is one of the errors that take strongest hold on the understanding; and it was only by ideas suggested by the French revolution, that he was reconciled to the desirableness of a government of the simplest construction. To the same event he owes the determination of mind which gave existence to this work.

Such was the preparation which encouraged him to undertake the present treatise. The direct execution may be dismissed in a few words. It was projected in the month of May 1791: the composition was begun in the following September, and has therefore occupied a space of sixteen months. This period was devoted to the purpose with unremitted ardour.* It were to be wished it had been longer; but it seemed as if no contemptible part of the utility of the work depended upon its early appearance.

The printing of the following treatise, as well as the composition, was influenced by the same principle, a desire to reconcile a certain degree of dispatch with the necessary deliberation. The printing was for that reason commenced, long before the composition was finished. Some disadvantages have arisen from this circumstance. The ideas of the author became more perspicuous and digested, as his enquiries advanced. The longer he considered the subject, the more accurately he seemed to understand it. This circumstance has led him into a few contradictions. The principal of these consists in an occasional inaccuracy of language, particularly in the first book, respecting the word government. He did not enter upon the work, without being aware that government by its very nature counteracts the improvement of individual mind; but he understood the full meaning of this proposition more completely as he proceeded, and saw more distinctly into the nature of the remedy. This, and a few other defects, under a different mode of preparation would have been avoided. The candid reader will make a suitable allowance. The author judges upon a review, that these defects are such as not materially to injure the object of the work, and that more has been gained than lost by the conduct he has pursued.

The period in which the work makes its appearance is singular. The people of England have assiduously been excited to declare their loyalty, and to mark every man as obnoxious who is not ready to sign the Shibboleth of the constitution.* Money is raised by voluntary subscription to defray the expence of prosecuting men who shall dare to promulgate heretical opinions, and thus to oppress them at once with the enmity of government and of individuals. This was an accident wholly unforeseen when the work was undertaken; and it will scarcely be supposed that such an accident could produce any alteration in the writer's designs. Every man, if we may believe the voice of rumour, is to be prosecuted who shall appeal to the people by the publication of any unconstitutional paper or pamphlet; and it is added, that men are to be prosecuted for any unguarded words that may be dropped in the warmth of conversation and debate. It is now to be tried whether, in addition to these alarming encroachments upon our liberty, a book is to fall under the arm of the civil power, which, beside the advantage of having for one of its express objects the dissuading from all tumult and violence, is by its very nature an appeal to men of study and reflexion. It is to be tried whether a project is formed for suppressing the activity of mind, and putting an end to the disquisitions of science. Respecting the event in a personal view the author has formed his resolution. Whatever conduct his countrymen may pursue, they will not be able to shake his tranquillity. The duty he is most bound to discharge is the assisting the progress of truth; and if he suffer in any respect for such a proceeding, there is certainly no vicissitude that can befal him, that can ever bring along with it a more satisfactory consolation.

But, exclusively of this precarious and unimportant consideration, it is the fortune of the present work to appear before a public that is panic struck, and impressed with the most dreadful apprehensions of such doctrines as are here delivered. All the prejudices of the human mind are in arms against it. This circumstance may appear to be of greater importance than the other. But it is the property of truth to be fearless, and to prove victorious over every adversary. It requires no great degree of fortitude, to look with indifference upon the false fire of the moment, and to foresee the calm period of reason which will succeed.

JANUARY 7, 1793

CONTENTS

BOOK VI. OF OPINION CONSIDERED AS A SUBJECT OF POLITICAL INSTITUTION

BOOK VII. OF CRIMES AND PUNISHMENTS

BOOK I
OF THE IMPORTANCE OF POLITICAL INSTITUTIONS

CHAPTER I
INTRODUCTION

The subject proposed.—System of indifference—of passive obedience—of liberty.—System of liberty extended.

THE question which first presents itself in an enquiry concerning institution, relates to the importance of the topic which is made the subject of enquiry. All men will grant that the happiness of the human species is the most desirable object for human science to promote; and that intellectual and moral happiness or pleasure is extremely to be preferred to those which are precarious and transitory. The methods which may be proposed for the attainment of this object, are various. If it could be proved that a sound political institution was of all others the most powerful engine for promoting individual good, or on the other hand that an erroneous and corrupt government was the most formidable adversary to the improvement of the species, it would follow that politics was the first and most important subject of human investigation.

The opinions of mankind in this respect have been divided. By one set of men it is affirmed, that the different degrees of excellence ascribed to different forms of government are rather imaginary than real; that in the great objects of superintendance no government will eminently fail; and that it is neither the duty nor the wisdom of an honest and industrious individual to busy himself with concerns so foreign to the sphere of his industry. A second class, in adopting the same principles, have given to them a different turn. Believing that all governments are nearly equal in their merit, they have regarded anarchy as the only political mischief that deserved to excite alarm, and have been the zealous and undistinguishing adversaries of all innovation. Neither of these classes has of course been inclined to ascribe to the science and practice of politics a pre-eminence over every other.

But the advocates of what is termed political liberty have always been numerous. They have placed this liberty principally in two articles; the security of our persons, and the security of our property. They have perceived that these objects could not be effected but by the impartial administration of general laws, and the investing in the people at large a certain power sufficient to give permanence to this administration. They have pleaded, some for a less and some for a greater degree of equality among the members of the community; and they have considered this equality as infringed or endangered by enormous taxation, and the prerogatives and privileges of monarchs and aristocratical bodies.

But, while they have been thus extensive in the object of their demand, they seem to have agreed with the two former classes in regarding politics as an object of subordinate importance, and only in a remote degree connected with moral improvement. They have been prompted in their exertions rather by a quick sense of justice and disdain of oppression, than by a consciousness of the intimate connection of the different parts of the social system, whether as it relates to the intercourse of individuals, or to the maxims and institutes of states and nations.[1]

It may however be reasonable to consider whether the science of politics be not of somewhat greater value than any of these reasoners have been inclined to suspect. It may fairly be questioned, whether government be not still more considerable in its incidental effects, than in those intended to be produced. Vice, for example, depends for its existence upon the existence of temptation. May not a good government strongly tend to extirpate, and a bad one to increase the mass of temptation? Again, vice depends for its existence upon the existence of error. May not a good government by taking away all restraints upon the enquiring mind hasten, and a bad one by its patronage of error procrastinate the discovery and establishment of truth? Let us consider the subject in this point of view. If it can be proved that the science of politics is thus unlimited in its importance, the advocates of liberty will have gained an additional recommendation, and its admirers will be incited with the greater eagerness to the investigation of its principles.

---

[1] These remarks will apply to the English writers on politics in general, from Sydney and Locke to the author of the *Rights of Man*. The more comprehensive view has been perspicuously treated by Rousseau and Helvetius.*

CHAPTER II

HISTORY OF POLITICAL SOCIETY

Frequency of war—among the ancients—among the moderns—the French—the English.—Causes of war.—Penal laws.—Despotism.— Deduction.—Enumeration of arguments.

WHILE we enquire whether government is capable of improvement, we shall do well to consider its present effects. It is an old observation, that the history of mankind is little else than the history of crimes. War has hitherto been considered as the inseparable ally of political institution. The earliest records of time are the annals of conquerors and heroes, a Bacchus, a Sesostris, a Semiramis and a Cyrus.* These princes led millions of men under their standard, and ravaged innumerable provinces. A small number only of their forces ever returned to their native homes, the rest having perished of diseases, hardships and misery. The evils they inflicted, and the mortality introduced in the countries against which their expeditions were directed, were certainly not less severe than those which their countrymen suffered. No sooner does history become more precise, than we are presented with the four great monarchies, that is, with four successful projects, by means of bloodshed, violence and murder, of enslaving mankind. The expeditions of Cambyses against Egypt, of Darius against the Scythians, and of Xerxes against the Greeks,* seem almost to set credibility at defiance by the fatal consequences with which they were attended. The conquests of Alexander cost innumerable lives, and the immortality of Cæsar is computed to have been purchased by the death of one million two hundred thousand men.* Indeed the Romans, by the long duration of their wars, and their inflexible adherence to their purpose, are to be ranked among the foremost destroyers of the human species. Their wars in Italy endured for more than four hundred years, and their contest for supremacy with the Carthaginians two hundred.* The Mithridatic war* began with a massacre of one hundred and fifty thousand Romans, and in three single actions of the war five hundred thousand men were lost by the eastern monarch. Sylla, his ferocious conqueror, next turned his arms against his country, and the struggle between him and Marius* was attended with proscriptions, butcheries and murders that knew no restraint from mercy and humanity. The Romans, at length, suffered the penalty of their iniquitous deeds; and the world was vexed for three hundred years by the irruptions of Goths, Vandals, Ostrogoths, Huns, and innumerable hordes of barbarians.

I forbear to detail the victorious progress of Mahomet and the pious expeditions of Charlemagne.* I will not enumerate the crusades against the infidels, the exploits of Aurungzebe, Gengiskan and Tamerlane, or the extensive murders of the Spaniards in the new world.* Let us examine the civilized and favoured quarter of Europe, or even those countries of Europe which are thought most enlightened.

France was wasted by successive battles during a whole century, for the question of the Salic law, and the claim of the Plantagenets. Scarcely was this contest terminated, before the religious wars broke out, some idea of which we may form from the siege of Rochelle, where of fifteen thousand persons shut up eleven thousand perished of hunger and misery; and from the massacre of Saint Bartholomew, in which the numbers assassinated were forty thousand. This quarrel was appeased by Henry the fourth, and succeeded by the thirty years war in Germany for superiority with the house of Austria, and afterwards by the military transactions of Louis the fourteenth.*

In England the war of Cressy and Agincourt only gave place to the civil war of York and Lancaster, and again after an interval to the war of Charles the first and his parliament.* No sooner was the constitution settled by the revolution, than we were engaged in a wide field of continental warfare by king William, the duke of Marlborough, Maria Theresa and the king of Prussia.*

And what are in most cases the pretexts upon which war is undertaken? What rational man could possibly have given himself the least disturbance for the sake of choosing whether Henry the sixth or Edward the fourth should have the style of king of England? What Englishman could reasonably have drawn his sword for the purpose of rendering his country an inferior dependency of France, as it must necessarily have been if the ambition of the Plantagenets had succeeded? What can be more deplorable than to see us first engage eight years in war rather than suffer the haughty Maria Theresa* to live with a diminished sovereignty or in a private station; and then eight years more to support the free-booter* who had taken advantage of her helpless condition?

The usual causes of war are excellently described by Swift. 'Sometimes the quarrel between two princes is to decide which of them shall dispossess a third of his dominions, where neither of them pretends to any right. Sometimes one prince quarrels with another, for fear the other should quarrel with him. Sometimes a war is entered upon because the enemy is too strong; and sometimes because he is too weak.

Sometimes our neighbours want the things which we have, or have the things which we want; and we both fight, till they take ours, or give us theirs. It is a very justifiable cause of war to invade a country after the people have been wasted by famine, destroyed by pestilence, or embroiled by factions among themselves. It is justifiable to enter into a war against our nearest ally, when one of his towns lies convenient for us, or a territory of land, that would render our dominions round and compact. If a prince sends forces into a nation where the people are poor and ignorant, he may lawfully put the half of them to death, and make slaves of the rest, in order to civilize and reduce them from their barbarous way of living. It is a very kingly, honourable and frequent practice, when one prince desires the assistance of another to secure him against an invasion, that the assistant, when he has driven out the invader, should seize on the dominions himself, and kill, imprison or banish the prince he came to relieve.'[1]

If we turn from the foreign transactions of states with each other, to the principles of their domestic policy, we shall not find much greater reason to be satisfied. A numerous class of mankind are held down in a state of abject penury, and are continually prompted by disappointment and distress to commit violence upon their more fortunate neighbours. The only mode which is employed to repress this violence, and to maintain the order and peace of society, is punishment. Whips, axes and gibbets, dungeons, chains and racks are the most approved and established methods of persuading men to obedience, and impressing upon their minds the lessons of reason. Hundreds of victims are annually sacrificed at the shrine of positive law and political institution.

Add to this the species of government which prevails over nine tenths of the globe, which is despotism: a government, as Mr. Locke justly observes, altogether 'vile and miserable,' and 'more to be deprecated than anarchy itself.'[2]

This account of the history and state of man is not a declamation, but an appeal to facts. He that considers it cannot possibly regard political

[1] Gulliver's Travels, Part IV. Ch. v.*
[2] Locke on Government, Book I. Ch. i. §. 1; and Book II. Ch. vii. §. 91. The words in the last place are: 'Wherever any two men are, who have no standing rule and common judge to appeal to on earth for the determination of controversies of right betwixt them, there they are still in *the state of nature*, and under all the inconveniences of it, with only this woeful difference to the subject, &c.'
Most of the above arguments may be found more at large in Burke's Vindication of Natural Society;* a treatise in which the evils of the existing political institutions are displayed with incomparable force of reasoning and lustre of eloquence, while the intention of the author was to shew that these evils were to be considered as trivial.

disquisition as a trifle, and government as a neutral and unimportant concern. I by no means call upon the reader implicitly to admit that these evils are capable of remedy, and that wars, executions and despotism can be extirpated out of the world. But I call upon him to consider whether they may be remedied. I would have him feel that civil policy is a topic upon which the severest investigation may laudably be employed.

If government be a subject, which, like mathematics, natural philosophy and morals, admits of argument and demonstration, then may we reasonably hope that men shall some time or other agree respecting it. If it comprehend every thing that is most important and interesting to man, it is probable that, when the theory is greatly advanced, the practice will not be wholly neglected. Men may one day feel that they are partakers of a common nature, and that true freedom and perfect equity, like food and air, are pregnant with benefit to every constitution. If there be the faintest hope that this shall be the final result, then certainly no subject can inspire to a sound mind such generous enthusiasm, such enlightened ardour and such invincible perseverance.

The probability of this improvement will be sufficiently established, if we consider, FIRST, that the moral characters of men are the result of their perceptions: and, SECONDLY, that of all the modes of operating upon mind government is the most considerable. In addition to these arguments it will be found, THIRDLY, that the good and ill effects of political institution are not less conspicuous in detail than in principle; and, FOURTHLY, that perfectibility is one of the most unequivocal characteristics of the human species, so that the political, as well as the intellectual state of man, may be presumed to be in a course of progressive improvement.

CHAPTER III

THE MORAL CHARACTERS OF MEN ORIGINATE IN THEIR PERCEPTIONS

No innate principles.—Objections to this assertion—from the early actions of infants—from the desire of self-preservation—from self-love—from pity—from the vices of children—tyranny—sullenness.—Conclusion.

WE bring into the world with us no innate principles: consequently we are neither virtuous nor vicious as we first come into existence. No truth can be more evident than this, to any man who will yield the subject an impartial consideration. Every principle is a proposition. Every proposition consists in the connection of at least two distinct ideas, which are affirmed to agree or disagree with each other. If therefore the principles be innate, the ideas must be so too. But nothing can be more incontrovertible, than that we do not bring pre-established ideas into the world with us.

Let the innate principle be, that virtue is a rule to which we are obliged to conform. Here are three great and leading ideas, not to mention subordinate ones, which it is necessary to form, before we can so much as understand the proposition.

What is virtue? Previously to our forming an idea corresponding to this general term, it seems necessary that we should have observed the several features by which virtue is distinguished, and the several subordinate articles of right conduct, that taken together, constitute that mass of practical judgments to which we give the denomination of virtue. Virtue may perhaps be defined, that species of operations of an intelligent being, which conduces to the benefit of intelligent beings in general, and is produced by a desire of that benefit. But taking for granted the universal admission of this definition, and this is no very defensible assumption, how widely have people of different ages and countries disagreed in the application of this general conception to particulars? a disagreement by no means compatible with the supposition that the sentiment is itself innate.

The next innate idea included in the above proposition, is that of a rule or standard, a generical measure with which individuals are to be compared, and their conformity or disagreement with which is to determine their value.

Lastly, there is the idea of obligation, its nature and source, the obliger and the sanction, the penalty and the reward.

Who is there in the present state of scientifical improvement, that will believe that this vast chain of perceptions and notions is something that we bring into the world with us, a mystical magazine, shut up in the human embryo, whose treasures are to be gradually unfolded as circumstances shall require? Who does not perceive that they are regularly generated in the mind by a series of impressions, and digested and arranged by association and reflexion?

Experience has by many been supposed adverse to these reasonings: but it will upon examination be found to be perfectly in harmony with them. The child at the moment of his birth is totally unprovided with ideas, except such as his mode of existence in the womb may have supplied. His first impressions are those of pleasure and pain. But he has no foresight of the tendency of any action to obtain either the one or the other, previously to experience.

A certain irritation of the palm of the hand will produce that contraction of the fingers, which accompanies the action of grasping. This contraction will at first be unaccompanied with design, the object will be grasped without any intention to retain it, and let go again without thought or observation. After a certain number of repetitions, the nature of the action will be perceived; it will be performed with a consciousness of its tendency; and even the hand stretched out upon the approach of any object that is desired. Present to the child, thus far instructed, a lighted candle. The sight of it will produce a pleasurable state of the organs of perception. He will stretch out his hand to the flame, and will have no apprehension of the pain of burning till he has felt the sensation.

At the age of maturity, the eyelids instantaneously close, when any substance, from which danger is apprehended, is advanced towards them; and this action is so spontaneous, as to be with great difficulty prevented by a grown person, though he should explicitly desire it. In infants there is no such propensity; and an object may be approached to their organs, however near and however suddenly, without producing this effect. Frowns will be totally indifferent to a child, who has never found them associated with the effects of anger. Fear itself is a species of foresight; and in no case exists till introduced by experience.

It has been said, that the desire of self-preservation is innate. I demand what is meant by this desire? Must we not understand by it, a preference of existence to non-existence? Do we prefer any thing but because it is apprehended to be good? It follows, that we cannot prefer existence, previously to our experience of the motives for preference it possesses. Indeed the ideas of life and death are exceedingly complicated, and very tardy in their formation. A child desires pleasure and loathes pain, long before he can have any imagination respecting the ceasing to exist.

Again, it has been said, that self-love is innate. But there cannot be an error more easy of detection. By the love of self we understand the approbation of pleasure, and dislike of pain: but this is only the faculty of perception under another name. Who ever denied that man was a percipient being? Who ever dreamed that there was a particular instinct necessary to render him percipient?

Pity has sometimes been supposed an instance of innate principle; particularly as it seems to arise more instantaneously in young persons, and persons of little refinement, than in others. But it was reasonable to expect, that threats and anger, circumstances that have been associated with our own sufferings, should excite painful feelings in us in the case of others, independently of any laboured analysis. The cries of distress, the appearance of agony or corporal infliction, irresistibly revive the memory of the pains accompanied by those symptoms in ourselves. Longer experience and observation enable us to separate the calamities of others and our own safety, the existence of pain in one subject and of pleasure or benefit in others, or in the same at a future period, more accurately than we could be expected to do previously to that experience.

Such then is universally the subject of human institution and education. We bring neither virtue nor vice with us at our entrance into the world. But the seeds of error are ordinarily sown so early as to pass with superficial observers for innate.

Our constitution prompts us to utter a cry at the unexpected sensation of pain. Infants early perceive the assistance they obtain from the volition of others; and they have at first no means of inviting that assistance but by an inarticulate cry. In this neutral and innocent circumstance, combined with the folly and imbecility of parents and nurses, we are presented with the first occasion of vice. Assistance is necessary, conducive to the existence, the health and the mental sanity of the infant. Empire in the infant over those who protect him is unnecessary. If we do not withhold our assistance precisely at the moment when it ceases to be requisite, if our compliance or our refusal be not in every case irrevocable, if we grant any thing to impatience, importunity or obstinacy, from that moment we become parties in the intellectual murder of our offspring.

In this case we instil into them the vices of a tyrant; but we are in equal danger of teaching them the vices of a slave. It is not till very late that mankind acquire the ideas of justice, retribution and morality, and these notions are far from existing in the minds of infants. Of consequence, when we strike, or when we rebuke them, we risk at least the exciting in them a sense of injury, and a feeling of resentment. Above all, sentiments of this sort cannot fail to be awakened, if our action be accompanied with symptoms of anger, cruelty, harshness or caprice. The same imbecility, that led us to inspire them with a spirit of tyranny by yielding to their importunities, afterwards dictates to us an inconsistent and capricious conduct, at one time denying them as absurdly, as at another we gratified them unreasonably. Who, that has observed the consequences of this treatment, how generally these mistakes are committed, how inseparable they are in some degree from the wisest and the best, will be surprised at the early indications of depravity in children?[1]

From these reasonings it sufficiently appears, that the moral qualities of men are the produce of the impressions made upon them, and that there is no instance of an original propensity to evil. Our virtues and vices may be traced to the incidents which make the history of our lives, and if these incidents could be divested of every improper tendency, vice would be extirpated from the world. The task may be difficult, may be of slow progress, and of hope undefined and uncertain. But hope will never desert it; and the man who is anxious for the benefit of his species, will willingly devote a portion of his activity to an enquiry into the mode of effecting this extirpation in whole or in part, an enquiry which promises much, if it do not in reality promise every thing.

CHAPTER IV

THREE PRINCIPAL CAUSES OF MORAL IMPROVEMENT
CONSIDERED

I. LITERATURE

*Benefits Of Literature.—Examples.—Essential Properties Of Literature.—
Its Defects.*

II. EDUCATION

Benefits of education.—Causes of its imbecility.

III. POLITICAL JUSTICE

*Benefits of political institution.—Universality of its influence—proved by
the mistakes of society—origin of evil.*

THERE are three principal causes by which the human mind is advanced towards a state of perfection; literature, or the diffusion of knowledge through the medium of discussion, whether written or oral; education, or a scheme for the early impression of right principles upon the hitherto unprejudiced mind; and political justice, or the adoption of any principle of morality and truth into the practice of a community. Let us take a momentary review of each of these.

---

[1] The arguments of this chapter are for the most part an abstract, the direct ones from Locke on the Human Understanding, those which relate to experience from Hartley's Observations on Man, and those respecting education from the Emile of J. J. Rousseau.*

I. LITERATURE

FEW engines can be more powerful, and at the same time more salutary in their tendency, than literature. Without enquiring for the present into the cause of this phenomenon, it is sufficiently evident in fact, that the human mind is strongly infected with prejudice and mistake. The various opinions prevailing in different countries and among different classes of men upon the same subject, are almost innumerable; and yet of all these opinions only one can be true. Now the effectual way for extirpating these prejudices and mistakes seems to be literature.

Literature has reconciled the whole thinking world respecting the great principles of the system of the universe, and extirpated upon this subject the dreams of romance and the dogmas of superstition. Literature has unfolded the nature of the human mind, and Locke and others have established certain maxims respecting man, as Newton has done respecting matter,* that are generally admitted for unquestionable. Discussion has ascertained with tolerable perspicuity the preference of liberty over slavery; and the Mainwarings, the Sibthorpes, and the Filmers,* the race of speculative reasoners in favour of despotism, are almost extinct. Local prejudice had introduced innumerable privileges and prohibitions upon the subject of trade; speculation has nearly ascertained that perfect freedom is most favourable to her prosperity. If in many instances the collation of evidence have failed to produce universal conviction, it must however be considered, that it has not failed to produce irrefragable argument, and that falshood would have been much shorter in duration, if it had not been protected and inforced by the authority of political government.

Indeed, if there be such a thing as truth, it must infallibly be struck out by the collision of mind with mind. The restless activity of intellect will for a time be fertile in paradox and error; but these will be only diurnals, while the truths that occasionally spring up, like sturdy plants, will defy the rigour of season and climate. In proportion as one reasoner compares his deductions with those of another, the weak places of his argument will be detected, the principles he too hastily adopted will be overthrown, and the judgments, in which his mind was exposed to no sinister influence, will be confirmed. All that is requisite in these discussions is unlimited speculation, and a sufficient variety of systems and opinions. While we only dispute about the best way of doing a thing in itself wrong, we shall indeed make but a trifling progress; but, when we are once persuaded that nothing is too sacred to be brought to the touchstone of examination, science will advance with rapid strides. Men, who turn their attention to the boundless field of enquiry, and still more who recollect the innumerable errors and caprices of mind, are apt to imagine that the labour is without benefit and endless. But this cannot be the case, if truth at last have any real existence. Errors will, during the whole period of their reign, combat each other; prejudices that have passed unsuspected for ages, will have their era of detection; but, if in any science we discover one solitary truth, it cannot be overthrown.

Such are the arguments that may be adduced in favour of literature. But, even should we admit them in their full force, and at the same time suppose that truth is the omnipotent artificer by which mind can infallibly be regulated, it would yet by no means sufficiently follow that literature is alone adequate to all the purposes of human improvement. Literature, and particularly that literature by which prejudice is superseded, and the mind is strung to a firmer tone, exists only as the portion of a few. The multitude, at least in the present state of human society, cannot partake of its illuminations. For that purpose it would be necessary, that the general system of policy should become favourable, that every individual should have leisure for reasoning and reflection, and that there should be no species of public institution, which, having falshood for its basis, should counteract their progress. This state of society, if it did not precede the general dissemination of truth, would at least be the immediate result of it.

But in representing this state of society as the ultimate result, we should incur an obvious fallacy. The discovery of truth is a pursuit of such vast extent, that it is scarcely possible to prescribe bounds to it. Those great lines, which seem at present to mark the limits of human understanding, will, like the mists that rise from a lake, retire farther and farther the more closely we approach them. A certain quantity of truth will be sufficient for the subversion of tyranny and usurpation; and this subversion, by a reflected force, will assist our understandings in the discovery of truth. In the mean time, it is not easy to define the exact portion of discovery that must necessarily precede political melioration. The period of partiality and injustice will be shortened, in proportion as political rectitude occupies a principal share in our disquisition. When the most considerable part of a nation, either for numbers or influence, becomes convinced of the flagrant absurdity of its institutions, the whole will soon be prepared tranquilly and by a sort of common consent to supersede them.

II. EDUCATION

BUT, if it appear that literature, unaided by the regularity of institution and discipline, is inadequate to the reformation of the species, it may perhaps be imagined, that education, commonly so called, is the best of all subsidiaries for making up its defects. Education may have the advantage of taking mind in its original state, a soil prepared for culture, and as yet uninfested with weeds; and it is a common and a reasonable opinion, that the task is much easier to plant right and virtuous dispositions in an unprejudiced understanding, than to root up the errors that have already become as it were a part of ourselves. If an erroneous and vicious education be, as it has been shewn to be, the source of all our depravity, an education, deprived of these errors, seems to present itself as the most natural exchange, and must necessarily render its subject virtuous and pure.

I will imagine the pupil never to have been made the victim of tyranny or the slave of caprice. He has never been permitted to triumph in the success of importunity, and cannot therefore well have become restless, inconstant, fantastical or unjust. He has been inured to ideas of equality and independence, and therefore is not passionate, haughty and overbearing. The perpetual witness of a temperate conduct and reasonable sentiments, he is not blinded with prejudice, is not liable to make a false estimate of things, and of consequence has no immoderate desires after wealth, and splendour, and the gratifications of luxury. Virtue has always been presented to him under the most attractive form, as the surest medium of success in every honourable pursuit, the never-failing consolation of disappointment, and infinitely superior in value to every other acquisition.

It cannot be doubted that such an education is calculated to produce very considerable effects. In the world indeed the pupil will become the spectator of scenes very different from what his preconceived ideas of virtue might have taught him to expect. Let us however admit it to be possible so to temper the mind, as to render it proof against the influence of example and the allurements of luxury. Still it may be reasonable to doubt of the sufficiency of education. How many instances may we expect to find, in which a plan has been carried into execution, so enlightened, unremitted and ardent, as to produce these extraordinary effects? Where must the preceptor himself have been educated, who shall thus elevate his pupil above all the errors of mankind? If the world teach an implicit deference to birth and riches and accidental distinctions, he will scarcely be exempt from this deference. If the world be full of intrigue and rivalship and selfishness, he will not be wholly disinterested. If falshood be with mankind at large reduced to a system, recommended by the prudent, commanded by the magistrate, inforced by the moralist,[1] and practised under a thousand forms, the individual will not always have the simplicity to be sincere, or the courage to be true. If prejudice have usurped the feat of knowledge, if law and religion and metaphysics and government be surrounded with mystery and artifice, he will not know the truth, and therefore cannot teach it; he will not possess the criterion, and therefore cannot furnish it to another. Again; if a man thus mighty, thus accomplished, thus superior to rivalship and comparison, can be found, who will consent to the profanation of employing him in cultivating the mind of a boy, when he should be instructing the world?

Education, in the sense in which it has commonly been understood, though in one view an engine of unlimited power, is exceedingly incompetent to the great business of reforming mankind. It performs its task weakly and in detail. The grand principles that the inventor seeks in his machines, and the philosopher in investigating the system of the universe, are such, as from a few simple data are sufficient to the production of a thousand events. But the education I have been describing is the reverse of this. It employs an immense combination of powers, and an endless chain of causes for the production of a single specimen. No task, which is not in its own nature impracticable, can easily be supposed more difficult, than that of counteracting universal error, and arming the youthful mind against the contagion of general example. The strongest mind that proposed this as its object, would scarcely undertake the forming more than one, or at most a very small number,

---

[1] The following passage is extracted from Lord Kaimes,* late one of the judges of the kingdom of Scotland.

'Custom-house oaths now a-days go for nothing. Not that the world grows more wicked, but because nobody lays any stress upon them. The duty on French wine is the same in Scotland and in England. But as we cannot afford to pay this high duty, the permission underhand to pay Spanish duty for French wine, is found more beneficial to the revenue than the rigour of the law. The oath however must be taken that the wine we import is Spanish, to entitle us to the ease of the Spanish duty. Such oaths at first were highly criminal because directly a fraud against the public; but now that the oath is only exacted for form's sake, without any faith intended to be given or received, it becomes very little different from saying in the way of civility, "I am, sir, your friend, or your obedient servant." '—Loose Hints upon Education, Appendix, p. 362. Edinburgh, 1781.

Archdeacon Paley* in a work, the seventh edition of which lies before me, and which is used as a text book in the university of Cambridge, speaks thus:

'There are falsehoods which are not lies; that is, which are not criminal; as—a servant's denying his master, a prisoner's pleading not guilty, an advocate asserting the justice, or his belief of the justice of his client's cause. In such instances no confidence is destroyed, because none was reposed.' Principles of Moral and Political Philosophy, Book III. Part I. Chap. xv. London, 1790.

of pupils. Where can a remedy be found for this fundamental disadvantage? where but in political justice, that all comprehensive scheme, that immediately applies to the removal of counteraction and contagion, that embraces millions in its grasp, and that educates in one school the preceptor and the pupil?

III. POLITICAL JUSTICE

THE benefits of political justice will best be understood, if we consider society in the most comprehensive view, taking into our estimate the erroneous institutions by which the human mind has been too often checked in its career, as well as those well founded opinions of public and individual interest, which perhaps need only to be clearly explained, in order to their being generally received.

Now in whatever light it be considered, we cannot avoid perceiving, first, that political institution is peculiarly strong in that very point in which the efficacy of education was deficient, the extent of its operation. That it in some way influences our conduct will hardly be disputed. It is sufficiently obvious that a despotic government is calculated to render men pliant, and a free one resolute and independent. All the effects that any principle adopted into the practice of a community may produce, it produces upon a comprehensive scale. It creates a similar bias in the whole, or a considerable part of the society. The motive it exhibits, the stimulus it begets, are operative, because they are fitted to produce effect upon mind. They will therefore inevitably influence all to whom they are equally addressed. Virtue, where virtue is the result, will cease to be a task of perpetual watchfulness and contention. It will neither be, nor appear to be, a sacrifice of our personal advantage to disinterested considerations. It will render those the confederates, support and security of our rectitude, who were before its most formidable enemies.

Again, an additional argument in favour of the efficacy of political institutions, arises from the extensive influence which certain false principles, engendered by an imperfect system of society, have been found to exert. Superstition, an immoderate fear of shame, a false calculation of interest, are errors that have been always attended with the most extensive consequences. How incredible at the present day do the effects of superstition exhibited in the middle ages, the horrors of excommunication and interdict,* and the humiliation of the greatest monarchs at the feet of the pope, appear? What can be more contrary to European modes than that dread of disgrace, which induces the Bramin widows of Indostan* to destroy themselves upon the funeral pile of their husbands? What more horribly immoral than the mistaken idea which leads multitudes in commercial countries to regard fraud, falshood and circumvention as the truest policy? But, however powerful these errors may be, the empire of truth, if once established, would be incomparably greater. The man, who is enslaved by shame, superstition or deceit, will be perpetually exposed to an internal war of opinions, disapproving by an involuntary censure the conduct he has been most persuaded to adopt. No mind can be so far alienated from truth, as not in the midst of its degeneracy to have incessant returns of a better principle. No system of society can be so thoroughly pervaded with mistake, as not frequently to suggest to us sentiments of virtue, liberty and justice. But truth is in all its branches harmonious and consistent.

The recollection of this circumstance induces me to add as a concluding observation, that it may reasonably be doubted whether error could ever be formidable or long-lived, if government did not lend it support. The nature of mind is adapted to the perception of ideas, their correspondence and difference. In the right discernment of these is its true element and most congenial pursuit. Error would indeed for a time have been the result of our partial perceptions; but, as our perceptions are continually changing, and continually becoming more definite and correct, our errors would have been momentary, and our judgments have hourly approached nearer to the truth. The doctrine of transubstantiation,* the belief that men were really eating flesh when they seemed to be eating bread, and drinking human blood when they seemed to be drinking wine, could never have maintained its empire so long, if it had not been reinforced by civil authority. Men would not have so long persuaded themselves that an old man elected by the intrigues of a conclave of cardinals, from the moment of that election became immaculate and infallible, if the persuasion had not been maintained by revenues, endowments and palaces. A system of government, that should lend no sanction to ideas of fanaticism and hypocrisy, would presently accustom its subjects to think justly upon topics of moral worth and importance. A state, that should abstain from imposing contradictory and impracticable oaths, and thus perpetually stimulating its members to concealment and perjury, would soon become distinguished for plain dealing and veracity. A country, in which places of dignity and confidence should cease to be at the disposal of faction, favour and interest, would not long be the residence of servility and deceit.

These remarks suggest to us the true answer to an obvious objection, that might otherwise present itself, to the conclusion to which these principles appear to lead. It might be said, that an erroneous government can never afford an adequate solution for the existence of moral evil, since government was itself the production of human intelligence, and therefore, if ill, must have been indebted for its ill qualities to some wrong which had previous existence.

The proposition asserted in this objection is undoubtedly true. All vice is nothing more than error and mistake reduced into practice, and adopted as the principle of our conduct. But error is perpetually hastening to its own detection. Vicious conduct is soon discovered to involve injurious consequences. Injustice therefore by its own nature is little fitted for a durable existence. But government 'lays its hand upon the spring there is in society, and puts a stop to its motion.'[1] It gives substance and permanence to our errors. It reverses the genuine propensities of mind, and, instead of suffering us to look forward, teaches us to look backward for perfection. It prompts us to seek the public welfare, not in innovation and improvement, but in a timid reverence for the decisions of our ancestors, as if it were the nature of mind always to degenerate, and never to advance.

CHAPTER V

INFLUENCE OF POLITICAL INSTITUTIONS EXEMPLIFIED

Robbery and fraud, two great vices in society—originate, 1. in extreme poverty—2. in the ostentation of the rich—3. in their tyranny—rendered permanent—1. by legislation—2. by the administration of law—3. by the inequality of conditions.

THE efficacy of political institutions will be rendered still more evident, if we enquire into the history of the most considerable vices at present existing in society; and if it can be shewn that they derive their inveteracy from political institution.

Two of the greatest abuses relative to the interior policy of nations, which at this time prevail in the world, will be allowed to consist in the irregular transfer of property, either first by violence, or secondly by fraud. If among the inhabitants of any country there existed no desire in one individual to possess himself of the substance of another, or no desire so vehement and restless, as to prompt him to acquire it by

[1] Logan, Philosophy of History, p. 69.*

means inconsistent with order and justice; undoubtedly in that country guilt could hardly be known but by report. If every man could with perfect facility obtain the necessaries of life, and, obtaining them, feel no uneasy craving after its superfluities, temptation would lose its power. Private interest would visibly accord with public good; and civil society become all that poetry has feigned of the golden age. Let us enquire into the principles to which these evils owe their existence, and the treatment by which they may be alleviated or remedied.

First then it is to be observed, that, in the most refined states of Europe, the inequality of property has arisen to an alarming height. Vast numbers of their inhabitants are deprived of almost every accommodation that can render life tolerable or secure. Their utmost industry scarcely suffices for their support. The women and children lean with an insupportable weight upon the efforts of the man, so that a large family has in the lower order of life become a proverbial expression for an uncommon degree of poverty and wretchedness. If sickness or some of those casualties which are perpetually incident to an active and laborious life, be superadded to these burthens, the distress is yet greater.

It seems to be agreed that in England there is less wretchedness and distress than in most of the kingdoms of the continent. In England the poors' rates amount to the sum of two millions sterling per annum. It has been calculated that one person in seven of the inhabitants of this country derives at some period of his life assistance from this fund. If to this we add the persons, who, from pride, a spirit of independence, or the want of a legal settlement, though in equal distress, receive no such assistance, the proportion will be considerably increased.

I lay no stress upon the accuracy of this calculation; the general fact is sufficient to give us an idea of the greatness of the abuse. The consequences that result are placed beyond the reach of contradiction. A perpetual struggle with the evils of poverty, if frequently ineffectual, must necessarily render many of the sufferers desperate. A painful feeling of their oppressed situation will itself deprive them of the power of surmounting it. The superiority of the rich, being thus unmercifully exercised, must inevitably expose them to reprisals; and the poor man will be induced to regard the state of society as a state of war, an unjust combination, not for protecting every man in his rights and securing to him the means of existence, but for engrossing all its advantages to a few favoured individuals, and reserving for the portion of the rest want, dependence and misery.

A second source of those destructive passions by which the peace of society is interrupted, is to be found in the luxury, the pageantry and magnificence with which enormous wealth is usually accompanied. Human beings are capable of encountering with chearfulness considerable hardships, when those hardships are impartially shared with the rest of the society, and they are not insulted with the spectacle of indolence and ease in others, no way deserving of greater advantages than themselves. But it is a bitter aggravation of their own calamity, to have the privileges of others forced on their observation, and, while they are perpetually and vainly endeavouring to secure for themselves and their families the poorest conveniences, to find others revelling in the fruits of their labours. This aggravation is assiduously administered to them under most of the political establishments at present in existence. There is a numerous class of individuals, who, though rich, have neither brilliant talents nor sublime virtues; and, however highly they may prize their education, their affability, their superior polish and the elegance of their manners, have a secret consciousness that they possess nothing by which they can so securely assert their pre-eminence and keep their inferiors at a distance, as the splendour of their equipage, the magnificence of their retinue and the sumptuousness of their entertainments. The poor man is struck with this exhibition; he feels his own miseries; he knows how unwearied are his efforts to obtain a slender pittance of this prodigal waste; and he mistakes opulence for felicity. He cannot persuade himself that an embroidered garment may frequently cover an aching heart.

A third disadvantage that is apt to connect poverty with discontent consists in the insolence and usurpation of the rich. If the poor man would in other respects compose himself in philosophic indifference, and, conscious that he possesses every thing that is truly honourable to man as fully as his rich neighbour, would look upon the rest as beneath his envy, his neighbour will not permit him to do so. He seems as if he could never be satisfied with his possessions unless he can make the spectacle of them grating to others; and that honest self-esteem, by which his inferior might otherwise arrive at apathy, is rendered the instrument of galling him with oppression and injustice. In many countries justice is avowedly made a subject of solicitation, and the man of the highest rank and most splendid connections almost infallibly carries his cause against the unprotected and friendless. In countries where this shameless practice is not established, justice is frequently a matter of expensive purchase, and the man with the longest purse is proverbially victorious. A consciousness of these facts must be expected to render the rich little cautious of offence in his dealings with the poor, and to inspire him with a temper overbearing, dictatorial and tyrannical. Nor does this indirect oppression satisfy his despotism. The rich are in all such countries directly or indirectly the legislators of the state; and of consequence are perpetually reducing oppression into a system, and depriving the poor of that little commonage of nature as it were, which might otherwise still have remained to them.

The opinions of individuals, and of consequence their desires, for desire is nothing but opinion maturing for action, will always be in a great degree regulated by the opinions of the community. But the manners prevailing in many countries are accurately calculated to impress a conviction, that integrity, virtue, understanding and industry are nothing, and that opulence is every thing. Does a man, whose exterior denotes indigence, expect to be well received in society, and especially by those who would be understood to dictate to the rest? Does he find or imagine himself in want of their assistance and favour? He is presently taught that no merits can atone for a mean appearance. The lesson that is read to him is, Go home, enrich yourself by whatever means, obtain those superfluities which are alone regarded as estimable, and you may then be secure of an amicable reception. Accordingly poverty in such countries is viewed as the greatest of demerits. It is escaped from with an eagerness that has no leisure for the scruples of honesty. It is concealed as the most indelible disgrace. While one man chooses the path of undistinguishing accumulation, another plunges into expences which are to impose him upon the world as more opulent than he is. He hastens to the reality of that penury, the appearance of which he dreads; and, together with his property, sacrifices the integrity, veracity and character which might have consoled him in his adversity.

Such are the causes, that, in different degrees under the different governments of the world, prompt mankind openly or secretly to encroach upon the property of each other. Let us consider how far they admit either of remedy or aggravation from political institution. Whatever tends to decrease the injuries attendant upon poverty, decreases at the same time the inordinate desire and the enormous accumulation of wealth. Wealth is not pursued for its own sake, and seldom for the sensual gratifications it can purchase, but for the same reasons that ordinarily prompt men to the acquisition of learning, eloquence and skill, for the love of distinction and fear of contempt. How few would prize the possession of riches, if they were condemned to enjoy their equipage, their palaces and their entertainments in solitude, with no eye to wonder at their magnificence, and no sordid observer ready to convert that wonder into an adulation of the owner? If admiration were not generally deemed the exclusive property of the rich, and contempt the constant lacquey of poverty, the love of gain would cease to be an universal passion. Let us consider in what respects political institution is rendered subservient to this passion.

First then, legislation is in almost every country grossly the favourer of the rich against the poor. Such is the character of the game laws,* by which the industrious rustic is forbidden to destroy the animal that preys upon the hopes of his future subsistence, or to supply himself with the food that unsought thrusts itself in his path. Such was the spirit of the late revenue laws of France,* which in several of their provisions fell exclusively upon the humble and industrious, and exempted from their operation those who were best able to support it. Thus in England the land tax at this moment produces half a million less than it did a century ago, while the taxes on consumption have experienced an addition of thirteen millions per annum during the same period. This is an attempt, whether effectual or no, to throw the burthen from the rich upon the poor, and as such is an exhibition of the spirit of legislation. Upon the same principle robbery and other offences, which the wealthier part of the community have no temptation to commit, are treated as capital crimes, and attended with the most rigorous, often the most inhuman punishments. The rich are encouraged to associate for the execution of the most partial and oppressive positive laws. Monopolies and patents are lavishly dispensed to such as are able to purchase them. While the most vigilant policy is employed to prevent combinations of the poor to fix the price of labour, and they are deprived of the benefit of that prudence and judgment which would select the scene of their industry.

Secondly, the administration of law is not less iniquitous than the spirit in which it is framed. Under the late government of France the office of judge was a matter of purchase, partly by an open price advanced to the crown, and partly by a secret douceur paid to the minister. He, who knew best how to manage his market in the retail trade of justice, could afford to purchase the good will of its functions at the highest price. To the client justice was avowedly made an object of personal solicitation, and a powerful friend, a handsome woman, or a proper present, were articles of much greater value than a good cause. In England the criminal law is administered with tolerable impartiality so far as regards the trial itself; but the number of capital offences, and of consequence the frequency of pardons, open even here a wide door to favour and abuse. In causes relating to property the practice of law is arrived at such a pitch as to render all justice ineffectual. The length of our chancery suits, the multiplied appeals from court to court, the enormous fees of counsel, attornies, secretaries, clerks, the drawing of briefs, bills, replications and rejoinders, and what has sometimes been called the glorious uncertainty of the law, render it often more advisable to resign a property than to contest it, and particularly exclude the impoverished claimant from the faintest hope of redress. Nothing certainly is more practicable than to secure to all questions of controversy a cheap and speedy decision, which, combined with the independence of the judges and a few obvious improvements in the construction of juries, would insure the equitable application of general rules to all characters and stations.

Thirdly, the inequality of conditions usually maintained by political institution, is calculated greatly to enhance the imagined excellence of wealth. In the ancient monarchies of the east, and in Turkey at the present day, an eminent station could scarcely fail to excite implicit deference. The timid inhabitant trembled before his superior; and would have thought it little less than blasphemy, to touch the veil drawn by the proud satrap* over his inglorious origin. The same principles were extensively prevalent under the feudal system. The vassal, who was regarded as a sort of live stock upon the estate, and knew of no appeal from the arbitrary fiat of his lord, would scarcely venture to suspect that he was of the same species. This however constituted an unnatural and violent situation. There is a propensity in man to look farther than the outside; and to come with a writ of enquiry into the title of the upstart and the successful. In England at the present day there are few poor men who do not console themselves, by the freedom of their animadversions upon their superiors. The new-fangled gentleman is by no means secure against having his tranquillity disturbed by their surly and pointed sarcasms. This propensity might easily be encouraged, and made conducive to the most salutary purposes. Every man might, as was the case in certain countries upon record, be inspired with the consciousness of citizenship, and be made to feel himself an active and efficient member of the great whole. The poor man would then perceive, that, if eclipsed, he could not be trampled upon; and he would no longer be stung with the furies of envy, resentment and despair.

CHAPTER VI

HUMAN INVENTIONS CAPABLE OF PERPETUAL IMPROVEMENT

Perfectibility of man—instanced, first, in language.—Its beginnings.— Abstraction.—Complexity of language.—Second instance: alphabetical writing.—Hieroglyphics at first universal.—Progressive deviations.— Application.

IF we would form to ourselves a solid estimate of political, or indeed of any other science, we ought not to confine our survey to that narrow portion of things which passes under our own immediate inspection, and rashly pronounce every thing that we have not ourselves seen, to be impossible. There is no characteristic of man, which seems at present at least so eminently to distinguish him, or to be of so much importance in every branch of moral science, as his perfectibility. Let us carry back our minds to man in his original state, a being capable of impressions and knowledge to an unbounded extent, but not having as yet received the one or cultivated the other; and let us contrast this being with all that science and genius have effected: and from hence we may form some idea what it is of which human nature is capable. It is to be remembered, that this being did not as now derive assistance from the communications of his fellows, nor had his feeble and crude conceptions assisted by the experience of successive centuries; but that in the state we are figuring all men were equally ignorant. The field of improvement was before them, but for every step in advance they were to be indebted to their untutored efforts. Nor is it of any consequence whether such was actually the progress of mind, or whether, as others teach, the progress was abridged, and man was immediately advanced half way to the end of his career by the interposition of the author of his nature. In any case it is an allowable and no unimproving speculation, to consider mind as it is in itself, and to enquire what would have been its history, if, immediately upon its production, it had been left to be acted upon by those ordinary laws of the universe with whose operation we are acquainted.

One of the acquisitions most evidently requisite as a preliminary to our present improvements is that of language. But it is impossible to conceive of an acquisition, that must have been in its origin more different from what at present it is found, or that less promised that copiousness and refinement it has since exhibited.

Its beginning was probably from those involuntary cries, which infants for example are found to utter in the earliest stages of their existence, and which, previously to the idea of exciting pity or procuring assistance, spontaneously arise from the operation of pain upon our animal frame. These cries, when actually uttered, become a subject of perception to him by whom they are uttered; and, being observed to be constantly associated with certain preliminary impressions and to excite the idea of those impressions in the hearer, may afterwards be repeated from reflection and the desire of relief. Eager desire to communicate any information to another, will also prompt us to utter some simple sound for the purpose of exciting attention: this sound will probably frequently recur to organs unpractised to variety, and will at length stand as it were by convention for the information intended to be conveyed. But the distance is extreme from these simple modes of communication, which we possess in common with some of the inferior animals, to all the analysis and abstraction which languages require.

Abstraction indeed, though as it is commonly understood it be one of the sublimest operations of mind, is in some sort coeval with and inseparable from the existence of mind. The next step to simple perception is that of comparison, or the coupling together of two ideas and the perception of their resemblances and differences. Without comparison there can be no preference, and without preference no action: though it must be acknowledged, that this comparison is an operation that may be performed by the mind without adverting to its nature, and that neither the brute nor the savage has any consciousness of the several steps of the intellectual progress. Comparison immediately leads to imperfect abstraction. The sensation of to-day is classed, if similar, with the sensation of yesterday, and an inference is made respecting the conduct to be adopted. Without this degree of abstraction the faint dawnings of language already described could never have existed. Abstraction, which was necessary to the first existence of language, is again assisted in its operations by language. That generalisation, which is implied in the very notion of thought, being thus embodied and rendered palpable, makes the mind acquainted with its own powers and creates a restless desire after farther progress.

But, though it be by no means impossible, to trace the causes that concurred to the production of language, and to prove them adequate to their effect, it does not the less appear that this is an acquisition of slow growth and inestimable value. The very steps, were we to pursue them, would appear like an endless labyrinth. The distance is immeasurable between the three or four vague and inarticulate sounds uttered by animals, and the copiousness of lexicography or the regularity of grammar. The general and special names by which things are at first complicated and afterwards divided, the names by which properties are separated from their substances and powers from both, the comprehensive distribution of parts of speech, verbs, adjectives and particles, the inflexions of words by which the change of their terminations changes their meaning through a variety of shadings, their concords and their governments, all of them present us with such a boundless catalogue of science, that he, who on the one hand did not know that the boundless task had been actually performed, or who on the other was not intimately acquainted with the progressive nature of mind, would pronounce the accomplishment of them impossible.

A second invention, well calculated to impress us with a sense of the progressive nature of man, is that of alphabetical writing. Hieroglyphical or picture writing appears at some time to have been universal, and the difficulty of conceiving the gradation from this to alphabetical is so great, as to have induced Hartley,* one of the most acute of all philosophical writers, to have recourse to miraculous interposition as the only adequate solution. In reality no problem can be imagined more operose, than that of decomposing the sounds of words into four and twenty simple elements or letters, and again finding these elements in all other words. When we have examined the subject a little more closely, and perceived the steps by which this labour was accomplished, perhaps the immensity of the labour will rather gain upon us, as he that shall have counted a million of units, will have a vaster idea upon the subject, than he that only considers them in the gross.

In China hieroglyphical writing has never been superseded by alphabetical, and this from the very nature of their language, which is considerably monosyllabic, the same found being made to signify a great variety of objects, by means of certain shadings of tone too delicate for any alphabet to be able to represent. They have however two kinds of writing, one for the learned, and another for the vulgar. The learned adhere closely to their hieroglyphical writing, representing every word by its corresponding picture; but the vulgar are frequent in their deviations from it.

Hieroglyphical writing and speech may indeed be considered in the first instance as two languages, running parallel to each other, but with no necessary connection. The picture and the word each of them represent the idea, one as immediately as the other. But, though independent, they will become accidentally associated; the picture at first imperfectly, and afterwards more constantly suggesting the idea of its correspondent sound. It is in this manner that the mercantile classes of China began to corrupt, as it is styled, their hieroglyphical writing. They had a word suppose of two syllables to write. The character appropriate to that word they were not acquainted with, or it failed to suggest itself to their memory. Each of the syllables however was a distinct word in the language, and the characters belonging to them perfectly familiar. The expedient that suggested itself was to write these two characters with a mark signifying their union, though in reality the characters had hitherto been appropriated to ideas of a different sort, wholly unconnected with that now intended to be conveyed. Thus a sort of rebus or chararde was produced. In other cases the word, though monosyllabic, was capable of being divided into two sounds, and the same process was employed. This is a first step towards alphabetical analysis. Some word, such as the interjection *O!* or the particle *A* is already a sound perfectly simple, and thus furnishes a first stone to the edifice. But, though these ideas may perhaps present us with a faint view of the manner in which an alphabet was produced, yet the actual production of a complete alphabet is perhaps of all human discoveries, that which required the most persevering reflection, the luckiest concurrence of circumstances, and the most patient and gradual progress.

Let us however suppose man to have gained the two first elements of knowledge, speaking and writing; let us trace him through all his subsequent improvements, through whatever constitutes the inequality between Newton and the ploughman, and indeed much more than this, since the most ignorant ploughman in civilised society is infinitely different from what he would have been, when stripped of all the benefits he has derived from literature and the arts. Let us survey the earth covered with the labours of man, houses, inclosures, harvests, manufactures, instruments, machines, together with all the wonders of painting, poetry, eloquence and philosophy.

Such was man in his original state, and such is man as we at present behold him. Is it possible for us to contemplate what he has already done, without being impressed with a strong presentiment of the improvements he has yet to accomplish? There is no science that is not capable of additions; there is no art that may not be carried to a still higher perfection. If this be true of all other sciences, why not of morals? If this be true of all other arts, why not of social institution? The very conception of this as possible, is in the highest degree encouraging. If we can still farther demonstrate it to be a part of the natural and regular progress of mind, our confidence and our hopes will then be complete. This is the temper with which we ought to engage in the study of political truth. Let us look back, that we may profit by the experience of mankind; but let us not look back, as if the wisdom of our ancestors was such as to leave no room for future improvement.

CHAPTER VII

OF THE OBJECTION TO THESE PRINCIPLES FROM THE INFLUENCE OF CLIMATE

PART I
OF MORAL AND PHYSICAL CAUSES

The question stated.—Provinces of sensation and reflection.—Moral causes frequently mistaken for physical.—Superiority of the former evident from the varieties of human character.—Operation of physical causes rare.—Fertility of reflection.—Physical causes in the first instance superior, afterwards moral.—Objection from the effect of breed in animals.—Conclusion.

THERE are certain propositions which may be considered indifferently, either as corollaries flowing from the principles already established, or as a source of new arguments against the validity of those principles. In the first view they are entitled to a clear and perspicuous statement, and in the second to a mature examination. For example:

The causes which appear to operate upon the human mind may be divided into two classes; perceptions, which are rendered directly a subject of reasoning, and regarded by the intellect as inducements to action; and perceptions, which act indirectly upon the mind, by rendering the animal frame gay, vigorous and elastic, or on the contrary sluggish, morbid and inactive. According to the system already established, the former of these are to be regarded as the whole, the latter being so comparatively inefficient and subordinate as to stand in the estimate as almost nothing. To many reasoners however they have by no means appeared of so trivial importance, and it may not be useless to examine for a moment the ideas they have formed, and the reasons which have induced them to ascribe so much to the meanest branch of the human constitution.

Impressions upon our senses may act either as physical or moral causes. Indisposition of the body operates upon the mind principally in the first of these ways, seeming without any formal deliberation of the understanding to incline us to dissatisfaction and indolence.

Corporal punishment affects us principally in the latter mode, since, though it directly introduces a painful state of the mind, it influences our conduct, only as it is reflected upon by the understanding, and converted into a motive of action.

It may be a curious speculation to examine how far these classes are distinct from each other. It cannot be denied but that sensation is of some moment in the affair. It possesses the initiative. It is that from which all the intellects with which we are acquainted date their operations. Its first effect upon mind does in the majority of cases precede reflection and choice. In some cases the impressions upon our senses are foreseen by us, and may consequently be resisted in the outset. But it would be a contradiction to affirm that they can always be foreseen. Foresight is itself the offspring of experience.

Meanwhile, though they can only in particular instances be foreseen, and of consequence completely forestalled, yet much of their effect is in all cases to be ascribed to deliberation and choice. 'I feel a painful sensation, and I persuade myself that it is wiser to submit, and thus cherish and second its influence, than to resist. I conceive myself unfortunate, oppressed by a combination of unfavourable accidents, and am rendered by this conception gloomy, discontented and wretched. I satisfy myself that my situation is such as to render exertion unreasonable, and believe that the attempt would produce nothing but abortive and fruitless torture. I remain listless, sluggish and inactive.'

How different would be the sum of my situation, if I were animated by sentiments of chearfulness, industry and courage? It has been said 'that a rainy day has been known to convert a man of valour into a coward.' How easily would this external disadvantage have been surmounted, if his mind had been more full of the benefits to arise from his valour, if the rainy day had been put in the balance with his wife and children, the most illustrious rewards to be bestowed upon himself, and freedom and felicity to be secured to his country? 'Indigestion,' we are told, 'perhaps a fit of the tooth-ach, renders a man incapable of strong thinking and spirited exertion.' How long would these be able to hold out against a sudden and unexpected piece of intelligence of the most delightful nature?

When operations of an injurious nature are inflicted on the body, and are encountered by the mind with unalterable firmness, what is the degree of pain which in such instances is suffered? Was the language of Anaxarchus merely a philosophical rant, 'Beat on, tyrant! Thou mayest destroy the shell of Anaxarchus, but thou canst not touch Anaxarchus himself?'* How much pain was really endured by Mutius Scævola and archbishop Cranmer, when each steadily held his hand to be devoured by the flames?* How much is endured by the savage Indians, who sing in the midst of tortures, and sarcastically provoke their tormentors to more ingenious barbarity?

The truth that seems to result from these considerations is, that indisposition only becomes formidable in proportion as it is seconded by the consent of the mind; that our communication with the material universe is at the mercy of our choice; and that the inability of the understanding for intellectual exertion is principally an affair of moral consideration, existing only in the degree in which it is deliberately preferred.

'The hero of to-day,' we are told, 'shall by an indigestion or a rainy atmosphere be converted into a coward to-morrow.' Waving the consideration of how far this fact where it exists is in reality of a moral and intellectual nature, let us examine to what degree a principle of this sort is the true index of human actions. We have already established it as a fundamental, that there are no innate ideas. Of consequence, if men were principally governed by external circumstances such as that of atmosphere, their characters and actions would be much alike. The same weather, that made you a coward, would make me so too, and an army would be defeated by a fog. Perhaps indeed this catastrophe would be prevented by the impartiality of the moisture, in proportion as the enemy advanced, which he necessarily must do, into the same atmosphere.

Every thing that checks the uniformity of this effect, and permanently distinguishes the character of one man from that of another, is to be traced to the association of ideas. But association is of the nature of reasoning. The principal, the most numerous and lasting of our associations, are intellectual, not accidental, built upon the resemblances and differences of things, not upon the contingency of their occurring in any given time or place. It is thus that one man appears courageous and another cowardly, one man vigorous and another dull, under the same or nearly the same external circumstances.

In reality the atmosphere, instead of considerably affecting the mass of mankind, affects in an eminent degree only a small part of that mass. The majority are either above or below it; are either too gross to feel strongly these minute variations, or too busy to be at leisure to attend to them. It is only a few, whose treatment has been tender enough to imbue them with extreme delicacy, and whose faculties are not roused by strong and unintermitted incitements, who can be thus blindly directed. If it should be said 'that the weather indeed is too great a trifle to produce these consequences, but that there are pains and interruptions which scarcely any man can withstand;' it may be answered, that these occur too seldom to be mistaken for the efficient principles of human character, that the system which determines our proceedings rises from a different source, and ordinarily returns when the pain or interruption has subsided.

There can be no question more interesting than that which we are now considering. Upon our decision in this case it depends, whether those persons act wisely who prescribe to themselves a certain discipline and are anxious to enrich their minds with science, or whether on the contrary it be better to trust every thing to the mercy of events. Is it possible that we should not perceive from the very nature of the thing the advantages which the wise man possesses over the foolish one, and that the points in which they resemble will be as nothing compared to those in which they differ? In those particulars in which our conduct is directed merely by external impressions we resemble the inferior animals; we differ from them in the greater facility with which we arrange our sensations, and compare, prefer and judge.

Out of a single sensation a great variety of reflections may be generated. Let the thing perceived be a material substance of certain regular dimensions. I perceive that it has an upper and a lower surface, I can therefore conceive of it as divided. I can conceive of the parts into which it is formed as moving towards and from each other, and hence I acquire the ideas of distance and space. I can conceive of them as striking against each other, and hence I derive the notion of impenetrability, gravity and momentum, the slowness, rapidity and direction of motion. Let the sensation be a pain in the head. I am led to reflect upon its causes, its seat, the structure of the parts in which it resides, the inconvenience it imposes, the consequences with which it may be attended, the remedies that may be applied and their effects, whether external or internal, material or intellectual.

It is true that the infant and inexperienced mind cannot thus analyse and conjure up dissertations of philosophy out of its most superior, afterwards moral, trivial sensations. Such a capacity infers a long series of preceding impressions. Mind is in its infancy nearly what these philosophers describe, the creature of contingencies. But the farther it advances, the more it individualises. Each man has habits and prejudices that are properly his own. He lives in a little universe of his own creating, or he communicates with the omnipresent and eternal volume of truth. With these he compares the successive perceptions of his mind, and upon these depend the conclusions he draws and the conduct he observes. Hence it inevitably follows, that physical causes, though of some consequence in the history of man, sink into nothing, when compared with the great and inexpressible operations of reflection. They are the prejudices we conceive or the judgments we form, our apprehensions of truth and falshood, that constitute the true basis of distinction between man and man. The difference between savage and savage indeed, in the first generation of the human species and in perfect solitude, can only be ascribed to the different impressions made upon their senses. But this difference would be almost imperceptible. The ideas of wisdom and folly would never have entered the human mind, if men, like beasts, derived neither good nor evil from the reflections and discoveries of their companions and ancestors.

Hence we are furnished with an answer to the analogical argument from the considerable effects that physical causes appear to produce upon brutes. 'Breed for example appears to be of unquestionable importance to the character and qualifications of horses and dogs; why should we not suppose this or certain other brute and occult causes to be equally efficacious in the case of men? How comes it that the races of animals perhaps never degenerate, if carefully cultivated; at the same time that we have no security against the wisest philosopher's begetting a dunce?'

I answer, that the existence of physical causes cannot be controverted. In the case of man their efficacy is swallowed up in the superior importance of reflection and science. In animals on the contrary they are left almost alone. If a race of negroes were taken, and maintained each man from his infancy, except so far as was necessary for the propagation of the species, in solitude; or even if they were excluded from an acquaintance with the improvements and imaginations of their ancestors, though permitted the society of each other, the operation of breed might perhaps be rendered as conspicuous among them, as in the different classes of horses and dogs. But the ideas they would otherwise receive from their parents and civilised or half-civilised neighbours would be innumerable: and, if the precautions above mentioned were unobserved, all parallel between the two cases would cease.

Such is the character of man considered as an individual. He is operated upon by exterior causes immediately, producing certain effects upon him independently of the exercise of reason; and he is operated upon by exterior causes immediately, their impressions furnishing him with materials for reflection, and assuming the form of motives to act or to refrain from acting. But the latter of these, at least so far as relates to man in a civilised state, may stand for the whole. He that would change the character of the individual, would miserably misapply his efforts, if he principally sought to effect this purpose by the operations of heat and cold, dryness and moisture upon the animal frame. The true instruments of moral influence, are desire and aversion, punishment and reward, the exhibition of general truth, and the development of those punishments and rewards, which wisdom and error by the very nature of the thing constantly bring along with them.

PART II
OF NATIONAL CHARACTERS

Character of the priesthood.—All nations capable of liberty.—The assertion illustrated.—Experience favours these reasonings.—Means of introducing liberty.

As is the character of the individual, so may we expect to find it with nations and great bodies of men. The operations of law and political institution will be important and interesting, the operations of climate trifling and unworthy of notice. Thus there are particular professions, such as that of the priesthood, which must always operate to the production of a particular character.

Priests are upon all occasions accustomed to have their opinions listened to with implicit deference; they will therefore be imperious, dogmatical and impatient of opposition. Their success with mankind depends upon the opinion of their superior innocence; they will therefore be particularly anxious about appearances, their deportment will be grave and their manners formal. The frank and ingenuous sallies of mind they will be obliged to suppress; the errors and irregularities into which they may be drawn they will be studious to conceal. They are obliged at set intervals to assume the exterior of an ardent devotion; but it is impossible that this should at all times be free from occasional coldness and distraction. Their importance is connected with their real or supposed mental superiority over the rest of mankind; they must therefore be patrons of prejudice and implicit faith. Their prosperity depends upon the reception of particular opinions in the world; they must therefore be enemies to freedom of enquiry; they must have a bias upon their minds impressed by something different from the force of evidence. Particular moral causes may in some instances limit, perhaps supersede the influence of general ones, and render some men superior to the character of their profession; but, exclusively of such exceptions, priests of all religions, of all climates and of all ages will have a striking similarity of manners and disposition. In the same manner we may rest assured that free men in whatever country will be firm, vigorous and spirited in proportion to their freedom, and that vassals and slaves will be ignorant, servile and unprincipled.

The truth of this axiom has indeed been pretty universally admitted; but it has been affirmed to be 'impossible to establish a free government in certain warm and effeminate climates.'* To enable us to judge of the reasonableness of this affirmation, let us consider what process would be necessary in order to introduce a free government into any country.

The answer to this question is to be found in the answer to that other, whether freedom have any real and solid advantages over slavery? If it have, then our mode of proceeding respecting it ought to be exactly parallel to that we should employ in recommending any other benefit. If I would persuade a man to accept a great estate, supposing that possession to be a real advantage; if I would induce him to select for his companion a beautiful and accomplished woman, or for his friend a wise, a brave and disinterested man; if I would persuade him to prefer ease to pain, and gratification to torture, what more is necessary, than that I should inform his understanding, and make him see these things in their true and genuine colours? Should I find it necessary to enquire first of what climate he was a native, and whether that were favourable to the possession of a great estate, a fine woman, or a generous friend?

The advantages of liberty over slavery are not less real, though unfortunately they are less palpable, than in the cases just enumerated. Every man has a confused sense of these advantages, but he has been taught to believe that men would tear each other to pieces, if they had not priests to direct their consciences, and lords to consult for their subsistence, and kings to steer them in safety through the inexplicable dangers of the political ocean. But whether they be misled by these or other prejudices, whatever be the fancied terror that induces them quietly to submit to have their hands bound behind them, and the scourge vibrated over their heads, all these are questions of reason. Truth may be presented to them in such irresistible evidence, perhaps by such just degrees familiarised to their apprehension, as ultimately to conquer the most obstinate prepossessions. Let the press find its way into Persia or Indostan,* let the political truths discovered by the best of the European sages be transfused into their language, and it is impossible that a few solitary converts should not be made. It is the property of truth to spread; and, exclusively of great national convulsions, its advocates in each succeeding age will be somewhat more numerous than in that which went before. The causes, which suspend its progress, arise, not from climate, but from the watchful and intolerant jealousy of despotic sovereigns.

Let us suppose then that the majority of a nation by however slow a progress are convinced of the desirableness, or, which amounts to the same, the practicability of freedom. The supposition would be parallel, if we were to imagine ten thousand men of sound intellect, shut up in a madhouse, and superintended by a set of three or four keepers. Hitherto they have been persuaded, for what absurdity has been too great for human intellect to entertain? that they were destitute of reason, and that the superintendence under which they were placed was necessary for their preservation. They have therefore submitted to whips and straw and bread and water, and perhaps imagined this tyranny to be a blessing. But a suspicion is at length by some means propagated among them, that all they have hitherto endured has been an imposition. The suspicion spreads, they reflect, they reason, the idea is communicated from one to another through the chinks of their cells, and at certain times when the vigilance of their keepers has not precluded them from the pleasures of mutual society. It becomes the clear perception, the settled persuasion of the majority of the persons confined.

What will be the consequence of this opinion? Will the influence of climate prevent them from embracing the obvious means of their happiness? Is there any human understanding that will not perceive a truth like this, when forcibly and repeatedly presented? Is there a mind that will conceive no indignation at so horrible a tyranny? In reality the chains fall off of themselves, when the magic of opinion is dissolved. When a great majority of any society are persuaded to secure any benefit to themselves, there is no need of tumult or violence to effect it. The effort would be to resist reason, not to obey it. The prisoners are collected in their common hall, and the keepers inform them that it is time to return to their cells. They have no longer the power to obey. They look at the impotence of their late masters, and smile at their presumption. They quietly leave the mansion where they were hitherto immured, and partake of the blessings of light and air like other men.

Let us compare this theory with the history of mankind. If the theory be true, we may expect to find the inhabitants of neighbouring provinces in different states, widely discriminated by the influence of government, and little assimilated by resemblance of climate. Thus the Gascons are the gayest people in all France; but the moment we pass the Pyrenees, we find the serious and saturnine character of the Spaniard. Thus the Athenians were lively, penetrating and ingenious, but the Thebans unpolished, phlegmatic and dull.—It would be reasonable to expect that different races of men, intermixed with each other, but differently governed, would afford a strong and visible contrast. Thus the Turks are brave, open and sincere, but the modern Greeks mean, cowardly and deceitful.——Wandering tribes closely connected among themselves, and having little sympathy with the people with whom they reside, may be expected to have great similarity of manners. Their situation renders them conspicuous, the faults of individuals reflect dishonour upon the whole, and their manners will be particularly sober and reputable, unless they should happen to labour under so peculiar an odium as to render all endeavour after reputation fruitless. Thus the Armenians in the East are as universally distinguished among the nations with whom they reside, as the Jews in Europe; but the Armenians are as much noted for probity, as the Jews for extortion.——What resemblance is there between the ancient and the modern Greeks, between the old Romans and the present inhabitants of Italy, between the Gauls and the French? Diodorus Siculus describes the Gauls as particularly given to taciturnity, and Aristotle* affirms that they are the only warlike nation who are negligent of women.

If on the contrary climate were principally concerned in forming the characters of nations, we might expect to find heat and cold producing an extraordinary effect upon men, as they do upon plants and inferior animals. But the reverse of this appears to be the fact. Is it supposed that the neighbourhood of the sun renders men gay, fantastic and ingenious? While the French, the Greeks and the Persians have been remarkable for their gaiety, the Spaniards, the Turks and the Chinese are not less distinguished by the seriousness of their deportment. It was the opinion of the ancients that the northern nations were incapable of civilisation and improvement; but the moderns have found that the English are not inferior in literary eminence to any nation in the world. Is it asserted, that the northern nations are more hardy and courageous, and that conquest has usually travelled from that to the opposite quarter? It would have been truer to say that conquest is usually made by poverty upon plenty. The Turks, who from the deserts of Tartary invaded the fertile provinces of the Roman empire, met the Saracens half way, who were advancing with similar views from the no less dreary deserts of Arabia. In their extreme perhaps heat and cold may determine the characters of nations, of the negroes for example on one side and the Laplanders on the other. Not but that in this very instance much may be ascribed to the wretchedness of a sterile climate on the one hand, and to the indolence consequent upon a spontaneous fertility on the other. As to what is more than this, the remedy has not yet been discovered. Physical causes have already appeared to be powerful, till moral ones can be brought into operation.

Has it been alledged that carnivorous nations are endowed with the greatest courage? The Swedes, whose nutriment is meagre and sparing, have ranked with the most distinguished modern nations in the operations of war.

It is usually said, that northern nations are most addicted to wine, and southern to women. Admitting this observation in its full force, it would only prove that climate may operate upon the grosser particles of our frame, not that it influences those finer organs upon which the operations of intellect depend. But the truth of the first of these remarks may well be doubted. The Greeks appear to have been sufficiently addicted to the pleasures of the bottle. Among the Persians no character was more coveted than that of a hard drinker. It is easy to obtain any thing of the negroes, even their wives and children, in exchange for liquor.

As to women the circumstance may be accounted for from moral causes. The heat of the climate obliges both sexes to go half naked. The animal arrives sooner at maturity in hot countries. And both these circumstances produce vigilance and jealousy, causes which inevitably tend to inflame the passions.[1]

The result of these reasonings is of the utmost importance to him who speculates upon principles of government. It is of little consequence what discoveries may be made in moral and political science, if, when we have ascertained most accurately what are the intellectual requisites that lead to wisdom and virtue, a blind and capricious principle is to intrude itself, and taint all our conclusions. Accordingly there have been writers on the subject of government, who, admitting, and even occasionally declaiming with enthusiasm upon the advantages of liberty and the equal claims of mankind to every social benefit, have yet concluded that the corruptions of despotism and the usurpations of aristocracy were congenial to certain ages and divisions of the world, and under proper limitations entitled to our approbation.

But this hypothesis will be found incapable of holding out against a moment's serious reflection. Can there be any state of mankind that renders them incapable of the exercise of reason? Can there be a period in which it is necessary to hold the human species in a condition of pupillage? If there be, it seems but reasonable that their superintendents and

---

[1] The majority of instances in the three preceding pages are taken from Hume's Essay on National Characters,* where this subject is treated with much ability. Essays, Vol. I, Part I, Essay xxi.

guardians, as in the case of infants of another sort, should provide for the means of their subsistence without calling upon them for the exertions of manual industry. Wherever men are competent to look the first duties of humanity in the face, and to provide for their defence against the invasions of hunger and the inclemencies of the sky, there they will out of all doubt be found equally capable of every other exertion that may be necessary to their security and welfare. Present to them a constitution which shall put them into a simple and intelligible method of directing their own affairs, adjudging their contests among themselves, and cherishing in their bosoms a manly sense of dignity, equality and independence, and you need not doubt that prosperity and virtue will be the result.

The real enemies of liberty in any country are not the people, but those higher orders who profit by a contrary system. Infuse just views of society into a certain number of the liberally educated and reflecting members; give to the people guides and instructors; and the business is done. This however is not to be accomplished but in a gradual manner, as will more fully appear in the sequel. The error lies, not in tolerating the worst forms of government for a time, but in supposing a change impracticable, and not incessantly looking forward to its accomplishment.

CHAPTER VIII

OF THE OBJECTION TO THESE PRINCIPLES FROM THE INFLUENCE OF LUXURY

The objection stated.—Source of this objection.—Refuted from mutability— from mortality—from sympathy—from the nature of truth.—The probability of perseverance considered.

THERE is another proposition relative to the subject, is less to be considered as an assertion distinct in itself, than as a particular branch of that which has just been discussed; I mean the proposition which affirms, 'that nations like individuals are subject to the phenomena of youth and old age, and that, when a people by luxury and depravation of manners have sunk into decrepitude, it is not in the power of legislation to restore them to vigour and innocence.'

This idea has partly been founded upon the romantic notions of pastoral life and the golden age. Innocence is not virtue. Virtue demands the active employment of an ardent mind in the promotion of the general good. No man can be eminently virtuous, who is not accustomed to an extensive range of reflection. He must see all the benefits to arise from a disinterested proceeding, and must understand the proper method of producing those benefits. Ignorance, the slothful habits and limited views of uncultivated life have not in them more of true virtue, though they may be more harmless, than luxury, vanity and extravagance. Individuals of exquisite feeling, whose disgust has been excited by the hardened selfishness or the unblushing corruption which have prevailed in their own times, have recurred in imagination to the forests of Norway or the bleak and uncomfortable Highlands of Scotland in search of a purer race of mankind. This imagination has been the offspring of disappointment, not the dictate of reason and philosophy.

It may be true, that ignorance is nearer than prejudice to the reception of wisdom, and that the absence of virtue is a condition more hopeful than the presence of its opposite. In this case it would have been juster to compare a nation sunk in luxury, to an individual with confirmed habits of wrong, than to an individual whom a debilitated constitution was bringing fast to the grave. But neither would that comparison have been fair and equitable.

The condition of nations is more fluctuating, and will be found less obstinate in its resistance to a consistent endeavour for their improvement, than that of individuals. In nations some of their members will be less confirmed in error than others. A certain number will be only in a very small degree indisposed to listen to the voice of truth. This number will perpetually increase. Every new convert will be the means of converting others. In proportion as the body of disciples is augmented, the modes of attack upon the prejudices of others will be varied, and suited to the variety of men's tempers and prepossessions.

Add to this that generations of men are perpetually going off the stage, while other generations succeed. The next generation will not have so many prejudices to subdue. Suppose a despotic nation by some revolution in its affairs to become possessed of a free constitution. The children of the present race will be bred in more firm and independent habits of thinking; the suppleness, the timidity and the vicious dexterity of their fathers will give place to an erect mien, and a clear and decisive judgment. The partial and imperfect change of character which was introduced at first, will in the succeeding age become more unalloyed and complete.

Lastly, the power of social institutions changing the character of nations is very different from and infinitely greater than any power which can ordinarily be brought to bear upon a solitary individual. Large bodies of men, when once they have been enlightened and persuaded, act with more vigour than solitary individuals. They animate the mutual exertions of each other, and the united forces of example and shame urge them to perseverance. The case is not of that customary sort where the power of reason only is tried in curing any person of his errors; but is as if he should be placed in an entirely new situation. His habits are broken through, and his motives of action changed. Instead of being perpetually recalled to vicious practices by the recurrence of his former connections, the whole society receives an impulse from the same cause that acts upon any individual. New ideas are suggested, and the surprise of novelty conspires with the approbation of truth to prevent men from falling back into imbecility and languor.

The question may in reality be reduced to an enquiry, whether the human understanding can be made the recipient of truth, whether it be possible for an effort so strenuous to exist as to make men aware of their true interests. For let this be granted, and the consequence is inevitable. It has already sufficiently appeared, that whatever is politically right or politically wrong, must be in all cases of no trivial consequence to the welfare of mankind. Monarchy for example will by all men be acknowledged to be attended with many disadvantages. It acts upon insufficient and partial information, it generates intrigue, corruption, adulation and servility. If it could be proved, that it produced no advantages in equal proportion, and that its abolition would not lead to mischief, anarchy and disorder, is there a nation upon the face of the earth to whom these propositions were rendered palpable, that would endure to submit to it? Is there a nation upon the face of the earth, that would submit to the impositions of its administration, the wars it occasions, and the lavish revenues by which it is maintained, if they knew it to be merely an excrescence and a disease in the order of society?

But it has been farther alledged, that, even should a luxurious nation be prompted by intolerable grievances and notorious usurpation to assert the just principles of human society, they would be unable to perpetuate them, and would soon be led back by their evil habits to their former vices and corruption: that is, they would be capable of the heroic energy that should expel the usurper, but not of the moderate resolution that should prevent his return. They would rouse themselves so far from their lethargy as to assume a new character and enter into different views; but, after having for some time acted upon their convictions, they would suddenly become incapable of understanding the truth of their principles and feeling their influence.

Men always act upon their apprehensions of preferableness. There are few errors of which they are guilty, which may not be resolved into a narrow and inadequate view of the alternative presented for their choice. Present pleasure may appear more certain and eligible than distant good. But they never choose evil as apprehended to be evil. Wherever a clear and unanswerable notion of any subject is presented to their view, a correspondent action or course of actions inevitably follows. Having thus gained one step in the acquisition of truth, it cannot easily be conceived of as lost. A body of men, having detected the injurious consequences of an evil under which they have long laboured, and having shaken it off, will scarcely voluntarily restore the mischief they have annihilated. Nothing can reconcile them to the revival of falshood, which does not obliterate their present conviction of truth.

BOOK II
PRINCIPLES OF SOCIETY

CHAPTER I
INTRODUCTION

Nature of the enquiry.—Mode of pursuing it.—Distinction between society and government.

MR. Locke begins his celebrated Treatise of Government with a refutation of the patriarchal scheme of sir Robert Filmer; and, having thus cleared his ground, proceeds to observe, that 'he, that will not give just occasion to think that all government in the world is the product only of force and violence, and that men live together by no other rules but that of beasts, must of necessity find out another rise of government, and another original of political power.'[1]* Accordingly he proceeds through the greater part of his treatise to reason abstractedly upon the probable history of the early ages of mankind, and concludes that no legitimate government could be built upon any other foundation than that of an original contract.

It is to be suspected that this great man, friend as he was to the liberty and the interests of mankind, intrepid and sagacious in his search after truth, has been guilty of an oversight in the first step of the investigation.

There are two modes, according to which we may enquire into the origin of society and government. We may either examine them historically, that is, consider in what manner they have or ought to have begun, as Mr. Locke has done; or we may examine them philosophically, that is, consider the moral principles upon which they depend. The first of these subjects is not without its use; but the second is of a higher order and more essential importance. The first is a question of form; the second of substance. It would be of trivial consequence practically considered, from what source any form of society flowed, and by what mode its principles were sanctioned, could we be always secure of their conformity to the dictates of truth and justice.

It is farther necessary before we enter upon the subject carefully to distinguish between society and government. Men associated at first

---

[1] Book II. Chap. I § I.

for the sake of mutual assistance. They did not foresee that any restraint would be necessary, to regulate the conduct of individual members of the society, towards each other, or towards the whole. The necessity of restraint grew out of the errors and perverseness of a few. An acute writer has expressed this idea with peculiar felicity. 'Society and government,' says he, 'are different in themselves, and have different origins. Society is produced by our wants, and government by our wickedness. Society is in every state a blessing; government even in its best state but a necessary evil.'[1]*

CHAPTER II

OF JUSTICE

Connection of politics and morals.—Extent and meaning of justice.—Subject of justice: mankind.—Its distribution measured by the capacity of its subject—by his usefulness.—Family affection considered.—Gratitude considered.—Objections: from ignorance—from utility.—An exception stated.—Degrees of justice.—Application.—Idea of political justice.

FROM what has been said it appears, that the subject of the present enquiry is strictly speaking a department of the science of morals. Morality is the source from which its fundamental axioms must be drawn, and they will be made somewhat clearer in the present instance, if we assume the term justice as a general appellation for all moral duty.

That this appellation is sufficiently expressive of the subject will appear, if we consider for a moment mercy, gratitude, temperance, or any of those duties which in looser speaking are contradistinguished from justice. Why should I pardon this criminal, remunerate this favour, abstain from this indulgence? If it partake of the nature of morality, it must be either right or wrong, just or unjust. It must tend to the benefit of the individual, either without intrenching upon, or with actual advantage to the mass of individuals. Either way it benefits the whole, because individuals are parts of the whole. Therefore to do it is just, and to forbear it is unjust. If justice have any meaning, it is just that I should contribute every thing in my power to the benefit of the whole.

Considerable light will probably be thrown upon our investigation, if, quitting for the present the political view, we examine justice merely

[1] Common Sense, p. 1.

as it exists among individuals. Justice is a rule of conduct originating in the connection of one percipient being with another. A comprehensive maxim which has been laid down upon the subject is, 'that we should love our neighbour as ourselves.' But this maxim, though possessing considerable merit as a popular principle, is not modelled with the strictness of philosophical accuracy.

In a loose and general view I and my neighbour are both of us men; and of consequence entitled to equal attention. But in reality it is probable that one of us is a being of more worth and importance than the other. A man is of more worth than a beast; because, being possessed of higher faculties, he is capable of a more refined and genuine happiness. In the same manner the illustrious archbishop of Cambray* was of more worth than his chambermaid, and there are few of us that would hesitate to pronounce, if his palace were in flames, and the life of only one of them could be preserved, which of the two ought to be preferred.

But there is another ground of preference, beside the private consideration of one of them being farther removed from the state of a mere animal. We are not connected with one or two percipient beings, but with a society, a nation, and in some sense with the whole family of mankind. Of consequence that life ought to be preferred which will be most conducive to the general good. In saving the life of Fenelon, suppose at the moment when he was conceiving the project of his immortal Telemachus, I should be promoting the benefit of thousands, who have been cured by the perusal of it of some error, vice and consequent unhappiness. Nay, my benefit would extend farther than this, for every individual thus cured has become a better member of society, and has contributed in his turn to the happiness, the information and improvement of others.

Supposing I had been myself the chambermaid, I ought to have chosen to die, rather than that Fenelon should have died. The life of Fenelon was really preferable to that of the chambermaid. But understanding is the faculty that perceives the truth of this and similar propositions; and justice is the principle that regulates my conduct accordingly. It would have been just in the chambermaid to have preferred the archbishop to herself. To have done otherwise would have been a breach of justice.

Supposing the chambermaid had been my wife, my mother or my benefactor. This would not alter the truth of the proposition. The life of Fenelon would still be more valuable than that of the chambermaid; and justice, pure, unadulterated justice, would still have preferred that which was most valuable. Justice would have taught me to save the life of Fenelon at the expence of the other. What magic is there in the pronoun 'my,' to overturn the decisions of everlasting truth? My wife or my mother may be a fool or a prostitute, malicious, lying or dishonest. If they be, of what consequence is it that they are mine?

'But my mother endured for me the pains of child bearing, and nourished me in the helplessness of infancy.' When she first subjected herself to the necessity of these cares, she was probably influenced by no particular motives of benevolence to her future offspring. Every voluntary benefit however entitles the bestower to some kindness and retribution. But why so? Because a voluntary benefit is an evidence of benevolent intention, that is, of virtue. It is the disposition of the mind, not the external action, that entitles to respect. But the merit of this disposition is equal, whether the benefit was conferred upon me or upon another. I and another man cannot both be right in preferring our own individual benefactor, for no man can be at the same time both better and worse than his neighbour. My benefactor ought to be esteemed, not because he bestowed a benefit upon me, but because he bestowed it upon a human being. His desert will be in exact proportion to the degree, in which that human being was worthy of the distinction conferred. Thus every view of the subject brings us back to the consideration of my neighbour's moral worth and his importance to the general weal, as the only standard to determine the treatment to which he is entitled. Gratitude therefore, a principle which has so often been the theme of the moralist and the poet, is no part either of justice or virtue. By gratitude I understand a sentiment, which would lead me to prefer one man to another, from some other consideration than that of his superior usefulness or worth: that is, which would make something true to me (for example this preferableness),which cannot be true to another man, and is not true in itself.[1]

It may be objected, 'that my relation, my companion, or my benefactor will of course in many instances obtain an uncommon: portion of my regard: for, not being universally capable of discriminating the comparative worth of different men, I shall inevitably judge most favourably of him, of whose virtues I have received the most unquestionable proofs; and thus shall be compelled to prefer the man of moral worth whom I know, to another who may possess, unknown to me, an essential superiority.'

---

[1] This argument respecting justice is stated with great clearness in an Essay on the Nature of True Virtue, by the Rev. Jonathan Edwards.* 12mo. Dilly.

This compulsion however is founded only in the present imperfection of human nature. It may serve as an apology for my error, but can never turn error into truth. It will always remain contrary to the strict and inflexible decisions of justice. The difficulty of conceiving this is owing merely to our confounding the disposition from which an action is chosen, with the action itself. The disposition, that would prefer virtue to vice and a greater degree of virtue to a less, is undoubtedly a subject of approbation; the erroneous exercise of this disposition by which a wrong object is selected, if unavoidable, is to be deplored, but can by no colouring and under no denomination be converted into right.[1]

It may in the second place be objected, 'that a mutual commerce of benefits tends to increase the mass of benevolent action, and that to increase the mass of benevolent action is to contribute to the general good.' Indeed! Is the general good promoted by falshood, by treating a man of one degree of worth, as if he had ten times that worth? or as if he were in any degree different from what he really is? Would not the most beneficial consequences result from a different plan; from my constantly and carefully enquiring into the deserts of all those with whom I am connected, and from their being sure, after a certain allowance for the fallibility of human judgment, of being treated by me exactly as they deserved? Who can tell what would be the effects of such a plan of conduct universally adopted?

There seems to be more truth in the argument, derived chiefly from the unequal distribution of property, in favour of my providing in ordinary cases for my wife and children, my brothers and relations, before I provide for strangers. As long as providing for individuals belongs to individuals, it seems as if there must be a certain distribution of the class needing superintendence and supply among the class affording it, that each man may have his claim and resource. But this argument, if admitted at all, is to be admitted with great caution. It belongs only to ordinary cases; and cases of a higher order or a more urgent necessity will perpetually occur, in competition with which these will be altogether impotent. We must be severely scrupulous in measuring out the quantity of supply; and, with respect to money in particular, must remember how little is yet understood of the true mode of employing it for the public benefit.

Having considered the persons with whom justice is conversant, let us next enquire into the degree in which we are obliged to consult the

---

[1] See this subject more copiously treated in the following chapter.

good of others. And here I say, that it is just that I should do all the good in my power. Does any person in distress apply to me for relief? It is my duty to grant it, and I commit a breach of duty in refusing. If this principle be not of universal application, it is because, in conferring a benefit upon an individual, I may in some instances inflict an injury of superior magnitude upon myself or society. Now the same justice, that binds me to any individual of my fellow men, binds me to the whole. If, while I confer a benefit upon one man, it appear, in striking an equitable balance, that I am injuring the whole, my action ceases to be right and becomes absolutely wrong. But how much am I bound to do for the general weal, that is, for the benefit of the individuals of whom the whole is composed? Every thing in my power. What to the neglect of the means of my own existence? No; for I am myself a part of the whole. Beside, it will rarely happen but that the project of doing for others every thing in my power, will demand for its execution the preservation of my own existence; or in other words, it will rarely happen but that I can do more good in twenty years than in one. If the extraordinary case should occur in which I can promote the general good by my death, more than by my life, justice requires that I should be content to die. In all other cases, it is just that I should be careful to maintain my body and my mind in the utmost vigour, and in the best condition for service.[1]

I will suppose for example that it is right for one man to possess a greater portion of property than another, either as the fruit of his industry, or the inheritance of his ancestors. Justice obliges him to regard this property as a trust, and calls upon him maturely to consider in what manner it may best be employed for the increase of liberty, knowledge and virtue. He has no right to dispose of a shilling of it at the will of his caprice. So far from being entitled to well earned applause for having employed some scanty pittance in the service of philanthropy, he is in the eye of justice a delinquent if he withhold any portion from that service. Nothing can be more incontrovertible. Could that portion have been better or more worthily employed? That it could is implied in the very terms of the proposition. Then it was just it should have been so employed.—In the same manner as my property, I hold my person as a trust in behalf of mankind. I am bound to employ my talents, my understanding, my strength and my time for the production of the greatest quantity of general good. Such are the declarations of justice, so great is the extent of my duty.

---

[1] Vide Appendix to this chapter, No. I.

But justice is reciprocal. If it be just that I should confer a benefit, it is just that another man should receive it, and, if I withhold from him that to which he is entitled, he may justly complain. My neighbour is in want of ten pounds that I can spare. There is no law of political institution that has been made to reach this case, and to transfer this property from me to him. But in the eye of simple justice, unless it can be shewn that the money can be more beneficently employed, his claim is as complete, as if he had my bond in his possession, or had supplied me with goods to the amount.[1]

To this it has sometimes been answered, 'that there is more than one person, that stands in need of the money I have to spare, and of consequence I must be at liberty to bestow it as I please.' I answer, if only one person offer himself to my knowledge or search, to me there is but one. Those others that I cannot find belong to other rich men to assist (rich men, I say, for every man is rich, who has more money than his just occasions demand), and not to me. If more than one person offer, I am obliged to balance their fitness, and conduct myself accordingly. It is scarcely possible to happen that two men shall be of exactly equal fitness, or that I shall be equally certain of the fitness of the one as of the other.

It is therefore impossible for me to confer upon any man a favour, I can only do him a right. Whatever deviates from the law of justice, even I will suppose in the too much done in favour of some individual or some part of the general whole, is so much subtracted from the general stock, is so much of absolute injustice.

The inference most clearly afforded by the preceding reasonings, is the competence of justice as a principle of deduction in all cases of moral enquiry. The reasonings themselves are rather of the nature of illustration and example, and any error that may be imputed to them in particulars, will not invalidate the general conclusion, the propriety of applying moral justice as a criterion in the investigation of political truth.

Society is nothing more than an aggregation of individuals. Its claims and its duties must be the aggregate of their claims and duties, the one no more precarious and arbitrary than the other. What has the society a right to require from me? The question is already answered: every thing that it is my duty to do. Any thing more? Certainly not. Can they change eternal truth, or subvert the nature of men and their actions?

[1] A spirited outline of these principles is sketched in Swift's Sermon on Mutual Subjection.*

Can they make it my duty to commit intemperance, to maltreat or assassinate my neighbour?—Again. What is it that the society is bound to do for its members? Every thing that can contribute to their welfare. But the nature of their welfare is defined by the nature of mind. That will most contribute to it, which enlarges the understanding, supplies incitements to virtue, fills us with a generous consciousness of our independence, and carefully removes whatever can impede our exertions.

Should it be affirmed, 'that it is not in the power of any political system to secure to us these advantages,' the conclusion I am drawing will still be incontrovertible. It is bound to contribute every thing it is able to these purposes, and no man was ever yet found hardy enough to affirm that it could do nothing. Suppose its influence in the utmost degree limited, there must be one method approaching nearer than any other to the desired object, and that method ought to be universally adopted. There is one thing that political institutions can assuredly do, they can avoid positively counteracting the true interests of their subjects. But all capricious rules and arbitrary distinctions do positively counteract them. There is scarcely any modification of society but has in it some degree of moral tendency. So far as it produces neither mischief nor benefit, it is good for nothing. So far as it tends to the improvement of the community, it ought to be universally adopted.

APPENDIX, No. I
OF SUICIDE

Motives of suicide: 1. escape from pain—2. benevolence.—Martyrdom considered.

THIS reasoning will explain to us the long disputed case of suicide. 'Have I a right under any circumstances to destroy myself in order to escape from pain or disgrace?' Probably not. It is perhaps impossible to imagine a situation, that shall exclude the possibility of future life, vigour and usefulness. The motive assigned for escape is eminently trivial, to avoid pain, which is a small inconvenience; or disgrace, which is an imaginary evil. The example of fortitude in enduring them, if there were no other consideration, would probably afford a better motive for continuing to live.

'Is there then no case in which suicide is a virtue?' What shall we think of the reasoning of Lycurgus, who, when he determined upon a voluntary death, remarked, 'that all the faculties a rational being possessed were capable of a moral use, and that, after having spent his life in the service of his country, a man ought, if possible, to render his death a source of additional benefit?'* This was the motive of the suicide of Codrus, Leonidas and Decius.* If the same motive prevailed in the much admired suicide of Cato,* if he were instigated by reasons purely benevolent, it is impossible not to applaud his intention, even if he were mistaken in the application.

The difficulty is to decide in any instance whether the recourse to a voluntary death can overbalance the usefulness I may exert in twenty or thirty years of additional life. But surely it would be precipitate to decide that there is no such instance. There is a proverb which affirms, 'that the blood of the martyrs is the seed of the church.'* It is commonly supposed that Junius Brutus did right in putting his sons to death* in the first year of the Roman republic, and that this action contributed more than any other cause, to generate that energy and virtue for which his country was afterwards so eminently distinguished. The death of Cato produced an effect somewhat similar to this. It was dwelt on with admiration by all the lovers of virtue under the subsequent tyrants of Rome. It seemed to be the lamp from which they caught the sacred flame. Who can tell how much it has contributed to revive that flame in after ages, when it seemed to have been so long extinct?

Let it be observed that all martyrs μάρτυρες are suicides by the very signification of the term. They die for a testimony μαρτύριο; that is, they have a motive for dying. But motives respect only our own voluntary acts, not the violence put upon us by another.

APPENDIX, No. II
OF DUELLING

Motives of duelling: 1. revenge—2. reputation for courage.—Fallacy of this motive.—Objection answered.—Illustration.

IT may be proper in this place to bestow a moment's consideration upon the trite, but very important case of duelling. A very short reflection will suffice to set it in its true light.

This detestable practice was originally invented by barbarians for the gratification of revenge. It was probably at that time thought a very happy project for reconciling the odiousness of malignity with the gallantry of courage.

But in this light it is now generally given up. Men of the best understanding who lend it their sanction, are unwillingly induced to do so, and engage in single combat merely that their reputation may sustain no slander.

Which of these two actions is the truest test of courage: the engaging in a practice which our judgment disapproves, because we cannot submit to the consequences of following that judgment; or the doing what we believe to be right, and chearfully encountering all the consequences that may be annexed to the practice of virtue? With what patience can a man of virtue think of cutting off the life of a fellow mortal, or of putting an abrupt close to all the generous projects he may himself conceive for the benefit of others, merely because he has not firmness enough to awe impertinence and falshood into silence?

'But the refusing a duel is an ambiguous action. Cowards may pretend principle to shelter themselves from a danger they dare not meet.'

This is partly true and partly false. There are few actions indeed that are not ambiguous, or that with the same general outline may not proceed from different motives. But the manner of doing them will sufficiently shew the principle from which they spring.

He, that would break through an universally received custom because he believes it to be wrong, must no doubt arm himself with fortitude. The point in which we chiefly fail, is in not accurately understanding our own intentions, and taking care beforehand to free ourselves from any alloy of weakness and error. He, who comes forward with no other idea in his mind but that of rectitude, and who expresses, with the simplicity and firmness which full conviction never fails to inspire, the views with which he is impressed, is in no danger of being mistaken for a coward. If he hesitate, it is because he has not an idea perfectly clear of the sentiment he intends to convey. If he be in any degree embarrassed, it is because he has not a feeling sufficiently generous and intrepid of the guilt of the action in which he is pressed to engage.

If there be any meaning in courage, its first ingredient must be the daring to speak the truth at all times, to all persons, and in every possible situation. What is it but the want of courage that should prevent me from saying, 'Sir, I ought to refuse your challenge. What I ought to do, that I dare do. Have I injured you? I will readily and without compulsion repair my injustice to the uttermost mite. Have you misconstrued me? State to me the particulars, and doubt not that what is true I will make appear to be true. Thus far I will go. But, though I should be branded for a coward by all mankind, I will not repair to a scene of deliberate murder. I will not do an act that I know to be flagitious. I will exercise my judgment upon every proposition that comes before me; the dictates of that judgment I will speak; and upon them I will form my conduct.' He that holds this language with a countenance in unison with his words, will never be suspected of acting from the impulse of fear.

CHAPTER III

OF DUTY

A difficulty stated.—Of absolute and practical virtue.—Impropriety of this distinction.—Universality of what is called practical virtue—instanced in robbery—in religious fanaticism.—The quality of an action distinct from the disposition with which it is performed—farther difficulty.—Meaning of the term, duty.—Application.—Inferences.

THERE is a difficulty of considerable magnitude as to the subject of the preceding chapter, founded upon the difference which may exist between abstract justice and my apprehensions of justice. When I do an act, wrong in itself, but which as to all the materials of judging extant to my understanding appears to be right, is my conduct virtuous or vicious?

Certain moralists have introduced a distinction upon this head between absolute and practical virtue. 'There is one species of virtue,' they say, 'which rises out of the nature of things and is immutable, and another which rises out of the views extant to my understanding. Thus for example suppose, I ought to worship Jesus Christ; but, having been bred in the religion of Mahomet, I ought to adhere to that religion, as long as its evidences shall appear to me conclusive. I am impannelled upon a jury to try a man arraigned for murder, and who is really innocent. Abstractedly considered, I ought to acquit him. But I am unacquainted with his innocence, and evidence is adduced such as to form the strongest presumption of his guilt. Demonstration in such cases is not to be attained; I am obliged in every concern of human life to act upon presumption; I ought therefore to convict him.'

It may be doubted however whether any good purpose is likely to be answered by employing the terms of abstract science in this versatile and uncertain manner. Morality is, if any thing can be, fixed and immutable; and there must surely be some strange deception that should induce us to give to an action eternally and unchangeably wrong, the epithets of rectitude, duty and virtue.

Nor have these moralists been thoroughly aware to what extent this admission would carry them. The human mind is incredibly subtle in inventing an apology for that to which its inclination leads. Nothing is so rare as pure and unmingled hypocrisy. There is no action of our lives which we were not ready at the time of adopting it to justify, unless so far as we were prevented by mere indolence and unconcern. There is scarcely any justification which we endeavour to pass upon others, which we do not with tolerable success pass upon ourselves. The distinction therefore which is here set up would go near to prove that every action of every human being is entitled to the appellation of virtuous.

There is perhaps no man that cannot recollect the time when he secretly called in question the arbitrary division of property established in human society, and felt inclined to appropriate to his use any thing the possession of which appeared to him desirable. It is probably in some such way that men are usually influenced in the perpetration of robbery. They persuade themselves of the comparative inutility of the property to its present possessor, and the inestimable advantage that would attend it in their hands. They believe that the transfer ought to be made. It is of no consequence that they are not consistent in these views, that the impressions of education speedily recur to their minds, and that in a season of adversity they readily confess the wickedness of their proceeding. It is not less true that they did what at the moment they thought to be right.

But there is another consideration that seems still more decisive in religious fanaticism of the subject before us. The worst actions, the most contrary to abstract justice and utility, have frequently been done from the most conscientious motives. Clement, Ravaillac, Damiens and Gerard* had their minds deeply penetrated with anxiety for the eternal welfare of mankind. For these objects they sacrificed their ease, and chearfully exposed themselves to tortures and death. It was benevolence probably that contributed to light the fires of Smithfield, and point the daggers of Saint Bartholomew.* The inventors of the Gunpowder Treason* were in general men remarkable for the sanctity of their lives and the severity of their manners. It is probable indeed, that some ambitious views, and some sentiments of hatred and abhorrence mixed with the benevolence and integrity of these persons. It is probable that no wrong action was ever committed from views entirely pure. But the deception they put upon themselves might nevertheless be complete. At all events their opinions upon the subject could not alter the real nature of the action.

The true solution of the question lies in observing, that the disposition with which an action is adopted is one thing, and the action itself another. A right action may be done from a wrong disposition; in that case we approve the action, but condemn the actor. A wrong action may be done from a right disposition; in that case we condemn the action, but approve the actor. If the disposition by which a man is governed have a systematical tendency to the benefit of his species, he cannot fail to obtain our esteem, however mistaken he may be in his conduct.

But what shall we say to the duty of a man under these circumstances? Calvin, we will suppose, was clearly and conscientiously persuaded that he ought to burn Servetus.* Ought he to have burned him or not? 'If he burned him, he did an action detestable in its own nature; if he refrained, he acted in opposition to the best judgment of his own understanding as to a point of moral obligation.' It is absurd however to say, that it was in any sense his duty to burn him. The most that can be admitted is, that his disposition was virtuous, and that in the circumstances in which he was placed an action greatly to be deplored flowed from that disposition by invincible necessity.

Shall we say then that it was the duty of Calvin, who did not understand the principles of toleration, to act upon a truth of which he was ignorant? Suppose that a person is to be tried at York next week for murder, and that my evidence would acquit him. Shall we say that it was my duty to go to York, though I knew nothing of the matter? Upon the same principles we might affirm that it is my duty to go from London to York in half an hour, as the trial will come on within that time; the impossibility not being more real in one case than in the other. Upon the same principles we might affirm, that it is my duty to be impeccable, omniscient and almighty.

Duty is a term the use of which seems to be to describe the mode in which any being may best be employed for the general good. It is limited in its extent by the extent of the capacity of that being. Now capacity varies in its idea in proportion as we vary our view of the subject to which it belongs. What I am capable of, if you consider me merely as a man, is one thing; what I am capable of as a man of a deformed figure, of weak understanding, of superstitious prejudices, or as the case may happen, is another. So much cannot be expected of me under these disadvantages, as if they were absent. But, if this be the true definition of duty, it is absurd to suppose in any case that an action injurious to the general welfare can be classed in the rank of duties.

To apply these observations to the cases that have been stated. Ignorance, so far as it goes, completely annihilates capacity. As I was uninformed of the trial at York, I could not be influenced by any consideration respecting it. But it is absurd to say that it was my duty to neglect a motive with which I was unacquainted. If you alledge, 'that Calvin was ignorant of the principles of toleration, and had no proper opportunity to learn them,' it follows that in burning Servetus he did not violate his duty, but it does not follow that it was his duty to burn him. Upon the supposition here stated duty is silent. Calvin was unacquainted with the principles of justice, and therefore could not practise them. The duty of no man can exceed his capacity; but then neither can in any case an act of injustice be of the nature of duty.

There are certain inferences that flow from this view of the subject, which it may be proper to mention. Nothing is more common than for individuals and societies of men to alledge that they have acted to the best of their judgment, that they have done their duty, and therefore that their conduct, even should it prove to be mistaken, is nevertheless virtuous. This appears to be an error. An action, though done with the best intention in the world, may have nothing in it of the nature of virtue. In reality the most essential part of virtue consists in the incessantly seeking to inform ourselves more accurately upon the subject of utility and right. Whoever is greatly misinformed respecting them, is indebted for his error to a defect in his philanthropy and zeal.

Secondly, since absolute virtue may be out of the power of a human being, it becomes us in the mean time to lay the greatest stress upon a virtuous disposition, which is not attended with the same ambiguity. A virtuous disposition is of the utmost consequence, since it will in the majority of instances be productive of virtuous actions; since it tends, in exact proportion to the quantity of virtue, to increase our discernment and improve our understanding; and since, if it were universally propagated, it would immediately lead to the great end of virtuous actions, the purest and most exquisite happiness of intelligent beings. But a virtuous disposition is principally generated by the uncontrolled exercise of private judgment, and the rigid conformity of every man to the dictates of his conscience.

CHAPTER IV

OF THE EQUALITY OF MANKIND

Physical   equality.—Objection.—Answers.—Moral   equality.—How limited.—Province of political justice.

THE equality of mankind is either physical or moral. Their physical equality may be considered either as it relates to the strength of the body or the faculties of the mind.

This part of the subject has been exposed to cavil and objection. It has been said, 'that the reverse of this equality is the result of our experience. Among the individuals of our species we actually find that there are not two alike. One man is strong and another weak. One man is wise and another foolish. All that exists in the world of the inequality of conditions is to be traced to this as their source. The strong man possesses power to subdue, and the weak stands in need of an ally to protect. The consequence is inevitable: the equality of conditions is a chimerical assumption, neither possible to be reduced into practice, nor desirable if it could be so reduced.'

Upon this statement two observations are to be made. First, this inequality was in its origin infinitely less than it is at present. In the uncultivated state of man diseases, effeminacy and luxury were little known, and of consequence the strength of every one much more nearly approached to the strength of his neighbour. In the uncultivated state of man the understandings of all were limited, their wants, their ideas and their views nearly upon a level. It was to be expected that in their first departure from this state great irregularities would introduce themselves; and it is the object of subsequent wisdom and improvement to mitigate these irregularities.

Secondly, notwithstanding the incroachments that have been made upon the equality of mankind, a great and substantial equality remains. There is no such disparity among the human race as to enable one man to hold several other men in subjection, except so far as they are willing to be subject. All government is founded in opinion.* Men at present live under any particular form, because they conceive it their interest to do so. One part indeed of a community or empire may be held in subjection by force; but this cannot be the personal force of their despot; it must be the force of another part of the community, who are of opinion that it is their interest to support his authority. Destroy this opinion, and the fabric which is built upon it falls to the ground. It follows therefore that all men are essentially independent.—So much for the physical equality.

The moral equality is still less open to reasonable exception. By moral equality I understand the propriety of applying one unalterable rule of justice to every case that may arise. This cannot be questioned but upon arguments that would subvert the very nature of virtue. 'Equality,' it has been affirmed, 'will always be an unintelligible fiction, so long as the capacities of men shall be unequal, and their pretended claims have neither guarantee nor sanction by which they can be inforced.'[1] But surely justice is sufficiently intelligible in its own nature, abstracted from the consideration whether it be or be not reduced into practice. Justice has relation to beings endowed with perception, and

---

[1] '*On a dit—que nous avions tous les mêmes droits. J'ignore ce que c'est que les mêmes droits, ou il y a inégalité de talens où de force, & nulle garantie, nulle sanction.*' Raynal, Revolution d'Amerique,* p. 34.

capable of pleasure and pain. Now it immediately results from the nature of such beings, independently of any arbitrary constitution, that pleasure is agreeable and pain odious, pleasure to be desired and pain to be obviated. It is therefore just and reasonable that such beings should contribute, so far as it lies in their power, to the pleasure and benefit of each other. Among pleasures some are more exquisite, more unalloyed and less precarious than others. It is just that these should be preferred.

From these simple principles we may deduce the moral equality of mankind. We are partakers of a common nature, and the same causes that contribute to the benefit of one contribute to the benefit of another. Our senses and faculties are of the same denomination. Our pleasures and pains will therefore be the same. We are all of us endowed with reason, able to compare, to judge and to infer. The improvement therefore which is to be desired for the one is to be desired for the other. We shall be provident for ourselves and useful to each other, in proportion as we rise above the atmosphere of prejudice. The same independence, the same freedom from any such restraint, as should prevent us from giving the reins to our own understanding, or from uttering upon all occasions whatever we think to be true, will conduce to the improvement of all. There are certain opportunities and a certain situation most advantageous to every human being, and it is just that these should be communicated to all, as nearly at least as the general economy will permit.

There is indeed one species of moral inequality parallel to the physical inequality that has been already described. The treatment to which men are entitled is to be measured by their merits and their virtues. That country would not be the seat of wisdom and reason, where the benefactor of his species was considered in the same point of view as their enemy. But in reality this distinction, so far from being adverse to equality in any tenable sense, is friendly to it, and is accordingly known by the appellation of equity, a term derived from the same origin. Though in some sense an exception, it tends to the same purpose to which the principle itself is indebted for its value. It is calculated to infuse into every bosom an emulation of excellence. The thing really to be desired is the removing as much as possible arbitrary distinctions, and leaving to talents and virtue the field of exertion unimpaired. We should endeavour to afford to all the same opportunities and the same encouragement, and to render justice the common interest and choice.

CHAPTER V

RIGHTS OF MAN

*The question stated.—Foundation of society.—Opposite rights impossible.
—Conclusion from these premises.—Discretion considered.—Rights of
kings.—Immoral consequences of the doctrine of rights.—Rights of communities.—Objections: 1. the right of mutual aid.—Explanation.—Origin
of the term, right.—2. rights of private judgment and of the press.—
Explanation—Reasons of this limitation upon the functions of the community:
1. the inutility of attempting restraint.—2. its pernicious tendency.
—Conclusion.*

THERE is no subject that has been discussed with more eagerness and
pertinacity than the rights of man. Has he any rights, or has he none?
Much may plausibly be alledged on both sides of this question; and in
the conclusion those reasoners appear to express themselves with the
greatest accuracy who embrace the negative. There is nothing that
has been of greater disservice to the cause of truth, than the hasty
and unguarded manner in which its advocates have sometimes defended
it: and it will be admitted to be peculiarly unfortunate, if the advocates
on one side of this question should be found to have the greatest quantity of truth, while their adversaries have expressed themselves in a
manner more consonant to reason and the nature of things. Where the
question has been so extremely darkened by an ambiguous use of
terms, it may at any rate be desirable to try, whether, by a patient and
severe investigation of the first principles of political society, it may be
placed in a light considerably different from the views of both parties.

Political society, as has already been observed, is founded in the principles of morality and justice. It is impossible for intellectual beings to
be brought into coalition and intercourse, with out a certain mode of
conduct, adapted to their nature and connection, immediately becoming a duty incumbent on the parties concerned. Men would never have
associated, if they had not imagined that in consequence of that
association they would mutually conduce to the advantage and happiness of each other. This is the real purpose, the genuine basis of their
intercourse; and, as far as this purpose is answered, so far does society
answer the end of its institution.

There is only one postulate more, that is necessary to bring us to a
conclusive mode of reasoning upon this subject. Whatever is meant by
the term right, for it will presently appear that the sense of the term

itself has never been clearly understood, there can neither be opposite rights, nor rights and duties hostile to each other. The rights of one man cannot clash with or be destructive of the rights of another; for this, instead of rendering the subject an important branch of truth and morality, as the advocates of the rights of man certainly understand it to be, would be to reduce it to a heap of unintelligible jargon and inconsistency. If one man have a right to be free, another man cannot have a right to make him a slave; if one man have a right to inflict chastisement upon me, I cannot have a right to withdraw myself from chastisement; if my neighbour have a right to a sum of money in my possession, I cannot have a right to retain it in my pocket.—It cannot be less incontrovertible, that I have no right to omit what my duty prescribes.

From hence it inevitably follows that men have no rights. By right, as the word is employed in this subject, has always been understood discretion, that is, a full and complete power of either doing a thing or omitting it, without the person's becoming liable to animadversion or censure from another, that is, in other words, without his incurring any degree of turpitude or guilt. Now in this sense I affirm that man has no rights, no discretionary power whatever.

It is commonly said, 'that a man has a right to the disposal of his fortune, a right to the employment of his time, a right to the uncontrolled choice of his profession or pursuits.' But this can never be consistently affirmed till it can be shewn that he has no duties, prescribing and limiting his mode of proceeding in all these respects. My neighbour has just as much right to put an end to my existence with dagger or poison, as to deny me that pecuniary assistance without which I must starve, or as to deny me that assistance without which my intellectual attainments or my moral exertions will be materially injured. He has just as much right to amuse himself with burning my house or torturing my children upon the rack, as to shut himself up in a cell careless about his fellow men, and to hide 'his talent in a napkin.'

If men have any rights, any discretionary powers, they must be in things of total indifference, as whether I sit on the right or on the left side of my fire, or dine on beef to day or tomorrow. Even these rights are much fewer than we are apt to imagine, since before they can be completely established, it must be proved that my choice on one side or the other can in no possible way contribute to the benefit or injury of myself or of any other person in the world. Those must indeed be rights well worth the contending for, the very essence of which consists in their absolute nugatoriness and inutility.

In reality nothing can appear more wonderful to a careful enquirer, than that two ideas so incompatible as man and rights should ever have been associated together. Certain it is, that one of them must be utterly exclusive and annihilatory of the other. Before we ascribe rights to man, we must conceive of him as a being endowed with intellect, and capable of discerning the differences and tendencies of things. But a being endowed with intellect, and capable of discerning the differences and tendencies of things, instantly becomes a moral being, and has duties incumbent on him to discharge: and duties and rights, as has already been shewn, are absolutely exclusive of each other.

It has been affirmed by the zealous advocates of liberty, 'that princes and magistrates have no rights;' and no position can be more incontrovertible. There is no situation of their lives that has not its correspondent duties. There is no power intrusted to them that they are not bound to exercise exclusively for the public good. It is strange that persons adopting this principle did not go a step farther, and perceive that the same restrictions were applicable to subjects and citizens.

Nor is the fallacy of this language more conspicuous than its immoral tendency. To this inaccurate and unjust use of the term right we owe it, that the miser, who accumulates to no end that which diffused would have conduced to the welfare of thousands, that the luxurious man who wallows in indulgence and sees numerous families around him pining in beggary, never fail to tell us of their rights, and to silence animadversion and quiet the censure of their own mind by reminding us, 'that they came fairly into possession of their wealth, that they owe no debts, and that of consequence no man has authority to enquire into their private manner of disposing of that which is their own.' A great majority of mankind are conscious that they stand in need of this sort of defence, and are therefore very ready to combine against the insolent intruder, who ventures to enquire into 'things that do not concern him.' They forget, that the wise man and the honest man, the friend of his country and his kind, is concerned for every thing by which they may be affected, and carries about with him a diploma, constituting him inquisitor general of the moral conduct of his neighbours, with a duty annexed to recal them to virtue, by every lesson that truth can enable him to read, and every punishment that plain speaking is competent to inflict.

It is scarcely necessary to add, that, if individuals have no rights, neither has society, which possesses nothing but what individuals have brought into a common stock. The absurdity of the common opinion, as applied to this subject, is still more glaring, if possible, than in the view in which we have already considered it. According to the usual sentiment every club assembling for any civil purpose, every congregation of religionists assembling for the worship of God, has a right to establish any provisions or ceremonies, no matter how ridiculous or detestable, provided they do not interfere with the freedom of others. Reason lies prostrate under their feet. They have a right to trample upon and insult her as they please. It is in the same spirit we have been told that every nation has a right to choose its form of government. A most acute, original and inestimable author was probably misled by the vulgar phraseology on this subject, when he asserted, that, 'at a time when neither the people of France nor the national assembly were troubling themselves about the affairs of England or the English parliament, Mr. Burke's conduct was unpardonable in commencing an unprovoked attack upon them.'[1]

There are various objections that suggest themselves to the theory which subverts the rights of men; and if the theory be true, they will probably appear in the result to be so far from really hostile to it, as to be found more fairly deducible from and consistent with its principles, than with any of those with which they have inadvertently been connected.

In the first place it has sometimes been alledged, and seems to result from the reasonings already adduced under the head of justice, that 'men have a right to the assistance and co-operation of their fellows in every honest pursuit.' But, when we assert this proposition, we mean something by the word right exceedingly different from what is commonly understood by the term. We do not understand something discretionary, which, if not voluntarily fulfilled, cannot be considered as a matter of claim. On the contrary every thing adduced upon that occasion was calculated to shew that it was a matter of strict claim; and perhaps something would be gained with respect to perspicuity, if we rather chose to distinguish it by that appellation, than by a name so much abused, and so ambiguous in its application, as the term right.

The true origin of this latter term is relative to the present state of political government, in which many of those actions which moral duty most strictly enjoins us are in no degree brought within the sphere of legislative sanction. Men uninfluenced by comprehensive principles of justice, commit every species of intemperance, are selfish, hardhearted, licentious and cruel, and maintain their right to all these caprices, because the laws of their country are silent with regard

---

[1] Rights of Man, page 1.*

to them. Philosophers and political enquirers have too frequently adopted the same principles with a certain degree of accommodation; though in fact men have no more right to these erroneous propensities in their most qualified sense, than they had to them originally in all their extravagance. It is true, that, under the forms of society now existing in the world, intemperance and the caprices of personal intercourse too frequently escape without animadversion. But in a more perfect form, though they may not fall under the cognisance of law, the offender will probably be so unequivocally reminded by the sincerity of his neighbours of the error he has committed, as to be in no danger of running away with the opinion that he had a right to commit it.

A second and more important objection to the doctrine I am maintaining is derived from the rights as they are called of private judgment, and the liberty of the press. But it may easily be shewn, that these, no more than the articles already mentioned, are rights of discretion. If they were, they would prove, that a man was strictly justifiable in publishing what he believed to be pernicious or false, and that it was a matter of perfect moral indifference whether he conformed to the religious rites of Confucius, of Mahomet,* or of Christ. The political freedom of conscience and of the press, so far from being as it is commonly supposed an extension, is a new case of the limitation of rights and discretion. Conscience and the press ought to be unrestrained, not because men have a right to deviate from the exact line that duty prescribes, but because society, the aggregate of individuals, has no right to assume the prerogative of an infallible judge, and to undertake authoritatively to prescribe to its members in matters of pure speculation.

One obvious reason against this assumption on the part of the society is the impossibility by any compulsatory method of bringing men to uniformity of opinion. The judgment we form upon topics of general truth, is or is imagined to be founded upon evidence: and, however it may be soothed by gentle applications to the betraying its impartiality, it is apt to repel with no little pertinacity whatever comes under the form of compulsion. Persecution cannot persuade the understanding, even when it subdues our resolution. It may make us hypocrites; but cannot make us converts. The government therefore, which is anxious above all things to imbue its subjects with integrity and virtue, will be the farthest in the world from discouraging them in the explicit avowal of their sentiments.

But there is another reason of a higher order. Man is not, as has been already shewn, a perfect being, but perfectible. No government, that has yet existed, or is likely presently to exist upon the face of the earth, is faultless. No government ought therefore pertinaciously to resist the change of its own institutions; and still less ought it to set up a standard upon the various topics of human speculation, to restrain the excursions of an inventive mind. It is only by giving a free scope to these excursions, that science, philosophy and morals have arrived at their present degree of perfection, or are capable of going on to that still greater perfection, in comparison of which all that has been already done will perhaps appear childish. But a proceeding, absolutely necessary for the purpose of exciting the mind to these salutary excursions, and still more necessary in order to give them their proper operation, consists in the unrestrained communication of men's thoughts and discoveries to each other. If every man have to begin again at the point from which his neighbour set out, the labour will be endless, and the progress in an unvarying circle. There is nothing that more eminently contributes to intellectual energy, than for every man to be habituated to follow without alarm the train of his speculations, and to utter without fear the conclusions that have suggested themselves to him.—But does all this imply that men have a right to act any thing but virtue, and to utter any thing but truth? Certainly not. It implies indeed that there are points with which society has no right to interfere, not that discretion and caprice are more free, or duty less strict upon these points, than upon any others with which human action is conversant.

CHAPTER VI

OF THE EXERCISE OF PRIVATE JUDGMENT

Foundation of virtue.—Human actions regulated: 1. by the nature of things.— 2. by positive institution.—Tendency of the latter: 1. to excite virtue.—Its equivocal character in this respect.—2. to inform the judgment.—Its inaptitude for that purpose.—Province of conscience considered.—Tendency of an interference with that province.—Recapitulation.—Arguments in favour of positive institution: 1. the necessity of repelling private injustice.—Objections: the uncertainty of evidence.—The diversity of motives—the unsuitableness of the means of correction—either to impress new sentiments—or to strengthen old ones.—Punishment for the sake of example considered.—Urgency of the case.—2. rebellion.—3. war.—Objections.—Reply.

To a rational being there can be but one rule of conduct, justice, and one mode of ascertaining that rule, the exercise of his understanding. If in any instance I be made the mechanical instrument of absolute violence, in that instance I fall under no description of moral conduct either good or bad. But, if, not being operated upon by absolute compulsion, I be wholly prompted by something that is frequently called by that name, and act from the hope of reward or the fear of punishment, my conduct is positively wrong.

Here however a distinction is to be made. Justice, as it was defined in a preceding chapter, is coincident with utility. I am myself a part of the great whole, and my happiness is a part of that complex view of things by which justice is regulated. The hope of reward therefore and the fear of punishment, confined within certain strict limits, are motives that ought to have influence with my mind.

There are two descriptions of tendency that may belong to any action, the tendency which it possesses by the necessary and universal laws of existence, and the tendency which results from the positive interference of some intelligent being. The nature of happiness and misery, pleasure and pain, is independent of all positive institution: that is, it is immutably true that whatever tends to procure a balance of the former is to be desired, and whatever tends to procure a balance of the latter is to be rejected. In like manner the promulgation of virtue, truth and political justice must always be right. There is perhaps no action of a rational being that has not some tendency to promote these objects, and consequently that has not a moral character founded in the abstract nature of things.

The tendency of positive institution is of two sorts, to furnish me with an additional motive to the practice of virtue or right, and to inform my understanding as to what actions are right and what actions are wrong. Much cannot be said in commendation of either of these tendencies.

First, positive institution may furnish me with an additional motive to the practice of virtue. I have an opportunity of contributing very essentially to the advantage of twenty individuals; they will be benefited, and no other persons will sustain a material injury. I ought to embrace this opportunity. Here let us suppose positive institution to interfere, and to annex some great personal reward to myself to the performance of my duty. This immediately changes the nature of the action. Before I preferred it for its intrinsic excellence. Now, so far as the positive institution operates, I prefer it, because some person has arbitrarily annexed to it a great weight of self-interest. But virtue, considered as the quality of an intelligent being, depends upon the disposition with which the action is accompanied. Under a positive institution then this very action, which is intrinsically virtuous, may, so far as relates to the agent, become vicious. The vicious man would before have neglected the advantage of these twenty individuals, because he would not bring a certain inconvenience or trouble upon himself. The same man with the same disposition will now promote their advantage, because his own welfare is concerned in it. Twenty, other things equal, is twenty times better than one. He that is not governed by the moral arithmetic of the case, or who acts from a disposition directly at war with that arithmetic, is unjust. In other words, morality requires that we should be attentive only to the tendency which belongs to any action by the necessary and universal laws of existence. This is what is meant by the principle, 'that we should do good, regardless of the consequences;' and by that other, 'that we may not do evil, from the prospect of good to result from it.' The case would have been rendered still more glaring, if, instead of the welfare of twenty, we had supposed the welfare of millions to have been concerned. In reality, whether the disparity be great or small, the inference ought to be the same.

Secondly, positive institution may inform my understanding as to what actions are right and what actions are wrong. Here it is proper for us to reflect upon the terms understanding and information. Understanding, particularly as it is concerned with moral subjects, is the percipient of truth. This is its proper sphere. Information, so far as it is genuine, is a portion detached from the great body of truth. You inform me, 'that Euclid* asserts the three angles of a plane triangle to be equal to two right angles.' Still I am unacquainted with the truth of this proposition. 'But Euclid has demonstrated it. His demonstration has existed for two thousand years, and during that term has proved satisfactory to every man by whom it has been understood.' I am nevertheless uninformed. The knowledge of truth lies in the perceived agreement or disagreement of the terms of a proposition. So long as I am unacquainted with the middle term by means of which they may be compared, so long as they are incommensurate to my understanding, you may have furnished me with a principle from which I may reason truly to farther consequences, but as to the principle itself I may strictly be said to know nothing about it.

Every proposition has an intrinsic evidence of its own. Every consequence has premises from which it flows; and upon them, and not upon any thing else, its validity depends. If you could work a miracle to prove, 'that the three angles of a triangle were equal to two right angles,' I should still know, that the proposition was either true or false previously to the exhibition of that miracle; and that there was no necessary connection between any one of its terms and the miracle exhibited. The miracle would take off my attention from the true question to a question altogether different, that of authority. By the authority adduced I might be prevailed on to yield an irregular assent to the proposition; but I could not properly be said to perceive its truth.

But this is not all. If it were, it might perhaps be regarded as a refinement foreign to the concerns of human life. Positive institutions do not content themselves with requiring my assent to certain propositions, in consideration of the respectable testimony by which they are inforced. This would amount to no more, than advice flowing from a respectable quarter, which after all I might reject, if it did not accord with the mature judgment of my own understanding. But in the very nature of these institutions there is included a sanction, a motive either of punishment or reward to induce me to obedience.

It is commonly said, 'that positive institutions ought to leave me perfectly free in matters of conscience, but may properly interfere with my conduct in civil concerns.' But this distinction seems to have been very lightly taken up. What sort of moralist must he be, who makes no conscience of what passes in his intercourse with other men? Such a distinction proceeds upon the supposition, 'that it is of great consequence whether I bow to the east or the west; whether I call the object of my worship Jehovah or Alla; whether I pay a priest in a surplice or a black coat. These are points in which an honest man ought to be rigid and inflexible. But as to those other, whether he shall be a tyrant, a slave or a free citizen; whether he shall bind himself with multiplied oaths impossible to be performed, or be a rigid observer of truth; whether he shall swear allegiance to a king *de jure* or a king *de facto*, to the best or the worst of all possible governments; respecting these points he may safely commit his conscience to the keeping of the civil magistrate.' In reality there are perhaps no concerns of a rational being, over which morality does not extend its province, and respecting which he is not bound to a conscientious proceeding.

I am satisfied at present, that a certain conduct, suppose it be a rigid attention to the confidence of private conversation, is incumbent upon me. You tell me, 'there are certain cases of such peculiar emergency as to supersede this rule.' Perhaps I think there are not. If I admit your proposition, a wide field of enquiry is opened, respecting what cases do or do not deserve to be considered as exceptions. It is little likely that we should agree respecting all these cases. How then does the law treat me, for my conscientious discharge of what I conceive to be my duty? Because I will not turn informer (which, it may be, I think an infamous

character) against my most valued friend, the law accuses me of mispri-
sion of treason, felony or murder, and perhaps hangs me. I believe a
certain individual to be a confirmed villain, and a most dangerous
member of society, and feel it to be my duty to warn others, perhaps the
public, against the effect of his vices. Because I publish what I know to
be true, the law convicts me of libel, *scandalum magnatum*,* and crimes
of I know not what complicated denomination.

If the evil stopped here, it would be well. If I only suffered a certain
calamity, suppose death, I could endure it. Death has hitherto been
the common lot of men, and I expect at some time or other to submit to
it. Human society must sooner or later be deprived of its individual
members, whether they be valuable, or whether they be inconsiderable.
But the punishment acts not only retrospectively upon me, but pro-
spectively upon my contemporaries and countrymen. My neighbour
entertains the same opinion respecting the conduct he ought to hold as
I did. But the executioner of public justice interposes with a powerful
argument, to convince him that he has mistaken the path of abstract
rectitude.

What sort of converts will be produced by this unfeeling logic?
'I have deeply reflected,' suppose, 'upon the nature of virtue, and am
convinced that a certain proceeding is incumbent on me. But the
hangman, supported by an act of parliament, assures me I am mistaken.' If I yield my opinion to his *dictum*, my action becomes modified,
and my character too. An influence like this is inconsistent with all generous magnanimity of spirit, all ardent impartiality in the discovery of
truth, and all inflexible perseverance in its assertion. Countries,
exposed to the perpetual interference of decrees instead of arguments,
exhibit within their boundaries the mere phantoms of men. We can
never judge from an observation of their inhabitants what men would
be, if they knew of no appeal from the tribunal of conscience, and if,
whatever they thought, they dared to speak, and dared to act.

At present there will perhaps occur to the majority of readers but
few instances of laws, which may be supposed to interfere with the conscientious discharge of duty. A considerable number will occur in the
course of the present enquiry. More would readily offer themselves to a
patient research. Men are so successfully reduced to a common standard by the operation of positive law, that in most countries they are
capable of little more than like parrots repeating each other. This
uniformity is capable of being produced in two ways, by energy of
mind and indefatigableness of enquiry, enabling a considerable number
to penetrate with equal success into the recesses of truth; and by

pusillanimity of temper and a frigid indifference to right and wrong, produced by the penalties which are suspended over such as shall disinterestedly enquire, and communicate and act upon the result of their enquiries. It is easy to perceive which of these is the cause of the uniformity that prevails in the present instance.

If there be any truth more unquestionable than the rest, it is, that every man is bound to the exertion of his faculties in the discovery of right, and to the carrying into effect all the right with which he is acquainted. It may be granted that an infallible standard, if it could be discovered, would be considerably beneficial. But this infallible standard itself would be of little use in human affairs, unless it had the property of reasoning as well as deciding, of enlightening the mind as well as constraining the body. If a man be in some cases obliged to prefer his own judgment, he is in all cases obliged to consult that judgment, before he can determine whether the matter in question be of the sort provided for or no. So that from this reasoning it ultimately appears, that no man is obliged to conform to any rule of conduct, farther than the rule is consistent with justice.

Such are the genuine principles of human society. Such would be the unconstrained concord of its members, in a state where every individual within the society, and every neighbour without, was capable of listening with sobriety to the dictates of reason. We shall not fail to be impressed with considerable regret, if, when we descend to the present mixed characters of mankind, we find ourselves obliged in any degree to depart from so simple and grand a principle. The universal exercise of private judgment is a doctrine so unspeakably beautiful, that the true politician will certainly resolve to interfere with it as sparingly and in as few instances as possible. Let us consider what are the emergencies that may be thought to demand an exception. They can only be briefly stated in this place, each of them requiring to be minutely examined in the subsequent stages of the enquiry.

In the first place then it seems necessary for some powerful arbitrator to interfere, where the proceedings of the individual threaten the most injurious consequences to his neighbours, and where the instant nature of the case will not accord with the uncertain progress of argument and conviction addressed to the mind of the offender. A man, suppose, has committed murder, or, to make the case more aggravated, several murders; and, having thus far over-stepped all those boundaries of innocence and guilt which restrain the generality of men, it is to be presumed from analogy that he may be led to the commission of other murders. At first it may appear to be no great infringement upon the exercise of private judgment, to put it under some degree of restraint, when it leads to the commission of atrocious crimes. There are however certain difficulties in the case which are worthy to be considered.

First, as soon as we admit the propriety of a rule such as that above stated, our next concern will be with the evidence, which shall lead to the acquittal or conviction of the person accused. Now it is well known, that no principles of evidence have yet been laid down that are infallible. Human affairs universally proceed upon presumption and probability. An eye-witness must identify the person of the offender, and in this he may be mistaken. We must necessarily be contented with presumptive proofs of his intention; and often are or imagine ourselves to be obliged to admit presumptive evidence of the fact itself. The consequence is inevitable. And surely it is no trivial evil, to subject an innocent man eventually, to the public award and the established punishment annexed to the most atrocious crimes.

Secondly, the same external action will admit of every possible shade of virtue or vice. One man shall commit murder, to remove a troublesome observer of his depraved dispositions, who will otherwise counteract and expose him to the world. A second, because he cannot bear the ingenuous sincerity with which he is told of his vices. A third, from his intolerable envy of superior merit. A fourth, because he knows his adversary meditates an act pregnant with extensive mischief, and he perceives no other mode by which its perpetration can be prevented. A fifth, in the actual defence of his father's life or his daughter's chastity. Each of these men, except perhaps the last, may act either from momentary impulse, or from any of the infinite shades and degrees of deliberation. Would you award one individual punishment to all these varieties of action? Can you pretend in each instance to ascertain the exact quantity of wrong and to invent a species of corporal punishment or restraint, equivalent to each? Strictly speaking no two men were ever guilty of the same crime; but here comes in positive law with its Procrustes's bed,* and levels all characters, and tramples upon all distinctions.

Thirdly, punishment is not the appropriate mode of correcting the errors of mankind. It will probably be admitted, that the only true end of punishment is correction. That question will be discussed in another part of the present enquiry. 'I have done something, which though wrong in itself, I believe to be right; or I have done something which I usually admit to be wrong; but my conviction upon the subject is not so clear and forcible, as to prevent my yielding to a powerful temptation.' There can be no doubt, that the proper way of conveying to my understanding a truth of which I am ignorant, or of impressing upon me a firmer persuasion of a truth with which I am acquainted, is by an appeal to my reason. Even an angry expostulation with me upon my conduct will but excite similar passions in me, and cloud instead of illuminate my understanding. There is certainly a way of expressing truth, with such benevolence as to command attention, and such evidence as to inforce conviction in all cases whatever.

Punishment inevitably excites in the sufferer, and ought to excite, a sense of injustice. Let its purpose be to convince me of the truth of a proposition, which I at present believe to be false. It is not abstractedly considered of the nature of an argument, and therefore it cannot begin with producing conviction. Punishment is a specious name, but is in reality nothing more than force put upon one being by another who happens to be stronger. Now strength apparently does not constitute justice, nor ought 'might,' according to a trite proverb, to 'overcome right.' The case of punishment, which we are now considering, is the case of you and I differing in opinion, and your telling me that you must be right, since you have a more brawny arm, or have applied your mind more to the acquiring skill in your weapons than I have.

But let us suppose, 'that I am convinced of my error, but that my conviction is superficial and fluctuating, and the object you propose is to render it durable and profound.' Ought it to be thus durable and profound? There are no doubt arguments and reasons calculated to render it so. Is it in reality problematical, and do you wish by the weight of your blows to make up for the deficiency of your logic? This can never be defended. An appeal to force must appear to both parties, in proportion to the soundness of their understanding, to be a confession of imbecility. He that has recourse to it, would have no occasion for this expedient, if he were sufficiently acquainted with the powers of that truth it is his office to communicate. If there be any man, who, in suffering punishment, is not conscious of injustice, he must have had his mind previously debased by slavery, and his sense of moral right and wrong blunted by a series of oppression.

The case is not altered for the better, if I suffer punishment, considered not for my own correction, but for an example to others. Upon this supposition a new difficulty is introduced, respecting the propriety of one man's being subjected to pain, for the sake of improving the character and eradicating the vices of another. The suffering is here also involuntary. Now, though will cannot alter the nature of justice, it must be admitted that the voluntary sufferer has at least one advantage over the involuntary, in the conscious liberality of his purpose. He that suffers, not for his own correction, but for the advantage of others, stands, so far as relates to that suffering, in the situation of an innocent person. If the suffering had relation to him personally as a vicious or imperfect character, it must have relation to him in respect either to the past or the future. It cannot have relation to him as to the past, for that is concluded and beyond the reach of alteration or remedy. By the supposition it has not relation to him but to others as to the future.

It ought to be observed in this place, that by innocence I do not understand virtue. Innocence is a sort of neutral character, and stands in the mid way between good and harm. Undoubtedly it were better, that a person useless to society should be destroyed than a man of eminent worth, and a person likely to prove injurious than either. I say likely to prove injurious; for the fault already committed, being irrevocable, ought not to enter into the account, and we have nothing to do but with the probability of its repetition. It is in this sense that the sufferer stands upon a level with many of those persons, who are usually denominated innocent.

It must also be allowed, that there are cases in which it is proper that innocent men should suffer for the public good. But this is a question of a very delicate nature, and the severe moralist will be very reluctant to condemn that man to die for the benefit of others, who is desirous to live.

As to every other circumstance in the case of him who is punished for an example to others, it remains precisely the same as when we supposed him to be punished for his own reformation. It is still an argument of the most exceptionable nature employed to correct the opinions of mankind. It is still a menace of violence made use of to persuade them of the truth or falshood of a proposition. It has little chance of making them wise, and can scarcely fail of making them timid, dissembling and corrupt.

Notwithstanding all these objections, it would be difficult to find a country, respecting which we could say, that the inhabitants might with safety be dismissed from the operation of punishment. So mixed is human character, so wild are its excursions, so calamitous and detestable are the errors into which it occasionally falls, that something more than argument seems necessary for their suppression. Human beings are such tyros in the art of reasoning, that the wisest of us often prove impotent in our attempts, where an instant effect was most powerfully wanted. While I stand still to reason with the thief, the assassin or the oppressor, they hasten to new scenes of devastation, and with unsparing violence confound all the principles of human society. I should obtain little success by the abolition of punishment, unless I could at the same time abolish those causes that generate temptation and make punishment necessary. Meanwhile the arguments already adduced may be sufficient to shew that punishment is always an evil, and to persuade us never to recur to it but from the most evident necessity.

The remaining cases in which it may seem requisite to have recourse to the general will of the society, and to supersede the private judgment of individuals, are, when we are called upon to counteract the hostilities of an internal enemy, or to repel the attacks of a foreign invader. Here as in the former instance the evils that arise from an usurpation upon private judgment are many and various. It is wrong that I should contribute in any mode to a proceeding, a war for example, that I believe to be unjust. Ought I to draw my sword, when the adversary appears to me to be employed in repelling a wanton aggression? The case seems not to be at all different, if I contribute my property, the produce it may be of my personal labour; though custom has reconciled us to the one rather than the other.

The consequences are a degradation of character and a relaxation of principle, in the person who is thus made the instrument of a transaction, which his judgment disapproves. In this case, as has been already stated generally, the human mind is compressed and unnerved, till it affords us scarcely the semblance of what it might otherwise have been. And, in addition to the general considerations in similar cases, it may be observed, that the frequent and obstinate wars which at present desolate the human race would be nearly extirpated, if they were supported only by the voluntary contributions of those by whom their principle was approved.

The objection, which has hitherto been permitted practically to supersede these reasonings, is the difficulty of conducting an affair, in the success of which millions may be interested, upon so precarious a support as that of private judgment. The men, with whom we are usually concerned in human society, are of so mixed a character, and a self-love of the narrowest kind is so deeply rooted in many of them, that it seems nearly unavoidable upon the scheme of voluntary contribution, that the most generous would pay a very ample proportion, while the mean and avaricious, though they contributed nothing, would come in for their full share of the benefit. He that would reconcile a perfect freedom in this respect with the interest of the whole, ought to propose at the same time the means of extirpating selfishness and vice. How far such a proposal is feasible will come hereafter to be considered.

BOOK III
PRINCIPLES OF GOVERNMENT

CHAPTER I
SYSTEMS OF POLITICAL WRITERS

The question stated.—First hypothesis: government founded in superior strength.—Second hypothesis: government jure divino.—Third hypothesis: the social contract.—The first hypothesis examined.—The second.—Criterion of divine right: 1. patriarchal descent—2. justice.

IT has appeared in the course of our reasonings upon the nature of society, that there are occasions in which it may be necessary, to supersede private judgment for the sake of public good, and to control the acts of the individual by an act to be performed in the name of the whole. It is therefore an interesting enquiry to ascertain in what manner such acts are to be originated, or in other words to ascertain the foundation of political government.

There are three hypotheses that have been principally maintained upon this subject. First, the system of force, according to which it is affirmed, 'that, inasmuch as it is necessary that the great mass of mankind should be held under the subjection of compulsory restraint, there can be no other criterion of that restraint, than the power of the individuals who lay claim to its exercise, the foundation of which power exists in the unequal degrees, in which corporal strength and intellectual sagacity are distributed among mankind.'

There is a second class of reasoners, who deduce the origin of all government from divine right, and affirm, 'that, as men derived their existence from an infinite creator at first, so are they still subject to his providential care, and of consequence owe allegiance to their civil governors, as to a power which he has thought fit to set over them.'

The third system is that which has been most usually maintained by the friends of equality and justice; the system according to which the individuals of any society are supposed to have entered into a contract with their governors or with each other, and which founds the rights of government in the consent of the governed.

The two first of these hypotheses may easily be dismissed. That of force appears to proceed upon the total negation of abstract and immutable justice, affirming every government to be right, that is possessed of power sufficient to inforce its decrees. It puts a violent termination upon all political science; and seems intended to persuade men, to sit down quietly under their present disadvantages, whatever they may be, and not exert themselves to discover a remedy for the evils they suffer. The second hypothesis is of an equivocal nature. It either coincides with the first, and affirms all existing power to be alike of divine derivation; or it must remain totally useless till a criterion can be found, to distinguish those governments which are approved by God, from those which cannot lay claim to that sanction. The criterion of patriarchal descent will be of no avail, till the true claimant and rightful heir can be discovered. If we make utility and justice the test of God's approbation, this hypothesis will be liable to little objection; but then on the other hand little will be gained by it, since those who have not introduced divine right into the argument, will yet readily grant, that a government which can be shewn to be agreeable to utility and justice, is a rightful government.

The third hypothesis demands a more careful examination. If any error have insinuated itself into the support of truth, it becomes of particular consequence to detect it. Nothing can be of more importance, than to separate prejudice and mistake on the one hand, from reason and demonstration on the other. Where-ever they have been confounded, the cause of truth must necessarily be a sufferer. That cause, so far from being injured by the dissolution of the unnatural alliance, may be expected to derive from that dissolution an eminent degree of prosperity and lustre.

CHAPTER II

OF THE SOCIAL CONTRACT

Queries proposed.—Who are the contracting parties?—What is the form of engagement?—Over how long a period does the contract extend?—To how great a variety of propositions?—Can it extend to laws hereafter to be made?—Addresses of adhesion considered.—Power of a majority.

UPON the first statement of the system of a social contract various difficulties present themselves. Who are the parties to this contract? For whom did they consent, for themselves only or for others? For how long a time is this contract to be considered as binding? If the consent of every individual be necessary, in what manner is that consent to be given? Is it to be tacit, or declared in express terms?

Little will be gained for the cause of equality and justice, if our ancestors, at the first institution of government, had a right indeed of choosing the system of regulations under which they thought proper to live, but at the same time could barter away the understandings and independence of all that came after them to the latest posterity. But, if the contract must be renewed in each successive generation, what periods must be fixed on for that purpose? And if I be obliged to submit to the established government till my turn comes to assent to it, upon what principle is that obligation founded? Surely not upon the contract into which my father entered before I was born?

Secondly, what is the nature of the consent, in consequence of which I am to be reckoned the subject of any particular government? It is usually said, 'that acquiescence is sufficient; and that this acquiescence is to be inferred from my living quietly under the protection of the laws.' But if this be true, an end is as effectually put to all political science, all discrimination of better and worse, as by any system invented by the most slavish sycophant that ever existed. Upon this hypothesis every government that is quietly submitted to is a lawful government, whether it be the usurpation of Cromwel or the tyranny of Caligula.* Acquiescence is frequently nothing more than a choice on the part of the individual of what he deems the least evil. In many cases it is not so much as this, since the peasant and the artisan, who form the bulk of a nation, however dissatisfied with the government of their country, seldom have it in their power to transport themselves to another. It is also to be observed upon the system of acquiescence, that it is in little agreement with the established opinions and practices of mankind. Thus what has been called the law of nations, lays least stress upon the allegiance of a foreigner settling among us, though his acquiescence is certainly most complete; while natives removing into an uninhabited region are claimed by the mother country, and removing into a neighbouring territory are punished by municipal law, if they take arms against the country in which they were born. Now surely acquiescence can scarcely be construed into consent, while the individuals concerned are wholly unapprised of the authority intended to be rested upon it.[1]

Mr. Locke, the great champion of the doctrine of an original contract, has been aware of this difficulty, and therefore observes, that 'a tacit consent indeed obliges a man to obey the laws of any government, as long as he has any possessions, or enjoyment of any part of the

---

[1] See Hume's Essays. Part II. Essay xii.*

dominions of that government; but nothing can make a man a member of the commonwealth, but his actually entering into it by positive engagement, and express promise and compact.'[1] A singular distinction; implying upon the face of it, that an acquiescence, such as has just been described, is sufficient to render a man amenable to the penal regulations of society; but that his own consent is necessary to entitle him to its privileges.

A third objection to the social contract will suggest itself, as soon as we attempt to ascertain the extent of the obligation, even supposing it to have been entered into in the most solemn manner by every member of the community. Allowing that I am called upon, at the period of my coming of age for example, to declare my assent or dissent to any system of opinions or any code of practical institutes; for how long a period does this declaration bind me? Am I precluded from better information for the whole course of my life? And, if not for my whole life, why for a year, a week or even an hour? If my deliberate judgment or my real sentiment be of no avail in the case, in what sense can it be affirmed that all lawful government is founded in my consent?

But the question of time is not the only difficulty. If you demand my assent to any proposition, it is necessary that the proposition should be stated simply and clearly. So numerous are the varieties of human understanding, in all cases where its independence and integrity are sufficiently preserved, that there is little chance of any two men coming to a precise agreement about ten successive propositions that are in their own nature open to debate. What then can be more absurd than to present to me the laws of England in fifty volumes folio, and call upon me to give an honest and uninfluenced vote upon their whole contents at once?

Can it extend to laws hereafter to be made? But the social contract, considered as the foundation of civil government, requires more of me than this. I am not only obliged to consent to all the laws that are actually upon record, but to all the laws that shall hereafter be made. It was under this view of the subject, that Rousseau, in tracing the consequences of the social contract, was led to assert, that 'the great body of the people, in whom the sovereign authority resides, can neither delegate nor resign it. The essence of that authority,' he adds, 'is the general will; and will cannot be represented. It must either be the same or another; there is no alternative. The deputies of the people cannot be its representatives; they are merely its attorneys.

---

[1] Treatise of Government. Book II. Ch. viii § 119, 122.

The laws, that the community does not ratify in person, are no laws, are nullities.'[1]

The difficulty here stated has been endeavoured to be provided against by some late advocates for liberty, in the way of addresses of adhesion; addresses, originating in the various districts and departments of a nation, and without which no regulation of constitutional importance is to be deemed valid. But this is a very inadequate and superficial remedy. The addressers of course have seldom any other remedy than that above described, of indiscriminate admission or rejection. There is an infinite difference between the first deliberation, and the subsequent exercise of a negative. The former is a real power, the latter is seldom more than the shadow of a power. Not to add, that addresses are a most precarious and equivocal mode of collecting the sense of a nation. They are usually voted in a tumultuous and summary manner; they are carried along by the tide of party; and the signatures annexed to them are obtained by indirect and accidental methods, while multitudes of bystanders, unless upon some extraordinary occasion, remain ignorant of or indifferent to the transaction.

Lastly, if government be founded in the consent of the people, it can have no power over any individual by whom that consent is refused. If a tacit consent be not sufficient, still less can I be deemed to have consented to a measure upon which I put an express negative. This immediately follows from the observations of Rousseau. If the people, or the individuals of whom the people is constituted, cannot delegate their authority to a representative; neither can any individual delegate his authority to a majority, in an assembly of which he is himself a member. The rules by which my actions shall be directed are matters of a consideration entirely personal; and no man can transfer to another the keeping of his conscience and the judging of his duties. But this brings us back to the point from which we set out. No consent of ours can divest us of our moral capacity. This is a species of property which we can neither barter nor resign; and of consequence it is impossible for any government to derive its authority from an original contract.

[1] '*La souveraineté ne peut être representée, par la même raison qu'elle ne peut être alienée; elle consiste essentiellement dans la volonté générale, et la volunté ne se represente point: elle est la même, ou elle est autre; il n'y a point de milieu. Les deputés du peuple ne sont donc point ses representans, ils ne sont que ses comissaires; ils ne peuvent rien conclure definitivement. Toute loi que le peuple en personne n'a pas ratifiée, est nulle; ce n'est point une loi.*' Du Contract Social.* Liv. III. Chap. xv.

CHAPTER III

OF PROMISES

The validity of promises examined.—Shown to be inconsistent with justice—to be foreign to the general good.—Of the expectation excited.—The fulfilling expectation does not imply the validity of a promise.—Conclusion.

THE whole principle of an original contract proceeds upon the obligation under which we are placed to observe our promises. The reasoning upon which it is founded is, 'that we have promised obedience to government, and therefore are bound to obey.' It may consequently be proper to enquire into the nature of this obligation to observe our promises.

We have already established justice as the sum of moral and political duty. Is justice then in its own nature precarious or immutable? Surely immutable. As long as men are men, the conduct I am bound to observe respecting them must remain the same. A good man must always be the proper object of my support and cooperation; vice of my censure; and the vicious man of instruction and reform.

What is it then to which the obligation of a promise applies? What I have promised is either right, or wrong, or indifferent. There are few articles of human conduct that fall under the latter class; and the greater shall be our improvements in moral science the fewer still will they appear. Omitting these, let us then consider only the two preceding classes. 'I have promised to do something just and right.' This certainly I ought to perform. Why? Not because I promised, but because justice prescribes it. 'I have promised to bestow a sum of money upon some good and respectable purpose. In the interval between the promise and my fulfilling it, a greater and nobler purpose offers itself, and calls with an imperious voice for my cooperation.' Which ought I to prefer? That which best deserves my preference. A promise can make no alteration in the case. I ought to be guided by the intrinsic merit of the objects, and not by any external and foreign consideration. No engagements of mine can change their intrinsic claims.

All this must be exceedingly plain to the reader who has followed me in my early reasonings upon the nature of justice. If every shilling of our property, every hour of our time and every faculty of our mind, have already received their destination from the principles of immutable justice, promises have no department left upon which for them to decide. Justice it appears therefore ought to be done, whether we have promised it or not. If we discover any thing to be unjust, we ought to abstain from it, with what ever solemnity we have engaged for its perpetration. We were erroneous and vicious when the promise was made; but this affords no sufficient reason for its performance.

But it will be said, 'if promises be not made, or when made be not fulfilled, how can the affairs of the world be carried on?' By rational and intelligent beings acting as if they were rational and intelligent. A promise would perhaps be sufficiently innocent, if it were understood merely as declaratory of intention, and not as precluding farther information. Even in this restrained sense however it is far from being generally necessary. Why should it be supposed that the affairs of the world would not go on sufficiently well, though my neighbour could no farther depend upon my assistance than it appeared rational to grant it? This would be a sufficient dependence if I were honest, nor would he if he were honest desire any thing more. If I were dishonest, if I could not be bound by the reason and justice of the case, it would afford him a slender additional dependence to call in the aid of a principle founded in prejudice and mistake: not to say, that, let it afford ever so great advantage in any particular case, the evil of the immoral precedent would outweigh the individual advantage.

It may be farther objected, 'that this principle might be sufficiently suited to a better and more perfect state of society, but that at present there are dishonest members of the community, who will not perform their duty, if they be not bound to it by some grosser motive, than the mere moral consideration.' Be it so. This is a question altogether different from that we have been examining. We are not now enquiring whether the community ought to animadvert upon the errors of its members. This animadversion the upright man is not backward to encounter, and willingly risks the penalty, which the society (for the society is more competent to ascertain the just amount of the penalty than the preceding caprice of the parties) has awarded in cases apparently similar, if he conceive that his duty requires from him that risk.

But to return to the case of promises. I shall be told, that, 'in choosing between two purposes about which to employ my money, my time or my talents, my promise may make an essential difference, and therefore having once been given ought to be fulfilled. The party to whom it was made has had expectations excited in him, which I ought not to disappoint; the party to whom I am under no engagement has no such disappointment to encounter.' What is this tenderness to which I am bound, this expectation I must not dare to disappoint? An expectation that I should do wrong, that I should prefer a less good to a greater, that

I should commit absolute evil; for such must be the result when the balance has been struck. 'But his expectation has altered the nature of his situation, has engaged him in undertakings from which he would otherwise have abstained.' Be it so. He and all other men will be taught to depend more upon their own exertions, and less upon the assistance of others, which caprice may refuse, or justice oblige me to withhold. He and all others will be taught to acquire such merit, and to engage in such pursuits, as shall oblige every honest man to come to their succour, if they should stand in need of assistance. The resolute execution of justice, without listening to that false pity, which, to do imaginary kindness to one, would lead us to injure the whole, would in a thousand ways increase the independence, the energies and the virtue of mankind.

Let us however suppose, 'that my conduct ought to be influenced by this previous expectation of the individual.' Let us suppose, 'that, in selecting an individual for a certain office, my choice ought not to be governed merely by the abstract fitness of the candidates, but that I ought to take into the account the extreme value of the appointment from certain circumstances to one of the candidates, and its comparative inutility to the other.' Let us farther suppose, 'that the expectation excited in one of them has led him into studies and pursuits to qualify himself for the office, which will be useless if he do not succeed to it; and that this is one of the considerations which ought to govern my determination.'—All this does not come up to what we have been taught respecting the obligation of a promise.

For, first, it may be observed, that it seems to be of little consequence in this statement, whether the expectation were excited by a direct promise or in some other manner, whether it were excited by a declaration of mine or of a third person, or lastly, whether it arose singly out of the reason of the case and the pure deductions and reflections of the expecter's mind. Upon every one of these suppositions his conduct, and the injury he may sustain from a disappointment, will remain the same. Here then all that has been commonly understood by the obligation of a promise is excluded. The motive to be attended to, flows from no solemn engagement of mine, but from an incidental consequence of my declaration, and which might just as easily have been the consequence of many other circumstances. The consideration by which it becomes me to be influenced is, not a regard for veracity, or a particular desire to preserve my integrity, both of which are in reality wholly unconcerned in the transaction, but an attention to the injury to be sustained by the losing candidate, whatever might be the original occasion of the conduct out of which the injury has proceeded.

Let us take an example of a still simpler nature. 'I live in Westminster; and I engage to meet the captain of a ship from Blackwal at the Royal Exchange.* My engagement is of the nature of information to him, that I shall be at the Exchange at a certain hour. He accordingly lays aside his other business, and comes thither to meet me.' This is a reason why I should not fail him unless for some very material cause. But it would seem as if the reason why I should not fail him would be equally cogent, if I knew from any other source that he would be there, and that a quantity of convenience equal to the quantity upon the former supposition would accrue from my meeting him. It may be said, 'that it is essential to various circumstances of human intercourse, that we should be able to depend on each other for a steady adherence to engagements of this sort.' The statement however would be somewhat more accurate if we said, 'that it was essential to various circumstances of human intercourse, that we should be known to bestow a steady attention upon the quantities of convenience or inconvenience, of good or evil, that might arise to others from our conduct.'

It is undoubtedly upon this hypothesis a part of our duty to make as few promises or declarations exciting appropriate expectations as possible. He who lightly gives to another the idea that he will govern himself in his future conduct, not by the views that shall be present to his mind when the conduct shall come to be determined on, but by the view he shall be able to take of it at some preceding period, is vicious in so doing. But the obligation he is under respecting his future conduct is, to act justly, and not, because he has committed one error, for that reason to become guilty of a second.

CHAPTER IV

OF POLITICAL AUTHORITY

Common deliberation the true foundation of government—proved from the equal claims of mankind—from the nature of our faculties—from the object of government—from the effects of common deliberation.—Delegation vindicated.—Difference between the doctrine here maintained and that of a social contract apparent—from the merely prospective nature of the former—from the nullity of promises—from the fallibility of deliberation.—Conclusion.

HAVING rejected the hypotheses that have most generally been adduced to account for the origin of government consistently with the principles of moral justice, let us enquire whether we may not arrive at the same object, by a simple investigation of the obvious reason of the case, without having recourse to any refinement of system or fiction of process.

Government then being introduced for the reasons already assigned, the first and most important principle that can be imagined relative to its form and structure, seems to be this; that, as government is a transaction in the name and for the benefit of the whole, every member of the community ought to have some share in its administration. The arguments in support of this proposition are various.

1. It has already appeared that there is no criterion perspicuously designating any one man or set of men to preside over the rest.
2. All men are partakers of the common faculty reason, and may be supposed to have some communication with the common preceptor truth. It would be wrong in an affair of such momentous concern, that any chance for additional wisdom should be rejected; nor can we tell in many cases till after the experiment how eminent any individual may one day be found in the business of guiding and deliberating for his fellows.
3. Government is a contrivance instituted for the security of individuals; and it seems both reasonable that each man should have a share in providing for his own security, and probable that partiality and cabal should by this means be most effectually excluded.
4. Lastly, to give each man a voice in the public concerns comes nearest to that admirable idea of which we should never lose sight, the uncontrolled exercise of private judgment. Each man would thus be inspired with a consciousness of his own importance, and the slavish feelings that shrink up the soul in the presence of an imagined superior would be unknown.

Admitting then the propriety of each man having a share in directing the affairs of the whole in the first instance, it seems necessary that he should concur, in electing a house of representatives, if he be the member of a large state; or, even in a small one, that he should assist in the appointment of officers and administrators; which implies, first, a delegation of authority to these officers, and, secondly, a tacit consent, or rather an admission of the necessity, that the questions to be debated should abide the decision of a majority.

But to this system of delegation the same objections may be urged, that were cited from Rousseau in the chapter of the Social Contract. It may be alleged that, 'if it be the business of every man to exercise his own judgment, he can in no instance surrender this function into the hands of another.'

To this objection it may be answered, first, that the parallel is by no means complete between an individual's exercise of his judgment in a case that is truly his own, and his exercise of his judgment in an article where the necessity and province of government are already admitted. Wherever there is a government, there must be a will superseding that of individuals. It is absurd to expect that every member of a society should agree with every other member in the various measures it may be found necessary to adopt. The same necessity, that requires the introduction of force to suppress injustice on the part of a few, requires that the sentiments of the majority should direct that force, and that the minority should either secede, or patiently wait for the period when the truth on the subject contested shall be generally understood.

Secondly, delegation is not, as at first sight it might appear to be, the act of one man committing to another a function, which strictly speaking it became him to exercise for himself. Delegation, in every instance in which it can be reconciled with justice, is an act which has for its object the general good. The individuals to whom the delegation is made, are either more likely from talents or leisure to perform the function in the most eligible manner, or at least there is some public interest requiring that it should be performed by one or a few persons, rather than by every individual for himself. This is the case, whether in that first and simplest of all delegations the prerogative of a majority, or in the election of a house of representatives, or in the appointment of public officers. Now all contest as to the person who shall exercise a certain function, and the propriety of resigning it, is frivolous, the moment it is decided how and by whom it can most advantageously be exercised. It is of no consequence that I am the parent of a child, when it has once been ascertained that the child will receive greater benefit by living under the superintendence of a stranger.

Lastly, it is a mistake to imagine that the propriety of restraining me when my conduct is injurious, rises out of any delegation of mine. The justice of employing force when every other means was insufficient, is even prior to the existence of society. Force ought never to be resorted to but in cases of absolute necessity; and, when such cases occur, it is the duty of every man to defend himself from violation. There is there-fore no delegation necessary on the part of the offender; but the community in the censure it exercises over him stands in the place of the injured party.

It may perhaps by some persons be imagined, that the doctrine here delivered of the justice of proceeding in common concerns by a common deliberation, is nearly coincident with that other doctrine which teaches that all lawful government derives its authority from a social contract. Let us consider what is the true difference between them.

In the first place, the doctrine of common deliberation is of a prospective, and not a retrospective nature. Is the question respecting some future measure to be adopted in behalf of the community? Here the obligation to deliberate in common presents itself, as eminently to be preferred to every other mode of deciding upon the interests of the whole. Is the question whether I shall yield obedience to any measure already promulgated? Here I have nothing to do with the consideration of how the measure originated; unless perhaps in a country where common deliberation has in some sort been admitted as a standing principle, and where the object may be to resist an innovation upon this principle. In the case of ship money under king Charles the first,* it was perhaps fair to resist the tax, even supposing it to be abstractedly a good one, upon account of the authority imposing it; though that reason might be insufficient, in a country unused to representative taxation.

Exclusively of this consideration, no measure is to be resisted on account of the irregularity of its derivation. If it be just, it is entitled both to my chearful submission and my zealous support. So far as it is deficient in justice, I am bound to resist. My situation in this respect is in no degree different from what it was previously to all organised government. Justice was at that time entitled to my assent, and injustice to my disapprobation. They can never cease to have the same claims upon me, till they shall cease to be distinguished by the same unalterable properties. The measure of my resistance will however vary with circumstances, and therefore will demand from us a separate examination.

Secondly, the distinction between the doctrine here advanced and that of a social contract will be better understood, if we recollect what has been said upon the nature and validity of promises. If promise be in all cases a fallacious mode of binding a man to a specific mode of action, then must the argument be in all cases impertinent, that I consented to such a decision, and am therefore bound to regulate myself accordingly. It is impossible to imagine a principle of more injurious tendency, than that which shall teach me to disarm my future wisdom by my past folly, and to consult for my direction the errors in which my ignorance has involved me, rather than the code of eternal truth. So far as consent has any validity, abstract justice becomes a matter of pure indifference: so far as justice deserves to be made the guide of my life, it is in vain to endeavour to share its authority with compacts and promises.

We have found the parallel to be in one respect incomplete between the exercise of these two functions, private judgment and common deliberation. In another respect the analogy is exceedingly striking, and considerable perspicuity will be given to our ideas of the latter by an illustration borrowed from the former. In the one case as in the other there is an obvious principle of justice in favour of the general exercise. No individual can arrive at any degree of moral or intellectual improvement, unless in the use of an independent judgment. No state can be well or happily administered, unless in the perpetual use of common deliberation respecting the measures it may be requisite to adopt. But, though the general exercise of these faculties be founded in immutable justice, justice will by no means uniformly vindicate the particular application of them. Private judgment and public deliberation are not themselves the standard of moral right and wrong; they are only the means of discovering right and wrong, and of comparing particular propositions with the standard of eternal truth.

Too much stress has undoubtedly been laid upon the idea, as of a grand and magnificent spectacle, of a nation deciding for itself upon some great public principle, and of the highest magistracy yielding its claims when the general voice has pronounced. The value of the whole must at last depend upon the quality of their decision. Truth cannot be made more true by the number of its votaries. Nor is the spectacle much less interesting, of a solitary individual bearing his undaunted testimony in favour of justice, though opposed by misguided millions. Within certain limits however the beauty of the exhibition must be acknowledged. That a nation should dare to vindicate its function of common deliberation, is a step gained, and a step that inevitably leads to an improvement of the character of individuals. That men should unite in the assertion of truth, is no unpleasing evidence of their virtue. Lastly, that an individual, however great may be his imaginary elevation, should be obliged to yield his personal pretensions to the sense of the community, at least bears the appearance of a practical confirmation of the great principle, that all private considerations must yield to the general good.

CHAPTER V

OF LEGISLATION

Society can declare and interpret, but cannot enact.—Its authority only executive.

HAVING thus far investigated the nature of political functions, it seems necessary that some explanation should be given in this place upon the subject of legislation. Who is it that has the authority to make laws? What are the characteristics by which that man or body of men is to be known, in whom the faculty is vested of legislating for the rest?

To these questions the answer is exceedingly simple: Legislation, as it has been usually understood, is not an affair of human competence. Reason is the only legislator, and her decrees are irrevocable and uniform. The functions of society extend, not to the making, but the interpreting of law; it cannot decree, it can only declare that, which the nature of things has already decreed, and the propriety of which irresistibly flows from the circumstances of the case. Montesquieu says, that 'in a free state every man will be his own legislator.'[1] This is not true, setting apart the functions of the community, unless in the limited sense already explained. It is the office of conscience to determine, 'not like an Asiatic cadi,* according to the ebbs and flows of his own passions, but like a British judge, who makes no new law, but faithfully declares that law which he finds already written.'[2]

The same distinction is to be made upon the subject of authority. All political power is strictly speaking executive. It has appeared to be necessary, with respect to men as we at present find them, that force should sometimes be employed in repressing injustice; and for the same reasons it appears that this force should as far as possible be vested in the community. To the public support of justice therefore the authority of the community extends. But no sooner does it wander in the smallest degree from the great line of justice, than its authority is at an end, it stands upon a level with the obscurest individual, and every man is bound to resist its decisions.

---

[1] '*Dans un état libre, tout home qui est censé avoir une ame libre, doit être gouverné par lui-même.' Esprit des Loix,* Liv. XI. Ch. vi.

[2] Sterne's Sermons*—'On a Good Conscience.'

CHAPTER VI

OF OBEDIENCE

Obedience not the correlative of authority.—No man bound to yield obedience to another.—Case of submission considered.—Foundation of obedience.—Usefulness of social communication.—Case of confidence considered.—Its limitations.—Mischief of unlimited confidence.—Subjection explained.

HAVING enquired into the just and legitimate source of authority, we will next turn our attention to what has usually been considered as its correlative, obedience. This has always been found a subject of peculiar difficulty, as well in relation to the measure and extent of obedience, as to the source of our obligation to obey.

The true solution will probably be found in the observation that obedience is by no means the proper correlative. The object of government, as has been already demonstrated, is the exertion of force. Now force can never be regarded as an appeal to the understanding; and therefore obedience, which is an act of the understanding or will, can have no legitimate connection with it. I am bound to submit to justice and truth, because they approve themselves to my judgment. I am bound to co-operate with government, as far as it appears to me to coincide with these principles. But I submit to government when I think it erroneous, merely because I have no remedy.

No truth can be more simple, at the same time that no truth has been more darkened by the glosses of interested individuals, than that one man can in no case be bound to yield obedience to any other man or set of men upon earth.

There is one rule to which we are universally bound to conform ourselves, justice, the treating every man precisely as his usefulness and worth demand, the acting under every circumstance in the manner that shall procure the greatest quantity of general good. When we have done thus, what province is there left to the disposal of obedience?

I am summoned to appear before the magistrate to answer for a libel, an imaginary crime, an act which perhaps I am convinced ought in no case to fall under the animadversion of law. I comply with this summons. My compliance proceeds, perhaps from a conviction that the arguments I shall exhibit in the court form the best resistance I can give to his injustice, or perhaps from perceiving that my non-compliance would frivolously and without real use interrupt the public tranquillity.

A quaker refuses to pay tithes.* He therefore suffers a tithe proctor to distrain upon his goods. In this action morally speaking he does wrong. The distinction he makes is the argument of a mind that delights in trifles. That which will be taken from me by force, it is no breach of morality to deliver with my own hand. The money which the robber extorts from me, I do not think it necessary to oblige him to take from my person. If I walk quietly to the gallows, this does not imply my consent to be hanged.

In all these cases there is a clear distinction between my compliance with justice and my compliance with injustice. I conform to the principles of justice, because I perceive them to be intrinsically and unalterably right. I yield to injustice, though I perceive that to which I yield to be abstractedly wrong, and only choose the least among inevitable evils.

The case of volition, as it is commonly termed, seems parallel to that of intellect. You present a certain proposition to my mind, to which you require my assent. If you accompany the proposition with evidence calculated to shew the agreement between the terms of which it consists, you may obtain my assent. If you accompany the proposition with authority, telling me that you have examined it and find it to be true, that thousands of wise and disinterested men have admitted it, that angels or Gods have affirmed it, I may assent to your authority; but, with respect to the proposition itself, my understanding of its reasonableness, my perception of that in the proposition which strictly speaking constitutes its truth or its falshood, remain just as they did. I believe something else, but I do not believe the proposition.

Just so in morals. I may be persuaded of the propriety of yielding compliance to a requisition the justice of which I cannot discern, as I may be persuaded to yield compliance to a requisition which I know to be unjust. But neither of these requisitions is strictly speaking a proper subject of obedience. Obedience seems rather to imply the unforced choice of the mind and assent of the judgment. But the compliance I yield to government, independently of my approbation of its measures, is of the same species as my compliance with a wild beast, that forces me to run north, when my judgment and inclination prompted me to go south.

But, though morality in its purest construction altogether excludes the idea of one man's yielding obedience to another, yet the greatest benefits will result from mutual communication. There is scarcely any man, whose communications will not sometimes enlighten my judgment and rectify my conduct. But the persons to whom it becomes me to pay particular attention in this respect, are not such as may exercise any particular magistracy, but such, whatever may be their station, as are wiser or better informed in any respect than myself.

There are two ways in which a man wiser than myself may be of use to me; by the communication of those arguments by which he is convinced of the truth of the judgments he has formed; and by the communication of the judgments themselves independent of argument. This last is of use only in respect to the narrowness of our own understandings, and the time that might be requisite for the acquisition of a science of which we are at present ignorant. On this account I am not to be blamed, if I employ a builder to construct me a house, or a mechanic to sink me a well; nor should I be liable to blame, if I worked in person under their direction. In this case, not having opportunity or ability to acquire the science myself, I trust to the science of another. I choose from the deliberation of my own judgment the end to be pursued; I am convinced that the end is good and commendable; and, having done this, I commit the selection of means to a person whose qualifications are superior to my own. The confidence reposed in this instance is precisely of the nature of delegation in general. No term surely can be more unapt than that of obedience, to express our duty towards the overseer we have appointed in our affairs.

Similar to the confidence I repose in a skilful mechanic is the attention which ought to be paid to the commander of an army. It is my duty in the first place to be satisfied of the goodness of the cause, of the propriety of the war, and of the truth of as many general propositions concerning the conduct of it, as can possibly be brought within the sphere of my understanding. It may well be doubted whether secrecy be in any degree necessary to the conduct of war. It may be doubted whether treachery and surprise are to be classed among the legitimate means of defeating our adversary. But after every deduction has been made for considerations of this sort, there will still remain cases, where something must be confided, as to the plan of a campaign or the arrangement of a battle, to the skill, so far as that skill really exists, of the commander. When he has explained both to the utmost of his ability, there may remain parts, the propriety of which I cannot fully comprehend, but which I have sufficient reason to confide to his judgment.

This doctrine however of limited obedience, or, as it may more properly be termed, of confidence and delegation, ought to be called into action as seldom as possible. Every man should discharge to the utmost practicable extent the duties which arise from his situation. If he gain as to the ability with which they may be discharged, when he delegates them to another, he loses with respect to the fidelity; every one being conscious of the sincerity of his own intention, and no one having equal proof of that of another. A virtuous man will not fail to perceive the obligation under which he is placed to exert his own understanding, and to judge for himself as widely as his circumstances will permit.

The abuse of the doctrine of confidence has been the source of more calamities to mankind than all the other errors of the human understanding. Depravity would have gained little ground in the world, if every man had been in the exercise of his independent judgment. The instrument by which extensive mischiefs have in all ages been perpetrated has been, the principle of many men being reduced to mere machines in the hands of a few. Man, while he consults his own understanding, is the ornament of the universe. Man, when he surrenders his reason, and becomes the partisan of implicit faith and passive obedience, is the most mischievous of all animals. Ceasing to examine every proposition that comes before him for the direction of his conduct, he is no longer the capable subject of moral instruction. He is, in the instant of submission, the blind instrument of every nefarious purpose of his principal; and, when left to himself, is open to the seduction of injustice, cruelty and profligacy.

These reasonings lead to a proper explanation of the word subject. If by the subject of any government we mean a person whose duty it is to obey, the true inference from the preceding principles is, that no government has any subjects. If on the contrary we mean a person, whom the government is bound to protect, or may justly restrain, the word is sufficiently admissible. This remark enables us to solve the long-disputed question, what it is that constitutes a man the subject of any government. Every man is in this sense a subject, whom the government is competent to protect on the one hand, or who on the other, by the violence of his proceedings, renders force requisite to prevent him from disturbing that community, for the preservation of whose peace the government is instituted.

APPENDIX

Moral principles frequently elucidated by incidental reflection—by incidental passages in various authors.—Example.

It will generally be found that, even where the truth upon any subject has been most industriously obscured, its occasional irradiations have not been wholly excluded. The mind has no sooner obtained evidence of any new truth, especially in the science of morals, but it recollects numerous intimations of that truth which have occasionally suggested themselves, and is astonished that a discovery which was perpetually upon the eve of being made, should have been kept at a distance so long.

This is eminently the case in the subject of which we are treating. Those numerous passages in poets, divines[1] and philosophers, which have placed our unalterable duty in the strongest contrast with the precarious authority of a superior, and have taught us to disclaim all subordination to the latter, have always been received by the ingenuous mind with a tumult of applause. There is indeed no species of composition, in which the seeds of a morality too perfect for our present improvements in science, may more reasonably be expected to discover themselves, than in works of imagination. When the mind shakes off the fetters of prescription and prejudice, when it boldly takes a flight into the world unknown, and employs itself in search of those grand and interesting principles which shall tend to impart to every reader the glow of enthusiasm, it is at such moments that the enquiring and philosophical reader may expect to be presented with the materials and rude sketches of intellectual improvement.[2]

Among the many passages from writers of every denomination that will readily suggest themselves under this head to a well informed mind, we may naturally recollect the spirited reasoning of young Norval in the tragedy of Douglas, when he is called upon by lord Randolph to state the particulars of a contest in which he is engaged, that lord Randolph may be able to decide between the disputants.

> 'Nay, my good lord, though I revere you much,
> My cause I plead not, nor demand your judgment.
> To the liege lord of my dear native land
> I owe a subject's homage; but even him

---

[1] 'Be not afraid of them that kill the body, and after that have no more that they can do.' Luke, Ch. XII. Ver. 4.

[2] This was the opinion of the celebrated Mr Turgot. 'He thought that the moral sentiments of mankind might be considerably strengthened, and the perception of them rendered more delicate and precise, either by frequent exercise, or the perpetually subjecting them to the anatomy of a pure and enlightened understanding. For this reason he considered romances as holding a place among the treatises of morality, and even as the only books in which he was aware of having seen moral principles treated in an impartial manner.' '*M. Turgot pensoit qu'on peut parvenir à fortifier dans les hommes leurs sentimens moraux, à les render plus délicatset plus justes, soit par l'exercice de ces sentimens, soit en apprenant àles soumettre à l'analyse d'une raison saine et éclairée. C'est par ce motif qu'il regardoit les romans comme des livres de morale, et meme, disoit-il, comme les seuls oùil eût vu de la morale.' Vie de M. Turgot,* par M. de Condorcet.

> And his high arbitration I reject.
> Within my bosom reigns another lord—
> Honour; sole judge and umpire of itself.'* Act IV.

Nothing can be more accurate than a considerable part of the philosophy of this passage. The term 'honour' indeed has been too much abused, and presents to the mind too fantastical an image, to be fairly descriptive of that principle by which the actions of every intellectual being ought to be regulated. The principle to which it behoves us to attend, is the internal decision of our own understanding; and nothing can be more evident than that the same reasoning, which led Norval to reject the authority of his sovereign in the quarrels and disputes in which he was engaged, ought to have led him to reject it as the regulator of any of his actions, and of consequence to abjure that homage which he sets out with reserving. Virtue cannot possibly be measured by the judgment and good pleasure of any man with whom we are concerned.

CHAPTER VII

OF FORMS OF GOVERNMENT

Argument in favour of a variety of forms—compared with the argument in favour of a variety of religious creeds.—That there is one best form of government proved—from the unity of truth—from the nature of man.— Objection from human weakness and prejudice.—Danger in establishing an imperfect code.—Manners of nations produced by their forms of government.— Gradual improvement necessary.—Simplicity chiefly to be desired.— Publication of truth the grand instrument—by individuals, not by government—the truth entire, and not by parcels.—Sort of progress to be desired.

A PROPOSITION that by many political reasoners has been vehemently maintained, is that of the propriety of instituting different political governments suited to the characters, the habits and prejudices of different nations. 'The English constitution,' say these reasoners, 'is adapted to the thoughtful, rough and unsubmitting character of this island race; the slowness and complication of Dutch formality to the phlegmatic Hollander; and the splendour of the *grand monarque** to the vivacity of Frenchmen. Among the ancients what could be better assorted than a pure democracy to the intellectual acuteness and impetuous energy of the Athenians; while the hardy and unpolished Spartan flourished much more under the rugged and inflexible discipline of Lycurgus? The great art of the legislator is to penetrate into the true character of the nation with whom he is concerned, and to discover the exact structure of government which is calculated to render that nation flourishing and happy.' Accordingly an Englishman who should reason upon these postulata might say, 'It is not necessary I should assert the English constitution to be the happiest and sublimest conception of the human mind; I do not enquire into the abstract excellence of that government under which France made herself illustrious for centuries. I contemplate with enthusiasm the venerable republics of Greece and Rome. But I am an enemy to the removing ancient landmarks, and disturbing with our crude devices the wisdom of ages. I regard with horror the Quixote plan,* that would reduce the irregular greatness of nations to the frigid and impracticable standard of metaphysical accuracy.'[1]

This question has been anticipated in various parts of the present work; but the argument is so popular and plausible to a superficial view, as justly to entitle it to a separate examination.

The idea bears some resemblance to one which was formerly insisted upon by certain latitudinarians in religion. 'It is impious,' said they, 'to endeavour to reduce all men to uniformity of opinion upon this subject. Men's minds are as various as their faces. God has made them so; and it is to be presumed that he is well pleased to be addressed in different languages, by different names, and with the consenting ardour of disagreeing sects.' Thus did these reasoners confound the majesty of truth with the deformity of falshood; and suppose that that being who was all truth, took delight in the errors, the absurdities, and the vices, for all falshood in some way or other engenders vice, of his creatures. At the same time they were employed in unnerving that activity of mind, which is the single source of human improvement. If truth and falshood be in reality upon a level, I shall be very weakly employed in a strenuous endeavour either to discover truth for myself, or to impress it upon others.

Truth is in reality single and uniform. There must in the nature of things be one best form of government, which all intellects, sufficiently

---

[1] These arguments bear some resemblance to those of Mr. Burke. It was not necessary that they should do so precisely, or that we should take advantage of the *argumentum ad hominem* built upon his fervent admiration of the English Constitution. Not to say that we shall feel ourselves more at ease in examining the question generally, than in a personal attack upon this illustrious and virtuous hero of the ancient model.

roused from the slumber of savage ignorance, will be irresistibly incited to approve. If an equal participation of the benefits of nature be good in itself, it must be good for you and me and all mankind. Despotism may be of use to keep human beings in ignorance, but can never conduce to render them wise or virtuous or happy. If the general tendency of despotism be injurious, every portion and fragment of it must be a noxious ingredient. Truth cannot be so variable, as to change its nature by crossing an arm of the sea, a petty brook or an ideal line, and become falshood. On the contrary it is at all times and in all places the same.

The subject of legislation is every where the same, man. The points in which human beings resemble are infinitely more considerable than those in which they differ. We have the same senses, the same inlets of pleasure and pain, the same faculty to reason, to judge and to infer. The same causes that make me happy will make you happy. We may differ in our opinions upon this subject at first, but this difference is only in prejudice, and is by no means invincible. An event may often conduce most to the benefit of a human being, which his erroneous judgment perhaps regarded with least complacency. A wise superintendent of affairs would press with steady attention the real advantage of those among whom he resided, careless of the temporary disapprobation he incurred, and which would last no longer than the partial and misguided apprehension from which it flowed.

Is there a country in which a prudent director of education would propose some other object for his labours than to make his pupil temperate and just and wise? Is there a climate that requires its inhabitants to be hard drinkers or horse-jockies or gamesters or bullies, rather than men? Can there be a corner of the world, where the lover of justice and truth would find himself out of his element and useless? If no; then liberty must be every where better than slavery, and the government of rectitude and impartiality better than the government of caprice.

But to this it may be objected that 'men may not be every where capable of liberty. A gift however valuable in itself, if it be intended to be beneficial, must be adapted to the capacity of the receiver. In human affairs every thing must be gradual; and it is contrary to every idea that experience furnishes of the nature of mind to expect to advance men to a state of perfection at once. It was in a spirit somewhat similar to this, that Solon, the Athenian lawgiver,* apologised for the imperfection of his code, saying, 'that he had not sought to promulgate such laws as were good in themselves, but such as his countrymen were able to bear.'

The experiment of Solon seems to be of a dangerous nature. A code, such as his, bid fair for permanence, and does not appear to have contained in it a principle of improvement. He did not meditate that gradual progress which was above described, nor contemplate in the Athenians of his own time, the root from which were to spring the possible Athenians of some future period, who might realise all that he was able to conceive of good sense, fortitude and virtue. His institutions were rather calculated to hold them down in perpetuity to one certain degree of excellence and no more.

This suggestion furnishes us with the real clue to that striking coincidence between the manners of a nation and the form of its government, which was mentioned in the beginning of the chapter, and which has furnished so capital an argument to the advocates for the local propriety of different forms of government. It was in reality somewhat illogical in these reasoners to employ this as an argument upon the subject, without previously ascertaining which of the two things was to be regarded as a cause and which as an effect, whether the government arose out of the manners of the nation, or the manners of the nation out of the government. The last of these statements appears upon the whole to be nearest to the fact. The government may be indebted for its existence to accident or force. Revolutions, as they have most frequently taken place in the world, are epochas, in which the temper and wishes of a nation are least consulted.[1] When it is otherwise, still the real effect of the government which is instituted, is to perpetuate propensities and sentiments, which without its operation would speedily have given place to other propensities. Upon every supposition, the existing correspondence between national character and national government will be found in a just consideration to arise out of the latter.

The principle of gradual improvement advanced in the last cited objection must be admitted for true; but then it is necessary, while we adopt it, that we should not suffer ourselves to act in direct opposition to it; and that we should choose the best and most powerful means for forwarding that improvement.

Man is in a state of perpetual progress. He must grow either better or worse, either correct his habits or confirm them. The government proposed must either increase our passions and prejudices by fanning the flame, or by gradually discouraging tend to extirpate them. In reality, it is sufficiently difficult to imagine a government that shall have the latter tendency. By its very nature political institution has a tendency to suspend the elasticity, and put an end to the advancement of mind. Every scheme for embodying imperfection must be injurious.

---

[1] See Hume's Essays. Part II. Essay xii.*

That which is to-day a considerable melioration, will at some future period, if preserved unaltered, appear a defect and disease in the body politic. It were earnestly to be desired that each man was wise enough to govern himself without the intervention of any compulsory restraint; and, since government even in its best state is an evil, the object principally to be aimed at is, that we should have as little of it as the general peace of human society will permit.

But the grand instrument for forwarding the improvement of mind is the publication of truth. Not the publication on the part of government; for it is infinitely difficult to discover infallibly what the truth is, especially upon controverted points, and government is as liable as individuals to be mistaken in this respect. In reality it is more liable; for the depositaries of government have a very obvious temptation to desire, by means of ignorance and implicit faith, to perpetuate the existing state of things. The only substantial method for the propagation of truth is discussion, so that the errors of one man may be detected by the acuteness and severe disquisition of his neighbours. All we have to demand from the officers of government, at least in their public character, is neutrality. The intervention of authority in a field proper to reasoning and demonstration is always injurious. If on the right side, it can only discredit truth, and call off the attention of men to a foreign consideration. If on the wrong, though it may not be able to suppress the spirit of enquiry, it will have a tendency to convert the calm pursuit of knowledge into passion and tumult.

'But in what manner shall the principles of truth be communicated so as best to lead to the practice? By shewing to man kind truth in all its evidence, or concealing one half of it? Shall they be initiated by a partial discovery, and thus led on by regular degrees to conclusions that would at first have wholly alienated their minds?'

This question will come to be more fully discussed in a following chapter. In the mean time let us only consider for the present the quantity of effect that may be expected from these two opposite plans.

An inhabitant of Turkey or Morocco may perhaps be of opinion, that the vesting power in the arbitrary will or caprice of an individual has in it more advantages than disadvantages. If I be desirous to change his opinion, should I undertake to recommend to him in animated language some modification of this caprice? I should attack it in its principle. If I do otherwise, I shall betray the strength of my cause. The principle opposite to his own, will not possess half the irresistible force which I could have given to it. His objections will assume vigour. The principle I am maintaining being half truth and half falshood, he will in every step of the contest possess an advantage in the offensive, of which, if he be sufficiently acute, I can never deprive him.

Now the principle I should have to explain of equal law and equal justice to the inhabitant of Morocco, would be as new to him, as any principle of the boldest political description that I could propagate in this country. Whatever apparent difference may exist between the two cases, may fairly be suspected to owe its existence to the imagination of the observer. The rule therefore which suggests itself in this case is fitted for universal application.

As to the improvements which are to be introduced into the political system, their quantity and their period must be determined by the degree of knowledge existing in any country, and the state of preparation of the public mind for the changes that are to be desired. Political renovation may strictly be considered as one of the stages in intellectual improvement. Literature and disquisition cannot of themselves be rendered sufficiently general; it will be only the cruder and grosser parts that can be expected to descend in their genuine form to the multitude; while those abstract and bold speculations, in which the value of literature principally consists, must necessarily continue the portion of the favoured few. It is here that social institution offers itself in aid of the abstruser powers of argumentative communication. As soon as any important truth has become established to a sufficient extent in the minds of the enterprising and the wise, it may tranquilly and with ease be rendered a part of the general system; since the uninstructed and the poor are never the strenuous supporters of those complicated systems by which oppression is maintained; and since they have an obvious interest in the practical introduction of simplicity and truth. One valuable principle being thus realised, prepares the way for the realising of more. It serves as a resting-place to the human mind in its great business of exploring the regions of truth, and gives it new alacrity and encouragement for farther exertions.

BOOK IV
MISCELLANEOUS PRINCIPLES

CHAPTER I
OF RESISTANCE

Every individual the judge of his own resistance.—Objection.—Answered
from the nature of government—from the modes of resistance.—1. Force
rarely to be employed—either where there is small prospect of success—or
where the prospect is great.—History of Charles the first estimated.—
2. Reasoning the legitimate mode.

IT has appeared in the course of our reasonings upon political authority, that every man is bound to resist every unjust proceeding on the
part of the community. But who is the judge of this injustice? The question answers itself: the private judgment of the individual. Were it not
so, the appeal would be nugatory, for we have no infallible judge to
whom to refer our controversies. He is obliged to consult his own
private judgment in this case, for the same reason that obliges him to
consult it in every other article of his conduct.

'But is not this position necessarily subversive of all government?
Can there be a power to rule, where no man is bound to obey; or at least
where every man is to consult his own understanding first, and then to
yield his concurrence no farther than he shall conceive the regulation
to be just? The very idea of government is that of an authority superseding private judgment; how then can the exercise of private judgment
be left entire? What degree of order is to be expected in a community,
where every man is taught to indulge his own speculations, and even to
resist the decision of the whole, whenever that decision is opposed to
the dictates of his own fancy?'

The true answer to these questions lies in the observation with which
we began our disquisition on government, that this boasted institution
is nothing more than a scheme for enforcing by brute violence the sense
of one man or set of men upon another, necessary to be employed in
certain cases of peculiar emergency. Supposing the question then to lie
merely between the force of the community on one part, and the force
with which any individual member should think it incumbent upon
him to resist their decisions on the other, it is sufficiently evident that a

certain kind of authority and supremacy would be the result. But this is not the true state of the question.

It is farther evident, that, though the duty of every man to exercise his private judgment be unalterable, yet so far as relates to practice, wherever government subsists, the exercise of private judgment is substantially intrenched upon. The force put by the community upon those who exercise rapine and injustice, and the influence of that force as a moral motive upon its members in general, are each of them exhibitions of an argument, not founded in general reason, but in the precarious interference of a fallible individual. Nor is this all. Without anticipating the question of the different kinds of resistance and the election that it may be our duty to make of one kind rather than another, it is certain in fact, that my conduct will be materially altered by the foresight that, if I act in a certain manner, I shall have the combined force of a number of individuals to oppose me. That government therefore is the best, which in no one instance interferes with the exercise of private judgment without absolute necessity.

The modes according to which an individual may oppose any measure which his judgment disapproves are of two sorts, action and speech. Shall he upon every occasion have recourse to the former? This it is absurd so much as to suppose. The object of every virtuous man is the general good. But how can he be said to promote the general good, who is ready to waste his active force upon every trivial occasion, and sacrifice his life without the chance of any public benefit?

'But he reserves himself,' I will suppose, 'for some great occasion; and then, careless as to success, which is a large object only to little minds, generously embarks in a cause where he has no hope but to perish. He becomes the martyr of truth. He believes that such an example will tend to impress the minds of his fellow men, and to rouse them from their lethargy.'

The question of martyrdom is of a difficult nature. I had rather convince men by my arguments, than seduce them by my example. It is scarcely possible for me to tell what opportunities for usefulness may offer themselves in the future years of my existence. Nor is it improbable in a general consideration that long and persevering services may be more advantageous than brilliant and transitory ones. The case being thus circumstanced, a truly wise man cannot fail to hesitate as to the idea of offering up his life a voluntary oblation.

Whenever martyrdom becomes an indispensible duty, when nothing can preserve him short of the clearest dereliction of principle and the most palpable desertion of truth, he will then meet it with perfect serenity. He did not avoid it before from any weakness of personal feeling. When it must be encountered, he knows that it is indebted for that lustre which has been so generally acknowledged among mankind, to the intrepidity of the sufferer. He knows that nothing is so essential to true virtue, as an utter disregard to individual advantage.

The objections that offer themselves to an exertion of actual force, where there are no hopes of success, are numerous. Such an exertion cannot be made without injury to the lives of more than a single individual. A certain number both of enemies and friends must be expected to be the victims of so wild an undertaking. It is regarded by contemporaries, and recorded by history as an intemperate ebullition of the passions; and serves rather as a beacon to deter others, than as a motive to animate them. It is not the frenzy of enthusiasm, but the calm, sagacious and deliberate effort of reason, to which truth must be indebted for its progress.

But let us suppose, 'that the prospect of success is considerable, and that there is reason to believe that resolute violence may in no long time accomplish its purpose.' Even here we may be allowed to hesitate. Force has already appeared to be an odious weapon; and, if the use of it be to be regretted in the hands of government, it does not change its nature though wielded by a band of patriots. If the cause we plead be the cause of truth, there is no doubt that by our reasonings, if sufficiently zealous and constant, the same purpose may be effected in a milder and more liberal way.[1]

In a word, it is proper to recollect here what has been established as to the doctrine of force in general, that it is in no case to be employed but where every other means is ineffectual. In the question therefore of resistance to government, force ought never to be introduced without the most imminent necessity; never but in circumstances similar to those of defending my life from a ruffian, where time can by no means be gained, and the consequences instantly to ensue are unquestionably fatal.

The history of king Charles the first furnishes an instructive example in both kinds. The original design of his opponents was that of confining his power within narrow and palpable limits. This object, after a struggle of many years, was fully accomplished by the parliament of 1640, without bloodshed (except indeed in the single instance of lord Strafford*) and without commotion. They next conceived the project of overturning the hierarchy and the monarchy of England, in

---

[1] See this case more fully discussed in the following chapter.

opposition to great numbers, and in the last point no doubt to a majority of their countrymen. Admitting these objects to have been in the utmost degree excellent, they ought not, for the purpose of obtaining them, to have precipitated the question to the extremity of a civil war.

'But, since force is scarcely under any circumstances to be employed, of what nature is that resistance which ought constantly to be given to every instance of injustice?' The resistance I am bound to employ is that of uttering the truth, of censuring in the most explicit manner every proceeding that I perceive to be adverse to the true interests of mankind. I am bound to disseminate without reserve all the principles with which I am acquainted, and which it may be of importance to mankind to know; and this duty it behoves me to practice upon every occasion and with the most persevering constancy. I must disclose the whole system of moral and political truth, without suppressing any part under the idea of its being too bold and paradoxical, and thus depriving the whole of that complete and irresistible evidence, without which its effects must always be feeble, partial and uncertain.

CHAPTER II

OF REVOLUTIONS

SECTION I
DUTIES OF A CITIZEN

Obligation to support the constitution of our country considered—must arise either from the reason of the case, or from a personal and local consideration.—The first examined.—The second.

No question can be more important than that which respects the best mode of effecting revolutions. Before we enter upon it however, it may be proper to remove a difficulty which has suggested itself to the minds of some men, how far we ought generally speaking to be the friends of revolution; or, in other words, whether it be justifiable in a man to be the enemy of the constitution of his country.

'We live,' it will be said, 'under the protection of this constitution; and protection, being a benefit conferred, obliges us to a reciprocation of support in return.'

To this it may be answered, first, that this protection is a very equivocal thing; and, till it can be shown that the vices, from the effects of which it protects us, are not for the most part the produce of that constitution, we shall never sufficiently understand the quantity of benefit it includes.

Secondly, gratitude, as has already been proved,[1] is a vice and not a virtue. Every man and every collection of men ought to be treated by us in a manner founded upon their intrinsic qualities and capacities, and not according to a rule which has existence only in relation to ourselves.

Add to this, thirdly, that no motive can be more equivocal than the gratitude here recommended. Gratitude to the constitution, an abstract idea, an imaginary existence, is altogether unintelligible. Affection to my countrymen will be much better proved, by my exertions to procure them a substantial benefit, than by my supporting a system which I believe to be fraught with injurious consequences.

He who calls upon me to support the constitution must found his requisition upon one of two principles. It has a claim upon my support either because it is good, or because it is British.

Against the requisition in the first sense there is nothing to object. All that is necessary is to prove the goodness which is ascribed to it. But perhaps it will be said, 'that, though not absolutely good, more mischief will result from an attempt to overturn it, than from maintaining it with its mixed character of partly right and partly wrong.' If this can be made evident, undoubtedly I ought to submit. Of this mischief however I can be no judge but in consequence of enquiry. To some the evils attendant on a revolution will appear greater, and to others less. Some will imagine that the vices with which the English constitution is pregnant are considerable, and some that it is nearly innocent. Before I can decide between these opposite opinions and balance the existing and the possible evils, I must examine for myself. But examination in its nature implies uncertainty of result. Were I to determine before I sat down on which side the decision should be, I could not strictly speaking be said to examine at all. He that desires a revolution for its own sake is to be regarded as a madman. He that desires it from a thorough conviction of its usefulness and necessity has a claim upon us for candour and respect.

As to the demand upon me for support to the English constitution, because it is English, there is little plausibility in this argument. It is of the same nature as the demand upon me to be a Christian, because I am a Briton, or a Mahometan, because I am a native of Turkey. Instead of being an expression of respect, it argues contempt of all government, religion and virtue, and every thing that is sacred among men. If there be such a thing as truth, it must be better than error. If there be such a

---

[1] Book II, chap. ii. p. 83.

faculty as reason, it ought to be exerted. But this demand makes truth a matter of absolute indifference, and forbids us the exercise of our reason. If men reason and reflect, it must necessarily happen that either the Englishman or the Turk will find his government to be odious and his religion false. For what purpose employ his reason, if he must for ever conceal the conclusions to which it leads him? How would man have arrived at his present attainments, if he had always been contented with the state of society in which he happened to be born? In a word, either reason is the curse of our species, and human nature is to be regarded with horror; or it becomes us to employ our understanding and to act upon it, and to follow truth wherever it may lead us. It cannot lead us to mischief, since utility, as it regards percipient beings, is the only basis of moral and political truth.

SECTION II

MODE OF EFFECTING REVOLUTIONS

Persuasion the proper instrument—not violence—nor resentment.—Lateness of event desirable.

To return to the enquiry respecting the mode of effecting revolutions. If no question can be more important, there is fortunately no question perhaps that admits of a more complete and satisfactory general answer. The revolutions of states, which a philanthropist would desire to witness, or in which he would willingly co-operate, consist principally in a change of sentiments and dispositions in the members of those states. The true instruments for changing the opinions of men are argument and persuasion. The best security for an advantageous issue is free and unrestricted discussion. In that field truth must always prove the successful champion. If then we would improve the social institutions of mankind, we must write, we must argue, we must converse. To this business there is no close; in this pursuit there should be no pause. Every method should be employed,—not so much positively to allure the attention of mankind, or persuasively to invite them to the adoption of our opinions,—as to remove every restraint upon thought, and to throw open the temple of science and the field of enquiry to all the world.

Those instruments will always be regarded by the discerning mind as suspicious, which may be employed with equal prospect of success on both sides of every question. This consideration should make us look with aversion upon all resources of violence. When we descend into the listed field,* we of course desert the vantage ground of truth, and commit the decision to uncertainty and caprice. The phalanx of reason is invulnerable; it advances with deliberate and determined pace; and nothing is able to resist it. But when we lay down our arguments, and take up our swords, the case is altered. Amidst the barbarous pomp of war and the clamorous din of civil brawls, who can tell whether the event shall be prosperous or miserable?

We must therefore carefully distinguish between informing the people and inflaming them. Indignation, resentment and fury are to be deprecated; and all we should ask is sober thought, clear discernment and intrepid discussion. Why were the revolutions of America and France a general concert of all orders and descriptions of men, without so much (if we bear in mind the multitudes concerned) as almost a dissentient voice; while the resistance against our Charles the first divided the nation into two equal parts? Because the latter was the affair of the seventeenth century, and the former happened in the close of the eighteenth. Because in the case of America and France philosophy had already developed some of the great principles of political truth, and Sydney and Locke and Montesquieu and Rousseau* had convinced a majority of reflecting and powerful minds of the evils of usurpation. If these revolutions had happened still later, not one drop of the blood of one citizen would have been shed by the hands of another, nor would the event have been marked so much perhaps as with one solitary instance of violence and confiscation.

There are two principles therefore which the man who desires the regeneration of his species ought ever to bear in mind, to regard the improvement of every hour as essential in the discovery and dissemination of truth, and willingly to suffer the lapse of years before he urges the reducing his theory into actual execution. With all his caution it is possible that the impetuous multitude will run before the still and quiet progress of reason; nor will he sternly pass sentence upon every revolution that shall by a few years have anticipated the term that wisdom would have prescribed. But, if his caution be firmly exerted, there is no doubt that he will supersede many abortive attempts, and considerably prolong the general tranquillity.

SECTION III
OF POLITICAL ASSOCIATIONS

Meaning of the term.—Associations objected to—1. from the sort of persons with whom a just revolution should originate—2. from the danger of tumult.— Objects of association.—In what cases admissible.—Argued for from the necessity to give weight to opinion—from their tendency to ascertain opinion.—Unnecessary for these purposes.—General inutility.— Concessions.—Importance of social communication.—Propriety of teaching resistance considered.

A QUESTION naturally suggests itself in this place respecting the propriety of associations among the people at large, for the purpose of effecting a change in their political institutions. It should be observed, that the associations here spoken of are voluntary confederacies of certain members of the society with each other, the tendency of which is to give weight to the opinions of the persons so associated, of which the opinions of the unconfederated and insulated part of the community are destitute. This question therefore has nothing in common with that other, whether in a well organized state every individual would not find his place in a deliberative as well as an elective capacity; the society being distributed into districts and departments, and each man possessing an importance, not measured by the capricious standard of some accidental confederacy, but by a rule impartially applied to every member of the community.

Relative then to political associations, as thus explained, there are two considerations, which, if they do not afford reason for undistinguishing condemnation, at least tend to diminish our anxiety to their introduction.

In the first place revolutions less originate in the energies of the people at large, than in the conceptions of persons of some degree of study and reflection. I say, originate, for it must be admitted, that they ought ultimately to be determined on by the choice of the whole nation. It is the property of truth to diffuse itself. The difficulty is to distinguish it in the first instance, and in the next to present it in that unequivocal form which shall enable it to command universal assent. This must necessarily be the task of a few. Society, as it at present exists in the world, will long be divided into two classes, those who have leisure for study, and those whose importunate necessities perpetually urge them to temporary industry. It is no doubt to be desired, that the latter class should be made as much as possible to partake of the privileges of the former. But we should be careful, while we listen to the undistinguishing demands of benevolence, that we do not occasion a greater mischief than that we undertake to cure. We should be upon our guard against an event the consequences of which are always to be feared, the propagating blind zeal, where we meant to propagate reason.

The studious and reflecting only can be expected to see deeply into future events. To conceive an order of society totally different from that which is now before our eyes, and to judge of the advantages that would accrue from its institution, are the prerogatives only of a few favoured minds. When these advantages have been unfolded by superior penetration, they cannot yet for some time be expected to be understood by the multitude. Time, reading and conversation are necessary to render them familiar. They must descend in regular gradation from the most thoughtful to the most unobservant. He, that begins with an appeal to the people, may be suspected to understand little of the true character of mind. A sinister design may gain by precipitation; but true wisdom is best adapted to a slow, unvarying, incessant progress.

Human affairs, through every link of the great chain of necessity, are admirably harmonised and adapted to each other. As the people form the last step in the progress of truth, they need least preparation to induce them to assert it. Their prejudices are few and upon the surface. They are the higher orders of society, that find, or imagine they find, their advantage in injustice, and are eager to invent arguments for its defence. In sophistry they first seek an excuse for their conduct, and then become the redoubted champions of those errors which they have been assiduous to cultivate. The vulgar have no such interest, and submit to the reign of injustice from habit only and the want of reflection. They do not want preparation to receive the truth, so much as examples to embody it. A very short catalogue of reasons is sufficient for them, when they see the generous and the wise resolved to assert the cause of justice. A very short period is long enough for them to imbibe the sentiments of patriotism and liberty.

Secondly, associations must be formed with great caution not to be allied to tumult. The conviviality of a feast may lead to the depredations of a riot. While the sympathy of opinion catches from man to man, especially in numerous meetings, and among persons whose passions have not been used to the curb of judgment, actions may be determined on, which solitary reflection would have rejected. There is nothing more barbarous, cruel and blood-thirsty, than the triumph of a mob. Sober thought should always prepare the way to the public assertion of truth. He, that would be the founder of a republic, should, like the first Brutus,* be insensible to the energies of the most imperious passions of our nature.

Upon this subject of associations an obvious distinction is to be made. Those, who are dissatisfied with the government of their country, may aim either at the correction of old errors, or the counteracting of new encroachments. Both these objects are legitimate. The wise and the virtuous man ought to see things precisely as they are, and judge of the actual constitution of his country with the same impartiality, as if he had simply read of it in the remotest page of history.

These two objects may be entitled to a different treatment. The first ought undoubtedly to proceed with a leisurely step and in all possible tranquillity. The second appears to require something more of activity. It is the characteristic of truth, to trust much to its own energy, and to resist invasion rather by the force of conviction than the force of arms. The individual oppressed seems however particularly entitled to our assistance, and this can best be afforded by the concurrence of many. The case may require an early and unequivocal display of opinion, and this perhaps will afford an apology for some sort of association, provided it be conducted with all possible attention to peaceableness and good order.

Few arguments can be of equal importance with that which we are here discussing. Few mistakes can be more to be deplored than that which should induce us to employ immoral and injurious methods for the support of a good cause. It may be alledged, 'that association is the only expedient for arming the sense of the country against the arts of its oppressors.' Why arm? Why spread a restless commotion over the face of a nation, which may lead to the most destructive consequences? Why seek to bestow upon truth a weight that is not her own? a weight that must always produce some obliquity, some blind and unenlightened zeal? In attempting prematurely to anticipate the conquest of truth, we shall infallibly give birth to deformity and abortion. If we have patience to wait her natural progress, and to assist her cause by no arguments that are not worthy of her, the event will be both certain and illustrious.

A similar answer will suggest itself to the objection, 'that associations are necessary unequivocally to ascertain the opinion of the people.' What sort of opinion is that, which thus stands in need of some sudden violence to oblige it to start from its hiding-place? The sentiments of mankind are then only equivocal in external appearance, when they are unformed and uncertain in the conception. When once the individual knows his own meaning, its symptoms will be clear and unequivocal. Be not precipitate. If the embryo sentiment at present existing in my mind be true, there is hope that it will gain strength by time. If you wish to assist its growth, let it be by instruction, not by attempting to pass that sentiment for mine which you only wish to be so. If the opinion of the people be not known to-day, it will not fail to shew itself to-morrow. If the opinion of the people be not known to-day, it is because that which you would have supposed to be their opinion is not sufficiently their opinion. You might as well think of hiding the inhabitants of England, concealing their towns and their cultivation, and making their country pass for a desert, as of concealing their real and deliberate sentiment.

These are the expedients of men who do not know that truth is omnipotent. It may appear to die for a time, but it will not fail to revive with fresh vigour. If it have ever failed to produce gradual conviction, it is because it has been told in a meagre, an obscure or a pusillanimous manner. Ten pages that should contain an absolute demonstration of the true interests of mankind in society could no otherwise be prevented from changing the face of the globe, than by the literal destruction of the paper on which they were written. It would become us to repeat their contents as widely as we were able; but, if we attempted any thing more than this, it would be a practical proof that we did not know they contained a demonstration.

Such are the reasonings that should decide upon our abstract opinion of every case of association that comes before us. But, though from hence it should sufficiently appear that association is scarcely in any case to be desired, there are considerations that should lead us sometimes to judge it with moderation and forbearance. There is one mode, according to which the benefit of mankind may best be promoted, and which ought always to be employed. But mankind are imperfect beings, and there are certain errors of his species which a wise man will be inclined to regard with indulgence. Associations, as a measure intrinsically wrong, he will endeavour at least to postpone as long as he can. But it must not be dissembled that in the crisis of a revolution they will sometimes be unavoidable. While opinion is advancing with silent step, imagination and zeal may be expected somewhat to outrun her progress. Wisdom will be anxious to hold them at bay; and, if her votaries be many, she will be able to do this long enough to prevent tragical consequences. But, when the cast is thrown, when the declaration is made and irrevocable, she will not fail, be the confusion greater or less, to take the side of truth, and forward her reign by the best means that the necessity of the case will admit.

But, though association, in the received sense of that term, must be granted to be an instrument of a very dangerous nature, it should be remembered that unreserved communication in a smaller circle, and especially among persons who are already awakened to the pursuit of truth, is of unquestionable advantage. There is at present in the world a cold reserve that keeps man at a distance from man. There is an art in the practice of which individuals communicate for ever, without any one telling his neighbour what estimate he should form of his attainments and character, how they ought to be employed, and how to be improved. There is a sort of domestic tactics, the object of which is to instruct us to elude curiosity, and to keep up the tenour of conversation, without the disclosure either of our feelings or our opinions. The philanthropist has no object more deeply at heart than the annihilation of this duplicity and reserve. No man can have much kindness for his species, who does not habituate himself to consider upon each successive occasion of social intercourse how that occasion may be most beneficently improved. Among the topics to which he will be anxious to awaken attention, politics will occupy a principal share.

Books have by their very nature but a limited operation; though, on account of their permanence, their methodical disquisition, and their easiness of access, they are entitled to the foremost place. But their efficacy ought not to engross our confidence. The number of those by whom reading is neglected is exceedingly great. Books to those by whom they are read have a sort of constitutional coldness. We review the arguments of an 'insolent innovator' with sullenness, and are unwilling to stretch our minds to take in all their force. It is with difficulty that we obtain the courage of striking into untrodden paths, and questioning tenets that have been generally received. But conversation accustoms us to hear a variety of sentiments, obliges us to exercise patience and attention, and gives freedom and elasticity to our mental disquisitions. A thinking man, if he will recollect his intellectual history, will find that he has derived inestimable advantage from the stimulus and surprise of colloquial suggestions; and, if he review the history of literature, will perceive that minds of great acuteness and ability have commonly existed in a cluster.

It follows that the promising of the best interests of mankind eminently depends upon the freedom of social communication. Let us imagine to ourselves a number of individuals, who, having first stored their minds with reading and reflection, proceed afterwards in candid and unreserved conversation to compare their ideas, to suggest their doubts, to remove their difficulties, and to cultivate a collected and striking manner of delivering their sentiments. Let us suppose these men, prepared by mutual intercourse, to go forth to the world, to explain with succinctness and simplicity, and in a manner well calculated to arrest attention, the true principles of society. Let us suppose their hearers instigated in their turn to repeat these truths to their companions. We shall then have an idea of knowledge as perpetually gaining ground, unaccompanied with peril in the means of its diffusion. Reason will spread itself, and not a brute and unintelligent sympathy. Discussion perhaps never exists with so much vigour and utility as in the conversation of two persons. It may be carried on with advantage in small and friendly societies. Does the fewness of their numbers imply the rarity of their existence? Far otherwise: the time perhaps will come when such institutions will be universal. Shew to mankind by a few examples the advantages of political discussion undebauched by political enmity and vehemence, and the beauty of the spectacle will soon render the example contagious. Every man will commune with his neighbour. Every man will be eager to tell and to hear what the interest of all requires them to know. The bolts and fortifications of the temple of truth will be removed. The craggy steep of science, which it was before difficult to ascend, will be levelled with the plain. Knowledge will be accessible to all. Wisdom will be the inheritance of man, from which none will be excluded but by their own heedlessness and prodigality. If these ideas cannot completely be realised, till the inequality of conditions and the tyranny of government are rendered somewhat less oppressive, this affords no reason against the setting afloat so generous a system. The improvement of individuals and the melioration of political institutions are destined mutually to produce and reproduce each other. Truth, and above all political truth, is not hard of acquisition, but from the superciliousness of its professors. It has been slow and tedious of improvement, because the study of it has been relegated to doctors and civilians. It has produced little effect upon the practice of mankind, because it has not been allowed a plain and direct appeal to their understandings. Remove these obstacles, render it the common property, bring it into daily use, and you may reasonably promise yourself consequences of the most inestimable value.

But these consequences are the property only of independent and impartial discussion. If once the unambitious and candid circles of enquiring men be swallowed up in the insatiate gulf of noisy assemblies, the opportunity of improvement is instantly annihilated. The happy varieties of sentiment which so eminently contribute to intellectual acuteness are lost. Activity of thought is shackled by the fear that our associates should disclaim us. A fallacious uniformity of opinion is produced, which no man espouses from conviction, but which carries all men along with a resistless tide. Clubs, in the old English sense, that is, the periodical meeting of small and independent circles, may be admitted to fall within the line of these principles. But they cease to be admissible, when united with the tremendous apparatus of articles of confederacy and committees of correspondence. Human beings should meet together, not to enforce, but to enquire. Truth disclaims the alliance of marshalled numbers.

It seems scarcely necessary to add, that the individuals who are engaged in the transactions here censured, have frequently been instigated by the best intentions, and informed with the most liberal views. It would be in the highest degree unjust, if their undertakings should be found of dangerous tendency, to involve the authors in indiscriminate censure for consequences which they did not foresee. But at the same time, in proportion to the purity of their views and the soundness of their principles, it were earnestly to be desired that they would seriously reflect on the means they employ. It would be deeply to be lamented, if those who were the truest friends to the welfare of mankind, should come, by the injudiciousness of their conduct, to rank among its enemies.

From what has been said it is sufficiently evident, that no alarm can be more groundless, than that of violence and precipitation from the enlightened advocates of political justice. There is however another objection which has been urged against them, built upon the supposed inexpediency of inculcating upon the people at large the propriety of occasional resistance to the authority of government. 'Obedience,' say these objectors 'is the rule; resistance the exception. Now what can be more preposterous, than perpetually to insist with all the pomp of eloquence upon an expedient, to which only an extreme necessity can oblige us to have recourse?'[1]

It has already been shewn that obedience, that is, a surrender of the understanding to the voice of authority, is a rule to which it can never be creditable to human beings to conform. Tranquillity indeed, a state in which a man shall least be disturbed in the exercise of his private judgment by the interposition of violence, is an object we should constantly endeavour to promote; but this tranquillity the principles here inculcated have little tendency to disturb.

---

[1] This argument, nearly in the words here employed, may be found in Hume's Essay on Passive Obedience. Essays, Part II, Essay xiii.

There is certainly no truth which it can be for the general interest to conceal. It must be confessed indeed, that a single truth may be so detached from the series to which it belongs, as, when separately told, to have the nature of falshood. But this is by no means the case in the present instance. To inform mankind of those general principles upon which all political institutions ought to be built, is not to diffuse partial information. To discover to them their true interests, and lead them to conceive of a state of society more uncorrupt and more equitable than that in which they live, is not to inculcate some rare exception to a general rule. If there be any government which must be indebted for its perpetuity to ignorance, that government is the curse of mankind. In proportion as men are made to understand their true interests, they will conduct themselves wisely, both when they act and when they forbear, and their conduct will therefore promise the most advantageous issue. He, whose mind has carefully been inured to the dictates of reason, is of all men least likely to convert into the rash and headstrong invader of the general weal.

SECTION IV
OF THE SPECIES OF REFORM TO BE DESIRED

Ought it to be partial or entire?—Truth may not be partially taught.—Partial reformation considered.—Objection.—Answer.—Partial reform indispensible.—Nature of a just revolution—how distant?

THERE is one more question which cannot fail occasionally to suggest itself to the advocate of social reformation. 'Ought we to desire to see this reformation introduced gradually or at once?' Neither side of this dilemma presents us with the proper expedient.

No project can be more injurious to the cause of truth, than that of presenting it imperfectly and by parcels to the attention of mankind. Seen in its just light, the effect produced cannot fail to be considerable; but, shewn in some partial and imperfect way, it will afford a thousand advantages to its adversaries. Many objections will seem plausible, which a full view of the subject would have dissipated. Whatever limits truth is error; and of consequence such a limited view cannot fail to include a considerable mixture of error. Many ideas may be excellent as parts of a great whole, which, when violently torn from their connection, will not only cease to be excellent, but may in some cases become positively injurious. In this war of posts and skirmishes victory will perpetually appear to be doubtful, and men will either be persuaded, that truth itself is of little value, or that human intellect is so narrow as to render the discovery of truth a hopeless pursuit.

It may be alledged, that 'one of the considerations of greatest influence in human affairs is that of the gradual decline of ill things to worse, till at length the mischief, having proceeded to its highest climax, can maintain itself no longer. The argument in favour of social improvement would lose much of its relative energy, if the opportunity of a secret comparison of possible good with actual evil were taken away. All partial reforms are of the nature of palliatives. They skin over the diseased part instead of extirpating the disease. By giving a small benefit, perhaps a benefit only in appearance, they cheat us of the superior good we ought to have demanded. By stripping error of a part of its enormities, they give it fresh vigour and a longer duration.'

We must be cautious however of pushing this argument too far. To suppose that truth stands in absolute need of a foil, or that she cannot produce full conviction by her native light, is a conception unworthy of her enlightened advocates. The true solution will probably be found in the accurately distinguishing the sources of reform. Whatever reform, general or partial, shall be suggested to the community at large by an unmutilated view of the subject, ought to be seen with some degree of complacency. But a reform, that shall be offered us by those whose interest is supposed to lie in the perpetuating of abuse, and the intention of which is rather to give permanence to error by divesting it of its most odious features, is little entitled to our countenance. The true principle of social improvement lies in the correcting public opinion. Whatever reform is stolen upon the community unregarded, and does not spontaneously flow from the energy of the general mind, is unworthy of congratulation. It is in this respect with nations as with individuals. He that quits a vicious habit, not from reason and conviction, but because his appetites no longer solicit him to its indulgence, does not deserve the epithet of virtuous. The object it becomes us to pursue is, to give vigour to public opinion, not to sink it into listlessness and indifference.

When partial reformation proceeds from its legitimate cause, the progress society has made in the acquisition of truth, it may frequently be entitled to our applause. Man is the creature of habits. Gradual improvement is a most conspicuous law of his nature. When therefore some considerable advantage is sufficiently understood by the community to induce them to desire its establishment, that establishment will afterwards react to the enlightening of intellect and the generating of virtue. It is natural for us to take our stand upon some leading truth, and from thence explore the regions we have still to traverse.

There is indeed a sense in which gradual improvement is the only alternative between reformation and no reformation. All human intellects are at sea upon the great ocean of infinite truth, and their voyage though attended with hourly advantage will never be at an end. If therefore we will stay till we shall have devised a reformation so complete, as shall need no farther reformation to render it more complete, we shall eternally remain in inaction. Whatever is fairly understood upon general principles by a considerable part of the community, and opposed by none or by a very few, may be considered as sufficiently ripe for execution.

To recapitulate the principal object of this chapter, I would once again repeat, that violence may suit the plan of any political partisan, rather than of him that pleads the cause of simple justice. There is even a sense in which the reform aimed at by the true politician may be affirmed to be less a gradual than an entire one, without contradicting the former position. The complete reformation that is wanted, is not instant but future reformation. It can in reality scarcely be considered as of the nature of action. It consists in an universal illumination. Men feel their situation, and the restraints, that shackled them before, vanish like a mere deception. When the true crisis shall come, not a sword will need to be drawn, not a finger to be lifted up. The adversaries will be too few and too feeble to dare to make a stand against the universal sense of mankind.

Nor do these ideas imply, as at first sight they might seem to imply, that the revolution is at an immeasurable distance. It is of the nature of human affairs that great changes should appear to be sudden, and great discoveries to be made unexpectedly, and as it were by accident. In forming the mind of a young person, in endeavouring to give a new bent to that of a person of maturer years, I shall for a long time seem to have produced little effect, and the fruits will shew themselves when I least expected them. The kingdom of truth comes not with ostentation. The seeds of virtue may appear to perish before they germinate.

To recur once more to the example of France, the works of her great political writers seemed for a long time to produce little prospect of any practical effect. Helvetius, one of the latest, in a work published after his death in 1771, laments in pathetic strains the hopeless condition of his country. 'In the history of every people,' says he, 'there are moments, in which, uncertain of the side they shall choose, and balanced between political good and evil, they feel a desire to be instructed; in which the soil, so to express myself, is in some manner prepared, and may easily be impregnated with the dew of truth. At such a moment the publication of a valuable book may give birth to the most auspicious reforms: but, when that moment is no more, the nation, become insensible to the best motives, is by the nature of its government plunged deeper and deeper in ignorance and stupidity. The soil of intellect is then hard and impenetrable; the rains may fall, may spread their moisture upon the surface, but the prospect of fertility is gone. Such is the condition of France. Her people are become the contempt of Europe. No salutary crisis shall ever restore them to liberty.'[1]

But in spite of these melancholy predictions, the work of renovation was in continual progress. The American revolution gave the finishing stroke, and only six years elapsed between the completion of American liberty and the commencement of the French revolution. Will a term longer than this be necessary, before France, the most refined and considerable nation in the world, will lead other nations to imitate and improve upon her plan? Let the true friend of man be incessant in the propagation of truth, and vigilant to counteract all the causes that might disturb the regularity of her progress, and he will have every reason to hope an early and a favourable event.

CHAPTER III

OF TYRANNICIDE

Diversity of opinions on this subject.—Argument in its vindication.—The destruction of a tyrant not a case of exception.—Consequences of tyrannicide.—Assassination described.—Importance of sincerity.

A QUESTION, connected with the mode of effecting revolutions, and which has been eagerly discussed among political reasoners, is that of tyrannicide. The moralists of antiquity warmly contended for the lawfulness of this practice; by the moderns it has generally been condemned.

The arguments in its favour are built upon a very obvious principle.

[1] *'Dans chaque nation il est des momens où les citoyens, incertains du parti qu'ils doivent prendre, et suspendus entre un bon et un mauvais gouvernement, éprouvent la soif de l'instruction, où les esprits, si je l'ose dire, préparés et ameublis peuvent être facilement pénétrés de la rosée de la vérité. Qu'en ce moment un bon ouvrage paroisse, il put opérer d'heureuse réformes: mails cet instant passé, les citoyens, insensibles à la gloire, sont par la forme de leur gouvernement invinciblement entraînés vers l'ignorance et l'abrutissement. Alors les esprits sont la terre endurcie: l'eau de la vérité y tombe, y coule, mais sans la féconder. Tel est l'état de la France. Cette nation avilie est aujourd'hui le mépris de l'Europe. Nulle crise salutaire ne lui rendra la liberté.' De l'Homme, Préface.**

'Justice ought universally to be administered. Upon lesser criminals it is done, or pretended to be done, by the laws of the community. But criminals by whom law is subverted, and who overturn the liberties of mankind, are out of the reach of the ordinary administration of justice. If justice be partially administered in subordinate cases, and the rich man be able to oppress the poor with impunity, it must be admitted that a few examples of this sort are insufficient to authorise the last appeal of human beings. But no man will deny that the case of the usurper and the despot is of the most atrocious nature. In this instance, all the provisions of civil policy being superseded, and justice poisoned at the source, every man is left to execute for himself the decrees of eternal equity.'

It may however be doubted whether the destruction of a tyrant be in any respect a case of exception from the rules proper to be observed upon ordinary occasions. The tyrant has certainly no particular sanctity annexed to his person, and may be killed with as little scruple as any other man, when the object is that of repelling immediate violence. In all other cases, the extirpation of the offender by a self-appointed authority, does not appear to be the proper mode of counteracting injustice.

For, first, either the nation, whose tyrant you would destroy, is ripe for the assertion and maintenance of its liberty, or it is not. If it be, the tyrant ought to be deposed with every appearance of publicity. Nothing can be more improper, than for an affair, interesting to the general weal, to be conducted as if it were an act of darkness and shame. It is an ill lesson we read to mankind, when a proceeding, built upon the broad basis of general justice, is permitted to shrink from public scrutiny. The pistol and the dagger may as easily be made the auxiliaries of vice as of virtue. To proscribe all violence, and neglect no means of information and impartiality, is the most effectual security we can have for an issue conformable to the voice of reason and truth.

If the nation be not ripe for a state of freedom, the man, who assumes to himself the right of interposing violence, may indeed shew the fervour of his conception, and gain a certain degree of notoriety. Fame he will not gain, for mankind at present regard an act of this sort with merited abhorrence; and he will inflict new calamities on his country. The consequences of tyrannicide are well known. If the attempt prove abortive, it renders the tyrant ten times more bloody, ferocious, and cruel than before. If it succeed, and the tyranny be restored, it produces the same effect upon his successors. In the climate of despotism some solitary virtues may spring up. But in the midst of plots and conspiracies there is neither truth, nor confidence, nor love, nor humanity.

Secondly, the true merits of the question will be still farther understood, if we reflect on the nature of assassination. The mistake, which has been incurred upon this subject, is to be imputed principally to the superficial view that has been taken of it. If its advocates had followed the conspirator through all his windings, and observed his perpetual alarm lest truth should become known, they would probably have been less indiscriminate in their applause. No action can be imagined more directly at war with a principle of ingenuousness and candour. Like all that is most odious in the catalogue of vices, it delights in obscurity. It shrinks from the penetrating eye of wisdom. It avoids all question, and hesitates and trembles before the questioner. It struggles for a tranquil gaiety, and is only complete where there is the most perfect hypocrisy. It changes the use of speech, and composes every feature the better to deceive. Imagine to yourself the conspirators, kneeling at the feet of Cæsar,* as they did the moment before they destroyed him. Not all the virtue of Brutus can save them from your indignation.

There cannot be a better instance than that of which we are treating, to prove the importance of general sincerity. We see in this example, that an action, which has been undertaken from the best motives, may by a defect in this particular tend to over-turn the very foundations of justice and happiness. Wherever there is assassination, there is an end to all confidence among men. Protests and asseverations go for nothing. No man presumes to know his neighbour's intention. The boundaries, that have hitherto served to divide virtue and vice, are gone. The true interests of mankind require, not their removal, but their confirmation. All morality proceeds upon the assumption of something evident and true, will grow and expand in proportion as these indications are more clear and unequivocal, and could not exist for a moment, if they were destroyed.

CHAPTER IV

OF THE CULTIVATION OF TRUTH

PERHAPS there cannot be a subject of greater political importance, or better calculated to lead us in safety through the mazes of controversy, than that of the value of truth. Truth may be considered by us, either abstractedly, as it relates to certain general and unchangeable principles, or practically, as it relates to the daily incidents and ordinary commerce of human life. In whichever of these views we consider it, the more deeply we meditate its nature and tendency, the more shall we be struck with its unrivalled importance.

SECTION I

OF ABSTRACT OR GENERAL TRUTH

Its importance as conducing—to our intellectual improvement—to our moral improvement.—Virtue the best source of happiness.—Proved by comparison—by its manner of adapting itself to all situations—by its undecaying excellence—cannot be effectually propagated but by a cultivated mind.—Importance of general truth to our political improvement.

ABSTRACTEDLY considered, it conduces to the perfection of our understandings, our virtue and our political institutions.

In the discovery and knowledge of truth is comprised all that which an impartial and reflecting mind is accustomed to admire. It is not possible for us seriously to doubt concerning the preference of a capacious and ardent intelligence over the limited perceptions of a brute. All that we can imagine of angels and Gods consists in superior wisdom. Do you say in power also? It will presently appear that wisdom is power. The truths of general nature, those truths which preceded, either substantially or in the nature of things, the particular existences that surround us, and are independent of them all, are inexhaustible. Is it possible that a knowledge of these truths, the truths of mathematics, of metaphysics and morals, the truths which, according to Plato's conception,[1] taught the creator of the world the nature of his materials, the result of his operations, the consequences of all possible systems in all their detail, should not exalt and elevate the mind? The truths of particular nature, the history of man, the characters and propensities of human beings, the process of our own minds, the capacity of our natures, are scarcely less valuable. The reason they are so will best appear if we consider, secondly, the tendency of truth in conducing to the perfection of our virtue.

Virtue cannot exist in an eminent degree, unaccompanied by an extensive survey of causes and their consequences, so that, having struck an accurate balance between the mixed benefits and injuries that for the present adhere to all human affairs, we may adopt that conduct which leads to the greatest possible advantage. If there be such a thing as virtue, it must admit of degrees. If it admit of degrees, he must be most virtuous, who chooses with the soundest judgment the greatest

---

[1] See the Parmenides.*

possible good of his species. But, in order to choose the greatest possible good, he must be deeply acquainted with the nature of man, its general features and its varieties. In order to execute it, he must have considered all the instruments for impressing mind, and the different modes of applying them, and must know exactly the proper moment for bringing them into action. In whatever light we consider virtue, whether we place it in the action or the disposition, its degree must be intimately connected with the degree of knowledge. No man can love virtue sufficiently, who has not an acute and lively perception of its beauty, and its tendency to produce the only solid and permanent happiness. What comparison can be made between the virtue of Socrates and that of a Hottentot or a Siberian? A humorous example how universally this truth has been perceived might be drawn from Tertullian, who, as a father of the church, was obliged to maintain the hollowness and insignificance of pagan virtues, and accordingly assures us, 'that the most ignorant peasant under the Christian dispensation possessed more real knowledge than the wisest of the ancient philosophers.'[1]

We shall be still more fully aware of the connection between virtue and knowledge, if we consider that the highest employment of virtue is to propagate itself. Virtue alone is happiness. The happiness of a brute that spends the greater part of his life in listlessness and sleep, is but one remove from the happiness of a plant that is full of sap, vigour and nutrition. The happiness of a man who pursues licentious pleasure is momentary, and his intervals of weariness and disgust perpetual. He speedily wears himself out in his specious career; and, every time that he employs the means of delight which his corporeal existence affords him, takes so much from his capacity of enjoyment. If he be wise enough like Epicurus* to perceive a part of these disadvantages, and to find in fresh herbs and the water of the spring the truest gratification of his appetite, he will be obliged to seek some addition to his stock of enjoyment, and like Epicurus to become benevolent out of pure sensuality. But the virtuous man has a perpetual source of enjoyment. The only reason on account of which the truth of this assertion was ever controverted, is, that men have not understood what it was that constituted virtue.

It is impossible that any situation can occur in which virtue cannot find room to expatiate. In society there is continual opportunity for its active employment. I cannot have intercourse with any human being who may not be the better for that intercourse. If he be already just and

---

[1] Apologia, Cap. xlvi.* See this subject farther pursued in Appendix, No. I.

virtuous, these qualities are improved by communication. It is from a similar principle that it has been observed that great geniuses have usually existed in a cluster, and have been awakened by the fire struck into them by their neighbours. If he be imperfect and erroneous, there must be always some prejudice I may contribute to destroy, some motive to delineate, some error to remove. If I be prejudiced and imperfect myself, it cannot however happen that my prejudices and imperfections shall be exactly coincident with his. I may therefore inform him of the truths that I know, and even by the collision of prejudices truth is elicited. It is impossible that I should strenuously apply myself to his mind with sincere motives of benevolence without some good being the result. Nor am I more at a loss in solitude. In solitude I may accumulate the materials of social benefit. No situation can be so desperate as to preclude these efforts. Voltaire, when shut up in the Bastille, and for ought he knew for life, deprived of books, of pens and of paper, arranged and in part executed the project of his Henriade.[1]

Another advantage of virtue in this personal view, is that, while sensual pleasure exhausts the frame, and passions often excited become frigid and callous, virtue has exactly the opposite propensities. Passions, in the usual acceptation of that term, having no absolute foundation in the nature of things, delight only by their novelty. But the more we are acquainted with virtue, the more estimable will it appear; and its field is as endless as the progress of mind. If an enlightened love of it be once excited in the mind, it is impossible that it should not continually increase. By its variety, by its activity it perpetually renovates itself, and renders the intellect in which it resides ever new and ever young.

All these reasonings are calculated to persuade us that the most precious boon we can bestow upon others is virtue, that the highest employment of virtue is to propagate itself. But, as virtue is inseparably connected with knowledge in my own mind, so can it only by knowledge be communicated to others. How can the virtue we have just been contemplating be created, but by infusing comprehensive views and communicating energetic truths? Now that man alone is qualified to give these views, and communicate these truths, who is himself pervaded with them.

Let us suppose for a moment virtuous dispositions as existing without knowledge or outrunning knowledge, the last of which is certainly possible, and we shall presently find how little such virtue is worthy to

---

[1] *Vie de Voltaire,** *par M**** (said to be the marquis de Villette). *A Geneve*, 1786. *Chap. iv.* This is probably the best history of this great man which has yet appeared.

be propagated. The most generous views will in such cases frequently lead to the most nefarious actions. A Calvin will burn Servetus, and a Digby generate the gunpowder treason.* But, to leave these extreme instances, in all cases where mistaken virtue leads to cruel and tyrannical actions, the mind will be soured and made putrescent by the actions it perpetrates. Truth, immortal and ever present truth, is so powerful, that, in spite of all his inveterate prejudices, the upright man will suspect himself, when he resolves upon an action that is at war with the plainest principles of morality. He will become melancholy, dissatisfied and anxious. His firmness will degenerate into obstinacy, and his justice into inexorable severity. The farther he pursues his system, the more erroneous will he become. The farther he pursues it, the less will he be satisfied with it. As truth is an endless source of tranquillity and delight, error will be a prolific fountain of new mistakes and new discontent.

As to the third point, the tendency of truth to the improvement of our political institutions, this is in reality the subject of the present volume, and has been particularly argued in some of the earlier divisions of the work. If politics be a science, the investigation of truth must be the means of unfolding it. If men resemble each other in more numerous and essential particulars than those in which they differ, if the best purposes that can be accomplished respecting them be to make them free and virtuous and wise, there must be one best method of advancing these common purposes, one best mode of social existence deducible from the principles of their nature. If truth be one, there must be one code of truths on the subject of our reciprocal duties. Nor is the investigation of truth only the best mode of arriving at the object of all political institutions, but it is also the best mode of introducing and establishing it. Discussion is the path that leads to discovery and demonstration. Motives ferment in the minds of great bodies of men till all is ripe for action. The more familiar the mind becomes with the ideas of which they consist and the propositions that express them, the more fully is it pervaded with their urgency and importance.

SECTION II
OF SINCERITY

Nature of this virtue.—Its effects—upon our own actions—upon our neighbours.—Its tendency to produce fortitude.—Effects of insincerity.—Character which sincerity would acquire to him who practiced it.—Objections.—Actions.—The fear of giving unnecessary pain.—Answer.—The desire of preserving my life.—This objection proves too much.—Answer.—Secrecy considered.—The secrets of others.—State secrets.—Secrets of philanthropy.

IT is evident in the last place, that a strict adherence to truth will have the best effect upon our minds in the ordinary commerce of life. This is the virtue which has commonly been known by the denomination of sincerity; and, whatever certain accommodating moralists may teach us, the value of sincerity will be in the highest degree obscured, when it is not complete. Real sincerity deposes me from all authority over the statement of facts. Similar to the duty which Tully* imposes upon the historian, it compels me not to dare 'to utter what is false, or conceal what is true.' It annihilates the bastard prudence, which would instruct me to give language to no sentiment that may be prejudicial to my interests. It extirpates the low and selfish principle, which would induce me to utter nothing 'to the disadvantage of him from whom I have received no injury.' It compels, me to regard the concerns of my species as my own concerns. What I know of truth, of morals, of religion, of government, it compels me to communicate. All the praise which a virtuous man and an honest action can merit, I am obliged to pay to the uttermost mite. I am obliged to give language to all the blame to which profligacy, venality, hypocrisy and circumvention are so justly entitled. I am not empowered to conceal any thing I know of myself, whether it tend to my honour or to my disgrace. I am obliged to treat every other man with equal frankness, without dreading the imputation of flattery on the one hand, without dreading his resentment and enmity on the other.

Did every man impose this law upon himself, he would be obliged to consider before he decided upon the commission of an equivocal action, whether he chose to be his own historian, to be the future narrator of the scene in which he was engaging. It has been justly observed that the popish practice of auricular confession has been attended with some salutary effects. How much better would it be, if, instead of a practice thus ambiguous, and which may be converted into so dangerous an engine of ecclesiastical despotism, every man would make the world his confessional, and the human species the keeper of his conscience?

How extensive an effect would be produced, if every man were sure of meeting in his neighbour the ingenuous censor, who would tell to himself, and publish to the world, his virtues, his good deeds, his meannesses and his follies? I have no right to reject any duty, because it is equally incumbent upon my neighbours, and they do not practise it. When I have discharged the whole of my duty, it is weakness and vice to make myself unhappy about the omissions of others. Nor is it possible to say how much good one man sufficiently rigid in his adherence to truth would effect. One such man, with genius, information and energy, might redeem a nation from vice.

The consequence to myself of telling every man the truth, regardless of personal danger or of injury to my interests in the world, would be uncommonly favourable. I should acquire a fortitude that would render me equal to the most trying situations, that would maintain my presence of mind entire in spite of unexpected occurrences, that would furnish me with extemporary arguments and wisdom, and endue my tongue with irresistible eloquence. Animated by the love of truth, my understanding would always be vigorous and alert, not as before frequently subject to listlessness, timidity and insipidity. Animated by the love of truth, and by a passion inseparable from its nature, and which is almost the same thing under another name, the love of my species, I should carefully seek for such topics as might most conduce to the benefit of my neighbours, anxiously watch the progress of mind, and incessantly labour for the extirpation of prejudice.

What is it that at this day enables a thousand errors to keep their station in the world, priestcraft, tests, bribery, war, cabal, and whatever else is the contempt and abhorrence of the enlightened and honest mind? Cowardice. Because, while vice walks erect with an unabashed countenance, men less vicious dare not paint her with that truth of colouring, which should at once confirm the innocent and reform the guilty. Because the majority of those who are not involved in the busy scene, and who, possessing some discernment, see that things are not altogether right, yet see in so frigid a way, and with so imperfect a view. Many, who detect the imposture, are yet absurd enough to imagine that imposture is necessary to keep the world in awe, and that truth being too weak to curb the turbulent passions of mankind, it is exceedingly proper to call in knavery and artifice as the abettors of her power. If every man to-day would tell all the truth he knows, three years hence there would be scarcely a falshood of any magnitude remaining in the civilised world.

There is no fear that the character here described should degenerate into ruggedness and brutality.[1] The motive by which it is animated affords a sufficient security against such consequences. 'I tell an unpleasant truth to my neighbour from a conviction that it is my duty. I am convinced it is my duty, because I perceive the communication is calculated for his benefit.' His benefit therefore is the motive of my proceeding, and with such a motive it is impossible I should not seek to communicate it in the most efficacious form, not rousing his resentment, but awakening his moral feelings and his energy. Meanwhile the happiest of all qualifications in order to render truth palatable, is that which rises spontaneously in the situation we have been considering. Truth according to the terms of the supposition is to be spoken from the love of truth. But the face, the voice, the gesture are so many indexes to the mind. It is scarcely possible therefore that the person with whom I am conversing should not perceive, that I am influenced by no malignity, acrimony and envy. In proportion as my motive is pure, at least after a few experiments, my manner will become unembarrassed. There will be frankness in my voice, fervour in my gesture, and kindness in my heart. That man's mind must be of a very perverse texture, that can convert a beneficent potion administered with no ungenerous retrospect, no selfish triumph, into rancour and aversion. There is an energy in the sincerity of a virtuous mind that nothing human can resist.

I stop not to consider the objections of the man who is immersed in worldly prospects and pursuits. He that does not know that virtue is better than riches or title must be convinced by arguments foreign to this place.

But it will be asked, 'What then, are painful truths to be disclosed to persons who are already in the most pitiable circumstances? Ought a woman that is dying of a fever to be informed of the fate of her husband whose skull has been fractured by a fall from his horse?'

The most that could possibly be conceded to a case like this, is, that this perhaps is not the moment to begin to treat like a rational being a person who has through the course of a long life been treated like an infant. But in reality there is a mode in which under such circumstances truth may safely be communicated; and, if it be not thus done, there is perpetual danger that it may be done in a blunter way by the heedless loquaciousness of a chambermaid, or the yet undebauched sincerity of an infant. How many arts of hypocrisy, stratagem and falshood must be employed to cover this pitiful secret? Truth was calculated in the nature of things to discipline the mind to fortitude, humanity and virtue.

---

[1] See a particular case of this sincerity discussed in Appendix, No. II.

Who are we, that we should subvert the nature of things and the system of the universe, that we should breed up a set of summer insects, upon which the breeze of sincerity may never blow, and the tempest of misfortune never beat?

'But truth may sometimes be fatal to him that speaks it. A man, who fought for the Pretender in the year 1745,* when the event happened that dispersed his companions, betook himself to solitary flight. He fell in with a party of loyalists who were seeking to apprehend him; but not knowing his person, they enquired of him for intelligence to guide them in their pursuit. He returned an answer calculated to cherish them in their mistake, and saved his life.'

This like the former is an extreme case; but the true answer will probably be found to be the same. If any one should question this, let him consider how far his approbation of the conduct of the person above cited would lead him. The rebels, as they were called, were treated in the period from which the example is drawn with the most illiberal injustice. This man, guided perhaps by the most magnanimous motives in what he had done, would have been put to an ignominious death. But, if he had a right to extricate himself by falshood, why not the wretch who has been guilty of forgery, who has deserved punishment, but who may now be conscious that he has in him materials and inclination to make a valuable member of society? Nor is the inclination an essential part of the supposition. Where-ever the materials exist, it will perhaps be found to be flagrantly unjust on the part of society to destroy them, instead of discovering the means by which they might be rendered innocent and useful. At this rate, a man has nothing to do but to commit one crime, in order to give him a right to commit a second which shall secure impunity to the first.

But why, when so many hundred individuals have been contented to become martyrs to the unintelligible principles of a pitiful sect, should not the one innocent man I have been describing be contented to offer himself up a victim at the shrine of veracity? Why should he purchase a few poor years of exile and misery by the commission of falshood? Had he surrendered himself to his pursuers, had he declared in the presence of his judges and his country, 'I, whom you think too wicked and degenerate to deserve even to live, have chosen rather to encounter your injustice than be guilty of an untruth: I would have escaped from your iniquity and tyranny if I had been able; but, hedged in on all sides, having no means of deliverance but in falshood, I chearfully submit to all that your malice can inflict rather than violate the majesty of truth:' would he not have done an honour to himself, and afforded an example to the world, that would have fully compensated the calamity of his untimely death? It is in all cases incumbent upon us to discharge our own duty, without being influenced by the enquiry whether other men will discharge or neglect theirs.

It must be remembered however that this is not the true jet of the argument. The stress does not lie upon the good he would have done: that is precarious. This heroic action, as it is to be feared has been the case with many others, might be consigned to oblivion. The object of true wisdom under the circumstances we are considering, is to weigh, not so much what is to be done, as what is to be avoided. We must not be guilty of insincerity. We must not seek to obtain a desirable object by vile means. We must prefer a general principle to the meretricious attractions of a particular deviation. We must perceive in the preservation of that general principle a balance of universal good, outweighing the benefit to arise in any instance from superseding it. It is by general principles that the business of the universe is carried on. If the laws of gravity and impulse did not make us know the consequences of our actions, we should be incapable of judgment and inference. Nor is this less true in morals. He that, having laid down to himself a plan of sincerity, is guilty of a single deviation, infects the whole, contaminates the frankness and magnanimity of his temper (for fortitude in the intrepidity of lying is baseness), and is less virtuous than the foe against whom he defends himself; for it is more virtuous in my neighbour to confide in my apparent honesty, than in me to abuse his confidence. In the case of martyrdom there are two things to be considered. It is an evil not wantonly to be incurred, for we know not what good yet remains for us to do. It is an evil not to be avoided at the expence of principle, for we should be upon our guard against setting an inordinate value upon our own efforts, and imagining that truth would die, if we were to be destroyed.

'But what becomes of the great duty of secrecy, which the incomparable Fenelon has made a capital branch in the education of his Telemachus?' It is annihilated. It becomes a truly virtuous man not to engage in any action of which he would be ashamed though all the world were spectator. Indeed Fenelon with all his ability has fallen into the most palpable inconsistency upon this subject. In Ithaca a considerable part of the merit of Telemachus consists in keeping his mother's secrets.[1] When he arrives in Tyre, he will not be persuaded to commit or suffer a deception, though his life was apparently at stake.[2]

What is it of which an honest man is commonly ashamed? Of

---

[1] *Télémaque.* Liv. XVI.   [2] Liv. III.

virtuous poverty, of doing menial offices for himself, of having raised himself by merit from a humble situation, and of a thousand particulars which in reality constitute his glory. With respect to actions of beneficence we cannot be too much upon our guard against a spirit of ostentation and the character that imperiously exacts the gratitude of its beneficiaries; but it is certainly an extreme weakness to desire to hide our deserts. So far from desiring to withhold from the world the knowledge of our good deeds, we ought to be forward to exhibit an attractive and illustrious example. We cannot determine to keep any thing secret without risking at the same time to commit a hundred artifices, quibbles, equivocations and falshoods.

But the secrets of others, 'have I a power over them?' Probably not: but you have a duty respecting them. The facts with which you are acquainted are a part of your possessions, and you are as much obliged respecting them as in any other case, to employ them for the public good. Have I no right to indulge in myself the caprice of concealing any of my affairs, and can another man have a right by his caprice to hedge up and restrain the path of my duty?—'But state secrets?' This perhaps is a subject that ought not to be anticipated. We shall have occasion to enquire how ministers of the concerns of a nation came by their right to equivocate, to juggle and over-reach, while private men are obliged to be ingenuous, direct and sincere.

There is one case of a singular nature that seems to deserve a separate examination; the case of secrets that are to be kept for the sake of mankind. Full justice is done to the affirmative side of this argument by Mr. Condorcet in his Life of Voltaire, where he is justifying this illustrious friend of mankind, for his gentleness and forbearance in asserting the liberties of the species. He first enumerates the incessant attacks of Voltaire upon superstition, hypocritical austerities and war; and then proceeds: 'It is true, the more men are enlightened, the more they will be free; but let us not put despots on their guard, and incite them to form a league against the progress of reason. Let us conceal from them the strict and eternal union that subsists between knowledge and liberty. Voltaire thought proper to paint superstition as the enemy of monarchy, to put kings and princes upon their guard against the gloomy ferocity and ambition of the priesthood, and to demonstrate that, were it not for the freedom of thought and investigation, there would be no security against the return of papal insolence, of proscriptions, assassinations and religious war. Had he taken the other side of the question, had he maintained, which is equally true, that superstition and ignorance are the support of despotism, he would only have anticipated truths for which the public were not ripe, and have seen a speedy end to his career. Truth taught by moderate degrees gradually enlarges the intellectual capacity, and insensibly prepares the equality and happiness of mankind; but taught without prudential restraint would either be nipped in the bud, or occasion national concussions in the world, that would be found premature and therefore abortive.'[1]

What a cowardly distrust do reasonings like these exhibit of the omnipotence of truth! With respect to personal safety, it will be found upon an accurate examination that Voltaire with all his ingenuity and stratagem was for sixty years together the object of perpetual, almost daily persecution from courts and ministers.[2] He was obliged to retire from country to country, and at last to take advantage of a residence upon the borders of two states with a habitation in each. His attempts to secure the patronage of princes led only to vicissitude and disgrace. If his plan had been more firm and direct, he would not have been less safe. Timidity, and an anxious endeavour to secure to ourselves a protector, invite persecution. With the advantages of Voltaire, with his talents and independence, he might have held the tyrants of the world in awe.

As to the progress of truth, it is not so precarious as its fearful friends may imagine. Mr. Condorcet has justly insinuated in the course of his argument, that 'in the invention of printing is contained the embryo, which in its maturity and vigour is destined to annihilate the slavery of the human race.'[3] Books, if proper precautions be employed, cannot be destroyed. Knowledge cannot be extirpated. Its progress is silent,

---

[1] '*Plus les hommes seront éclairés, plus ils seront libres.—Mais n'avertissons point les oppresseurs de former une ligue contre la raison, cachons leur l'étroite et nécessaire unions des lumières et de la liberté.—Quel sera donc le devoir d'un philosophe?—Il éclairera les gouvernemens sur tout ce qu'ils ont à craindre des prêtres.—Ils sera voir que sans la liberté de penser le même esprit dans la clergé ramènerait les mêmes assassinats, les mêmes supplices, les mêmes proscriptions, les mêmes guerres civiles.—Au lieu de montrer que la superstition est l'appui du despotisme, avant que la raison ait rassemblé assez de force, il prouvera qu'elle est l'ennemie des rois.—Tel est l'esprit de tous les ouvrages de Voltaire.—Que des hommes, inférieurs à lui, ne voyent pas que si Voltaire eût fait autrement, ni Montesquieu ni Rousseau n'auraient pu écrire leurs ouvrages, que l'Europe serait encore superstitieuse, et resterait longtems esclave.—En attaquant les oppresseurs avant d'avoir éclairé les citoyens, on risque de perdre la liberté et d'étouffer la raison. L'histoire offre la preuve de cette vérité. Combien de fois, malgré les généreux efforts des amis de la liberté, une seule bataille n'a-t-elle pas réduit des nations à une servitude de plusieurs siècles!—Pourquoi ne pas profiter de cette expérience funeste, et savoir attendre des progrès des lumières une liberté plus réelle, plus durable et plus paisible?*'

[2] *Vie de Voltaire, Par M****, throughout.*

[3] '*Peut-être avant l'invention de l'imprimerie était-il impossible à se soustraire au joug.*'

but infallible; and he is the most useful soldier in this war, who accumulates in an unperishable form the greatest mass of truth.

As truth has nothing to fear from her enemies, she needs not have any thing to fear from her friends. The man, who publishes the sublimest discoveries, is not of all others the most likely to inflame the vulgar, and hurry the great question of human happiness to a premature crisis. The object to be pursued undoubtedly is, the gradual improvement of mind. But this end will be better answered by exhibiting as much truth as possible, enlightening a few, and suffering knowledge to expand in the proportion which the laws of nature and necessity prescribe, than by any artificial plan of piecemeal communication that we can invent. There is in the nature of things a gradation in discovery and a progress in improvement, which do not need to be assisted by the stratagems of their votaries. In a word, there cannot be a more unworthy idea, than that truth and virtue should be under the necessity of seeking alliance with concealment. The man, who would artfully draw me into a little, that by so doing he may unawares surprise me into much, I infallibly regard as an impostor. Will truth, contracted into some petty sphere and shorn of its beams, acquire additional evidence? Rather let me trust to its omnipotence, to its congeniality with the nature of intellect, to its direct and irresistible tendency to produce liberty, and happiness, and virtue. Let me fear that I have not enough of it, that my views are too narrow to produce impression, and anxiously endeavour to add to my stock; not apprehend that, exhibited in its noon-day brightness, its lustre and genial nature should not be universally confessed.[1]

---

[1] See this subject farther pursued in Appendix, No. III.

APPENDIX, No. I
OF THE CONNEXION BETWEEN UNDERSTANDING AND VIRTUE

Can eminent virtue exist unconnected with talents?—Nature of virtue.—It is the offspring.—Of understanding.—It generates understanding.—Illustration from other pursuits—love—ambition—applied.

Can eminent talents exist unconnected with virtue?—Argument in the affirmative from analogy—in the negative from the universality of moral speculation—from the nature of vice as founded in mistake.—The argument balanced.—Importance of a sense of justice.—Its connexion with talents.—Illiberality with which men of talents are usually treated.

A PROPOSITION which, however evident in itself, seems never to have been considered with the attention it deserves, is that which affirms the connexion between understanding and virtue. Can an honest ploughman be as virtuous as Cato? Is a man of weak intellects and narrow education as capable of moral excellence as the sublimest genius or the mind most stored with information and science?

To determine these questions it is necessary we should recollect the nature of virtue. Considered as a personal quality it consists in the disposition of the mind, and may be defined a desire to promote the benefit of intelligent beings in general, the quantity of virtue being as the quantity of desire. Now desire is another name for preference, or a perception of the excellence real or supposed of any object. I say real or supposed, for an object totally destitute of real and intrinsic excellence, may become an object of desire by means of the imaginary excellence that is ascribed to it. Nor is this the only mistake to which human intelligences are liable. We may desire an object of absolute excellence, not for its real and genuine recommendations, but for some fictitious attractions we may impute to it. This is always in some degree the case, when a beneficial action is performed from an ill motive.

How far is this mistake compatible with real virtue? If I desire the benefit of intelligent beings, not from a clear and distinct perception of what it is in which their benefit consists, but from the unexamined lessons of education, from the physical effect of sympathy, or from any species of zeal unallied to and incommensurate with knowledge, can this desire be admitted for virtuous? Nothing seems more inconsistent with our ideas of virtue. A virtuous preference is the preference of an object for the sake of certain beneficial qualities which really belong to that object. To attribute virtue to any other species of preference would be the same as to suppose that an accidental effect of my conduct, which was altogether out of my view at the time of adopting it, might entitle me to the appellation of virtuous.

Hence it appears, first, that virtue consists in a desire of the benefit of the species: and, secondly, that that desire only can be denominated virtuous, which flows from a distinct perception of the value, and consequently of the nature, of the thing desired. But how extensive must be the capacity that comprehends the full value of that benefit which is the object of virtue! It must begin with a collective idea of the human species. It must discriminate, among all the different causes that produce a pleasurable state of mind, that which produces the most exquisite and durable pleasure. Eminent virtue requires that I should have a grand view of the tendency of knowledge to produce happiness, and of just political institution to favour the progress of knowledge. It demands that I should perceive in what manner social intercourse may be made conducive to virtue and felicity, and imagine the unspeakable advantages that may arise from a coincidence and succession of generous efforts. These things are necessary, not merely for the purpose of enabling me to employ my virtuous disposition in the best manner, but also for the purpose of giving to that disposition a just animation and vigour. God, according to the ideas usually conceived of that being, is more benevolent than man, because he has a constant and clear perception of the nature of that end which his providence pursues.

A farther proof that a powerful understanding is inseparable from eminent virtue will suggest itself, if we recollect that earnest desire never fails to generate capacity.

This proposition has been beautifully illustrated by the poets, when they have represented the passion of love as immediately leading in the breast of the lover to the attainment of many arduous accomplishments. It unlocks his tongue, and enables him to plead the cause of his passion with insinuating eloquence. It renders his conversation pleasing and his manners graceful. Does he desire to express his feelings in the language of verse? It dictates to him the most natural and pathetic strains, and supplies him with a just and interesting language which the man of mere reflection and science has often fought for in vain.

No picture can be more truly founded in a knowledge of human nature than this. The history of all eminent talents is of a similar kind. Did Themistocles desire to eclipse the trophies of the battle of Marathon?* The uneasiness of this desire would not let him sleep, and all his thoughts were occupied with the invention of means to accomplish the purpose he had chosen. It is a well known maxim in the forming of juvenile minds, that the instruction, which is communicated by mere constraint, makes a slow and feeble impression; but that, when once you have inspired the mind with a love for its object, the scene and the progress are entirely altered. The uneasiness of mind which earnest desire produces, doubles our intellectual activity; and as surely carries us forward with increased velocity towards our goal, as the expectation of a reward of ten thousand pounds would prompt me to walk from London to York with firmer resolution and in a shorter time.

Let the object be for a person uninstructed in the rudiments of drawing to make a copy of some celebrated statue. At first, we will suppose, his attempt shall be mean and unsuccessful. If his desire be feeble, he will be deterred by the miscarriage of this essay. If his desire be ardent and invincible, he will return to the attack. He will derive instruction from his failure. He will examine where and why he miscarried. He will study his model with a more curious eye. He will perceive that he failed principally from the loose and undigested idea he had formed of the object before him. It will no longer stand in his mind as one general mass, but he will analyse it, bestowing upon each part in succession a separate consideration.

The case is similar in virtue as in science. If I have conceived an earnest desire of being a benefactor of my species, I shall no doubt find out a channel in which for my desire to operate, and shall be quick-sighted in discovering the defects or comparative littleness of the plan I have chosen. But the choice of an excellent plan for the accomplishment of an important purpose, and the exertion of a mind perpetually watchful to remove its defects, imply considerable understanding. The farther I am engaged in the pursuit of this plan the more will my capacity increase. If my mind flag and be discouraged in the pursuit, it will not be merely want of understanding, but want of desire. My desire and my virtue will be less, than those of the man, who goes on with unremitted constancy in the same career.

Thus far we have only been considering how impossible it is that eminent virtue should exist in a weak understanding, and it is surprising that such a proposition should ever have been contested. It is a curious question to examine, how far the converse of this proposition is true, and in what degree eminent talents are compatible with the absence of virtue.

From the arguments already adduced it appears that virtuous desire is another name for a clear and distinct perception of the nature and value of the object of virtue. Hence it seems most natural to conclude, that, though understanding, or strong percipient power is the indispensible prerequisite of virtue, yet it is necessary that this power should be fixed upon this object, in order to its producing the desired effect. Thus it is in art. Without genius no man ever was a poet; but it is necessary that general capacity should have been directed to this particular channel, for poetical excellence to be the result.

There is however some difference between the two cases. Poetry is the business of a few, virtue and vice are the affairs of all men. To every intellect that exists one or other of these qualities must properly belong. It must be granted that, where every other circumstance is equal, that man will be most virtuous, whose understanding has been most actively employed in the study of virtue. But morality has been in a certain degree an object of attention to all men. No person ever failed more or less to apply the standard of just and unjust to his own actions and those of others; and this has of course been generally done with most ingenuity by men of the greatest capacity.

It must farther be remembered that a vicious conduct is always the result of narrow views. A man of powerful capacity and extensive observation is least likely to commit the mistake, either of seeing himself as the only object of importance in the universe, or of conceiving that his own advantage may best be promoted by trampling on that of others. Liberal accomplishments are surely in some degree connected with liberal principles. He, who takes into his view a whole nation as the subjects of his operation or the instruments of his greatness, may naturally be expected to entertain some kindness for the whole. He, whose mind is habitually elevated to magnificent conceptions, is not likely to sink without strong reluctance into those sordid pursuits, which engross so large a portion of mankind.

But, though these general maxims must be admitted for true, and would incline us to hope for a constant union between eminent talents and great virtues, there are other considerations which present a strong drawback upon so agreeable an expectation. It is sufficiently evident that morality in some degree enters into the reflections of all mankind. But it is equally evident, that it may enter for more or for less; and that there will be men of the highest talents, who have their attention diverted to other objects, and by whom it will be meditated upon with less earnestness, than it may sometimes be by other men who are in a general view their inferiors. The human mind is in some cases so tenacious of its errors, and so ingenious in the invention of a sophistry by which they may be vindicated, as to frustrate expectations of virtue in other respects the best founded.

From the whole of the subject it seems to appear, that men of talents, even when they are erroneous, are not destitute of virtue, and that there is a degree of guilt of which they are incapable. There is no ingredient that so essentially contributes to a virtuous character as a sense of justice. Philanthropy, as contradistinguished to justice, is rather an unreflecting feeling, than a rational principle. It leads to an absurd indulgence, which is frequently more injurious than beneficial even to the individual it proposes to favour. It leads to a blind partiality, inflicting calamity without remorse upon many perhaps, in order to promote the imagined interest of a few. But justice measures by one inflexible standard the claims of all, weighs their opposite pretensions, and seeks to diffuse happiness, because happiness is the fit and reasonable adjunct of a conscious being. Wherever therefore a strong sense of justice exists, it is common and reasonable to say, that in that mind exists considerable virtue, though the individual from an unfortunate concurrence of circumstances may with all his great qualities be the instrument of a very small portion of benefit. Can great intellectual energy exist without a strong sense of justice?

It has no doubt resulted from a train of speculation similar to this, that poetical readers have commonly remarked Milton's devil to be a being of considerable virtue.* It must be admitted that his energies centered too much in personal regards. But why did he rebel against his maker? It was, as he himself informs us, because he saw no sufficient reason for that extreme inequality of rank and power which the creator assumed. It was because prescription and precedent form no adequate ground for implicit faith. After his fall, why did he still cherish the spirit of opposition? From a persuasion that he was hardly and injuriously treated. He was not discouraged by the apparent inequality of the contest: because a sense of reason and justice was stronger in his mind, than a sense of brute force: because he had much of the feelings of an Epictetus or a Cato,* and little of those of a slave. He bore his torments with fortitude, because he disdained to be subdued by despotic power. He sought revenge, because he could not think with tameness of the unexpostulating authority that assumed to dispose of him. How beneficial and illustrious might the temper from which these qualities flowed have proved with a small diversity of situation!

Let us descend from these imaginary existences to real history. We shall find that even Cæsar and Alexander* had their virtues. There is great reason to believe, that, however mistaken was their system of conduct, they imagined it reconcileable and even conducive to the general good. If they had desired the general good more earnestly, they would have understood better how to promote it.

Upon the whole it appears, that great talents are great energies, and that great energies cannot flow but from a powerful sense of fitness and justice. A man of uncommon genius is a man of high passions and lofty design; and our passions will be found in the last analysis to have their surest foundation in a sentiment of justice. If a man be of an aspiring and ambitious temper, it is because at present he finds himself out of his place, and wishes to be in it. Even the lover imagines that his qualities or his passion give him a title superior to that of other men. If I accumulate wealth, it is because I think that the most rational plan of life cannot be secured without it; and, if I dedicate my energies to sensual pleasures, it is that I regard other pursuits as irrational and visionary. All our passions would die in the moment they were conceived, were it not for this reinforcement. A man of quick resentment, of strong feelings, and who pertinaciously resists every thing that he regards as an unjust assumption, may be considered as having in him the seeds of eminence. Nor is it easily to be conceived that such a man should not proceed from a sense of justice to some degree of benevolence; as Milton's hero felt real compassion and sympathy for his partners in misfortune.

If these reasonings are to be admitted, what judgment shall we form of the decision of doctor Johnson,* who, speaking of a certain obscure translator of the odes of Pindar, says, that he was 'one of the few poets to whom death needed not to be terrible?'[1] Let it be remembered that the error is by no means peculiar to doctor Johnson, though there are few instances in which it is carried to a more violent extreme, than in the general tenour of the work from which this quotation is taken. It was natural to expect that there would be a combination among the multitude to pull down intellectual eminence. Ambition is common to all men; and those, who are unable to rise to distinction, are at least willing to reduce others to their own standard. No man can completely understand the character of him with whom he has no sympathy of views, and we may be allowed to revile what we do not understand. But it is deeply to be regretted that men of talents should so often have entered into this combination. Who does not recollect with pain the vulgar abuse that Swift has thrown upon Dryden, and the mutual jealousies and animosities of Rousseau and Voltaire,* men who ought to have co-operated for the salvation of the world?

[1] Lives of the Poets: Life of West.

APPENDIX, No. II
OF THE MODE OF EXCLUDING VISITORS

Its impropriety argued—from the situation in which it places, 1. the visitor—2. the servant.—Objections:—pretended necessity of this practice, 1. to preserve us from intrusion—2. to free us from disagreeable acquaintance.—Characters of the honest and dishonest man in this respect compared.

THIS principle respecting the observation of truth in the common intercourses of life cannot perhaps be better illustrated, than from the familiar and trivial case, as it is commonly supposed to be, of a master directing his servant to say he is not at home, as a means of freeing him from the intrusion of impertinent guests. No question of morality can be foreign to the science of politics; nor will those few pages of the present work be found perhaps the least valuable, which here and in other places[1] are dedicated to the refutation of errors, that by their extensive influence have perverted the foundation of moral and political justice.

Let us first, according to the well known axiom of morality, put ourselves in the place of the person whom this answer excludes. It seldom happens but that he is able, if he be in possession of any discernment, to discover with tolerable accuracy whether the answer he receives be true or false. There are a thousand petty circumstances by which falshood continually detects itself. The countenance and the voice of the servant, unless long practised indeed in this lesson of deceit, his cold and reserved manner in the one case, and his free, ingenuous and unembarrassed air in the other, will almost always speak a language less ambiguous than his lips. But let us suppose only that we vehemently suspect the truth. It is not intended to keep us in ignorance of the existence of such a practice. He that adopts it, is willing to avow in general terms that such is his system, or he makes out a case for himself much less favourable than I was making out for him. The visitor then who receives this answer, feels in spite of himself a contempt for the prevarication of the person he visits. I appeal to the feelings of every man in the situation described, and I have no doubt that he will find this to be their true state in the first instance, however he may have a set of sophistical reasonings at hand by which he may in a few minutes reason down the first movements of indignation. He feels that the trouble he has taken and the civility he intended intitled him at least to truth in return.

[1] Vide Appendices to Book II, Chap. II.

Having put ourselves in the place of the visitor, let us next put ourselves in the place of the poor despised servant. Let us suppose that we are ourselves destined as sons or husbands to give this answer that our father or our wife is not at home, when he or she is really in the house. Should we not feel our tongues contaminated with the base plebeian lie? Would it be a sufficient opiate to our consciences to say that 'such is the practice, and it is well understood?' It never can be understood: its very intention is, not to be understood. We say that 'we have certain arguments that prove the practice to be innocent.' Are servants only competent to understand these arguments? Surely we ought best to be able to understand our own arguments, and yet we shrink with abhorrence from the idea of personally acting upon them.

Whatever sophistry we may have to excuse our error, nothing is more certain than that our servants understand the lesson we teach them to be a lie. It is accompanied by all the retinue of falshood. Before it can be gracefully practised, the servant must be no mean proficient in the mysteries of hypocrisy. By the easy impudence with which it is uttered, he best answers the purpose of his master, or in other words the purpose of deceit. By the easy impudence with which it is uttered, he best stifles the upbraidings of his own mind, and conceals from others the shame imposed on him by his despotic task-master. Before this can be sufficiently done, he must have discarded the ingenuous frankness by means of which the thoughts find easy commerce with the tongue, and the clear and undisguised countenance which ought to be the faithful mirror of the mind. Do you think, when he has learned this degenerate lesson in one instance, that it will produce no unfavourable effects upon his general conduct? Surely, if we will practise vice, we ought at least to have the magnanimity to practise it in person, not cowardlike corrupt the principles of another, and oblige him to do that which we have not the honesty to dare to do for ourselves.

But it is said, 'that this lie is necessary, and that the intercourse of human society cannot be carried on without it.' What, is it not as easy to say, 'I am engaged,' or 'indisposed,' or as the case may happen, as 'I am not at home?' Are these answers more insulting, than the universally suspected answer, the notorious hypocrisy of 'I am not at home?'

The purpose indeed for which this answer is usually employed is a deceit of another kind. Every man has in the catalogue of his acquaintance some that he particularly loves, and others to whom he is indifferent, or perhaps worse than indifferent. This answer leaves the latter to suppose, if they please, that they are in the class of the former.

And what is the benefit to result from this indiscriminate, undistinguishing manner of treating our neighbours? Whatever benefit it be, it
no doubt exists in considerable vigour in the present state of polished
society, where forms perpetually intrude to cut off all intercourse
between the feelings of mankind; and I can scarcely tell a man on the
one hand 'that I esteem his character and honour his virtues,' or on the
other 'that he is fallen into an error which will be of prejudicial consequence to him,' without trampling upon all the barriers of politeness.
But is all this right? Is not the esteem or the disapprobation of others
among the most powerful incentives to virtue or punishments of vice?
Can we even understand virtue and vice half so well as we otherwise
should, if we be unacquainted with the feelings of our neighbours
respecting them? If there be in the list of our acquaintance any person
whom we particularly dislike, it usually happens that it is for some
moral fault that we perceive or think we perceive in him. Why should
he be kept in ignorance of our opinion respecting him, and prevented
from the opportunity either of amendment or vindication? If he be
too wise or too foolish, too virtuous or too vicious for us, why should
he not be ingenuously told of his mistake in his intended kindness to
us, rather than be suffered to find it out by six months enquiry from our
servants?

   This leads us to yet one more argument in favour of this disingenuous practice. We are told, 'there is no other by which we can rid ourselves of disagreeable acquaintance.' How long shall this be one of the
effects of polished society, to persuade us that we are incapable of doing
the most trivial offices for ourselves? You may as well tell me, 'that it is
a matter of indispensible necessity to have a valet to put on my stockings.' In reality the existence of these troublesome visitors is owing to
the hypocrisy of politeness. It is that we wear the same indiscriminate
smile, the same appearance of cordiality and complacence to all our
acquaintance. Ought we to do thus? Are virtue and excellence entitled
to no distinctions? For the trouble of these impertinent visits we may
thank ourselves. If we practised no deceit, if we assumed no atom of
cordiality and esteem we did not feel, we should be little pestered with
these buzzing intruders. But one species of falshood involves us in
another; and he, that pleads for these lying answers to our visitors, in
reality pleads the cause of a cowardice, that dares not deny to vice the
distinction and kindness that are exclusively due to virtue.

   The man who acted upon this system would be very far removed
from a Cynic.* The conduct of men formed upon the fashionable
system is a perpetual contradiction. At one moment they fawn upon us

with a servility that dishonours the dignity of man, and at another treat us with a neglect, a sarcastic insolence, and a supercilious disdain, that are felt as the severest cruelty, by him who has not the firmness to regard them with neglect. The conduct of the genuine moralist is equable and uniform. He loves all mankind, he desires the benefit of all, and this love and this desire are legible in his conduct. Does he remind us of our faults? It is with no mixture of asperity, selfish disdain and insolent superiority. Of consequence it is scarcely possible he should wound. Few indeed are those effeminate valetudinarians, who recoil from the advice, when they distinguish the motive. But, were it otherwise, the injury is nothing. Those who feel themselves incapable of suffering the most benevolent plain dealing, would derive least benefit from the prescription, and they avoid the physician. Thus is he delivered, without harshness, hypocrisy and deceit, from those whose intercourse he had least reason to desire; and the more his character is understood, the more his acquaintance will be select, his company being chiefly sought by the ingenuous, the well disposed, and those who are desirous of improvement.

APPENDIX, No. III
SUBJECT OF SINCERITY RESUMED

A case proposed.—Arguments in favour of concealment.—Previous question: is truth in general to be partially communicated?—Customary effects of sincerity—of insincerity—upon him who practices it—1. the suspension of improvement—2. misanthropy—3. disingenuity—upon the spectators.—Sincerity delineated—its general importance.—Application.— Duty respecting the choice of a residence.

To enable us more accurately to judge of the extent of the obligation to be sincere, let us suppose, 'that I am resident, as a native or otherwise, in the kingdom of Portugal,* and that I am of opinion that the establishment, civil and religious, of that country is in a high degree injurious to the welfare and improvement of the inhabitants.' Ought I explicitly to declare the sentiments I entertain? To this question I answer, that 'my immediate duty is to seek for myself a different residence.'

The arguments in favour of concealment in this case are obvious. 'That country is subject to a high degree of despotism, and, if I delivered my sentiments in this frank manner, especially if along with this I were ardent and indefatigable in endeavouring to proselyte the inhabitants, my sincerity would not be endured. In that country the institution of the holy inquisition still flourishes, and the fathers of this venerable court would find means effectually to silence me, before I had well opened my commission. The inhabitants, wholly unaccustomed to such bold assertions as those I uttered, would feel their pious ears inexpressibly shocked, and the martyrdom I endured, instead of producing the good effects with which martyrdom is sometimes attended, would soon be forgotten, and, as long as it was remembered, would be remembered only with execrations of my memory. If on the contrary I concealed my sentiments, I might spend a long life in acts of substantial benevolence. If I concealed them in part, I might perhaps by a prudent and gradual disclosure effect that revolution in the opinions of the inhabitants, which by my precipitation in the other case I defeated in the outset. These arguments in favour of concealment are not built upon cowardice and selfishness, or upon a recollection of the horrible tortures to which I should be subjected. They flow from considerations of philanthropy, and an endeavour fairly to estimate in what mode my exertions may be rendered most conducive to the general good.'

Before we enter upon their direct examination, it may be proper to premise some general observations. In the first place, let us calmly enquire whether the instance here stated be of the nature of an exception or a rule. 'Ought I universally to tell only a small part of the truth at a time, careful not to shock the prejudices of my hearers, and thus lead them imperceptibly to conclusions which would have revolted them at first; or am I to practise this method only, where the risk is great, and my life may be the forfeit?' It would seem as if truth were a sacred deposit, which I had no right to deal out in shreds to my fellow men, just as my temper or my prudence should dictate. It would seem as if it were an unworthy artifice, by an ingenious arrangement of my materials to trick men into a conclusion, to which frankness, ingenuity and sincerity would never have conducted them. It would seem as if the shock I am so careful to avoid were favourable to the health and robust constitution of mind; and that, though I might in this way produce least temporary effect, the ultimate result would afford a balance greatly in favour of undisguised sincerity.

A second preliminary proper to be introduced in this place consists in a recollection of the general effects of sincerity and insincerity, the reasons for which the one is commonly laudable and the other to be blamed, independently of the subjects about which they may be employed. Sincerity is laudable, on account of the firmness and energy of character it never fails to produce. 'An upright man,' it has sometimes been said, 'ought to carry his heart in his hand.' He ought to have an ingenuousness which shrinks from no examination. The commerce between his tongue and his heart is uniform. Whatever he speaks you can depend upon to be the truth and the whole truth. The designs he has formed he employs no artifice to conceal. He tells you in the first instance: 'This is the proposition I mean to demonstrate. I put you upon your guard. I will not take you by surprise. If what I affirm be the truth, it will bear your scrutiny. If it were error, I could have recourse to no means more equivocal, than that of concealing in every step of the process the object in which my exertions were intended to terminate.'

Insincerity is to be blamed, because it has an immediate tendency to vitiate the integrity of character. 'I must conceal the opinions I entertain,' suppose, 'from the holy father inquisitor.' What method shall I employ for this purpose? Shall I hide them as an impenetrable secret from all the world? If this be the system I adopt, the consequence is an instant and immediate end to the improvement of my mind. It is by the efforts of a daring temper that improvements and discoveries are made. The seeds of discovery are scattered in every thinking mind, but they are too frequently starved by the ungenial soil upon which they fall. Every man suspects the absurdity of kings and lords, and the injustice of that glaring and oppressive inequality which subsists in most civilised countries. But he dares not let his mind loose in so adventurous a subject. If I tell my thoughts, I derive from the act of communication encouragement to proceed. I perceive in what manner they are received by others, and this perception acts by rebound upon my own progress. If they be received cordially, I derive new encouragement from the approbation of others. If they be received with opposition and distrust, I am induced to revise them. I detect their errors, or I strengthen my arguments, and add new truths to those which I had previously accumulated. What can excite me to the pursuit of discovery, if I know that I am never to communicate my discoveries? It is in the nature of things impossible, that the man, who has determined with himself never to utter the truths he knows, should be an intrepid and indefatigable thinker. The link which binds together the inward and the outward man is indissoluble; and he, that is not bold in speech, will never be ardent and unprejudiced in enquiry. Add to this, that conscious disguise has the worst effect upon the temper, and converts virtue, which ought to be frank, social and ingenuous, into a solitary, morose and misanthropical principle.

But let us conceive that the method I employ to protect myself from persecution is different from that above stated. Let us suppose that I communicate my sentiments, but with caution and reserve. This system involves with it an endless train of falshood, duplicity and tergiversation. When I communicate my sentiments, it is under the inviolable seal of secrecy. If my zeal carry me any great lengths, and my love of truth be ardent, I shall wish to communicate it as far as the bounds of prudence will possibly admit, and it will be strange if in a course of years I do not commit one mistake in my calculation. My grand secret is betrayed, and suspicion is excited in the breast of the father inquisitor. What shall I do now? I must, I suppose, stoutly deny the fact. I must compose my features into a consistent expression of the most natural ignorance and surprise, happy if I have made such progress in the arts of hypocrisy and falshood, as to put the change upon the wild beast who is ready to devour me. The most consummate impostor is upon this hypothesis the man of most perfect virtue.

But this is not all. My character for benevolence being well known, I am likely to be surrounded by persons of good humoured indiscretion rather than by inveterate enemies. Of every man who questions me about my real sentiments I must determine first, whether he simply wish to be informed, or whether his design be to betray me. The character of virtue seems in its own nature to be that of firm and unalterable resolution, confident in its own integrity. But the character that results from this system begins in hesitation, and ends in disgrace. I am questioned whether such be my real sentiments. I deny it. My questioner returns to the charge with an, 'Oh, but I heard it from such a one, and he was present when you delivered them.' What am I to do now? Am I to asperse the character of the honest reporter of my words? Am I to make an impotent effort to get rid of the charge; and, instead of establishing my character for orthodoxy, astonish my informer with my cool and intrepid effrontery?

Insincerity has the worst effect both upon him who practises, and upon them who behold it. It deprives virtue of that conscious magnanimity and ease, which ought ever to be ranked among its noblest effects. It requires the perpetual exercise of presence of mind, not for the purpose of telling the most useful truths in the best manner, but in order to invent a consistent catalogue of lies, and to utter them with a countenance at war with every thing that is passing in my heart. It destroys that confidence on the part of my hearers, which ought to be inseparable from virtue. They cannot all of them be expected to understand the deep plan of benevolence and the total neglect of all selfish and timid considerations by which I am supposing my conduct to be regulated. But they can all see my duplicity and tergiversation. They all know that I excel the most consummate impostor in the coolness with which I can utter falshood, and the craft with which I can support it.

Sincerity has sometimes been brought into disrepute by the absurd system according to which it has been pursued, and still oftener by the whimsical picture which the adversaries of undistinguishing sincerity have made of it. It is not necessary that I should stop every person that I meet in the street to inform him of my sentiments. It is not necessary that I should perpetually talk to the vulgar and illiterate of the deepest and sublimest truths. All that is necessary is, that I should practise no concealment, that I should preserve my disposition and character untainted. Whoever questions me, it is necessary that I should have no secrets or reserves, but be always ready to return a frank and explicit answer. When I undertake by argument to establish any principle, it is necessary that I should employ no circuitous methods, but clearly state in the first instance the object I have in view. Having satisfied this original duty, I may fairly call upon my hearer for the exercise of his patience. 'It is true,' I may say, 'that the opinion I deliver will appear shocking to your prejudices, but I will now deliberately and minutely assign the reasons upon which it is founded. If they appear satisfactory, receive; if they be inconclusive, reject it.' This is the ground work of sincerity. The superstructure is the propagation of every important truth, because it conduces to the improvement of man whether individually or collectively; and the telling all I know of myself and of my neighbour, because strict justice and unequivocal publicity are the best security for every virtue.

Sincerity then, in ordinary cases at least, seems to be of so much importance, that it is my duty first to consider how to preserve my sincerity untainted, and afterwards to select the best means in my power in each particular situation, of benefiting mankind. Sincerity is one of those paramount and general rules, which is never to give way to the affair of the day. I may imagine perhaps that falshood and deceit may be most beneficial in some particular instances, as I might imagine upon the subject of a preceding chapter, that it would be virtuous to plant my dagger in the heart of a tyrant. But we should be cautious of indulging our imaginations in these instances. The great law of always employing ingenuous and honourable means seems to be of more importance than the exterminating any local and temporary evils. I well know in the present case what good will result from a frank and undisguised principle of action, and what evil from deceit, duplicity and falshood. But I am much less certain of the good that will arise under particular circumstances from a neglect of these principles.

Having thus unfolded the true ground of reasoning upon this subject, we will return to the question respecting the conduct to be observed by the reformer in Portugal.

And here the true answer will perhaps be found to be that which has been above delivered, that a person so far enlightened upon these subjects, ought by no consideration to be prevailed upon to settle in Portugal; and, if he were there already, ought to quit the country with all convenient speed. His efforts in Portugal would probably be vain; but there is some other country in which they will be attended with the happiest consequences.

It may be objected, 'that some person must begin the work of reformation in Portugal, and why should it not be the individual of whom we are treating?' But the answer is, that, in the sense supposed in this objection, it is not necessary that any body should begin. These great and daring truths ought to be published in England, France and other countries; and the dissemination that will attend them here, will produce a report and afford an example, which after some time may prepare them a favourable reception there.

The great chain of causes from which every event in the universe takes its rise, has sufficiently provided for the gradual instruction of mankind, without its being necessary that individuals should violate their principles and sacrifice their integrity to accomplish it. Perhaps there never was a mind that so far outran the rest of the species, but that there was some country in which the man that possessed it might safely tell all he knew. The same causes that ripen the mind of the individual are acting generally, ripening similar minds, and giving a certain degree of similar impression to whole ages and countries. There exist perhaps at this very moment in Portugal, or soon will exist, minds, which, though mere children in science compared with their gigantic neighbours in a more favoured soil, are yet accurately adapted to the improvement of their countrymen. If by any sport of nature an exotic should spring up, let him be transplanted to a climate that will prove more favourable to his vigour and utility. Add to this, that, when we are inclined to set an inordinate value upon our own importance, it may be reasonable to suspect that we are influenced by some lurking principle of timidity or vanity. It is by no means certain that the individual ever yet existed, whose life was of so much value to the community, as to be worth preserving at so great an expence, as that of his sincerity.

CHAPTER V

OF FREE WILL AND NECESSITY

Importance of the question.—Definition of necessity.—Why supposed to exist in the operations of the material universe.—The case of the operations of mind is parallel.—Indications of necessity—in history—in our judgments of character—in our schemes of policy—in our ideas of moral discipline.—Objection from the fallibility of our expectations in human conduct.—Answer.—Origin and universality of the sentiment of free will.—The sentiment of necessity also universal.—The truth of this sentiment argued from the nature of volition.— Hypothesis of free will examined.—Self-determination.—indifference.— The will not a distinct faculty.—Free will disadvantageous to its possessor.—Of no service to morality.

HAVING now finished the theoretical part of our enquiry, far as appeared to be necessary to afford a foundation for our reasoning respecting the different provisions of political institution, we might directly proceed to the consideration of those provisions. It will not however be useless to pause in this place, in order to consider those general principles of the human mind, which are most intimately connected with the topics of political reasoning.[1]

None of these principles seems to be of greater importance than that which affirms that all actions are necessary.

Most of the reasonings upon which we have hitherto been employed, though perhaps constantly built upon this doctrine as a postulate, will yet by their intrinsic evidence, however inconsistently with his opinion upon this primary topic, be admitted by the advocate of free will. But it ought not to be the present design of political enquirers to treat the questions that may present themselves superficially. It will be found upon maturer reflection that this doctrine of moral necessity includes in it consequences of the highest moment, and leads to a bold and comprehensive view of man in society, which cannot possibly be entertained by him who has embraced the opposite opinion. Severe method would have required that this proposition should have been established in the first instance, as an indispensible foundation of moral reasoning of every sort. But there are well disposed persons, who notwithstanding

---

[1] The reader, who is indisposed to abstruse speculations, will find the other members of the enquiry sufficiently connected, without an express reference to the remaining part of the present book.

the evidence with which it is attended, have been alarmed at its consequences; and it was perhaps proper, in compliance with their mistake, to shew that the moral reasonings of this work did not stand in need of this support, in any other sense than moral reasonings do upon every other subject.

To the right understanding of any arguments that may be adduced under this head, it is requisite that we should have a clear idea of the meaning of the term necessity. He who affirms that all actions are necessary, means, that, if we form a just and complete view of all the circumstances in which a living or intelligent being is placed, we shall find that he could not in any moment of his existence have acted otherwise than he has acted. According to this assertion there is in the transactions of mind nothing loose, precarious and uncertain. Upon this question the advocate of liberty in the philosophical sense must join issue. He must, if he mean any thing, deny this certainty of conjunction between moral antecedents and consequents. Where all is constant and invariable, and the events that arise uniformly flow from the circumstances in which they originate, there can be no liberty.

It is acknowledged that in the events of the material universe everything is subjected to this necessity. The tendency of investigation and enquiry relatively to this topic of human knowledge has been, more effectually to exclude chance, as our improvements extended. Let us consider what is the species of evidence that has satisfied philosophers upon this point. Their only valid ground of reasoning has been from experience. The argument which has induced mankind to conceive of the universe as governed by certain laws, and to entertain the idea of necessary connexion between successive events, has been an observed similarity in the order of succession. If, when we had once remarked two events succeeding each other, we had never had occasion to see that individual succession repeated; if we saw innumerable events in perpetual progression without any apparent order, so that all our observation would not enable us, when we beheld one, to pronounce that another of such a particular class might be expected to follow; we should never have conceived of the existence of necessary connexion, or have had an idea corresponding to the term cause.

Hence it follows that all that strictly speaking we know of the material universe is this succession of events. Uniform succession irresistibly forces upon the mind the idea of abstract connexion. When we see the sun constantly rise in the morning and set at night, and have had occasion to observe this phenomenon invariably taking place through the whole period of our existence, we cannot avoid believing that there is some cause producing this uniformity of event. But the principle or virtue by which one event is conjoined to another we never see.

Let us take some familiar illustrations of this truth. Can it be imagined that any man by the inspection and analysis of gunpowder would have been enabled, previously to experience, to predict its explosion? Would he previously to experience have been enabled to predict, that one piece of marble having a flat and polished surface might with facility be protruded along another in a horizontal, but would with considerable pertinacity resist separation in a perpendicular direction? The simplest phenomena of the most hourly occurrence were originally placed at an equal distance from human sagacity.

There is a certain degree of obscurity incident to this subject arising from the following circumstance. All human knowledge is the result of perception. We know nothing of any substance but by experience. If it produced no effects, it would be no subject of human intelligence. We collect a considerable number of these effects, and, by their perceived uniformity having reduced them into general classes, form a general idea annexed to the subject that produces them. It must be admitted, that a definition of any substance, that is, any thing that deserves to be called knowledge respecting it, will enable us to predict some of its future possible effects, and that for this plain reason, that definition is prediction under another name. But, though, when we have gained the idea of impenetrability as a general phenomenon of matter, we can predict some of its effects, there are others which we cannot predict: or in other words, we know none of its effects but such as we have actually remarked, added to an expectation that similar events will arise under similar circumstances, proportioned to the constancy with which they have been observed to take place in our past experience. Finding as we do by repeated experiments, that material substances have the property of resistance, and that one substance in a state of rest, when impelled by another, passes into a state of motion, we are still in want of more particular observation to enable us to predict the specific effects that will follow from this impulse in each of the bodies. Enquire of a man who knows nothing more of matter than its general property of impenetrability, what will be the result of one ball of matter impinging upon another, and you will soon find how little this general property can inform him of the particular laws of motion. We suppose him to know that it will communicate motion to the second ball. But what quantity of motion will it communicate? What effects will the impulse produce upon the impelling ball? Will it continue to move in the same direction?

will it recoil in the opposite direction? will it fly off obliquely, or will it subside into a state of rest? All these events will appear equally probable to him whom a series of observations upon the past has not instructed as to what he is to expect from the future.

From these remarks we may sufficiently collect what is the species of knowledge we possess respecting the laws of the material universe. No experiments we are able to make, no reasonings we are able to deduce, can ever instruct us in the principle of causation, or shew us for what reason it is that one event has, in every instance in which it has been known to occur, been the precursor of another event of a certain given description. Yet we reasonably believe that these events are bound together by a perfect necessity, and exclude from our ideas of matter and motion the supposition of chance or an uncaused event. Association of ideas obliges us, after having seen two events perpetually conjoined, to pass, as soon as one of them occurs, to the recollection of the other: and, in cases where this transition never deceives us, but the ideal succession is always found to be an exact copy of the future event, it is impossible that this species of foresight should not convert into a general foundation of reasoning. We cannot take a single step upon this subject, which does not partake of the species of operation we denominate abstraction. Till we have been led to consider the rising of the sun to-morrow as an incident of the same species as its rising today, we cannot deduce from it similar consequences. It is the business of science to carry this task of generalisation to its farthest extent, and to reduce the diversified events of the universe to a small number of original principles.

Let us proceed to apply these reasonings concerning matter to the illustration of the theory of mind. Is it possible in this latter theory, as in the former subject, to discover any general principles? Can intellect be made a topic of science? Are we able to reduce the multiplied phenomena of mind to any certain standard of reasoning? If the affirmative of these questions be conceded, the inevitable consequence appears to be, that mind, as well as matter, exhibits a constant conjunction of events, and affords a reasonable presumption to the necessary connexion of those events. It is of no importance that we cannot see the ground of that connexion, or imagine how propositions and reasoning, when presented to the mind of a percipient being, are able by necessary consequence to generate volition and animal motion; for, if there be any truth in the above reasonings, we are equally incapable of perceiving the ground of connexion between any two events in the material universe, the common and received opinion that we do perceive such ground of connexion being in reality nothing more than a vulgar prejudice.

That mind is a topic of science may be argued from all those branches of literature and enquiry which have mind for their subject. What species of amusement or instruction would history afford us, if there were no ground of inference from moral causes to effects, if certain temptations and inducements did not in all ages and climates produce a certain series of actions, if we were unable to trace connexion and a principle of unity in men's tempers, propensities and transactions? The amusement would be inferior to that which we derive from the perusal of a chronological table, where events have no order but that of time; since, however the chronologist may neglect to mark the internal connexion between successive transactions, the mind of the reader is busied in supplying that connexion from memory or imagination: but the very idea of such connexion would never have suggested itself, if we had never found the source of that idea in experience. The instruction arising from the perusal of history would be absolutely none; since instruction implies in its very nature the classing and generalising of objects. But, upon the supposition on which we are arguing, all objects would be unconnected and disjunct, without the possibility of affording any grounds of reasoning or principles of science.

The idea correspondent to the term character inevitably includes in it the assumption of necessary connexion. The character of any man is the result of a long series of impressions communicated to his mind, and modifying it in a certain manner, so as to enable us, from a number of these modifications and impressions being given, to predict his conduct. Hence arise his temper and habits, respecting which we reasonably conclude, that they will not be abruptly superseded and reversed; and that, if they ever be reversed, it will not be accidentally, but in consequence of some strong reason persuading, or some extraordinary event modifying his mind. If there were not this original and essential connexion between motives and actions, and, which forms one particular branch of this principle, between men's past and future actions, there could be no such thing as character, or as a ground of inference enabling us to predict what men would be from what they have been.

From the same idea of necessary connexion arise all the schemes of policy, in consequence of which men propose to themselves by a certain plan of conduct to prevail upon others to become the tools and instruments of their purposes. All the arts of courtship and flattery, of playing upon men's hopes and fears, proceed upon the supposition that mind is subject to certain laws, and that, provided we be skilful and assiduous enough in applying the cause, the effect will inevitably follow.

Lastly, the idea of moral discipline proceeds entirely upon this principle. If I carefully persuade, exhort, and exhibit motives to another, it is because I believe that motives have a tendency to influence his conduct. If I reward or punish him, either with a view to his own improvement or as an example to others, it is because I have been led to believe that rewards and punishments are calculated in their own nature to affect the sentiments and practices of mankind.

There is but one conceivable objection against the inference from these premises to the necessity of human actions. It may be alledged, that 'though there is a real connexion between motives and actions, yet that this connexion may not amount to a certainty, and that of consequence the mind still retains an inherent activity by which it can at pleasure dissolve this connexion. Thus for example, when I address argument and persuasion to my neighbour to induce him to adopt a certain species of conduct, I do it not with a certain expectation of success, and am not utterly disappointed if all my efforts fail of their effect. I make a reserve for a certain faculty of liberty he is supposed to possess, which may at last counteract the best digested projects.'

But in this objection there is nothing peculiar to the case of mind. It is just so in matter. I see a part only of the premises, and therefore can pronounce only with uncertainty upon the conclusion. A philosophical experiment, which has succeeded a hundred times, may altogether fail upon the next trial. But what does the philosopher conclude from this? Not that there is a liberty of choice in his retort and his materials, by which they baffle the best formed expectations. Not that the connexion between effects and causes is imperfect, and that part of the effect happens from no cause at all. But that there was some other cause concerned whose operation he did not perceive, but which a fresh investigation will probably lay open to him. When the science of the material universe was in its infancy, men were sufficiently prompt to refer events to accident and chance; but the farther they have extended their enquiries and observation, the more reason they have found to conclude that every thing takes place according to necessary and universal laws.

The case is exactly parallel with respect to mind. The politician and the philosopher, however they may speculatively entertain the opinion of free will, never think of introducing it into their scheme of accounting for events. If an incident turn out otherwise than they expected, they take it for granted, that there was some unobserved bias, some habit of thinking, some prejudice of education, some singular association of ideas, that disappointed their prediction; and, if they be of an active and enterprising temper, they return, like the natural philosopher, to search out the secret spring of this unlooked for event.

The reflections into which we have entered upon the doctrine of causes, not only afford us a simple and impressive argument in favour of the doctrine of necessity, but suggest a very obvious reason why the doctrine opposite to this has been in a certain degree the general opinion of mankind. It has appeared that the idea of necessary connexion between events of any sort is the lesson of experience, and the vulgar never arrive at the universal application of this principle even to the phenomena of the material universe. In the easiest and most familiar instances, such as the impinging of one ball of matter upon another and its consequences, they willingly admit the interference of chance, or an event uncaused. In this instance however, as both the impulse and its effects are subjects of observation to the senses, they readily imagine that they perceive the absolute principle which causes motion to be communicated from the first ball to the second. Now the very same prejudice and precipitate conclusion, which induce them to believe that they discover the principle of motion in objects of sense, act in an opposite direction with respect to such objects as cannot be subjected to the examination of sense. The manner in which an idea or proposition suggested to the mind of a percipient being produces animal motion they never see; and therefore readily conclude that there is no necessary connexion between these events.

But, if the vulgar will universally be found to be the advocates of free will, they are not less strongly, however inconsistently, impressed with the belief of the doctrine of necessity. It is a well known and a just observation, that, were it not for the existence of general laws to which the events of the material universe always conform, man could never have been either a reasoning or a moral being. The most considerable actions of our lives are directed by foresight. It is because he foresees the regular succession of the seasons, that the farmer sows his field, and after the expiration of a certain term expects a crop. There would be no kindness in my administering food to the hungry, and no injustice in my thrusting a drawn sword against the bosom of my friend, if it were not the established quality of food to nourish, and of a sword to wound.

But the regularity of events in the material universe will not of itself afford a sufficient foundation of morality and prudence. The voluntary conduct of our neighbours enters for a share into almost all those calculations upon which our own plans and determinations are founded. If voluntary conduct, as well as material impulse, were not subjected to general laws, included in the system of cause and effect, and a legitimate topic of prediction and foresight, the certainty of events in the material universe would be productive of little benefit. But in reality the mind passes from one of these topics of speculation to the other, without accurately distributing them into classes, or imagining that there is any difference in the certainty with which they are attended. Hence it appears that the most uninstructed peasant or artisan is practically a necessarian. The farmer calculates as securely upon the inclination of mankind to buy his corn when it is brought into the market, as upon the tendency of the seasons to ripen it. The labourer no more suspects that his employer will alter his mind and not pay him his daily wages, than he suspects that his tools will refuse to perform those functions today, in which they were yesterday employed with success.[1]

Another argument in favour of the doctrine of necessity, not less clear and irresistible than that from the consideration of cause and effect, will arise from any consistent explication that can be given of the nature of voluntary motion. The motions of the animal system distribute themselves into two great classes, voluntary and involuntary. Involuntary motion, whether it be conceived to take place independently of the mind, or to be the result of thought and perception, is so called, because the consequences of that motion, either in whole or in part, did not enter into the view of the mind when the motion commenced. Thus the cries of a new-born infant are not less involuntary than the circulation of the blood; it being impossible that the sounds first resulting from a certain agitation of the animal frame should be foreseen, since foresight is the fruit of experience.

From these observations we may deduce a rational and consistent account of the nature of volition. Voluntary motion is that which is accompanied with foresight, and flows from intention and design. Volition is that state of an intellectual being, in which, the mind being affected in a certain manner by the apprehension of an end to be accomplished, a certain motion of the organs and members of the animal frame is found to be produced.

Here then the advocates of intellectual liberty have a clear dilemma proposed to their choice. They must ascribe this freedom, this imperfect connexion of effects and causes, either to our voluntary or our involuntary motions. They have already made their determination. They are aware that to ascribe freedom to that which is involuntary, even if the assumption could be maintained, would be altogether foreign to the

[1] The reader will find the substance of the above arguments in a more diffusive form in Hume's Enquiry concerning Human Understanding,* being the third part of his Essays.

great subjects of moral, theological or political enquiry. Man would not
be in any degree more of an agent or an accountable being, though it
could be proved that all his involuntary motions sprung up in a fortuit-
ous and capricious manner.

But on the other hand to ascribe freedom to our voluntary actions is
an express contradiction in terms. No motion is voluntary any farther
than it is accompanied with intention and design, and flows from the
apprehension of an end to be accomplished. So far as it flows in any
degree from another source, so far it is involuntary. The new-born infant
foresees nothing, therefore all his motions are involuntary. A person
arrived at maturity takes an extensive survey of the consequences of his
actions, therefore he is eminently a voluntary and rational being. If any
part of my conduct be destitute of all foresight of the effects to result,
who is there that ascribes to it depravity and vice? Xerxes acted just as
soberly as such a reasoner, when he caused his attendants to inflict a
thousand lashes on the waves of the Hellespont.*

The truth of the doctrine of necessity will be still more evident, if we
consider the absurdity of the opposite hypothesis. One of its principal
ingredients is self determination. Liberty in an imperfect and popular
sense is ascribed to the motions of the animal system, when they result
from the foresight and deliberation of the intellect, and not from external compulsion. It is in this sense that the word is commonly used in
moral and political reasoning. Philosophical reasoners therefore, who
have desired to vindicate the property of freedom, not only to our
external motions, but to the acts of the mind, have been obliged to
repeat this process. Our external actions are then said to be free, when
they truly result from the determination of the mind. If our volitions,
or internal acts be also free, they must in like manner result from the
determination of the mind, or in other words, 'the mind in adopting
them' must be 'self determined.' Now nothing can be more evident
than that that in which the mind exercises its freedom, must be an act
of the mind. Liberty therefore according to this hypothesis consists in
this, that every choice we make has been chosen by us, and every act of
the mind been preceded and produced by an act of the mind. This is so
true, that in reality the ultimate act is not styled free from any quality
of its own, but because the mind in adopting it was self determined,
that is, because it was preceded by another act. The ultimate act resulted
completely from the determination that was its precursor. It was itself
necessary; and, if we would look for freedom, it must be in the preceding act. But in that preceding act also, if the mind were free, it was self
determined, that is, this volition was chosen by a preceding volition,

and by the same reasoning this also by another antecedent to itself. All the acts except the first were necessary, and followed each other as inevitably as the links of a chain do, when the first link is drawn forward. But then neither was this first act free, unless the mind in adopting it were self determined, that is, unless this act were chosen by a preceding act. Trace back the chain as far as you please, every act at which you arrive is necessary. That act, which gives the character of freedom to the whole, can never be discovered; and, if it could, in its own nature includes a contradiction.

Another idea which belongs to the hypothesis of self determination, is, that the mind is not necessarily inclined this way or that by the motives which are presented to it, by the clearness or obscurity with which they are apprehended, or by the temper and character which preceding habits may have generated; but that by its inherent activity it is equally capable of proceeding either way, and passes to its determination from a previous state of absolute indifference. Now what sort of activity is that which is equally inclined to all kinds of actions? Let us suppose a particle of matter endowed with an inherent propensity to motion. This propensity must either be to move in one particular direction, and then it must for ever move in that direction unless counteracted by some external impression; or it must have an equal tendency to all directions, and then the result must be a state of perpetual rest.

The absurdity of this consequence is so evident, that the advocates of intellectual liberty have endeavoured to destroy its force by means of a distinction. 'Motive,' it has been said, 'is indeed the occasion, the *sine qua non* of volition, but it has no inherent power to compel volition. Its influence depends upon the free and unconstrained surrender of the mind. Between opposite motives and considerations the mind can choose as it pleases, and by its determination can convert the motive which is weak and insufficient in the comparison into the strongest.' But this hypothesis will be found exceedingly inadequate to the purpose for which it is produced. Motives must either have a necessary and irresistible influence, or they can have no influence at all.

For, first, it must be remembered, that the ground or reason of any event, of whatever nature it be, must be contained among the circumstances which precede that event. The mind is supposed to be in a state of previous indifference, and therefore cannot be, in itself considered, the source of the particular choice that is made. There is a motive on one side and a motive on the other: and between these lie the true ground and reason of preference. But, wherever there is tendency to preference, there may be degrees of tendency. If the degrees be equal, preference cannot follow: it is equivalent to the putting equal weights into the opposite scales of a balance. If one of them have a greater tendency to preference than the other, that which has the greatest tendency must ultimately prevail. When two things are balanced against each other, so much amount may be conceived to be struck off from each side as exists in the smaller sum, and the overplus that belongs to the greater is all that truly enters into the consideration.

Add to this, secondly, that, if motive have not a necessary influence, it is altogether superfluous. The mind cannot first choose to be influenced by a motive, and afterwards submit to its operation: for in that case the preference would belong wholly to this previous volition. The determination would in reality be complete in the first instance; and the motive, which came in afterwards, might be the pretext, but could not be the true source of the proceeding.[1]

Lastly, it may be observed upon the hypothesis of free will, that the whole system is built upon a distinction where there is no difference, to wit, a distinction between the intellectual and active powers of the mind. A mysterious philosophy taught men to suppose, that, when the understanding had perceived any object to be desirable, there was need of some distinct power to put the body in motion. But reason finds no ground for this supposition; nor is it possible to conceive, that, in the case of an intellectual faculty placed in an aptly organised body, preference can exist, together with a consciousness, gained from experience, of our power to obtain the object preferred, without a certain motion of the animal frame being the necessary result. We need only attend to the obvious meaning of the terms in order to perceive that the will is merely, as it has been happily termed, the last act of the understanding, one of the different cases of the association of ideas. What indeed is preference, but a perception of something that really inheres or is supposed to inhere in the objects themselves? It is the judgment, true or erroneous, which the mind makes respecting such things as are brought into comparison with each other. If this had been sufficiently attended to, the freedom of the will would never have been gravely maintained by philosophical writers, since no man ever imagined that we were free to feel or not to feel an impression made upon our organs, and to believe or not to believe a proposition demonstrated to our understanding.

It must be unnecessary to add any thing farther on this head, unless it be a momentary recollection of the sort of benefit that freedom of the

---

[1] The argument from the impossibility of free will is treated with great force of reasoning in Jonathan Edwards's *Enquiry into the Freedom of the Will*.*

will would confer upon us, supposing it to be possible. Man being, as we have now found him to be, a simple substance, governed by the apprehensions of his understanding, nothing farther is requisite but the improvement of his reasoning faculty, to make him virtuous and happy. But, did he possess a faculty independent of the understanding, and capable of resisting from mere caprice the most powerful arguments, the best education and the most sedulous instruction might be of no use to him. This freedom we shall easily perceive to be his bane and his curse; and the only hope of lasting benefit to the species would be, by drawing closer the connexion between the external motions and the understanding, wholly to extirpate it. The virtuous man, in proportion to his improvement, will be under the constant influence of fixed and invariable principles; and such a being as we conceive God to be, can never in any one instance have exercised this liberty, that is, can never have acted in a foolish and tyrannical manner. Freedom of the will is absurdly represented as necessary to render the mind susceptible of moral principles; but in reality, so far as we act with liberty, so far as we are independent of motives, our conduct is as independent of morality as it is of reason, nor is it possible that we should deserve either praise or blame for a proceeding thus capricious and indisciplinable.

CHAPTER VI

INFERENCES FROM THE DOCTRINE OF NECESSITY

Idea it suggests to us of the universe.—Influence on our moral ideas—action— virtue—exertion—persuasion—exhortation—ardour—complacence   and aversion—punishment—repentance—praise and bland blame—intellectual tranquillity.—Language of necessity recommended.

CONSIDERING then the doctrine of moral necessity as sufficiently established, let us proceed to the consequences that are to be deduced from it. This view of things presents us with an idea of the universe as connected and cemented in all its parts, nothing in the boundless progress of things being capable of happening otherwise than it has actually happened. In the life of every human being there is a chain of causes, generated in that eternity which preceded his birth, and going on in regular procession through the whole period of his existence, in consequence of which it was impossible for him to act in any instance otherwise than he has acted.

    The contrary of this having been the conception of the mass of mankind in all ages, and the ideas of contingency and accident having perpetually obtruded themselves, the established language of morality has been universally tinctured with this error. It will therefore be of no trivial importance to enquire how much of this language is founded in the truth of things, and how much of what is expressed by it is purely imaginary. Accuracy of language is the indispensible prerequisite of sound knowledge, and without attention to that subject we can never ascertain the extent and importance of the consequences of necessity.

First then it appears, that, in the emphatical and refined sense in which the word has sometimes been used, there is no such thing as action. Man is in no case strictly speaking the beginner of any event or series of events that takes place in the universe, but only the vehicle through which certain causes operate, which causes, if he were supposed not to exist, would cease to operate. Action however, in its more simple and obvious sense, is sufficiently real, and exists equally both in mind and in matter. When a ball upon a billiard board is struck by a person playing, and afterwards impinges upon a second ball, the ball which was first in motion is said to act upon the second, though it operate in the strictest conformity to the impression it received, and the motion it communicates be precisely determined by the circumstances of the case. Exactly similar to this, upon the principles already explained, are the actions of the human mind. Mind is a real cause, an indispensible link in the great chain of the universe; but not, as has sometimes been supposed, a cause of that paramount description, as to supersede all necessities, and be itself subject to no laws and methods of operation. Upon the hypothesis of a God, it is not the choice, apprehension or judgment of that being, so properly as the truth which was the foundation of that judgment, that has been the source of all contingent and particular existences. His existence, if necessary, was necessary only as the sensorium* of truth and the medium of its operation.

Is this view of things incompatible with the existence of virtue?

If by virtue we understand the operation of an intelligent being in the exercise of an optional power, so that under the same precise circumstances it might or might not have taken place, undoubtedly it will annihilate it.

But the doctrine of necessity does not overturn the nature of things. Happiness and misery, wisdom and error will still be distinct from each other, and there will still be a connexion between them. Wherever there is distinction there is ground for preference and desire, or on the contrary for neglect and aversion. Happiness and wisdom will be objects worthy to be desired, misery and error worthy to be disliked. If therefore by virtue we mean that principle which asserts the preference of the former over the latter, its reality will remain undiminished by the doctrine of necessity.

Virtue, if we would speak accurately, ought to be considered by us in the first instance objectively, rather than as modifying any particular beings. It is a system of general advantage, in their aptitude or inaptitude to which lies the value or worthlessness of all particular existences. This aptitude is in intelligent beings usually termed capacity or power. Now power in the sense of the hypothesis of liberty is altogether chimerical. But power in the sense in which it is sometimes affirmed of inanimate substances, is equally true of those which are animate. A candlestick has the power or capacity of retaining a candle in a perpendicular direction. A knife has a capacity of cutting. In the same manner a human being has a capacity of walking: though it may be no more true of him, than of the inanimate substance, that he has the power of exercising or not exercising that capacity. Again, there are different degrees as well as different classes of capacity. One knife is better adapted for the purposes of cutting than another.

Now there are two considerations relative to any particular being, that excite our approbation, and this whether the being be possessed of consciousness or no. These considerations are capacity and the application of that capacity. We approve of a sharp knife rather than a blunt one, because its capacity is greater. We approve of its being employed in carving food, rather than in maiming men or other animals, because that application of its capacity is preferable. But all approbation or preference is relative to utility or general good. A knife is as capable as a man of being employed in the purposes of virtue, and the one is no more free than the other as to its employment. The mode in which a knife is made subservient to these purposes is by material impulse. The mode in which a man is made subservient is by inducement and persuasion. But both are equally the affair of necessity. The man differs from the knife, just as the iron candlestick differs from the brass one; he has one more way of being acted upon. This additional way in man is motive, in the candlestick is magnetism.

But virtue has another sense, in which it is analogous to duty. The virtue of a human being is the application of his capacity to the general good; his duty is the best possible application of that capacity. The words thus explained are to be considered as rather similar to grammatical distinction, than to real and philosophical difference. Thus in Latin *bonus* is *good* as affirmed of a man, *bona* is *good* as affirmed of a woman. In the same manner we can as easily conceive of the capacity of an inanimate as of an animate substance being applied to the general good, and as accurately describe the best possible application of the one as of the other. There is no essential difference between the two cases. But we call the latter virtue and duty, and not the former. These words may in a popular sense be considered as either masculine or feminine, but never neuter.

But, if the doctrine of necessity do not annihilate virtue, it tends to introduce a great change into our ideas respecting it. According to this doctrine it will be absurd for a man to say, 'I will exert myself,' 'I will take care to remember,' or even 'I will do this.' All these expressions imply as if man was or could be something else than what motives make him. Man is in reality a passive, and not an active being. In another sense however he is sufficiently capable of exertion. The operations of his mind may be laborious, like those of the wheel of a heavy machine in ascending a hill, may even tend to wear out the substance of the shell in which it acts, without in the smallest degree impeaching its passive character. If we were constantly aware of this, our minds would not glow less ardently with the love of truth, justice, happiness and mankind. We should have a firmness and simplicity in our conduct, not wasting itself in fruitless struggles and regrets, not hurried along with infantine impatience, but seeing events with their consequences, and calmly and unreservedly given up to the influence of those comprehensive views which this doctrine inspires.

As to our conduct towards others in instances where we were concerned to improve and meliorate their minds, we should address our representations and remonstrances to them with double confidence. The believer in free will can expostulate with or correct his pupil with faint and uncertain hopes, conscious that the clearest exhibition of truth is impotent, when brought into contest with the unhearing and indisciplinable faculty of will; or in reality, if he were consistent, secure that it could produce no effect at all. The necessarian on the contrary employs real antecedents, and has a right to expect real effects.

But, though he would represent, he would not exhort, for this is a term without a meaning. He would suggest motives to the mind, but he would not call upon it to comply, as if it had a power to comply or not to comply. His office would consist of two parts, the exhibition of motives to the pursuit of a certain end, and the delineation of the easiest and most effectual way of attaining that end.

There is no better scheme for enabling us to perceive how far any idea that has been connected with the hypothesis of liberty has a real foundation, than to translate the usual mode of expressing it into the language of necessity. Suppose the idea of exhortation so translated to stand thus: 'To enable any arguments I may suggest to you to make a suitable impression it is necessary that they should be fairly considered. I proceed therefore to evince to you the importance of attention, knowing, that, if I can make this importance sufficiently manifest attention will inevitably follow.' I should however be far better employed in enforcing directly the truth I am desirous to impress, than in having recourse to this circuitous mode of treating attention as if it were a separate faculty. Attention will in reality always be proportionate to our apprehension of the importance of the subject before us.

At first sight it may appear as if, the moment I was satisfied that exertion on my part was no better than a fiction, and that I was the passive instrument of causes exterior to myself, I should become indifferent to the objects which had hitherto interested me the most deeply, and lose all that inflexible perseverance, which seems inseparable from great undertakings. But this cannot be the true state of the case. The more I resign myself to the influence of truth, the clearer will be my perception of it. The less I am interrupted by questions of liberty and caprice, of attention and indolence, the more uniform will be my constancy. Nothing could be more unreasonable than that the sentiment of necessity should produce in me a spirit of neutrality and indifference. The more certain is the connexion between effects and causes, the more chearfulness should I feel in yielding to painful and laborious employments.

It is common for men impressed with the opinion of free will to entertain resentment, indignation and anger against those who fall into the commission of vice. How much of these feelings is just, and how much erroneous? The difference between virtue and vice will equally remain upon the opposite hypothesis. Vice therefore must be an object of rejection and virtue of preference; the one must be approved and the other disapproved. But our disapprobation of vice will be of the same nature as our disapprobation of an infectious distemper.

One of the reasons why we are accustomed to regard the murderer with more acute feelings of displeasure than the knife he employs, is that we find a more dangerous property, and greater cause for apprehension, in the one than in the other. The knife is only accidentally an object of terror, but against the murderer we can never be enough upon our guard. In the same manner we regard the middle of a busy street with less complacency as a place for walking than the side, and the ridge of a house with more aversion than either. Independently therefore of the idea of freedom, mankind in general find in the enormously vicious a sufficient motive of antipathy and disgust. With the addition of that idea, it is no wonder that they should be prompted to expressions of the most intemperate abhorrence.

These feelings obviously lead to the prevailing conceptions on the subject of punishment. The doctrine of necessity would teach us to class punishment in the list of the means we possess of reforming error. The more the human mind can be shewn to be under the influence of motive, the more certain it is that punishment will produce a great and unequivocal effect. But the doctrine of necessity will teach us to look upon punishment with no complacence, and at all times to prefer the most direct means of encountering error, which is the development of truth. Whenever punishment is employed under this system, it will be employed, not for any intrinsic recommendation it possesses, but just so far as it shall appear to conduce to general utility.

On the contrary it is usually imagined, that, independently of the utility of punishment, there is proper desert in the criminal, a certain fitness in the nature of things that renders pain the suitable concomitant of vice. It is therefore frequently said, that it is not enough that a murderer should be transported to a desert island, where there should be no danger that his malignant propensities should ever again have opportunity to act; but that it is also right the indignation of mankind against him should express itself in the infliction of some actual ignominy and pain. On the contrary, under the system of necessity the ideas of guilt, crime, desert and accountableness have no place.

Correlative to the feelings of resentment, indignation and anger against the offences of others, are those of repentance, contrition and sorrow for our own. As long as we admit of an essential difference between virtue and vice, no doubt all erroneous conduct whether of ourselves or others will be regarded with disapprobation. But it will in both cases be considered, under the system of necessity, as a link in the great chain of events which could not have been otherwise than it is. We shall therefore no more be disposed to repent of our own faults than of the faults of others. It will be proper to view them both as actions, injurious to the public good, and the repetition of which is to be deprecated. Amidst our present imperfections it will perhaps be useful to recollect what is the error by which we are most easily seduced. But in proportion as our views extend, we shall find motives enough to the practice of virtue, without any partial retrospect to ourselves, or recollection of our own propensities and habits.

In the ideas annexed to the words resentment and repentance there is some mixture of true judgment and a sound conception of the nature of things. There is perhaps still more justice in the notions conveyed by praise and blame, though these also are for the most part founded in the hypothesis of liberty. When I speak of a beautiful landscape or an agreeable sensation, I employ the language of panegyric. I employ it still more emphatically, when I speak of a good action; because I am conscious that panegyric has a tendency to procure a repetition of such actions. So far as praise implies nothing more than this, it perfectly accords with the severest philosophy. So far as it implies that the man could have abstained from the virtuous action I applaud, it belongs only to the delusive system of liberty.

A farther consequence of the doctrine of necessity is its tendency to make us survey all events with a tranquil and placid temper, and approve and disapprove without impeachment to our self possession. It is true, that events may be contingent as to any knowledge we possess respecting them, however certain they are in themselves. Thus the advocate of liberty knows that his relation was either lost or saved in the great storm that happened two months ago; he regards this event as past and certain, and yet he does not fail to be anxious about it. But it is not less true, that all anxiety and perturbation imply an imperfect sense of contingency, and a feeling as if our efforts could make some alteration in the event. When the person recollects with clearness that the event is over, his mind grows composed; but presently he feels as if it were in the power of God or man to alter it, and his distress is renewed. All that is more than this is the impatience of curiosity; but philosophy and reason have an evident tendency to prevent an useless curiosity from disturbing our peace. He therefore who regards all things past, present and to come as links of an indissoluble chain, will, as often as he recollects this comprehensive view, be superior to the tumult of passion; and will reflect upon the moral concerns of mankind with the same clearness of perception, the same unalterable firmness of judgment, and the same tranquillity as we are accustomed to do upon the truths of geometry.

It would be of infinite importance to the cause of science and virtue to express ourselves upon all occasions in the language of necessity. The contrary language is perpetually intruding, and it is difficult to speak two sentences upon any topic connected with human action without it. The expressions of both hypotheses are mixed in inextricable confusion, just as the belief of both hypotheses, however incompatible, will be found to exist in all uninstructed minds. The reformation of which I speak would probably be found exceedingly practicable in itself; though, such is the subtlety of error, that we should at first find several revisals and much laborious study necessary before it could be perfectly weeded out. This must be the author's apology for not having attempted in the present work what he recommends to others. Objects of more immediate importance demanded his attention, and engrossed his faculties.

CHAPTER VII

OF THE MECHANISM OF THE HUMAN MIND

Nature of mechanism—its classes, material and intellectual.—Material system, or of vibrations.—The intellectual system most probable—from the consideration that thought would otherwise be a superfluity—from the established principles of reasoning from effects to causes.—Objections refuted.—Thoughts which produce animal motion may be—1. Involuntary. All animal motions were first involuntary.—2. Unattended with consciousness.—The mind cannot have more than one thought at any one time.—Objection to this assertion from the case of complex ideas—from various mental operations—as comparison—apprehension—rapidity of the succession of ideas.—Application.—Duration measured by consciousness.—3. A distinct thought to each motion may be unnecessary.—Apparent from the complexity of sensible impressions.—The mind always thinks.—Conclusion.—The theory applied to the phenomenon of walking—to the circulation of the blood.—Of motion in general.—Of dreams.

THE doctrine of necessity being admitted, it follows that the theory of the human mind is properly, like the theory of every other series of events with which we are acquainted, a system of mechanism; understanding by mechanism nothing more than a regular connexion of phenomena without any uncertainty of event, so that every incident requires a specific cause, and could be no otherwise in any respect than as the cause determined it to be.

But there are two sorts of mechanism capable of being applied to the solution of this case, one which has for its medium only matter and motion, the other which has for its medium thought. Which of these is to be regarded as most probable?

According to the first we may conceive the human body to be so constituted as to be susceptible of vibrations, in the same manner as the strings of a musical instrument are susceptible of vibrations. These vibrations, having begun upon the surface of the body, are conveyed to the brain; and, in a manner that is equally the result of construction, produce a second set of vibrations beginning in the brain, and conveyed to the different organs or members of the body. Thus it may be supposed, that a piece of iron considerably heated is applied to the body of an infant, and that the report of this uneasiness, or irritation and separation of parts being conveyed to the brain, vents itself again in a shrill and piercing cry. It is in this manner that we are apt to imagine certain convulsive and spasmodic affections to take place in the body. The case, as here described, is similar to that of the bag of a pair of bagpipes, which, being pressed in a certain manner, utters a groan, without any thing more being necessary to account for this phenomenon, than the known laws of matter and motion. Let us add to these vibrations a system of associations to be carried on by traces to be made upon the medullary substance of the brain, by means of which past and present impressions are connected according to certain laws, as the traces happen to approach or run into each other; and we have then a complete scheme for accounting in a certain way for all the phenomena of human action. It is to be observed, that, according to this system, mind or perception is altogether unnecessary to explain the appearances. It might for other reasons be desirable or wise, in the author of the universe for example, to introduce a thinking substance or a power of perception as a spectator of the process. But this percipient power is altogether neutral, having no concern either as a medium or otherwise in producing the events.[1]

The intellectual system most probable: The second system, which represents thought as the medium of operation, is not less a system of mechanism, according to the doctrine of necessity, than the other, but it is a mechanism of a totally different kind.

There are various reasons calculated to persuade us that this last hypothesis is the most probable. No inconsiderable argument may be derived from the singular and important nature of that property of human beings, which we term thought; which it is surely somewhat violent to strike out of our system as a mere superfluity.

A second reason still more decisive than the former, arises from the constancy with which thought in innumerable instances accompanies the functions of this mechanism. Now this constancy of conjunction has been shewn to be the only ground we have in any imaginable subject for

---

[1] The above will be found to be a tolerably accurate description of the hypothesis of the celebrated Hartley.* It was unnecessary to quote his words, as it would be foreign to the plan of the present work to enter into a refutation of any individual writer. The sagacity of Hartley, in having pointed out the necessary connexion of the phenomena of mind, and shewn the practicability of reducing its different operations to a simple principle, cannot be too highly applauded. The reasonings of the present chapter, if true, may be considered as giving farther stability to his principal doctrine by freeing it from the scheme of material automatism with which it was unnecessarily clogged.

inferring necessary connexion, or that species of relation which exists between cause and effect. We cannot therefore reject the principle which supposes thought to have an efficient share in the mechanism of man, but upon grounds that would vitiate all our reasonings from effects to causes.

It may be objected, 'that, though this contiguity of event argues necessary connexion, yet the connexion may be exactly the reverse of what is here stated, motion being in all instances the cause, and thought never any thing more than an effect.' But this is contrary to every thing we know of the system of the universe, in which each event appears to be alternately both the one and the other, nothing terminating in itself, but every thing leading on to an endless chain of consequences.

It would be equally vain to object, 'that we are unable to conceive how thought can have any tendency to produce motion in the animal system;' since it has just appeared that this ignorance is by no means peculiar to the subject before us. We are universally unable to perceive the ground of necessary connexion.

It being then sufficiently clear that there are cogent reasons to persuade us that thought is the medium through which the motions of the animal system are generally carried on, let us proceed to consider what is the nature of those thoughts by which the limbs and organs of our body are set in motion. It will then probably be found, that the difficulties which have clogged the intellectual hypothesis, are principally founded in erroneous notions derived from the system of liberty; as if there were any essential difference between those thoughts which are the medium of generating motion, and thoughts in general.

First, thought may be the source of animal motion, without partaking in any degree of volition, or design. It is certain that there is a great variety of motions in the animal system, which are in every view of the subject involuntary. Such, for example, are the cries of an infant, when it is first impressed with the sensation of pain. Such must be all those motions which flowed from sensation previously to experience. Volition implies that something which is the subject of volition, is regarded as desirable; but we cannot desire any thing, till we have an idea corresponding to the term futurity. Volition implies intention, or design; but we cannot design any thing, till we have the expectation that the existence of that thing is in some way connected with the means employed to produce it. An infant, when he has observed that a voice exciting compassion is the result of certain previous emotions, may have the idea of that voice predominant in his mind during the train of emotions that produce it. But this could not have been the case the first time it was uttered. In the first motions of the animal system, nothing of any sort could possibly be foreseen, and therefore nothing of any sort could be intended. Yet in the very instances here produced the motions have sensation or thought for their constant concomitant; and therefore all the arguments, which have been already alledged, remain in full force to prove that thought is the medium of their production.

Nor will this appear very extraordinary, if we consider the nature of volition itself. In volition, if the doctrine of necessity be true, the mind is altogether passive. Two ideas present themselves in some way connected with each other; and a perception of preferableness necessarily follows. An object having certain desirable qualities, is perceived to be within my reach; and my hand is necessarily stretched out with an intention to obtain it. If a perception of preferableness and a perception of desirableness irresistibly lead to animal motion, why may not the mere perception of pain? All that the adversary of automatism is concerned to maintain is, that thought is an essential link in the chain; and that, the moment it is taken away, the links that were before it have no longer any tendency to produce motion in the links that were after it. It is possible, that, as a numerous class of motions have their constant origin in thought, so there may be no thoughts altogether unattended with motion.

Here it may be proper to observe, that, from the principles already delivered, it follows that all the original motions of the animal system are involuntary. In proportion however as we obtain experience, they are successively made the subjects of reflection and foresight; and of consequence become many of them the themes of intention and design, that is, become voluntary. We shall presently have occasion to suspect that motions, which were at first involuntary, and afterwards by experience and association are made voluntary, may in the process of intellectual operation be made involuntary again.—But to proceed.

Secondly, thought may be the source of animal motion, and yet be unattended with consciousness. This is undoubtedly a distinction of considerable refinement, depending upon the precise meaning of words; and, if any person should choose to express himself differently on the subject, it would be useless obstinately to dispute that difference with him. By the consciousness which accompanies any thought there seems to be something implied distinct from the thought itself. Consciousness is a sort of supplementary reflection, by which the mind not only has the thought, but adverts to its own situation and observes that it has it. Consciousness therefore, however nice the distinction, seems to be a second thought.

In order to ascertain whether every thought be attended with consciousness, it may be proper to consider whether the mind can ever have more than one thought at any one time. Now this seems altogether contrary to the very nature of mind. My present thought is that to which my present attention is yielded; but I cannot attend to several things at once. This assertion appears to be of the nature of an intuitive axiom; and experience is perpetually reminding us of its truth. In comparing two objects we frequently endeavour as it were to draw them together in the mind, but we seem to be obliged to pass successively from the one to the other.

But this principle, though apparently supported both by reason and experience, is not unattended with difficulties. The first is that which arises from the case of complex ideas. This will best be apprehended if we examine it as relates to visible objects. 'Let us suppose that I am at present employed in the act of reading. I appear to take in whole words and indeed clusters of words by a single act of the mind. But let it be granted for a moment that I see each letter successively. Yet each letter is made up of parts: the letter D for example of a right line and a curve, and each of these lines of the successive addition or fluxion of points. If I consider the line as a whole, yet its extension is one thing, and its terminations another. I could not see the letter if the black line that describes it and the white surface that bounds it were not each of them in the view of my organ. There must therefore, as it should seem, upon the hypothesis above stated, be an infinite succession of ideas in the mind, before it could apprehend the simplest objects with which we are conversant. But we have no feeling of any such thing, but rather of the precise contrary. Thousands of human beings go out of the world without ever apprehending that lines are composed of the addition or fluxion of points. An hypothesis therefore, that is in direct opposition to so many apparent facts, must have a very uncommon portion of evidence to sustain it, if indeed it can be sustained at all.'

The true answer to this objection seems to be the following. The mind can apprehend only a single idea at once, but that idea needs not be in every sense of the word a simple idea. The mind can apprehend two or more objects at a single effort, but it cannot apprehend them as two. There seems no sufficient reason to deny that all those objects which are painted at once upon the retina of the eye, produce a joint and simultaneous impression upon the mind. But they are not immediately conceived by the mind as many, but as one: so soon as the idea suggests itself that they are made up of parts, these parts cannot be considered by us otherwise than successively. The resolution of objects into their simple elements, is an operation of science and improvement; but it is altogether foreign to our first and original conceptions. In all cases the operation is rather analytical than synthetical, rather that of resolution than composition. We do not begin with the successive perception of elementary parts till we have obtained an idea of a whole; but, beginning with a whole, are capable of reducing it into its elements.

The second difficulty is of a much subtler nature. It consists in the seeming 'impossibility of performing any mental operation, such as comparison for example, which has relation to two or more ideas, if we have not both ideas before us at once, if one of them be completely vanished and gone, before the other begins to exist.' The cause of this difficulty seems to lie in the mistake of supposing that there is a real interval between the two ideas. It will perhaps be found upon an accurate examination, that, though we cannot have two ideas at once, yet it is not just to say, that the first has perished before the second begins to exist. The instant that connects them, is of no real magnitude, and produces no real division. The mind is always full. It is this instant therefore that is the true point of comparison.

It may be objected, 'that this cannot be a just representation, since comparison is rather a matter of retrospect deciding between two ideas that have been completely apprehended, than a perception which occurs in the middle, before the second has been yet observed.' To this objection experience will perhaps be found to furnish the true answer. We find in fact that we cannot compare two objects till we have passed and repassed them in the mind.

'Supposing this account of the operation of the mind in comparison to be admitted, yet what shall we say to a complex sentence containing twenty ideas, the sense of which I fully apprehend at a single hearing, nay, even in some cases by that time one half of it has been uttered?'

The mere task of understanding what is affirmed to us is of a very different nature from that of comparison, or any other species of judgment that is to be formed concerning this affirmation. When a number of ideas are presented in a train, though in one sense there be variety, yet in another there is unity. First, there is the unity of uninterrupted succession, the perennial flow as of a stream, where the drop indeed that succeeds is numerically distinct from that which went before, but there is no cessation. Secondly, there is the unity of method. The mind apprehends, as the discourse proceeds, a strict association, from similarity or some other source, between each idea as it follows in the process, and that which went before it.

The faculty of understanding the different parts of a discourse in their connexion with each other, simple as it appears, is in reality of gradual and slow acquisition. We are by various causes excluded from a minute observation of the progress of the infant mind, and therefore do not readily conceive by how imperceptible advances it arrives at a quickness of apprehension relative to the simplest sentences. But we more easily remark its subsequent improvement, and perceive how long it is before it can apprehend a discourse of any length or a sentence of any abstraction.

Nothing is more certain than the possibility of my perceiving the sort of relation that exists between the different parts of a methodical discourse, for example, Mr. Burke's Speech upon Oeconomical Reform,* though it be impossible for me after the severest attention to consider the several parts otherwise than successively. I have a latent feeling of this relation as the discourse proceeds, but I cannot give a firm judgment respecting it otherwise than by retrospect. It may however be suspected that, even in the case of simple apprehension, an accurate attention to the operations of mind would show, that we scarcely in any instance hear a single sentence, without returning again and again upon the steps of the speaker, and drawing more closely in our minds the preceding members of his period, before he arrives at its conclusion; though even this exertion of mind, subtle as it is, be not of itself thought sufficient to authorise us to give a judgment upon the whole. There may perhaps be cases where the apprehension is more instantaneous. A similar exception appears to take place even in some cases of judgment or comparison. A new association, or a connecting of two ideas by means of a middle term, which were never brought into this relation before, is a task of such a nature, that the strongest mind feels some sense of effort in the operation. But, where the judgment accurately speaking is already made, the operation is in a manner instantaneous. If you say, that a melon is a larger fruit than a cherry, I immediately assent. The judgment, though perhaps never applied to this individual subject, may be said to have been made by me long before. If again you tell me that Cæsar was a worse man than Alexander, I instantly apprehend your meaning; but, unless I have upon some former occasion considered the question, I can neither assent nor dissent till after some reflection.

But, if the principle here stated be true, how infinitely rapid must be the succession of ideas? While I am speaking no two ideas are in my mind at the same time, and yet with what facility do I pass from one to another? If my discourse be argumentative, how often do I pass the topics of which it consists in review before I utter them, and even while

I am speaking continue the review at intervals without producing any pause in my discourse? How many other sensations are perceived by me during this period, without so much as interrupting, that is, without materially diverting the train of my ideas? My eye successively remarks a thousand objects that present themselves. My mind wanders to the different parts of my body, and receives a sensation from the chair upon which I sit, from the table upon which I lean; from the pinching of a shoe, from a singing in my ear, a pain in my head, or an irritation of the breast. When these most perceptibly occur, my mind passes from one to another, without feeling the minutest obstacle, or being in any degree distracted by their multiplicity. From this cursory view of the subject it appears that we have a multitude of different successive perceptions in every moment of our existence.[1]

Consciousness, as it has been above defined, appears to be one of the departments of memory. Now the nature of memory, so far as it relates to the subject of which we are treating, is exceedingly obvious. An infinite number of thoughts passed through my mind in the last five minutes of my existence. How many of them am I now able to recollect? How many of them shall I recollect to-morrow? One impression after another is perpetually effacing from this intellectual register. Some of them may with great attention and effort be revived; others obtrude themselves uncalled for; and a third sort are perhaps out of the reach of any power of thought to reproduce, as having never left their traces behind them for a moment. If the memory be capable of so many variations and degrees of intensity, may there not be some cases with which it never connects itself? If the succession of thoughts be so inexpressibly rapid, may they not pass over some topics with so delicate a touch, as to elude the supplement of consciousness?

It seems to be consciousness, rather than the succession of ideas, that measures time to the mind. The succession of ideas is in all cases exceedingly rapid, and it is by no means clear that it can be accelerated. We find it impracticable in the experiment to retain any idea in our minds unvaried for any perceptible duration. Continual flux appears to take place in every part of the universe. It is perhaps a law of our nature, that thoughts shall at all times succeed to each other with equal rapidity. Yet time seems to our apprehension to flow now with a precipitated and

---

[1] An attempt has been made to calculate these, but there is no reason to believe that the calculation deserves to be considered as a standard of truth. Sensations leave their images behind them, some for a longer and some for a shorter time; so that, in two different instances, the calculation is in one case eight, and in another three hundred and twenty to a second. See Watson on Time,* Ch. II.

now with a tardy course. The indolent man reclines for hours in the shade; and, though his mind be perpetually at work, the silent lapse of duration is unobserved. But, when acute pain or uneasy expectation obliges consciousness to recur with unusual force, the time then appears insupportably long. Indeed it is a contradiction in terms to suppose that the succession of thoughts, where there is nothing that perceptibly links them together, where they totally elude or instantly vanish from the memory, can be a measure of time to the mind. That there is such a state of mind in some cases assuming a permanent form, has been so much the general opinion of mankind, that it has obtained a name, and is called reverie. It is probable from what has been said that thoughts of reverie, understanding by that appellation thoughts untransmitted to the memory, perpetually take their turn with our more express and digested thoughts, even in the most active scenes of our life.

Lastly, thought may be the source of animal motion, and yet there may be no need of a distinct thought producing each individual motion. This is a very important point in the subject before us. In uttering a cry for example, the number of muscles and articulations of the body concerned in this operation is very great; shall we say that the infant has a distinct thought for each motion of these articulations?

The answer to this question will be considerably facilitated, if we recollect the manner in which the impressions are blended, which we receive from external objects. The sense of feeling is diffused over every part of my body, I feel the different substances that support me, the pen I guide, various affections and petty irregularities in different parts of my frame, nay, the very air that environs me. But all these impressions are absolutely simultaneous, and I can have only one perception at once. Out of these various impressions, the most powerful, or that which has the greatest advantage to solicit my attention, overcomes and drives out the rest; or, which not less frequently happens, some idea of association suggested by the last preceding idea wholly withdraws my attention from every external object. It is probable however that this perception is imperceptibly modified by the miniature impressions that accompany it, just as we actually find that the very same ideas presented to a sick man, take a peculiar tinge, that renders them exceedingly different from what they are in the mind of a man in health. It has been already shown, that, though there is nothing less frequent than the apprehending of a simple idea, yet every idea, however complex, offers itself to the mind under the conception of unity. The blending of numerous impressions into one perception is a law of our nature, and the customary train of our perceptions is entirely of this denomination.

Mean while it deserves to be remarked by the way, that, at the very time that the most methodical series of perceptions is going on in the mind, there is another set of perceptions, or rather many sets playing an under or intermediate part; and, though these perpetually modify each other, yet the manner in which it is done is in an eminent degree minute and unobserved.

These remarks furnish us with an answer to the long disputed question, whether the mind always thinks? It appears that innumerable impressions are perpetually made upon our body, and the only way, in which the slightest of these is prevented from conveying a distinct report to the mind, is in consequence of its being overpowered by some more considerable impression. It cannot therefore be alledged, 'that, as one impression is found to be overpowered by another while we wake, the strongest only of the simultaneous impressions furnishing an idea to the mind; so the whole set of simultaneous impressions during sleep may be overpowered by some indisposition of the sensorium, and entirely fail of its effect.' For, first, the cases are altogether different. From the explication above given it appeared, that not one of the impressions was really lost, but tended, though in a very limited degree, to modify the predominant impression. Secondly, nothing can be more unintelligible than this indisposition. Were it of the nature which the objection requires, sleep ought to cease of its own accord after the expiration of a certain term, but to be incapable of interruption from any experiment I might make upon the sleeper. To what purpose call or shake him? Shall we say, that it requires an impression of a certain magnitude to excite the sensorium? But a clock shall strike in the room and not wake him, when a voice of a much lower key produces that effect. What is the precise degree of magnitude necessary? We actually find the ineffectual calls that are addressed to us, as well as various other sounds, occasionally mixing with our dreams, without our being aware from whence this new perception arose.

To apply these observations. If a number of impressions may come blended to the mind, so as to make up one thought or perception, why may not one thought, in cases where the mind acts as a cause, produce a variety of motions? It has already been shown that there is no essential difference between the two cases. The mind is completely passive in both. Is there any sufficient reason to show, that, though it be possible for one substance considered as the recipient of effects to be the subject of a variety of simultaneous impressions, yet it is impossible for one substance considered as a cause to produce a variety of simultaneous motions? If it be granted that there is not, if the mere modification of a thought designing a motion in chief, may produce a secondary motion, then it must perhaps farther be confessed possible for that modification which my first thought produced in my second, to carry on the motion, even though the second thought be upon a subject altogether different.

The consequences, which seem deducible from this theory of mind, are sufficiently memorable. By showing the extreme subtlety and simplicity of thought, it removes many of the difficulties that might otherwise rest upon its finer and more evanescent operations. If thought, in order to be the cause of animal motion, need not have either the nature of volition, or the concomitant of consciousness, and if a single thought may become a complex cause and produce a variety of motions, it will then become exceedingly difficult to trace its operations, or to discover any circumstances in a particular instance of animal motion, which can sufficiently indicate that thought was not the principle of its production, and by that means supersede the force of the general arguments adduced in the beginning of this chapter. Hence therefore it appears that all those motions which are observed to exist in substances having perception, and which are not to be discovered in substances of any other species, may reasonably be suspected to have thought, the distinguishing peculiarity of such substances, for their cause.

There are various classes of motion which will fall under this definition, beside those already enumerated. An example of one of these classes suggests itself in the phenomenon of walking. An attentive observer will perceive various symptoms calculated to persuade him, that every step he takes during the longest journey is the production of thought. Walking is in all cases originally a voluntary motion. In a child when he learns to walk, in a rope dancer when he begins to practise that particular exercise, the distinct determination of mind preceding each step is sufficiently perceptible. It may be absurd to say, that a long series of motions can be the result of so many express volitions, when these supposed volitions leave no trace in the memory. But it is not unreasonable to believe, that a species of motion which began in express design, may, though it ceases to be the subject of conscious attention, owe its continuance to a continued series of thoughts flowing in that direction, and that, if life were taken away, material impulse would not carry on the exercise for a moment. We actually find, that, when our thoughts in a train are more than commonly earnest, our pace slackens, and sometimes our going forward is wholly suspended, particularly in any less common species of walking, such as that of descending a flight of stairs. In ascending the case is still more difficult, and accordingly we are accustomed wholly to suspend the regular progress of reflection during that operation.

Another class of motions of a still subtler nature, are the regular motions of the animal economy, such as the circulation of the blood, and the pulsation of the heart. Are thought and perception the medium of these motions? We have the same argument here as in the former instances, conjunction of event. When thought begins, these motions also begin; and, when it ceases, they are at an end. They are therefore either the cause or effect of percipiency, or mind; but we shall be inclined to embrace the latter side of this dilemma, when we recollect that we are probably acquainted with many instances in which thought is the immediate cause of motions, which scarcely yield in subtlety to these; but that, as to the origin of thought, we are wholly uninformed. Add to this, that there are probably no motions of the animal economy, which we do not find it in the power of volition, and still more of our involuntary sensations, to hasten or retard.

It is far from certain that the phenomenon of motion can any where exist where there is not thought. Motion may be distributed into four classes; the simpler motions which result from what are called the essential properties of matter and the laws of impulse; the more complex ones which cannot be accounted for by the assumption of these laws, such as gravitation, elasticity, electricity and magnetism; and the motions of the vegetable and animal systems. Each of these seems farther than that which preceded it from being able to be accounted for by any thing we understand of the nature of matter.

Some light may be derived from what has been here advanced upon the phenomenon of dreams. 'In sleep we sometimes imagine' for example 'that we read long passages from books, or hear a long oration from a speaker. In all cases scenes and incidents pass before us that in various ways excite our passions and interest our feelings. Is it possible that these should be the unconscious production of our own minds?'

It has already appeared, that volition is the accidental, and by no means the necessary concomitant, even of those thoughts which are most active and efficient in the producing of motion. It is therefore no more to be wondered at that the mind should be busied in the composition of books which it appears to read, than that a train of thoughts of any other kind should pass through it without a consciousness of its being the author. In fact we perpetually annex wrong and erroneous ideas to this phrase, that we are the authors. Though mind be a real and efficient cause, it is in no case a first cause. It is the medium through which operations are produced. Ideas succeed each other in our sensorium according to certain necessary laws. The most powerful impression, either from without or from within, constantly gets the better of all its competitors, and forcibly drives out the preceding thought, till it is in the same irresistible manner driven out by its successor.

CHAPTER VIII

OF THE PRINCIPLE OF VIRTUE

Hypotheses of benevolence and self love—superiority of the former.—Action is either voluntary or involuntary.—Nature of the first of these classes.—Argument that results from it.—Voluntary action has a real existence—consequence of that existence.—Experimental view of the subject.—Suppositions suggested by the advocates of self love—that we calculate upon all occasions the advantage to accrue to us.—Falseness of this supposition.—Supposition of a contrary sort.—We do not calculate what would be the uneasiness to result from our refraining to act—either in relieving distress—or in adding to the stock of general good.—Uneasiness an accidental member of the process.—The suppositions inconsistently blended.—Scheme of self love recommended from the propensity of mind to abbreviate its process—from the simplicity that obtains in the natures of things.—Hypothesis of self love incompatible with virtue.—Conclusion.—Importance of the question.—Application.

THE subject of intellectual mechanism suggested itself as the most suitable introduction to an enquiry into the moral principles of human conduct. Having first ascertained that thought is the real and efficient source of animal motion, it remains to be considered what is the nature of those particular thoughts in which the moral conduct of man originates.

Upon this question there are two opinions. By some it is supposed that the human mind is of a temper considerably ductile, so that, as we in certain instances evidently propose our own advantage for the object of our pursuit, so we are capable no less sincerely and directly in other instances of desiring the benefit of our neighbour. By others it is affirmed, that we are incapable of acting but from the prospect or stimulant of personal advantage, and that, when our conduct appears most retrograde from this object, the principle from which it flows is Superiority of the former secretly the same. It shall be the business of this chapter to prove that the former hypothesis is conformable to truth.

It is to be presumed from the arguments of the preceding chapter, that there exist in the theory of the human mind two classes of action, voluntary and involuntary. The last of these we have minutely investigated. It has sufficiently appeared that there are certain motions of the animal system, which have sensation or thought for their medium of production, and at the same time arise, to have recourse to a usual mode of expression, spontaneously, without foresight of or a direct reflecting on the result which is to follow. But, if we admit the existence of this phenomenon, there does not seem less reason to admit the existence of the other class of action above enumerated, which is accompanied in its operation with a foresight of its result, and to which that foresight serves as the reason and cause of existence.

Voluntary action cannot proceed from all perceptions indiscriminately, but only from perceptions of a peculiar class, viz. such perceptions as are accompanied with the idea of something as true respecting them, something which may be affirmed or denied. One of the first inferences therefore from the doctrine of voluntary action, is the existence of the understanding as a faculty distinct from sensation, or, to speak more accurately, the possibility of employing the general capacity of perception, not merely as the vehicle of distinct ideas, but as the medium of connecting two or more ideas together. This particular habit, when it has once been created, gradually extends itself to every province of the mind, till at length it is impossible for any thing to make a clear and distinct impression upon the sensorium, without its being followed with some judgment of the mind concerning it.

It is thus that man becomes a moral being. He is no farther so than he is capable of connecting and comparing ideas, of making propositions concerning them, and of foreseeing certain consequences as the result of certain motions of the animal system.

But, if the foresight of certain consequences to result may be the sufficient reason of action, that is, if there be such a thing as volition, then every foresight of that kind has a tendency to action. If the perception of something as true, joined with the consciousness of my capacity to act upon this truth, be of itself sufficient to produce motion in the animal system, then every perception so accompanied has a tendency to motion. To apply this to the subject before us.

I perceive a certain agreeable food, I perceive in myself an appetite which this food is adapted to gratify, and these perceptions are accompanied with a consciousness of my power to appropriate this food. If no other consideration exist in my mind beyond those which have just been stated, a certain motion of the animal system irresistibly follows.

Suppose now that the person about whose appetites these propositions are conversant, is not myself but another. This variation cannot materially alter the case. Still there remain all the circumstances necessary to generate motion. I perceive the food, I am acquainted with the wants of the person in question, and I am conscious of my power of administering to them. Nothing more is necessary in order to produce a certain movement of my body. Therefore, if, as in the former case, no other consideration exist in my mind, a certain motion of the animal system irresistibly follows. Therefore, if ten thousand other considerations exist, yet there was in this, separately considered, a tendency to motion. That which, when alone, must inevitably produce motion, must, however accompanied, retain its internal character.

Let us however suppose, which seems the only consistent mode of supporting the doctrine of self love, 'that there is no such thing practically considered as volition, that man never acts from a foresight of consequences, but always continues to act, as we have proved him to act at first, from the mere impulse of pain, and precisely in the manner to which that impulse prompts him, without the rational faculty having any tendency to prolong, to check or to regulate his actions.' What an incredible picture does this exhibit to us of the human mind? We form to ourselves, for this cannot be disputed, opinions, we measure the tendency of means to the promotion of ends, we compare the value of different objects, and we imagine our conduct to be influenced by the judgments we are induced to make. We perceive the preferableness of one thing to another, we desire, we chuse; all this cannot be denied. But all this is a vain apparatus; and the whole system of our conduct proceeds, uninfluenced by our apprehension of the relative value of objects, and our foresight of consequences favourable or adverse.

There is no other alternative. Once admit the understanding to an efficient share in the business, and there is no reason that can possibly be assigned, why every topic, which is the object of human understanding, should not have its portion of efficiency. Once admit that we act upon the apprehension of something that may be affirmed or denied respecting an idea, and we shall be compelled to acknowledge that every proposition including in it the notion of preferableness or the contrary, of better or worse, will, so far as it falls within the compass of our power real or supposed to effect, afford a motive inducing, though with different degrees of energy, to animal motion. But this is directly contrary to the theory of self love. They who maintain that self love is the only spring of action, say in effect, not only that no action is disinterested, but that no disinterested consideration contributes in any degree as an inducement to action. If I relieve the virtuous distress of the best of men, I am influenced according to them by no particle of love for the individual or compassion for his distress, but exclusively by the desire of procuring gratification to myself.

Let us consider this case a little more closely. If I perceive either that my prosperity or existence must be sacrificed to those of twenty men as good as myself, or theirs to mine, surely this affords some small inducement to adopt the former part of the alternative. It may not be successful, but does it excite no wish however fleeting, no regret however ineffectual? The decision of the question is in reality an affair of arithmetic; is there no human being that was ever competent to understand it? The value of a man is his usefulness; has no man ever believed that another's capacity for usefulness was equal to his own? I am as 40, consequently the others are as 800; if the 40 were not myself, I should perceive that it was less than 800; is it possible I should not perceive it, when the case becomes my own?

But the advocates for the system of self love generally admit, 'that it is possible for a man to sacrifice his own existence in order to preserve that of twenty others;' but they affirm, 'that in so doing he acts from personal interest. He perceives that it is better for him to die with the consciousness of an heroic action, than live with the remorse of having declined it.' That is, here is an action attended with various recommendations, the advantage to arise to twenty men, their tranquillity and happiness through a long period of remaining existence, the benefits they will not fail to confer on thousands of their contemporaries, and through them on millions of posterity, and lastly his own escape from remorse and momentary exultation in the performance of an act of virtue. From all these motives he selects the last, the former he wholly disregards, and adopts a conduct of the highest generosity from no view but to his own advantage. Abstractedly and impartially considered, and putting self as such out of the question, this is its least recommendation, and he is absolutely and unlimitedly callous to all the rest.

Considering then the system of disinterestedness as sufficiently established in theory, let us compare it with the lessons of experience. There are two different hypotheses by which this theory is opposed; the one affirming 'that in every thing we do, we employ, previously to the choice of the mind, a calculation by which we determine how far the thing to be done will conduce to our own advantage;' the other ascribing our actions 'to the same blind and unintelligent principle, by which, when a child cries, he frequently utters a sound unexpected by himself, but which inevitably results from a certain connexion of an organized body with an irritated mind.'

How far does experience agree with the first of these hypotheses? Surely nothing can be more contrary to any thing we are able to observe of ourselves, than to imagine, that in every act, of pity suppose, we estimate the quantity of benefit to arise to ourselves, before we yield to the emotion. It might be said indeed, that the mind is very subtle in its operations, and that, a certain train of reasoning having been rendered familiar to us, we pass it over in our reflections with a rapidity that leaves no trace in the memory. But this, though true, will contribute little to relieve the system we are considering, since it unfortunately happens that our first emotions of pity are least capable of being accounted for in this way.

To understand this let us begin with the case of an infant. Before he can feel sympathy, he must have been led by a series of observations to perceive that his nurse for example, is a being possessed of consciousness, and susceptible like himself of the impressions of pleasure and pain. Having supplied him with this previous knowledge, let us suppose his nurse to fall from a flight of stairs and break her leg. He will probably feel some concern for the accident; he will understand the meaning of her cries, similar to those he has been accustomed to utter in distress; and he will discover some wish to relieve her. Pity is perhaps first introduced by a mechanical impression upon the organs, in consequence of which the cries uttered by another prompt the child without direct design to utter cries of his own. These are at first unaccompanied with compassion, but they naturally induce the mind of the infant to yield attention to the appearance which thus impressed him.

In the relief he wishes to communicate is he prompted by reflecting on the pleasures of generosity? This is by the supposition the first benevolent emotion he has experienced, and previously to experience it is impossible he should foresee the pleasures of benevolence. Shall we suppose that he is influenced by other selfish considerations? He considers, that, if his nurse die, he will be in danger of perishing; and that, if she be lame, he will be deprived of his airings. Is it possible that any man should believe, that, in the instantaneous impulse of sympathy, the child is guided by these remote considerations? Indeed it was unnecessary to have instanced in an action apparently benevolent, since it is equally clear that our most familiar actions are inconsistent with this explanation. We do not so much as eat and drink, from the recollection that these functions are necessary to our support.

The second of the two hypotheses enumerated, is diametrically the reverse of the first. As the former represented all human actions as proceeding from a very remote deduction of the intellect, the latter considers the whole as merely physical. In its literal sense, as has already been seen, nothing can be more incompatible with experience. Its advocates therefore are obliged to modify their original assumption, and to say, not that we act merely from sensation, but that sensation affords the basis for reflection; and that, though we be capable of conducting ourselves by system and foresight, yet the only topic to which we can apply that foresight is the removal of pain. In reality all that which is regularly adapted to the accomplishment of a certain purpose, must be admitted to flow from the dictates of reflection. The tear starts, the cry is uttered at the prompting of sensation only, but we cannot lift a finger to relieve except as we are commanded by the understanding.

Here then we are presented with the commencement of a new series. If uneasiness be still the source of the phenomena, at least it is now under a different form. Before, a certain emotion was produced, respecting which no intention was extant in the mind. Now an action or a series of actions is adopted with a certain view and leading to a certain end. This end is said to be the removal of uneasiness. Whether it be or no is a question which recollection in many cases is competent to enable us to decide. If we frequently deceive ourselves as to the motive by which we are prompted to act, this is chiefly owing to vanity, a desire of imputing to ourselves, or being understood by the world to act from a principle more elevated than that which truly belongs to us. But this idea is least prevalent with children and savages, and of consequence they ought to be most completely aware that the project they have conceived is that of removing uneasiness. It seems to be an uncommon refinement in absurdity to say, that the end we really pursue is one to which we are in no instance conscious; that our action is wholly derived from an unperceived influence, and the view extant in the understanding altogether impotent and unconcerned.

In the case we have just examined uneasiness is the first step in the process; in others which might be stated uneasiness is not the first step. 'In the pursuit' suppose 'of a chemical process I accidentally discover a circumstance, which may be of great benefit to mankind. I instantly quit the object I was originally pursuing, prosecute this discovery, and communicate it to the world.' In the former proceeding a sensation of pain was the initiative, and put my intellectual powers into action. In the present case the perception of truth is the original mover. Whatever uneasiness may be supposed to exist, rendering me anxious for the publication of this benefit, is the consequence of the perception. The uneasiness would never have existed if the perception had not gone before it.

But it has been said, 'that, though the perception of truth in this case goes first, the pain was not less indispensible in the process, since, without that, action would never have followed. Action is the child of desire, and a cold and uninteresting decision of the understanding would for ever have laid dormant in the mind.' Granting that pain in a certain modified degree is a constant step in the process, it may nevertheless be denied that it is in the strictest sense of the word indispensible. To perceive that I ought to publish a certain discovery, is to perceive that publishing is preferable to not publishing it. But to perceive a preference is to prefer, and to prefer is to choose. The process is in this case complete, and pain, in the sense in which it comes in at all, is merely an accident. Why do I feel pain in the neglect of an act of benevolence, but because benevolence is judged by me to be a conduct which it becomes me to adopt? Does the understanding wait to enquire what advantage will result from the propositions, that two and two make four, or that such and such causes will contribute to the happiness of my neighbour, before it is capable of perceiving them to be true?

The same principle which is applied here, is not less applicable to fame, wealth and power, in a word to all those pursuits which engage the reflecting and speculative part of the civilised world. None of these objects would ever have been pursued, if the decisions of the intellect had not gone first, and informed us that they were worthy to be pursued.

Neither of the two hypotheses we have been examining would perhaps have been reckoned so much as plausible in themselves, if they had not been blended together by the inadvertence of their supporters. The advocates of self love have been aware, that the mere sensitive impulse of pain would account for a very small part of the history of man; and they have therefore insensibly elided from the consideration of uneasiness to be removed, to that of interest to be promoted. They have confounded the two cases of sensation and reflection; and, taking it for granted in the latter that private gratification was the object universally pursued, have concluded that they were accounting for all human actions from one principle. In reality no two principles can be more distinct, than the impulse of uneasiness, which has very improperly been denominated the love of ourselves, and that deliberate self love, by which of set design we pursue our own advantage. One circumstance only they have in common, that of representing us as incapable of understanding any proposition, till we have in some way or other connected it with personal interest. This is certainly a just representation of their consequences; since, if I were capable of understanding the naked proposition, that my neighbour stood in need, of a candle for instance to be removed from one end of a room to the other, this would be a reason of action, a motive, either strong or weak, either predominant or the contrary. But, if this consideration entered for any thing into the ground of my proceeding, the whole would not be resolvable into self love.

An hypothesis, which has been thought to have some tendency to relieve the difficulties of the system of self love, is that 'of the mind's reasoning out for itself certain general principles, which are a sort of resting-places in the process, to which it afterwards recurs, and upon which it acts, without being at the trouble in each instance of application, of repeating the reasons upon which the general principle was founded. Thus in geometry, as we proceed to the higher branches, we perpetually refer to the earlier propositions as established and certain, without having at the time in our minds perhaps the smallest recollection of the way in which those early propositions were demonstrated.' But this representation, though true, has very little tendency to decide in the subject before us. It is still true, that, if I be capable of understanding a proposition as it relates to the interest of my neighbour, any reasoning about the proposition by which it is indirectly connected with my own interest, is unnecessary to put me into a state of action. It is still true, that my action has a direct and an indirect tendency; and, till it can be shown that there is something in the nature of mind that unfits it for entertaining the direct purpose, an unprejudiced enquirer will be very little disposed universally to have recourse to that which is indirect.

The hypothesis of self love seems to have been originally invented from a love of 'that simplicity, which appears to be the ultimate term in all grand discoveries relative to the system of the universe.' But simplicity, though well deserving our approbation, can scarcely of itself be a sufficient support for any opinion. The simplicity however in this case is more apparent than real. Not to repeat what has been said relative to the coalition of two hypotheses very incongruous in their own nature, there is little genuine simplicity in a scheme, that represents us as perpetually acting from a motive which we least suspected, and seeks by a circuitous and intricate method for a recommendation of little intrinsic value, rejecting in all cases the great and obvious reason which the first view of the subject suggested. True simplicity is altogether on the side of the opposite system, which represents man as capable of being governed by the nature of the thing, and of acting from the motive which he supposes to influence him; which requires nothing but perception to account for all the phenomena of mind, and, when a reason exciting to action is apprehended, does not seek for an additional principle to open a communication between the judgment and the choice.

There is one observation more, which, though it be not so conclusive as some of those which have been mentioned, ought not to be omitted.

If self love be the only principle of action, there can be no such thing as virtue. Virtue is a principle in the mind, by which we are enabled to form a true estimate of the pretensions of different reasons inviting us to preference. He, that makes a false estimate, and prefers a trivial and partial good to an important and comprehensive one, is vicious. It is in the disposition and view of the mind, and not in the good which may accidentally and unintentionally result, that virtue consists. Judas's act in betraying Christ, according to the Christian system, may be regarded as a real and essential cause conducing to the salvation of mankind. Yet Judas's act was not virtuous, but vicious. He thought only of the forty pieces of silver, the price of his treachery, and neglected every consideration of public utility and justice. Just so in the case stated early in the present chapter, the public benefactor, absolutely and strictly speaking, prefers forty to eight hundred or eight hundred millions. So far as relates to the real merits of the case, his own advantage or pleasure is a very insignificant consideration, and the benefit to be produced, suppose to a world, is inestimable. Yet he falsely and unjustly prefers the first, and regards the latter, abstractedly considered, as nothing. If there be such a thing as justice, if I have a real and absolute value, upon which truth can decide, and which can be compared with what is greater or less, then, according to this system, the best action that ever was performed, may, for any thing we know, have been the action in the whole world of the most exquisite and deliberate injustice. Nay, it could not have been otherwise, since it produced the greatest good, and therefore was the individual instance in which the greatest good was most directly postponed to personal gratification.

Nor will this objection be much relieved by the system already alluded to of resting-places, enabling a man in a certain degree to forget the narrow and selfish principles in which his conduct originated. It can scarcely be questioned, that the motives which induced a man to adopt his system of conduct, and without which he never would have adopted it, are of more importance, than the thoughtlessness and inattention by which they are forgotten, in deciding upon the morality of his character.

From this train of reasoning the result is, that men are capable of understanding the beauty of virtue, and the claims of other men upon their benevolence; and, understanding them, that these views, as well as every other perception of the intellect, are of the nature of motives, sometimes overpowered by other considerations, and sometimes overpowering them, but always in their own nature capable of exciting to action, when not counteracted by pleas of a different sort. Men are capable no doubt of preferring an inferior interest of their own to a superior interest of other people; but to this preference it is perhaps necessary, that they should imagine the benefit to themselves to be great and the injury to others comparatively small, or else that they should have embraced the pernicious opinion that the general good is best served by each man's applying himself exclusively to his personal advantage.

There is no doctrine in which the generous and elevated mind rests with more satisfaction, than in that of which we are treating. If it be false, it is no doubt incumbent upon us to make the best of the small remnant of good that remains. But it is a heartless prospect for the moralist, who, when he has done all, has no hope to persuade mankind to one atom of real affection towards any one individual of their species. We may be made indeed the instruments of good, but in a way less honourable, than that in which a frame of wood or a sheet of paper may be made the instrument of good. The wood or the paper are at least neutral. But we are drawn into the service with affections of a diametrically opposite direction. When we do the most benevolent action, it is with a view only to our own advantage, and with the most sovereign and unreserved neglect of that of others. We are instruments of good, just in the same manner as bad men are said to be the instruments of providence, even when their inclinations are most refractory to its decrees. In this sense we may admire the system of the universe, where public utility results from each man's contempt of that utility, and where the most beneficial actions of those, whom we have been accustomed to term the best men, are only instances in which justice and the real merits of the case are most flagrantly violated. But we can think with little complacence of the individuals of whom this universe is composed. It is no wonder that philosophers, whose system has taught them to look upon their fellow men as thus perverse and unjust, have been frequently cold, phlegmatic and unanimated. It is no wonder that Rousseau, the most benevolent of all these philosophers, and who most escaped the general contagion, has been driven to place the perfection of all virtue in doing no injury.[1] Neither philosophy nor morality nor politics will ever show like themselves, till man shall be acknowledged for what he really is, a being capable of justice, virtue and benevolence, and who needs not always to be led to a philanthropical conduct by foreign and frivolous considerations.

---

[1] '*La plus sublime vertu est négative; elles nous instruit de ne jamais faire du mal à personne.*' Emile, Liv. II.*

The system of disinterested benevolence proves to us, that it is possible to be virtuous, and not merely to talk of virtue; that all which has been said by philosophers and moralists respecting impartial justice is not an unmeaning rant; and that, when we call upon mankind to divest themselves of selfish and personal considerations, we call upon them for something which they are able to practise. An idea like this reconciles us to our species; teaches us to regard with enlightened admiration the men who have appeared to lose the feeling of their personal existence in the pursuit of general advantage; and gives us reason to expect, that, as men collectively advance in science and useful institution, they will proceed more and more to consolidate their private judgment and their individual will with abstract justice and the unmixed approbation of general happiness.

What are the inferences that ought to be made from this doctrine with respect to political institution? Certainly not that the interest of the individual ought to be made incompatible with the part he is expected to take in the interest of the whole. This is neither desirable, nor even possible. But that social institution needs not despair of seeing men influenced by other and better motives. The legislator is bound to recollect that the true perfection of mind consists in disinterestedness. He should regard it as the ultimate object of his exertions, to induce men to estimate themselves at their true value, and neither to grant to themselves nor claim from others a higher consideration than they justly deserve. Above all he should be careful not to add to the vigour of the selfish passions. He should gradually wean men from contemplating their own benefit in all that they do, and induce them to view with complacency the advantage that is to result to others.

The last perfection of this feeling consists in that state of mind which bids us rejoice as fully in the good that is done by others, as if it were done by ourselves. The truly wise man will be actuated neither by interest nor ambition, the love of honour nor the love of fame. He has no emulation. He is not made uneasy by a comparison of his own attainments with those of others, but by a comparison with the standard of right. He has a duty indeed obliging him to seek the good of the whole; but that good is his only object. If that good be effected by another hand, he feels no disappointment. All men are his fellow labourers, but he is the rival of no man. Like Pedaretus in ancient story,* he exclaims: 'I also have endeavoured to deserve; but there are three hundred citizens in Sparta better than myself, and I rejoice.'

CHAPTER IX

OF THE TENDENCY OF VIRTUE

It is the road to happiness—to the esteem and affection of others.—Objection from misconstruction and calumny.—Answer.—Virtue compared with other modes of procuring esteem.—Vice and not virtue is the subject of oblo-quy—instanced in the base alloy with which our virtues are mixed—in arrogance and ostentation—in the vices in which persons of moral excellence allow themselves.—The virtuous man only has friends.—Virtue the road to prosperity and success in the world—applied to commercial transactions—to cases that depend upon patronage.—Apparent exception where the dependent is employed as the instrument of vice.—Virtue compared with other modes of becoming prosperous.—Source of the disrepute of virtue in this respect.—Concession.—Case where convenient vice bids fair for concealment.—Chance of detection.—Indolence—apprehensiveness—and depravity the offspring of vice.

HAVING endeavoured to establish the theory of virtue upon its true principle, and to shew that self interest is neither its basis in justice and truth, nor by any means necessary to incite us to the practice, it may not be improper to consider in what degree public interest is coincident with private, and by that means at once to remove one of the entice-ments and apologies of vice, and afford an additional encouragement and direction to the true politician.

In the first place then, there appears to be sufficient reason to believe, that the practice of virtue is the true road to individual happiness. Many of the reasons which might be adduced in this place have been anticipated in the chapter of the Cultivation of Truth. Virtue is a source of happiness that does not pall in the enjoyment, and of which no man can deprive us.[1] The essence of virtue consists in the seeing every thing in its true light, and estimating every thing at its intrinsic value. No man therefore, so far as he is virtuous, can be in danger to become a prey to sorrow and discontent. He will habituate himself, respecting every species of conduct and temper, to look at its absolute utility, and to tolerate none from which benefit cannot arise either to himself or others. Nor will this be so difficult a task as it is commonly imagined. The man, who is accustomed upon every occasion to consult his reason, will speedily find a habit of this nature growing upon him, till

[1] Ch. IV. p. 233.

the just and dispassionate value of every incident that befals him will come at length spontaneously to suggest itself. Those evils which prejudice has taught so great a part of mankind to regard with horror, will appear to his understanding disarmed of their terrors. Poverty, obloquy and disgrace will be judged by him to be very trivial misfortunes. Few conditions can be so destitute as to deprive us of the means of obtaining for ourselves a subsistence. The reasonable mind perceives at once the possibility of this and the best method of executing it; and it needs no great stretch of understanding to decide, that real happiness does not consist in luxurious accommodations. With respect to obloquy and disgrace, the wise man may lament the tendency they possess to narrow the sphere of his usefulness; but he will readily perceive, that, separately from this consideration, they are no evils. My real value depends upon the qualities that are properly my own, and cannot be diminished by the slander and contempt of the whole world. Even bodily pain loses much of its sting, when it is encountered by a chearful, a composed, and a determined spirit. To all these negative advantages of virtue, we may add the positive satisfaction of a mind conscious of rectitude, rejoicing in the good of the whole, and perpetually exerted for the promotion of that good.

There are indeed some extreme cases of the election of a virtuous conduct, respecting which it is difficult to pronounce. Was it Regulus's interest to return to Carthage to a tormenting death,* rather than save his life by persuading the Roman senate to an exchange of prisoners? Probably it was. Probably, with the exquisite feeling of duty with which Regulus was animated, a life that was to be perpetually haunted with the recollection of his having omitted the noblest opportunity of public service, was not worth his purchase. His reasoning, so far as related to personal interest, might be like that of Cato in the play:*

> 'A day, an hour, of virtuous liberty
> Is worth a whole eternity in bondage.'[1]

Secondly, virtue not only leads to the happiness of him who practises it, but to the esteem and affection of others. Nothing can be more

---

[1] The first of the three heads discussed in this chapter is inserted chiefly for the sake of method, few persons having really doubted that virtue is the most genuine source of individual tranquillity and happiness. It is therefore dismissed with all practicable brevity. The two remaining heads had a stronger claim to discussion. It unfortunately happens to be the generally received opinion, that rigid virtue is neither the surest road to other men's approbation and esteem, nor the most probable means of securing our external prosperity. If the author had known of any work at present existing, that had appeared to him to place this subject in any degree in its true light, he would have omitted the reasonings of this chapter.

indisputable, than that the direct road to the esteem of mankind, is by doing things worthy of their esteem. The most artful scheme for passing things upon others for somewhat different from what they really are, is in momentary danger of detection; and it would be an egregious mistake to suppose, that men esteem any thing but what comes to them under the appearance of virtue. No man ever existed of a taste so depraved as to feel real approbation of another, for the artfulness of his flattery, or the cunning with which he over-reached his neighbours.

There is indeed one disadvantage that occurs under this head, consisting in this circumstance, 'that no man truly admires what he does not understand. Now, in order thoroughly to comprehend the value of any mental effort, whether of a purely intellectual or moral nature, it is perhaps necessary that the genius or virtue of the spectator should be equal to that of him by whom it is made. It is an inevitable law of our nature, that we should in a great measure judge of others by ourselves, and form our standard of human nature by an investigation of our own minds. That, respecting which we feel a clear and distinct conviction that we are ourselves incapable, we are prone to suspect to be mere show and deception in others. We are the more inclined to this, because we feel their virtues to be a reproach to our indolence, and therefore are little disposed to make a liberal estimate of them.'

But, though there be some truth in these observations, they have frequently been made much too indiscriminate, by the misanthropy and impatience of those, who have conceived their estimation with their neighbours or the world to fall greatly short of their merit. It must be admitted that mankind are reluctant to acknowledge a wisdom or a virtue superior to their own; but this reluctance is by no means invincible. It is absurd to suppose that no man believes himself the inferior of his neighbour, or that, when he reads the plays of Shakespeare, the philosophy of Rousseau, or the actions of Cato, he says, 'I am as skilful, as wise, or as virtuous as this man.' It would be still more absurd to suppose that men may not in a considerable degree perceive the beauty of passages they could never have written, and actions they would never have performed.

It is true that men of high moral excellence are seldom estimated at their true value, especially by their contemporaries. But the question does not relate to this point, but to that other, whether they be not esteemed more than persons of any other description, and of consequence whether virtue be not the best road to esteem? Now, let a specious appearance be maintained with ever so much uniformity of success, it is perpetually in danger of detection. It will always want something of animation, of consistency and firmness that true virtue would produce. The imitation will never come up to the life. That temporising and compliance, which are careful not to contradict too much the prejudices of mankind, and in which the principal advantage of a merely exterior virtue consists, will always bear something suspicious about them. Men do not love him who is perpetually courting their applause. They do not give with a liberal spirit what is sought with too unwearied an assiduity. But their praise is involuntarily extorted, by him who is not so anxious to obtain success, as to deserve it.

If men of virtue be frequently misinterpreted or misunderstood, this is in a great degree to be ascribed to the imperfection of their virtue and the errors of their conduct. True virtue should hold no commerce with art. We ought not to be so desirous to exhibit our virtue to advantage, as to give it free scope and suffer it to exhibit itself. Art is nearly allied to selfishness; and true virtue has already been shown to be perfectly disinterested. The mind should be fixed only on the object pursued, and not upon the gracefulness or gallantry of the pursuit. We should be upon all occasions perfectly ingenuous, expressing with simplicity the sentiments of our heart, and speaking of ourselves, when that may be necessary, neither with ostentation and arrogance on the one hand, nor with the frequently applauded lies of a cowardlike humility on the other. There is a charm in sincerity that nothing can resist. If once a man could be perfectly frank, open and firm in all his words and actions, it would be impossible for that man to be misinterpreted.

Another fruitful source of misrepresentation has appeared to be envy. But, if we be regarded with envy, it may be suspected to be in a great measure our own fault. He will always be envied most, who is most arrogant, and whose mind most frequently recurs to his own attainments and the inferiority of others. Our virtues would seldom be contemplated with an uneasy sense of reproach, if they were perfectly unassuming. Any degree of ostentation in their less corrupted neighbour, as it humbles the vanity of mankind, must be expected to excite in them a desire of retaliation. But he whose virtues flow from philanthropy alone, whose heart expands with benevolence and good will, and who has no desire to make his superiority felt, will at all times have many friends and few enemies.

Virtue has also frequently been subject to misrepresentation from a farther circumstance which is most properly chargeable upon the sufferers, and that is, the inequality of their actions. It is no wonder, if we first rouse the angry passions of mankind by our arrogance, and then render our motives suspected by a certain mixture of art in the exhibition of our characters, that the follies and vices we commit, if they be of a glaring kind, should too often furnish a triumphant argument to support against us the accusation of hypocrisy and deceit. It unfortunately happens, that, when men of an ardent spirit fall into error, their errors are inevitably conspicuous. It happens, that men, who have dedicated the flower of their strength to laudable purposes, too often think they have a right to indulge in relaxations unworthy of the energy of their characters. They would surely avoid this fatal mistake, if they duly reflected, that it is not their individual character only that is at stake, but that they are injuring the cause of justice and general good. Prudential and timid virtues, unalloyed with imprudent and thoughtless vices, are best understood by the vulgar. Their reign indeed is short; they triumph only for a day: but that they are transitory is of little avail, while those who are most worthy of lasting esteem, wantonly barter it for gratifications, contemptible in themselves, and fatally important in their effects.

But to return to the comparison between the esteem and affection that accrue from virtue, and from any other plan of conduct. The produce in the latter case must always be in a considerable degree barren, and of very short duration. Whether the good name acquired by virtue be more or less, virtue will appear in the end to be the only mode for its acquisition. He who merits the esteem of his neighbours and fellow citizens, will at least be understood by a few. Instances might be adduced in which persons instigated by the purest motives have been eminently unpopular. But there is perhaps no instance in which such men have not had a few friends of tried and zealous attachment. There is no friendship but this. No man was ever attached to an individual but for the good qualities he ascribed to him; and the degree of attachment will always bear some proportion to the eminence of the qualities. Who would ever have redeemed the life of a knave at the expence of his own? And how many instances do there occur of such heroic friendship where the character was truly illustrious?

In the third place, virtue will probably be found the securest road to outward prosperity and success in the world, according to the old maxim, 'that honesty is the best policy.' It is indeed natural to suppose that a good name should eminently contribute to our success. This is evident even in the humblest walks of life. That tradesman, other things equal, will always be most prosperous, who is most fair and equitable in his dealings. Which is most likely to succeed, he who never gives expectations that he cannot fulfil, or who is perpetually disappointing his customers? he who is contented with a reasonable profit, or who is ever upon the watch to outwit those with whom he deals? he who puts one constant price upon his commodities, or who takes whatever he can get, favouring a suspicious customer unreasonably, and extorting with merciless avarice from an easy one? in a word, he who wishes to keep the persons with whom he is concerned in present good humour, or who would give them permanent satisfaction?

There is no doubt, that, though the former may obtain by his artifices a momentary success, the latter will in the sequel be generally preferred. Men are not so blind to their own interest as they have sometimes been represented, and they will soon feel the advantage of dealing with the person upon whom they can depend. We do not love to be perpetually upon our guard against an enemy, and for ever prying into the tricks and subterfuges of a depraved heart.

But what shall we say to those cases in which advancement depends upon patronage? There are two circumstances under this head which seem to form an exception to the rule above delivered. The first is that of a patron, whose vicious and imperfect character renders the co-operation of vicious men necessary to his pursuits, whom therefore he will be contented to reward, even while he despises. The second is that of an office, and it is to be feared such offices exist, which may require a compliant and corrupt character in the person who is to fill it, and for the obtaining of which vice of a certain sort is a necessary recommendation.

It must no doubt be admitted as to this subject in general, that, so far as relates to success in the world, vicious men will often prove fortunate. But it may reasonably be questioned, whether vice be in the first instance the most likely road to fortune. The candidates for this equivocal species of preferment may be numerous. An individual cannot distinguish himself in the crowd but by a portion of ability, which it may well be supposed would not have been unsuccessful in the career of virtue. After all, not every candidate, not even every skilful candidate, will be victorious. There is always a struggle in the breast of the patron between contempt and a corrupt motive; and, where there is struggle, the decision will sometimes be on the side which the client least desires. Even when fortune seems to have overtaken him, his situation is still precarious. His success is founded upon a local and mutable basis; his patron may desert him, may be deprived of his power or his life; and the client, who, after having sacrificed every principle to his hopes of advantage, misses his aim, or is cut short in his career, is in all cases a subject of derision. A bad eminence is always unstable; and, if we could sum up the numbers of those who have sacrificed their virtue to their ambition, we should probably find that a great majority of them had egregiously miscarried in their calculation.

In the mean time, if we turn to the other side of the estimate, we shall in the first place inevitably suspect that esteem must lead to some of the fruits of esteem. But, exclusively of this consideration, if there be offices for which vice of a certain sort is a necessary qualification, there are also undoubtedly a multitude of offices which cannot be well discharged but by a man of integrity. The patron, though he would perhaps willingly provide for his pander or his parasite at the expence of his country, will not be inclined to trust a man of accommodating principles with the superintendence of his fortune or the education of his child. With the exception of the two cases that have been stated, integrity, as it is the first qualification for discharging a function with propriety, will always occupy a foremost place in the recommendation of the client. The employer, whose object is the real interest of himself, his friends or his country, will have a powerful motive inducing him to prefer the honest candidate. Ability may be almost equally requisite; but ability and virtue, if we should choose to suppose that there is no necessary alliance between them, will at least by no person be thought exclusive of each other. If a knave may in some cases obtain an employment of trust and real importance, it is vehemently to be suspected that this would not have happened, if an honest man of equal ability had been at hand. Add to this that virtue is perpetually gaining ground upon us. The more it is tried, and the more it is known, the more will it be respected. It is to the man of real virtue, whose character is not brought into suspicion by the equivocal nature of some of his proceedings, whose virtue consists in benevolence, equanimity and justice, that all will have recourse, when they have the success of the affair in which they are concerned deeply at heart.

Nothing has tended more to bring honesty as an instrument of success into general disrepute, than the sort of complaint that is frequently heard from such as are unsuccessful. These men will naturally have recourse to the most specious topic of self consolation, and there is none that more obviously suggests itself than the supposition that they failed through their too much virtue. Thus the man of rugged temper who is perpetually insulting the foibles of others, the timid man who is incapable of embracing at once a perilous alternative, the scrupulous man who knows not what to admit or reject and is always undetermined upon his course of action, and a thousand others, are forward to impute their miscarriage to their integrity, though strictly speaking it was in every one of these cases to be ascribed to their vices.

There is another consideration which deserves to be taken into account in this estimate. There is a degree of virtue which would probably render me disinclined to fill many eminent stations, to be a great lawyer, a great senator, or a great minister. The functions of these situations in the present state of mankind are of so equivocal a nature, that a man, whose moral views are in the highest degree sublime, will perhaps find in himself little forwardness to exercise them. He will perhaps conceive that in a private station, unincumbered with engagements, unwarped by the sinister motives that high office will not fail to present, he may render more lasting services to mankind. But surely it is no very formidable objection to say, that honesty will prevent a man from acquiring what he has no wish to acquire.

A case of somewhat a different nature has been suggested, and it has been asked, 'Whether honesty be the best road to success, where the violation of it bids fair for perpetual concealment? Fortune has led me to the military profession, I lack advancement, but promotions in the army are customarily made by purchase. Thus circumstanced, I find by accident a sum of money, in secreting which I am in little danger of detection, and I apply this sum to purchase me a commission. Should I have more effectually promoted my worldly success by a more scrupulous conduct?'

The answer to this question ought probably to be affirmative. In the first place we are to consider the chance of detection. The direct tendency of the laws of the material universe is such, as to force the more considerable and interesting actions of human beings into publicity. No man can render himself invisible. The most artful conspirator cannot sufficiently provide against a thousand petty circumstances, that will lead, if not to conviction, at least to presumption against him. Who is there that would wish to have fastened upon him the suspicion of a base and disingenuous procedure? This feature in human affairs is so remarkable, as to have furnished topics to the literary industry of former centuries, and to have been interpreted God's revenge against the unjust. Suppose that in this case I found the money dropped in a field. Will the owner have no suspicion where he lost it? Will no human being have observed that I was near the spot at the questionable period? The chances are certainly against me, and a mere balance of chance would probably have been sufficient to prove that honesty is the best policy. The bare circumstance of my suddenly possessing a sum of money without visible means of acquiring it, a circumstance to which the attention of my neighbours is always sufficiently alive, would cast an unpleasant stain upon my character. How often has the well contrived train of the politician, triumphing in the inscrutability of his wisdom, been baffled by the most trivial accidents? Since therefore, 'the race is not to the swift, nor the battle to the strong,' the truest wisdom is to act so as to fear no detection.

There are other circumstances which tend to establish the same proposition. The man, who depends upon his courage, his ability, or his amiable character for recommendation, will perpetually cultivate these. His constancy will be unwearied; and, conscious of the integrity of his means, his spirit will be intrepid and erect. The progress of this man, if his ardour be sufficiently great to inspire him with ability, and to render him quick sighted to the detection of his mistakes, will be incessant. But the man who has employed foul means, will depend partly upon them, and cannot be so fervent in the cultivation of the true. If he always escape detection, he will always fear it, and this will sully the clearness of his spirit. Vice cannot compare with virtue in its tendency to individual happiness. This is not the subject we are considering in this place; but this will apply to our subject. Remorse, uneasiness and confusion of mind are calculated to prevent me from perceiving the true point of projection in my affairs, and detract much from the probability of my rising to eminence in any profession.

Lastly, the man who has once yielded to a dishonest temptation, will yield to it again. He has lost the consistency of character and disdain of vice, which were his firmest securities. He that says, 'I will be dishonest now, and dishonest no more,' forgets some of the most obvious and characteristic features of the human mind. If he escape suspicion in the first instance, he will only disgrace himself more foully in the second: if the remorse and degradation of spirit arising from one base action could perish, they would be fixed and invigorated by other base actions growing out of the first.

BOOK V

OF LEGISLATIVE AND EXECUTIVE POWER

CHAPTER I

INTRODUCTION

Retrospect of principles already established.—Distribution of the remaining subjects.—Subject of the present book.—Forms of government.—Method of examination to be adopted.

IN the preceding divisions of this work the ground has been sufficiently cleared to enable us to proceed with considerable explicitness and satisfaction to the practical detail of political institution. It has appeared that an enquiry concerning the principles and conduct of social intercourse is the most important topic upon which the mind of man can be exercised;[1] that upon those principles well or ill conceived, and the manner in which they are executed, the vices and virtues of individuals depend[2] that political institution to be good must have its sole foundation in the rules of immutable justice;[3] and that those rules, uniform in their nature, are equally applicable to the whole human race.[4]

The different topics of political institution cannot perhaps be more perspicuously distributed than under the four following heads: provisions for general administration; provisions for the intellectual and moral improvement of individuals; provisions for the administration of criminal justice; and provisions for the regulation of property. Under each of these heads it will be our business, in proportion as we adhere to the great and comprehensive principles already established, rather to clear away abuses than to recommend farther and more precise regulations, rather to simplify than to complicate. Above all we should not forget, that government is an evil, an usurpation upon the private judgment and individual conscience of mankind; and that, however we may be obliged to admit it as a necessary evil for the present, it behoves us, as the friends of reason and the human species, to admit as little of it as possible, and carefully to observe whether, in consequence of

---

[1] Book I.
[2] Book I.
[3] Book II, Chap. II.
[4] Book I, Chap VII, VIII. Book III, Chap. VII.

the gradual illumination of the human mind, that little may not hereafter be diminished.

And first we are to consider the different provisions that may be made for general administration; including under the phrase general administration all that shall be found necessary of what has usually been denominated legislative and executive power. Legislation has already appeared to be a term not applicable to human society.[1] Men cannot do more than declare and interpret law; nor can there be an authority so paramount, as to have the prerogative of making that to be law, which abstract and immutable justice had not made to be law previously to that interposition. But it might notwithstanding this be found necessary, that there should be an authority empowered to declare those general principles, by which the equity of the community will be regulated, in particular cases upon which it may be compelled to decide. The question concerning the reality and extent of this necessity it is proper to reserve for after consideration. Executive power consists of two very distinct parts: general deliberations relative to particular emergencies, which, so far as practicability is concerned, may be exercised either by one individual or a body of individuals, such as peace and war, taxation,[2] and the selection of proper periods for convoking deliberative assemblies: and particular functions, such as those of financial detail, or minute superintendence, which cannot be exercised unless by one or at most by a small number of persons.

In reviewing these several branches of authority, and considering the persons to whom they may be most properly confided, we cannot do better than adopt the ordinary distribution of forms of government into monarchy, aristocracy and democracy. Under each of these heads we may enquire into the merits of their respective principles, first absolutely, and upon the hypothesis of their standing singly for the whole administration; and secondly, in a limited view, upon the supposition of their constituting one branch only of the system of government. It is usually alike incident to them all to confide the minuter branches of executive detail to inferior agents.

One thing more it is necessary to premise. The merits of each of the three heads I have enumerated are to be considered negatively. The corporate duties of mankind are the result of their irregularities and follies in their individual capacity. If they had no imperfection, or

---

[1] Book III, Chap. V.
[2] I state the article of taxation as a branch of executive government, since it is not, like law or the declaration of law, a promulgation of some general principle, but is a temporary regulation for some particular emergence.

if men were so constituted as to be sufficiently and sufficiently early corrected by persuasion alone, society would cease from its functions. Of consequence, of the three forms of government and their compositions that is the best, which shall least impede the activity and application of our intellectual powers. It was in the recollection of this truth that I have preferred the term political institution to that of government, the former appearing to be sufficiently expressive of that relative form, whatever it be, into which individuals would fall, when there was no need of force to direct them into their proper channel, and were no refractory members to correct.

CHAPTER II

OF EDUCATION, THE EDUCATION OF A PRINCE

Nature of monarchy delineated.—School of adversity.—Tendency of superfluity to inspire effeminacy—to deprive us of the benefit of experience— illustrated in the case of princes.—Manner in which they are addressed.—Inefficacy of the instruction bestowed upon them.

FIRST then of monarchy; and we will first suppose the succession to the monarchy to be hereditary. In this case we have the additional advantage of considering this distinguished mortal, who is thus set over the heads of the rest of his species, from the period of his birth.

The abstract idea of a king is of an extremely momentous and extraordinary nature; and, though the idea has by the accident of education been rendered familiar to us from our infancy, yet perhaps the majority of readers can recollect the period, when it struck them with astonishment and confounded their powers of apprehension. It being sufficiently evident that some species of government was necessary, and that individuals must concede a part of that sacred and important privilege by which each man is constituted judge of his own words and actions, for the sake of general good, it was next requisite to consider what expedients might be substituted in the room of this original claim. One of these expedients has been monarchy. It was the interest of each individual that his individuality should be invaded as rarely as possible; that no invasion should be permitted to flow from wanton caprice, from sinister and disingenuous views, or from the instigation of anger, partiality and passion; and that this bank, severely levied upon the peculium* of each member of the society, should be administered with frugality and discretion. It was therefore without doubt a very bold adventure to commit this precious deposit to the custody of a single man. If we contemplate the human powers whether of body or mind, we shall find them much better suited to the superintendence of our private concerns and to the administering occasional assistance to others, than to the accepting the formal trust of superintending the affairs and watching for the happiness of millions. If we recollect the physical and moral equality of mankind, it will appear a very violent usurpation upon this principle to place one individual at so vast an interval from the rest of his species. Let us then consider how such persons are usually educated, or may be expected to be educated, and how well they are prepared for this illustrious office.

It is a common opinion that adversity is the school in which all extraordinary virtue must be formed. Henry the fourth of France and Elizabeth of England experienced a long series of calamities before they were elevated to a throne.* Alfred,* of whom the obscure chronicles of a barbarous age record such superior virtues, passed through the vicissitudes of a vagabond and a fugitive. Even the mixed, and upon the whole the vicious, yet accomplished, characters of Frederic and Alexander,* were not formed without the interference of injustice and persecution.

This hypothesis however seems to have been pushed too far. It is no more reasonable to suppose that virtue cannot be matured without injustice, than to believe, which has been another prevailing opinion, that human happiness cannot be secured without imposture and deceit. Both these errors have a common source, a distrust of the omnipotence of truth. If their advocates had reflected more deeply upon the nature of the human mind, they would have perceived that all our voluntary actions are judgments of the understanding, and that actions of the most judicious and useful nature must infallibly flow from a real and genuine conviction of truth.

But, though the exaggerated opinion here stated of the usefulness of adversity be erroneous, it is, like many other of our errors, allied to important truth. If adversity be not necessary, it must be allowed that prosperity is pernicious. Not a genuine and philosophical prosperity, which requires no more than sound health with a sound intellect, the capacity of procuring for ourselves by a moderate and well regulated industry the means of subsistence, virtue and wisdom: but prosperity as it is usually understood, that is, a competence, provided for us by the caprice of human institution, inviting our bodies to indolence, and our minds to lethargy; and still more prosperity, as it is understood in the case of noblemen and princes, that is, a superfluity of wealth, which deprives us of all intercourse with our fellow men upon equal terms, and makes us prisoners of state, gratified indeed with baubles and splendour, but shut out from the real benefits of society and the perception of truth. If truth be so intrinsically powerful as to make adversity unnecessary to excite our attention to it, it is nevertheless certain that luxury and wealth have the most fatal effects in distorting it. If it require no foreign aid to assist its energies, we ought however to be upon our guard against principles and situations the tendency of which may be perpetually to counteract it.

Nor is this all. One of the most essential ingredients of virtue is fortitude. It was the plan of many of the Grecian philosophers, and most of all of Diogenes,* to show to mankind how very limited was the supply that our necessities required, and how little dependent our real welfare and prosperity were upon the caprice of others. Among innumerable incidents upon record that illustrate this principle, a single one may suffice to suggest to our minds its general spirit. Diogenes had a slave whose name was Menas, and Menas thought proper upon some occasion to elope. 'Ha!' said the philosopher, 'can Menas live without Diogenes, and cannot Diogenes live without Menas?' There can be no lesson more important than that which is thus conveyed. The man that does not know himself not to be at the mercy of other men, that does not feel that he is invulnerable to all the vicissitudes of fortune, is incapable of a constant and inflexible virtue. He, to whom the rest of his species can reasonably look up with confidence, must be firm, because his mind is filled with the excellence of the object he pursues; and chearful, because he knows that it is out of the power of events to injure him. If any one should choose to imagine that this idea of virtue is strained too high, yet all must allow that no man can be entitled to our confidence, who trembles at every wind, who can endure no adversity, and whose very existence is linked to the artificial character he sustains. Nothing can more reasonably excite our contempt, than a man who, if he were once reduced to the genuine and simple condition of man, would be reduced to despair, and find himself incapable of consulting and providing for his own subsistence. Fortitude is a habit of mind that grows out of a sense of our own independence. If there be a man, who dares not even trust his own imagination with the fancied change of his circumstances, he must necessarily be effeminate, irresolute and temporising. He that loves sensuality or ostentation better than virtue, may be entitled to our pity, but a madman only would entrust to his disposal any thing that was dear to him.

Again, the only means by which truth, however immutable in its own nature, can be communicated to the human mind is through the inlet of the senses. It is perhaps impossible that a man shut up in a cabinet can ever be wise. If we would acquire knowledge, we must open our eyes, and contemplate the universe. Till we are acquainted with the meaning of terms and the nature of the objects around us, we cannot understand the propositions that may be formed concerning them. Till we are acquainted with the nature of the objects around us, we cannot compare them with the principles we have formed, and understand the modes of employing them. There are other ways of attaining wisdom and ability beside the school of adversity, but there is no way of attaining them but through the medium of experience. That is, experience brings in the materials with which intellect works; for it must be granted that a man of limited experience will often be more capable than he who has gone through the greatest variety of scenes; or rather perhaps, that one man may collect more experience in a sphere of a few miles square, than another who has sailed round the world.

To conceive truly the value of experience we must recollect the infinite improvements the human mind has received in a long series of ages, and how an enlightened European differs from a solitary savage. However multifarious are these improvements, there are but two ways in which they can be appropriated by any individual; either at second hand by books and conversation, or at first hand by our own observations of men and things. The improvement we receive in the first of these modes is unlimited; but it will not do alone. We cannot understand books, till we have seen the subjects of which they treat.

He that knows the mind of man, must have observed it for himself; he that knows it most intimately, must have observed it in its greatest variety of situations. He must have seen it without disguise, when no exterior situation puts a curb upon its passions, and induces the individual to exhibit a studied, not a spontaneous character. He must have seen men in their unguarded moments, when the eagerness of temporary resentment tips their tongue with fire, when they are animated and dilated by hope, when they are tortured and anatomised by despair, when the soul pours out its inmost self into the bosom of an equal and a friend. Lastly, he must himself have been an actor in the scene, have had his own passions brought into play, have known the anxiety of expectation and the transport of success, or he will feel and understand about as much of what he sees, as mankind in general would of the transactions of the vitriolised inhabitants of the planet Mercury, or the salamanders that live in the sun.*—Such is the education of the true philosopher, the genuine politician, the friend and benefactor of human kind.

What is the education of a prince? Its first quality is extreme tenderness. The winds of heaven are not permitted to blow upon him. He is dressed and undressed by his lacqueys and valets. His wants are carefully anticipated; his desires without any effort of his profusely supplied. His health is of too much importance to the community to permit him to exert any considerable effort either of body or mind. He must not hear the voice of reprimand or blame. In all things it is first of all to be remembered that he is a prince, that is, some rare and precious creature, but not of human kind.

As he is the heir to a throne, it is never forgotten by those about him, that considerable importance is to be annexed to his favour or his displeasure. Accordingly they never express themselves in his presence frankly and naturally, either respecting him or themselves. They are supporting a part. They play under a mask. Their own fortune and emolument is always uppermost in their minds, at the same time that they are anxious to appear generous, disinterested and sincere. All his caprices are to be complied with. All his gratifications are to be studied. They find him a depraved and sordid mortal; they judge of his appetites and capacities by their own; and the gratifications they recommend serve to sink him deeper in folly and vice.

What is the result of such an education? Having never experienced contradiction, the young prince is arrogant and presumptuous. Having always been accustomed to the slaves of necessity or the slaves of choice, he does not understand even the meaning of the word freedom. His temper is insolent, and impatient of parley and expostulation. Knowing nothing, he believes himself sovereignly informed, and runs headlong into danger, not from firmness and courage, but from the most egregious wilfulness and vanity. Like Pyrrho* among the ancient philosophers, if his attendants were at a distance, and he trusted himself alone in the open air, he would perhaps be run over by the next coach, or fall down the first precipice. His violence and presumption are strikingly contrasted with the extreme timidity of his disposition. The first opposition terrifies him, the first difficulty seen and understood appears insuperable. He trembles at a shadow, and at the very semblance of adversity is dissolved into tears. It has accordingly been observed that princes are commonly superstitious beyond the rate of common mortals.

Above all, simple, unqualified truth is a stranger to his ear. It either never approaches; or is so unexpected a guest should once appear, it meets with so cold a reception, as to afford little encouragement to a second visit. The longer he has been accustomed to falshood and flattery, the more grating will it sound. The longer he has been accustomed to falshood and flattery, the more terrible will the task appear to him, to change his tastes, and discard his favourites. He will either place a blind confidence in all men, or, having detected the insincerity of those who were most agreeable to him, will conclude that all men are knavish and designing. As a consequence of this last opinion, he will become indifferent to mankind, callous to their sufferings, and will believe that even the virtuous are knaves under a craftier mask. Such is the education of an individual, who is destined to superintend the affairs and watch for the happiness of millions.

In this picture are indeed contained all those features which naturally constitute the education of a prince, into the conducting of which no person of energy and virtue has by accident been introduced. In real life it will be variously modified, but the majority of the features, unless in very rare instances, will remain the same. In no case can the education of a friend and benefactor of human kind, as sketched in a preceding page, by any speculative contrivance be communicated.

Nor is there any difficulty in accounting for this universal miscarriage. The wisest preceptor thus circumstanced must labour under insuperable disadvantages. No situation can be so unnatural as that of a prince, so difficult to be understood by him who occupies it, so irresistibly propelling the mind to mistake. The first ideas it suggests are of a tranquillising and soporific nature. It fills him with the opinion of his secretly possessing some inherent advantage over the rest of his species, by which he is formed to command and they to obey. If you assure him of the contrary, you can expect only an imperfect and temporary credit; for facts, which in this case depose against you, speak a language more emphatic and intelligible than words. If it were not as he supposes, why should every one that approaches be eager to serve him? The sordid and selfish motives by which they are really animated he is very late in detecting. It may even be doubted whether the individual, who was never led to put the professions of others to the test by his real wants, has in any instance been completely aware of the little credit that is often due to them. A prince finds himself courted and adored long before he can have acquired a merit entitling him to such distinctions. By what arguments can you persuade him laboriously to pursue what appears so completely superfluous? How can you induce him to be dissatisfied with his present acquisitions, while every other person assures him that his accomplishments are admirable and his mind a mirror of sagacity? How will you persuade him who finds all his wishes anticipated, to engage in any arduous undertaking, or propose any distant object for his ambition?

But, even should you succeed in this, his pursuits may be expected to be either mischievous or useless. His understanding is distorted; and the basis of all morality, the recollection that other men are beings of the same order with himself, is extirpated. It would be unreasonable to expect from him any thing generous and humane. Unfortunate as he is, his situation is continually propelling him to vice, and destroying the germs of integrity and virtue before they are unfolded. If sensibility begin to discover itself, it is immediately poisoned by the blighting winds of flattery. Amusement and sensuality call with an imperious voice, and will not allow him time to feel. Artificial as is the character he fills, even should he aspire to fame, it will be by the artificial methods of false refinement, or the barbarous inventions of usurpation and conquest, not by the plain and unornamented road of benevolence.

Some idea of the methods usually pursued, and the effects produced in the education of a prince, may be collected from a late publication of the celebrated madame de Genlis, in which she gives an account of her own proceedings in relation to the children of the duke d'Orleans.* She thus describes the features of their disposition and habits at the time they were committed to her care. 'The duke de Valois (the eldest) is frequently coarse in his manners and ignoble in his expressions. He finds a great deal of humour in describing mean and common objects by vulgar expressions; and all this seasoned with the proverbial fertility of Sancho Panza himself, and set off with a loud forced laugh. His prate is eternal, nor does he suspect but that it must be an exquisite gratification to any one to be entertained with it; and he frequently heightens the jest by a falshood uttered in the gravest manner imaginable. Neither he nor his brother has the least regard for any body but himself; they are selfish and grasping to an extreme, considering every thing that is done for them as their due, and imagining that they are in no respect obliged to consult the happiness of others. The slightest reproof is beyond measure shocking to them, and the indignation they conceive at it immediately vents itself in sullenness or tears. They are in an uncommon degree effeminate, afraid of the wind or the cold, unable to run or to leap, or even so much as to walk at a round pace, or for more than half an hour together. The duke de Valois has an extreme terror of dogs, to such a degree as to turn pale and shriek out at the sight of one.' 'When the children of the duke d'Orleans were committed to my care, they had been accustomed in winter to wear under-waistcoats, two pair of stockings, gloves, muffs, &c. The eldest, who was eight years of age, never came down stairs without being supported by the arm of one or two persons; the domestics were obliged to render them the meanest services, and, for a cold or any slight indisposition, sat up with them for nights together.'[1]

Madame de Genlis, a woman of uncommon talents and comprehensive views, though herself infected with a considerable number of errors, corrected these defects in the young princes. But few princes have the good fortune to be educated by a mind so powerful and wise as that of madame de Genlis, and we may safely take our standard for the average calculation rather from her predecessors than herself. She forms the exception; they the rule. Even were it otherwise, we have already seen what it is that a preceptor can do in the education of a prince. Nor should it be forgotten that these were not of the class of princes destined to a throne.

CHAPTER III

PRIVATE LIFE OF A PRINCE

Principles by which he is influenced—irresponsibility—impatience of control—habits of dissipation—ignorance—dislike of truth—dislike of justice—pitiable situation of princes.

Such is the culture; the fruit that it produces may easily be conjectured. The fashion which is given to the mind in youth, it ordinarily retains in age; and it is with ordinary cases only that the present

---

[1] '*M. de Valois a encore des manières bein déesagéables, des expressions gnobles, & de tems en tems le plus mauvais ton. A présent qu'il est à sonaise avec moi, il me débite avec confiance toutes les gentillesses qu'on lui a aprprises. Tout cela assaisonné de tous les proverbes de Sancho, et d'un gros rire forcé, qui n'est pas le moindre de ses désagréments. En outre, it est très bavarde, grand conteur, & il ment souvent pour se divertir; avec cla la plus grande indifférence pur M. &Mde. De Chartres, n'y pensant jamais, le voyant froidement, ne désirant point les voir.—Ils étoient l'un &l'autre de la plus grande impolitesse,* oui & non *tout court, ou un signe de tête, peu reconnoissant, parcequ'ils croient qu'il n'est point de soins, d'attentions, ni d'égards qu'on ne les doive. Il n'étoit pas possible de les reprendre sans les mettre au désespoir; dans ce cas, toujours des pleurs ou de l'humeur. Its étoient très douillets, craignant le vent, le froid, ne pouvant, non seulement ni courir ni sauter, mais même ni marcher d'un bon pas, &plus d'une demi-heure. Et M. le duc de Valois ayant une peur affreuse des chiens au point de pâlir & et de crier quand il en voyoit un.*'

Quand on m's remis ceux que j'ai élevés, ils avoient l'habitude de porter en hiver de gillets, des double paires de bays, des grand manchone &c. L'aîné, qui avoit huit ans, ne déscendoit jamais un escalier sans s'appuyer sur le bras d'une ou deux personnes. On obligeoit des domestiques de ces enfans à leur rendre les services les plus vils: pour un rhume, pour une légère incommodité, ces domestiques passoient sans cesse les nuits, &c.'

Leçons d'une Gouvernante à ses Eleves, par Mde. De Sillery Brulart (ci-devant comtesse de Genlis), Tome II.

argument is concerned. If there have been kings, as there have been other men, in the forming of whom particular have outweighed general causes, the recollection of such exceptions has little to do with the question, whether monarchy be generally speaking a benefit or an evil. Nature has no particular mould of which she forms the intellects of princes; monarchy is certainly not *jure divino*;* and of consequence, whatever system we may adopt upon the subject of natural talents, the ordinary rate of kings will possess at best but the ordinary rate of human understanding. In what has been said, and in what remains to say, we are not to fix our minds upon prodigies, but to think of the species as it is usually found.

But, though education for the most part determines the character of the future man, it may not be useless to follow the disquisition a little farther. Education in one sense is the affair of youth, but in a stricter and more accurate sense the education of an intellectual being can terminate only with his life. Every incident that befals us is the parent of a sentiment, and either confirms or counteracts the preconceptions of the mind.

Now the causes that acted upon kings in their minority, continue to act upon them in their maturer years. Every thing is carefully kept out of sight that may remind them they are men. Every means is employed that can persuade them that they are of a different species of beings, and subject to different laws of existence. 'A king,' such at least is the maxim of absolute monarchies, 'though obliged by a rigid system of duties, is accountable for his discharge of those duties only to God.' That is, exposed to a hundred fold more seductions than ordinary men, he has not like them the checks of a visible constitution of things, perpetually through the medium of the senses making their way to the mind. He is taught to believe himself superior to the restraints that bind ordinary men, and subject to a rule peculiarly his own. Every thing is trusted to the motives of an invisible world; which, whatever may be the estimate to which they are entitled in the view of philosophy, mankind are not now to learn are weakly felt by those who are immerged in splendour or affairs, and have little chance of success in contending with the impressions of sense and the allurements of visible objects.

It is a maxim generally received in the world 'that every king is a despot in his heart,' and the maxim can seldom fail to be verified in the experiment. A limited monarch and an absolute monarch, though in many respects different, approach in more points than they separate. A monarch, strictly without limitation, is perhaps a phenomenon that never yet existed. All countries have possessed some check upon despotism, which to their deluded imaginations appeared a sufficient security for their independence. All kings have possessed such a portion of luxury and ease, have been so far surrounded with servility and falshood, and to such a degree exempt from personal responsibility, as to destroy the natural and wholesome complexion of the human mind. Being placed so high, they find but one step between them and the summit of social authority, and they cannot but eagerly desire to gain that step. Having so frequent occasions of seeing their behest implicitly obeyed, being trained in so long a scene of adulation and servility, it is impossible they should not feel some indignation at the honest firmness that sets limits to their omnipotence. But to say, 'that every king is a despot in his heart,' will presently be shown to be the same thing as to say, that every king is by unavoidable necessity the enemy of the human race.

The principal source of virtuous conduct is to recollect the absent. He that takes into his estimate present things alone, will be the perpetual slave of sensuality and selfishness. He will have no principle by which to restrain appetite, or to employ himself in just and benevolent pursuits. The cause of virtue and innocence, however urgent, will no sooner cease to be heard, than it will be forgotten. Accordingly nothing is found more favourable to the attainment of moral excellence than meditation: nothing more inimical than an uninterrupted succession of amusements. It would be absurd to expect from kings the recollection of virtue in exile or disgrace. It has generally been observed, that even for the loss of a flatterer or a favourite they speedily console themselves. Image after image so speedily succeed in their sensorium, that no one of them leaves a durable impression. A circumstance which contributes to this moral insensibility, is the effeminacy and cowardice which grow out of perpetual indulgence. Their minds spontaneously shrink from painful ideas, from motives that would awaken them to effort, and reflections that would demand severity of disquisition.

What situation can be more unfortunate than that of a stranger, who cannot speak our language, knows nothing of our manners and customs, and enters into the busy scene of our affairs, without one friend to advise with or assist him? If any thing is to be got by such a man, we may depend upon seeing him instantly surrounded with a group of thieves, sharpers and extortioners. They will make him swallow the most incredible stories, will impose upon him in every article of his necessities or his commerce, and he will leave the country at last, as unfriended and in as absolute ignorance as he entered it. Such a stranger is a king; but with this difference, that the foreigner, if he be a man of sagacity and penetration, may make his way through this crowd of intruders, and discover a set of persons worthy of his confidence, which can scarcely in any case happen to a king. He is placed in a vortex peculiarly his own. He is surrounded with an atmosphere through which it is impossible for him to discover the true colours and figure of things. The persons that are near him are in a cabal and conspiracy of their own, and there is nothing about which they are more anxious than to keep truth from approaching him. The man, who is not accessible to every comer, who delivers up his person into the custody of another, and may, for any thing that he can tell, be precluded from that very intercourse and knowledge it is most important for him to possess, whatever name he may bear, is in reality a prisoner.

Whatever the arbitrary institutions of men may pretend, the more powerful institutions of nature forbid one man to transact the affairs and provide for the welfare of millions. A king soon finds the necessity of entrusting his functions to the administration of his servants. He acquires the habit of seeing with their eyes and acting with their hands. He finds the necessity of confiding implicitly in their fidelity. Like a man long shut up in a dungeon, his organs are not strong enough to bear the irradiation of truth. Accustomed to receive information of the feelings and sentiments of mankind through the medium of another person, he cannot bear directly to converse with business and affairs. Whoever would detach his confidence from his present favourites, and induce him to pass over again in scrutiny the principles and data upon which he has already determined, requires of him too painful a task. He hastens from his informer to communicate the accusation to his favourite, and the tongue that has been accustomed to gain credit, easily varnishes over this new discovery. He flies from uncertainty, anxiety and doubt to his routine of amusements; or amusement presents itself, is importunate to be received, and presently obliterates the tale that overspread the mind with melancholy and suspicion. Much has been said of intrigue and duplicity. They have been alledged to intrude themselves into the walks of commerce, to haunt the intercourse of men of letters, and to rend the petty concerns of a village with faction. But, wherever else they may be strangers, in courts they undoubtedly find a congenial climate. The intrusive talebearer, who carries knowledge to the ear of kings, is within that circle an object of general abhorrence. The favourite marks him for his victim; and the inactive and unimpassioned temper of the monarch soon resigns him to the vindictive importunity of his adversary. It is in the contemplation of these circumstances that Fenelon has remarked that 'kings are the most unfortunate and the most misled of all human beings.'[1]

But in reality were they in possession of purer sources of information, it would be to little purpose. Royalty inevitably allies itself to vice. Virtue, in proportion as it has taken possession of any character, is just, consistent and sincere. But kings, debauched by their education, ruined by their situation, cannot endure an intercourse with these attributes. Sincerity, that would tell them of their errors and remind them of their cowardice; justice, that, uninfluenced by the trappings of majesty, would estimate the man at his true desert; consistency, that no temptation would induce to part with its principles; are odious and intolerable in their eyes. From such intruders they hasten to men of a pliant character, who will flatter their mistakes, put a false varnish on their actions, and be visited by no impertinent scruples in assisting the indulgence of their appetites. There is scarcely in human nature an inflexibility that can resist perpetual flattery and compliance. The virtues that grow up among us are cultured in the open soil of equality, not in the artificial climate of greatness. We need the winds to harden, as much as the heat to cherish us. Many a mind, that promised well in its outset, has been found incapable to stand the test of perpetual indulgence and ease, without one shock to waken, and one calamity to stop it in its smooth career.

Monarchy is in reality so unnatural an institution, that mankind have at all times strongly suspected it was unfriendly to their happiness. The power of truth upon important topics is such, that it may rather be said to be obscured than obliterated; and falshood has scarcely ever been so successful, as not to have had a restless and powerful antagonist in the heart of its votaries. The man who with difficulty earns his scanty subsistence, cannot behold the ostentatious splendour of a king; without being visited by some sense of injustice. He inevitably questions in his mind the utility of an officer whose services are hired at so enormous a price. If he consider the subject with any degree of accuracy, he is led to perceive, and that with sufficient surprise, that a king is nothing more than a common mortal, exceeded by many and equalled by more in every requisite of strength, capacity and virtue. He feels therefore that nothing can be more groundless and unjust than the supposing that one such man as this is the fittest and most competent instrument for regulating the affairs of nations.

---

[1] '*Les plus malheureux & les plus aveugles de tousles homes.*' *Télémaque, Liv. XIII.* More forcible and impressive description is scarcely any where to be found, than that of the evils inseparable from monarchial government, contained in this and the following book of Fenelon's work.

These reflections are so unavoidable that kings themselves have often been aware of the danger to their imaginary happiness with which they are pregnant. They have sometimes been alarmed with the progress of thinking, and oftener regarded the ease and prosperity of their subjects as a source of terror and apprehension. They justly consider their functions as a sort of public exhibition, the success of which depends upon the credulity of the spectators, and which good sense and courage would speedily bring to a termination. Hence the well known maxims of monarchical government, that ease is the parent of rebellion, and that it is necessary to keep the people in a state of poverty and endurance in order to render them submissive. Hence it has been the perpetual complaint of despotism, that 'the restive knaves are overrun with ease, and plenty ever is the nurse of faction.'[1] Hence it has been the lesson perpetually read to monarchs: 'Render your subjects prosperous, and they will speedily refuse to labour; they will become stubborn, proud, unsubmissive to the yoke, and ripe for revolt. It is impotence and misery that alone will render them supple, and prevent them from rebelling against the dictates of authority.'[2]

It is a common and vulgar observation that the state of a king is greatly to be pitied. 'All his actions are hemmed in with anxiety and doubt. He cannot, like other men, indulge the gay and careless hilarity of his mind; but is obliged, if he be of an honest and conscientious disposition, to consider how necessary the time, which he is thoughtlessly giving to amusement, may be to the relief of a worthy and oppressed individual; how many benefits might in a thousand instances result from his interference; how many a guileless and undesigning heart might be cheared by his justice. The conduct of kings is the subject of the severest criticism, which the very nature of their situation disables them to encounter. A thousand things are done in their name in which they have no participation; a thousand stories are so disguised to their ear as to render the truth absolutely undiscoverable; and the king is the general scape-goat, loaded with the offences of all his dependents.'

No picture can be more just, judicious and humane than that which is thus exhibited. Why then should the advocates of antimonarchical principles be considered as the enemies of kings? They would relieve

---

[1] Tragedy of Jane Shore, Act III.*

[2] '*Si vous mettez les peoples dans l'abòndance, ils ne travailleront plus, ils deviendront fiers, indolciles, et seront toujours prêts à se revolter: il n'y a que la foiblesse et la misere qui les rendent souples, et qui les empéchent de resister à l'autorité.*' Télémaque, Liv. XIII.

them from 'a load would sink a navy, too much honour.'[1] They would exalt them to the happy and enviable condition of private individuals. In reality nothing can be more iniquitous and cruel than to impose upon a man the unnatural office of a king. It is not less inequitable towards him that exercises it, than towards them who are subjected to it. Kings, if they understood their own interests, would be the first to espouse these principles, the most eager to listen to them, the most fervent in expressing their esteem of the men who undertake to impress upon their species this important truth.

CHAPTER IV

OF A VIRTUOUS DESPOTISM

Supposed excellence of this form of government controverted—from the narrowness of human powers.—Case of a vicious administration—of a virtuous administration intended to be formed.—Monarchy not adapted to the government of large states.

THERE is a principle frequently maintained upon this subject, which is well entitled to our impartial consideration. It is granted by those who espouse it, 'that absolute monarchy, from the imperfection of those by whom it is administered, is most frequently attended with evil;' but they assert, 'that it is the best and most desirable of all forms under a good and virtuous prince. It is exposed,' say they, 'to the fate of all excellent natures, and from the best thing frequently, if corrupted, becomes the worst.' This remark is certainly not very decisive of the general question, so long as any weight shall be attributed to the arguments which have been adduced to evince what sort of character and disposition may be ordinarily expected in princes. It may however be allowed, if true, to create in the mind a sort of partial retrospect to this happy and perfect despotism; and, if it can be shown to be false, it will render the argument for the abolition of monarchy, so far as it is concerned, more entire and complete.

Now, whatever dispositions any man may possess in favour of the welfare of others, two things are necessary to give them validity; discernment and power. I can promote the welfare of a few persons, because I can be sufficiently informed of their circumstances. I can promote the welfare of many in certain general articles, because for

---

[1] Shakespeare: Henry the Eighth, Act III.*

this purpose it is only necessary that I should be informed of the nature of the human mind as such, not of the personal situation of the individuals concerned. But for one man to undertake to administer the affairs of millions, to supply, not general principles and perspicuous reasoning, but particular application, and measures adapted to the necessities of the moment, is of all undertakings the most extravagant and absurd.

The most natural and obvious of all proceedings is for each man to be the sovereign arbiter of his own concerns. If the imperfection, the narrow views and the mistakes of human beings render this in certain cases inexpedient and impracticable, the next resource is to call in the opinion of his peers, persons who from their vicinity may be presumed to have some general knowledge of the case, and who have leisure and means minutely to investigate the merits of the question. It cannot reasonably be doubted, that the same expedient which men employed in their civil and criminal concerns, would by uninstructed mortals be adopted in the assessment of taxes, in the deliberations of commerce, and in every other article in which their common interests were involved, only generalising the deliberative assembly or pannel in proportion to the generality of the question to be decided.

Monarchy, instead of referring every question to the persons concerned or their neighbours, refers it to a single individual placed at the greatest distance possible from the ordinary members of the society. Instead of distributing the causes to be judged into as many parcels as they would conveniently admit for the sake of providing leisure and opportunities of examination, it draws them to a single centre, and renders enquiry and examination impossible. A despot, however virtuously disposed, is obliged to act in the dark, to derive his knowledge from other men's information, and to execute his behests by other men's instrumentality. Monarchy seems to be a species of government proscribed by the nature of man; and those persons, who furnished their despot with integrity and virtue, forgot to add omniscience and omnipotence, qualities not less necessary to fit him for the office they had provided.

Let us suppose this honest and incorruptible despot to be served by ministers, avaricious, hypocritical and interested. What will the people gain by the good intentions of their monarch? He will mean them the greatest benefits, but he will be altogether unacquainted with their situation, their character and their wants. The information he receives will frequently be found the very reverse of the truth. He will be taught that one individual is highly meritorious and a proper subject of reward, whose only merit is the profligate cruelty with which he has served the purposes of his administration. He will be taught that another is the pest of the community, who is indebted for this report to the steady virtue with which he has traversed and defeated the wickedness of government. He will mean the greatest benefits to his people; but when he prescribes something calculated for their advantage, his servants under pretence of complying shall in reality perpetrate diametrically the reverse. Nothing will be more dangerous than to endeavour to remove the obscurity with which his ministers surround him. The man, who attempts so hardy a task, will become the incessant object of their hatred. Though the sovereign should be ever so severely just, the time will come when his observation will be laid asleep, while malice and revenge are ever vigilant. Could he unfold the secrets of his prison houses of state, he would find men committed in his name whose crimes he never knew, whose names he never heard of, perhaps men whom he honoured and esteemed. Such is the history of the benevolent and philanthropic despots whom memory has recorded; and the conclusion from the whole is, that, wherever despotism exists, there it will always be attended with the evils of despotism, capricious measures and arbitrary infliction.

'But will not a wise king take care to provide himself with good and virtuous servants?' Undoubtedly he will effect a part of this, but he cannot supersede the essential natures of things. He that executes any office as a deputy will never discharge it in the same perfection as if he were the principal. Either the minister must be the author of the plans which he carries into effect, and then it is of little consequence, except so far as relates to his integrity in the choice of his servants, what sort of mortal the sovereign shall be found; or he must play a subordinate part, and then it is impossible to transfuse into his mind the perspicacity and energy of his master. Wherever despotism exists, it cannot remain in a single hand, but must be transmitted whole and entire through all the progressive links of authority. To render despotism auspicious and benign it is necessary, not only that the sovereign should possess every human excellence, but that all his officers should be men of penetrating genius and unspotted virtue. If they fall short of this, they will, like the ministers of Elizabeth, be sometimes specious profligates,[1] and sometimes men, who, however admirably adapted for business, consult on many occasions exclusively their private advantage, worship the rising sun, enter into vindictive cabals, and cuff down

---

[1] Dudley earl of Leicester.*

new fledged merit.[1] Wherever the continuity is broken, the flood of vice will bear down all before it. One weak or disingenuous man will be the source of unbounded mischief. It is the nature of monarchy under all its forms to confide greatly in the discretion of individuals. It provides no resource for maintaining and diffusing the spirit of justice. Every thing rests upon the permanence and extent of influence of personal virtue.

Another position, not less generally asserted than that of the desirableness of a virtuous despotism, is, 'that republicanism is a species of government practicable only in a small state, while monarchy is best fitted to embrace the concerns of a vast and flourishing empire.' The reverse of this, so far at least as relates to monarchy, appears at first sight to be the truth. The competence of any government cannot be measured by a purer standard, than the extent and accuracy of its information. In this respect monarchy appears in all cases to be wretchedly deficient; but, if it can ever be admitted, it must surely be in those narrow and limited instances where an individual can with least absurdity be supposed to be acquainted with the affairs and interests of the whole.

CHAPTER V

OF COURTS AND MINISTERS

Systematical monopoly of confidence.—Character of ministers—of their dependents.—Venality of courts.—Universality of this principle.

WE shall be better enabled to judge of the dispositions with which information is communicated and measures are executed in monarchical countries, if we reflect upon another of the evil consequences attendant upon this species of government, the existence and corruption of courts.

The character of this, as well as of every other human institution, arises out of the circumstances with which it is surrounded. Ministers and favourites are a sort of people who have a state prisoner in their custody, the whole management of whose understanding and actions they can easily engross. This they completely effect with a weak and credulous master, nor can the most cautious and penetrating entirely elude their machinations. They unavoidably desire to continue in the administration of his functions, whether it be emolument, or the love of homage, or any more generous motive by which they are attached to it.

---

[1] Cecil earl of Salisbury,* lord treasurer; Howard earl of Nottingham,* lord admiral, &c.

But the more they are confided in by the sovereign, the greater will be the permanence of their situation; and the more exclusive is their possession of his ear, the more implicit will be his confidence. The wisest of mortals are liable to error; the most judicious projects are open to specious and superficial objections; and it can rarely happen but a minister will find his ease and security in excluding as much as possible other and opposite advisers, whose acuteness and ingenuity are perhaps additionally whetted by a desire to succeed to his office.

Ministers become a sort of miniature kings in their turn. Though they have the greatest opportunity of observing the impotence and unmeaningness of the character, they yet envy it. It is their trade perpetually to extol the dignity and importance of the master they serve; and men cannot long anxiously endeavour to convince others of the truth of any proposition without becoming half convinced of it themselves. They feel themselves dependent for all that they most ardently desire upon this man's arbitrary will; but a sense of inferiority is perhaps the never failing parent of emulation or envy. They assimilate themselves therefore of choice to a man to whose circumstances their own are considerably similar.

In reality the requisites, without which monarchical government cannot be preserved in existence, are by no means sufficiently supplied by the mere intervention of ministers. There must be the ministers of ministers, and a long bead roll of subordination descending by tedious and complicated steps. Each of these lives on the smile of the minister, as he lives on the smile of the sovereign. Each of these has his petty interests to manage, and his empire to employ under the guise of servility. Each imitates the vices of his superior, and exacts from others the adulation he is obliged to pay.

It has already appeared that a king is necessarily and almost unavoidably a despot in his heart. He has been used to hear those things only which were adapted to give him pleasure; and it is with a grating and uneasy sensation that he listens to communications of a different sort. He has been used to unhesitating compliance; and it is with difficulty he can digest expostulation and opposition. Of consequence the honest and virtuous character, whose principles are clear and unshaken, is least qualified for his service; he must either explain away the severity of his principles, or he must give place to a more crafty and temporising politician. The temporising politician expects the same pliability in others that he exhibits in himself; and the fault which he can least forgive is an ill timed and inauspicious scrupulosity.

Expecting this compliance from all the coadjutors and instruments of his designs, he soon comes to set it up as a standard by which to judge of the merit of all other men. He is deaf to every recommendation but that of a fitness for the secret service of government, or a tendency to promote his interest and extend the sphere of his influence. The worst man with this argument in his favour will seem worthy of encouragement; the best man who has no advocate but virtue to plead for him will be treated with superciliousness and neglect. It is true the genuine criterion of human desert can never be superseded and reversed. But it will appear to be reversed, and appearance will produce many of the effects of reality. To obtain honour it will be thought necessary to pay a servile court to administration, to bear with unaltered patience their contumely and scorn, to flatter their vices, and render ourselves useful to their private gratification. To obtain honour it will be thought necessary by assiduity and intrigue to make to ourselves a party, to procure the recommendation of lords and the good word of women of pleasure and clerks in office. To obtain honour it will be thought necessary to merit disgrace. The whole scene consists in hollowness, duplicity and falshood. The minister speaks fair to the man he despises, and the slave pretends a generous attachment, while he thinks of nothing but his personal interest. That these principles are interspersed under the worst governments with occasional deviations into better it would be folly to deny; that they do not form the great prevailing features wherever a court and a monarch are to be found it would be madness to assert.

The fundamental disadvantage of such a form of government is, that it renders things of the most essential importance subject through successive gradations to the caprice of individuals. The suffrage of a body of electors will always bear a resemblance more or less remote to the public sentiment. The suffrage of an individual will depend upon caprice, personal convenience or pecuniary corruption. If the king be himself inaccessible to injustice, if the minister disdain a bribe, yet the fundamental evil remains, that kings and ministers, fallible themselves, must upon a thousand occasions depend upon the recommendation of others. Who will answer for these through all their classes, officers of state and deputies of department, humble friends and officious valets, wives and daughters, concubines and confessors?

It is supposed by many, that the existence of permanent hereditary distinction is necessary to the maintenance of order among beings so imperfect as the human species. But it is allowed by all, that permanent hereditary distinction is a fiction of policy, not an ordinance of immutable truth. Wherever it exists, the human mind, so far as relates to political society, is prevented from settling upon its true foundation. There is a perpetual struggle between the genuine sentiments of under- standing, which tell us that all this is an imposition, and the imperious voice of government, which bids us, Reverence and obey. In this un- equal contest, alarm and apprehension will perpetually haunt the minds of those who exercise usurped power. In this artificial state of man powerful engines must be employed to prevent him from rising to his true level. It is the business of the governors to persuade the gov- erned, that it is their interest to be slaves. They have no other means by which to create this fictitious interest, but those which they derive from the perverted understandings and burdened property of the public, to be returned in titles, ribbands and bribes. Hence that system of univer- sal corruption without which monarchy could not exist.

It has sometimes been supposed that corruption is particularly inci- dent to a mixed government. 'In such a government the people possess a certain portion of freedom; privilege finds its place as well as pre- rogative; a certain sturdiness of manner and consciousness of inde- pendence are the natives of these countries. The country gentleman will not abjure the dictates of his judgment without a valuable consid- eration. There is here more than one road to success; popular favour is as sure a means of advancement as courtly patronage. In despotic coun- tries the people may be driven like sheep; however unfortunate is their condition, they know of no other, and they submit to it as an inevitable calamity. Their characteristic feature is a torpid dullness in which all the energies of man are forgotten. But in a country calling itself free the minds of the inhabitants are in a perturbed and restless state, and extraordinary means must be employed to calm their vehemence.' It has sometimes happened to men whose hearts have been pervaded with the love of virtue, of which pecuniary prostitution is the most odious corruption, to prefer, while they have contemplated this picture, an acknowledged despotism to a state of specious and imperfect liberty.

But this picture is not accurate. As much of it as relates to a mixed government must be acknowledged to be true. But the features of despot- ism are much too favourably touched. Whether privilege be conceded by the forms of the constitution or no, a whole nation cannot be kept ignorant of its force. No people were ever yet so sunk in stupidity as to imagine one man, because he bore the appellation of a king, literally equal to a million. In a whole nation, as monarchical nations at least must be expected to be constituted, there will be nobility and yeomanry, rich and poor. There will be persons who by their situation, or their wealth, or their talents, form a middle rank between the monarch and the vulgar, and who by their confederacies and their intrigues can hold the throne in awe. These men must be bought or defied. There is no disposition that clings so close to despotism as incessant terror and alarm. What else gave birth to the armies of spies and the numerous state prisons under the late government of France? The eye of the tyrant is never closed. How numerous are the precautions and jealousies that these terrors dictate? No man can go out or come into the country but he is watched. The press must issue no productions that have not the imprimatur of government. All coffee houses and places of public resort are objects of attention. Twenty people cannot be collected together, unless for the purposes of superstition, but it is immediately suspected that they may be conferring about their rights. Is it to be supposed, that, where the means of jealousy are employed, the means of corruption will be forgotten? Were it so indeed, the case would not be much improved. No picture can be more disgustful, no state of mankind more depressing, than that in which a whole nation is held in obedience by the mere operation of fear, in which all that is most eminent among them, and that should give example to the rest, is prevented under the severest penalties from expressing its real sentiments, and by necessary consequence from forming any sentiments that are worthy to be expressed. But in reality fear was never employed for these purposes alone. No tyrant was ever so unsocial as to have no confederates in his guilt. This monstrous edifice will always be found supported by all the various instruments for perverting the human character, severity, menaces, blandishments, professions and bribes. To this it is in a great degree owing that monarchy is so very costly an establishment. It is the business of the despot to distribute his lottery of seduction into as many prizes as possible. Among the consequences of a pecuniary polity these are to be reckoned the foremost, that every man is supposed to have his price, and that, the corruption being managed in an underhand manner, many a man, who appears a patriot, may be really a hireling; by which means virtue itself is brought into discredit, is either regarded as mere folly and romance, or observed with doubt and suspicion, as the cloke of vices which are only the more humiliating the more they are concealed.

CHAPTER VI

OF SUBJECTS

Monarchy founded in imposture.—Kings not entitled to superiority—inadequate to the functions they possess.—Means by which the imposture is maintained—1. splendour—2. exaggeration.—This imposture generates—1. indifference to merit—2. indifference to truth—3. artificial desires—4. pusillanimity.—Moral incredulity of monarchical countries.—Injustice of luxury—of the inordinate admiration of wealth.

LET us proceed to consider the moral effects which the institution of monarchical government is calculated to produce upon the inhabitants of the countries in which it flourishes. And here it must be laid down as a first principle that monarchy is founded in imposture. It is false that kings are entitled to the eminence they obtain. They possess no intrinsic superiority over their subjects. The line of distinction that is drawn is the offspring of pretence, an indirect means employed for effecting certain purposes, and not the offspring of truth. It tramples upon the genuine nature of things, and depends for its support upon this argument, 'that, were it not for impositions of a similar nature, mankind would be miserable.'

Secondly, it is false that kings can discharge the functions of royalty. They pretend to superintend the affairs of millions, and they are necessarily unacquainted with these affairs. The senses of kings are constructed like those of other men, they can neither see nor hear what is transacted in their absence. They pretend to administer the affairs of millions, and they possess no such supernatural powers as should enable them to act at a distance. They are nothing of what they would persuade us to believe them. The king is often ignorant of that of which half the inhabitants of his dominions are informed. His prerogatives are administered by others, and the lowest clerk in office is frequently to this and that individual more effectually the sovereign than the king himself. He knows nothing of what is solemnly transacted in his name.

To conduct this imposture with success it is necessary to bring over to its party our eyes and our ears. Accordingly kings are always exhibited with all the splendour of ornament, attendance and equipage. They live amidst a sumptuousness of expence; and this not merely to gratify their appetites, but as a necessary instrument of policy. The most fatal opinion that could lay hold upon the minds of their subjects is that kings are but men. Accordingly they are carefully withdrawn from the profaneness of vulgar inspection; and, when they are exhibited, it is with every artifice that may dazzle our sense and mislead our judgment.

The imposture does not stop with our eyes, but addresses itself to our ears. Hence the inflated style of regal formality. The name of the king every where obtrudes itself upon us. It would seem as if every thing in the country, the lands, the houses, the furniture and the inhabitants were his property. Our estates are the king's dominions. Our bodies and minds are his subjects. Our representatives are his parliament. Our courts of law are his deputies. All magistrates throughout the realm are the king's officers. His name occupies the foremost place in all statutes and decrees. He is the prosecutor of every criminal. He is 'Our Sovereign Lord the King.' Were it possible that he should die, 'the fountain of our blood, the means by which we live,' would be gone: every political function would be suspended. It is therefore one of the fundamental principles of monarchical government that 'the king cannot die.' Our moral principles accommodate themselves to our veracity: and accordingly the sum of our political duties (the most important of all duties) is loyalty; to be true and faithful to the king; to honour a man, whom it may be we ought to despise; and to obey; that is, to acknowledge no immutable criterion of justice and injustice.

What must be the effects of this machine upon the moral principles of mankind? Undoubtedly we cannot trifle with the principles of morality and truth with impunity. However gravely the imposture may be carried on, it is impossible but that the real state of the case should be strongly suspected. Man in a state of society, if undebauched by falshoods like these, which confound the nature of right and wrong, is not ignorant of what it is in which merit consists. He knows that one man is not superior to another except so far as he is wiser or better. Accordingly these are the distinctions to which he aspires for himself. These are the qualities he honours and applauds in another, and which therefore the feelings of each man instigate his neighbour to acquire. But what a revolution is introduced among these original and undebauched sentiments by the arbitrary distinctions which monarchy engenders? We still retain in our minds the standard of merit, but it daily grows more feeble and powerless, we are persuaded to think that it is of no real use in the transactions of the world, and presently lay it aside as Utopian and visionary.

Consequences equally injurious are produced by the hyperbolical pretensions of monarchy. There is a simplicity in truth that refuses alliance with this impudent mysticism. No man is entirely ignorant of the

nature of man. He will not indeed be incredulous to a degree of energy
and rectitude that may exceed the standard of his preconceived ideas.
But for one man to pretend to think and act for a nation of his fellows
is so preposterous as to set credibility at defiance. Is he persuaded that
the imposition is salutary? He willingly assumes the right of introducing
similar falsehoods into his private affairs. He becomes convinced that
veneration for truth is to be classed among our errors and prejudices,
and that, so far from being, as it pretends to be, in all cases salutary, it
would lead, if ingenuously practised, to the destruction of mankind.

Again, if kings were exhibited simply as they are in themselves to the
inspection of mankind, the salutary prejudice, as it has been called,
which teaches us to venerate them, would speedily be extinct: it has
therefore been found necessary to surround them with luxury and
expence. Thus are luxury and expence made the standard of honour,
and of consequence the topics of anxiety and envy. However fatal this
sentiment may be to the morality and happiness of mankind, it is one
of those illusions which monarchical government is eager to cherish. In
reality, the first principle of virtuous feeling, as has been elsewhere said,
is the love of independence. He that would be just must before all
things estimate the objects about him at their true value. But the principle in regal states has been to think your father the wisest of men
because he is your father,[1] and your king the foremost of his species
because he is a king. The standard of intellectual merit is no longer the
man but his title. To be drawn in a coach of state by eight milk-white
horses is the highest of all human claims to our veneration. The fame
principle inevitably runs through every order of the state, and men
desire wealth under a monarchical government, for the same reason
that under other circumstances they would have desired virtue.

Let us suppose an individual who by severe labour earns a scanty
subsistence, to become by accident or curiosity a spectator of the pomp
of a royal progress. Is it possible that he should not mentally apostro-
phise this elevated mortal, and ask, 'What has made thee to differ from
me?' If no such sentiment pass through his mind, it is a proof that the
corrupt institutions of society have already divested him of all sense

[1] 'The persons whom you ought to love infinitely more than me, are those to whom
you are indebted for your existence.' 'Their conduct ought to regulate yours and be the
standard of your sentiments.' 'The respect we owe to our father and mother is a sort of
worship, as the phrase *filial piety* implies.' '*Ce que vous devez aimer avant moi sans aucune
comparison, ce sont ceux à qui vouz devez la vie.*' '*Leur conduite doit regler la vôitre et fixer
votre opinion.*' '*Le respect que nous devons à votre père et à notre mere est une* culte, *comme
l'exprime le mot* piété filiale.' *Leçons d'une Gouvernante, Tome I.**

of justice. The more simple and direct is his character, the more certainly will these sentiments occur. What answer shall we return to his enquiry? That the well being of society requires men to be treated otherwise than according to their intrinsic merit? Whether he be satisfied with this answer or no, will he not aspire to possess that (which in this instance is wealth) to which the policy of mankind has annexed such high distinction? Is it not indispensible, that, before he believes in the rectitude of this institution, his original feelings of right and wrong should be wholly reversed? If it be indispensible, then let the advocate of the monarchical system ingenuously declare, that, according to that system, the interest of society in the first instance requires the total subversion of all principles of moral truth and justice.

With this view let us again recollect the maxim adopted in monarchical countries, 'that the king never dies.' Thus with true oriental extravagance we salute this imbecil mortal, 'O king, live for ever!' Why do we this? Because upon his existence the existence of the state depends. In his name the courts of law are opened. If his political capacity be suspended for a moment, the centre to which all public business is linked, is destroyed. In such countries every thing is uniform: the ceremony is all, and the substance nothing. In the riots in the year 1780* the mace of the house of lords was proposed to be sent into the passages by the terror of its appearance to quiet the confusion; but it was observed that, if the mace should be rudely detained by the rioters, the whole would be thrown into anarchy. Business would be at a stand, their insignia, and with their insignia their legislative and deliberative functions be gone. Who can expect firmness and energy in a country, where every thing is made to depend not upon justice, public interest and reason, but upon a piece of gilded wood? What conscious dignity and virtue can there be among a people, who, if deprived of the imaginary guidance of one vulgar mortal, are taught to believe that their faculties are benumbed, and all their joints unstrung?

Lastly, one of the most essential ingredients in a virtuous character is undaunted firmness; and nothing can more powerfully tend to destroy this principle than the spirit of a monarchical government. The first lesson of virtue is, Fear no man; the first lesson of such a constitution is, Fear the king. The first lesson of virtue is, Obey no man;[1] the first lesson of monarchy is, Obey the king. The true interest of mind demands the annihilation of all factitious and imaginary distinctions; it is inseparable from monarchy to support and render them more

---

[1] Book III, Chap. VI.

palpable than ever. He that cannot speak to the proudest despot with a consciousness that he is a man speaking to a man, and a determination to yield him no superiority to which his inherent qualifications do not entitle him, is wholly incapable of sublime virtue. How many such men are bred within the pale of monarchy? How long would monarchy maintain its ground in a nation of such men? Surely it would be the wisdom of society, instead of conjuring up a thousand phantoms to induce us into error, instead of surrounding us with a thousand fears to deprive us of true energy, to remove every obstacle and smooth the path of improvement.

Virtue was never yet held in much honour and esteem in a monarchical country. It is the inclination and the interest of courtiers and kings to bring it into disrepute; and they are but too successful in the attempt. Virtue is in their conception arrogant, intrusive, unmanageable and stubborn. It is an assumed outside, by which those who pretend to it intend to gratify their rude tempers or their secret views. Within the circle of monarchy virtue is always regarded with dishonourable incredulity. The philosophical system which affirms self love to be the first mover of all our actions* and the falsity of human virtues, is the growth of these countries.[1] Why is it that the language of integrity and public spirit is constantly regarded among us as hypocrisy? It was not always thus. It was not till the usurpation of Cæsar, that books were written by the tyrant and his partisans to prove that Cato* was no better than a snarling pretender.[2]

There is a farther consideration, which has seldom been adverted to upon this subject, but which seems to be of no inconsiderable importance. In our definition of justice it appeared that our debt to our fellow men extended to all the efforts we could make for their welfare, and all the relief we could supply to their necessities. Not a talent do we possess, not a moment of time, not a shilling of property, for which we are not responsible at the tribunal of the public, which we are not obliged to pay into the general bank of common advantage. Of every one of these things there is an employment which is best, and that best justice obliges us to select. But how extensive is the consequence of this principle with respect to the luxuries and ostentation of human life? Are there many of these luxuries that will stand the test, and approve themselves upon examination to be the best objects upon which our

---

[1] *Maximes, par M. le Duc de la Rochefoucault: De la Fousseté des Vertus Humaines, par M. Esprit.*

[2] See Plutarch's Lives;* Lives of Caesar and Cicero: *Ciceronis Epistola ad Atticum, Lib. XL, XLI.*

property can be employed? Will it often come out to be true, that hundreds of individuals ought to be subjected to the severest and most incessant labour, that one man may spend in idleness what would afford to the general mass ease, leisure, and consequently wisdom?

Whoever frequents the habitation of the luxurious will speedily be infected with the vices of luxury. The ministers and attendants of a sovereign, accustomed to the trappings of magnificence, will turn with disdain from the merit that is obscured with the clouds of adversity. In vain may virtue plead, in vain may talents solicit distinction, if poverty seem to the fastidious sense of the man in place to envelop them as it were with its noisome effluvia. The very lacquey knows how to repel unfortunate merit from the great man's door.

Here then we are presented with the lesson which is loudly and perpetually read through all the haunts of monarchy. Money is the great requisite for the want of which nothing can atone. Distinction, the homage and esteem of mankind, are to be bought, not earned. The rich man need not trouble himself to invite them, they come unbidden to his surly door. Rarely indeed does it happen, that there is any crime that gold cannot expiate, any baseness and meanness of character that wealth cannot cover with oblivion. Money therefore is the only object worthy of your pursuit, and it is of little importance by what sinister and unmanly means, so it be but obtained.

It is true that virtue and talents do not stand in need of the great man's assistance, and might, if they did but know their worth, repay his scorn with a just and enlightened pity. But unfortunately they are too often ignorant of their strength, and adopt the errors they see universally espoused in the world. Were it otherwise, they would indeed be happier, but the general manners would probably remain the same. The general manners are fashioned by the form and spirit of the national government; and, if in extraordinary cases they become discordant, they speedily subvert it.

The evils indeed that arise out of avarice, an inordinate admiration of wealth and an intemperate pursuit of it, are so obvious, that they have constituted a perpetual topic of lamentation and complaint. The object in this place is to consider how far they are extended and aggravated by a monarchical government, that is, by a constitution the very essence of which is to accumulate enormous wealth upon a single head, and to render the ostentation of splendour the chosen instrument for securing honour and veneration. The object is to consider in what degree the luxury of courts, the effeminate softness of favourites, the system, never to be separated from the monarchical form, of putting men's approbation and good word at a price, of individuals buying the favour of government, and government buying the favour of individuals, is injurious to the moral improvement of mankind. As long as the unvarying practice of courts is cabal, and as long as the unvarying tendency of cabal is to bear down talents, and discourage virtue, to recommend cunning in the room of sincerity, a servile and supple disposition in preference to firmness and inflexibility, a convenient morality as better than a strict one, and the study of the red book of promotion rather than the study of general welfare, so long will monarchy be the bitterest and most potent of all the adversaries of the true interests of mankind.

CHAPTER VII
OF ELECTIVE MONARCHY

Disorders attendant on such an election.—Election is intended either to provide a man of great or of moderate talents.—Consequences of the first—of the second.—Can elective and hereditary monarchy be combined?

Having considered the nature of monarchy in general, it is incumbent on us to examine how far its mischiefs may be qualified by rendering the monarchy elective.

One of the most obvious objections to this remedy is the difficulty that attends upon the conduct of such an election. There are machines that are too mighty for the human hand to conduct; there are proceedings that are too gigantic and unwieldy for human institutions to regulate. The distance between the mass of mankind and a sovereign is so immense, the trust to be confided so inestimably great, the temptations of the object to be decided on so alluring, as to set every passion that can vex the mind in tumultuous conflict. Election will therefore either dwindle into an empty form, a *congé à élire** with the successful candidate's name at full length in the conclusion, an election perpetually continued in the same family, perhaps in the same lineal order of descent; or will become the signal of a thousand calamities, foreign cabal and domestic war. These evils have been so generally understood, that elective monarchy in the strict sense of that appellation has very few advocates.

Rousseau, who in his advice to the Polish nation appears to be one of those few, that is, one of those who without loving monarchy conceive an elective sovereignty greatly preferable to an hereditary one, endeavours to provide against the disorders of an election by introducing into it a species of sortition.[1] In another part of the present enquiry it will be our business to examine how far chance and the decision by lot are compatible with the principles either of sound morality or sober reason. For the present it will be sufficient to say, that the project of Rousseau will probably fall under one part of the following dilemma, and of consequence will be refuted by the same arguments that bear upon the mode of election in its most obvious idea.

The design with which election can be introduced into the constitution of a monarchy must either be that of raising to the kingly office a man of superlative talents and uncommon genius, or of providing a moderate portion of wisdom and good intention for the discharge of these functions, and preventing them from falling to the lot of persons of notorious imbecility. To the first of these designs it will be objected by many, 'that genius is frequently nothing more in the hands of its possessor than an instrument for accomplishing the most pernicious intentions.' And, though in this assertion there is much partial and mistaken exaggeration, it cannot however be denied that genius, such as we find it amidst the present imperfections of mankind, is compatible with very serious and essential errors. If then genius can by temptations of various sorts be led into practical mistake, may we not reasonably entertain a fear respecting the effect of that situation which of all others is most pregnant with temptation? If considerations of inferior note be apt to mislead the mind, what shall we think of this most intoxicating draught, of a condition superior to restraint, stripped of all those accidents and vicissitudes from which the morality of human beings has flowed, with no salutary check, with no intellectual warfare where mind meets mind on equal terms, but perpetually surrounded with sycophants, servants and dependents? To suppose a mind in which genius and virtue are united and permanent, is also undoubtedly to suppose something which no calculation will teach us to expect should offer upon every vacancy. And, if the man could be found, we must imagine to ourselves electors almost as virtuous as the elected, or else error and prejudice, faction and intrigue will render his election at least precarious, perhaps improbable. Add to this that it is sufficiently evident from the unalterable evils of monarchy already enumerated, and which I shall presently have occasion to recapitulate, that the first act of sovereignty in a virtuous monarch, whose discernment was equal to his virtue, would be to annihilate the constitution, which had raised him to a throne.

---

[1] *Considérations sur le Gouvernement de Pologne, Chap. VIII.**

But we will suppose the purpose of instituting an elective monarchy not to be that of constantly filling the throne with a man of sublime genius, but merely to prevent the sovereignty from falling to the lot of persons of notorious mental imbecility. Such is the strange and pernicious nature of monarchy, that it may be doubted whether this be a benefit. Wherever monarchy exists, courts and administrations must, as long as men can see only with their eyes and act only with their hands, be its constant attendants. But these have already appeared to be institutions so mischievous, that perhaps one of the greatest injuries that can be done to mankind is to persuade them of their innocence. Under the most virtuous despot favour and intrigue, the unjust exaltation of one man and depression of another will not fail to exist. Under the most virtuous despot the true spring there is in mind, the desire to possess merit, and the consciousness that merit will not fail to make itself perceived by those around it, and through their esteem to rise to its proper sphere, will be cut off; and mean and factitious motives be substituted in its room. Of what consequence is it that my merit is perceived by mortals who have no power to advance it? The monarch, shut up in his sanctuary and surrounded with formalities, will never hear of it. How should he? Can he know what is passing in the remote corners of his kingdom? Can he trace the first timid blossoms of genius and virtue? The people themselves will lose their discernment of these things, because they will perceive their discernment to be powerless in effects. The offspring of mind is daily sacrificed by hecatombs to the genius of monarchy. The seeds of reason and truth become barren and unproductive in this unwholesome climate. And the example perpetually exhibited of the preference of wealth and craft over integrity and talents, produces the most powerful effects upon that mass of mankind, who at first sight may appear least concerned in the objects of generous ambition. This mischief, to whatever it amounts, becomes more strongly fastened upon us under a good monarch than under a bad one. In the latter case it only restrains our efforts by violence, in the former it seduces our understandings. To palliate the defects and skin over the deformity of what is fundamentally wrong, is certainly very perilous, perhaps very fatal to the best interests of mankind.

A question has been started, whether it be possible to blend elective and hereditary monarchy, and the constitution of England has been cited as an example of this possibility. What was it that the parliament effected at the revolution, and when they settled the succession upon the house of Hanover?* They elected not an individual, but a new race of men to fill the throne of these kingdoms. They gave a practical instance of their power upon extraordinary emergencies to change the succession. At the same time however that they effected this in action, they denied it in words. They employed the strongest expressions that language could furnish to bind themselves, their heirs and posterity for ever to adhere to this settlement.* They considered the present as an emergence, which, taking into the account the precautions and restrictions they had provided, could never occur again.

In reality what sort of sovereignty is that which is partly hereditary and partly elective? That the accession of a family or race of men should originally be a matter of election has nothing particular in it. All government is founded in opinion; and undoubtedly some sort of election, made by a body of electors more or less extensive, originated every new establishment. To whom in this amphibious government does the sovereignty belong upon the death of the first possessor? To his heirs and descendants. What sort of choice shall that be considered, which is made of a man half a century before he begins to exist? By what designation does he succeed? Undoubtedly by that of hereditary descent. A king of England therefore holds his crown independently, or, as it has been energetically expressed, 'in contempt' of the choice of the people.[1]

CHAPTER VIII

OF LIMITED MONARCHY

Liable to most of the preceding objections—to farther objections peculiar to itself.—Responsibility considered.—Maxim, that the king can do no wrong.— Functions of a limited monarch.—Impossibility of maintaining the neutrality required.—Of the dismission of ministers.—Responsibility of ministers.— Appointment of ministers, its importance—its difficulties.—Recapitulation.— Strength and weakness of the human species.

I PROCEED to consider monarchy, not as it exists in countries where it is unlimited and despotic, but, as in certain instances it has appeared, a branch merely of the general constitution.

Here it is only necessary to recollect the objections which applied to it in its unqualified state, in order to perceive that they bear upon it with the same explicitness, if not with equal force, under every possible modification. Still the government is founded in falsehood, affirming

---

[1] This argument is stated with great copiousness and irresistible force of reasoning by Mr Burke towards the beginning of his Reflections on the Revolution in France.

that a certain individual is eminently qualified for an important situation, whose qualifications are perhaps scarcely superior to those of the meanest member of the community. Still the government is founded in injustice, because it raises one man for a permanent duration over the heads of the rest of the community, not for any moral recommendation he possesses, but arbitrarily and by accident. Still it reads a constant and powerful lesson of immorality to the people at large, exhibiting pomp and splendour and magnificence instead of virtue, as the index to general veneration and esteem. The individual is, not less than in the most absolute monarchy, unfitted by his education to become either respectable or useful. He is unjustly and cruelly placed in a situation that engenders ignorance, weakness and presumption, after having been stripped in his infancy of all the energies that should defend him against the inroads of these adversaries. Finally, his existence implies that of a train of courtiers and a series of intrigue, of servility, secret influence, capricious partialities and pecuniary corruption. So true is the observation of Montesquieu, that 'we must not expect under a monarchy to find the people virtuous.'[1]

But if we consider the question more narrowly, we shall perhaps find, that limited monarchy has other absurdities and vices which are peculiarly its own. In an absolute sovereignty the king may if he please be his own minister; but in a limited one a ministry and a cabinet are essential parts of the constitution. In an absolute sovereignty princes are acknowledged to be responsible only to God; but in a limited one there is a responsibility of a very different nature. In a limited monarchy there are checks, one branch of the government counteracting the excesses of another, and a check without responsibility is the most flagrant of all contradictions.

There is no subject that deserves to be more maturely considered than this of responsibility. To be responsible is to be liable to be called into an open judicature, where the accuser and the defendant produce their allegations and evidence on equal terms. Every thing short of this is mockery. Every thing that would give to either party any other influence than that of truth and virtue is subversive of the great ends of justice. He that is arraigned of any crime must descend a private individual to the level plain of justice. If he can bias the sentiments of his judges by his possession of power, or by any compromise previous to his resignation, or by the mere sympathy excited in his successors, who

---

[1] '*Il n'est pas rare qu'il y ait des princes vertueux: mais il est très difficile dans une monarchie que le peuple le soit.*' Esprit des Loix, Liv III, Chap. V.

will not be severe in their censures, lest they should be treated with severity in return, he cannot truly be said to be responsible at all. From the honest insolence of despotism we may perhaps promise ourselves better effects, than from the hypocritical disclaimers of a limited government. Nothing can be more pernicious than falshood, and no falshood can be more palpable than that which pretends to put a weapon into the hands of the general interest, which constantly proves blunt and powerless in the very act to strike.

It was a confused feeling of these truths, that introduced into limited monarchies the principle 'that the king can do no wrong.' Observe the peculiar consistency of this proceeding. Consider what a specimen it affords us of plain dealing, frankness and unalterable sincerity. An individual is first appointed, and endowed with the most momentous prerogatives, and then it is pretended that, not he, but other men are answerable for the abuse of these prerogatives. This pretence may appear tolerable to men bred among the fictions of law, but justice, truth and virtue revolt from it with indignation.

Having first invented this fiction, it becomes the business of such constitutions as nearly as possible to realise it. A ministry must be regularly formed; they must concert together; and the measures they execute must originate in their own discretion. The king must be reduced as nearly as possible to a cypher. So far as he fails to be completely so, the constitution must be imperfect.

What sort of figure is it that this miserable wretch exhibits in the face of the world? Every thing is with great parade transacted in his name. He assumes all the inflated and oriental style which has been already described, and which indeed was upon that occasion transcribed from the practice of a limited monarchy. We find him like Pharaoh's frogs 'in our houses and upon our beds, in our ovens and our kneading troughs.'*

Now observe the man himself to whom all this importance is annexed. To be idle is the abstract of all his duties. He is paid an immense revenue only to dance and to eat, to wear a scarlet robe and a crown. He may not choose any one of his measures. He must listen with docility to the consultations of his ministers, and sanction with a ready assent whatever they determine. He must not hear any other advisers, for they are his known and constitutional counsellors. He must not express to any man his opinion, for that would be a sinister and unconstitutional interference. To be absolutely perfect he must have no opinion, but be the vacant and colourless mirror by which theirs is reflected. He speaks, for they have taught him what he should say; he affixes his signature, for they inform him that it is necessary and proper.

A limited monarchy in the articles I have described might be executed with great facility and applause, if a king were what such a constitution endeavours to render him, a mere puppet regulated by pullies and wires. But it is perhaps the most egregious and palpable of all political mistakes to imagine that we can reduce a human being to this state of neutrality and torpor. He will not exert any useful and true activity, but he will be far from passive. The more he is excluded from that energy that characterises wisdom and virtue, the more depraved and unreasonable will he be in his caprices. Is any promotion vacant, and do we expect that he will never think of bestowing it on a favourite, or of proving by an occasional election of his own that he really exists? This promotion may happen to be of the utmost importance to the public welfare; or, if not;—every promotion unmeritedly given is pernicious to national virtue, and an upright minister will refuse to assent to it. A king does not fail to hear his power and prerogatives extolled, and he will no doubt at some time wish to essay their reality in an unprovoked war against a foreign nation or against his own citizens.

To suppose that a king and his ministers should through a period of years agree in their genuine sentiments upon every public topic, is what human nature in no degree authorises. This is to attribute to the king talents equal to those of the most enlightened statesmen, or at least to imagine him capable of understanding all their projects, and comprehending all their views. It is to suppose him unspoiled by education, undebauched by rank, and with a mind ingenuously disposed to receive the impartial lessons of truth.

'But, if they disagree, the king can choose other ministers.' We shall presently have occasion to consider this prerogative in a general view; let us for the present examine it in its application to the differences that may occur between the sovereign and his servants. It is an engine for ever suspended over the heads of the latter to persuade them to depart from the sternness of their integrity. The compliance that the king demands from them is perhaps at first but small; and the minister, strongly pressed, thinks it better to sacrifice his opinion in this inferior point than to sacrifice his office. One compliance of this sort leads on to another, and he that began perhaps only with the preference of an unworthy candidate for distinction ends with the most atrocious political guilt. The more we consider this point, the greater will its magnitude appear. It will rarely happen but that the minister will be more dependent for his existence on the king, than the king upon his minister. When it is otherwise, there will be a mutual compromise, and both in turn will part with every thing that is firm, generous, independent and honourable in man.

And in the mean time what becomes of responsibility? The measures are mixed and confounded as to their source, beyond the power of human ingenuity to unravel. Responsibility is in reality impossible. 'Far otherwise,' cries the advocate of monarchical government: 'it is true that the measures are partly those of the king and partly those of the minister, but the minister is responsible for all.' Where is the justice of that? It were better to leave guilt wholly without censure, than to condemn a man for crimes of which he is innocent. In this case the grand criminal escapes with impunity, and the severity of the law falls wholly upon his coadjutors. The coadjutors receive that treatment which constitutes the essence of all bad policy: punishment is profusely menaced against them, and antidote is wholly forgotten. They are propelled to vice by irresistible temptations, the love of power and the desire to retain it; and then censured with a rigour altogether disproportioned to their fault. The vital principle of the society is tainted with injustice, and the same neglect of equity and partial respect of persons will extend itself over the whole.

I proceed to consider that prerogative in limited monarchy, which, whatever others may be given or denied, is inseparable from its substance, the prerogative of the king to nominate to public offices. If any thing be of importance, surely this must be of importance, that such a nomination be made with wisdom and integrity, that the fittest persons be appointed to the highest trusts the state has to confer, that an honest and generous ambition be cherished, and that men who shall most ardently qualify themselves for the care of the public welfare be secure of having the largest share in its superintendence.

This nomination is a most arduous task, and requires the wariest circumspection. It approaches more nearly than any other affair of political society to the exercise of discretion. In all other cases the line of rectitude seems visible and distinct. Justice in the contests of individuals, justice in questions of peace and war, justice in the ordination of law, will not obstinately withdraw itself from the research of an impartial and judicious enquirer. But to observe the various portions of capacity scattered through a nation, and minutely to decide among the qualifications of innumerable pretenders, must after all our accuracy be committed to some degree of uncertainty.

The first difficulty that occurs is to discover those whom genius and ability have made in the best sense candidates for the office. Ability is not always intrusive; talents are often to be found in the remoteness of a village, or the obscurity of a garret. And, though self consciousness and self possession are to a certain degree the attributes of genius, yet there are many things beside false modesty, that may teach its possessor to shun the air of a court.

Of all men a king is least qualified to penetrate these recesses, and discover merit in its hiding place. Encumbered with forms, he cannot mix at large in the society of his species. He is too much engrossed with the semblance of business or a succession of amusements to have leisure for such observations as should afford a just estimate of men's characters. In reality the task is too mighty for any individual, and the benefit can only be secured by the mode of election.

Other disadvantages attendant on this prerogative of choosing his own ministers it is needless to enumerate. If enough have not been already said to explain the character of a monarch as growing out of the functions with which he is invested, a laboured repetition in this place would be both tedious and vain. If there be any dependence to be placed upon the operation of moral causes, a king will in almost every instance be found among the most undiscriminating, the most deceived, the least informed and the least heroically disinterested of mankind.

Such then is the genuine and uncontrovertible scene of a mixed monarchy. An individual placed at the summit of the edifice, the centre and the fountain of honour, and who is neutral, or must seem neutral in the current transactions of his government. This is the first lesson of honour, virtue and truth, which mixed monarchy reads to its subjects. Next to the king come his administration and the tribe of courtiers; men driven by a fatal necessity to be corrupt, intriguing and venal; selected for their trust by the most ignorant and ill informed of their countrymen; made solely accountable for measures of which they cannot solely be the authors; threatened, if dishonest, with the vengeance of an injured people; and, if honest, with the surer vengeance of their sovereign's displeasure. The rest of the nation, the subjects at large—

Was ever a name so fraught with degradation and meanness as this of subjects? I am, it seems, by the very place of my birth become a subject. Of what, or whom? Can an honest man consider himself as the subject of any thing but the laws of justice? Can he acknowledge a superior, or hold himself bound to submit his judgment to the will of another, not less liable than himself to prejudice and error? Such is the idol that monarchy worships in lieu of the divinity of truth and the sacred obligation of public good. It is of little consequence whether we vow fidelity to the king and the nation, or to the nation and the king, so long as the king intrudes himself to tarnish and undermine the true simplicity, the altar of virtue.

Are mere names beneath our notice, and will they produce no sinister influence upon the mind? May we bend the knee before the shrine of vanity and folly without injury? Far otherwise. Mind had its beginning in sensation, and it depends upon words and symbols for the progress of its associations. The true good man must not only have a heart resolved, but a front erect. We cannot practise abjection, hypocrisy and meanness, without becoming degraded in other men's eyes and in our own. We cannot 'bow the head in the temple of Rimmon,'* without in some degree apostatising from the divinity of truth. He that calls a king a man, will perpetually hear from his own mouth the lesson, that he is unfit for the trust reposed in him: he that calls him by any sublimer appellation, is hastening fast into the most palpable and dangerous errors.

But perhaps 'mankind are so weak and imbecil, that it is in vain to expect from the change of their institutions the improvement of their character.' Who made them weak and imbecil? Previously to human institutions they had certainly none of this defect. Man considered in himself is merely a being capable of impression, a recipient of perceptions. What is there in this abstract character that precludes him from advancement? We have a faint discovery in individuals at present of what our nature is capable: why should individuals be fit for so much, and the species for nothing? Is there any thing in the structure of the globe that forbids us to be virtuous? If no, if nearly all our impressions of right and wrong flow from our intercourse with each other, why may not that intercourse be susceptible of modification and amendment? It is the most cowardly of all systems that would represent the discovery of truth as useless, and teach us that, when discovered, it is our wisdom to leave the mass of our species in error.

There is not in reality the smallest room for scepticism respecting the omnipotence of truth. Truth is the pebble in the lake; and however slowly in the present case the circles succeed each other, they will infallibly go on till they overspread the surface. No order of mankind will for ever remain ignorant of the principles of justice, equality and public good. No sooner will they understand them, than they will perceive the coincidence of virtue and public good with private interest: nor will any erroneous establishment be able effectually to support itself against general opinion. In this contest sophistry will vanish, and mischievous institutions sink quietly into neglect. Truth will bring down all her forces, mankind will be her army, and oppression, injustice, monarchy and vice will tumble into a common ruin.

CHAPTER IX

OF A PRESIDENT WITH REGAL POWERS

Enumeration of powers—that of appointing to inferior offices—of pardoning offences—of convoking deliberative assemblies—of affixing a veto to their decrees.—Conclusion.—The title of king estimated—monarchical and aristocratical systems, similarity of their effects.

STILL monarchy it seems has one refuge left. 'We will not,' say some men, 'have an hereditary monarchy, we acknowledge that to be an enormous injustice. We are not contented with an elective monarchy, we are not contented with a limited one. We admit the office however reduced, if the tenure be for life, to be an intolerable grievance. But why not have kings, as we have magistrates and legislative assemblies, renewable by frequent elections? We may then change the holder of the office as often as we please.'

Let us not be seduced by a mere plausibility of phrase, nor employ words without having reflected on their meaning. What are we to understand by the appellation, a king? If the office have any meaning, it seems reasonable that the man who holds it, should possess the privilege, either of appointing to certain employments at his own discretion, or of remitting the decrees of criminal justice, or of convoking and dismissing popular assemblies, or of affixing and refusing his sanction to the decrees of those assemblies. Most of these privileges may claim a respectable authority in the powers delegated to their president by the United States of America.

Let us however bring these ideas to the touchstone of reason. Nothing can appear more adventurous than the reposing, unless in cases of absolute necessity, the decision of any affair of importance to the public, in the breast of one man. But this necessity will scarcely be alledged in any of the articles just enumerated. What advantage does one man possess over a society or council of men in any of these respects? The disadvantages under which he labours are obvious. He is more easily corrupted, and more easily misled. He cannot possess so many advantages for obtaining accurate information. He is abundantly more liable to the attacks of passion and caprice, of unfounded antipathy to one man and partiality to another, of uncharitable censure or blind idolatry. He cannot be always upon his guard; there will be moments in which the most exemplary vigilance is liable to surprise. Meanwhile we are placing the subject in much too favourable a light. We are supposing his intentions to be upright and just; but the contrary of this will be more frequently the truth. Where powers beyond the capacity of human nature are intrusted, vices the disgrace of human nature will be engendered. Add to this, that the same reasons, which prove that government, wherever it exists, should be directed by the sense of the people at large, equally prove that, wherever public officers are necessary, the sense of the whole, or of a body of men most nearly approaching in spirit to the whole, ought to decide on their pretensions.

These objections are applicable to the most innocent of the privileges above enumerated, that of appointing to the exercise of certain employments. The case will be still worse if we consider the other privileges. We shall have occasion hereafter to examine the propriety of pardoning offences, considered independently of the persons in whom that power is vested: but, in the mean time, can any thing be more intolerable than for a single individual to be authorised, without assigning a reason, or assigning a reason upon which no one is allowed to pronounce, to supersede the grave decisions of a court of justice, founded upon a careful and public examination of evidence? Can any thing be more unjust than for a single individual to assume the function of informing a nation when they are to deliberate, and when they are to cease from deliberation?

The remaining privilege is of too iniquitous a nature to be an object of much terror. It is not in the compass of credibility to conceive, that any people would remain quiet spectators, while the sense of one man was openly and undisguisedly set against the sense of the national representative in frequent assembly, and suffered to overpower it. Two or three direct instances of the exercise of this negative could not fail to annihilate it for ever. Accordingly, wherever it is supposed to exist, we find it softened and nourished by the genial dew of pecuniary corruption; either rendered unnecessary beforehand by a sinister application to the frailty of individual members, or disarmed and made palatable in the sequel by a copious effusion of venal emollients. If it can in any case be endured, it must be in countries where the degenerate representative no longer possesses the sympathy of the public, and the haughty president is made sacred, by the blood of an exalted ancestry which flows through his veins, or the holy oil which the representatives of the Most High have poured on his head. A common mortal, periodically selected by his fellow-citizens to watch over their interests, can never be supposed to possess this stupendous virtue.

If there be any truth in these reasonings, it inevitably follows that there are no important functions of general superintendence that can justly be delegated to a single individual. If the office of a president be necessary, either in a deliberative assembly or an administrative council, supposing such a council to exist, his employment will have relation to the order of their proceedings, and by no means consist in the arbitrary preferring and carrying into effect his private decision. A king, if unvarying usage can have given meaning to a word, designs a man upon whose single discretion some part of the public interest is made to depend. What use can there be for such a man in an unperverted and well ordered state? With respect to its internal affairs certainly none. How far the office can be of advantage in our transactions with foreign governments we shall hereafter have occasion to decide.

Let us beware by an unjustifiable perversion of terms of confounding the common understanding of mankind. A king is the well known and standing appellation for an office, which, if there be any truth in the arguments of the preceding chapters, has been the bane and the grave of human virtue. Why endeavour to purify and exorcise what is entitled only to execration? Why not suffer the term to be as well understood and as cordially detested, as the once honourable appellation of tyrant* afterwards was among the Greeks? Why not suffer it to rest a perpetual monument of the folly, the cowardice and misery of our species?

In proceeding from the examination of monarchical to that of aristocratical government, it is impossible not to remark that there are several disadvantages common to both. One of these is the creation of a separate interest. The benefit of the governed is made to lie on one side, and the benefit of the governors on the other. It is to no purpose to say that individual interest accurately understood will always be found to coincide with general, if it appear in practice, that the opinions and errors of mankind are perpetually separating them and placing them in opposition to each other. The more the governors are fixed in a sphere distinct and distant from the governed, the more will this error be cherished. Theory, in order to produce an adequate effect upon the mind, should be favoured, not counteracted, by practice. What principle in human nature is more universally confessed than self love, that is, than a propensity to think individually of a private interest, to discriminate and divide objects which the laws of the universe have indissolubly united? None, unless it be the *esprit de corps*, the tendency of bodies of men to aggrandise themselves, a spirit, which, though less ardent than self love, is still more vigilant, and not exposed to the accidents of sleep, indisposition and mortality. Thus it appears that, of all impulses to a narrow, self-interested conduct, those afforded by monarchy and aristocracy are the greatest.

Nor must we be too hasty and undistinguishing in applying the principle, that individual interest accurately understood will always be found to coincide with general. Relatively to individuals considered as men it is true; relatively to individuals considered as lords and kings it is false. The man will be served by the sacrifice of all his little peculium to the public interest, but the king will be annihilated. The first sacrifice that justice demands at the hand of monarchy and aristocracy, is that of their immunities and prerogatives. Public interest dictates the laborious dissemination of truth and the impartial administration of justice. Kings and lords subsist only under favour of error and oppression. They will therefore resist the progress of knowledge and illumination; the moment the deceit is dispelled, their occupation is gone.

In thus concluding however we are taking for granted that aristocracy will be found an arbitrary and pernicious institution, as monarchy has already appeared to be. It is time that we should enquire in what degree this is actually the case.

CHAPTER X

OF HEREDITARY DISTINCTION

Birth considered as a physical cause—as a moral cause.—Aristocratical estimate of the human species.—Education of the great.—Recapitulation.

A PRINCIPLE deeply interwoven with both monarchy and aristocracy in their most flourishing state, but most deeply with the latter, is that of hereditary preheminence. No principle can present a deeper insult upon reason and justice. Examine the new born son of a peer and a mechanic. Has nature designated in different lineaments their future fortune? Is one of them born with callous hands and an ungainly form? Can you trace in the other the early promise of genius and understanding, of virtue and honour? We have been told indeed that 'nature will break out,'[1] and that

'The eaglet of a valiant nest will quickly tower
Up to the region of his fire;'*

and the tale was once believed. But mankind will not soon again be persuaded, that one lineage of human creatures produces beauty and virtue, and another vice.

---

[1] Tragedy of Douglas, Act iii.

An assertion thus bold and unfounded will quickly be refuted if we consider the question *a priori*. Mind is the creature of sensation; we have no other inlet of knowledge. What are the sensations that the lord experiences in his mother's womb, by which his mind is made different from that of the peasant? Is there any variation in the finer reticulated substance of the brain, by which the lord is adapted to receive clearer and stronger impressions than the husbandman or the smith?

'But a generous blood circulates in his heart and enriches his veins.' What are we to understand by this hypothesis? Men's actions are the creatures of their perceptions. He that apprehends most strongly will act most intrepidly. He, in whose mind truth is most distinctly impressed, who, understanding its nature, is best aware of its value, will speak with the most heart-felt persuasion, and write with the greatest brilliancy and energy. By intrepidity and firmness in action we must either understand the judicious and deliberate constancy of a Regulus or a Cato,* or the brute courage of a private soldier, which is still an affair of mind, consisting in a slight estimate of life which affords him few pleasures, and a thoughtless and stupid oblivion of danger. What has the blood to do with this?——Health is undoubtedly in most cases the prerequisite of the best exertions of mind. But health itself is a mere negation, the absence of disease. A man must have experienced or imagined the inconveniences of sickness, before he can derive positive pleasure from the enjoyment of health. Again, however extravagant we may be in our estimate of the benefit of health, is it true in fact that the lord enjoys a more vigorous health, experiences a more uniform chearfulness, and is less a prey to weariness and languor than the rustic? High birth may inspire high thoughts as a moral cause; but is it credible that it should operate instinctively and when its existence is unknown, while, with every external advantage to assist, the noblest families so often produce the most degenerate sons? Into its value then as a moral cause let us proceed to enquire.

The persuasion of its excellence in this respect is an opinion probably as old as the institution of nobility itself. The very etymology of the word expressing this particular form of government is built upon this idea. It is called aristocracy or the government of the best αριςοι. In the writings of Cicero and the speeches of the Roman senate this order of men is styled the *'optimates,'** the 'virtuous,' the 'liberal,' and the 'honest.' It is taken for granted, 'that the multitude is an unruly beast, with no sense of honour or principle, guided by sordid interest or not less sordid appetite, envious, tyrannical, inconstant and unjust.' From hence they deduced as a consequence, 'the necessity of maintaining an order of men of liberal education and elevated sentiments, who should either engross the government of the humbler and more numerous class incapable of governing themselves, or at least should be placed as a rigid guard upon their excesses, with powers adequate to their correction and restraint.' The greater part of these reasonings will fall under our examination when we consider the disadvantages of democracy. So much as relates to the excellence of aristocracy it is necessary at present to discuss.

The whole proceeds upon a supposition that, 'if nobility should not, as its hereditary constitution might seem to imply, be found originally superior to the ordinary rate of mortals, it is at least rendered eminently so by the power of education. Men, who grow up in unpolished ignorance and barbarism, and are chilled with the icy touch of poverty, must necessarily be exposed to a thousand sources of corruption, and cannot have that delicate sense of rectitude and honour, which literature and manly refinement are found to bestow. It is under the auspices of indulgence and ease that civilisation is engendered. A nation must have surmounted the disadvantages of a first establishment, and have arrived at some degree of leisure and prosperity, before the love of letters can take root among them. It is in individuals as in large bodies of men. A few exceptions will occur; but, bating these, it can hardly be expected that men, who are compelled in every day by laborious corporal efforts to provide for the necessities of the day, should arrive at great expansion of mind and comprehensiveness of thinking.'

In certain parts of this argument there is considerable truth. The real philosopher will be the last man to deny the power and importance of education. It is therefore necessary, either that a system should be discovered for securing leisure and prosperity to every member of the community, or that a paramount influence and authority should be given to the liberal and the wise over the illiterate and ignorant. Now, supposing for the present that the former of these measures is impossible, it may yet be reasonable to enquire whether aristocracy be the most judicious scheme for obtaining the latter. Some light may be collected on this subject from what has already appeared respecting education under the head of monarchy.

Education is much, but opulent education is of all its modes the least efficacious. The education of words is not to be despised, but the education of things is on no account to be dispensed with. The former is of admirable use in inforcing and developing the latter; but, when taken alone, it is pedantry and not learning, a body without a soul. Whatever may be the abstract perfection of which mind is capable, we seem at present frequently to need being excited, in the case of any uncommon effort, by motives that address themselves to the individual. But so far as relates to these motives, the lower classes of mankind, had they sufficient leisure, have greatly the advantage of the higher. The plebeian must be the maker of his own fortune; the lord finds his already made. The plebeian must expect to find himself neglected and despised in proportion as he is remiss in cultivating the objects of esteem; the lord will always be surrounded with sycophants and slaves. The lord therefore has no motive to industry and exertion; no stimulus to rouse him from the lethargic, 'oblivious pool,' out of which every finite intellect originally rose. It must indeed be confessed, that truth does not need the alliance of circumstances, and that a man may arrive at the temple of fame by other pathways than those of misery and distress. But the lord does not content himself with excluding the spur of adversity: he goes farther than this, and provides himself with fruitful sources of effeminacy and error. Man cannot offend with impunity against the great principle of universal good. He that accumulates to himself luxuries and titles and wealth to the injury of the whole, becomes degraded from the rank of man; and, however he may be admired by the multitude, is pitied by the wise and wearisome to himself. Hence it appears, that to elect men to the rank of nobility is to elect them to a post of moral danger and a means of depravity; but that to constitute them hereditarily noble is to preclude them, bating a few extraordinary accidents, from all the causes that generate ability and virtue.

The reasonings we have here repeated upon the subject of hereditary distinction are so obvious, that nothing can be a stronger instance of the power of prejudice instilled in early youth, than the fact of their having been at any time called in question. If we can in this manner produce an hereditary legislator, why not an hereditary moralist or an hereditary poet?[1] In reality an attempt in either of these kinds would be more rational and feasible than in the other. From birth as a physical cause it sufficiently appears that little can be expected: and, for education, it is practicable in a certain degree, nor is it easy to set limits to that degree, to infuse poetical or philosophical emulation into a youthful mind; but wealth is the fatal blast that destroys the hopes of a future harvest. There was once indeed a gallant kind of virtue, that, by irresistibly seizing the senses, seemed to communicate extensively to young men of birth, the mixed and equivocal accomplishments of chivalry; but, since the subjects of moral emulation have been turned from personal prowess

---

[1] See Paine's Rights of Man.*

to the energies of intellect, and especially since the field of that emulation has been more widely opened to the species, the lists have been almost uniformly occupied by those, whose narrow circumstances have goaded them to ambition, or whose undebauched habits and situation in life have rescued them from the poison of flattery and effeminate indulgence.

CHAPTER XI

MORAL EFFECTS OF ARISTOCRACY

Importance of practical justice.—Species of injustice which aristocracy creates.—Estimate of the injury produced.—Examples.

THERE is one thing, more than all the rest, of importance to the well being of mankind, justice. Can there be any thing problematical or paradoxical in this fundamental principle, that all injustice is injury; and a thousand times more injurious by its effects in perverting the understanding and overturning our calculations of the future, than by the immediate calamity it may produce?

All moral science may be reduced to this one head, calculation of the future. We cannot reasonably expect virtue from the multitude of mankind, if they be induced by the perverseness of the conductors of human affairs to believe that it is not their interest to be virtuous. But this is not the point upon which the question turns. Virtue, is nothing else but the pursuit of general good. Justice, is the standard which discriminates the advantage of the many and of the few, of the whole and a part. If this first and most important of all subjects be involved in obscurity, how shall the well being of mankind be substantially promoted? The most benevolent of our species will be engaged in crusades of error; while the cooler and more phlegmatic spectators, discerning no evident clue that should guide them amidst the labyrinth, sit down in selfish neutrality, and leave the complicated scene to produce its own denouement.

It is true that human affairs can never be reduced to that state of depravation as to reverse the nature of justice. Virtue will always be the interest of the individual as well as of the public. Immediate virtue will always be beneficial to the present age, as well as to their posterity. But, though the depravation cannot rise to this excess, it will be abundantly sufficient to obscure the understanding, and mislead the conduct. Human beings will never be so virtuous as they might easily be made, till justice be the spectacle perpetually presented to their view, and injustice be wondered at as a prodigy.

Of all the principles of justice there is none so material to the moral rectitude of mankind as this, that no man can be distinguished but by his personal merit. Why not endeavour to reduce to practice so simple and sublime a lesson? When a man has proved himself a benefactor to the public, when he has already by laudable perseverance cultivated in himself talents, which need only encouragement and public favour to bring them to maturity, let that man be honoured. In a state of society where fictitious distinctions are unknown, it is impossible he should not be honoured. But that a man should be looked up to with servility and awe, because the king has bestowed on him a spurious name, or decorated him with a ribband; that another should wallow in luxury, because his ancestor three centuries ago bled in the quarrel of Lancaster or York; do we imagine that these iniquities can be practised without injury?

Let those who entertain this opinion converse a little with the lower orders of mankind. They will perceive that the unfortunate wretch, who with unremitted labour finds himself incapable adequately to feed and clothe his family, has a sense of injustice rankling at his heart.

> 'One whom distress has spited with the world,
> Is he whom tempting fiends would pitch upon
> To do such deeds, as make the prosperous men
> Lift up their hands and wonder who could do them.'[1]

Such is the education of the human species. Such is the fabric of political society.

But let us suppose that their sense of injustice were less acute than it is here described, what favourable inference can be drawn from that? Is not the injustice real? If the minds of men be so withered and stupefied by the constancy with which it is practised, that they do not feel the rigour that grinds them into nothing, how does that improve the picture?

Let us for a moment give the reins to reflexion, and endeavour accurately to conceive the state of mankind where justice should form the public and general principle. In that case our moral feelings would assume a firm and wholesome tone, for they would not be perpetually counteracted by examples that weakened their energy and confounded their clearness. Men would be fearless, because they would know that there were no legal snares lying in wait for their lives. They would be courageous, because no man would be pressed to the earth that another might enjoy immoderate luxury, because every one would be secure of

---

[1] Tragedy of Douglas,* Act iii.

the just reward of his industry and prize of his exertions. Jealousy and hatred would cease, for they are the offspring of injustice. Every man would speak truth with his neighbour, for there would be no temptation to falshood and deceit. Mind would find its level, for there would be every thing to encourage and to animate. Science would be unspeakably improved, for understanding would convert into a real power, no longer an *ignis fatuus*,* shining and expiring by turns, and leading us into sloughs of sophistry, false science and specious mistake. All men would be disposed to avow their dispositions and actions: none would endeavour to suppress the just eulogium of his neighbour, for, so long as there were tongues to record, the suppression would be impossible; none fear to detect the misconduct of his neighbour, for there would be no laws converting the sincere expression of our convictions into a libel.

Let us fairly consider for a moment what is the amount of injustice included in the institution of aristocracy. I am born, suppose, a Polish prince with an income of £300,000 per annum. You are born a manorial serf or a Creolian negro, by the law of your birth attached to the soil, and transferable by barter or otherwise to twenty successive lords. In vain shall be your most generous efforts and your unwearied industry to free yourself from the intolerable yoke. Doomed by the law of your birth to wait at the gates of the palace you must never enter, to sleep under a ruined weather-beaten roof, while your master sleeps under canopies of state, to feed on putrefied offals while the world is ransacked for delicacies for his table, to labour without moderation or limit under a parching sun while he basks in perpetual sloth, and to be rewarded at last with contempt, reprimand, stripes and mutilation. In fact the case is worse than this. I could endure all that injustice or caprice could inflict, provided I possessed in the resource of a firm mind the power of looking down with pity on my tyrant, and of knowing that I had that within, that sacred character of truth, virtue and fortitude, which all his injustice could not reach. But a slave and a serf are condemned to stupidity and vice, as well as to calamity.

Is all this nothing? Is all this necessary for the maintenance of civil order? Let it be recollected that for this distinction there is not the smallest foundation in the nature of things, that, as we have already said, there is no particular mould for the construction of lords, and that they are born neither better nor worse than the poorest of their dependents. It is this structure of aristocracy in all its sanctuaries and fragments against which reason and philosophy have declared war. It is alike unjust, whether we consider it in the casts of India, the villainage of the feudal system, or the despotism of the patricians of ancient Rome dragging their debtors into personal servitude to expiate loans they could not repay. Mankind will never be in an eminent degree virtuous and happy, till each man shall possess that portion of distinction and no more, to which he is entitled by his personal merits. The dissolution of aristocracy is equally the interest of the oppressor and the oppressed. The one will be delivered from the listlessness of tyranny, and the other from the brutalising operation of servitude. How long shall we be told in vain, 'that mediocrity of fortune is the true rampart of personal happiness?'

CHAPTER XII

OF TITLES

Their origin and history.— Their miserable absurdity.— Truth the only adequate reward of merit.

THE case of mere titles is so absurd that it would deserve to be treated only with ridicule, were it not for the serious mischiefs it imposes on mankind. The feudal system was a ferocious monster devouring wherever it came all that the friend of humanity regards with attachment and love. The system of titles appears under a different form. The monster is at length destroyed, and they who followed in his train, and fattened upon the carcasses of those he slew, have stuffed his skin, and by exhibiting it hope still to terrify mankind into patience and pusillanimity. The system of the Northern invaders, however odious, escaped the ridicule of the system of titles. When the feudal chieftains assumed a geographical appellation, it was from some place really subject to their authority; and there was no more absurdity in the style they assumed, than in our calling a man at present the governor of Tangiers or the governor of Gibraltar. The commander in chief or the sovereign did not then give an empty name; he conferred an earldom or a barony, a substantial tract of land, with houses and men, and producing a real revenue. He now grants nothing but the privilege of calling yourself Tom who were beforetime called Will; and, to add to the absurdity, your new appellation is borrowed from some place perhaps you never saw, or some country you never visited. The style however is the same; we are still earls and barons, governors of provinces and commanders of forts, and that with the same evident propriety as the elector of Hanover and arch treasurer of the empire styles himself king of France.*

Can there be any thing more ludicrous, than that the man, who was yesterday Mr St. John, the most eloquent speaker of the British house of commons, the most penetrating thinker, the umpire of maddening parties, the restorer of peace to bleeding and exhausted Europe, should be to-day lord Bolingbroke?* In what is he become greater and more venerable than he was? In the pretended favour of a stupid and besotted woman, who always hated him, as she uniformly hated talents and virtue, though for her own interest she was obliged to endure him.

The friends of a man upon whom a title has recently been conferred, must either be wholly blinded by the partiality of friendship not to feel the ridicule of his situation, or completely debased by the parasitical spirit of dependence not to betray their feelings. Every time they essay to speak, they are in danger of blundering upon the inglorious appellations of Mr and Sir.[1] Every time their tongue faulters with unconfirmed practice, the question rushes upon them with irresistible force, 'What change has my old friend undergone; in what is he wiser or better, happier or more honourable?' The first week of a new title is a perpetual war of the feelings in every spectator, the genuine dictates of common sense against the arbitrary institutions of society. To make the farce more perfect these titles are subject to perpetual fluctuations, and the man who is to-day earl of Kensington, will to-morrow resign with unblushing effrontery all appearance of character and honour to be called marquis of Kew. History labours under the Gothic and unintelligible burden; no mortal patience can connect the different stories of him who is to-day lord Kimbolton, and to-morrow earl of Manchester; to-day earl of Mulgrave, and to-morrow marquis of Normanby and duke of Buckinghamshire.*

The absurdity of these titles strikes us the more, because they are usually the reward of intrigue and corruption. But, were it otherwise, still they would be unworthy of the adherents of reason and justice. When we speak of Mr St. John,* as of the man, who by his eloquence swayed contending parties, who withdrew the conquering sword from suffering France, and gave forty years of peace and calm pursuit of the arts of life and wisdom to mankind, we speak of something eminently great. Can any title express these merits? Is not truth the consecrated and single vehicle of justice? Is not the plain and simple truth worth all the cunning substitutions in the world? Could an oaken garland or a gilded coronet have added one atom to his real greatness? Garlands and coronets may be bestowed on the unworthy and prostituted to the intriguing. Till mankind be satisfied with the naked statement of what

---

[1] In reality these appellations are little less absurd than those by which they are superseded.

they really perceive, till they confess virtue to be then most illustrious when she most disdains the aid of ornament, they will never arrive at that manly justice of sentiment, at which they are destined one day to arrive. By this scheme of naked truth, virtue will be every day a gainer; every succeeding observer will more fully do her justice, while vice, deprived of that varnish with which she delighted to gloss her actions, of that gaudy exhibition which may be made alike by every pretender, will speedily sink into unheeded contempt.

CHAPTER XIII

OF THE ARISTOCRATICAL CHARACTER

Intolerance of aristocracy—dependent for its success upon the ignorance of the multitude.—Precautions necessary for its support.—Different kinds of aristocracy.—Aristocracy of the romans: its virtues—its vices.—Aristocratical distribution of property—regulations by which it is maintained—avarice it engenders.—Argument against innovation from the present happy establishment of affairs considered.—Conclusion.

ARISTOCRACY in its proper signification implies neither less nor more than a scheme for rendering more permanent and visible by the interference of political institution the inequality of mankind. Aristocracy, like monarchy, is founded in falshood, the offspring of art foreign to the real nature of things, and must therefore, like monarchy, be supported by artifice and false pretences. Its empire however is founded in principles more gloomy and unsocial than those of monarchy. The monarch often thinks it advisable to employ blandishments and courtship with his barons and officers; but the lord deems it sufficient to rule with a rod of iron.

Both depend for their perpetuity upon ignorance. Could they, like Omar, destroy the productions of profane reasoning, and persuade mankind that the Alcoran* contained every thing which it became them to study, they might then renew their lease of empire. But here again aristocracy displays its superior harshness. Monarchy admits of a certain degree of monkish learning among its followers. But aristocracy holds a stricter hand. Should the lower ranks of society once come to be generally taught to write and read, its power would be at an end. To make men serfs and villains it is indispensibly necessary to make them brutes. This is a question which has long been canvassed with great eagerness and avidity. The resolute advocates of the old system have with no contemptible foresight opposed this alarming innovation. In their well known observation, 'that a servant who has been taught to write and read ceases to be any longer a passive machine,' is contained the embryo from which it would be easy to explain the whole philosophy of human society.

And who is there that can reflect with patience upon the malevolent contrivances of these insolent usurpers, contrivances the end of which is to keep the human species in a state of endless degradation? It is in the subjects we are here examining that the celebrated maxim of 'many made for one' is brought to the real test. Those reasoners were no doubt wise in their generation, who two centuries ago conceived alarm at the blasphemous doctrine, 'that government was instituted for the benefit of the governed, and, if it proposed to itself any other object, was no better than an usurpation.'* It will perpetually be found that the men, who in every age have been the earliest to give the alarm of innovation, and have been ridiculed on that account as bigoted and timid, were in reality persons of more than common discernment, who saw, though but imperfectly, in the rude principle the inferences to which it inevitably led. It is time that men of reflexion should choose between the two alternatives: either to go back fairly and without reserve to the primitive principles of tyranny; or, adopting any one of the axioms opposite to these, however neutral it may at first appear, not feebly and ignorantly to shut their eyes upon its countless host of consequences.

It is not necessary to enter into a methodical disquisition of the different species of aristocracy, since, if the above reasonings have any force, they are equally cogent against them all. Aristocracy may vest its prerogatives principally in the individual, as in Poland; or entirely restrict them to the nobles in their corporate capacity, as in Venice. The former will be more tumultuous and disorderly; the latter more jealous, intolerant and severe. The magistrates may either recruit their body by election among themselves, as in Holland;* or by the choice of the people, as in ancient Rome.*

The aristocracy of ancient Rome was incomparably the most venerable and illustrious that ever existed upon the face of the earth. It may not therefore be improper to contemplate in them the degree of excellence to which aristocracy may be raised. They included in their institution some of the benefits of democracy, as generally speaking no man became a member of the senate, but in consequence of his being elected by the people to the superior magistracies. It was reasonable therefore to expect that the majority of the members would possess some degree of capacity. They were not like modern aristocratical assemblies, in which, as primogeniture and not selection decides upon their prerogatives, we shall commonly seek in vain for capacity, except in a few of the lords of recent creation. As the plebeians were long restrained from looking for candidates except among the patricians, that is, the posterity of senators, it was reasonable to suppose that the most eminent talents would be confined to that order. A circumstance which contributed to this was the monopoly of liberal education and the cultivation of the mind, a monopoly which the art of printing has at length fully destroyed. Accordingly all the great literary ornaments of Rome were either patricians, or of the equestrian order, or their immediate dependents. The plebeians, though in their corporate capacity they possessed for some centuries the virtues of sincerity, intrepidity, love of justice and of the public, could never boast of any of those individual characters in their party that reflect lustre on mankind, except the two Gracchi:* while the patricians told of Brutus, Valerius, Coriolanus, Cincinnatus, Camillus, Fabricius, Regulus, the Fabii, the Decii, the Scipios, Lucullus, Marcellus, Cato, Cicero,* and innumerable others. With this retrospect continually suggested to their minds it was almost venial for the stern heroes of Rome and the last illustrious martyrs of the republic to entertain aristocratical sentiments.

Let us however consider impartially this aristocracy, so incomparably superior to any other of ancient or modern times. Upon the first institution of the republic, the people possessed scarcely any authority except in the election of magistrates, and even here their intrinsic importance was eluded by the mode of arranging the assembly, so that the whole decision vested in the richer classes of the community. No magistrates of any description were elected but from among the patricians. All causes were judged by the patricians, and from their judgment there was no appeal. The patricians intermarried among themselves, and thus formed a republic of narrow extent in the midst of the nominal one, which was held by them in a state of abject servitude. The idea which purified these usurpations in the minds of the usurpers, was, 'that the vulgar are essentially coarse, groveling and ignorant, and that there can be no security for the empire of justice and consistency but in the decided ascendancy of the liberal.' Thus, even while they opposed the essential interests of mankind, they were animated with public spirit and an unbounded enthusiasm of virtue. But it is not less true that they did oppose the essential interests of mankind. What can be more extraordinary than the declamations of Appius Claudius* in this style, at once for the moral greatness of mind by which they were dictated, and the cruel intolerance they were intended to inforce? It is inexpressibly painful to see so much virtue through successive ages employed in counteracting the justest requisitions. The result was, that the patricians, notwithstanding their immeasurable superiority in abilities, were obliged to yield one by one the exclusions to which they so obstinately clung. In the interval they were led to have recourse to the most odious methods of counteraction; and every man among them contended who should be loudest in applause of the nefarious murder of the Gracchi. If the Romans were distinguished for so many virtues, constituted as they were, what might they not have been but for the iniquity of aristocratical usurpation? The indelible blemish of their history, the love of conquest, originated in the same cause. Their wars, through every period of the republic, were nothing more than the contrivance of the patricians, to divert their countrymen from attending to the sentiments of unalterable truth, by leading them to scenes of conquest and carnage. They understood the art, common to all governments, of confounding the understandings of the multitude, and persuading them that the most unprovoked hostilities were merely the dictates of necessary defence.

The principle of aristocracy is founded in the extreme inequality of conditions. No man can be an useful member of society, except so far as his talents are employed in a manner conducive to the general advantage. In every society the produce, the means of contributing to the necessities and conveniencies of its members, is of a certain amount. In every society the bulk at least of its members contribute by their personal exertions to the creation of this produce. What can be more reasonable and just, than that the produce itself should with some degree of equality be shared among them? What more injurious than the accumulating upon a few every means of superfluity and luxury, to the total destruction of the ease, and plain, but plentiful, subsistence of the many? It may be calculated that the king even of a limited monarchy, receives as the salary of his office, an income equivalent to the labour of fifty thousand men.[1] Let us set out in our estimate from this point, and figure to ourselves the shares of his counsellors, his nobles, the wealthy commoners by whom the nobility will be emulated, their kindred and dependents. Is it any wonder that in such countries the lower orders of the community are exhausted by all the hardships of penury and immoderate fatigue? When we see the wealth of a province spread upon the great man's table, can we be surprised that his neighbours have not bread to satiate the cravings of hunger?

---

[1] Taking the average price of labour at one shilling per diem.

Is this a state of human beings that must be considered as the last improvement of political wisdom? In such a state it is impossible that eminent virtue should not be exceedingly rare. The higher and the lower classes will be alike corrupted by their unnatural situation. But to pass over the higher class for the present, what can be more evident than the tendency of want to contract the intellectual powers? The situation which the wise man would desire for himself and for those in whose welfare he was interested, would be a situation of alternate labour and relaxation, labour that should not exhaust the frame, and relaxation that was in no danger to degenerate into indolence. Thus industry and activity would be cherished, the frame preserved in a healthful tone, and the mind accustomed to meditation and reflection. But this would be the situation of the whole human species, if the supply of our wants were equally distributed. Can any system be more worthy of our disapprobation than that which converts nineteen-twentieths of them into beasts of burden, annihilates so much thought, renders impossible so much virtue and extirpates so much happiness?

But it may be alledged, 'that this argument is foreign to the subject of aristocracy; the inequality of conditions being the inevitable consequence of the institution of property.' It is true that many disadvantages flow out of this institution in its simplest form; but these disadvantages, to whatever they may amount, are greatly aggravated by the operations of aristocracy. Aristocracy turns the stream of property out of its natural channel, and forwards with the most assiduous care its accumulation in the hands of a very few persons. The doctrines of primogeniture and entails, as well as the immense volumes of the laws of transfer and inheritance which have infested every part of Europe, were produced for this express purpose.

At the same time that it has endeavoured to render the acquisition of permanent property difficult, aristocracy has greatly increased the excitements to that acquisition. All men are accustomed to conceive a thirst after distinction and pre-eminence, but they do not all fix upon wealth as the object of this passion, but variously upon skill in any particular art, grace, learning, talents, wisdom and virtue. Nor does it appear that these latter objects are pursued by their votaries with less assiduity, than wealth is pursued by those who are anxious to acquire it. Wealth would be still less capable of being mistaken for the universal passion, were it not rendered by political institution, more than by its natural influence, the road to honour and respect.

There is no mistake more thoroughly to be deplored on this subject, than that of persons, sitting at their ease and surrounded with all the conveniences of life, who are apt to exclaim, 'We find things very well as they are;' and to inveigh bitterly against all projects of reform, as 'the romances of visionary men, and the declamations of those who are never to be satisfied.' Is it well, that so large a part of the community should be kept in abject penury, rendered stupid with ignorance and disgustful with vice, perpetuated in nakedness and hunger, goaded to the commission of crimes, and made victims to the merciless laws which the rich have instituted to oppress them? Is it sedition to enquire whether this state of things may not be exchanged for a better? Or can there be any thing more disgraceful to ourselves than to exclaim that 'All is well,' merely because we are at our ease, regardless of the misery, degradation and vice that may be occasioned in others?

There is one argument to which the advocates of monarchy and aristocracy always have recourse when driven from every other pretence; the mischievous nature of democracy. 'However imperfect the two former of these institutions may be in themselves, they are found necessary,' we are told, 'as accommodations to the imperfection of human nature.' It is for the reader who has considered the arguments of the preceding chapters to decide, how far it is probable that circumstances can occur, which should make it our duty to submit to these complicated evils. Meanwhile let us proceed to examine that democracy of which so alarming a picture has uniformly been exhibited.

CHAPTER XIV
GENERAL FEATURES OF DEMOCRACY

Definition.—Supposed evils of this form of government—ascendancy of the ignorant—of the crafty—inconstancy—rash confidence—groundless suspicion.—Merits and defects of democracy compared.—Its moral tendency.—Tendency of truth.—Representation.

DEMOCRACY is a system of government according to which every member of society is considered as a man and nothing more. So far as positive regulation is concerned, if indeed that can with any propriety be termed regulation which is the mere recognition of the simplest of all principles, every man is regarded as equal. Talents and wealth, wherever they exist, will not fail to obtain a certain degree of influence, without requiring any positive institution of society to second their operation.

But there are certain disadvantages that may seem the necessary result of democratical equality. In political society it is reasonable to suppose that the wise will be outnumbered by the unwise, and it will be inferred 'that the welfare of the whole will therefore be at the mercy of ignorance and folly.' It is true that the ignorant will generally be sufficiently willing to be guided by the judicious, 'but their very ignorance will incapacitate them from discerning the merit of their guides. The turbulent and crafty demagogue will often possess greater advantages for inveigling their judgment, than the man who with purer intentions may possess a less brilliant talent. Add to this, that the demagogue has a never failing resource in the ruling imperfection of human nature, that of preferring the specious present to the substantial future. This is what is usually termed, playing upon the passions of mankind. Political truth has hitherto proved an enigma, that all the wit of man has been insufficient to solve. Is it to be supposed that the uninstructed multitude should always be able to resist the artful sophistry and captivating eloquence that will be employed to darken it? Will it not often happen that the schemes proposed by the ambitious disturber will possess a meretricious attraction, which the severe and sober project of the discerning statesman shall be unable to compensate?

'One of the most fruitful sources of human happiness is to be found in the steady and uniform operation of certain fixed principles. But it is the characteristic of a democracy to be wavering and inconstant. The philosopher only, who has deeply meditated his principles, is inflexible in his adherence to them. The mass of mankind, as they have never arranged their reflections into system, are at the mercy of every momentary impulse, and liable to change with every wind. But this inconstancy is directly the reverse of every idea of political justice.

'Nor is this all. Democracy is a monstrous and unwieldy vessel launched upon the sea of human passions without ballast. Liberty in this unlimited form is in danger to be lost almost as soon as it is obtained. The ambitious man finds nothing in this scheme of human affairs to set bounds to his desires. He has only to dazzle and deceive the multitude in order to rise to absolute power.

'A farther ill consequence flows out of this circumstance. The multitude, conscious of their weakness in this respect, will, in proportion to their love of liberty and equality, be perpetually suspicious and uneasy. Has any man displayed uncommon virtues or rendered eminent services to his country? He will presently be charged with secretly aiming at the tyranny. Various circumstances will come in aid of this accusation, the general love of novelty, envy of superior merit, and the incapacity of the multitude to understand the motives and character of those who so far excel them. Like the Athenian, they will be tired of hearing Aristides constantly called the Just.* Thus will merit be too frequently the victim of ignorance and envy. Thus will all that is liberal and refined, whatever the human mind in its highest state of improvement is able to conceive, be often overpowered by the turbulence of unbridled passion and the rude dictates of savage folly.'

If this picture must inevitably be realised wherever democratical principles are established, the state of human nature would be peculiarly unfortunate. No form of government can be devised which does not partake of monarchy, aristocracy or democracy. We have taken a copious survey of the two former, and it would seem impossible that greater or more inveterate mischiefs can be inflicted on mankind, than those which are inflicted by them. No portrait of injustice, degradation and vice can be exhibited, that can surpass the fair and inevitable inferences from the principle upon which they are built. If then democracy could by any arguments be brought down to a level with such monstrous institutions as these, in which there is neither integrity nor reason, our prospects of the future happiness of mankind would indeed be deplorable.

But this is impossible. Supposing that we should even be obliged to take democracy with all the disadvantages that were ever annexed to it, and that no remedy could be discovered for any of its defects, it would be still greatly preferable to the exclusive system of other forms. Let us take Athens with all its turbulence and instability; with the popular and temperate usurpations of Pisistratus and Pericles;* with their monstrous ostracism, by which with undisguised injustice they were accustomed periodically to banish some eminent citizen without the imputation of a crime; with the imprisonment of Miltiades, the exile of Aristides and the murder of Phocion:*—with all these errors on its head, it is incontrovertible that Athens exhibited a more illustrious and enviable spectacle than all the monarchies and aristocracies that ever existed. Who would reject the gallant love of virtue and independence, because it was accompanied with some irregularities? Who would pass an unreserved condemnation upon their penetrating mind, their quick discernment and their ardent feeling, because they were subject occasionally to be intemperate and impetuous? Shall we compare a people of such incredible achievements, such exquisite refinement, gay without insensibility and splendid without intemperance, in the midst of whom grew up the greatest poets, the noblest artists, the most finished orators and political writers, and the most disinterested philosophers the world ever saw,—shall we compare this chosen seat of patriotism, independence and generous virtue, with the torpid and selfish realms of monarchy and aristocracy? All is not happiness that looks tranquillity. Better were a portion of turbulence and fluctuation, than that unwholesome calm which is a stranger to virtue.

In the estimate that is usually made of democracy, one of the most flagrant sources of error lies in our taking mankind such as monarchy and aristocracy have made them, and from thence judging how fit they are to legislate for themselves. Monarchy and aristocracy would be no evils, if their tendency were not to undermine the virtues and the understandings of their subjects. The thing most necessary is to remove all those restraints which hold mind back from its natural flight. Implicit faith, blind submission to authority, timid fear, a distrust of our powers, an inattention to our own importance and the good purposes we are able to effect, these are the chief obstacles to human improvement. Democracy restores to man a consciousness of his value, teaches him by the removal of authority and oppression to listen only to the dictates of reason, gives him confidence to treat all other men as his fellow beings, and induces him to regard them no longer as enemies against whom to be upon his guard, but as brethren whom it becomes him to assist. The citizen of a democratical state, when he looks upon the miserable oppression and injustice that prevail in the countries around him, cannot but entertain an inexpressible esteem for the advantages he enjoys, and the most unalterable determination at all hazards to preserve them. The influence of democracy upon the sentiments of its members is altogether of the negative sort, but its consequences are inestimable. Nothing can be more unreasonable than to argue from men as we now find them, to men as they may hereafter be made. Strict and accurate reasoning, instead of suffering us to be surprised that Athens did so much, would at first induce us to wonder that she retained so many imperfections.

The road to the improvement of mankind is in the utmost degree simple, to speak and act the truth. If the Athenians had had more of this, it is impossible they should have been so flagrantly erroneous. To tell the truth in all cases without reserve, to administer justice without partiality, are principles which, when once rigorously adopted, are of all others the most prolific. They enlighten the understanding, give energy to the judgment, and strip misrepresentation of its speciousness and plausibility. In Athens men suffered themselves to be dazzled by splendour and show. If the error in their constitution which led to this defect can be discovered, if a form of political society can be devised in which men shall be accustomed to judge strictly and soberly, and habitually exercised to the plainness and simplicity of truth, democracy would in that society cease from the turbulence, instability, fickleness and violence that have too often characterised it. Nothing can be more certain than the omnipotence of truth, or, in other words, than the connexion between the judgment and the outward behaviour. If science be capable of perpetual improvement, men will also be capable of perpetually advancing in practical wisdom and justice. Once establish the perfectibility of man, and it will inevitably follow that we are advancing to a state, in which truth will be too well known to be easily mistaken, and justice too habitually practiced to be voluntarily counteracted. Nor shall we see reason to think upon severe reflection, that this state is so distant as we might at first be inclined to imagine. Error is principally indebted for its permanence to social institution. Did we leave individuals to the progress of their own minds, without endeavouring to regulate them by any species of public foundation, mankind would in no very long period convert to the obedience of truth. The contest between truth and falsehood is of itself too unequal, for the former to stand in need of support from any political ally. The more it be discovered, especially that part of it which relates to man in society, the more simple and self evident will it appear; and it will be found impossible any otherwise to account for its having been so long concealed, than from the pernicious influence of positive institution.

There is another obvious consideration that has frequently been alledged to account for the imperfection of ancient democracies, which is worthy of our attention, though it be not so important as the argument which has just been stated. The ancients were unaccustomed to the idea of deputed, or representative assemblies; and it is reasonable to suppose that affairs might often be transacted with the utmost order in such assemblies, which might be productive of much tumult and confusion, if submitted to the personal discussion of the citizens at large.[1] By this happy expedient we secure many of the pretended benefits of aristocracy, as well as the real benefits of democracy. The discussion of national affairs is brought before persons of superior education and wisdom: we may conceive of them, not only as the appointed medium of the sentiments of their constituents, but as authorised upon certain occasions to act on their part, in the same manner as an unlearned parent delegates his authority over his child to a preceptor of greater

---

[1] The general grounds of this institution have been stated, Book III, Chap. IV. The exceptions which limit its value, will be seen in the twenty-third chapter of the previous book.

accomplishments than himself. This idea within proper limits might be entitled to our approbation, provided the elector had the wisdom not to relax in the exercise of his own understanding in all his political concerns, exerted his censorial power over his representative, and were accustomed, if the representative were unable after the fullest explanation to bring him over to his opinion, to transfer his deputation to another.

The true value of the system of representation is as follows. It is not reasonable to doubt that mankind, whether acting by themselves or their representatives, might in no long time be enabled to contemplate the subjects offered to their examination with calmness and true discernment, provided no positive obstacles were thrown in their way by the errors and imperfection of their political institutions. This is the principle in which the sound political philosopher will rest with the most perfect satisfaction. But, should it ultimately appear that representation, and not the intervention of popular assemblies, is the mode which reason prescribes, then an error in this preliminary question, will of course infer errors in the practice which is built upon it. We cannot make one false step, without involving ourselves in a series of mistakes and ill consequences that must be expected to grow out of it.

Such are the general features of democratical government: but this is a subject of too much importance to be dismissed without the fullest examination of every thing that may enable us to decide upon its merits. We will proceed to consider the farther objections that have been alledged against it.

CHAPTER XV

OF POLITICAL IMPOSTURE

Importance of this topic.—Example in the doctrine of eternal punishment— its inutility argued—from history—from the nature of mind.—Second example: the religious sanction of a legislative system.—This idea is 1. in strict construction impracticable—2. injurious.—Third example: principle of political order.—Vice has no essential advantage over virtue.—Imposture unnecessary to the cause of justice—not adapted to the nature of man.

ALL the arguments that have been employed to prove the insufficiency of democracy grow out of this one root, the supposed necessity of deception and prejudice for restraining the turbulence of human passions. Without the assumption of this principle the argument could not be sustained for a moment. The direct and decisive answer would be, 'Are kings and lords intrinsically wiser and better than their humbler neighbours? Can there be any solid ground of distinction except what is founded in personal merit? Are not men, really and strictly considered, equal, except so far as what is personal and inalienable makes them to differ?' To these questions there can be but one reply, 'Such is the order of reason and absolute truth, but artificial distinctions are necessary for the happiness of mankind. Without deception and prejudice the turbulence of human passions cannot be restrained.' Let us then examine the merits of this theory; and these will best be illustrated by an instance.

It has been held by some divines and some politicians, that the doctrine which teaches that men will be eternally tormented in another world for their errors and misconduct in this, is 'in its own nature unreasonable and absurd, but that it is nevertheless necessary, to keep mankind in awe. Do we not see,' say they, 'that notwithstanding this terrible denunciation the world is overrun with vice? What then would be the case, if the irregular passions of mankind were set free from their present restraint, and they had not the fear of this retribution before their eyes?'

This argument seems to be founded in a singular inattention to the dictates of history and experience, as well as to those of reason. The ancient Greeks and Romans had nothing of this dreadful apparatus of fire and brimstone,* and a torment 'the smoke of which ascends for ever and ever.'* Their religion was less personal than political. They confided in the Gods as protectors of the state, and this inspired them with invincible courage. In periods of public calamity they found a ready consolation in expiatory sacrifices to appease the anger of the Gods. The attention of these beings was conceived to be principally directed to the ceremonial of religion, and very little to the moral excellencies and defects of their votaries, which were supposed to be sufficiently provided for by the inevitable tendency of moral excellence or defect to increase or diminish individual happiness. If their systems included the doctrine of a future existence, little attention was paid by them to the connecting the moral deserts of individuals in this life with their comparative situation in another. The same defect ran through the systems of the Persians, the Egyptians, the Celts, the Phenicians, the Jews, and indeed every system which has not been in some manner or other the offspring of the Christian. If we were to form our judgment of these nations by the above argument, we should expect to find every individual among them cutting his neighbour's throat, and hackneyed in the commission of every enormity without measure and without remorse. But they were in reality as susceptible of the regulations of government and the order of society, as those whose imaginations have been most artfully terrified by the threats of future retribution, and some of them were much more generous, determined and attached to the public weal.

Nothing can be more contrary to a just observation of the nature of the human mind, than to suppose that these speculative tenets have much influence in making mankind more virtuous than they would otherwise be found. Human beings are placed in the midst of a system of things, all the parts of which are strictly connected with each other, and exhibit a sympathy and unison by means of which the whole is rendered intelligible and as it were palpable to the mind. The respect I shall obtain and the happiness I shall enjoy for the remainder of my life are topics of which my mind has a complete comprehension. I understand the value of plenty, liberty and truth to myself and my fellow men. I perceive that these things and a certain conduct intending them are connected, in the visible system of the world, and not by the supernatural interposition of an invisible director. But all that can be told me of a future world, a world of spirits or of glorified bodies, where the employments are spiritual and the first cause is to be rendered a subject of immediate perception, or of a scene of retribution, where the mind, doomed to everlasting inactivity, shall be wholly a prey to the upbraidings of remorse and the sarcasms of devils, is so foreign to the system of things with which I am acquainted, that my mind in vain endeavours to believe or to understand it. If doctrines like these occupy the habitual reflections of any, it is not of the lawless, the violent and ungovernable, but of the sober and conscientious, persuading them passively to submit to despotism and injustice, that they may receive the recompense of their patience hereafter. This objection is equally applicable to every species of deception. Fables may amuse the imagination; but can never stand in the place of reason and judgment as the principles of human conduct.—Let us proceed to a second instance.

It is affirmed by Rousseau in his treatise of the Social Contract, 'that no legislator could ever establish a grand political system without having recourse to religious imposture. To render a people who are yet to receive the impressions of political wisdom susceptible of the evidence of that wisdom, would be to convert the effect of civilisation into the cause. The legislator ought not to employ force and cannot employ reasoning; he is therefore obliged to have recourse to authority of a different sort, which may draw without compulsion, and persuade without conviction.'[1]

These are the dreams of a fertile conception, busy in the erection of imaginary systems. To a rational mind that project would seem to promise little substantial benefit, which set out from so erroneous a principle. To terrify men into the reception of a system the reasonableness of which they were unable to perceive, is surely a very indirect method of rendering them sober, judicious, fearless and happy.

In reality no grand political system ever was introduced in the manner Rousseau describes. Lycurgus, as he observes, obtained the sanction of the oracle at Delphi to the constitution he had established. But was it by an appeal to Apollo that he persuaded the Spartans to renounce the use of money, to consent to an equal division of land, and to adopt various other regulations* the most contrary to their preconceived prejudices? No; it was by an appeal to their understandings, in the midst of long debate and perpetual counteraction, and through the

[1] '*Pour qu'un peuple naissant pût gouter les saines maxims de la politique & suivre les regles fondamentales de la raison de l'état, il faudrai qu l'effet put devenir la cause; que l'esprit social, qui doit être l'ouvrage de l'institution, présidât à l'institution méme, & que les homes fussent, avant les lois, ce qu'ils doivent devenir par ells. Ainsi donc le législateur ne pouvant employer ni la orce ni la raisonnement; c'est une nécessité qu'il recourse à une autorité d'un autre ordre, qui puisse entraîner sans violence et persuader sans convaincre.*' Du Contrat Social, Liv.II. Chap. VIII.

Having frequently quoted Rousseau in the course of this work, it may be allowable to say one word of his general merits as a moral and political writer. He has been subjected to perpetual ridicule for the extravagance of the proposition with which he began his literary career; that the savage state was the genuine and proper condition of man. It is however by a very slight mistake that he missed the opposite opinion which it is the business of the present work to establish. It is sufficiently observable that, where he describes the enthusiastic influx of truth that first make him a moral and political writer (in his second letter to Malesherbes*), he does not so much as mention his fundamental error, but only the just principles that led him into it. He was the first to teach that the imperfections of government were the only permanent sources of the vices of mankind; and this principle was adopted from him by Helvetius and others. But he saw further than this, that government, however reformed, was little capable of affording solid benefit to mankind, which they did not. This principle has since (probably without any assistance from the writings of Rousseau) been expressed with great perspicuity and energy, but not developed by Mr. Thomas Paine in the first page of his Common Sense.

Rousseau, notwithstanding his great genius, was full of weakness and prejudice. His *Emile* is upon the whole to be regarded as the principal reservoir of philosophical truth as yet existing in the world, but with a perpetual mixture of absurdity and mistake. In his writings expressly political, *Du Contrat Social* and *Considérations sur la Pologne*, the unrivalled superiority of his genius appears to desert him. To his merits as a reasoner we should not to forget to add, that the term eloquence is more precisely descriptive of his mode of composition, than that of any other writer that has ever existed.

inflexibility of his courage and resolution, that he at last attained his purpose. Lycurgus thought proper, after the whole was concluded, to obtain the sanction of the oracle, conceiving that it became him to neglect no method of substantiating the benefit he had conferred on his countrymen. It is indeed hardly possible to persuade a society of men to adopt any system without convincing them that it is their wisdom to adopt it. It is difficult to conceive of a society of such miserable dupes as to receive a code, without any imagination that it is reasonable or wise or just, but upon this single recommendation that it is delivered to them from the Gods. The only reasonable, and infinitely the most efficacious method of changing the institutions of any people, is by creating in them a general opinion of their erroneousness and insufficiency.

But, if it be indeed impracticable to persuade men into the adoption of any system, without employing as our principal argument the intrinsic rectitude of that system, what is the argument which he would desire to use, who had most at heart the welfare and improvement of the persons concerned? Would he begin by teaching them to reason well, or to reason ill? by unnerving their mind with prejudice, or new stringing it with truth? How many arts, and how noxious to those towards whom we employ them, are necessary, if we would successfully deceive? We must not only leave their reason in indolence at first, but endeavour to supersede its exertion in any future instance. If men be for the present kept right by prejudice, what will become of them hereafter, if by any future penetration or any accidental discovery this prejudice shall be annihilated? Detection is not always the fruit of systematical improvement, but may be effected by some solitary exertion of the faculty or some luminous and irresistible argument, while every thing else remains as it was. If we would first deceive, and then maintain our deception unimpaired, we shall need penal statutes, and licensers of the press, and hired ministers of falshood and imposture. Admirable modes these for the propagation of wisdom and virtue!

There is another case similar to that stated by Rousseau, upon which much stress has been laid by political writers. 'Obedience,' say they, 'must either be courted or compelled. We must either make a judicious use of the prejudices and the ignorance of mankind, or be contented to have no hold upon them but their fears, and maintain social order entirely by the severity of punishment. To dispense us from this painful necessity, authority ought carefully to be invested with a sort of magic persuasion. Citizens should serve their country, not with a frigid submission that scrupulously weighs its duties, but with an enthusiasm that places its honour in its loyalty. For this reason our governors and superiors must not be spoken of with levity. They must be considered, independently of their individual character, as deriving a sacredness from their office. They must be accompanied with splendour and veneration. Advantage must be taken of the imperfection of mankind. We ought to gain over their judgments through the medium of their senses, and not leave the conclusions to be drawn, to the uncertain process of immature reason.'[1]

This is still the same argument under another form. It takes for granted that reason is inadequate to teach us our duty; and of consequence recommends an equivocal engine, which may with equal ease be employed in the service of justice and injustice, but would surely appear somewhat more in its place in the service of the latter. It is injustice that stands most in need of superstition and mystery, and will most frequently be a gainer by the imposition. This hypothesis proceeds upon an assumption, which young men sometimes impute to their parents and preceptors. It says, 'Mankind must be kept in ignorance: if they know vice, they will love it too well; if they perceive the charms of error, they will never return to the simplicity of truth.' And, strange as it may appear, this barefaced and unplausible argument has been the foundation of a very popular and generally received hypothesis. It has taught politicians to believe that a people once sunk into decrepitude, as it has been termed, could never afterwards be endued with purity and vigour.[2]

Is it certain that there is no alternative between deceit and unrelenting severity? Does our duty contain no inherent recommendations? If it be not our own interest that we should be temperate and virtuous, whose interest is it? Political institution, as has abundantly appeared in the course of this work, and will still farther appear as we go forward, has been too frequently the parent of temptations to error and vice of a thousand different denominations. It would be well, if legislators, instead of contriving farther deceptions and enchantments to retain us in our duty, would remove the impostures which at present corrupt our hearts and engender at once artificial wants and real distress. There would be less need, under the system of plain, unornamented truth, than under theirs, that 'every visto should be terminated with the gallows.'[3]

---

[1] This argument is the great common place of Mr Burke's Reflections on the Revolution in France, of several successive productions of Mr Necker,* and of a multitude of other works upon the subject of government.

[2] Book I, Chap. VIII.

[3] Burke's Reflections.*

Why deceive me? It is either my wisdom to do the thing you require of me, or it is not. The reasons for doing it are either sufficient or insufficient. If sufficient, why should not they be the machine to govern my understanding? Shall I most improve while I am governed by false reasons, by imposture and artifice, which, were I a little wiser, I should know were of no value in whatever cause they may be employed; or, while my understanding grows every day sounder and stronger by perpetual communication with truth? If the reasons for what you demand of me be insufficient, why should I comply? It is strongly to be suspected that that regulation, which dares not rest upon its own reasonableness, conduces to the benefit of a few at the expence of the many. Imposture was surely invented by him, who thought more of securing dignity to himself, than of prevailing on mankind to consent to their own welfare. That which you require of me is wise, no farther than it is reasonable. Why endeavour to persuade me that it is more wise, more essential than it really is, or that it is wise for any other reason than the true? Why divide men into two classes, one of which is to think and reason for the whole, and the other to take the conclusions of their superiors on trust? This distinction is not founded in the nature of things; there is no such inherent difference between man and man as it thinks proper to suppose. The reasons that should convince us that virtue is better than vice are neither complicated nor abstruse; and the less they be tampered with by the injudicious interference of political institution, the more will they come home to the understanding and approve themselves to the judgment of every man.

Nor is the distinction less injurious, than it is unfounded. The two classes which it creates, must be more and less than man. It is too much to expect of the former, while we consign to them an unnatural monopoly, that they should rigidly consult for the good of the whole. It is an iniquitous requisition upon the latter, that they should never employ their understandings, never penetrate into the essences of things, but always rest in a deceitful appearance. It is iniquitous, that we should seek to withhold from them the principles of simple truth, and exert ourselves to keep alive their fond and infantine mistakes. The time must probably come when the deceit shall vanish; and then the impostures of monarchy and aristocracy will no longer be able to maintain their ground. The change will at that time be most auspicious, if we honestly inculcate the truth now, secure that men's minds will grow strong enough to endure the practice, in proportion as their understanding of the theory excites them to demand it.

CHAPTER XVI

OF THE CAUSES OF WAR

Offensive war contrary to the nature of democracy.—Defensive war exceed-
ingly rare.—Erroneousness of the ideas commonly annexed to the phrase,
our country.—Nature of war delineated.—Insufficient causes of war—the
acquiring a healthful and vigorous tone to the public mind—the putting a
termination upon private insults—the menaces or preparations of our
neighbours—the dangerous consequences of concession.—Two legitimate
causes of war.

EXCLUSIVELY of those objections which have been urged against the
democratical system as it relates to the internal management of affairs,
there are others upon which considerable stress has been laid in relation to the transactions of a state with foreign powers, to war and peace,
to treaties of alliance and commerce.

There is indeed an eminent difference with respect to these between
the democratical system and all others. It is perhaps impossible to shew
that a single war ever did or could have taken place in the history of
mankind, that did not in some way originate with those two great political monopolies, monarchy and aristocracy. This might have formed an
additional article in the catalogue of evils to which they have given
birth, little inferior to any of those we have enumerated. But nothing
could be more superfluous than to seek to overcharge a subject the
evidence of which is irresistible.

What could be the source of misunderstanding between states,
where no man or body of men found encouragement to the accumulation of privileges to himself at the expence of the rest? A people among
whom equality reigned, would possess every thing they wanted, where
they possessed the means of subsistence. Why should they pursue
additional wealth or territory? These would lose their value the moment
they became the property of all. No man can cultivate more than a
certain portion of land. Money is representative, and not real wealth. If
every man in the society possessed a double portion of money, bread
and every other commodity would sell at double their present price,
and the relative situation of each individual would be just what it had
been before. War and conquest cannot be beneficial to the community.
Their tendency is to elevate a few at the expence of the rest, and consequently they will never be undertaken but where the many are the
instruments of the few. But this cannot happen in a democracy, till the

democracy shall become such only in name. If expedients can be devised for maintaining this species of government in its purity, or if there be any thing in the nature of wisdom and intellectual improvement which has a tendency daily to make truth prevail more over falshood, the principle of offensive war will be extirpated. But this principle enters into the very essence of monarchy and aristocracy.

Meanwhile, though the principle of offensive war be incompatible with the genius of democracy, a democratical state may be placed in the neighbourhood of states whose government is less equal, and therefore it will be proper to enquire into the supposed disadvantages which the democratical state may sustain in the contest. The only species of war in which it can consistently be engaged, will be that, the object of which is to repel wanton invasion. Such invasions will be little likely frequently to occur. For what purpose should a corrupt state attack a country, which has no feature in common with itself upon which to build a misunderstanding, and which presents in the very nature of its government a pledge of its own inoffensiveness and neutrality? Add to which, it will presently appear that this state, which yields the fewest incitements to provoke an attack, will prove a very impracticable adversary to those by whom an attack shall be commenced.

One of the most essential principles of political justice is diametrically the reverse of that which impostors and patriots have too frequently agreed to recommend. Their perpetual exhortation has been, 'Love your country. Sink the personal existence of individuals in the existence of the community. Make little account of the particular men of whom the society consists, but aim at the general wealth, prosperity and glory. Purify your mind from the gross ideas of sense, and elevate it to the single contemplation of that abstract individual of which particular men are so many detached members, valuable only for the place they fill.'[1]

The lessons of reason on this head are precisely opposite. 'Society is an ideal existence, and not on its own account entitled to the smallest regard. The wealth, prosperity and glory of the whole are unintelligible chimeras. Set no value on any thing, but in proportion as you are convinced of its tendency to make individual men happy and virtuous. Benefit by every practicable mode man wherever he exists; but be not deceived by the specious idea of affording services to a body of men, for which no individual man is the better. Society was instituted, not for the sake of glory, not to furnish splendid materials for the page

---

[1] *Du Contrat Social*, &c. &c. &c.

of history, but for the benefit of its members. The love of our country, if we would speak accurately, is another of those specious illusions, which have been invented by impostors in order to render the multitude the blind instruments of their crooked designs.'

Meanwhile let us beware of passing from one injurious extreme to another. Much of what has been usually understood by the love of our country is highly excellent and valuable, though perhaps nothing that can be brought within the strict interpretation of the phrase. A wise man will not fail to be the votary of liberty and equality. He will be ready to exert himself in their defence wherever they exist. It cannot be a matter of indifference to him, when his own liberty and that of other men with whose excellence and capabilities he has the best opportunity of being acquainted, are involved in the event of the struggle to be made. But his attachment will be to the cause, and not to the country. Wherever there are men who understand the value of political justice and are prepared to assert it, that is his country. Wherever he can most contribute to the diffusion of these principles and the real happiness of mankind, that is his country. Nor does he desire for any country any other benefit than justice.

To apply these principles to the subject of war. And, before that application can be adequately made, it is necessary to recollect for a moment the force of the term.

Because individuals were liable to error, and suffered their apprehensions of justice to be perverted by a bias in favour of themselves, government was instituted. Because nations were susceptible of a similar weakness, and could find no sufficient umpire to whom to appeal, war was introduced. Men were induced deliberately to seek each other's lives, and to adjudge the controversies between them, not according to the dictates of reason and justice, but as either should prove most successful in devastation and murder. This was no doubt in the first instance the extremity of exasperation and rage. But it has since been converted into a trade. One part of the nation pays another part to murder and be murdered in their stead; and the most trivial causes, a supposed insult or a sally of youthful ambition, have sufficed to deluge provinces with blood.

We can have no adequate idea of this evil, unless we visit, at least in imagination, a field of battle. Here men deliberately destroy each other by thousands without any resentment against or even knowledge of each other. The plain is strewed with death in all its various forms. Anguish and wounds display the diversified modes in which they can torment the human frame. Towns are burned, ships are blown up in the air while the mangled limbs descend on every side, the fields are laid desolate, the wives of the inhabitants exposed to brutal insult, and their children driven forth to hunger and nakedness. It would be despicable to mention, along with these scenes of horror, and the total subversion of all ideas of moral justice they must occasion in the auditors and spectators, the immense treasures which are wrung in the form of taxes from those inhabitants whose residence is at a distance from the scene.

After this enumeration we may venture to enquire what are the justifiable causes and rules of war.

It is not a justifiable reason, 'that we imagine our own people would be rendered more cordial and orderly, if we could find a neighbour with whom to quarrel, and who might serve as a touchstone to try the characters and dispositions of individuals among ourselves.'[1] We are not at liberty to have recourse to the most complicated and atrocious of all mischiefs, in the way of an experiment.

It is not a justifiable reason, 'that we have been exposed to certain insults, and that tyrants perhaps have delighted in treating with contempt the citizens of our happy state who have visited their dominions.' Government ought to protect the tranquillity of those who reside within the sphere of its functions; but, if individuals think proper to visit other countries, they must then be delivered over to the protection of general reason. Some proportion must be observed between the evil of which we complain, and the evil which the nature of the proposed remedy inevitably includes.

It is not a justifiable reason, 'that our neighbour is preparing or menacing hostilities.' If we be obliged to prepare in our turn, the inconvenience is only equal; and it is not to be believed, that a despotic country is capable of more exertion than a free one, when the task incumbent on the latter is indispensible precaution.

It has sometimes been held to be sound reasoning upon this subject, 'that we ought not to yield little things, which may not in themselves be

---

[1] The reader will easily perceive that the pretences by which the people of France were instigated to a declaration of war in April 1792 were in the author's mind in this place. Nor will a few lines be mispent in this note in stating the judgment of the impartial observer upon the wantonness with which they have appeared ready upon different occasions to proceed to extremities.* If policy were in question, it might be doubted, whether the confederacy of kings would ever have been brought into action against them, had it not been for their precipitation; and it might be asked, what impression they must expect to be made upon the minds of other states by their intemperate commission of hostility? But that strict justice, which prescribes to us, never by a hasty interference to determine the doubtful balance in favour of murder, is a superior consideration, in comparison with which policy is unworthy so much as to be named.

sufficiently valuable to authorise this tremendous appeal, because a disposition to yield only invites farther experiments.'[1] Far otherwise; at least when the character of such a nation is sufficiently understood. A people that will not contend for nominal and trivial objects, that maintains the precise line of unalterable justice, and that does not fail to be moved at the moment that it ought to be moved, is not the people that its neighbours will delight to urge to extremities.

'The vindication of national honour' is a very insufficient reason for hostilities. True honour is to be found only in integrity and justice. It has been doubted how far a view to reputation ought in matters of inferior moment to be permitted to influence the conduct of individuals; but, let the case of individuals be decided as it may, reputation, considered as a separate motive in the instance of nations, can never be justifiable. In individuals it seems as if I might, consistently with the utmost real integrity, be so misconstrued and misrepresented by others, as to render my efforts at usefulness almost always abortive. But this reason does not apply to the case of nations. Their real story cannot easily be suppressed. Usefulness and public spirit in relation to them chiefly belong to the transactions of their members among themselves; and their influence in the transactions of neighbouring nations is a consideration evidently subordinate. The question which respects the justifiable causes of war, would be liable to few difficulties, if we were accustomed, along with the word, strongly to call up to our minds the thing which that word is intended to represent.

Accurately considered, there can probably be but two justifiable causes of war, and one of them is among those which the logic of sovereigns and the law of nations, as it has been termed, proscribe: these are the defence of our own liberty and of the liberty of others. The well known objection to the latter of these cases, is, 'that one nation ought not to interfere in the internal transactions of another;' and we can only wonder that so absurd an objection should have been admitted so long. The true principle, under favour of which this false one has been permitted to pass current, is, 'that no people and no individual are fit for the possession of any immunity, till they understand the nature of that immunity, and desire to possess it.' It may therefore be an unjustifiable undertaking to force a nation to be free. But, when the people themselves desire it, it is virtue and duty to assist them in the acquisition. This principle is capable of being abused by men of ambition and intrigue; but, accurately considered, the very same argument that

---

[1] This pretence is sustained in Paley's Moral and Political Philosophy, Book VI, Chap. XII.

should induce me to exert myself for the liberties of my own country, is equally cogent, so far as my opportunities and ability extend, with respect to the liberties of any other country. But the morality that ought to govern the conduct of individuals and of nations is in all cases the same.

CHAPTER XVII

OF THE OBJECT OF WAR

The repelling an invader.—Not reformation—not restraint—not indemnification.—Nothing can be a sufficient object of war that is not a sufficient cause for beginning it.—Reflections on the balance of power.

LET us pass from the causes to the objects of war. As defence is the only legitimate cause, the object pursued, reasoning from this principle, will be circumscribed within very narrow limits. It can extend no farther than the repelling the enemy from our borders. It is perhaps desirable that, in addition to this, he should afford some proof that he does not propose immediately to renew his invasion; but this, though desirable, affords no sufficient apology for the continuance of hostilities. Declarations of war and treaties of peace are inventions of a barbarous age, and would never have grown into established usages, if war had customarily gone no farther than to the limits of defence.

It will hereafter appear that what has been termed the criminal justice of nations within themselves, has only two legitimate objects, restraint and reformation. Neither of these objects applies to the case of war between independent states; and therefore ideas of criminal justice are altogether foreign to this subject. War, as we have already seen, perhaps never originates on the offending side in the sentiments of a nation, but of a comparatively small number of individuals: and, if it were other-- wise, it is not in a reciprocation of hostilities that good sense would teach us to look for the means of reform.

Restraint appears to be sometimes necessary with respect to the offenders that exist in the midst of a community, because it is the property of such offenders to assault us with unexpected violence; but nations cannot move with such secrecy as to make an unforeseen attack an object of considerable apprehension. The only effectual means of restraint in this last case is by disabling, impoverishing and depopulating the country of our adversaries; and, if we recollected that they were men as well as ourselves, and the great mass of them innocent of the quarrel against us, we should be little likely to consider these expedients with complacency.

Indemnification is another object of war which the same mode of reasoning will not fail to condemn. The true culprits can never be discovered, and the attempt would only serve to confound the innocent and the guilty: not to mention that, nations having no common umpire, the reverting, in the conclusion of every war, to the justice of the original quarrel and the indemnification to which the parties were entitled, would be a means of rendering the controversy endless. The question respecting the justifiable objects of war would be liable to few difficulties, if we laid it down as a maxim, that, as often as the principle or object of a war already in existence was changed, this was to be considered as equivalent to the commencement of a new war. This maxim impartially applied would not fail to condemn objects of prevention, indemnification and restraint.

The celebrated topic of the balance of power is a mixed consideration, having sometimes been proposed as the cause for beginning a war, and sometimes as an object to be pursued in a war already begun. A war, undertaken to maintain the balance of power, may be either of defence, as to protect a people who are oppressed, or of prevention to counteract new acquisitions, or to reduce the magnitude of old possessions. We shall be in little danger of error however, if we pronounce wars undertaken to maintain the balance of power to be universally unjust. If any people be oppressed, it is our duty, as we have already said, as far as our ability extends, to fly to their succour. But it would be well if in such cases we called our interference by the name which justice prescribes, and sought against the injustice, and not the power. All hostilities against a neighbouring people, because they are powerful, or because we impute to them evil designs which they have not yet begun to carry in execution, are an enormous violation of every principle of morality. If one nation chuse to be governed by the sovereign or an individual allied to the sovereign of another, as seems to have been the case of the people of Spain upon the extinction of the elder branch of the house of Austria, we may endeavour to enlighten them on the subject of government and imbue them with principles of liberty, but it is an execrable piece of tyranny to tell them, 'You shall exchange the despot you love for the despot you hate, on account of certain remote consequences we apprehend from the accession of the former.' The pretence of the balance of power has in a multitude of instances served as a veil to the intrigue of courts, but it would be easy to show that the present independence of the different states of Europe has in no instance been materially supported by the wars undertaken for that purpose. The fascination of a people desiring to become the appendage of a splendid despotism can rarely occur, and might perhaps easily be counteracted by peaceable means and the dissemination of a few of the most obvious truths. The defence of a people struggling with oppression must always be just, with this single limitation, that the entering into it without urgent need on their part, would unnecessarily spread the calamities of war, and diminish those energies, the exertion of which would contribute to their virtue and happiness. Add to this, that the object itself, the independence of the different states of Europe, is of an equivocal nature. The despotism, which at present prevails among them, is certainly not so excellent as to make us very anxious for its preservation. The press is an engine of so admirable a nature for the destruction of despotism, as to elude the sagacity perhaps of the most vigilant police; and the internal checks upon freedom in a mighty empire and distant provinces, can scarcely be expected to be equally active with those of a petty tyrant. The reasoning will surely be good with respect to war, which has already been employed upon the subject of government, that an instrument, evil in its own nature, ought never to be selected as the means of promoting our purpose, in any case in which selection can be practised.

CHAPTER XVIII

OF THE CONDUCT OF WAR

Offensive operations.—Fortifications.—General action.—Stratagem.— Military contributions.—Capture of mercantile vessels.—Naval war.— Humanity.—Military obedience.—Foreign possessions.

ANOTHER topic respecting war, which it is of importance to consider in this place, relates to the mode of conducting it. Upon this article our judgments will be greatly facilitated by a recollection of the principles already established, first, that no war is justifiable but a war purely defensive; and secondly, that a war already begun is liable to change its character in this respect, the moment the object pursued in it becomes in any degree varied. From these principles it follows as a direct corollary, that it is never allowable to make an expedition into the provinces of the enemy, unless for the purpose of assisting its oppressed inhabitants. It is scarcely necessary to add that all false casuistry respecting the application of this exception would be particularly odious; and that it is better undisguisedly to avow the corrupt principles of policy by which we conduct ourselves, than hypocritically to claim the praise of better principles, which we fail not to wrest to the justification of whatever we desire. The case of relieving the inhabitants of our enemy's territory and their desire of obtaining relief ought to be extremely unequivocal; we shall be in great danger of misapprehension on the subject, when the question comes under the form of immediate benefit to ourselves; and above all we must recollect that human blood is not to be shed upon a precarious experiment.

The little advantages of war that might be gained by offensive operations will be abundantly compensated, by the character of magnanimous forbearance that a rigid adherence to defence will exhibit, and the effects that character will produce upon foreign nations and upon our own people. Great unanimity at home can scarcely fail to be the effect of severe political justice. The enemy who penetrates into our country, wherever he meets a man, will meet a foe. Every obstacle will oppose itself to his progress, while every thing will be friendly and assisting to our own forces. He will scarcely be able to procure the slightest intelligence, or understand in any case his relative situation. The principles of defensive war are so simple as to procure an almost infallible success. Fortifications are a very equivocal species of protection, and will oftener be of advantage to the enemy, by being first taken, and then converted into magazines for his armies. A moving force on the contrary, if it only hovered about his march, and avoided general action, would always preserve the real superiority. The great engine of military success or miscarriage, is the article of provisions; and the farther the enemy advanced into our country, the more easy would it be to cut off his supply; at the same time that, so long as we avoided general action, any decisive success on his part would be impossible. These principles, if rigidly practised, would soon be so well understood, that the entering in a hostile manner the country of a neighbouring nation would come to be regarded as the infallible destruction of the invading army. Perhaps no people were ever conquered at their own doors, unless they were first betrayed either by divisions among themselves or by the abject degeneracy of their character. The more we come to understand of the nature of justice, the more it will show itself to be stronger than a host of foes. Men, whose bosoms are truly pervaded with this principle, cannot perhaps be other than invincible. Among the various examples of excellence in almost every department that ancient Greece has bequeathed us, the most conspicuous is her resistance with a handful of men against three millions of invaders.

One branch of the art of war, as well as of every other human art, has hitherto consisted in deceit. If the principles of this work be built upon a sufficiently solid basis, the practice of deceit ought in all instances to be condemned, whether it proceed from false tenderness to our friends, or from a desire to hasten the downfal of injustice. Vice is neither the most allowable nor effectual weapon with which to contend against vice. Deceit is not less deceit, whether the falshood be formed into words or be conveyed through the medium of fictitious appearances. We should no more allow ourselves to mislead the enemy by false intelligence or treacherous ambuscade, than by the breach of our declarations, or feigned demonstrations of friendship. There is no essential difference between throwing open our arms to embrace them, and advancing towards them with neutral colours or covering ourselves with a defile or a wood. By the practice of surprise and deceit we shall oftenest cut off their straggling parties and shed most blood. By an open display of our force we shall prevent detachments from being made, shall intercept the possibility of supply without unnecessary bloodshed, and there seems no reason to believe that our ultimate success will be less certain. Why should war be made the science of disingenuousness and mystery, when the plain dictates of good sense would answer all its legitimate purposes? The first principle of defence is firmness and vigilance. The second perhaps, which is not less immediately connected with the end to be attained, is frankness and the open disclosure of our purpose even to our enemies. What astonishment, admiration and terror would this conduct excite in those with whom we had to contend? What confidence and magnanimity would accompany it in our own bosoms? Why should not war, as a step towards its complete abolition, be brought to such perfection, as that the purposes of the enemy might be utterly baffled without firing a musket or drawing a sword?

Another corollary not less inevitable from the principles which have been delivered, is that the operations of war should be limited as accurately as possible to the generating no farther evils than defence inevitably requires. Ferocity ought carefully to be banished from it. Calamity should as entirely as possible be prevented to every individual who is not actually in arms, and whose fate has no immediate reference to the event of the war. This principle condemns the levying military contributions, and the capture of mercantile vessels. Each of these atrocities would be in another way precluded by the doctrine of simple defence. We should scarcely think of levying such contributions, if we never attempted to pass the limits of our own territory; and every species of naval war would perhaps be proscribed.

The utmost benevolence ought to be practised towards our enemies. We should refrain from the unnecessary destruction of a single life, and afford every humane accommodation to the unfortunate. The bulk of those against whom we have to contend are comparatively speaking innocent of the projected injustice. Those by whom it has been most assiduously fostered are entitled to our kindness as men, and to our compassion as mistaken. It has already appeared that all the ends of punishment are foreign to the business of war. It has appeared that the genuine melioration of war, in consequence of which it may be expected absolutely to cease, is by gradually disarming it of its ferocity. The horrors of war have sometimes been apologised by a supposition that the more intolerable it was made, the more quickly would it cease to infest the world. But the direct contrary of this is the truth. Severities do but beget severities in return. It is a most mistaken way of teaching men to feel that they are brothers, by imbuing their minds with unrelenting hatred. The truly just man cannot feel animosity, and is therefore little likely to act as if he did.

Having examined the conduct of war as it respects our enemies let us next consider it in relation to the various descriptions of persons by whom it is to be supported. We have seen how little a just and upright war stands in need of secrecy. The plans for conducting a campaign, instead of being, as artifice and ambition have hitherto made them, inextricably complicated, will probably be reduced to two or three variations, suited to the different circumstances that can possibly occur in a war of simple defence. The better these plans are known to the enemy, the more advantageous will it be to the resisting party. Hence it follows that the principles of implicit faith and military obedience will be no longer necessary. Soldiers will cease to be machines. The essential circumstance that constitutes men machines in this sense of the word, is not the uniformity of their motions, when they see the reasonableness of that uniformity. It is their performing any motion, or engaging in any action, the object and utility of which they do not clearly understand. It is true that in every state of human society there will be men of an intellectual capacity much superior to their neighbours. But defensive war, and probably every other species of operation in which it will be necessary that many individuals should act in concert, will perhaps be found so simple in their operations, as not to exceed the apprehension of the most common capacities. It is ardently to be desired that the time should arrive, when no man should lend his assistance to any operation, without at the same time exercising his judgment respecting the honesty and the expected event of that operation.

The principles here delivered on the conduct of war lead the mind to a very interesting subject, that of foreign and distant territories. Whatever may be the value of these principles considered in themselves, they become altogether nugatory the moment the idea of foreign dependencies is admitted. But in reality what argument possessing the smallest degree of plausibility can be alledged in favour of that idea? The mode in which dependencies are acquired, must be either conquest, cession or colonization. The first of these no true moralist or politician will attempt to defend. The second is to be considered as the same thing in substance as the first, but with less openness and ingenuity. Colonization, which is by much the most specious pretence, is however no more than a pretence. Are these provinces held in a state of dependence for our own sake or for theirs? If for our own, we must recollect this is still an usurpation, and that justice requires we should yield to others what we demand for ourselves, the privilege of being governed by the dictates of their own reason. If for theirs, they must be told, that it is the business of associations of men to defend themselves, or, if that be impracticable, to look for support to the confederation of their neighbours. They must be told, that defence against foreign enemies is a very inferior consideration, and that no people were ever either wise or happy who were not left to the fair development of their inherent powers. Can any thing be more absurd than for the West India islands for example to be defended by fleets and armies to be transported across the Atlantic? The support of a mother country extended to her colonies, is much oftener a means of involving them in danger, than of contributing to their security. The connexion is maintained by vanity on one side and prejudice on the other. If they must sink into a degrading state of dependence, how will they be the worse in belonging to one state rather than another? Perhaps the first step towards putting a stop to this fruitful source of war, would be to annihilate that monopoly of trade which all enlightened reasoners at present agree to condemn, and to throw open the ports of our colonies to all the world. The principle which will not fail to lead us right upon this subject of foreign dependencies, as well as upon a thousand others, is, that that attribute, however splendid, is not really beneficial to a nation, that is not beneficial to the great mass of individuals of which the nation consists.

CHAPTER XIX

OF MILITARY ESTABLISHMENTS AND TREATIES

A country may look for its defence either to a standing army or an universal militia.—The former condemned.—The latter objected to as of immoral tendency—as unnecessary—either in respect to courage—or discipline.—Of a commander.—Of treaties.

THE last topic which it may be necessary to examine as to the subject of war, is the conduct it becomes us to observe respecting it in a time of peace. This article may be distributed into two heads, military establishments and treaties of alliance.

If military establishments in time of peace be judged proper, their purpose may be effected either by consigning the practice of military discipline to a certain part of the community, or by making every man whose age is suitable for that purpose a soldier.*

The preferableness of the latter of these methods to the former is obvious. The man that is merely a soldier, must always be uncommonly depraved. War in his case inevitably degenerates from the necessary precautions of a personal defence, into a trade by which a man sells his skill in murder and the safety of his existence for a pecuniary recompense. The man that is merely a soldier, ceases to be, in the same sense as his neighbours, a citizen. He is cut off from the rest of the community, and has sentiments and a rule of judgment peculiar to himself. He considers his countrymen as indebted to him for their security; and, by an unavoidable transition of reasoning, believes that in a double sense they are at his mercy. On the other hand that every citizen should exercise in his turn the functions of a soldier, seems peculiarly favourable to that confidence in himself and in the resources of his country, which it is so desirable he should entertain. It is congenial to that equality, which must subsist in an eminent degree before mankind in general can be either virtuous or wise. And it seems to multiply the powers of defence in a country, so as to render the idea of its falling under the yoke of an enemy in the utmost degree improbable.

There are reasons however that oblige us to doubt respecting the propriety of cultivating under any form the system of military discipline in time of peace. It is in this respect with nations as it is with individuals. The man that with a pistol bullet is sure of his mark, or that excels his contemporaries in the exercise of the sword, can hardly escape those obliquities of understanding which these accomplishments are calculated to nourish. It is not to be expected that he should entertain all that confidence in reason and distaste of violence which severe truth prescribes. It is beyond all controversy that war, though the practice of it under the present state of the human species may in some instances be unavoidable, is an idea pregnant with calamity and vice. It cannot be a matter of indifference, for the human mind to be systematically familiarised to thoughts of murder and desolation. The disciple of mere reason would not fail at the sight of a musket or a sword to be impressed with sentiments of abhorrence. Why expel these sentiments? Why connect the discipline of death with ideas of festivity and splendour; which will inevitably happen, if the citizens, without oppression, are accustomed to be drawn out to encampments and reviews? Is it possible that he who has not learned to murder his neighbour with a grace, is imperfect in the trade of man?

If it be replied, 'that the generating of error is not inseparable from military discipline, and that men may at some time be sufficiently guarded against the abuse, even while they are taught the use of arms;' it will be found upon reflection that this argument is of little weight. Though error be not unalterably connected with the science of arms, it will for a long time remain so. When men are sufficiently improved to be able to handle familiarly and with application of mind the instruments of death without injury, they will also be sufficiently improved to be able to master any study with much greater facility than at present, and consequently the cultivation of the art military in time of peace will have still fewer inducements to recommend it to our choice.—To apply these considerations to the present situation of mankind.

We have already seen that the system of a standing army is altogether indefensible, and that an universal militia is a much more formidable defence, as well as infinitely more agreeable to the principles of justice and political happiness. It remains to be seen what would be the real situation of a nation surrounded by other nations in the midst of which standing armies were maintained, which should nevertheless upon principle wholly neglect the art military in seasons of peace. In such a nation it will probably be admitted, that, so far as relates to mere numbers, an army may be raised upon the spur of occasion, nearly as soon as in a nation the citizens of which had been taught to be soldiers. But this army, though numerous, would be in want of many of those principles of combination and activity which are of material importance in a day of battle. There is indeed included in the supposition, that the internal state of this people is more equal and free than that of the people by whom they are invaded. This will infallibly be the case in a comparison between a people with a standing army and a people without one; between a people who can be brought blindly and wickedly to the invasion of their peaceful neighbours, and a people who will not be induced to fight but in their own defence. The latter therefore will be obliged to compare the state of society and government in their own country and among their neighbours, and will not fail to be impressed with great ardour in defence of the inestimable advantages they possess. Ardour, even in the day of battle, might prove sufficient. A body of men, however undisciplined, whom nothing could induce to quit the field, would infallibly be victorious over their veteran adversaries, who, under the circumstances of the case, could not possibly have an accurate conception of the object for which they were fighting, and therefore could not entertain an invincible love for it. It is not certain that activity and discipline opposed to ardour, have even a tendency to turn the balance of slaughter against the party that wants them. Their great advantage consists in their power over the imagination to astonish, to terrify and confound. An intrepid courage in the party thus assailed would soon convert them from sources of despair into objects of contempt.

But it would be extremely unwise in us to have no other resource but in the chance of this intrepidity. A resource much surer and more agreeable to justice is in recollecting that the war of which we treat is a war of defence. Battle is not the object of such a war. An army, which, like that of Fabius,* by keeping on the hills, or by whatever other means, rendered it impracticable for the enemy to force them to an engagement, might look with scorn upon his impotent efforts to enslave the country. One advantage included in such a system of war is, that, as its very essence is protraction, the defending army might in a short time be rendered as skilful as the assailants. Discipline, like every other art, has been represented by vain and interested men as surrounded with imaginary difficulties, but is in reality exceedingly simple; and would be learned much more effectually in the midst of real war than in the puppet show exhibitions of a period of peace.

It is desirable indeed that we should have a commander of considerable skill, or rather of considerable wisdom, to reduce this patient and indefatigable system into practice. This is of much more importance than the mere discipline of the ranks. But the nature of military wisdom has been greatly misrepresented. Experience in this, as well as in other arts, has been unreasonably magnified, and the general power of a cultivated mind been thrown into shade. It will probably be no long time before this quackery of professional men will be thoroughly exploded.

How perpetually do we meet with those whom experience finds incorrigible; while it is recorded of one of the greatest generals of antiquity, that he set out for his appointment wholly unacquainted with his art, and was indebted for that skill, which broke out immediately upon his arrival, to the assiduousness of his enquiries, and a careful examination of those writers by whom the art had most successfully been illustrated?[1] At all events it will be admitted, that the maintenance of a standing army or the perpetual discipline of a nation is a very dear price to pay for the purchase of a general, as well as that the purchase would be extremely precarious, if we were even persuaded to consent to the condition. It may perhaps be true, though this is not altogether clear, that a nation by whom military discipline was wholly neglected would be exposed to some disadvantage. In that case it becomes us to weigh the neglect and cultivation together, and to cast the balance on that side to which upon mature examination it shall appear to belong.

A second article which belongs to the military system in a season of peace is that of treaties of alliance. This subject may easily be dispatched. Treaties of alliance are in all cases wrong, in the first place, because all absolute promises are wrong, and neither individuals nor bodies of men ought to preclude themselves from the benefit of future improvement and deliberation. Secondly, they are wrong, because they are in all cases nugatory. Governments, and public men, will not, and ought not to hold themselves bound to the injury of the concerns they conduct, because a parchment, to which they or their predecessors were a party, requires it at their hands. If the concert demanded in time of need, approve itself to their judgment or correspond with their inclination, it will be yielded, though they were under no previous engagement for that purpose. Treaties of alliance serve to no other end, than to exhibit by their violation an appearance of profligacy and vice, which unfortunately becomes too often a powerful encouragement to the inconsistency of individuals. Add to this, that, if alliances were engines as powerful, as they are really impotent, they could seldom be of use to a nation uniformly adhering to the principles of justice. They would be useless, because they are in reality ill calculated for any other purposes than those of ambition. They might be pernicious, because it would be beneficial for nations as for individuals to look for resources at home, instead of depending upon the precarious compassion of their neighbours.

---

[1] *Ciceronis Lucullus, sive Academicorum Liber Secundus, init.**

CHAPTER XX

OF DEMOCRACY AS CONNECTED WITH THE TRANSACTIONS OF WAR

External affairs are of subordinate consideration.—Application.—Farther objections to democracy—1. it is incompatible with secrecy—this proved to be an excellence—2. its movements are too slow—3. too precipitate.—Evils of anarchy considered.

HAVING thus endeavoured to reduce the subject of war to its true principles, it is time that we should recur to the maxim delivered at our entrance upon this subject, that individuals are every thing, and society, abstracted from the individuals of which it is composed, nothing. An immediate consequence of this maxim is, that the internal affairs of the society are entitled to our principal attention, and the external are matters of inferior and subordinate consideration. The internal affairs are subjects of perpetual and hourly concern, the external are periodical and precarious only. That every man should be impressed with the consciousness of his independence, and rescued from the influence of extreme want and artificial desires, are purposes the most interesting that can suggest themselves to the human mind; but the life of man might pass, in a state uncorrupted by ideal passions, without its tranquillity being so much as once disturbed by foreign invasions. The influence that a certain number of millions, born under the same climate with ourselves, and known by the common appellation of English or French, shall possess over the administrative councils of their neighbour millions, is a circumstance of much too airy and distant consideration, to deserve to be made a principal object in the institutions of any people. The best influence we can exert is that of a sage and upright example.

If therefore it should appear that of these two articles, internal and external affairs, one must in some degree be sacrificed to the other, and that a democracy will in certain respects be less fitted for the affairs of war than some other species of government, good sense would not hesitate between these alternatives. We should have sufficient reason to be satisfied, if, together with the benefits of justice and virtue at home, we had no reason to despair of our safety from abroad. A confidence in this article will seldom deceive us, if our countrymen, however little trained to formal rules and the uniformity of mechanism, have studied the profession of man, understand his attributes and his nature, and have their necks unbroken to the yoke of blind credulity and abject submission. Such men, inured, as we are now supposing them, to a rational state of society, will be full of calm confidence and penetrating activity, and these qualities will stand them in stead of a thousand lessons in the school of military mechanism. If democracy can be proved adequate to wars of defence, and other governments be better fitted for wars of a different sort, this would be an argument, not of its imperfection, but its merit.

It has been one of the objections to the ability of a democracy in war, 'that it cannot keep secrets. The legislative assembly, whether it possess the initiative, or a power of control only, in executive affairs, will be perpetually calling for papers, plans and information, cross examining ministers, and sifting the policy and the justice of public undertakings. How shall we be able to cope with an enemy, if he know precisely the points we mean to attack, the state of our fortifications, and the strength and weakness of our armies? How shall we manage our treaties with skill and address, if he be informed precisely of the sentiments of our mind and have access to the instructions of our ambassadors?'

It happens in this instance, that that which the objection attacks as the vice of democracy, is one of its most essential excellencies. The trick of a mysterious carriage is the prolific parent of every vice; and it is an eminent advantage incident to democracy, that, though the proclivity of mind has hitherto reconciled this species of administration in some degree to the keeping of secrets, yet its inherent tendency is to annihilate them. Why should disingenuity and concealment be more virtuous or more beneficial in nations than in individuals? Why should that, which every man of an elevated mind would disdain in his personal character, be entitled to more lenity and toleration, if undertaken by him as a minister of state? Who is there that sees not, that this inextricable labyrinth was artfully invented, lest the people should understand their own affairs, and, understanding, become inclined to conduct them? With respect to treaties, it is to be suspected that they are in all instances superfluous. But, if public engagements ought to be entered into, what essential difference is there between the governments of two countries endeavouring to overreach each other, and the buyer and seller in any private transaction adopting a similar proceeding?

This whole system proceeds upon the idea of national grandeur and glory, as if in reality these words had any specific meaning. These contemptible objects, these airy names, have from the earliest page of history been made the ostensible colour for the most pernicious undertakings. Let us take a specimen of their value from the most innocent and laudable pursuits. If I aspire to be a great poet, a great historian, so far as I am influenced by the dictates of reason, it is that I may be useful to mankind, and not that I may do honour to my country. Is Newton the better because he was an Englishman, or Galileo* the worse because he was an Italian? Who can endure to put this high sounding nonsense in the balance against the best interests of mankind, which will always suffer a mortal wound, when dexterity, artifice and concealment are made topics of admiration and applause? The understanding and the virtues of mankind will always keep pace with the manly simplicity of their designs and the undisguised integrity of their hearts.

It has farther been objected to a democratical state in its transactions with foreign powers, 'that it is incapable of those rapid and decisive proceedings, which in some situations have so eminent a tendency to ensure success.' If by this objection it be understood that a democratical state is ill fitted for dexterity and surprise, the rapidity of an assassin, it has already received a sufficient answer. If it be meant that the regularity of its proceedings may ill accord with the impatience of a neighbouring despot, and, like the Jews of old, we desire a king 'that we may be like the other nations,' this is a very unreasonable requisition. A just and impartial reasoner will be little desirous to see his country figure high in the diplomatical roll, deeply involved in the intrigues of nations, and assiduously courted by foreign princes as the instrument of their purposes. A more groundless and absurd passion cannot seize upon any people than that of glory, the preferring their influence in the affairs of Europe to their internal happiness and virtue, for these objects will perpetually counteract and clash with each other.

But democracy is by no means necessarily of a phlegmatic character, or obliged to take every proposition that is made to it, *ad referendum*, for the consideration of certain primary assemblies, like the states of Holland. The first principle in the institution of government itself, is the necessity, under the present imperfections of mankind, of having some man or body of men to act on the part of the whole. Wherever government subsists, the authority of the individual must be in some degree superseded. It does not therefore seem unreasonable for a representative national assembly to exercise in certain cases a discretionary power. Those privileges, which are vested in individuals selected out of the mass by the voice of their fellows, and who will speedily return to a private station, are by no means liable to the same objections, as the exclusive and unaccommodating privileges of an aristocracy. Representation, together with many disadvantages, has this benefit, that it is able impartially and with discernment to call upon the most enlightened part of the nation to deliberate for the whole, and may thus generate a degree of wisdom, a refined penetration of sentiment, which it would have been unreasonable to expect as the result of primary assemblies.

A third objection more frequently offered against democratical government is, 'that it is incapable of that mature and deliberate proceeding which is alone suitable to the decision of such important concerns. Multitudes of men have appeared subject to fits of occasional insanity: they act from the influence of rage, suspicion and despair: they are liable to be hurried into the most unjustifiable extremes by the artful practices of an impostor.' One of the most obvious answers to this objection is, that we must not judge of a sovereign people by the example of the rude multitude in despotic states. We must not judge of men born to the exercise of rational functions, by the example of men rendered mad with oppression, and drunk with the acquisition of new born power. Another answer is, that for all men to share the privileges of all is the law of our nature and the dictate of justice. The case in this instance is parallel to that of an individual in his private concerns. It is true that, while each man is master of his own affairs, he is liable to all the starts of passion. He is attacked by the allurements of temptation and the tempest of rage, and may be guilty of the most fatal errors, before reflection and judgment come forward to his aid. But this is no sufficient reason for depriving men of the direction of their own concerns. We should endeavour to make them wise, and not to make them slaves. The depriving men of their self-government is in the first place unjust, while in the second this self-government, imperfect as it is, will be found more salutary than any thing that can be substituted in its place.

The nature of anarchy has never been sufficiently understood. It is undoubtedly a horrible calamity, but it is less horrible than despotism. Where anarchy has slain its hundreds, despotism has sacrificed millions upon millions, with this only effect, to perpetuate the ignorance, the vices and the misery of mankind. Anarchy is a short lived mischief, while despotism is all but immortal. It is unquestionably a dreadful remedy, for the people to yield to all their furious passions, till the spectacle of their effects gives strength to recovering reason: but, though it be a dreadful remedy, it is a sure one. No idea can be supposed, more pregnant with absurdity, than that of a whole people taking arms against each other till they are all exterminated. It is to despotism that anarchy is indebted for its sting. If despotism were not ever watchful for its prey, and mercilessly prepared to take advantage of the errors of mankind, this ferment, like so many others, being left to itself, would subside into an even, clear and delightful calm. Reason is at all times progressive. Nothing can give permanence to error, that does not convert it into an establishment, and arm it with powers to resist an invasion.

CHAPTER XXI

OF THE COMPOSITION OF GOVERNMENT

Houses of assembly.—*This institution unjust.*—*Deliberate proceeding the proper antidote.*—*Separation of legislative and executive power consid-ered.*—*Superior importance of the latter.*—*Functions of ministers.*

ONE of the articles which has been most eagerly insisted on by the advocates of complexity in political institutions, is that of 'checks, by which a rash proceeding may be prevented, and the provisions under which mankind have hitherto lived with tranquillity, may not be reversed without mature deliberation.' We will suppose that the evils of monarchy and aristocracy are by this time too notorious to incline the speculative enquirer to seek for a remedy in either of these. 'Yet it is possible, without the institution of privileged orders, to find means that may answer a similar purpose in this respect. The representatives of the people may be distributed for example into two assemblies; they may be chosen with this particular view to constitute an upper and a lower house, and may be distinguished from each other, either by various qualifications of age or fortune, or by being chosen by a greater or smaller number of electors, or for a shorter or longer term.'

To every inconvenience that experience can produce or imagination suggest there is probably an appropriate remedy. This remedy may either be sought in the dictates of reason or in artificial combinations encroaching upon those dictates. Which are we to prefer? There is no doubt that the institution of two houses of assembly is contrary to the primary dictates of reason and justice. How shall a nation be governed? Agreeably to the opinions of its inhabitants, or in opposition to them? Agreeably to them undoubtedly. Not, as we cannot too often repeat, because their opinion is a standard of truth, but because, however erro-neous that opinion may be, we can do no better. There is no effectual way of improving the institutions of any people, but by enlightening their understandings. He that endeavours to maintain the authority of any sentiment, not by argument, but by force, may intend a benefit, but really inflicts an extreme injury. To suppose that truth can be instilled through any medium but that of its intrinsic evidence, is the most flagrant of all errors. He that believes the most fundamental proposition through the influence of authority, does not believe a truth, but a falshood. The proposition itself he does not understand, for thoroughly to understand it, is to perceive the degree of evidence with which it is accompanied; thoroughly to understand; it is to know the full meaning of its terms, and, by necessary consequence, to perceive in what respects they agree or disagree with each other. All that he believes is, that it is very proper he should submit to usurpation and injustice.

It was imputed to the late government of France, that, when they called an assembly of notables in 1787,* they contrived, by dividing the assembly into seven distinct corps, and not allowing them to vote otherwise than in these corps, that the vote of fifty persons should be capable of operating as if they were a majority in an assembly of one hundred and forty-four. It would have been still worse, if it had been ordained that no measure should be considered as the measure of the assembly, unless it were adopted by the unanimous voice of all the corps: eleven persons might then, in voting a negative, have operated as a majority of one hundred and forty-four. This may serve as a specimen of the effects of distributing a representative national assembly into two or more houses. Nor should we suffer ourselves to be deceived under the pretence of the innocence of a negative in comparison with an affirmative. In a country in which universal truth was already established, there would be little need of a representative assembly. In a country into whose institutions error has insinuated itself, a negative upon the repeal of those errors is the real affirmative.

The institution of two houses of assembly is the direct method to divide a nation against itself. One of these houses will in a greater or less degree be the asylum of usurpation, monopoly and privilege. Parties would expire as soon as they were born, in a country where opposition of sentiments and a struggle of interests were not allowed to assume the formalities of distinct institution.

Meanwhile a species of check perfectly simple, and which appears sufficiently adequate to the purpose, suggests itself in the idea of a slow and deliberate proceeding which the representative assembly should prescribe to itself. Perhaps no proceeding of this assembly should have the force of a general regulation till it had undergone five or six successive discussions in the assembly, or till the expiration of one month from the period of its being proposed. Something like this is the order of the English house of commons,* nor does it appear to be by any means among the worst features of our constitution. A system like this would be sufficiently analogous to the proceedings of a wise individual, who certainly would not wish to determine upon the most important concerns of his life without a severe examination, and still less would omit this examination, if his decision were destined to be a rule for the conduct and a criterion to determine upon the rectitude of other men.

Perhaps, as we have said, this slow and gradual proceeding ought in no instance to be dispensed with by the national representative assembly. This seems to be the true line between the functions of the assembly and its ministers. It would give a character of gravity and good sense to this central authority, that would tend eminently to fix the confidence of the citizens in its wisdom and justice. The mere votes of the assembly, as distinguished from its acts and decrees, might serve as an encouragement to the public functionaries, and as affording a certain degree of hope respecting the speedy cure of those evils of which the public might complain; but they should never be allowed to be pleaded as the legal justification of any action. A precaution like this would not only tend to prevent the fatal consequences of any precipitate judgment of the assembly within itself, but of tumult and disorder from without. An artful demagogue would find it much more easy to work up the people into a fit of momentary insanity, than to retain them in it for a month in opposition to the efforts of their real friends to undeceive them. Meanwhile the consent of the assembly to take their demand into consideration might reasonably be expected to moderate their violence.

Scarcely any plausible argument can be adduced in favour of what has been denominated by political writers a division of powers. Nothing can seem less reasonable, than to prescribe any positive limits to the topics of deliberation in an assembly adequately representing the people; or peremptorily to forbid them the exercise of functions, the depositaries of which are placed under their inspection and censure. Perhaps upon any emergence, totally unforeseen at the time of their election, and uncommonly important, they would prove their wisdom by calling upon the people to elect a new assembly with a direct view to that emergence. But the emergence, as we shall have occasion more fully to observe in the sequel, cannot with any propriety be prejudged, and a rule laid down for their conduct by a body prior to or distinct from themselves. The distinction of legislative and executive powers, however intelligible in theory, will by no means authorise their separation in practice.

Legislation, that is, the authoritative enunciation of abstract or general propositions, is a function of equivocal nature, and will never be exercised in a pure state of society, or a state approaching to purity, but with great caution and unwillingness. It is the most absolute of the functions of government, and government itself is a remedy that inevitably brings its own evils along with it. Administration on the other hand is a principle of perpetual application. So long as men shall see reason to act in a corporate capacity, they will always have occasions of temporary emergency for which to provide. In proportion as they advance in social improvement, executive power will, comparatively speaking, become every thing, and legislative nothing. Even at present, can there be any articles of greater importance than those of peace and war, taxation, and the selection of proper periods for the meeting of deliberative assemblies, which, as was observed in the commencement of the present book, are articles of temporary regulation?[1] Is it decent, can it be just, that these prerogatives should be exercised by any power less than the supreme, or be decided by any authority but that which most adequately represents the voice of the nation? This principle ought beyond question to be extended universally. There can be no just reason for excluding the national representative from the exercise of any function, the exercise of which on the part of the society is at all necessary.

The functions therefore of ministers and magistrates commonly so called, do not relate to any particular topic, respecting which they have a right exclusive of the representative assembly. They do not relate to any supposed necessity for secrecy; for secrets are always pernicious, and, most of all, secrets relating to the interests of any society, which are to be concealed from the members of that society. It is the duty of the assembly to desire information without reserve for themselves and the public upon every subject of general importance, and it is the duty of ministers and others to communicate such information, though it should not be expressly desired. The utility therefore of ministerial functions being less than nothing in these respects, there are only two classes of utility that remain to them; particular functions, such as those of financial detail or minute superintendence, which cannot be exercised unless by one or at most by a small number of persons;[2] and measures, proportioned to the demand of those necessities which will not admit of delay, and subject to the revision and censure of the deliberative assembly. The latter of these classes will perpetually diminish

---

[1] Chap. I, pp. 205–6.   [2] Ibid.

as men advance in improvement; nor can any thing be of greater importance than the reduction of that discretionary power in an individual, which may greatly affect the interests or fetter the deliberations of the many.

CHAPTER XXII

OF THE FUTURE HISTORY OF POLITICAL SOCIETIES

Quantity of administration necessary to be maintained.—Objects of administration: national glory—rivalship of nations.—Inferences: 1. complication of government unnecessary—2. extensive territory superfluous—3. constraint, its limitations.—Project of government: police—defence.

WE have now endeavoured to deduce certain general principles upon most of the subjects of legislative and executive power. But there is one very important topic which remains to be discussed. How much of either of these powers does the benefit of society require us to maintain?

We have already seen that the only legitimate object of political institution is the advantage of individuals. All that cannot be brought home to them, national wealth, prosperity and glory, can be advantageous only to those self interested impostors, who, from the earliest accounts of time, have confounded the understandings of mankind the more securely to sink them in debasement and misery.

The desire to gain a more extensive territory, to conquer or to hold in awe our neighbouring states, to surpass them in arts or arms, is a desire founded in prejudice and error. Power is not happiness. Security and peace are more to be desired than a name at which nations tremble. Mankind are brethren. We associate in a particular district or under a particular climate, because association is necessary to our internal tranquillity, or to defend us against the wanton attacks of a common enemy. But the rivalship of nations is a creature of the imagination. If riches be our object, riches can only be created by commerce; and the greater is our neighbour's capacity to buy, the greater will be our opportunity to sell. The prosperity of all is the interest of all.

The more accurately we understand our own advantage, the less shall we be disposed to disturb the peace of our neighbour. The same principle is applicable to him in return. It becomes us therefore to desire that he may be wise. But wisdom is the growth of equality and independence, not of injury and oppression. If oppression had been the school of wisdom, the improvement of mankind would have been inestimable, for they have been in that school for many thousand years. We ought therefore to desire that our neighbour should be independent. We ought to desire that he should be free; for wars do not originate in the unbiassed propensities of nations, but in the cabals of government and the propensities that governments inspire into the people at large. If our neighbour invade our territory, all we should desire is to repel him from it; and for that purpose it is not necessary we should surpass him in prowess, since upon our own ground his match is unequal. Not to say that to conceive a nation attacked by another, so long as its own conduct is sober, equitable and moderate, is an exceedingly improbable supposition.

Where nations are not brought into avowed hostility, all jealousy between them is an unintelligible chimera. I reside upon a certain spot, because that residence is most conducive to my happiness or usefulness. I am interested in the political justice and virtue of my species, because they are men, that is, creatures eminently capable of justice and virtue; and I have perhaps additional reason to interest myself for those who live under the same government as myself, because I am better qualified to understand their claims, and more capable of exerting myself in their behalf. But I can certainly have no interest in the infliction of pain upon others, unless so far as they are expressly engaged in acts of injustice. The object of sound policy and morality is to draw men nearer to each other, not to separate them; to unite their interests, not to oppose them.

Individuals cannot have too frequent or unlimited intercourse with each other; but societies of men have no interests to explain and adjust, except so far as error and violence may render explanation necessary. This consideration annihilates at once the principal objects of that mysterious and crooked policy which has hitherto occupied the attention of governments. Before this principle officers of the army and the navy, ambassadors and negociators, and all the train of artifices that has been invented to hold other nations at bay, to penetrate their secrets, to traverse their machinations, to form alliances and counter alliances, sink into nothing. The expence of government is annihilated, and together with its expence the means of subduing and undermining the determination of its subjects.

Another of the great opprobriums of political science is at the same time completely removed, that extent of territory subject to one head, respecting which philosophers and moralists have alternately disputed whether it be most unfit for a monarchy or for a democratical government. The appearance which mankind in a future state of improvement may be expected to assume, is a policy that in different countries will wear a similar form, because we have all the same faculties and the same wants; but a policy the independent branches of which will extend their authority over a small territory, because neighbours are best informed of each other's concerns, and are perfectly equal to their adjustment. No recommendation can be imagined of an extensive rather than a limited territory, except that of external security.

Whatever evils are included in the abstract idea of government, are all of them extremely aggravated by the extensiveness of its jurisdiction, and softened under circumstances of an opposite species. Ambition, which may be no less formidable than a pestilence in the former, has no room to unfold itself in the latter. Popular commotion is like the waves of the sea, capable where the surface is large of producing the most tragical effects, but mild and innocuous when confined within the circuit of an humble lake. Sobriety and equity are the obvious characteristics of a limited circle.

It may indeed be objected, 'that great talents are the offspring of great passions, and that in the quiet mediocrity of a petty republic the powers of intellect may be expected to subside into inactivity.' This objection, if true, would be entitled to the most serious consideration. But it is to be considered that, upon the hypothesis here advanced, the whole human species would constitute in one sense one great republic, and the prospects of him who desired to act beneficially upon a great surface of mind, would become more animating than ever. During the period in which this state was growing but not yet complete, the comparison of the blessings we enjoyed with the iniquities practising among our neighbours would afford an additional stimulus to exertion.[1]

Ambition and tumult are evils that arise out of government in an indirect manner, in consequence of the habits which government introduces of material action extending itself over multitudes of men. There are other evils inseparable from its existence. The objects of government are the suppression of violence, either external or internal, which might otherwise destroy or bring into jeopardy the well being of the community or its members; and the means it employs is violence of a more regulated kind. For this purpose the concentration of individual forces becomes necessary, and the method in which this concentration is usually obtained, is also constraint. The evils of constraint have been considered on a former occasion.[2] Constraint employed against

[1] This objection will be copiously discussed in the eighth book of the present work.
[2] Book II, Chap. VI.

delinquents or persons to whom delinquency is imputed, is by no means without its mischiefs. Constraint employed by the majority of a society against the minority who may differ from them upon some question of public good, is calculated at first sight at least to excite a still greater disapprobation.

Both of these exertions may indeed appear to rest upon the same principle. Vice is unquestionably no more than error of judgment, and nothing can justify an attempt to correct it by force but the extreme necessity of the case.[1] The minority, if erroneous, fall under precisely the same general description, though their error may not be of equal magnitude. But the necessity of the case can seldom be equally impressive. If the idea of secession for example were somewhat more familiarised to the conceptions of mankind, it could seldom happen that the secession of the minority could in any degree compare in mischievous tendency with the hostility of a criminal offending against the most obvious principles of social justice. The cases are parallel to those of offensive and defensive war. In putting constraint upon a minority, we yield to a suspicious temper that tells us the opposing party may hereafter in some way injure us, and we will anticipate his injury. In putting constraint upon a criminal, we seem to repel an enemy who has entered our territory and refuses to quit it.

Government can have no more than two legitimate purposes, the suppression of injustice against individuals within the community, and the common defence against external invasion. The first of these purposes, which alone can have an uninterrupted claim upon us, is sufficiently answered by an association of such an extent as to afford room for the institution of a jury, to decide upon the offences of individuals within the community, and upon the questions and controversies respecting property which may chance to arise. It might be easy indeed for an offender to escape from the limits of so petty a jurisdiction; and it might seem necessary at first that the neighbouring parishes or jurisdictions should be governed in a similar manner, or at least should be willing, whatever was their form of government, to co-operate with us in the removal or reformation of an offender, whose present habits were alike injurious to us and to them. But there will be no need of any express compact, and still less of any common centre of authority, for this purpose. General justice and mutual interest are found more capable of binding men than signatures and seals. In the mean time all necessity for causing the punishment of the crime to pursue the

[1] Book II, Chap. VI. Book IV, Chap. VI.

criminal, would soon at least cease, if it ever existed. The motives to offence would become rare: its aggravations few: and rigour superfluous. The principal object of punishment is restraint upon a dangerous member of the community; and the end of this restraint would be answered, by the general inspection that is exercised by the members of a limited circle over the conduct of each other, and by the gravity and good sense that would characterise the censures of men, from whom all mystery and empiricism were banished. No individual would be hardy enough in the cause of vice, to defy the general consent of sober judgment that would surround him. It would carry despair to his mind, or, which is better, it would carry conviction. He would be obliged, by a force not less irresistible than whips and chains, to reform his conduct.

In this sketch is contained the rude outline of political government. Controversies between parish and parish would be in an eminent degree unreasonable, since, if any question arose, about limits for example, justice would presently teach us that the individual who cultivates any portion of land, is the properest person to decide to which district he would belong. No association of men, so long as they adhered to the principles of reason, could possibly have any interest in extending their territory. If we would produce attachment in our associates, we can adopt no surer method than that of practising the dictates of equity and moderation; and, if this failed in any instance, it could only fail with him who, to whatever society he belonged, would prove an unworthy member. The duty of any society to punish offenders is not dependent upon the hypothetical consent of the offender to be punished, but upon the duty of necessary defence.

But however irrational might be the controversy of parish with parish in such a state of society, it would not be the less possible. For such extraordinary emergencies therefore provision ought to be made. These emergencies are similar in their nature to those of foreign invasion. They can only be provided against by the concert of several districts, declaring and, if needful, inforcing the dictates of justice.

One of the most obvious remarks that suggests itself upon these two cases, of hostility between district and district, and of foreign invasion which the interest of all calls upon them jointly to repel, is, that it is their nature to be only of occasional recurrence, and that therefore the provisions to be made respecting them need not be in the strictest sense of perpetual operation. In other words, the permanence of a national assembly, as it has hitherto been practised in France, cannot be necessary in a period of tranquillity, and may perhaps be pernicious.

That we may form a more accurate judgment of this, let us recollect some of the principal features that enter into the constitution of a national assembly.

CHAPTER XXIII

OF NATIONAL ASSEMBLIES

They produce a fictitious unanimity—an unnatural uniformity of opinion.—Causes of this uniformity.—Consequences of the mode of decision by vote—1. perversion of reason—2. contentious disputes—3. the triumph of ignorance and vice.—Society incapable of acting from itself—of being well conducted by others.—Conclusion.—Modification of democracy that results from these considerations.

In the first place the existence of a national assembly introduces the evils of a fictitious unanimity. The public, guided by such an assembly, acts with concert, or else the assembly is a nugatory excrescence. But it is impossible that this unanimity can really exist. The individuals who constitute a nation, cannot take into consideration a variety of important questions, without forming different sentiments respecting them. In reality all matters that are brought before such an assembly are decided by a majority of votes, and the minority, after having exposed with all the power of eloquence and force of reasoning of which they are capable the injustice and folly of the measures adopted, are obliged in a certain sense to assist in carrying them into execution. Nothing can more directly contribute to the depravation of the human understanding and character. It inevitably renders mankind timid, dissembling and corrupt. He that is not accustomed exclusively to act upon the dictates of his own understanding, must fall infinitely short of that energy and simplicity of which our nature is capable. He that contributes his personal exertions or his property to the support of a cause which he believes to be unjust, will quickly lose that accurate discrimination and nice sensibility of moral rectitude which are the principal ornaments of reason.

Secondly, the existence of national councils produces a certain species of real unanimity, unnatural in its character, and pernicious in its effects. The genuine and wholesome state of mind is, to be unloosed from shackles, and to expand every fibre of its frame according to the independent and individual impressions of truth upon that mind. How great would be the progress of intellectual improvement, if men were unfettered by the prejudices of education, unseduced by the influence of a corrupt state of society, and accustomed to yield without fear to the guidance of truth, however unexplored might be the regions and unexpected the conclusions to which she conducted us? We cannot advance in the voyage of happiness, unless we be wholly at large upon the stream that would carry us thither: the anchor, that we at first looked upon as the instrument of our safety, will at last appear to be the means of detaining our progress. Unanimity of a certain species will be the result of perfect freedom of enquiry, and this unanimity would, in a state of perfect freedom, become hourly more conspicuous. But the unanimity, that results from men's having a visible standard by which to adjust their sentiments, is deceitful and pernicious.

In numerous assemblies a thousand motives influence our judgments, independently of reason and evidence. Every man looks forward to the effects which the opinions he avows will produce on his success. Every man connects himself with some sect or party. The activity of his thought is shackled at every turn by the fear that his associates may disclaim him. This effect is strikingly visible in the present state of the British parliament, where men, whose faculties are comprehensive almost beyond all former example, are induced by these motives sincerely to espouse the most contemptible and clearly exploded errors.

Thirdly, the debates of a national assembly are distorted from their reasonable tenour by the necessity of their being uniformly terminated by a vote. Debate and discussion are in their own nature highly conducive to intellectual improvement; but they lose this salutary character the moment they are subjected to this unfortunate condition. What can be more unreasonable, than to demand, that argument, the usual quality of which is gradually and imperceptibly to enlighten the mind, should declare its effect in the close of a single conversation? No sooner does this circumstance occur than the whole scene changes its character. The orator no longer enquires after permanent conviction, but transitory effect. He seeks rather to take advantage of our prejudices than to enlighten our judgment. That which might otherwise have been a scene of philosophic and moral enquiry, is changed into wrangling, tumult and precipitation.

Another circumstance that arises out of the decision by vote, is the necessity of constructing a form of words that shall best meet the sentiments and be adapted to the preconceived ideas of a multitude of men. What can be conceived of at once more ludicrous and disgraceful, than the spectacle of a set of rational beings employed for hours together in weighing particles and adjusting commas? Such is the scene that is perpetually witnessed in clubs and private societies. In parliaments this sort of business is usually adjusted before the measure becomes a subject of public inspection. But it does not the less exist; and sometimes it occurs in the other mode, so that, when numerous amendments have been made to suit the corrupt interest of imperious pretenders, the Herculean task remains at last to reduce the chaos into a grammatical and intelligible form.

The whole is then wound up with that intolerable insult upon all reason and justice, the deciding upon truth by the casting up of numbers. Thus every thing that we have been accustomed to esteem most sacred, is determined, at best by the weakest heads in the assembly, but, as it not less frequently happens, by the most corrupt and dishonourable intentions.

In the last place, national assemblies will by no means be thought to deserve our direct approbation, if we recollect for a moment the absurdity of that fiction by which society is considered, as it has been termed, as a moral individual. It is in vain that we endeavour to counteract the immutable laws of necessity. A multitude of men after all our ingenuity will still remain no more than a multitude of men. Nothing can intellectually unite them short of equal capacity and identical perception. So long as the varieties of mind shall remain, the force of society can no otherwise be concentrated, than by one man for a shorter or a longer term taking the lead of the rest, and employing their force, whether material or dependent on the weight of their character, in a mechanical manner, just as he would employ the force of a tool or a machine. All government corresponds in a certain degree to what the Greeks denominated a tyranny. The difference is, that in despotic countries mind is depressed by an uniform usurpation; while in republics it preserves a greater portion of its activity, and the usurpation more easily conforms itself to the fluctuations of opinion.

The pretence of collective wisdom is the most palpable of all impostures. The acts of the society can never rise above the suggestions of this or that individual who is a member of it. Let us enquire whether society, considered as an agent, can really become the equal of certain individuals of whom it is composed. And here, without staying to examine what ground we have to expect that the wisest member of the society will actually take the lead in it, we find two obvious reasons to persuade us that, whatever be the degree of wisdom inherent in him that really superintends, the acts which he performs in the name of the society will be both less virtuous and less able, than under other circumstances they might be expected to be. In the first place, there are few men who, with the consciousness of being able to cover their responsibility under the name of a society, will not venture upon measures, less direct in their motives, or less justifiable in the experiment, than they would have chosen to adopt in their own persons. Secondly, men who act under the name of a society, are deprived of that activity and energy which may belong to them in their individual character. They have a multitude of followers to draw after them, whose humours they must consult, and to whose slowness of apprehension they must accommodate themselves. It is for this reason that we frequently see men of the most elevated genius dwindle into vulgar leaders, when they become involved in the busy scenes of public life.

From these reasonings we are sufficiently authorised to conclude, that national assemblies, or in other words assemblies instituted for the joint purpose of adjusting the differences between district and district, and of consulting respecting the best mode of repelling foreign invasion, however necessary to be had recourse to upon certain occasions, ought to be employed as sparingly as the nature of the case will admit. They should either never be elected but upon extraordinary emergencies, like the dictator of the ancient Romans,* or else sit periodically, one day for example in a year, with a power of continuing their sessions within a certain limit; to hear the complaints and representations of their constituents. The former of these modes is greatly to be preferred. Several of the reasons already adduced are calculated to show, that election itself is of a nature not to be employed but when the occasion demands it. There would be no difficulty in suggesting expedients relative to the regular originating of national assemblies. It would be most suitable to past habits and experience, that a general election should take place whenever a certain number of districts demanded it. It would be most agreeable to rigid simplicity and equity that an assembly of two or two hundred districts should take place, in exact proportion to the number of districts by whom that measure was desired.

It cannot reasonably be denied that all the objections which have been most loudly reiterated against democracy, become null in an application to the form of government which has now been delineated. Here is no opening for tumult, for the tyranny of a multitude drunk with unlimited power, for political ambition on the part of the few, or restless jealousy and precaution on the part of the many. Here no demagogue would find a suitable occasion for rendering the multitude the blind instrument of his purposes. Men in such a state of society would understand their happiness and cherish it. The true reason why the mass of mankind has so often been made the dupe of knaves, has been the mysterious and complicated nature of the social system. Once annihilate the quackery of government, and the most homebred understanding will be prepared to scorn the shallow artifices of the state juggler that would mislead him.

CHAPTER XXIV

OF THE DISSOLUTION OF GOVERNMENT

Political authority of a national assembly—of juries.—Consequence from the whole.

IT remains for us to consider what is the degree of authority necessary to be vested in such a modified species of national assembly as we have admitted into our system. Are they to issue their commands to the different members of the confederacy? Or is it sufficient that they should invite them to co-operate for the common advantage, and by arguments and addresses convince them of the reasonableness of the measures they propose? The former of these would at first be necessary. The latter would afterwards become sufficient. The Amphictyonic council of Greece* possessed no authority but that which derived from its personal character. In proportion as the spirit of party was extirpated, as the restlessness of public commotion subsided, and as the political machine became simple, the voice of reason would be secure to be heard. An appeal by the assembly to the several districts would not fail to obtain the approbation of all reasonable men, unless it contained in it something so evidently questionable, as to make it perhaps desirable that it should prove abortive.

This remark leads us one step farther. Why should not the same distinction between commands and invitations, which we have just made in the case of national assemblies, be applied to the particular assemblies or juries of the several districts? At first, we will suppose, that some degree of authority and violence would be necessary. But this necessity does not arise out of the nature of man, but out of the institutions by which he has already been corrupted. Man is not originally vicious. He would not refuse to listen, or to be convinced by the expostulations that are addressed to him, had he not been accustomed to regard them as hypocritical, and to conceive that, while his neighbour, his parent and his political governor pretended to be actuated by a pure regard to his interest, they were in reality, at the expence of his, promoting their own. Such are the fatal effects of mysteriousness and complexity. Simplify the social system in the manner which every motive but those of usurpation and ambition powerfully recommends; render the plain dictates of justice level to every capacity; remove the necessity of implicit faith; and the whole species will become reasonable and virtuous. It will then be sufficient for juries to recommend a certain mode of adjusting controversies, without assuming the prerogative of dictating that adjustment. It will then be sufficient for them to invite offenders to forsake their errors. If their expostulations proved in a few instances ineffectual, the evils arising out of this circumstance would be of less importance, than those which proceed from the perpetual violation of the exercise of private judgment. But in reality no evils would arise, for, where the empire of reason was so universally acknowledged, the offender would either readily yield to the expostulations of authority; or, if he resisted, though suffering no personal molestation, he would feel so uneasy under the unequivocal disapprobation and observant eye of public judgment, as willingly to remove to a society more congenial to his errors.

The reader has probably anticipated me in the ultimate conclusion, from these remarks. If juries might at length cease to decide and be contented to invite, if force might gradually be withdrawn and reason trusted alone, shall we not one day find that juries themselves and every other species of public institution, may be laid aside as unnecessary? Will not the reasonings of one wise man be as effectual as those of twelve? Will not the competence of one individual to instruct his neighbours be a matter of sufficient notoriety, without the formality of an election? Will there be many vices to correct and much obstinacy to conquer? This is one of the most memorable stages of human improvement. With what delight must every well informed friend of mankind look forward to the auspicious period, the dissolution of political government, of that brute engine, which has been the only perennial cause of the vices of mankind, and which, as has abundantly appeared in the progress of the present work, has mischiefs of various sorts incorporated with its substance, and no otherwise to be removed than by its utter annihilation!

BOOK VI

OF OPINION CONSIDERED AS A SUBJECT
OF POLITICAL INSTITUTION

CHAPTER I

GENERAL EFFECTS OF THE POLITICAL
SUPERINTENDENCE OF OPINION

*Arguments in favour of this superintendence.—Answer.—The exertions of
society in its corporate capacity are, 1. unwise—2. incapable of proper
effect.—Of sumptuary laws, agrarian laws and rewards.—Political degeneracy not incurable.—3. superfluous—in commerce—in speculative enquiry—
in morality.—4. pernicious—as undermining intellectual capacity—as sus-
pending intellectual improvement—contrary to the nature of morality—to
the nature of mind.—Conclusion.*

A PRINCIPLE, which has entered deeply into the systems of the writers
on political law, is that of the duty of governments to watch over the
manners of the people. 'Government,' say they, 'plays the part of an
unnatural step-mother, not of an affectionate parent, when she is
contented by rigorous punishments to avenge the commission of a
crime, while she is wholly inattentive beforehand to imbue the mind
with those virtuous principles, which might have rendered punishment
unnecessary. It is the business of a sage and patriotic magistracy to have
its attention ever alive to the sentiments of the people, to encourage
such as are favourable to virtue, and to check in the bud such as may
lead to disorder and corruption. How long shall government be
employed to display its terrors, without ever having recourse to the
gentleness of invitation? How long shall she deal in retrospect and censure to the utter neglect of prevention and remedy?' These reasonings
have in some respects gained additional strength by means of the latest
improvements and clearest views upon the subject of political truth.
It has been rendered more evident than in any former period, that government, instead of being an object of secondary consideration, has
been the principal vehicle of extensive and permanent evil to mankind.
It was natural therefore to say, 'since government can produce so much
positive mischief, surely it can do some positive good.'

But these views, however specious and agreeable they may in the first instance appear, are liable to very serious question. If we would not be seduced by visionary good, we ought here more than ever, to recollect the principles that have repeatedly been insisted upon and illustrated in this work, 'that government is in all cases an evil,' and 'that it ought to be introduced as sparingly as possible.' Nothing can be more unquestionable than that the manners and opinions of mankind are of the utmost consequence to the general welfare. But it does not follow that government is the instrument by which they are to be fashioned.

One of the reasons that may lead us to doubt of its fitness for this purpose, is to be drawn from the view we have already taken of society considered as an agent.[1] A multitude of men may be feigned to be an individual, but they cannot become a real individual. The acts which go under the name of the society, are really the acts now of one single person and now of another. The men who by turns usurp the name of the whole, perpetually act under the pressure of incumbrances that deprive them of their true energy. They are fettered by the prejudices, the humours, the weakness and the vice of those with whom they act; and, after a thousand sacrifices to these contemptible interests, their project comes out at last distorted in every joint, abortive and monstrous. Society therefore in its corporate capacity can by no means be busy and intrusive with impunity, since its acts must be expected to be deficient in wisdom.

Secondly, they will not be less deficient in efficacy than they are in wisdom. The object at which we are supposing them to aim, is to improve the opinions, and through them the manners of mankind; for manners are nothing else but opinions carried out into action: such as is the fountain, such will be the streams that are supplied from it. But what is it upon which opinion must be founded? Surely upon evidence, upon the perceptions of the understanding. Has society then any particular advantage in its corporate capacity for illuminating the understanding? Can it convey into its addresses and expostulations a compound or sublimate of the wisdom of all its members, superior in quality to the individual wisdom of any? If so, why have not societies of men written treatises of morality, of the philosophy of nature, or the philosophy of mind? Why have all the great steps of human improvement been the work of individuals?

If then society considered as an agent have no particular advantage for enlightening the understanding, the real difference between the *dicta* of society and the *dicta* of individuals must be looked for in the

---

[1] Book V, Chap. XXIII, p. 303.

article of authority. But is authority a proper instrument for influencing the opinions and manners of men? If laws were a sufficient means for the reformation of error and vice, it is not to be believed but that the world long ere this would have become the seat of every virtue. Nothing can be more easy than to command men to be just and good, to love their neighbours, to practise universal sincerity, to be content with a little, and to resist the enticements of avarice and ambition. But, when you have done, will the characters of men be altered by your precepts? These commands have been issued for thousands of years; and, if it had been decreed that every man should be hanged that violated them, it is vehemently to be suspected that this would not have secured their influence.

But it will be answered, 'that laws need not deal thus in generals, but may descend to particular provisions calculated to secure their success. We may institute sumptuary laws, limiting the expence of our citizens in dress and food. We may institute agrarian laws, forbidding any man to possess more than a certain annual revenue. We may proclaim prizes as the reward of acts of justice, benevolence and public virtue.' And, when we have done this, how far are we really advanced in our career? If the people be previously inclined to moderation in expence, the laws are a superfluous parade. If they are not inclined, who shall execute them, or prevent their evasion? It is the misfortune in these cases that regulations cannot be executed but by individuals of that very people they are meant to restrain. If the nation at large be infested with vice, who shall secure us a succession of magistrates that are free from the contagion? Even if we could surmount this difficulty, still it would be vain. Vice is ever more ingenious in evasion, than authority in detection. It is absurd to imagine that any law can be executed, that directly contradicts the propensities and spirit of the nation. If vigilance were able fully to countermine the subterfuges of art, the magistrates, who thus pertinaciously adhered to the practice of their duty, would not fail to be torn in pieces.

What can be more contrary to the most rational principles of human intercourse than the inquisitorial spirit which such regulations imply? Who shall enter into my house, scrutinise my expenditure and count the dishes upon my table? Who shall detect the stratagems I employ to cover my real possession of an enormous income, while I seem to receive but a small one? Not that there is really any thing unjust and unbecoming, as has been too often supposed, in my neighbour's animadverting with the utmost freedom upon my personal conduct. But that such regulations include a system of petty watchfulness and inspection; not contenting themselves with animadversion whenever the occasion is presented, but making it the business of one man constantly to pry into the proceedings of another, the whole depending upon the uniformity with which this is done; creating a perpetual struggle between the restless curiosity of the first, and the artful concealment of the second. By what motives will you make a man an informer? If by public spirit and philanthropy inciting him to brave obloquy and resentment for the sake of duty, will sumptuary laws be very necessary among a people thus far advanced in virtue? If by sinister and indirect considerations, will not the vices you propagate be more dangerous than the vices you suppress?

Such must be the case in extensive governments: in governments of smaller dimensions opinion would be all sufficient; the inspection of every man over the conduct of his neighbours, when unstained with caprice, would constitute a censorship of the more irresistible nature. But the force of this censorship would depend upon its freedom, not following the positive dictates of law, but the spontaneous decisions of the understanding.

Again, in the distribution of rewards who shall secure us against error, partiality and intrigue, converting that which was meant for the support of virtue into a new engine for her ruin? Not to add, that prizes are a very feeble instrument for the generation of excellence, always inadequate to its reward where it really exists, always in danger of being bestowed on its semblance, continually misleading the understanding by foreign and degenerate motives of avarice and vanity.

In truth, the whole system of such regulations is a perpetual struggle against the laws of nature and necessity. Mind will in all instances be swayed by its own views and propensities. No project can be more absurd, than that of reversing these propensities by the interposition of authority. He that should command a conflagration to cease or a tempest to be still, would not display more ignorance of the system of the universe, than he, who, with a code of regulations, whether general or minute, that he has framed in his closet, expects to restore a corrupt and luxurious people to temperance and virtue.

The force of this argument respecting the inefficacy of regulations has often been felt, and the conclusions that are deduced from it have been in a high degree discouraging. 'The character of nations,' it has been said, 'is unalterable, or at least, when once debauched, can never be recovered to purity. Laws are an empty name, when the manners of the people are become corrupt. In vain shall the wisest legislator attempt the reformation of his country, when the torrent of profligacy and vice has once broken down the bounds of moderation. There is no longer any instrument left for the restoration of simplicity and frugality. It is useless to declaim against the evils that arise from inequality of riches and rank, where this inequality has already gained an establishment. A generous spirit will admire the exertions of a Cato and a Brutus;* but a calculating spirit will condemn them, as inflicting useless torture upon a patient whose disease is irremediable. It was from a view of this truth that the poets derived their fictions respecting the early history of mankind; well aware that, when luxury was introduced and the springs of mind unbent, it would be a vain expectation that should hope to recal men from passion to reason, and from effeminacy to energy.[1] But this conclusion from the inefficacy of regulations is so far from being valid, that in reality,*

A third objection to the positive interference of society in its corporate capacity for the propagation of truth and virtue is, that such interference is altogether unnecessary. Truth and virtue are competent to fight their own battles. They do not need to be nursed and patronised by the hand of power.

The mistake which has been made in this case, is similar to the mistake which is now universally exploded upon the subject of commerce. It was long supposed that, if any nation desired to extend its trade, the thing most immediately necessary was for government to interfere, and institute protecting duties, bounties and monopolies. It is now well known that commerce never flourishes so much, as when it is delivered from the guardianship of legislators and ministers, and is built upon the principle, not of forcing other people to buy our commodities dear when they might purchase them elsewhere cheaper and better, but of ourselves feeling the necessity of recommending them by their intrinsic advantages. Nothing can be at once so unreasonable and hopeless, as to attempt by positive regulations to disarm the unalterable laws of the universe.

The same truth which has been felt under the article of commerce, has also made a considerable progress as to the subjects of speculative enquiry. Formerly it was thought that the true religion was to be defended by acts of uniformity, and that one of the principal duties of the magistrate was to watch the progress of heresy. It was truly judged that the connexion between error and vice is of the most intimate nature, and it was concluded that no means could be more effectual to prevent men from deviating into error, than to check their wanderings

[1] Book I, Chap. VIII.

by the scourge of authority. Thus writers, whose political views in other respects have been uncommonly enlarged, have told us 'that men ought indeed to be permitted to think as they please, but not to propagate their pernicious opinions; as they may be permitted to keep poisons in their closet, but not to offer them to sale under the denomination of cordials.'[1] Or, if humanity have forbidden them to recommend the extirpation of a sect which has already got footing in a country, they have however earnestly advised the magistrate to give no quarter to any new extravagance that might be attempted to be introduced.[2]—The reign of these two errors respecting commerce and theoretical speculation is nearly at an end, and it is reasonable to believe that the idea of teaching virtue through the instrumentality of government will not long survive them.

All that is to be asked on the part of government in behalf of morality and virtue is a clear stage upon which for them to exert their own energies, and perhaps some restraint for the present upon the violent disturbers of the peace of society, that the efforts of these principles may be allowed to go on uninterrupted to their natural conclusion. Who ever saw an instance in which error unaided by power was victorious over truth? Who is there so absurd as to believe, that with equal arms truth can be ultimately defeated? Hitherto every instrument of menace or influence has been employed to counteract her. Has she made no progress?—Has the mind of man the capacity to chuse falshood and reject truth, when her evidence is fairly presented? When it has been once thus presented and has gained a few converts, does she ever fail to go on perpetually increasing the number of her votaries? Exclusively of the fatal interference of government, and the violent irruptions of barbarism threatening to sweep her from the face of the earth, has not this been in all instances the history of science?

Nor are these observations less true in their application to the manners and morals of mankind. Do not men always act in the manner which they esteem best upon the whole or most conducive to their interest? Is it possible then that evidence of what is best or what is most beneficial can be thrown away upon them? The real history of the changes of character they experience in this respect is this. Truth for a long time spreads itself unobserved. Those who are the first to embrace it are little aware of the extraordinary effects with which it is pregnant. But it goes on to be studied and illustrated. It perpetually increases in

[1] Gulliver's Travels, Part II, Chap. VI.*
[2] *Mably,* de la Législation, Liv IV, Chap. III: des Etats Unis d'Amerique, Lettre III.

clearness and amplitude of evidence. The number of those by whom it is embraced is gradually enlarged. If it have relation to their practical interests, if it show them that they may be a thousand times more happy and free than at present, it is impossible that in its perpetual increase of evidence and energy, it should not at last break the bounds of speculation, and become an animating principle of action. What can be more absurd than the opinion, which has so long prevailed, 'that justice and an equal distribution of the means of happiness may appear ever so clearly to be the only reasonable foundation of political society, without ever having any chance of being reduced into practice? that oppression and misery are draughts of so intoxicating a nature, that, when once tasted, we can never afterwards refuse to partake of them? that vice has so many advantages over virtue, that the reasonableness and wisdom of the latter, however powerfully exhibited, can never obtain a hold upon our affections?'

While therefore we decry the efficacy of unassisted laws, we are far from throwing any discouragement by that means upon the prospect of social improvement. The true tendency of this view of the subject is to suggest indeed a different, but a more consistent and promising method by which this improvement is to be produced. The legitimate instrument of effecting political reformation is truth. Let truth be incessantly studied, illustrated and propagated, and the effect is inevitable. Let us not vainly endeavour by laws and regulations to anticipate the future dictates of the general mind, but calmly wait till the harvest of opinion is ripe. Let no new practice in politics be introduced, and no old one anxiously superseded, till called for by the public voice. The task, which for the present should wholly occupy the friend of man, is enquiry, instruction, discussion. The time may come when his task shall be of another sort. Error, being completely detected, may indeed sink into unnoticed oblivion, without one partisan to interrupt her fall. This would inevitably be the event, were it not for the restlessness and inconsiderate impetuosity of mankind. But the event may be otherwise. Political change, by advancing too rapidly to its crisis, may become attended with commotion and hazard; and it will then be incumbent on him actively to assist in unfolding the catastrophe. The evils of anarchy have been shown to be much less than they are ordinarily supposed;[1] but, whatever be their amount, the friend of man will not, when they arise, timidly shrink from the post of danger. He will on the contrary by social emanations of wisdom endeavour to guide the understandings of the people at large to the perception of felicity.

[1]   Book V, Chap. XX, p. 291.

In the fourth place the interference of an organised society for the purpose of influencing opinions and manners, is not only useless, but pernicious. We have already found that such interference is in one view of the subject ineffectual. But here a distinction is to be made. Considered with a view to the introduction of any favourable changes in the state of society, it is altogether impotent. But, though it be inadequate to change, it is powerful to prolong. This property in political regulation is so far from being doubtful, that to it alone we are to ascribe all the calamities that government has inflicted on mankind. When regulation coincides with the habits and propensities of mankind at the time it is introduced, it will be found sufficiently capable of maintaining those habits and propensities in the greater part unaltered for centuries. In this view it is doubly pernicious.

To understand this more accurately, let us apply it to the case of rewards, which has always been a favourite topic with the advocates of an improved legislation. How often have we been told, 'that talents and virtues would spring up spontaneously in a country, one of the objects of whose constitution should be to secure to them an adequate reward?' Now to judge of the propriety of this aphorism we should begin with recollecting that the discerning of merit is an individual, and not a social capacity. What can be more reasonable than that each man for himself should estimate the merits of his neighbour? To endeavour to institute a general judgment in the name of the whole, and to melt down the different opinions of mankind into one common opinion, appears at first sight so monstrous an attempt, that it is impossible to augur well of its consequences. Will this judgment be wise, reasonable or just? Wherever each man is accustomed to decide for himself, and the appeal of merit is immediately to the opinion of its contemporaries, there, were it not for the false bias of some positive institution, we might expect a genuine ardour in him who aspired to excellence, creating and receiving impressions in the judgment of an impartial audience. We might expect the judgment of the auditors to ripen by perpetual exercise, and mind, ever curious and awake, continually to approach nearer to the standard of truth. What do we gain in compensation for this, by setting up authority as the general oracle, from which the active mind is to inform itself what sort of excellence it should seek to acquire, and the public at large what judgment they should pronounce upon the efforts of their contemporaries? What should we think of an act of parliament appointing some particular individual president of the court of criticism, and judge in the last resort of the literary merit of dramatic compositions? Is there any solid reason why we should expect better things, from authority usurping the examination of moral or political excellence?

Nothing can be more unreasonable than the attempt to retain men in one common opinion by the dictate of authority. The opinion thus obtruded upon the minds of the public is not their real opinion; it is only a project by which they are rendered incapable of forming an opinion. Whenever government assumes to deliver us from the trouble of thinking for ourselves, the only consequences it produces are those of torpor and imbecility. Wherever truth stands in the mind unaccompanied by the evidence upon which it depends, it cannot properly be said to be apprehended at all. Mind is in this case robbed of its essential character and genuine employment, and along with them must be expected to lose all that which is capable of rendering its operations salutary and admirable. Either mankind will resist the assumptions of authority undertaking to superintend their opinions, and then these assumptions will produce no more than an ineffectual struggle; or they will submit, and then the effects will be injurious. He that in any degree consigns to another the task of dictating his opinions and his conduct, will cease to enquire for himself, or his enquiries will be languid and inanimate.

Regulations will originally be instituted in favour either of falshood or truth. In the first case no rational enquirer will pretend to alledge any thing in their defence; but, even should truth be their object, yet such is their nature, that they infallibly defeat the very purpose they were intended to serve. Truth, when originally presented to the mind, is powerful and invigorating; but, when attempted to be perpetuated by political institution, becomes flaccid and lifeless. Truth in its unpatronised state strengthens and improves the understanding; because in that state it is embraced only so far as it is perceived to be truth. But truth, when recommended by authority, is weakly and irresolutely embraced. The opinions I entertain are no longer properly my own; I repeat them as a lesson appropriated by rote, but I do not strictly speaking understand them, and I am not able to assign the evidence upon which they rest. My mind is weakened, while it is pretended to be improved. Instead of the firmness of independence, I am taught to bow to authority I know not why. Persons thus trammelled, are not strictly speaking capable of a single virtue. The first duty of man is to take none of the principles of conduct upon trust, to do nothing without a clear and individual conviction that it is right to be done. He that resigns his understanding upon one particular topic, will not exercise it vigorously upon others. If he be right in any instance, it will be inadvertently and

by chance. A consciousness of the degradation to which he is subjected
will perpetually haunt him; or at least he will want the consciousness
that accrues from independent consideration, and will therefore equally
want that intrepid perseverance, that calm self approbation that grows
out of independence. Such beings are the mere dwarfs and mockery of
men, their efforts comparatively pusillanimous, and the vigour with
which they should execute their purposes, superficial and hollow.

Strangers to conviction, they will never be able to distinguish
between prejudice and reason. Nor is this the worst. Even when the
glimpses of enquiry suggest themselves, they will not dare to yield to
the temptation. To what purpose enquire, when the law has told me
what to believe and what must be the termination of my enquiries?
Even when opinion properly so called suggests itself, I am compelled,
if it differ in any degree from the established system, to shut my eyes,
and loudly profess my adherence where I doubt the most. This compulsion may exist in many different degrees. But, supposing it to amount
to no more than a very slight temptation to be insincere, what judgment
must we form of such a regulation either in a moral or intellectual view?
of a regulation, inviting men to the profession of certain opinions by
the proffer of a reward, and deterring them from a severe examination
of their justice by penalties and disabilities? A system like this does
not content itself with habitually unnerving the mind of the great mass
of mankind through all its ranks, but provides for its own continuance
by debauching or terrifying the few individuals, who, in the midst
of the general emasculation, might retain their curiosity and love of
enterprise. We may judge how pernicious it is in its operation in this
respect by the long reign of papal usurpation in the dark ages, and the
many attacks upon it that were suppressed, previously to the successful
one of Luther. Even yet, how few are there that venture to examine into
the foundation of Mahometanism and Christianity, or the effects of monarchy and aristocratical institution, in countries where those systems are
established by law? Supposing men were free from persecution for
their hostilities in this respect, yet the investigation could never be
impartial, while so many allurements are held out, inviting men to a
decision in one particular way.

To these considerations it should be added, that what is right under
certain circumstances to-day, may by an alteration in those circumstances become wrong to-morrow. Right and wrong are the result of
certain relations, and those relations are founded in the respective
qualities of the beings to whom they belong. Change those qualities,
and the relations become altogether different. The treatment that I am

bound to bestow upon any one depends upon my capacity and his circumstances. Increase the first, or vary the second, and I am bound to a different treatment. I am bound at present to subject an individual to forcible restraint, because I am not wise enough by reason alone to change his vicious propensities. The moment I can render myself wise enough, I ought to confine myself to the latter mode. It is perhaps right to suffer the negroes in the West Indies to continue in slavery, till they can be gradually prepared for a state of liberty. Universally it is a fundamental principle in sound political science, that a nation is best fitted for the amendment of its civil government by being made to understand and desire the advantage of that amendment, and the moment it is so understood and desired it ought to be introduced. But, if there be any truth in these views, nothing can be more adverse to reason or inconsistent with the nature of man, than positive regulations tending to continue a certain mode of proceeding when its utility is gone.

If we would be still more completely aware of the pernicious tendency of positive institutions, we ought in the last place explicitly to contrast the nature of mind and the nature of government. It is one of the most unquestionable properties of mind to be susceptible of perpetual improvement. It is the inalienable tendency of positive institution, to retain that with which it is conversant for ever in the same state. Is then the perfectibility of understanding an attribute of trivial importance? Can we recollect with coldness and indifference the advantages with which this quality is pregnant to the latest posterity? And how are these advantages to be secured? By incessant industry, by a curiosity never to be disheartened or fatigued, by a spirit of enquiry to which a sublime and philanthropic mind will allow no pause. The circumstance of all others most necessary, is that we should never stand still, that every thing most interesting to the general welfare, wholly delivered from restraint, should be in a state of change, moderate and as it were imperceptible, but continual. Is there any thing that can look with a more malignant aspect upon the general welfare, than an institution tending to give permanence to certain systems and opinions? Such institutions are two ways pernicious; first, which is most material, because they render all the future advances of mind infinitely tedious and operose; secondly, because, by violently confining the stream of reflexion, and holding it for a time in an unnatural state, they compel it at last to rush forward with impetuosity, and thus occasion calamities, which, were it free from restraint, would be found extremely foreign to its nature. Is it to be believed that, if the interference of positive institution were out of the question, the progress of mind in past ages would have been so slow, as to have struck the majority of ingenuous observers with despair? The science of Greece and Rome upon the subjects of political justice was in many respects extremely imperfect: yet could we have been so long in appropriating their discoveries, had not the allurements of reward and the menace of persecution united to induce us, not to trust to the first and fair verdict of our own understandings?

The just conclusion from the above reasonings is nothing more than a confirmation, with some difference in the mode of application, of the fundamental principle, that government is little capable of affording benefit of the first importance to mankind. It is calculated to induce us to lament, not the apathy and indifference, but the inauspicious activity of government. It incites us to look for the moral improvement of the species, not in the multiplying of regulations, but in their repeal. It teaches us that truth and virtue, like commerce, will then flourish most, when least subjected to the mistaken guardianship of authority and laws. This maxim will rise upon us in its importance, in proportion as we connect it with the numerous departments of political justice to which it will be found to have relation. As fast as it shall be adopted into the practical system of mankind, it will go on to deliver us from a weight intolerable to mind, and in the highest degree inimical to the progress of truth.

CHAPTER II

OF RELIGIOUS ESTABLISHMENTS

Their general tendency.—Effects on the clergy: they introduce, 1. implicit faith—2. hypocrisy: topics by which an adherence to them is vindicated.— Effects on the laity.—Application.

ONE of the most striking instances of the injurious effects of the political patronage of opinion, as it at present exists in the world, is to be found in the system of religious conformity. Let us take our example from the church of England, by the constitution of which subscription is required from its clergy to thirty-nine articles* of precise and dogmatical assertion upon almost every subject of moral and metaphysical enquiry. Here then we have to consider the whole honours and revenues of the church, from the archbishop who takes precedence next after the princes of the blood royal to the meanest curate in the nation, as employed in support of a system of blind submission and abject hypocrisy. Is there one man through this numerous hierarchy that is at liberty to think for himself? Is there one man among them that can lay his hand upon his heart, and declare, upon his honour and conscience, that his emoluments have no effect in influencing his judgment? The declaration is literally impossible. The most that an honest man under such circumstances can say is, 'I hope not; I endeavour to be impartial.'

First, the system of religious conformity is a system of blind submission. In every country possessing a religious establishment, the state, from a benevolent care it may be for the manners and opinions of its subjects, publicly encourages a numerous class of men to the study of morality and virtue. What institution, we might naturally be led to enquire, can be more favourable to public happiness? Morality and virtue are the most interesting topics of human speculation; and the best effects might be expected to result from the circumstance of many persons, perpetually receiving the most liberal education, and setting themselves apart, for the express cultivation of these topics. But unfortunately these very men are fettered in the outset by having a code of propositions put into their hands, in a conformity to which all their enquiries must terminate. The natural tendency of science is to increase from age to age, and proceed from the humblest beginnings to the most admirable conclusions. But care is taken in the present case to anticipate these conclusions, and to bind men by promises and penalties not to improve upon the wisdom of their ancestors. The plan is to guard against degeneracy and decline, but never to advance. It is founded in the most sovereign ignorance of the nature of mind, which never fails to do either the one or the other.

Secondly, the tendency of a code of religious conformity is to topics by which an adherence to them is vindicated. To understand this it may be useful to recollect the various subterfuges that have been invented by ingenious men to apologise for the subscription of the English clergy. It is observable by the way that the articles of the church are founded upon the creed of the Calvinists, though for one hundred and fifty years past it has been accounted disreputable among the clergy to be of any other than the opposite, or Arminian tenets.* Volumes have been written to prove that, while these articles express predestinarian sentiments,* they are capable of a different construction, and that the subscriber has a right to take advantage of that construction. Divines of another class have rested their arguments upon the known good character and benevolent intentions of the first reformers, and have concluded that they could never intend to tyrannise over the consciences of men, or preclude the result of farther information. Lastly, there are many who have treated the articles as articles of peace, and inferred that, though you did not believe, you might allow yourself in the disingenuity of subscribing them, provided you added to it the farther guilt of constantly refraining to oppose what you considered as an adulteration of divine truth.

It would perhaps be regarded as incredible, if it rested upon the evidence of history alone, that a whole body of men, set apart as the instructors of mankind, weaned as they are expected to be from temporal ambition, and maintained from the supposition that the existence of human virtue and divine truth depends on their exertions, should with one consent employ themselves in a casuistry, the object of which is to prove the propriety of a man's declaring his assent to what he does not believe. These men either credit their own subterfuges, or they do not. If they do not, what can be expected from men so unprincipled and profligate? With what front can they exhort other men to virtue, with the brand of vice upon their own foreheads? If they do, what must be their portion of moral sensibility and discernment? Can we believe that men shall enter upon their profession with so notorious a perversion of reason and truth, and that no consequences will flow from it to infect their general character? Rather, can we fail to compare their unnatural and unfortunate state, with the profound wisdom and determined virtue which their industry and exertions would unquestionably have produced, if they had been left to their genuine operation? They are like the victims of Circe,* to whom human understanding was preserved entire, that they might more exquisitely feel their degraded condition. They are incited to study and to a thirst after knowledge, at the same time that the fruits of knowledge are constantly withheld from their unsuccessful attempts. They are held up to their contemporaries as the professors of truth, and political institution tyrannically commands them, in all the varieties of understanding and succession of ages, to model themselves to one common standard.

Such are the effects that a code of religious conformity produces upon the clergy themselves; let us consider the effects that are produced upon their countrymen. They are bid to look for instruction and morality to a denomination of men, formal, embarrassed and hypocritical, in whom the main spring of intellect is unbent and incapable of action. If the people be not blinded with religious zeal, they will discover and despise the imperfections of their spiritual guides. If they be so blinded, they will not the less transplant into their own characters the imbecil and unworthy spirit they are not able to detect. Is virtue so deficient in attractions as to be incapable of gaining adherents to her standard? Far otherwise. Nothing can bring the wisdom of a just and pure conduct into question, but the circumstance of its being recommended to us from an equivocal quarter. The most malicious enemy of mankind could not have invented a scheme more destructive of their true happiness, than that of hiring at the expence of the state a body of men, whose business it should seem to be to dupe their contemporaries into the practice of virtue.

One of the lessons that powerful facts are perpetually reading to the inhabitants of such countries, is that of duplicity and prevarication in an order of men, which, if it exist at all, ought to exist only for reverence. Do you think that this prevarication is not a subject of general notoriety? Do you think that the first idea that rises to the understanding of the multitude at sight of a clergyman, is not that of a man who inculcates certain propositions, not so properly because he thinks them true or thinks them interesting, as because he is hired to the employment? Whatever instruction a code of religious uniformity may fail to convey, there is one that it always communicates, the wisdom of estimating an unreserved and disinterested sincerity at a very cheap rate. Such are the effects that are produced by political institution, at a time when it most zealously intends with parental care to guard its subjects from seduction and depravity.

These arguments do not apply to any particular articles and creeds, but to the very notion of ecclesiastical establishments in general. Wherever the state sets apart a certain revenue for the support of religion, it will infallibly be given to the adherents of some particular opinions, and will operate in the manner of prizes to induce men at all events to embrace and profess those opinions. Undoubtedly, if I think it right to have a spiritual instructor to guide me in my researches and at stated intervals to remind me of my duty, I ought to be at liberty to take the proper steps to supply myself in this respect. A priest, who thus derives his mission from the unbiassed judgment of his parishioners, will stand a chance to possess beforehand and independently of corrupt influence the requisites they demand. But why should I be compelled to contribute to the support of an institution, whether I approve of it or no? If public worship be conformable to reason, reason without doubt will prove adequate to its vindication and support. If it be from God, it is profanation to imagine that it stands in need of the alliance of the state. It must be in an eminent degree artificial and exotic, if it be incapable of preserving itself in existence, otherwise than by the inauspicious interference of political institution.

CHAPTER III

OF THE SUPPRESSION OF ERRONEOUS OPINION
IN RELIGION AND GOVERNMENT

Of heresy.—Arguments by which the suppression of heresy is recommended.—
Answer.—Ignorance not necessary to make men virtuous.—Difference of
opinion not subversive of public security.—Reason, and not force, the proper
corrective of sophistry.—Absurdity of the attempt to restrain thought—to
restrain the freedom of speech.—Consequences that would result.—Fallibility
of the men by whom authority is exercised.—Of erroneous opinions in
government.—Iniquity of the attempt to restrain them.—Tendency of
unlimited political discussion.

THE same views which have prevailed for the introduction of religious
establishments, have inevitably led to the idea of provisions against the
rise and progress of heresy. No arguments can be adduced in favour
of the political patronage of truth, that will not be equally cogent in
behalf of the political discouragement of error. Nay, they will, of the
two, be most cogent in the latter case; for error and misrepresentation
are the irreconcilable enemies of virtue, and if authority were the true
mean to disarm them, there would then at least be no need of positive
provisions to assist the triumph of truth. It has however happened that
this argument, though more tenable, has had fewer adherents. Men are
more easily reconciled to abuse in the distribution of rewards, than in
the infliction of penalties. It will not therefore be requisite laboriously
to insist upon the refutation of this principle; its discussion is principally necessary for the sake of method.

Various arguments have been alledged in defence of this. 'The importance of opinion as a general proposition is notorious and unquestionable.
Ought not political institution to take under its inspection that root
from which all our actions are ultimately derived? The opinions of men
must be expected to be as various as their education and their temper:
ought not government to exert its foresight to prevent this discord from
breaking out into anarchy and violence? There is no proposition so
absurd or so hostile to morality and public good, as not to have found
its votaries: will there be no danger in suffering these eccentricities to
proceed unmolested, and every perverter of truth and justice to make
as many converts as he is able? It has been found indeed a hopeless task
to endeavour to extirpate by violence errors already established; but is
it not the duty of government to prevent their ascendancy, to check the

growth of their adherents and the introduction of heresies hitherto unknown? Can those persons, to whom the care of the general welfare is confided, or who are fitted by their situation or their talents to suggest proper regulations to the adoption of the community, be justified in conniving at the spread of such extravagant and pernicious opinions as strike at the root of order and morality? Simplicity of mind and an understanding undebauched with sophistry have ever been the characteristics of a people among whom virtue has flourished: ought not government to exert itself to exclude the inroad of qualities opposite to these? It is thus that the friends of moral justice have ever contemplated with horror the progress of infidelity and latitudinarian principles. It was thus that the elder Cato* viewed with grief the importation into his own country of that plausible and loquacious philosophy by which Greece had already been corrupted.'[1]

There are several trains of reflexion which these reasonings suggest. None of them can be more important than that which may assist us in detecting the error of the elder Cato, and of other persons who have been the zealous but mistaken advocates of virtue. Ignorance is not necessary to render men virtuous. If it were, we might reasonably conclude that virtue was an imposture, and that it was our duty to free ourselves from its shackles. The cultivation of the understanding has no tendency to corrupt the heart. A man who should possess all the science of Newton and all the genius of Shakespeare,* would not on that account be a bad man. Want of great and comprehensive views had as considerable a share as benevolence in the grief of Cato. It is like the taking to pieces an imperfect machine in order by reconstructing it to enchance its value. An uninformed and timid spectator would be frightened at the temerity of the artist, at the confused heap of pins and wheels that were laid aside at random, and would take it for granted that nothing but destruction would be the consequence. But he would be disappointed. It is thus that the extravagant sallies of mind are the prelude of the highest wisdom, and that the dreams of Ptolemy* were destined to precede the discoveries of Newton.

The event cannot be other than favourable. Mind would else cease to be mind. It would be more plausible to say that the perpetual cultivation of the understanding will terminate in madness, than that it will terminate in vice. As long as enquiry is suffered to proceed, and science to improve, our knowledge is perpetually increased. Shall we know

---

[1] The reader will consider this as the language of the objectors. The most eminent of the Greek philosophers were in reality distinguished from all other teachers, by the fortitude with which they conformed to the precepts they taught.

every thing else, and nothing of ourselves? Shall we become clear sighted and penetrating in all other subjects, without increasing our penetration upon the subject of man? Is vice most truly allied to wisdom or to folly? Can mankind perpetually increase in wisdom, without increasing in the knowledge of what it is wise for them to do? Can a man have a clear discernment, unclouded with any remains of former mistake, that this is the action he ought to perform, most conducive to his own interest and to the general good, most delightful at the instant and satisfactory in the review, most agreeable to reason, justice and the nature of things, and refrain from performing it? Every system which has been constructed relative to the nature of superior beings and Gods, amidst all its other errors has reasoned truly upon these topics, and taught that the increase of wisdom and knowledge led, not to malignity and tyranny, but to benevolence and justice.

Secondly, it is a mistake to suppose that speculative differences of opinion threaten materially to disturb the peace of society. It is only when they are enabled to arm themselves with the authority of government, to form parties in the state, and to struggle for that political ascendancy which is too frequently exerted in support of or in opposition to some particular creed, that they become dangerous. Wherever government is wise enough to maintain an inflexible neutrality, these jarring sects are always found to live together with sufficient harmony. The very means that have been employed for the preservation of order, have been the only means that have led to its disturbance. The moment government resolves to admit of no regulations oppressive to either party, controversy finds its level, and appeals to argument and reason, instead of appealing to the sword or the stake. The moment government descends to wear the badge of a sect, religious war is commenced, the world is disgraced with inexpiable broils and deluged with blood.

Thirdly, the injustice of punishing men for their opinions and arguments will be still more visible, if we reflect a little on the nature of punishment. Punishment is one of those classes of coercion, the multiplication of which is so much to be deprecated, and which nothing but the most urgent necessity can in any case justify. That necessity is commonly admitted to exist, where a man has proved by his unjust actions the injuriousness of his character, and where the injury, the repetition of which is to be apprehended, is of such a nature as to be committed before we can have sufficient notice to guard ourselves against it. But no such necessity can possibly exist in the case of false opinions and perverse arguments. Does any man assert falsehood? Nothing farther can be desired than that it should be confronted with truth. Does he bewilder us with sophistry? Introduce the light of reason, and his deceptions will vanish. There is in this case a clear line of distinction. In the only admissible province of punishment force it is true is introduced, but it is only in return for force previously exerted. Where argument therefore, erroneous statements and misrepresentation alone are employed, it is by argument only that they must be encountered. We should not be creatures of a rational and intellectual nature, if the victory of truth over error were not ultimately certain.

To enable us to conceive properly of the value of laws for the punishment of heresy, let us suppose a country to be sufficiently provided with such laws, and observe the result. The object is to prevent men from entertaining certain opinions, or in other words from thinking in a certain way. What can be more absurd than to undertake to put fetters upon the subtlety of thought? How frequently does the individual who desires to restrain it in himself, fail in the attempt? Add to this, that prohibition and menace in this respect do but give new restlessness to the curiosity of the mind. I must not think of the possibility, that there is no God; that the stupendous miracles of Moses and Christ were never really performed; that the dogmas of the Athanasian creed* are erroneous. I must shut my eyes, and run blindly into all the opinions, religious and political, that my ancestors regarded as sacred. Will this in all instances be possible?

There is another consideration, trite indeed, but the triteness of which is an additional argument of its truth. Swift says* 'Men ought to be permitted to think as they please, but not to propagate their pernicious opinions.'[1] The obvious answer to this is, 'We are much obliged to him: how would he be able to punish our heresy, even if he desired it, so long as it was concealed?' The attempt to punish opinion is absurd: we may be silent respecting our conclusions, if we please; the train of thinking by which those conclusions are generated cannot fail to be silent.

'But, if men be not punished for their thoughts, they may be punished for uttering those thoughts.' No. This is not less impossible than the other. By what arguments will you persuade every man in the nation to exercise the trade of an informer? By what arguments will you persuade my bosom friend, with whom I repose all the thoughts of my heart, to repair immediately from my company to a magistrate, in order to procure my commitment for so doing to the prisons of the inquisition? In countries where this is attempted, there will be a perpetual struggle,

---

[1] See above, Chap. I, p. 312.

the government endeavouring to pry into our most secret transactions, and the people busy to countermine, to outwit and to detest their superintendents.

But the most valuable consideration which this part of the subject suggests, is, supposing all this were done, what judgment must we form of the people among whom it is done? Though all this cannot, yet much may be performed; though the embryo cannot be annihilated, it may be prevented from ever expanding itself into the dimensions of a man. The arguments by which we were supposing a system for the restraint of opinion to be recommended, were arguments derived from a benevolent anxiety for the virtue of mankind, and to prevent their degeneracy. Will this end be accomplished? Let us contrast a nation of men, daring to think, to speak and to act what they believe to be right, and fettered with no spurious motives to dissuade them from right, with a nation that fears to speak, and fears to think upon the most interesting subjects of human enquiry. Can any spectacle be more degrading than this timidity? Can men in whom mind is thus annihilated be capable of any good or valuable purpose? Can this most abject of all slaveries be the genuine state, the true perfection of the human species?

Another argument, though it has often been stated to the world, deserves to be mentioned in this place. Governments, no more than individual men, are infallible. The cabinets of princes and the parliaments of kingdoms, if there be any truth in considerations already stated,[1] are often less likely to be right in their conclusions than the theorist in his closet. But, dismissing the estimate of greater and less, it was to be presumed from the principles of human nature, and is found true in fact, that cabinets and parliaments are liable to vary from each other in opinion. What system of religion or government has not in its turn been patronised by national authority? The consequence therefore of admitting this authority is, not merely attributing to government a right to impose some, but any or all opinions upon the community. Are Paganism and Christianity, the religions of Mahomet, Zoroaster and Confucius,* are monarchy and aristocracy in all their forms equally worthy to be perpetuated among mankind? Is it quite certain that the greatest of all human calamities is change? Must we never hope for any advance, any improvement? Have no revolution in government, and no reformation in religion been productive of more benefit than disadvantage? There is no species of reasoning in defence of the suppression of heresy which may not be brought back to this monstrous principle,

---

[1] Book V, Chap. XXIII, p. 303.

that the knowlege of truth and the introduction of right principles of policy, are circumstances altogether indifferent to the welfare of mankind.

The same reasonings that are here employed against the forcible suppression of religious heresy, will be found equally valid with respect to political. The first circumstance that will not fail to suggest itself to every reflecting mind, is, What sort of constitution must that be which must never be examined? whose excellencies must be the constant topic of eulogium, but respecting which we must never permit ourselves to enquire in what they consist? Can it be the interest of society to proscribe all investigation respecting the wisdom of its regulations? Or must our debates be occupied with provisions of temporary convenience; and are we forbid to ask, whether there may not be something fundamentally wrong in the design of the structure? Reason and good sense will not fail to augur ill of that system of things which is too sacred to be looked into; and to suspect that there must be something essentially weak that thus shrinks from the eye of curiosity. Add to which, that, however we may doubt of the importance of religious disputes, nothing can less reasonably be exposed to question than that the happiness of mankind is essentially connected with the improvement of political science.

'But will not demagogues and declaimers lead to the subversion of all order, and introduce the most dreadful calamities?' What is the state they will introduce? Monarchy and aristocracy are some of the most extensive and lasting mischiefs that have yet afflicted mankind. Will these demagogues persuade their hearers to institute a new dynasty of hereditary despots to oppress them? Will they persuade them to create out of their own body a set of feudal chiefs to hold their brethren in the most barbarous slavery? They would probably find the most copious eloquence inadequate to these purposes. The arguments of declaimers will not produce an extensive and striking alteration in political opinions, except so far as they are built upon a basis of irresistible truth. Even if the people were in some degree intemperate in carrying the conclusions of these reasoners into practice, the mischiefs they would inflict would be inexpressibly trivial, compared with those which are hourly perpetrated by the most cold blooded despotism. But in reality the duty of government in these cases is to be mild and equitable. Arguments alone will not have the power, unassisted by the sense or the recollection of oppression or treachery, to hurry the people into excesses. Excesses are never the offspring of reason, are never the offspring of misrepresentation only, but of power endeavouring to stifle reason and traverse the common sense of mankind.

CHAPTER IV

OF TESTS

Their supposed advantages are attended with injustice—are nugatory.—
Illustration.—Their disadvantages—they ensnare.—example.—Second
example.—They are an usurpation.—Influence of tests on the latitudinar-
ian—on the purist.—Conclusion.

THE majority of the arguments above employed on the subject of penal
laws in matters of opinion are equally applicable to tests, religious
and political. The distinction between prizes and penalties, between
greater and less, is little worthy of our attention, if any discouragement
extended to the curiosity of intellect, and any authoritative countenan-
ance afforded to one set of opinions in preference to another, be in its
own nature unjust, and evidently hostile to the general good.

Leaving out of the consideration religious tests, as being already
sufficiently elucidated in the preceding discussion,[1] let us attend for a
moment to an article which has had its advocates among men of considerable liberality, the supposed propriety of political tests. 'What, shall
we have no federal oaths, no oaths of fidelity to the nation, the law and
the republic? How in that case shall we ever distinguish between the
enemies and the friends of freedom?'

Certainly there cannot be a method devised at once more ineffectual
and iniquitous than a federal oath. What is the language that in strictness of interpretation belongs to the act of the legislature imposing this
oath? To one party it says, 'We know very well that you are our friends;
the oath as it relates to you we acknowledge to be altogether superfluous; nevertheless you must take it, as a cover to our indirect purposes
in imposing it upon persons whose views are less unequivocal than
yours.' To the other party it says, 'It is vehemently suspected that you
are inimical to the cause in which we are engaged; this suspicion is
either true or false; if false, we ought not to suspect you, and much less
ought we to put you to this invidious and nugatory purgation; if true,
you will either candidly confess your difference, or dishonestly prevari-
cate: be candid, and we will indignantly banish you; be dishonest, and
we will receive you as bosom friends.'

Those who say this however promise too much. Duty and common
sense oblige us to watch the man we suspect, even though he should

[1] Chap. II.

swear he is innocent. Would not the same precautions which we are still obliged to employ to secure us against his duplicity, have sufficiently answered our purpose without putting him to his purgation? Are there no methods by which we can find out whether a man be the proper subject in whom to repose an important trust without putting the question to himself? Will not he, who is so dangerous an enemy that we cannot suffer him at large, discover his enmity by his conduct, without reducing us to the painful necessity of tempting him to an act of prevarication? If he be so subtle a hypocrite that all our vigilance cannot detect him, will he scruple to add to his other crimes the crime of perjury?

Whether the test we impose be merely intended to operate as an exclusion from office, or to any more considerable disadvantage, the disability it introduces is still in the nature of a punishment. It treats the individual in question as an unsound member of society, as distinguished in an unfavourable sense from the multitude of his countrymen, and possessing certain attributes detrimental to the general good. In the eye of reason human nature is capable of no other guilt than this.[1] Society is authorised to animadvert upon a certain individual, in the case of murder for example, not because he has done an action that he might have avoided, not because he was sufficiently informed of the better and obstinately chose the worse; for this is impossible, every man necessarily does that which he at the time apprehends to be best: but because his habits and character render him dangerous to society, in the same sense as a wolf or a blight would be dangerous.[2] It must no doubt be an emergency of no common magnitude, that can justify a people in putting a mark of displeasure upon a man for the opinions he entertains, be they what they may. But, taking for granted for the present the reasonableness of this proceeding, it would certainly be just as equitable for the government to administer to the man accused for murder an oath of purgation, as to the man accused of disaffection to the established order of society. There cannot be a principle of justice clearer than this, that no man can be called on in order to punishment to accuse himself.

These reasonings being particularly applicable to a people in a state of revolution like the French, it may perhaps be allowable to take from their revolution an example of the injurious and ensnaring effects with which tests and oaths of fidelity are usually attended. It was required of all men to swear 'that they would be faithful to the nation, the law and

---

[1]   Book IV, Chap. VI.   [2]   Book IV, Chap. VI.

the king.' In what sense can they be said to have adhered to their oath, who, twelve months after their constitution had been established on its new basis, have taken a second oath, declaratory of their everlasting abjuration of monarchy?* What sort of effect, favourable or unfavourable? must this precarious mutability in their solemn appeals to heaven have upon the minds of those by whom they are made?

And this leads us from the consideration of the supposed advantages of tests religious and political, to their real disadvantages. The first of these disadvantages consists in the impossibility of constructing a test in such a manner, as to suit the various opinions of those upon whom it is imposed, and not to be liable to reasonable objection. When the law was repealed imposing upon the dissenting clergy of England a subscription with certain reservations to the articles of the established church, an attempt was made to invent an unexceptionable test that might be substituted in its room. This test simply affirmed, 'that the books of the Old and New Testament in the opinion of the person who took it contained a revelation from God;' and it was supposed that no Christian could scruple such a declaration. But is it impossible that I should be a Christian, and yet doubt of the canonical authority of the amatory eclogues of Solomon, or of certain other books contained in a selection that was originally made in a very arbitrary manner?* 'Still however I may take the test, with a persuasion that the books of the Old and New Testament contain a revelation from God, and something more.' In the same sense I might take it, even if the Alcoran, the Talmud and the sacred books of the Hindoos* were added to the list. What sort of influence will be produced upon the mind that is accustomed to this looseness of construction in its most solemn engagements?

Let us examine with the same view the federal oath of the French, proclaiming the determination of the swearer 'to be faithful to the nation, the law and the king.'* Fidelity to three several interests which may in various cases be placed in opposition to each other will appear at first sight to be no very reasonable engagement. The propriety of vowing fidelity to the king has already been brought to the trial and received its condemnation.[1] Fidelity to the law is an engagement of so complicated a nature, as to strike terror into every mind of serious reflection. It is impossible that a system of law the composition of men should ever be presented to such a mind, that shall appear altogether faultless. But, with respect to laws that appear to me to be unjust, I am bound to every sort of hostility short of open violence, I am bound to exert

---

[1] Book V, Chap. II–VIII.

myself incessantly in proportion to the magnitude of the injustice for their abolition. Fidelity to the nation is an engagement scarcely less equivocal. I have a paramount engagement to the cause of justice and the benefit of the human race. If the nation undertake what is unjust, fidelity in that undertaking is a crime. If it undertake what is just, it is my duty to promote its success, not because I am one of its citizens, but because such is the command of justice.

Add to this what has been already said upon the subject of obedience,[1] and it will be sufficiently evident that all tests are the offspring of usurpation. Government has in no case a right to issue its commands, and therefore cannot command me to take a certain oath. Its only legal functions are, to impose upon me a certain degree of restraint whenever I manifest by my actions a temper detrimental to the community, and to invite me to a certain contribution for purposes conducive to the general interest.

It may be alledged with respect to the French federal oath, as well as with respect to the religious test before cited, that it may be taken with a certain laxity of interpretation. When I swear fidelity to the law, I may mean only that there are certain parts of it that I approve. When I swear fidelity to the nation, the law and the king, I may mean so far only as these three authorities shall agree with each other, and all of them agree with the general welfare of mankind. In a word the final result of this laxity of interpretation explains the oath to mean, 'I swear that I believe it is my duty to do every thing that appears to me to be just.' Who can look without indignation and regret at this prostitution of language? Who can think without horror of the consequences of the public and perpetual lesson of duplicity which is thus read to mankind?

But, supposing there should be certain members of the community simple and uninstructed enough to conceive that an oath contained some real obligation, and did not leave the duty of the person to whom it was administered precisely where it found it, what is the lesson that would be read to such members? They would listen with horror to the man who endeavoured to persuade them that they owed no fidelity to the nation, the law and the king, as to one who was instigating them to sacrilege. They would tell him that it was too late, and that they must not allow themselves to hear his arguments. They would perhaps have heard enough before their alarm commenced, to make them look with envy on the happy state of this man, who was free to listen to the communications of others without terror, who could give a loose to his

---

[1] Book III, Chap. VI.

thoughts, and intrepidly follow the course of his enquiries wherever they led him. For themselves they had promised to think no more for the rest of their lives. Compliance indeed in this case is impossible; but will a vow of inviolable adherence to a certain constitution have no effect in checking the vigour of their contemplations and the elasticity of their minds?

We put a miserable deception upon ourselves, when we promise ourselves the most favourable effects from the abolition of monarchy and aristocracy, and retain this wretched system of tests, overturning in the apprehensions of mankind at large the fundamental distinctions of justice and injustice. Sincerity is not less essential than equality to the well being of mankind. A government, that is perpetually furnishing motives to Jesuitism and hypocrisy,* is not less abhorrent to right reason, than a government of orders and hereditary distinction. It is not easy to imagine how soon men would become frank, explicit in their declarations, and unreserved in their manners, were there no positive institutions inculcating upon them the necessity of falshood and disguise. Nor is it possible for any language to describe the inexhaustible benefits that would arise from the universal practice of sincerity.

CHAPTER V

OF OATHS

Oaths of office and duty—their absurdity—their immoral consequences.—Oaths of evidence: less atrocious.—Opinion of the liberal and resolved respecting them.—Their essential features: contempt of veracity—false morality.—Their particular structure—abstract principles assumed by them to be true—their inconsistency with these principles.

THE same arguments that prove the injustice of tests, may be applied universally to all oaths of duty and office. If I entered upon the office without an oath, what would be my duty? Can the oath that is imposed upon me make any alteration in my duty? If not, does not the very act of imposing it, by implication assert a falshood? Will this falshood, the assertion that a direct engagement has a tendency to create a duty, have no injurious effect upon a majority of the persons concerned? What is the true criterion that I shall faithfully discharge the office that is conferred upon me? Surely my past life, and not any protestations I may be compelled to make. If my life have been unimpeachable, this compulsion is an unmerited insult; if it have been otherwise, it is something worse.

It is with no common disapprobation that we recollect the prostitution of oaths which marks the history of modern European countries, and particularly of our own. This is one of the means that government employs to discharge itself of its proper functions, by making each man security for himself. It is one of the means that legislators have provided to cover the inefficiency and absurdity of their regulations, by making individuals promise the execution of that which the police is not able to execute. It holds out in one hand the temptation to do wrong, and in the other the obligation imposed not to be influenced by that temptation. It compels a man to engage not only for his own conduct, but for that of all his dependents. It obliges certain officers (churchwardens in particular*) to promise an inspection beyond the limits of human faculties, and to engage for a proceeding on the part of those under their jurisdiction, which they neither intend nor are expected to inforce. Will it be believed in after ages that every considerable trader in exciseable articles in this country is induced by the constitution of its government to reconcile his mind to the guilt of perjury, as to the condition upon which he is accustomed to exercise his profession?

There remains only one species of oaths to be considered, which have found their advocates among persons sufficiently enlightened to reject every other species of oath, I mean, oaths administered to a witness in a court of justice. These are certainly free from many of the objections that apply to oaths of fidelity, duty or office. They do not call upon a man to declare his assent to a certain proposition which the legislator has prepared for his acceptance; they only require him solemnly to pledge himself to the truth of assertions, dictated by his own apprehension of things, and expressed in his own words. They do not require him to engage for something future, and of consequence to shut up his mind against farther information as to what his conduct in that future ought to be; but merely to pledge his veracity to the apprehended order of things past.

These considerations palliate the evil, but do not convert it into good. Wherever men of uncommon energy and dignity of mind have existed, they have felt the degradation of binding their assertions with an oath. The English constitution recognises in a partial and imperfect manner the force of this principle, and therefore provides that, while the common herd of mankind shall be obliged to swear to the truth, nothing more shall be required from the order of nobles than a declaration upon honour. Will reason justify this distinction?

Can there be a practice more pregnant with false morality than that of administering oaths in a court of justice? The language it expressly holds is, 'You are not to be believed upon your mere word;' and there are few men firm enough resolutely to preserve themselves from contamination, when they are accustomed upon the most solemn occasions to be treated with contempt. To the unthinking it comes like a plenary indulgence to the occasional tampering with veracity in affairs of daily occurrence, that they are not upon their oath; and we may affirm without risk of error, that there is no cause of insincerity, prevarication and falshood more powerful, than the practice of administering oaths in a court of justice. It treats veracity in the affairs of common life as a thing unworthy to be regarded. It takes for granted that no man, at least no man of plebeian rank, is to be credited upon his bare affirmation; and what it takes for granted it has an irresistible tendency to produce.

Add to this a feature that runs through all the abuses of political institution, it inverts the eternal principles of morality. Why is it that I am bound to be more especially careful of what I affirm in a court of justice? Because the subsistence, the honest reputation or the life of a fellow man may be materially affected by it. All these genuine motives are by the contrivance of human institution thrown into shade, and we are expected to speak the truth, only because government demands it of us upon oath, and at the times in which government has thought proper or recollected to administer this oath. All attempts to strengthen the obligations of morality by fictitious and spurious motives, will in the sequel be found to have no tendency but to relax them.

Men will never act with that liberal justice and conscious integrity which is their highest ornament, till they come to understand what men are. He that contaminates his lips with an oath, must have been thoroughly fortified with previous moral instruction, if he be able afterwards to understand the beauty of an easy and simple integrity. If our political institutors had been but half so judicious in perceiving the manner in which excellence and worth were to be generated, as they have been ingenious and indefatigable in the means of depraving mankind, the world, instead of a slaughter house, would have been a paradise.

Let us leave for a moment the general consideration of the principle of oaths, to reflect upon their particular structure and the precise meaning of the term. They take for granted in the first place the existence of an invisible governor of the world, and the propriety of our addressing petitions to him, both which a man may deny, and yet continue a good member of society. What is the situation in which the institution of which we treat places this man? But we must not suffer ourselves to be stopped by trivial considerations.—Oaths are also so constructed as to take for granted the religious system of the country whatever it may happen to be.

Now what are the words with which we are taught in this instance with these principles, to address the creator of the universe? 'So help me God, and the contents of his holy word.' It is the language of imprecation. I pray him to pour down his everlasting wrath and curse upon me, if I utter a lie.—It were to be wished that the name of that man were recorded, who first invented this mode of binding men to veracity. He had surely himself but very light and contemptuous notions of the Supreme Being, who could thus tempt men to insult him, by braving his justice. If it be our duty to invoke his blessing, yet there must surely be something insupportably profane in wantonly and unnecessarily putting all that he is able to inflict upon us upon conditions.

CHAPTER VI

OF LIBELS

Public libels.—Injustice of an attempt to prescribe the method in which public questions shall be discussed—its pusillanimity.—Invitations to tumult.—Private libels.—Reasons in favour of their being subjected to restraint.—Answer.—1. It is necessary the truth should be told.—Salutary effects of the unrestrained investigation of character.—Objection: freedom of speech would be productive of calumny, not of justice.—Answer.—Future history of libel.—2. It is necessary men should be taught to be sincere.— Extent of the evil which arises from a command to be insincere.—The mind spontaneously shrinks from the prosecution of a libel.—Conclusion.

IN the examination already bestowed upon the article of heresy political and religious,[1] we have anticipated one of the two heads of the law of libel; and, if the arguments there adduced be admitted for valid, it will follow that no punishment can justly be awarded against any writing or words derogatory to religion or political government.

It is impossible to establish any solid ground of distinction upon this subject, or to lay down rules in conformity to which the argument must be treated. It is impossible to tell me, when I am penetrated with the magnitude of the subject, that I must be logical and not eloquent; or when I feel the absurdity of the theory I am combating, that I must not express it in terms that may produce feelings of ridicule in my readers.

---

[1] Chap. III.

It were better to forbid me the discussion of the subject altogether, than forbid me to describe it in the manner I conceive to be most suitable to its merits. It would be a most tyrannical species of candour to tell me, 'You may write against the system we patronise, provided you will write in an imbecil and ineffectual manner; you may enquire and investigate as much as you please, provided, when you undertake to communicate the result, you carefully check your ardour, and be upon your guard that you do not convey any of your own feelings to your readers.' Add to this, that rules of distinction, as they are absurd in relation to the dissidents, will prove a continual instrument of usurpation and injustice to the ruling party. No reasonings will appear fair to them, but such as are futile. If I speak with energy, they will deem me inflammatory; and if I describe censurable proceedings in plain and homely, but pointed language, they will cry out upon me as a buffoon.

It must be truly a lamentable case, if truth, favoured by the many and patronised by the great, should prove too weak to enter the lists with falshood. It is self evident, that that which will stand the test of examination, cannot need the support of penal statutes. After our adversaries have exhausted their eloquence and exerted themselves to mislead us, truth has a clear, nervous and simple story to tell, which, if force be excluded on all sides, will not fail to put down their arts. Misrepresentation will speedily vanish, if the friends of truth be but half as alert as the advocates of falshood. Surely then it is a most ungracious plea to offer, 'We are too idle to reason with you, we are therefore determined to silence you by force.' So long as the adversaries of justice confine themselves to expostulation, there can be no ground for serious alarm. As soon as they begin to act with violence and riot, it will then be time enough to encounter them with force.

There is however one particular class of libel that seems to demand a separate consideration. A libel may either not confine itself to any species of illustration of religion or government, or it may leave illustration entirely out of its view. Its object may be to invite a multitude of persons to assemble, as the first step towards acts of violence. A public libel is any species of writing in which the wisdom of some established system is controverted; and it cannot be denied that a dispassionate and severe demonstration of its injustice tends, not less than the most alarming tumult, to the destruction of such institutions. But writing and speech are the proper and becoming methods of operating changes in human society, and tumult is an improper and equivocal method. In the case then of the specific preparations of riot, it should seem that the regular force of the society may lawfully interfere. But this interference may be of two kinds. It may consist of precautions to counteract all tumultuous concourse, or it may arraign the individual for the offence he has committed against the peace of the community. The first of these seems sufficiently commendable and wise, and would, if vigilantly exerted, be in almost all cases adequate to the purpose. The second is attended with some difficulty. A libel the avowed intention of which is to lead to immediate violence, is altogether different from a publication in which the general merits of any institution are treated with the utmost freedom, and may well be supposed to fall under different rules. The difficulty here arises only from the consideration of the general nature of punishment, which is abhorrent to the true principles of mind, and ought to be restrained within as narrow limits as possible, if not instantly abolished.[1] A distinction to which observation and experience in cases of judicial proceeding have uniformly led, is that between crimes that exist only in intention, and overt acts. So far as prevention only is concerned, the former would seem in many cases not less entitled to the animadversion of society than the latter; but the evidence of intention usually rests upon circumstances equivocal and minute, and the friend of justice will tremble to erect any grave proceeding upon so uncertain a basis.—It might be added, that he who says that every honest citizen of London ought to repair to St. George's Fields to-morrow in arms,* only says what he thinks is best to be done, and what the laws of sincerity oblige him to utter. But this argument is of a general nature, and applies to every thing that is denominated crime, not to the supposed crime of inflammatory invitations in particular. He that performs any action, does that which he thinks is best to be done; and, if the peace of society make it necessary that he should be restrained from this by threats of violence, the necessity is of a very painful nature.—It should be remembered that the whole of these reasonings suppose that the tumult is an evil, and will produce more disadvantage than benefit, which is no doubt frequently, but may not be always, the case. It cannot be too often recollected, that there is in no case a right of doing wrong, a right to punish for a meritorious action. Every government, as well as every individual, must follow their own apprehensions of justice, at the peril of being mistaken, unjust and consequently vicious.[2]—These reasonings on exhortations to tumult, will also be found applicable with slight variation to incendiary letters addressed to private persons.

But the law of libel, as we have already said, distributes itself into

---

[1] See the following Book.   [2] Book II, Chap. III.

two heads, libels against public establishments and measures, and libels against private character. Those who have been willing to admit that the first ought to pass unpunished, have generally asserted the propriety of counteracting the latter by censures and penalties. It shall be the business of the remainder of this chapter to show that they were erroneous in their decision.

The arguments upon which their decision is built must be allowed to be both popular and impressive. 'There is no external possession more solid or more valuable than an honest fame. My property, in goods or estate, is appropriated only by convention. Its value is for the most part the creature of a debauched imagination; and, if I were sufficiently wise and philosophical, he that deprived me of it would do me very little injury. He that inflicts a stab upon my character is a much more formidable enemy. It is a very serious inconvenience that my countrymen should regard me as destitute of principle and honesty. If the mischief were entirely to myself, it is not possible to be regarded with levity. I must be void of all sense of justice, if I were callous to the contempt and detestation of the world. I must cease to be a man, if I were unaffected by the calumny that deprived me of the friend I loved, and left me perhaps without one bosom in which to repose my sympathies. But this is not all. The same stroke that annihilates my character, extremely abridges, if it do not annihilate, my usefulness. It is in vain that I would exert my good intentions and my talents for the assistance of others, if my motives be perpetually misinterpreted. Men will not listen to the arguments of him they despise; he will be spurned during life, and execrated as long as his memory endures. What then are we to conclude but that to an injury, greater than robbery, greater perhaps than murder, we ought to award an exemplary punishment?'

The answer to this statement may be given in the form of an illustration of two propositions: first, that it is necessary the truth should be told; secondly, that it is necessary men should be taught to be sincere.

First, it is necessary the truth should be told. How can this ever be done, if I be forbidden to speak upon more than one side of the question? The case is here exactly similar to the case of religion and political establishment. If we must always hear the praise of things as they are, and allow no man to urge an objection, we may be lulled into torpid tranquillity, but we can never be wise.

If a veil of partial favour is to be drawn over the errors of mankind, it is easy to perceive whether virtue or vice will be the gainer. There is no terror that comes home to the heart of vice, like the terror of being exhibited to the public eye. On the contrary there is no reward worthy to be bestowed upon eminent virtue but this one, the plain, unvarnished proclamation of its excellence in the face of the world.

If the unrestrained discussion of abstract enquiry be of the highest importance to mankind, the unrestrained investigation of character is scarcely less to be cultivated. If truth were universally told of men's dispositions and actions, gibbets and wheels might be dismissed from the face of the earth. The knave unmasked would be obliged to turn honest in his own defence. Nay, no man would have time to grow a knave. Truth would follow him in his first irresolute essays, and public disapprobation arrest him in the commencement of his career.

There are many men at present who pass for virtuous, that tremble at the boldness of a project like this. They would be detected in their effeminacy and imbecility. Their imbecility is the growth of that inauspicious secrecy, which national manners and political institutions at present draw over the actions of individuals. If truth were spoken without reserve, there would be no such men in existence. Men would act with clearness and decision, if they had no hopes in concealment, if they saw at every turn that the eye of the world was upon them. How great would be the magnanimity of the man who was always sure to be observed, sure to be judged with discernment, and to be treated with justice? Feebleness of character would hourly lose its influence in the breast of those over whom it now domineers. They would feel themselves perpetually urged with an auspicious violence to assume manners more worthy of the form they bore.

To these reasonings it may perhaps be rejoined, 'This indeed is an interesting picture. If truth could be universally told, the effects would no doubt be of the most excellent nature; but the expectation is to be regarded as visionary.'

Not so: the discovery of individual and personal truth is to be effected in the same manner as the discovery of general truth, by discussion. From the collision of disagreeing accounts justice and reason will be produced. Mankind seldom think much of any particular subject, without coming to think right at last.

'What, and is it to be supposed, that mankind will have the discernment and the justice of their own accord to reject the libel?' Yes; libels do not at present deceive mankind, from their intrinsic power, but from the restraint under which they labour. The man who from his dungeon is brought to the light of day, cannot accurately distinguish colours; but he that has suffered no confinement, feels no difficulty in the operation. Such is the state of mankind at present: they are not exercised to employ their judgment, and therefore they are deficient in judgment.

The most improbable tale now makes a deep impression; but then men would be accustomed to speculate upon the possibilities of human action.

At first it may be, if all restraint upon the freedom of writing and speech were removed, and men were encouraged to declare what they thought as publicly as possible, every press would be burdened with an inundation of scandal. But the stories by their very multiplicity would defeat themselves. No one man, if the lie were successful, would become the object of universal persecution. In a short time the reader, accustomed to the dissection of character, would acquire discrimination. He would either detect the imposition by its internal absurdity, or at least would attribute to the story no farther weight, than that to which its evidence entitled it.

Libel, like every other human concern, would soon find its level, if it were delivered from the injurious interference of political institution. The libeller, that is, he who utters an unfounded calumny, either invents the story he tells, or delivers it with a degree of assurance to which the evidence that has offered itself to him is by no means entitled. In each case he would meet with his proper punishment in the judgment of the world. The consequences of his error would fall back upon himself. He would either pass for a malignant accuser, or for a rash and headlong censurer. Anonymous scandal would be almost impossible in a state where nothing was concealed. But, if it were attempted, it would be wholly pointless, since, where there could be no honest and rational excuse for concealment, the desire to be concealed would prove the baseness of the motive.

Secondly, force ought not to intervene for the suppression of private libels, because men ought to learn to be sincere. There is no branch of virtue more essential than that which consists in giving language to our thoughts. He that is accustomed to utter what he knows to be false or to suppress what he knows to be true, is in a perpetual state of degradation. If I have had particular opportunity to observe any man's vices, justice will not fail to suggest to me that I ought to admonish him of his errors, and to warn those whom his errors might injure. There may be very sufficient ground for my representing him as a vicious man, though I may be totally unable to establish his vices so as to make him a proper subject of judicial punishment. Nay, it cannot be otherwise; for I ought to describe his character exactly such as it appears to be, whether it be virtuous, or vicious, or of an ambiguous nature. Ambiguity would presently cease, if every man avowed his sentiments. It is here as in the intercourses of friendship: a timely explanation seldom fails to heal a broil; misunderstandings would not grow considerable, were we not in the habit of brooding over imaginary wrongs.

Laws for the suppression of private libels are properly speaking laws to restrain men from the practice of sincerity. They create a warfare between the genuine dictates of unbiassed private judgment and the apparent sense of the community, throwing obscurity upon the principles of virtue, and inspiring an indifference to the practice. This is one of those consequences of political institution that presents itself at every moment: morality is rendered the victim of uncertainty and doubt. Contradictory systems of conduct contend with each other for the preference, and I become indifferent to them all. How is it possible that I should imbibe the divine enthusiasm of benevolence and justice, when I am prevented from discerning what it is in which they consist? Other laws assume for the topic of their animadversion actions of unfrequent occurrence. But the law of libels usurps the office of directing me in my daily duties, and, by perpetually menacing me with the scourge of punishment, undertakes to render me habitually a coward, continually governed by the basest and most unprincipled motives.

Courage consists more in this circumstance than in any other, the daring to speak every thing, the uttering of which may conduce to good. Actions, the performance of which requires an inflexible resolution, call upon us but seldom; but the virtuous economy of speech is our perpetual affair. Every moralist can tell us that morality eminently consists in 'the government of the tongue.' But this branch of morality has long been inverted. Instead of studying what we shall tell, we are taught to consider what we shall conceal. Instead of an active virtue, 'going about doing good,' we are instructed to believe that the chief end of man is to do no mischief. Instead of fortitude, we are carefully imbued with maxims of artifice and cunning, misnamed prudence.

Let us contrast the character of those men with whom we are accustomed to converse, with the character of men such as they ought to be, and will be. On the one side we perceive a perpetual caution, that shrinks from the observing eye, that conceals with a thousand folds the genuine emotions of the heart, and that renders us unwilling to approach the men that we suppose accustomed to read it, and to tell what they read. Such characters as ours are the mere shadows of men, with a specious outside perhaps, but destitute of substance and soul. Oh, when shall we arrive at the land of realities, when men shall be known for what they are, by energy of thought and intrepidity of action! It is fortitude, that must render a man superior alike to caresses and threats, enable him to derive his happiness from within, and accustom him to be upon all occasions prompt to assist and to inform. Every thing therefore favourable to fortitude must be of inestimable value; every thing that inculcates dissimulation worthy of our perpetual abhorrence.

There is one thing more that is of importance to be observed upon this subject of libel, which is, the good effects that would spring from every man's being accustomed to encounter falshood with its only proper antidote, truth. After all the arguments that have been industriously accumulated to justify prosecution for libel, every man that will retire into himself, will feel himself convinced of their insufficiency. The modes in which an innocent and a guilty man would repel an accusation against them might be expected to be opposite; but the law of libel confounds them. He that was conscious of his rectitude, and undebauched by ill systems of government, would say to his adversary, 'Publish what you please against me, I have truth on my side, and will confound your misrepresentations.' His sense of fitness and justice would not permit him to say, 'I will have recourse to the only means that are congenial to guilt, I will compel you to be silent.' A man, urged by indignation and impatience, may commence a prosecution against his accuser; but he may be assured, the world, that is a disinterested spectator, feels no cordiality for his proceedings. The language of their sentiments upon such occasions is, 'What! he dares not even let us hear what can be said against him.'

The arguments in favour of justice, however different may be the views under which it is considered, perpetually run parallel to each other. The recommendations under this head are precisely the same as those under the preceding, the generation of activity and fortitude. The tendency of all false systems of political institution is to render the mind lethargic and torpid. Were we accustomed not to recur either to public or individual force but upon occasions that unequivocally justified their employment, we should then come to have some respect for reason, for we should know its power. How great must be the difference between him who answers me with a writ of summons or a challenge, and him who employs the sword and the shield of truth alone? He knows that force only is to be encountered with force, and allegation with allegation; and he scorns to change places with the offender by being the first to break the peace. He does that which, were it not for the degenerate habits of society, would scarcely deserve the name of courage, dares to meet upon equal ground, with the sacred armour of truth, an adversary who possesses only the perishable weapons of falshood. He calls up his understanding; and does not despair of baffling the shallow pretences of calumny. He calls up his firmness; and knows that a plain story, every word of which is marked with the emphasis of sincerity, will carry conviction to every hearer. It were absurd to expect that truth should be cultivated, so long as we are accustomed to believe that it is an impotent incumbrance. It would be impossible to neglect it, if we knew that it was as impenetrable as adamant, and as lasting as the world.

CHAPTER VII

OF CONSTITUTIONS

Distinction of regulations constituent and legislative.—Supposed character of permanence that ought to be given to the former—inconsistent with the nature of man.—Source of the error.—Remark.—Absurdity of the system of permanence.—Its futility.—Mode to be pursued in framing a constitution.—Constituent laws not more important than others.—In what manner the consent of the districts is to be declared.—Tendency of the principle which requires this consent.—It would reduce the number of constitutional articles—parcel out the legislative power—and produce the gradual extinction of law.—Objection.—Answer.

An article intimately connected with the political consideration of opinion is suggested to us by a doctrine which has lately been taught relatively to constitutions. It has been said that the laws of every regular state naturally distribute themselves under two heads, fundamental and adscititious,* laws, the object of which is the distribution of political power and directing the permanent forms according to which public business is to be conducted; and laws, the result of the deliberations of powers already constituted. This distinction being established in the first instance, it has been inferred, that these laws are of very unequal importance, and that of consequence those of the first class ought to be originated with much greater solemnity, and to be declared much less susceptible of variation than those of the second. The French national assembly of 1789 pushed this principle to the greatest extremity, and seemed desirous of providing every imaginable security for rendering the work they had formed immortal. It could not be touched upon any account under the term of ten years; every alteration it was to receive must be recognised as necessary by two successive national assemblies of the ordinary kind;* after these formalities an assembly of revision was to be elected, and they to be forbidden to touch the constitution in any other points than those which had been previously marked out for their consideration.

It is easy to perceive that these precautions are in direct hostility with the principles established in this work. 'Man and for ever!' was the motto of the labours of this assembly. Just broken loose from the thick darkness of an absolute monarchy, they assumed to prescribe lessons of wisdom to all future ages. They seem not so much as to have dreamed of that purification of intellect, that climax of improvement, which may very probably be the destiny of posterity. The true state of man, as has been already demonstrated, is, not to have his opinions bound down in the fetters of an eternal quietism, but flexible and unrestrained to yield with facility to the impressions of increasing truth. That form of society will appear most perfect to an enlightened mind, which is least founded in a principle of permanence. But, if this view of the subject be just, the idea of giving permanence to what is called the constitution of any government, and rendering one class of laws, under the appellation of fundamental, less susceptible of change than another, must be founded in misapprehension and error.

The error probably originally sprung out of the forms of political monopoly which we see established over the whole civilised world. Government could not justly derive in the first instance but from the choice of the people; or, to speak more accurately (for the former principle, however popular and specious, is in reality false), government ought to be adjusted in its provisions to the prevailing apprehensions of justice and truth. But we see government at present administered either in whole or in part by a king and a body of noblesse; and we reasonably say that the laws made by these authorities are one thing, and the laws from which they derived their existence another. But we do not consider that these authorities, however originated, are in their own nature unjust. If we had never seen arbitrary and capricious forms of government, we should probably never have thought of cutting off certain laws from the code under the name of constitutional. When we behold certain individuals or bodies of men exercising an exclusive superintendence over the affairs of a nation, we inevitably ask how they came by their authority, and the answer is, By the constitution. But, if we saw no power existing in the state but that of the people, having a body of representatives, and a certain number of official secretaries and clerks acting in their behalf, subject to their revisal, and renewable at their pleasure, the question, how the people came by this authority, would never have suggested itself.

A celebrated objection that has been urged against the governments of modern Europe is that they have no constitutions.[1] If by this objection it be understood, that they have no written code bearing this appellation, and that their constitutions have been less an instantaneous than a gradual production, the criticism seems to be rather verbal, than of essential moment. In any other sense it is to be suspected that the remark would amount to an eulogium, but an eulogium to which they are certainly by no means entitled.

But to return to the question of permanence. Whether we admit or reject the distinction between constitutional and ordinary legislation, it is not less true that the power of a people to change their constitution morally considered, must be strictly and universally coeval with the existence of a constitution. The language of permanence in this case is the greatest of all absurdities. It is to say to a nation, 'Are you convinced that something is right, perhaps immediately necessary, to be done? It shall be done ten years hence.'

The folly of this system may be farther elucidated, if farther elucidation be necessary, from the following dilemma. Either a people must be governed according to their own apprehensions of justice and truth, or they must not. The last of these assertions cannot be avowed, but upon the unequivocal principles of tyranny. But, if the first be true, then it is just as absurd to say to a nation, This government, which you chose nine years ago, is the legitimate government, and the government which your present sentiments approve the illegitimate; as to insist upon their being governed by the *dicta* of their remotest ancestors, or even of the most insolent usurper.

It is extremely probable that a national assembly chosen in the ordinary forms, is just as much empowered to change the fundamental laws, as to change any of the least important branches of legislation. This function would never perhaps be dangerous but in a country that still preserved a portion of monarchy or aristocracy, and in such a country a principle of permanence would be found a very feeble antidote against the danger. The true principle upon the subject is, that no assembly, though chosen with the most unexampled solemnity, has a power to impose any regulations contrary to the public apprehension of right; and a very ordinary authority, fairly originated, will be sufficient to facilitate the harmonious adoption of a change that is dictated by national opinion. The distinction of constitutional and ordinary topics will always appear in practice unintelligible and vexatious. The assemblies of more frequent recurrence will find themselves arrested in the

---

[1] Rights of Man.*

intention of conferring any eminent benefit on their country, by the apprehension that they shall invade the constitution. In a country where the people are habituated to sentiments of equality and where no political monopoly is tolerated, there is little danger that any national assembly should be disposed to inforce a pernicious change, and there is still less that the people should submit to the injury, or not possess the means easily and with small interruption of public tranquillity to avert it. The language of reason on this subject is, 'Give us equality and justice, but no constitution. Suffer us to follow without restraint the dictates of our own judgment, and to change our forms of social order as fast as we improve in understanding and knowledge.'

The opinion upon this head most popular in France at the time that the national convention entered upon its functions, was that the business of the convention extended only to the presenting a draught of a constitution, to be submitted in the sequel to the approbation of the districts, and then only to be considered as law.* This opinion is well deserving of a serious examination.

The first idea that suggests itself respecting it is, that, if constitutional laws ought to be subjected to the revision of the districts, then all laws ought to undergo the same process, understanding by laws all declarations of a general principle to be applied to particular cases as they may happen to occur, and even including all provisions for individual emergencies that will admit of the delay incident to the revision in question. It is an egregious mistake to imagine that the importance of these articles is in a descending ratio from fundamental to ordinary, and from ordinary to particular. It is possible for the most odious injustice to be perpetrated by the best constituted assembly. A law rendering it capital to oppose the doctrine of transubstantiation, would be more injurious to the public welfare, than a law changing the duration of the national representative, from two years, to one year or to three. Taxation has been shown to be an article rather of executive than legislative administration;[1] and yet a very oppressive and unequal tax would be scarcely less ruinous than any single measure that could possibly be devised.

It may farther be remarked that an approbation demanded from the districts to certain constitutional articles, whether more or less numerous, will be either real or delusive according to the mode adopted for that purpose. If the districts be required to decide upon these articles by a simple affirmative or negative, it will then be delusive. It is

[1] Book V, Chap. I.

impossible for any man or body of men, in the due exercise of their understanding, to decide upon any complicated system in that manner. It can scarcely happen but that there will be some things that they will approve and some that they will disapprove. On the other hand, if the articles be unlimitedly proposed for discussion in the districts, a transaction will be begun to which it is not easy to foresee a termination. Some districts will object to certain articles; and, if these articles be modelled to obtain their approbation, it is possible that the very alteration introduced to please one part of the community, may render the code less acceptable to another. How are we to be assured that the dissidents will not set up a separate government for themselves? The reasons that might be offered to persuade a minority of districts to yield to the sense of a majority, are by no means so perspicuous and forcible, as those which sometimes persuade the minority of members in a given assembly to that species of concession.

It is desirable in all cases of the practical adoption of any given principle, that we should fully understand the meaning of the principle, and perceive the conclusions to which it inevitably leads. This principle of a consent of districts has an immediate tendency, by a salutary gradation perhaps, to lead to the dissolution of all government. What then can be more absurd, than to see it embraced by those very men, who are at the same time advocates for the complete legislative unity of a great empire? It is founded upon the same basis as the principle of private judgment, which it is to be hoped will speedily supersede the possibility of the action of society in a collective capacity. It is desirable that the most important acts of the national representatives should be subject to the approbation or rejection of the districts whose representatives they are, for exactly the same reason as it is desirable, that the acts of the districts themselves should, as speedily as practicability will admit, be in force only so far as relates to the individuals by whom those acts are approved.

The first consequence that would result, not from the delusive, but the real establishment of this principle, would be the reduction of the constitution to a very small number of articles.* The impracticability of obtaining the deliberate approbation of a great number of districts to a very complicated code, would speedily manifest itself. In reality the constitution of a state governed either in whole or in part by a political monopoly, must necessarily be complicated. But what need of complexity in a country where the people are destined to govern themselves? The whole constitution of such a country ought scarcely to exceed two articles; first, a scheme for the division of the whole into parts equal in their population, and, secondly, the fixing of stated periods for the election of a national assembly: not to say that the latter of these articles may very probably be dispensed with.

A second consequence that results from the principle of which we are treating is as follows. It has already appeared, that the reason is no less cogent for submitting important legislative articles to the revisal of the districts, than for submitting the constitutional articles themselves. But after a few experiments of this sort, it cannot fail to suggest itself, that the mode of sending laws to the districts for their revision, unless in cases essential to the general safety, is a proceeding unnecessarily circuitous, and that it would be better, in as many instances as possible, to suffer the districts to make laws for themselves without the intervention of the national assembly. The justness of this consequence is implicitly assumed in the preceding paragraph, while we stated the very narrow bounds within which the constitution of an empire, such as that of France for example, might be circumscribed. In reality, provided the country were divided into convenient districts with a power of sending representatives to the general assembly, it does not appear that any ill consequences would ensue to the common cause from these districts being permitted to regulate their internal affairs, in conformity to their own apprehensions of justice. Thus, that which was at first a great empire with legislative unity, would speedily be transformed into a confederacy of lesser republics, with a general congress or Amphictyonic council,* answering the purpose of a point of cooperation upon extraordinary occasions. The ideas of a great empire and legislative unity are plainly the barbarous remains of the days of military heroism. In proportion as political power is brought home to the citizens, and simplified into something of the nature of parish regulation, the danger of misunderstanding and rivalship will be nearly annihilated. In proportion as the science of government is divested of its present mysterious appearances, social truth will become obvious, and the districts pliant and flexible to the dictates of reason.

A third consequence sufficiently memorable from the same principle is the gradual extinction of law. A great assembly, collected from the different provinces of an extensive territory, and constituted the sole legislator of those by whom the territory is inhabited, immediately conjures up to itself an idea of the vast multitude of laws that are necessary for regulating the concerns of those whom it represents. A large city, impelled by the principles of commercial jealousy, is not slow to digest the volume of its by-laws and exclusive privileges. But the inhabitants of a small parish, living with some degree of that simplicity which best corresponds with the real nature and wants of a human being, would soon be led to suspect that general laws were unnecessary, and would adjudge the causes that came before them, not according to certain axioms previously written, but according to the circumstances and demand of each particular cause.—It was proper that this consequence should be mentioned in this place. The benefits that will arise from the abolition of law will come to be considered in detail in the following book.

The principal objection that is usually made to the idea of confederacy considered as the substitute of legislative unity, is the possibility that arises of the members of the confederacy detaching themselves from the support of the public cause. To give this objection every advantage, let us suppose that the seat of the confederacy, like France, is placed in the midst of surrounding nations, and that the governments of these nations are anxious by every means of artifice and violence to suppress the insolent spirit of liberty that has started up among this neighbour people. It is to be believed that even under these circumstances the danger is more imaginary than real. The national assembly, being precluded by the supposition from the use of force against the malcontent districts, is obliged to confine itself to expostulation; and it is sufficiently observable that our powers of expostulation are tenfold increased the moment our hopes are confined to expostulation alone. They have to describe with the utmost perspicuity and simplicity the benefits of independence; to convince the public at large, that all they intend is to enable every district, and as far as possible every individual, to pursue unmolested their own ideas of propriety; and that under their auspices there shall be no tyranny, no arbitrary punishments, such as proceed from the jealousy of councils and courts, no exactions, almost no taxation. Some ideas respecting this last subject will speedily occur. It is not possible but that, in a country rescued from the inveterate evils of despotism, the love of liberty should be considerably diffused. The adherents therefore of the public cause will be many: the malcontents few. If a small number of districts were so far blinded as to be willing to surrender themselves to oppression and slavery, it is probable they would soon repent. Their desertion would inspire the more enlightened and courageous with additional energy. It would be a glorious spectacle to see the champions of the cause of truth declaring that they desired none but willing supporters. It is not possible that so magnanimous a principle should not contribute more to the advantage than the injury of their cause.

CHAPTER VIII

OF NATIONAL EDUCATION

Arguments in its favour.—Answer.—1. It produces permanence of opinion.—Nature of prejudice and judgment described.—2. It requires uniformity of operation.—3. It is the mirror and tool of national government.—The right of punishing not founded in the previous function of instructing.

A MODE in which government has been accustomed to interfere for the purpose of influencing opinion, is by the superintendence it has in a greater or less degree exerted in the article of education. It is worthy of observation that the idea of this superintendence has obtained the countenance of several of the most zealous advocates of political reform. The question relative to its propriety or impropriety is entitled on that account to the more deliberate examination.

The arguments in its favour have been already anticipated. 'Can it be justifiable in those persons, who are appointed to the functions of magistracy, and whose duty it is to consult for the public welfare, to neglect the cultivation of the infant mind, and to suffer its future excellence or depravity to be at the disposal of fortune? Is it possible for patriotism and the love of the public to be made the characteristic of a whole people in any other way so successfully, as by rendering the early communication of these virtues a national concern? If the education of our youth be entirely confided to the prudence of their parents or the accidental benevolence of private individuals, will it not be a necessary consequence, that some will be educated to virtue, others to vice, and others again entirely neglected?' To these considerations it has been added, 'That the maxim which has prevailed in the majority of civilised countries, that ignorance of the law is no apology for the breach of it, is in the highest degree iniquitous; and that government cannot justly punish us for our crimes when committed, unless it have forewarned us against their commission, which cannot be adequately done without something of the nature of public education.'

The propriety or impropriety of any project for this purpose must be determined by the general consideration of its beneficial or injurious tendency. If the exertions of the magistrate in behalf of any system of instruction will stand the test as conducive to the public service, undoubtedly he cannot be justified in neglecting them. If on the contrary they conduce to injury, it is wrong and unjustifiable that they should be made.

The injuries that result from a system of national education are, in the first place, that all public establishments include in them the idea of permanence. They endeavour it may be to secure and to diffuse whatever of advantageous to society is already known, but they forget that more remains to be known. If they realised the most substantial benefits at the time of their introduction, they must inevitably become less and less useful as they increased in duration. But to describe them as useless is a very feeble expression of their demerits. They actively restrain the flights of mind, and fix it in the belief of exploded errors. It has commonly been observed of universities and extensive establishments for the purpose of education, that the knowledge taught there, is a century behind the knowledge which exists among the unshackled and unprejudiced members of the same political community. The moment any scheme of proceeding gains a permanent establishment, it becomes impressed as one of its characteristic features with an aversion to change. Some violent concussion may oblige its conductors to change an old system of philosophy for a system less obsolete; and they are then as pertinaciously attached to this second doctrine as they were to the first. Real intellectual improvement demands that mind should as speedily as possible be advanced to the height of knowledge already existing among the enlightened members of the community, and start from thence in the pursuit of farther acquisitions. But public education has always expended its energies in the support of prejudice; it teaches its pupils, not the fortitude that shall bring every proposition to the test of examination, but the art of vindicating such tenets as may chance to be previously established. We study Aristotle or Thomas Aquinas or Bellarmine or chief justice Coke, not that we may detect their errors, but that our minds may be fully impregnated with their absurdities.* This feature runs through every species of public establishment; and even in the petty institution of Sunday schools, the chief lessons that are taught, are a superstitious veneration for the church of England, and to bow to every man in a handsome coat. All this is directly contrary to the true interest of mind. All this must be unlearned, before we can begin to be wise.

It is the characteristic of mind to be capable of improvement. An individual surrenders the best attribute of man, the moment he resolves to adhere to certain fixed principles, for reasons not now present to his mind, but which formerly were. The instant in which he shuts upon himself the career of enquiry, is the instant of his intellectual decease. He is no longer a man; he is the ghost of departed man. There can be no scheme more egregiously stamped with folly, than that of separating a tenet from the evidence upon which its validity depends. If I cease from the habit of being able to recal this evidence, my belief is no longer a perception, but a prejudice: it may influence me like a prejudice; but cannot animate me like a real apprehension of truth. The difference between the man thus guided, and the man that keeps his mind perpetually alive, is the difference between cowardice and fortitude. The man who is in the best sense an intellectual being, delights to recollect the reasons that have convinced him, to repeat them to others, that they may produce conviction in them, and stand more distinct and explicit in his own mind; and he adds to this a willingness to examine objections, because he takes no pride in consistent error. The man who is not capable of this salutary exercise, to what valuable purpose can he be employed? Hence it appears that no vice can be more destructive than that which teaches us to regard any judgment as final, and not open to review. The same principle that applies to individuals applies to communities. There is no proposition, at present apprehended to be true, so valuable as to justify the introduction of an establishment for the purpose of inculcating it on mankind. Refer them to reading, to conversation, to meditation; but teach them neither creeds nor catechisms, neither moral nor political.

Secondly, the idea of national education is founded in an inattention to the nature of mind. Whatever each man does for himself is done well; whatever his neighbours or his country undertake to do for him is done ill. It is our wisdom to incite men to act for themselves, not to retain them in a state of perpetual pupillage. He that learns because he desires to learn, will listen to the instructions he receives, and apprehend their meaning. He that teaches because he desires to teach, will discharge his occupation with enthusiasm and energy. But the moment political institution undertakes to assign to every man his place, the functions of all will be discharged with supineness and indifference. Universities and expensive establishments have long been remarked for formal dulness. Civil policy has given me the power to appropriate my estate to certain theoretical purposes; but it is an idle presumption to think I can entail my views, as I can entail my fortune. Remove all those obstacles which prevent men from seeing and restrain them from pursuing their real advantage, but do not absurdly undertake to relieve them from the activity which this pursuit requires. What I earn, what I acquire only because I desire to acquire it, I estimate at its true value; but what is thrust upon me may make me indolent, but cannot make me respectable. It is extreme folly to endeavour to secure to others, independently of exertion on their part, the means of being happy.—This whole proposition of a national education, is founded upon a supposition which has been repeatedly refuted in this work, but which has recurred upon us in a thousand forms, that unpatronised truth is inadequate to the purpose of enlightening mankind.

Thirdly, the project of a national education ought uniformly to be discouraged on account of its obvious alliance with national government. This is an alliance of a more formidable nature, than the old and much contested alliance of church and state. Before we put so powerful a machine under the direction of so ambiguous an agent, it behoves us to consider well what it is that we do. Government will not fail to employ it to strengthen its hands, and perpetuate its institutions. If we could even suppose the agents of government not to propose to themselves an object, which will be apt to appear in their eyes, not merely innocent, but meritorious; the evil would not the less happen. Their views as institutors of a system of education, will not fail to be analogous to their views in their political capacity: the data upon which their conduct as statesmen is vindicated, will be the data upon which their instructions are founded. It is not true that our youth ought to be instructed to venerate the constitution, however excellent; they should be instructed to venerate truth; and the constitution only so far as it corresponded with their independent deductions of truth. Had the scheme of a national education been adopted when despotism was most triumphant, it is not to be believed that it could have for ever stifled the voice of truth. But it would have been the most formidable and profound contrivance for that purpose that imagination can suggest. Still, in the countries where liberty chiefly prevails, it is reasonably to be assumed that there are important errors, and a national education has the most direct tendency to perpetuate those errors, and to form all minds upon one model.

It is not easy to say whether the remark, 'that government cannot justly punish offenders, unless it have previously informed them what is virtue and what is offence,' be entitled to a separate answer. It is to be hoped that mankind will never have to learn so important a lesson through so corrupt a channel. Government may reasonably and equitably presume that men who live in society know that enormous crimes are injurious to the public weal, without its being necessary to announce them as such, by laws to be proclaimed by heralds, or expounded by curates. It has been alledged that 'mere reason may teach me not to strike my neighbour; but will never forbid my sending a sack of wool from England, or printing the French constitution in Spain.'* This objection leads to the true distinction upon the subject. All real crimes are capable of being discerned without the teaching of law. All supposed crimes, not capable of being so discerned, are truly and unalterably innocent. It is true that my own understanding would never have told me that the exportation of wool was a vice: neither do I believe it is a vice now that a law has been made affirming it. It is a feeble and contemptible remedy for iniquitous punishments, to signify to mankind beforehand that you intend to inflict them. Nay, the remedy is worse than the evil: destroy me if you please; but do not endeavour by a national education to destroy in my understanding the discernment of justice and injustice. The idea of such an education, or even perhaps of the necessity of a written law, would never have occurred, if government and jurisprudence had never attempted the arbitrary conversion of innocence into guilt.

CHAPTER IX

OF PENSIONS AND SALARIES

Reasons by which they are vindicated.—Labour in its usual acceptation and labour for the public compared.—Immoral effects of the institution of salaries.—Source from which they are derived—unnecessary for the subsistence of the public functionary—for dignity.—Salaries of inferior officers— may also be superseded.—Taxation.—Qualifications.

AN article which deserves the maturest consideration, and by means of which political institution does not fail to produce the most important influence upon opinion, is that of the mode of rewarding public services. The mode which has obtained in all European countries is that of pecuniary reward. He who is employed to act in behalf of the public, is recompensed with a salary. He who retires from that employment, is recompensed with a pension. The arguments in support of this system are well known. It has been remarked, 'that it may indeed be creditable to individuals to be willing to serve their country without a reward, but that it is a becoming pride on the part of the public, to refuse to receive as an alms that for which they are well able to pay. If one man, animated by the most disinterested motives, be permitted to serve the public upon these terms, another will assume the exterior of disinterestedness, as a step towards the gratification of a sinister ambition. If men be not openly and directly paid for the services they perform, we may rest assured that they will pay themselves by ways ten thousand times more injurious. He who devotes himself to the public, ought to devote himself entire: he will therefore be injured in his personal fortune, and ought to be replaced. Add to this, that the servants of the public ought by their appearances and mode of living to command respect both from their own countrymen and from foreigners; and that this circumstance will require an expence for which it is the duty of their country to provide.'[1]

Before this argument can be sufficiently estimated, it will be necessary for us to consider the analogy between labour in its most usual acceptation and labour for the public service, what are the points in which they resemble and in which they differ. If I cultivate a field the produce of which is necessary for my subsistence, this is an innocent and laudable action, the first object it proposes is my own emolument, and it cannot be unreasonable that that object should be much in my contemplation while the labour is performing. If I cultivate a field the produce of which is not necessary to my subsistence, but which I propose to give in barter for a garment, the case then becomes different. The action here does not properly speaking begin in myself. Its immediate object is to provide food for another; and it seems to be in some degree a perversion of intellect, that causes me to place in an inferior point of view the inherent quality of the action, and to do that which is in the first instance benevolent, from a partial retrospect to my own advantage. Still the perversion here, at least to our habits of reflecting and judging, does not appear violent. The action differs only in form from that which is direct. I employ that labour in cultivating a field, which must otherwise be employed in manufacturing a garment. The garment I propose to myself as the end of my labour. We are not apt to conceive of this species of barter and trade as greatly injurious to our moral discernment.

But then this is an action in the slightest degree indirect. It does not follow, because we are induced to do some actions immediately beneficial to others from a selfish motive, that we can admit of this in all instances with impunity. It does not follow, because we are sometimes inclined to be selfish, that we must never be generous. The love of our neighbour is the great ornament of a moral nature. The perception of truth is the most solid improvement of an intellectual nature. He that sees nothing in the universe deserving of regard but himself, is a consummate stranger to the dictates of immutable reason. He that is not influenced in his conduct by the real and inherent natures of things, is

[1] The substance of these arguments may be found in Mr. Burke's Speech on Oeconomical Reform.*

rational to no purpose. Admitting that it is venial to do some actions immediately beneficial to my neighbour from a partial retrospect to myself, surely there must be other actions in which I ought to forget, or endeavour to forget myself. This duty is most obligatory in actions most extensive in their consequences. If a thousand men be to be benefited, I ought to recollect that I am only an atom in the comparison, and to reason accordingly.

These considerations may qualify us to decide upon the article of pensions and salaries. Surely it ought not to be the end of a good political institution to increase our selfishness, instead of suffering it to dwindle and decay. If we pay an ample salary to him who is employed in the public service, how are we sure that he will not have more regard to the salary than to the public? If we pay a small salary, yet the very existence of such a payment will oblige men to compare the work performed and the reward bestowed; and all the consequence that will result will be to drive the best men from the service of their country, a service first degraded by being paid, and then paid with an ill-timed parsimony. Whether the salary be large or small, if a salary exist, many will desire the office for the sake of its appendage. Functions the most extensive in their consequences will be converted into a trade. How humiliating will it be to the functionary himself, amidst the complication and subtlety of motives, to doubt whether the salary were not one of his inducements to the accepting the office? If he stand acquitted to himself, it is however still to be regretted, that grounds should be afforded to his countrymen, which tempt them to misinterpret his views.

Another consideration of great weight in this instance is that of the source from which salaries are derived: from the public revenue, from taxes imposed upon the community. But there is no practicable mode of collecting the superfluities of the community. Taxation, to be strictly equal, if it demand from the man of an hundred a year ten pounds, ought to demand from the man of a thousand a year nine hundred and ten. Taxation will always be unequal and oppressive, wresting the hard earned morsel from the gripe of the peasant, and sparing him most whose superfluities most defy the limits of justice. I will not say that the man of clear discernment and an independent mind would rather starve than be subsisted at the public cost: but I will say, that it is scarcely possible to devise any expedient for his subsistence that he would not rather accept.

Meanwhile the difficulty under this head is by no means insuperable. The majority of the persons chosen for public employment, under any situation of mankind approaching to the present, will possess a personal fortune adequate to their support. Those selected from a different class, will probably be selected for extraordinary talents, which will naturally lead to extraordinary resources. It has been deemed dishonourable to subsist upon private liberality; but this dishonour is produced only by the difficulty of reconciling this mode of subsistence and intellectual independence. It is free from many of the objections that have been urged against a public stipend. I ought to receive your superfluity as my due, while I am employed in affairs more important than that of earning a subsistence; but at the same time to receive it with a total indifference to personal advantage, taking only precisely what is necessary for the supply of my wants. He that listens to the dictates of justice and turns a deaf ear to the dictates of pride, will wish that the constitution of his country should cast him for support on the virtue of individuals, rather than provide for his support at the public expence. That virtue will, in this as in all other instances, increase, the more it is called into action. 'But what if he have a wife and children?' Let many aid him, if the aid of one be insufficient. Let him do in his lifetime what Eudamidas did at his decease, bequeath his daughter to be subsisted by one friend, and his mother by another.* This is the only true taxation, which he that is able, and thinks himself able, assesses on himself, not which he endeavours to discharge upon the shoulders of the poor. It is a striking example of the power of venal governments in generating prejudice, that this scheme of serving the public functions without salaries, so common among the ancient republicans, should by liberal minded men of the present day be deemed impracticable. It is not to be believed that those readers who already pant for the abolition of government and regulations in all their branches, should hesitate respecting so easy an advance towards this desirable object. Nor let us imagine that the safety of the community will depend upon the services of an individual. In the country in which individuals fit for the public service are rare, the post of honour will be his, not that fills an official situation, but that from his closet endeavours to waken the sleeping virtues of mankind. In the country where they are frequent, it will not be difficult by the short duration of the employment to compensate for the slenderness of the means of him that fills it. It is not easy to describe the advantages that must result from this proceeding. The public functionary would in every article of his charge recollect the motives of public spirit and benevolence. He would hourly improve in the energy and disinterestedness of his character. The habits created by a frugal fare and a chearful poverty, not hid as now in obscure retreats, but held forth to public view, and honoured with public esteem, would speedily pervade the community, and auspiciously prepare them for still farther improvements.

The objection, 'that it is necessary for him who acts on the part of the public to make a certain figure, and to live in a style calculated to excite respect,' does not deserve a separate answer. The whole spirit of this treatise is in direct hostility to this objection. If therefore it have not been answered already, it would be vain to attempt an answer in this place. It is recorded of the burghers of the Netherlands who conspired to throw off the Austrian yoke,* that they came to the place of consultation each man with his knapsack of provisions: who is there that feels inclined to despise this simplicity and honourable poverty? The abolition of salaries would doubtless render necessary the simplification and abridgment of public business. This would be a benefit and not a disadvantage.

It will farther be objected that there are certain functionaries in the lower departments of government, such as clerks and tax-gatherers, whose employment is perpetual, and whose subsistence ought for that reason to be made the result of their employment. If this objection were admitted, its consequences would be of subordinate importance. The office of a clerk or a tax-gatherer is considerably similar to those of mere barter and trade; and therefore to degrade it altogether to their level, would have little resemblance to the fixing such a degradation upon offices that demand the most elevated mind. The annexation of a stipend to such employments, if considered only as a matter of temporary accommodation, might perhaps be endured.

But the exception, if admitted, ought to be admitted with great caution. He that is employed in an affair of public necessity, ought to feel, while he discharges it, its true character. We should never allow ourselves to undertake an office of a public nature, without feeling ourselves animated with a public zeal. We shall otherwise discharge our trust with comparative coldness and neglect. Nor is this all. The abolition of salaries would lead to the abolition of those offices to which salaries are thought necessary. If we had neither foreign wars nor domestic stipends, taxation would be almost unknown; and, if we had no taxes to collect, we should want no clerks to keep an account of them. In the simple scheme of political institution which reason dictates, we could scarcely have any burdensome offices to discharge; and, if we had any that were so in their abstract nature, they might be rendered light by the perpetual rotation of their holders.

If we have no salaries, for a still stronger reason we ought to have no pecuniary qualifications, or in other words no regulation requiring the possession of a certain property, as a condition to the right of electing or the capacity of being elected. It is an uncommon strain of tyranny to call upon men to appoint for themselves a delegate, and at the same time forbid them to appoint exactly the man whom they may judge fittest for the office. Qualification in both kinds is the most flagrant injustice. It asserts the man to be of less value than his property. It furnishes to the candidate a new stimulus to the accumulation of wealth; and this passion, when once set in motion, is not easily allayed. It tells him, 'Your intellectual and moral qualifications may be of the highest order; but you have not enough of the means of luxury and vice.' To the non-elector it holds the most detestable language. It says, 'You are poor; you are unfortunate; the institutions of society oblige you to be the perpetual witness of other men's superfluity: because you are sunk thus low, we will trample you yet lower; you shall not even be reckoned in the lists for a man, you shall be passed by as one of whom society makes no account, and whose welfare and moral existence she disdains to recollect.'

CHAPTER X

OF THE MODES OF DECIDING A QUESTION ON THE PART OF THE COMMUNITY

Decision by lot, its origin—founded in the system of discretionary rights—implies the desertion of duty.—Decision by ballot—inculcates timidity—and hypocrisy.—Decision by vote, its recommendations.

WHAT has been here said upon the subject of qualifications, naturally leads to a few important observations upon the three principal modes of conducting election, by sortition, by ballot or by vote.*

The idea of sortition was first introduced by the dictates of superstition. It was supposed that, when human reason piously acknowledged its insufficiency, the Gods, pleased with so unfeigned a homage, interfered to guide the decision. This imagination is now exploded. Every man who pretends to philosophy will confess that, wherever sortition is introduced, the decision is exclusively guided by the laws of impulse and gravitation.—Strictly speaking there is no such thing as contingence. But, so far as relates to the exercise of apprehension and judgment on the particular question to be determined, all decision by lot is the decision of contingence. The operations of impulse and gravitation either proceed from a blind and unconscious principle; or, if they proceed from mind, it is mind executing general laws, and not temporising with every variation of human caprice.

All reference of public questions and elections to lot includes in it two evils, moral misapprehension and cowardice. There is no situation in which we can be placed that has not its correspondent duties. There is no alternative that can be offered to our choice, that does not include in it a better and a worse. The idea of sortition derives from the same root as the idea of discretionary rights. Men, undebauched by the lessons of superstition, would never have recourse to the decision by lot, were they not impressed with the notion of indifference, that they had a right to do any one of two or more things offered to their choice; and that of consequence, in order to rid themselves of uncertainty and doubt, it was sufficiently allowable to refer the decision of certain matters to accident. It is of great importance that this idea should be extirpated. Mind will never arrive at the true tone of energy, till we feel that moral liberty and discretion are mere creatures of the imagination, that in all cases our duty is precise, and the path of justice single and direct.

But, supposing us convinced of this principle, if we afterwards desert it, this is the most contemptible cowardice. Our desertion either arises from our want of energy to enquire, to compare and to decide, or from our want of fortitude to despise the inconveniences that might attend upon our compliance with what our judgment dictates.

Ballot is a mode of decision still more censurable than sortition. It is scarcely possible to conceive of a political institution that includes a more direct and explicit patronage of vice. It has been said, 'that ballot may in certain cases be necessary to enable a man of a feeble character to act with ease and independence, and to prevent bribery, corrupt influence and faction.' Vice is an ill remedy to apply to the diminution of vice. A feeble and irresolute character might before be accidental; ballot is a contrivance to render it permanent, and to scatter its seeds over a wider surface. The true cure for a want of constancy and public spirit is to inspire firmness, not to inspire timidity. Truth, if communicated to the mind with perspicuity, is a sufficient basis for virtue. To tell men that it is necessary they should form their decision by ballot, is to tell them that it is necessary they should be vicious.

If sortition taught us to desert our duty, ballot teaches us to draw a veil of concealment over our performance of it. It points out to us a method of acting unobserved. It incites us to make a mystery of our sentiments. If it did this in the most trivial article, it would not be easy to bring the mischief it would produce within the limits of calculation.

But it dictates this conduct in our most important concerns. It calls upon us to discharge our duty to the public with the most virtuous constancy; but at the same time directs us to hide our discharge of it. One of the most admirable principles in the structure of the material universe, is its tendency to prevent us from withdrawing ourselves from the consequences of our own actions. Political institution that should attempt to counteract this principle, would be the only true impiety. How can a man have the love of the public in his heart, without the dictates of that love flowing to his lips? When we direct men to act with secrecy, we direct them to act with frigidity. Virtue will always be an unusual spectacle among men, till they shall have learned to be at all times ready to avow their actions and assign the reasons upon which they are founded.

If then sortition and ballot be institutions pregnant with vice, it follows, that all social decisions should be made by open vote; that, wherever we have a function to discharge, we should reflect on the mode in which it ought to be discharged; and that, whatever conduct we are persuaded to adopt, especially in affairs of general concern, should be adopted in the face of the world.

BOOK VII
OF CRIMES AND PUNISHMENTS

CHAPTER I

LIMITATIONS OF THE DOCTRINE OF PUNISHMENT
WHICH RESULT FROM THE PRINCIPLES OF MORALITY

Definition of punishment.—Nature of crime.—Retributive justice not independent and absolute—not to be vindicated from the system of nature.—Desert a chimerical property.—Conclusion.

THE subject of punishment is perhaps the most fundamental in the science of politics. Men associated for the sake of mutual protection and benefit. It has already appeared, that the internal affairs of such associations are of infinitely greater importance than their external.[1] It has appeared that the action of society in conferring rewards and superintending opinion is of pernicious effect.[2] Hence it follows that government, or the action of the society in its corporate capacity, can scarcely be of any utility, except so far as it is requisite for the suppression of force by force; for the prevention of the hostile attack of one member of the society upon the person or property of another, which prevention is usually called by the name of criminal justice, or punishment.

Before we can properly judge of the necessity or urgency of this action of government, it will be of some importance to consider the precise import of the word punishment. I may employ force to counteract the hostility that is actually committing on me. I may employ force to compel any member of the society to occupy the post that I conceive most conducive to the general advantage, either in the mode of impressing soldiers and sailors, or by obliging a military officer or a minister of state to accept or retain his appointment. I may put an innocent man to death for the common good, either because he is infected with a pestilential disease, or because some oracle has declared it essential to the public safety. None of these, though they consist in the exertion of force for some moral purpose, comes within the import of the word punishment. Punishment is generally used to signify the voluntary infliction of evil upon a vicious being, not merely because the public

---

[1] Book V, Chap. XX.   [2] Book V, Chap. XII. Book VI, *passim.*

advantage demands it, but because there is apprehended to be a certain fitness and propriety in the nature of things, that render suffering, abstractedly from the benefit to result, the suitable concomitant of vice.

The justice of punishment therefore, in the strict import of the word, can only be a deduction from the hypothesis of freewill, and must be false, if human actions be necessary. Mind, as was sufficiently apparent when we treated of that subject,[1] is an agent, in no other sense than matter is an agent. It operates and is operated upon, and the nature, the force and line of direction of the first, is exactly in proportion to the nature, force and line of direction of the second. Morality in a rational and designing mind is not essentially different from morality in an inanimate substance. A man of certain intellectual habits is fitted to be an assassin, a dagger of a certain form is fitted to be his instrument. The one or the other excites a greater degree of disapprobation, in proportion as its fitness for mischievous purposes appears to be more inherent and direct. I view a dagger on this account with more disapprobation than a knife, which is perhaps equally adapted for the purposes of the assassin; because the dagger has few or no beneficial uses to weigh against those that are hurtful, and because it has a tendency by means of association to the exciting of evil thoughts. I view the assassin with more disapprobation than the dagger, because he is more to be feared, and it is more difficult to change his vicious structure or take from him his capacity to injure. The man is propelled to act by necessary causes and irresistible motives, which, having once occurred, are likely to occur again. The dagger has no quality adapted to the contraction of habits, and, though it have committed a thousand murders, is not at all more likely (unless so far as those murders, being known, may operate as a slight associated motive with the possessor) to commit murder again. Except in the articles here specified, the two cases are exactly parallel. The assassin cannot help the murder he commits any more than the dagger.

These arguments are merely calculated to set in a more perspicuous light a principle, which is admitted by many by whom the doctrine of necessity has never been examined; that the only measure of equity is utility, and whatever is not attended with any beneficial purpose, is not just. This is so evident a proposition that few reasonable and reflecting minds will be found inclined to reject it. Why do I inflict suffering on another? If neither for his own benefit nor the benefit of others, can that be right? Will resentment, the mere indignation and horror I have

---

[1] Book IV, Chap. VI.

conceived against vice, justify me in putting a being to useless torture? 'But suppose I only put an end to his existence.' What, with no prospect of benefit either to himself or others? The reason the mind easily reconciles itself to this supposition is, that we conceive existence to be less a blessing than a curse to a being incorrigibly vicious. But in that case the supposition does not fall within the terms of the question: I am in reality conferring a benefit. It has been asked, 'If we conceive to ourselves two beings, each of them solitary, but the first virtuous and the second vicious, the first inclined to the highest acts of benevolence, if his situation were changed for the social, the second to malignity, tyranny and injustice, do we not feel that the first is entitled to felicity in preference to the second?' If there be any difficulty in the question, it is wholly caused by the extravagance of the supposition. No being can be either virtuous or vicious who has no opportunity of influencing the happiness of others. He may indeed, though now solitary, recollect or imagine a social state; but this sentiment and the propensities it generates can scarcely be vigorous, unless he have hopes of being at some future time restored to that state. The true solitaire cannot be considered as a moral being, unless the morality we contemplate be that which has relation to his own permanent advantage. But, if that be our meaning, punishment, unless for reform, is peculiarly absurd. His conduct is vicious, because it has a tendency to render him miserable: shall we inflict calamity upon him, for this reason only because he has already inflicted calamity upon himself? It is difficult for us to imagine to ourselves a solitary intellectual being, whom no future accident shall ever render social. It is difficult for us to separate even in idea virtue and vice from happiness and misery; and of consequence not to imagine that, when we bestow a benefit upon virtue, we bestow it where it will turn to account; and, when we bestow a benefit upon vice, we bestow it where it will be unproductive. For these reasons the question of a solitary being will always be extravagant and unintelligible, but will never convince.

It has sometimes been alledged that the very course of nature has annexed suffering to vice, and has thus led us to the idea of punishment. Arguments of this sort must be listened to with great caution. It was by reasonings of a similar nature that our ancestors justified the practice of religious persecution: 'Heretics and unbelievers are the objects of God's indignation; it must therefore be meritorious in us to mal-treat those whom God has cursed.' We know too little of the system of the universe, are too liable to error respecting it, and see too small a portion of the whole, to entitle us to form our moral principles upon an imitation of what we conceive to be the course of nature.

It is an extreme error to suppose that the course of nature is something arbitrarily adjusted by a designing mind. Let us once conceive a system of percipient beings to exist, and all that we know of the history of man follows from that conception as so many inevitable consequences. Mind beginning to exist must have begun from ignorance, must have received idea after idea, must have been liable to erroneous conclusions from imperfect conceptions. We say that the system of the universe has annexed happiness to virtue and pain to vice. We should speak more accurately if we said, that virtue would not be virtue nor vice be vice, if this connection could cease. The office of the principle, whether mind or whatever else, to which the universe owes its existence, is less that of fabricating than conducting; is not the creation of truth, and the connecting ideas and propositions which had no original relation to each other, but the rendering truth, the nature of which is unalterable, an active and vivifying principle. It cannot therefore be good reasoning to say, the system of nature annexes unhappiness to vice, or in other words vice brings its own punishment along with it, therefore it would be unjust in us not by a positive interference to render that punishment double.

Thus it appears, whether we enter philosophically into the principle of human actions, or merely analyse the ideas of rectitude and justice which have the universal consent of mankind, that, accurately speaking, there is no such thing as desert. It cannot be just that we should inflict suffering on any man, except so far as it tends to good. Hence it follows that the strict acceptation of the word punishment by no means accords with any sound principles of reasoning. It is right that I should inflict suffering, in every case where it can be clearly shown that such infliction will produce an overbalance of good. But this infliction bears no reference to the mere innocence or guilt of the person upon whom it is made. An innocent man is the proper subject of it, if it tend to good. A guilty man is the proper subject of it under no other point of view. To punish him upon any hypothesis for what is past and irrecoverable and for the consideration of that only, must be ranked among the wildest conceptions of untutored barbarism. Every man upon whom discipline is administered, is to be considered as to the rationale of this discipline as innocent. Xerxes was not more unreasonable when he lashed the waves of the sea,* than that man would be who inflicted suffering on his fellow, from a view to the past, and not from a view to the future.

It is of the utmost importance that we should bear these ideas constantly in mind during our whole examination of the theory of punishment. This theory would in the past transactions of mankind have been totally different, if they had divested themselves of all emotions of anger and resentment; if they had considered the man who torments another for what he has done, as upon par with the child who beats the table; if they had figured to their imagination, and then properly estimated, the man, who should shut up in prison some atrocious criminal, and afterwards torture him at stated periods, merely in consideration of the abstract congruity of crime and punishment, without any possible benefit to others or to himself; if they had regarded infliction as that which was to be regulated solely by a dispassionate calculation of the future, without suffering the past, in itself considered, for a moment to enter into the account.

CHAPTER II

GENERAL DISADVANTAGES OF COERCION

Conscience in matters of religion considered—in the conduct of life.—Best practicable criterion of duty—not the decision of other men—but of our own understanding.—Tendency of coercion.—Its various classes considered.

HAVING thus precluded all ideas of punishment or retribution strictly so called, it belongs to us in the farther discussion of this interesting subject, to think merely of that coercion, which has usually been employed against persons convicted of past injurious action, for the purpose of preventing future mischief. And here we will first consider what is the quantity of evil which accrues from all such coercion, and secondly examine the cogency of the various reasons by which this coercion is recommended. It will not be possible wholly to avoid the repetition of some of the reasons which occurred in the preliminary discussion of the exercise of private judgment.[1] But those reasonings will now be extended, and derive additional advantage from a fuller arrangement.

It is commonly said that no man ought to be compelled in conscience in matters of religion considered: matters of religion to act contrary to the dictates of his conscience. Religion is a principle which the practice of all ages has deeply impressed upon the mind. He that discharges what his own apprehensions prescribe to him on the subject, stands approved to the tribunal of his own mind, and, conscious of rectitude in his intercourse with the author of nature, cannot fail to obtain the

---

[1] Book II, Chap. VI.

greatest of those advantages, whatever may be their amount, which religion has to bestow. It is in vain that I endeavour by persecuting statutes to compel him to resign a false religion for a true. Arguments may convince, but persecution cannot. The new religion, which I oblige him to profess contrary to his conviction, however pure and holy it may be in its own nature, has no benefits in store for him. The sublimest worship becomes transformed into a source of corruption, when it is not consecrated by the testimony of a pure conscience. Truth is the second object in this respect, integrity of heart is the first: or rather a proposition, that in its abstract nature is truth itself, converts into rank falshood and mortal poison, if it be professed with the lips only, and abjured by the understanding. It is then the foul garb of hypocrisy. Instead of elevating the mind above sordid temptations, it perpetually reminds the worshipper of the abject pusillanimity to which he has yielded. Instead of filling him with sacred confidence, it overwhelms with confusion and remorse.

The inference that has been made from these reasonings is, that criminal law is eminently misapplied in affairs of religion, and that its true province is civil misdemeanours. But this inference is false. It is only by an unaccountable perversion of reason, that men have been induced to affirm that religion is the sacred province of conscience, and that moral duty may be left undefined to the decision of the magistrate. What, is it of no consequence whether I be the benefactor of my species, or their bitterest enemy? whether I be an informer, or a robber, or a murderer? whether I be employed as a soldier to extirpate my fellow beings, or be called upon as a citizen to contribute my property to their extirpation? whether I tell the truth with that firmness and unreserve which ardent philanthropy will not fail to inspire, or suppress science lest I be convicted of blasphemy, and fact lest I be convicted of a libel? whether I contribute my efforts for the furtherance of political justice, or quietly submit to the exile of a family of whose claims I am an advocate, or to the subversion of liberty for which every man should be ready to die? Nothing can be more clear, than that the value of religion, or of any other species of abstract opinion, lies in its moral tendency. If I should be ready to set at nought the civil power for the sake of that which is the means, how much more when it rises in contradiction to the end?

Of all human concerns morality is the most interesting. It is the perpetual associate of our transactions: there is no situation in which we can be placed, no alternative that can be presented to our choice, respecting which duty is silent. 'What is the standard of morality and duty?' Justice. Not the arbitrary decrees that are in force in a particular climate; but those laws of eternal reason that are equally obligatory wherever man is to be found. 'But the rules of justice often appear to us obscure, doubtful and contradictory; what criterion shall be applied to deliver us from uncertainty?' There are but two criterions not the decisions of other men: possible, the decisions of other men's wisdom, and the decisions of our own understanding. Which of these is conformable to the nature of man? Can we surrender our own understandings? However we may strain after implicit faith, will not conscience in spite of ourselves whisper us, 'This decree is equitable, and this decree is founded in mistake?' Will there not be in the minds of the votaries of superstition, a perpetual dissatisfaction, a desire to believe what is dictated to them, accompanied with a want of that in which belief consists, evidence and conviction? If we could surrender our understandings, what sort of beings should we become? By the terms of the proposition we should not be rational: the nature of things would prevent us from being moral, for morality is the judgment of reason, employed in determining on the effects to result from the different kinds of conduct we may observe.

Hence it follows that there is no criterion of duty to any man but in the exercise of his private judgment. Whatever attempts to prescribe to his conduct, and to deter him from any course of action by penalties and threats, is an execrable tyranny. There may be some men of such inflexible virtue as to set human ordinances at defiance. It is generally believed that there are others so depraved, that, were it not for penalties and threats, the whole order of society would be subverted by their excesses. But what will become of the great mass of mankind, who are neither so virtuous as the first, nor so degenerate as the second? They are successfully converted by positive laws into latitudinarians and cowards. They yield like wax to the impression that is made upon them. Directed to infer the precepts of duty from the *dicta* of the magistrate, they are too timid to resist, and too short sighted to detect the imposition. It is thus that the mass of mankind have been condemned to a tedious imbecility.

There is no criterion of duty to any man but in the exercise of his private judgment. Has coercion any tendency to enlighten the judgment? Certainly not. Judgment is the perceived agreement or disagreement of two ideas, the perceived truth or falshood of any proposition. Nothing can aid this perception, that does not set the ideas in a clearer light, that does not afford new evidence of the substantialness or unsubstantialness of the proposition. The direct tendency of coercion is to set our understanding and our fears, our duty and our weakness at variance with each other. And how poor spirited a refuge does coercion afford? If what you require of me is duty, are there no reasons that will prove it to be such? If you understand more of eternal justice than I, and are thereby fitted to instruct me, cannot you convey the superior knowledge you possess from your understanding into mine? Will you set your wit against one who is intellectually a child, and because you are better informed than I, assume, not to be my preceptor, but my tyrant? Am I not a rational being? Could I resist your arguments, if they were demonstrative? The odious system of coercion, first annihilates the understanding of the subject, and then of him that adopts it. Dressed in the supine prerogatives of a master, he is excused from cultivating the faculties of a man. What would not man have been, long before this, if the proudest of us had no hopes but in argument, if he knew of no resort beyond, and if he were obliged to sharpen his faculties, and collect his powers, as the only means of effecting his purposes?

Let us reflect for a moment upon the species of argument, if argument it is to be called, that coercion employs. It avers to its victim that he must necessarily be in the wrong, because I am more vigorous and more cunning than he. Will vigour and cunning be always on the side of truth? Every such exertion implies in its nature a species of contest. This contest may be decided before it is brought to open trial by the despair of one of the parties. But it is not always so. The thief that by main force surmounts the strength of his pursuers, or by stratagem and ingenuity escapes from their toils, so far as this argument is valid, proves the justice of his cause. Who can refrain from indignation when he sees justice thus miserably prostituted? Who does not feel, the moment the contest begins, the full extent of the absurdity that this appeal includes? It is not easy to decide which of the two is most deeply to be deplored, the magistracy, the representative of the social system, that declares war against one of its members, in the behalf of justice, or in the behalf of oppression. In the first we see truth throwing aside her native arms and her intrinsic advantage, and putting herself upon a level with falshood. In the second we see falshood confident in the casual advantage she possesses, artfully extinguishing the new born light that would shame her in the midst of her usurped authority. The exhibition in both is that of an infant crushed in the merciless grasp of a giant. No sophistry can be more palpable than that which pretends to bring the two parties to an impartial hearing. Observe the consistency of this reasoning. We first vindicate political coercion, because the criminal has committed an offence against the community at large, and then pretend, while we bring him to the bar of the community, the offended party, that we bring him before an impartial umpire. Thus in England, the king by his attorney is the prosecutor, and the king by his representative is the judge.* How long shall such odious inconsistencies impose on mankind? The pursuit commenced against the supposed offender is the *posse comitatus*,* the armed force of the whole, drawn out in such portions as may be judged necessary; and when seven millions of men have got one poor, unassisted individual in their power, they are then at leisure to torture or to kill him, and to make his agonies a spectacle to glut their ferocity.

The argument against political coercion is equally good against the infliction of private penalties between master and slave, and between parent and child. There was in reality, not only more of gallantry, but more of reason in the Gothic system of trial by duel, than in these. The trial of force is over in these, as we have already said, before the exertion of force is begun. All that remains is the leisurely infliction of torture, my power to inflict it being placed in my joints and my sinews. This whole argument may be subjected to an irresistible dilemma. The right of the parent over his child lies either in his superior strength or his superior reason. If in his strength, we have only to apply this right universally, in order to drive all morality out of the world. If in his reason, in that reason let him confide. It is a poor argument of my superior reason, that I am unable to make justice be apprehended and felt in the most necessary cases, without the intervention of blows.

Let us consider the effect that coercion produces upon the mind of him against whom it is employed. It cannot begin with convincing; it is no argument. It begins with producing the sensation of pain, and the sentiment of distaste. It begins with violently alienating the mind from the truth with which we wish it to be impressed. It includes in it a tacit confession of imbecility. If he who employs coercion against me could mould me to his purposes by argument, no doubt he would. He pretends to punish me because his argument is important, but he really punishes me because his argument is weak.

CHAPTER III

OF THE PURPOSES OF COERCION

Nature of defence considered.—Coercion for restraint—for reformation.— Supposed uses of adversity—defective—unnecessary.—Coercion for example—1. Nugatory.—The necessity of political coercion arises from the defects of political institution.—2. Unjust.—Unfeeling character of this species of coercion.

PROCEED we to consider three principal ends that coercion proposes to itself, restraint, reformation and example. Under each of these heads the arguments on the affirmative side must be allowed to be cogent, not irresistible. Under each of them considerations will occur, that will oblige us to doubt universally of the propriety of coercion. In this examination I shall take it for granted that the persons with whom I am reasoning allow, that the ends of restraint and example may be sufficiently answered in consistency with the end of reformation, that is, without the punishment of death. To those by whom this is not allowed in the first instance, the subsequent reasonings will only apply with additional force.

The first and most innocent of all the classes of coercion is that which is employed in repelling actual force. This has but little to do with any species of political institution, but may nevertheless deserve to be first considered. In this case I am employed (suppose, for example, a drawn sword is pointed at my own breast or that of another, with threats of instant destruction) in preventing a mischief that seems about inevitably to ensue. In this case there appears to be no time for experiments. And yet even here meditation will not leave us without our difficulties. The powers of reason and truth are yet unfathomed. That truth which one man cannot communicate in less than a year, another can communicate in a fortnight. The shortest term may have an understanding commensurate to it. When Marius said with a stern voice and a commanding countenance to the soldier that was sent down into his dungeon to assassinate him, 'Wretch, have you the temerity to kill Marius!'* and with these few words drove him to flight; it was, that he had so energetic an idea compressed in his mind, as to make its way with irresistible force to the mind of his executioner. If there were falshood and prejudice mixed with this idea, can we believe that truth is not more powerful than they? It would be well for the human species, if they were all in this respect like Marius, all accustomed to place an intrepid confidence in the single energy of intellect. Who shall say what there is that would be impossible to men with these habits? Who shall say how far the whole species might be improved, were they accustomed to despise force in others, and did they refuse to employ it for themselves?

But the coercion we are here considering is exceedingly different. It is employed against an individual whose violence is over. He is at present engaged in no hostility against the community or any of its members. He is quietly pursuing those occupations which are beneficial to himself, and injurious to none. Upon what pretence is this man to be the subject of violence? For restraint? Restraint from what? 'From some future injury which it is to be feared he will commit.' This is the very argument which has been employed to justify the most execrable of all tyrannies. By what reasonings have the inquisition, the employment of spies and the various kinds of public censure directed against opinion been vindicated? Because there is an intimate connexion between men's opinions and their conduct: because immoral sentiments lead by a very probable consequence to immoral actions. There is not more reason, in many cases at least, to apprehend that the man who has once committed robbery will commit it again, than the man who dissipates his property at the gaming-table, or who is accustomed to profess that upon any emergency he will not scruple to have recourse to this expedient. Nothing can be more obvious than that, whatever precautions may be allowable with respect to the future, justice will reluctantly class among these precautions any violence to be committed on my neighbour. Nor are they oftener unjust than they are superfluous. Why not arm myself with vigilance and energy, instead of locking up every man whom my imagination may bid me fear, that I may spend my days in undisturbed inactivity? If communities, instead of aspiring, as they have hitherto done, to embrace a vast territory, and to glut their vanity with ideas of empire, were contented with a small district with a proviso of confederation in cases of necessity, every individual would then live under the public eye, and the disapprobation of his neighbours, a species of coercion, not derived from the caprice of men, but from the system of the universe, would inevitably oblige him either to reform or to emigrate.—The sum of the argument under this head is, that all coercion for the sake of restraint is punishment upon suspicion, a species of punishment, the most abhorrent to reason, and arbitrary in its application, that can be devised.

The second object which coercion may be imagined to propose to itself is reformation. We have already seen various objections that may be offered to it in this point of view. Coercion cannot convince, cannot conciliate, but on the contrary alienates the mind of him against whom it is employed. Coercion has nothing in common with reason, and therefore can have no proper tendency to the generation of virtue. Reason is omnipotent: if my conduct be wrong, a very simple statement, flowing from a clear and comprehensive view, will make it appear to be such; nor is there any perverseness that can resist the evidence of which truth is capable.

But to this it may be answered, 'that this view of the subject may indeed be abstractedly true, but that it is not true relative to the present imperfection of human faculties. The grand requisite for the reformation and improvement of the human species, seems to consist in the rousing of the mind. It is for this reason that the school of adversity has so often been considered as the school of virtue. In an even course of easy and prosperous circumstances the faculties sleep. But, when great and urgent occasion is presented, it should seem that the mind rises to the level of the occasion. Difficulties awaken vigour and engender strength; and it will frequently happen that the more you check and oppress me, the more will my faculties swell, till they burst all the obstacles of oppression.'

The opinion of the excellence of adversity is built upon a very obvious mistake. If we will divest ourselves of paradox and singularity, we shall perceive that adversity is a bad thing, but that there is something else that is worse. Mind can neither exist nor be improved without the reception of ideas. It will improve more in a calamitous, than a torpid state. A man will sometimes be found wiser at the end of his career, who has been treated with severity, than with neglect. But because severity is one way of generating thought, it does not follow that it is the best.

It has already been shown that coercion absolutely considered is injustice. Can injustice be the best mode of disseminating principles of equity and reason? Oppression exercised to a certain extent is the most ruinous of all things. What is it but this, that has habituated mankind to so much ignorance and vice for so many thousand years? Can that which in its genuine and unlimited state is the worst, become by a certain modification and diluting the best of all things? All coercion sours the mind. He that suffers it, is practically persuaded of the want of a philanthropy sufficiently enlarged in those with whom he is most intimately connected. He feels that justice prevails only with great limitations, and that he cannot depend upon being treated with justice. The lesson which coercion reads to him is, 'Submit to force, and abjure reason. Be not directed by the convictions of your understanding, but by the basest part of your nature, the dread of present pain, and the pusillanimous terror of the injustice of others.' It was thus Elizabeth of England and Frederic of Prussia were educated in the school of adversity. The way in which they profited by this discipline was by finding resources in their own minds, enabling them to regard unmoved the violence that was employed against them. Can this be the best possible mode of forming men to virtue? If it be, perhaps it is farther requisite that the coercion we use should be flagrantly unjust, since the improvement seems to lie not in submission, but resistance.

But it is certain that truth is adequate to awaken the mind without the aid of adversity. Truth does not consist in a certain number of unconnected propositions, but in evidence that shows their reality and their value. If I apprehend the value of any pursuit, shall I not engage in it? If I apprehend it clearly, shall I not engage in it zealously? If you would awaken my mind in the most effectual manner, tell me the truth with energy. For that purpose, thoroughly understand it yourself, impregnate your mind with its evidence, and speak from the clearness of your view, and the fulness of conviction. Were we accustomed to an education, in which truth was never neglected from indolence, or told in a way treacherous to its excellence, in which the preceptor subjected himself to the perpetual discipline of finding the way to communicate it with brevity and force, but without prejudice and acrimony, it cannot be doubted, but such an education would be much more effectual for the improvement of the mind, than all the modes of angry or benevolent coercion that can be devised.

The last object which coercion proposes is example. Had legislators confined their views to reformation and restraint, their exertions of power, though mistaken, would still have borne the stamp of humanity. But, the moment vengeance presented itself as a stimulus on the one side, or the exhibition of a terrible example on the other, no barbarity was then thought too great. Ingenious cruelty was busied to find new means of torturing the victim, or of rendering the spectacle impressive and horrible.

It has long since been observed that this system of policy constantly fails of its purpose. Farther refinements in barbarity produce a certain impression so long as they are new, but this impression soon vanishes, and the whole scope of a gloomy invention is exhausted in vain.[1] The reason of this phenomenon is that, whatever may be the force with which novelty strikes the imagination, the unchangeable principles of

---

[1] *Beccaria, Dei Delitti e delle Pene.**

reason speedily recur, and assert their indestructible empire. We feel the emergencies to which we are exposed, and we feel, or we think we feel, the dictates of truth directing to their relief. Whatever ideas we form in opposition to the mandates of law, we draw, with sincerity, though it may be with some mixture of mistake, from the unalterable conditions of our existence. We compare them with the despotism which society exercises in its corporate capacity, and the more frequent is our comparison, the greater are our murmurs and indignation against the injustice to which we are exposed. But indignation is not a sentiment that conciliates; barbarity possesses none of the attributes of persuasion. It may terrify; but it cannot produce in us candour and docility. Thus ulcerated with injustice, our distresses, our temptations, and all the eloquence of feeling present themselves again and again. Is it any wonder they should prove victorious?

With what repugnance shall we contemplate the present forms of human society, if we recollect that the evils which they thus mercilessly avenge, owe their existence to the vices of those very forms? It is a well known principle of speculative truth, that true self love and social prescribe to us exactly the same species of conduct.[1] Why is this acknowledged in speculation and perpetually contradicted in practice? Is there any innate perverseness in man that continually hurries him to his own destruction? This is impossible; for man is thought, and, till thought began, he had no propensities either to good or evil. My propensities are the fruit of the impressions that have been made upon me, the good always preponderating, because the inherent nature of things is more powerful than any human institutions. The original sin of the worst men, is in the perverseness of these institutions, the opposition they produce between public and private good, the monopoly they create of advantages which reason directs to be left in common. What then can be more shameless than for society to make an example of those whom she has goaded to the breach of order, instead of amending her own institutions, which, by straining order into tyranny, produced the mischief? Who can tell how rapid would be our progress towards the total annihilation of civil delinquency, if we did but enter upon the business of reform in the right manner?

Coercion for example, is liable to all the same objections as coercion for restraint or reformation, and to certain other objections peculiar to itself. It is employed against a person not now in the commission of offence, and of whom we can only suspect that he ever will offend.

---

[1] Book IV, Chap. IX.

It supersedes argument, reason and conviction, and requires us to think such a species of conduct our duty, because such is the good pleasure of our superiors, and because, as we are taught by the example in question, they will make us rue our stubbornness if we think otherwise. In addition to this it is to be remembered that, when I am made to suffer as an example to others, I am treated myself with supercilious neglect, as if I were totally incapable of feeling and morality. If you inflict pain upon me, you are either just or unjust. If you be just, it should seem necessary that there should be something in me that makes me the fit subject of pain, either desert, which is absurd, or mischief I may be expected to perpetrate, or lastly a tendency to reformation. If any of these be the reason why the suffering I undergo is just, then example is out of the question: it may be an incidental consequence of the procedure, but it can form no part of its principle. It must surely be a very inartificial and injudicious scheme for guiding the sentiments of mankind; to fix upon an individual as a subject of torture or death, respecting whom this treatment has no direct fitness, merely that we may bid others look on, and derive instruction from his misery. This argument will derive additional force from the reasonings of the following chapter.

CHAPTER IV

OF THE APPLICATION OF COERCION

Delinquency and coercion incommensurable—external action no proper subject of criminal animadversion—how far capable of proof.—Iniquity of this standard in a moral—and in a political view.—Propriety of a retribution to be measured by the intention of the offender considered.—Such a project would overturn criminal law—would abolish coercion.— Inscrutability, 1. Of motives—doubtfulness of history—declarations of sufferers.—2. Of the future conduct of the offender—uncertainty of evidence—either of the facts—or the intention.—Disadvantages of the defendant in a criminal suit.

A FARTHER consideration, calculated to show, not only the absurdity of coercion for example, but the iniquity of coercion in general, is, that delinquency and coercion are in all cases incommensurable. No standard of delinquency ever has been or ever can be discovered. No two crimes were ever alike; and therefore the reducing them explicitly or implicitly to general classes, which the very idea of example implies, is absurd. Nor is it less absurd to attempt to proportion the degree of suffering to the degree of delinquency, when the latter can never be discovered. Let us endeavour to clear in the most satisfactory manner the truth of these propositions.

Man, like every other machine the operations of which can be made the object of our senses, may be said, relatively, not absolutely speaking, to consist of two parts, the external and the internal. The form which his actions assume is one thing; the principle from which they flow is another. With the former it is possible we should be acquainted; respecting the latter there is no species of evidence that can adequately inform us. Shall we proportion the degree of suffering to the former or the latter, to the injury sustained by the community, or to the quantity of ill intention conceived by the offender? Some philosophers, sensible of the inscrutability of intention, have declared in favour of our attending to nothing but the injury sustained. The humane and benevolent Beccaria has treated this as a truth of the utmost importance, 'unfortunately neglected by the majority of political institutors, and preserved only in the dispassionate speculation of philosophers.'[1]

It is true that we may in many instances be tolerably informed respecting external actions, and that there will at first sight appear to be no great difficulty in reducing them to general rules. Murder, according to this system, will be the exertion of any species of action affecting my neighbour, so as that the consequences terminate in death. The difficulties of the magistrate are much abridged upon this principle, though they are by no means annihilated. It is well known how many subtle disquisitions, ludicrous or tragical according to the temper with which we view them, have been introduced to determine in each particular instance, whether the action were or were not the real occasion of the death. It never can be demonstratively ascertained.

But, dismissing this difficulty, how complicated is the iniquity of treating all instances alike, in which one man has occasioned the death of another? Shall we abolish the imperfect distinctions, which the most odious tyrannies have hitherto thought themselves compelled to admit, between chance medley, manslaughter and malice prepense?* Shall we inflict on the man who, in endeavouring to save the life of a drowning fellow creature, oversets a boat and occasions the death of a second, the same suffering, as on him who from gloomy and vicious habits is incited to the murder of his benefactor? In reality the injury sustained by the

---

[1] '*Questa è una di quelle palpabili verità, che per una maravigliosa combinazione di circostanze non sono con decisa sicurezza conosciute, che da alcuni pochi pensatori uomini d'ogni nazione, e d'ogni secolo.*' Dei Delitti e delle Pene.*

community is by no means the same in these two cases; the injury sustained by the community is to be measured by the antisocial dispositions of the offender, and, if that were the right view of the subject, by the encouragement afforded to similar dispositions from his impunity. But this leads us at once from the external action to the unlimited consideration of the intention of the actor. The iniquity of the written laws of society is of precisely the same nature, though not of so atrocious a degree, in the confusion they actually introduce between varied intentions, as if this confusion were unlimited. The delinquencies recited upon a former occasion, of 'one man that commits murder, to remove a troublesome observer of his depraved dispositions, who will otherwise counteract and expose him to the world; a second, because he cannot bear the ingenuous sincerity with which he is told of his vices; a third, from his intolerable envy of superior merit; a fourth, because he knows that his adversary meditates an act pregnant with extensive mischief, and perceives no other mode by which its perpetration can be prevented; a fifth, in defence of his father's life or his daughter's chastity; and any of these, either from momentary impulse, or any of the infinite shades of deliberation;'[1]—are delinquencies all of them unequal, and entitled to a very different censure in the court of reason. Can a system that levels these inequalities, and confounds these differences, be productive of good? That we may render men beneficent towards each other, shall we subvert the very nature of right and wrong? Or is not this system, from whatever pretences introduced, calculated in the most powerful manner to produce general injury? Can there be a more flagrant injury than to inscribe as we do in effect upon our courts of judgment, 'This is the Hall of Justice, in which the principles of right and wrong are daily and systematically slighted, and offences of a thousand different magnitudes are confounded together, by the insolent supineness of the legislator, and the unfeeling selfishness of those who have engrossed the produce of the general labour to their sole emolument!'

But suppose, secondly, that we were to take the intention of the offender, and the future injury to be apprehended, as the standard of infliction. This would no doubt be a considerable improvement. This would be the true mode of reconciling coercion and justice, if for reasons already assigned they were not in their own nature incompatible. It is earnestly to be desired that this mode of administring retribution should be seriously attempted. It is to be hoped that men will one day attempt to establish an accurate criterion, and not go on for ever, as

---

[1] Book II, Chap. VI, p. 78.

they have hitherto done, with a sovereign contempt of equity and reason. This attempt would lead by a very obvious process to the abolition of all coercion.

It would immediately lead to the abolition of all criminal law. An enlightened and reasonable judicature would have recourse, in order to decide upon the cause before them, to no code but the code of reason. They would feel the absurdity of other men's teaching them what they should think, and pretending to understand the case before it happened, better than they who had all the circumstances of the case under their inspection. They would feel the absurdity of bringing every error to be compared with a certain number of measures previously invented, and compelling it to agree with one of them. But we shall shortly have occasion to return to this topic.[1]

The greatest advantage that would result from men's determining to govern themselves in the suffering to be inflicted by the motives of the offender and the future injury to be apprehended, would consist in their being taught how vain and iniquitous it is in them to attempt to wield the rod of retribution. Who is it that in his sober reason will pretend to assign the motives that influenced me in any article of my conduct, and upon them to found a grave, perhaps a capital, penalty against me? The attempt would be presumptuous and absurd, even though the individual who was to judge me, had made the longest observation of my character, and been most intimately acquainted with the series of my actions. How often does a man deceive himself in the motives of his conduct, and assign it to one principle when it in reality proceeds from another? Can we expect that a mere spectator should form a judgment sufficiently correct, when he who has all the sources of information in his hands, is nevertheless mistaken? Is it not to this hour a dispute among philosophers whether I be capable of doing good to my neighbour for his own sake? 'To ascertain the intention of a man it is necessary to be precisely informed of the actual impression of the objects upon his senses, and of the previous disposition of his mind, both of which vary in different persons, and even in the same person at different times, with a rapidity commensurate to the succession of ideas, passions and circumstances.'[2] Meanwhile the individuals, whose office it is to judge of this inscrutable mystery, are possessed of no

---

[1] Chap. VIII.

[2] '*Questa [l'intenzione] dipende dalla impressione attuale degli oggetti, et dalla precedente disposizione della mente: esse variano in tutti gli uomini e in ciascun nomo colla velocissima successione idee, delle passioni, e delle circostanze.*' He adds, '*Sarebbe dunque necessario formare non solo un codice particolare per ciascun cittadino, ma una nuova legge ad ogni delitto.*'*

previous knowledge, utter strangers to the person accused, and collecting their only lights from the information of two or three ignorant and prejudiced witnesses.

What a vast train of actual and possible motives enter into the history of a man, who has been incited to destroy the life of another? Can you tell how much in these there was of apprehended justice and how much of inordinate selfishness? how much of sudden passion, and how much of rooted depravity? how much of intolerable provocation, and how much of spontaneous wrong? how much of that sudden insanity which hurries the mind into a certain action by a sort of incontinence of nature almost without any assignable motive, and how much of incurable habit? Consider the uncertainty of history. Do we not still dispute whether Cicero were more a vain or a virtuous man, whether the heroes of ancient Rome were impelled by vain glory or disinterested benevolence, whether Voltaire were the stain of his species, or their most generous and intrepid benefactor? Upon these subjects moderate men perpetually quote upon us the impenetrableness of the human heart. Will moderate men pretend that we have not an hundred times more evidence upon which to found our judgment in these cases, than in that of the man who was tried last week at the Old Bailey?* This part of the subject will be put in a striking light, if we recollect the narratives that have been written by condemned criminals. In how different a light do they place the transactions that proved fatal to them, from the construction that was put upon them by their judges? And yet these narratives were written under the most awful circumstances, and many of them without the least hope of mitigating their fate, and with marks of the deepest sincerity. Who will say that the judge with his slender pittance of information was more competent to decide upon the motives, than the prisoner after the severest scrutiny of his own mind? How few are the trials which an humane and a just man can read, terminating in a verdict of guilty, without feeling an uncontrolable repugnance against the verdict? If there be any sight more humiliating than all others, it is that of a miserable victim acknowledging the justice of a sentence, against which every enlightened reasoner exclaims with horror.

But this is not all. The motive, when ascertained, is only a subordinate part of the question. The point upon which only society can equitably animadvert, if it had any jurisdiction in the case, is a point, if possible, still more inscrutable than that of which we have been treating. A legal inquisition into the minds of men, considered by itself, all rational enquirers have agreed to condemn. What we want to ascertain is, not the intention of the offender, but the chance of his offending again.

For this purpose we reasonably enquire first into his intention. But, when we have found this, our task is but begun. This is one of our materials, to enable us to calculate the probability of his repeating his offence, or being imitated by others. Was this an habitual state of his mind, or was it a crisis in his history likely to remain an unique? What effect has experience produced on him, or what likelihood is there that the uneasiness and suffering that attend the perpetration of eminent wrong may have worked a salutary change in his mind? Will he hereafter be placed in circumstances that shall propel him to the same enormity? Precaution is in the nature of things a step in the highest degree precarious. Precaution that consists in inflicting injury on another, will at all times be odious to an equitable mind. Meanwhile be it observed, that all which has been said upon the uncertainty of crime, tends to aggravate the injustice of coercion for the sake of example. Since the crime upon which I animadvert in one man can never be the same as the crime of another, it is as if I should award a grievous penalty against persons with one eye, to prevent any man in future from putting out his eyes by design.

One more argument calculated to prove the absurdity of the attempt to proportion delinquency and suffering to each other may be derived from the imperfection of evidence. The veracity of witnesses will be to an impartial spectator a subject of continual doubt. Their competence, so far as relates to just observation and accuracy of understanding, will be still more doubtful. Absolute impartiality it would be absurd to expect from them. How much will every word and every action come distorted by the medium through which it is transmitted? The guilt of a man, to speak in the phraseology of law, may be proved either by direct or circumstantial evidence. I am found near to the body of a man newly murdered. I come out of his apartment with a bloody knife in my hand or with blood upon my clothes. If, under these circumstances and unexpectedly charged with murder, I falter in my speech or betray perturbation in my countenance, this is an additional proof. Who does not know that there is not a man in England, however blameless a life he may lead, who is secure that he shall not end it at the gallows? This is one of the most obvious and universal blessings that civil government has to bestow. In what is called direct evidence, it is necessary to identify the person of the offender. How many instances are there upon record of persons condemned upon this evidence, who after their death have been proved entirely innocent? Sir Walter Raleigh, when a prisoner in the Tower, heard some high words accompanied with blows under his window. He enquired of several eye witnesses who entered his apartment in succession, into the nature of the transaction. But the story they told varied in such material circumstances, that he could form no just idea of what had been done. He applied this to prove the vanity of history.* The parallel would have been more striking if he had applied it to criminal suits.

But supposing the external action, the first part of the question to be ascertained, we have next to discover through the same garbled and confused medium the intention. How few men should I choose to entrust with the drawing up a narrative of some delicate and interesting transaction of my life? How few, though, corporally speaking, they were witnesses of what was done, would justly describe my motives, and properly report and interpret my words? And yet in an affair, that involves my life, my fame and my future usefulness, I am obliged to trust to any vulgar and casual observer.

A man properly confident in the force of truth, would consider a public libel upon his character as a trivial misfortune. But a criminal trial in a court of justice is inexpressibly different. Few men, thus circumstanced, can retain the necessary presence of mind and freedom from embarrassment. But, if they do, it is with a cold and unwilling ear that their tale is heard. If the crime charged against them be atrocious, they are half condemned in the passions of mankind, before their cause is brought to a trial. All that is interesting to them is decided amidst the first burst of indignation; and it is well if their story be impartially estimated, ten years after their body has mouldered in the grave. Why, if a considerable time elapse between the trial and the execution, do we find the severity of the public changed into compassion? For the same reason that a master, if he do not beat his slave in the moment of resentment, often feels a repugnance to the beating him at all. Not so much, as is commonly supposed, from forgetfulness of the offence, as that the sentiments of reason have time to recur, and he feels in a confused and indefinite manner the injustice of coercion. Thus every consideration tends to show, that a man tried for a crime is a poor deserted individual with the whole force of the community conspiring his ruin. The culprit that escapes, however conscious of innocence, lifts up his hands with astonishment, and can scarcely believe his senses, having such mighty odds against him. It is easy for a man who desires to shake off an imputation under which he labours, to talk of being put on his trial; but no man ever seriously wished for this ordeal, who knew what a trial was.

CHAPTER V

OF COERCION CONSIDERED AS A TEMPORARY EXPEDIENT

Arguments in its favour.—Answer.—It cannot fit men for a better order of society.—The true remedy to private injustice described—is adapted to immediate practice.—Duty of the community in this respect.—Duty of individuals.—Illustration from the case of war—of individual defence.—Application.—Disadvantages of anarchy—want of security—of progressive enquiry.—Correspondent disadvantages of despotism.—Anarchy awakens, despotism depresses the mind.—Final result of anarchy—how determined.—Supposed purposes of coercion in a temporary view.—Reformation—example—restraint.—Conclusion.

THUS much for the general merits of coercion considered as an instrument to be applied in the government of men. It is time that we should enquire into the arguments by which it may be apologised as a temporary expedient. No introduction seemed more proper to this enquiry than such a review of the subject upon a comprehensive scale; that the reader might be inspired with a suitable repugnance against so pernicious a system, and prepared firmly to resist its admission in all cases where its necessity cannot be clearly demonstrated.

The arguments in favour of coercion as a temporary expedient are obvious. It may be alledged that, 'however suitable an entire immunity in this respect may be to the nature of mind absolutely considered, it is impracticable with regard to men as we now find them. The human species is at present infected with a thousand vices, the offspring of established injustice. They are full of factitious appetites and perverse habits: headstrong in evil, inveterate in selfishness, without sympathy and forbearance for the welfare of others. In time they may become accommodated to the lessons of reason; but at present they would be found deaf to her mandates, and eager to commit every species of injustice.'

One of the remarks that most irresistibly suggest themselves upon this statement is, that coercion has no proper tendency to prepare men for a state in which coercion shall cease. It is absurd to expect that force should begin to do that which it is the office of truth to finish, should fit men by severity and violence to enter with more favourable auspices into the schools of reason.

But, to omit this gross misrepresentation in behalf of the supposed utility of coercion, it is of importance in the first place to observe that there is a complete and unanswerable remedy to those evils the cure of which has hitherto been sought in coercion, that is within the reach of every community whenever they shall be persuaded to adopt it. There is a state of society, the outline of which has been already sketched,[1] that by the mere simplicity of its structure would infallibly lead to the extermination of offence: a state, in which temptation would be almost unknown, truth brought down to the level of all apprehensions, and vice sufficiently checked by the general discountenance and sober condemnation of every spectator. Such are the consequences that would necessarily spring from an abolition of the craft and mystery of governing; while on the other hand the innumerable murders that are daily committed under the sanction of legal forms, are solely to be ascribed to the pernicious notion of an extensive territory; to the dreams of glory, empire and national greatness, which have hitherto proved the bane of the human species, without producing solid benefit and happiness to a single individual.

Another observation which this consideration immediately suggests, is, that it is not, as the objection supposed, by any means necessary, that mankind should pass through a state of purification, and be freed from the vicious propensities which ill constituted governments have implanted, before they can be dismissed from the coercion to which they are at present subjected. In that case their state would indeed be hopeless, if it were necessary that the cure should be effected, before we were at liberty to discard those practices to which the disease owes its most alarming symptoms. But it is the characteristic of a well formed society, not only to maintain in its members those virtues with which they are already indued, but to extirpate their errors, and render them benevolent and just to each other. It frees us from the influence of those phantoms which before misled us, shows us our true advantage as consisting in independence and integrity, and binds us by the general consent of our fellow citizens to the dictates of reason, more strongly than with fetters of iron. It is not to the sound of intellectual health that the remedy so urgently addresses itself, as to those who are infected with diseases of the mind. The ill propensities of mankind no otherwise tend to postpone the abolition of coercion, than as they prevent them from perceiving the advantages of political simplicity. The moment in which they can be persuaded to adopt any rational plan for this abolition, is the moment in which the abolition ought to be effected.

A farther consequence that may be deduced from the principles that have here been delivered, is that coercion of a municipal kind can in no

---

[1] Book V, Chap. XXII, pp. 299–300.

case be the duty of the community. The community is always competent to change its institutions, and thus to extirpate offence in a way
infinitely more rational and just than that of coercion. If in this sense
coercion has been deemed necessary as a temporary expedient, the
opinion admits of satisfactory refutation. Coercion can at no time,
either permanently or provisionally, make part of any political system
that is built upon the principles of reason.

But, though in this sense coercion cannot be admitted so much as a
temporary expedient, there is another sense in which it must be so
admitted. Coercion exercised in the name of the state upon its respective members cannot be the duty of the community; but coercion
may be the duty of individuals within the community. The duty of individuals is, in the first place, to display with all possible perspicuity the
advantages of an improved state of society, and to be indefatigable in
detecting the imperfections of the constitution under which they live.
But, in the second place, it behoves them to recollect, that their efforts
cannot be expected to meet with instant success, that the progress of
knowledge has in all cases been gradual, and that their obligation to
promote the welfare of society during the intermediate period is not
less real, than their obligation to promote its future and permanent
advantage. In reality the future advantage cannot be effectually pro-
cured, if we be inattentive to the present security. But, as long as nations
shall be so far mistaken as to endure a complex government and an
extensive territory, coercion will be indispensibly necessary to general
security. It is therefore the duty of individuals to take an active share
upon occasion, in so much coercion, and in such parts of the existing
system, as shall be sufficient to prevent the inroad of universal violence
and tumult. It is unworthy of a rational enquirer to say, 'these things
are necessary, but I am not obliged to take my share in them.' If they be
necessary, they are necessary for the general good; of consequence are
virtuous, and what no just man will refuse to perform.

The duty of individuals is in this respect similar to the duty of independent communities upon the subject of war. It is well known what has
been the prevailing policy of princes under this head. Princes, especially
the most active and enterprising among them, are seized with an
inextinguishable rage for augmenting their dominions. The most innocent and inoffensive conduct on the part of their neighbours is an insufficient security against their ambition. They indeed seek to disguise
their violence under plausible pretences; but it is well known that,
where no such pretences occur, they are not on that account disposed
to drop their pursuit. Let us suppose then a land of freemen invaded by

one of these despots. What conduct does it behove them to adopt? We are not yet wise enough to make the sword drop out of the hands of our oppressors by the mere force of reason. Were we resolved, like quakers, neither to oppose nor obey them,* much bloodshed might perhaps be avoided: but a more lasting evil would result. They would fix garrisons in our country, and torment us with perpetual injustice. Supposing even it were granted that, if the invaded nation should conduct itself with unalterable constancy upon the principles of reason, the invaders would become tired of their fruitless usurpation, it would prove but little. At present we have to do, not with nations of philosophers, but with nations of men whose virtues are alloyed with weakness, fluctuation and inconstancy. At present it is our duty to consult respecting the procedure which to such nations would be attended with the most favourable result. It is therefore proper that we should choose the least calamitous mode of obliging the enemy speedily to withdraw himself from our territories.

The case of individual defence is of the same nature. It does not appear that any advantage can result from my forbearance, adequate to the disadvantages of my suffering my own life or that of another, a peculiarly valuable member of the community as it may happen, to become a prey to the first ruffian who inclines to destroy it. Forbearance in this case will be the conduct of a singular individual, and its effect may very probably be trifling. Hence it appears, that I ought to arrest the villain in the execution of his designs, though at the expence of a certain degree of coercion.

The case of an offender, who appears to be hardened in guilt, and to trade in the violation of social security, is clearly parallel to these. I ought to take up arms against the despot by whom my country is invaded, because my capacity does not enable me by arguments to prevail on him to desist, and because my countrymen will not preserve their intellectual independence in the midst of oppression. For the same reason I ought to take up arms against the domestic spoiler, because I am unable either to persuade him to desist, or the community to adopt a just political institution, by means of which security might be maintained consistently with the abolition of coercion.

To understand the full extent of this duty it is incumbent upon us to remark that anarchy as it is usually understood, and a well conceived form of society without government, are exceedingly different from each other. If the government of Great Britain were dissolved to-morrow, unless that dissolution were the result of consistent and digested views of political justice previously disseminated among the inhabitants, it would be very far from leading to the abolition of violence. Individuals, freed from the terrors by which they had been accustomed to be restrained, and not yet placed under the happier and more rational restraint of public inspection, or convinced of the wisdom of reciprocal forbearance, would break out into acts of injustice, while other individuals, who desired only that this irregularity should cease, would find themselves obliged to associate for its forcible suppression. We should have all the evils attached to a regular government, at the same time that we were deprived of that tranquillity and leisure which are its only advantages.

It may not be useless in this place to consider more accurately than we have hitherto done the evils of anarchy. Such a review will afford us a criterion by which to discern, as well the comparative value of different institutions, as the precise degree of coercion which must be employed for the exclusion of universal violence and tumult.

Anarchy in its own nature is an evil of short duration. The more horrible are the mischiefs it inflicts, the more does it hasten to a close. But it is nevertheless necessary that we should consider both what is the quantity of mischief it produces in a given period, and what is the scene in which it promises to close. The first victim that is sacrificed at its shrine is personal security. Every man who has a secret foe, ought to dread the dagger of that foe. There is no doubt that in the worst anarchy multitudes of men will sleep in happy obscurity. But woe to him who by whatever means excites the envy, the jealousy or the suspicion of his neighbour! Unbridled ferocity instantly marks him for its prey. This is indeed the principal evil of such a state, that the wisest, the brightest, the most generous and bold will often be most exposed to an immature fate. In such a state we must bid farewel to the patient lucubrations of the philosopher and the labour of the midnight oil. All is here, like the society in which it exists, impatient and headlong. Mind will frequently burst forth, but its appearance will be like the corruscations of the meteor, not like the mild illumination of the sun. Men, who start forth into sudden energy, will resemble in temper the state that brought them to this unlooked for greatness. They will be rigorous, unfeeling and fierce; and their ungoverned passions will often not stop at equality, but incite them to grasp at power.

With all these evils, we must not hastily conclude, that the mischiefs of anarchy are worse than those which government is qualified to produce. With respect to personal security anarchy is certainly not worse than despotism, with this difference that despotism is as perennial as anarchy is transitory. Despotism, as it existed under the Roman emperors, marked out wealth for its victim, and the guilt of being rich never failed to convict the accused of every other crime. This despotism continued for centuries. Despotism, as it has existed in modern Europe, has been ever full of jealousy and intrigue, a tool to the rage of courtiers and the resentment of women. He that dared utter a word against the tyrant, or endeavour to instruct his countrymen in their interests, was never secure that the next moment would not conduct him to a dungeon. Here despotism wreaked her vengeance at leisure, and forty years of misery and solitude were sometimes insufficient to satiate her fury. Nor was this all. An usurpation that defied all the rules of justice, was obliged to purchase its own safety by assisting tyranny through all its subordinate ranks. Hence the rights of nobility, of feudal vassalage, of primogeniture, of fines and inheritance. When the philosophy of law shall be properly understood, the true key to its spirit and its history will be found, not, as some men have fondly imagined, in a desire to secure the happiness of mankind, but in the venal compact by which superior tyrants have purchased the countenance and alliance of the inferior.

There is one point remaining in which anarchy and despotism are strongly contrasted with each other. Anarchy awakens mind, diffuses energy and enterprize through the community, though it does not effect this in the best manner, as its fruits, forced into ripeness, must not be expected to have the vigorous stamina of true excellence. But in despotism mind is trampled into an equality of the most odious sort. Every thing that promises greatness is destined to fall under the exterminating hand of suspicion and envy. In despotism there is no encouragement to excellence. Mind delights to expatiate in a field where every species of eminence is within its reach. A scheme of policy, under which all men are fixed in classes or levelled with the dust, affords it no encouragement to enter on its career. The inhabitants of such countries are but a more vicious species of brutes. Oppression stimulates them to mischief and piracy, and superior force of mind often displays itself only in deeper treachery or more daring injustice.

One of the most interesting questions in relation to anarchy is that of the manner in which it may be expected to terminate. The possibilities as to this termination are as wide as the various schemes of society which the human imagination can conceive. Anarchy may and has terminated in despotism; and in that case the introduction of anarchy will only serve to afflict us with variety of evils. It may lead to a modification of despotism, a milder and more equitable government than that which has gone before. And it does not seem impossible that it should lead to the best form of human society, that the most penetrating philosopher is able to conceive. Nay, it has something in it that suggests the likeness, a distorted and tremendous likeness, of true liberty. Anarchy has commonly been generated by the hatred of oppression. It is accompanied with a spirit of independence. It disengages men from prejudice and implicit faith, and in a certain degree incites them to an impartial scrutiny into the reason of their actions.

The scene in which anarchy shall terminate principally depends upon the state of mind by which it has been preceded. All mankind were in a state of anarchy, that is, without government, previously to their being in a state of policy. It would not be difficult to find in the history of almost every country a period of anarchy. The people of England were in a state of anarchy immediately before the Restoration.* The Roman people were in a state of anarchy at the moment of their secession to the Sacred Mountain.* Hence it follows that anarchy is neither so good nor so ill a thing in relation to its consequences, as it has sometimes been represented.

It is not reasonable to expect that a short period of anarchy should do the work of a long period of investigation and philosophy. When we say, that it disengages men from prejudice and implicit faith, this must be understood with much allowance. It tends to loosen the hold of these vermin upon the mind, but it does not instantly convert ordinary men into philosophers. Some prejudices, that were never fully incorporated with the intellectual habit, it destroys; but other prejudices it arms with fury, and converts into instruments of vengeance.

Little good can be expected from any species of anarchy that should subsist for instance among American savages. In order to anarchy being rendered a seed plot of future justice, reflexion and enquiry must have gone before, the regions of philosophy must have been penetrated, and political truth have opened her school to mankind. It is for this reason that the revolutions of the present age (for every total revolution is a species of anarchy) promise much happier effects than the revolutions of any former period. For the same reason the more anarchy can be held at bay, the more fortunate will it be for mankind. Falshood may gain by precipitating the crisis; but a genuine and enlightened philanthropy will wait with unaltered patience for the harvest of instruction. The arrival of that harvest may be slow, but it is infallible. If vigilance and wisdom be successful in their present opposition to anarchy, every benefit will be ultimately obtained, untarnished with violence, and unstained with blood.

These observations are calculated to lead us to an accurate estimate of the mischiefs of anarchy, and prove that there are forms of coercion and government more injurious in their tendency than the absence of organisation itself. They also prove that there are other forms of government which deserve in ordinary cases to be preferred to anarchy. Now it is incontrovertibly clear that, where one of two evils is inevitable, the wise and just man will choose the least. Of consequence the wise and just man, being unable as yet to introduce the form of society which his understanding approves, will contribute to the support of so much coercion, as is necessary to exclude what is worse, anarchy.

If then constraint as the antagonist of constraint must in certain cases and under temporary circumstances be admitted, it is an interesting enquiry to ascertain which of the three ends of coercion already enumerated must be proposed by the individuals by whom coercion is employed. And here it will be sufficient very briefly to recollect the reasonings that have been stated under each of these heads.

It cannot be reformation. To reform a man is to change the sentiments of his mind. Sentiments may be changed either for the better or the worse. They can only be changed by the operation of falshood or the operation of truth. Punishment we have already found, at least so far as relates to the individual, is injustice. The infliction of stripes upon my body can throw no new light upon the question between us. I can perceive in them nothing but your passion, your ignorance and your mistake. If you have any new light to offer, any cogent arguments to introduce; they will not fail, if adequately presented, to produce their effect. If you be partially informed, stripes will not supply the deficiency of your arguments. Whatever be the extent or narrowness of your wisdom, it is the only instrument by which you can hope to add to mine. You cannot give that which you do not possess. When all is done, I have nothing but the truths you told me by which to derive light to my understanding. The violence with which the communication of them was accompanied, may prepossess me against giving them an impartial hearing, but cannot, and certainly ought not, to make their evidence appear greater than your statement was able to make it.—These arguments are conclusive against coercion as an instrument of private or individual education.

But considering the subject in a political view it may be said, 'that, however strong may be the ideas I am able to communicate to a man in order to his reformation, he may be restless and impatient of expostulation, and of consequence it may be necessary to retain him by force, till I can properly have instilled these ideas into his mind.' It must be remembered that the idea here is not that of precaution to prevent the mischiefs he might perpetrate in the mean time, for that belongs to another of the three ends of coercion, that of restraint. But, separately from this idea, the argument is peculiarly weak. If the truths I have to communicate be of an energetic and impressive nature, if they stand forward perspicuous and distinct in my own mind, it will be strange if they do not at the outset excite curiosity and attention in him to whom they are addressed. It is my duty to choose a proper season at which to communicate them, and not to betray the cause of truth by an ill timed impatience. This prudence I should infallibly exercise, if my object were to obtain something interesting to myself; why should I be less quick sighted when I plead the cause of justice and eternal reason? It is a miserable way of preparing a man for conviction, to compel him by violence to hear an expostulation which he is eager to avoid. These arguments prove, not that we should lose sight of reformation, if coercion for any other reason appear to be necessary; but that reformation cannot reasonably be made the object of coercion.

Coercion for the sake of example is a theory that can never be justly maintained. The coercion proposed to be employed, considered absolutely, is either right or wrong. If it be right, it should be employed for its own intrinsic recommendations. If it be wrong, what sort of example does it display? To do a thing for the sake of example, is in other words to do a thing to-day, in order to prove that I will do a similar thing to-morrow. This must always be a subordinate consideration. No argument has been so grossly abused as this of example. We found it under the subject of war[1] employed to prove the propriety of my doing a thing otherwise wrong, in order to convince the opposite party that I should, when occasion offered, do something else that was right. He will display the best example, who carefully studies the principles of justice, and assiduously practises them. A better effect will be produced in human society by my conscientious adherence to them, than by my anxiety to create a specific expectation respecting my future conduct. This argument will be still farther inforced, if we recollect what has already been said respecting the inexhaustible differences of different cases, and the impossibility of reducing them to general rules.

The third object of coercion according to the enumeration already made is restraint. If coercion be in any case to be admitted, this is the only object it can reasonably propose to itself. The serious objections to which even in this point of view it is liable have been stated in another

---

[1] Book V, Chap. XVI, p. 275.

stage of the enquiry:[1] the amount of the necessity tending to supersede these objections has also been considered.

The subject of this chapter is of greater importance, in proportion to the length of time that may possibly elapse, before any considerable part of mankind shall be persuaded to exchange the present complexity of political institution for a mode which shall supersede the necessity of coercion. It is highly unworthy of the cause of truth to suppose, that during this interval I have no active duties to perform, that I am not obliged to co-operate for the present welfare of the community, as well as for its future regeneration. The temporary obligation that arises out of this circumstance exactly corresponds with what was formerly delivered on the subject of duty. Duty is the best possible application of a given power to the promotion of the general good.[2] But my power depends upon the disposition of the men by whom I am surrounded. If I were inlisted in an army of cowards, it might be my duty to retreat, though absolutely considered it should have been the duty of the army to come to blows. Under every possible circumstance it is my duty to advance the general good by the best means which the circumstances under which I am placed will admit.

CHAPTER VI

SCALE OF COERCION

Its sphere described.—Its several classes.—Death with torture.—Death absolutely.—Origin of this policy—in the corruptness of political institutions—in the inhumanity of the institutors.—Corporal punishment.—Its absurdity—its atrociousness.—Privation of freedom.—Duty of reforming our neighbour an inferior consideration in this case.—Its place defined.—Modes of restraint.—Indiscriminate imprisonment.—Solitary imprisonment.—Its severity.—Its moral effects.—Slavery.—Banishment.—1. Simple banishment.—2. Transportation.—3. Colonisation.—This project has miscarried from unkindness—from officiousness.—Its permanent evils.—Recapitulation.

It is time to proceed to the consideration of certain inferences that may be deduced from the theory of coercion which has now been delivered; nor can any thing be of greater importance than these inferences will be found to the virtue, the happiness and improvement of mankind.

---

[1] Chap. III.   [2] Book IV, Chap. VI, p. 167.

And, first, it evidently follows that coercion is an act of painful necessity, inconsistent with the true character and genius of mind, the practice of which is temporarily imposed upon us by the corruption and ignorance that reign among mankind. Nothing can be more absurd than to look to it as a source of improvement. It contributes to the generation of excellence, just as much as the keeper of the course contributes to the fleetness of the race. Nothing can be more unjust than to have recourse to it, but upon the most undeniable emergency. Instead of multiplying occasions of coercion, and applying it as the remedy of every moral evil, the true politician will anxiously confine it within the narrowest limits, and perpetually seek to diminish the occasions of its employment. There is but one reason by which it can in any case be apologised, and that is, where the suffering the offender to be at large shall be notoriously injurious to the public security.

Secondly, the consideration of restraint as the only justifiable ground of coercion, will furnish us with a simple and satisfactory criterion by which to measure the justice of the suffering inflicted.

The infliction of a lingering and tormenting death cannot be vindicated upon this hypothesis; for such infliction can only be dictated by sentiments of resentment on the one hand, or by the desire to exhibit a terrible example on the other.

To deprive an offender of his life in any manner will appear to be unjust, since it will always be sufficiently practicable without this to prevent him from farther offence. Privation of life, though by no means the greatest injury that can be inflicted, must always be considered as a very serious injury; since it puts a perpetual close upon the prospects of the sufferer, as to all the enjoyments, the virtues and the excellence of a human being.

In the story of those whom the merciless laws of Europe devote to destruction, we sometimes meet with persons who subsequently to their offence have succeeded to a plentiful inheritance, or who for some other reason seem to have had the fairest prospects of tranquillity and happiness opened upon them. Their story with a little accommodation may be considered as the story of every offender. If there be any man whom it may be necessary for the safety of the whole to put under restraint, this circumstance is a powerful plea to the humanity and justice of the leading members of the community in his behalf. This is the man who most stands in need of their assistance. If they treated him with kindness instead of supercilious and unfeeling neglect, if they made him understand with how much reluctance they had been induced to employ the force of the society against him, if they presented truth to his mind with calmness, perspicuity and benevolence, if they employed those precautions which an humane disposition would not fail to suggest, to keep from him the motives of corruption and obstinacy, his reformation would be almost infallible. These are the prospects to which his wants and his misfortunes powerfully entitle him; and it is from these prospects that the hand of the executioner cuts him off for ever.

It is a mistake to suppose that this treatment of criminals tends to multiply crimes. On the contrary few men would enter upon a course of violence with the certainty of being obliged by a slow and patient process to amputate their errors. It is the uncertainty of punishment under the existing forms that multiplies crimes. Remove this uncertainty, and it would be as reasonable to expect that a man would wilfully break his leg, for the sake of being cured by a skilful surgeon. Whatever gentleness the intellectual physician may display, it is not to be believed that men can part with rooted habits of injustice and vice without the sensation of considerable pain.

The true reasons in consequence of which these forlorn and deserted members of the community are brought to an ignominious death, are, first, the peculiar iniquity of the civil institutions of that community, and, secondly, the supineness and apathy of their superiors. In republican and simple forms of government punishments are rare, the punishment of death is almost unknown. On the other hand the more there is in any country of inequality and oppression, the more punishments are multiplied. The more the institutions of society contradict the genuine sentiments of the human mind, the more severely is it necessary to avenge their violation. At the same time the rich and titled members of the community, proud of their fancied eminence, behold with total unconcern the destruction of the destitute and the wretched, disdaining to recollect that, if there be any intrinsic difference between them, it is the offspring of their different circumstances, and that the man whom they now so much despise, would have been as accomplished and susceptible as they, if they had only changed situations. When we behold a string of poor wretches brought out for execution, justice will present to our affrighted fancy all the hopes and possibilities which are thus brutally extinguished, the genius, the daring invention, the unshrinking firmness, the tender charities and ardent benevolence, which have occasionally under this system been sacrificed at the shrine of torpid luxury and unrelenting avarice.

The species of suffering commonly known by the appellation of corporal punishment is also proscribed by the system above established.

Corporal punishment, unless so far as it is intended for example, appears in one respect in a very ludicrous point of view. It is an expeditious mode of proceeding, which has been invented in order to compress the effect of much reasoning and long confinement, that might otherwise have been necessary, into a very short compass. In another view it is not possible to express the abhorrence it ought to create. The genuine propensity of man is to venerate mind in his fellow man. With what delight do we contemplate the progress of intellect, its efforts for the discovery of truth, the harvest of virtue that springs up under the genial influence of instruction, the wisdom that is generated through the medium of unrestricted communication? How completely do violence and corporal infliction reverse the scene? From this moment all the wholesome avenues of mind are closed, and on every side we see them guarded with a train of disgraceful passions, hatred, revenge, despotism, cruelty, hypocrisy, conspiracy and cowardice. Man becomes the enemy of man; the stronger are seized with the lust of unbridled domination, and the weaker shrink with hopeless disgust from the approach of a fellow. With what feelings must an enlightened observer contemplate the furrow of a lash imprinted upon the body of a man? What heart beats not in unison with the sublime law of antiquity, 'Thou shalt not inflict stripes upon the body of a Roman?'* There is but one alternative in this case on the part of the sufferer. Either his mind must be subdued by the arbitrary dictates of the superior (for to him all is arbitrary that does not stand approved to the judgment of his own understanding); he will be governed by something that is not reason, and ashamed of something that is not disgrace; or else every pang he endures will excite the honest indignation of his heart and fix the clear disapprobation of his intellect, will produce contempt and alienation, against his punisher.

The justice of coercion is built upon this simple principle: Every man is bound to employ such means as shall suggest themselves for preventing evils subversive of general security, it being first ascertained, either by experience or reasoning, that all milder methods are inadequate to the exigence of the case. The conclusion from this principle is, that we are bound under certain urgent circumstances to deprive the offender of the liberty he has abused. Farther than this no circumstance can authorise us. He whose person is imprisoned (if that be the right kind of seclusion) cannot interrupt the peace of his fellows; and the infliction of farther evil, when his power to injure is removed, is the wild and unauthorised dictate of vengeance and rage, the wanton sport of unquestioned superiority.

When indeed the person of the offender has been first seized, there is a farther duty incumbent on his punisher, the duty of reforming him. But this makes no part of the direct consideration. The duty of every man to contribute to the intellectual health of his neighbour is of general application. Beside which it is proper to recollect what has been already demonstrated, that coercion of no sort is among the legitimate means of reformation. Restrain the offender as long as the safety of the community prescribes it, for this is just. Restrain him not an instant from a simple view to his own improvement, for this is contrary to reason and morality.

Meanwhile there is one circumstance by means of which restraint and reformation are closely connected. The person of the offender is to be restrained as long as the public safety would be endangered by his liberation. But the public safety will cease to be endangered, as soon as his propensities and dispositions have undergone a change. The connection which thus results from the nature of things, renders it necessary that, in deciding upon the species of restraint to be imposed, these two circumstances be considered jointly, how the personal liberty of the offender may be least intrenched upon, and how his reformation may be best promoted.

The most common method pursued in depriving the offender of the liberty he has abused is to erect a public jail in which offenders of every description are thrust together, and left to form among themselves what species of society they can. Various circumstances contribute to imbue them with habits of indolence and vice, and to discourage industry; and no effort is made to remove or soften these circumstances. It cannot be necessary to expatiate upon the atrociousness of this system. Jails are to a proverb seminaries of vice; and he must be an uncommon proficient in the passion and the practice of injustice, or a man of sublime virtue, who does not come out of them a much worse man than he entered.

An active observer of mankind,[1] with the purest intentions, and who had paid a very particular attention to this subject, was struck with the mischievous tendency of the reigning system, and called the attention of the public to a scheme of solitary imprisonment. But this, though free from the defects of the established mode, is liable to very weighty objections.

It must strike every reflecting mind as uncommonly tyrannical and severe. It cannot therefore be admitted into the system of mild coercion

[1] Mr Howard.*

which forms the topic of our enquiry. Man is a social animal. How far he is necessarily so will appear, if we consider the sum of advantages resulting from the social, and of which he would be deprived in the solitary state. But, independently of his original structure, he is eminently social by his habits. Will you deprive the man you imprison, of paper and books, of tools and amusements? One of the arguments in favour of solitary imprisonment is, that it is necessary the offender should be called off from his wrong habits of thinking, and obliged to enter into himself. This the advocates of solitary imprisonment probably believe will be most effectually done, the fewer be the avocations of the prisoner. But let us suppose that he is indulged in these particulars, and only deprived of society. How many men are there that can derive amusement from books? We are in this respect the creatures of habit, and it is scarcely to be expected from ordinary men that they should mould themselves to any species of employment, to which in their youth they were wholly strangers. But he that is most fond of study has his moments when study pleases no longer. The soul yearns with inexpressible longings for the society of its like. Because the public safety unwillingly commands the confinement of an offender, must he for that reason never light up his countenance with a smile? Who can tell the sufferings of him who is condemned to uninterrupted solitude? Who can tell that this is not, to the majority of mankind, the bitterest torment that human ingenuity can inflict? No doubt a mind truly sublime would conquer this inconvenience: but the powers of such a mind do not enter into the present question.

From the examination of solitary imprisonment in itself considered, we are naturally led to enquire into its real tendency as to the article of reformation. To be virtuous it is requisite that we should consider men and their relation to each other. As a preliminary to this study is it necessary that we should be shut out from the society of men? Shall we be most effectually formed to justice, benevolence and prudence in our intercourse with each other, in a state of solitude? Will not our selfish and unsocial dispositions be perpetually increased? What temptation has he to think of benevolence or justice who has no opportunity to exercise it? The true soil in which atrocious crimes are found to germinate, is a gloomy and morose disposition. Will his heart become much either softened or expanded, who breathes the atmosphere of a dungeon? Surely it would be better in this respect to imitate the system of the universe, and, if we would teach justice and humanity, transplant those we would teach into a natural and reasonable state of society. Solitude absolutely considered may instigate us to serve ourselves, but not to serve our neighbours. Solitude, imposed under too few limitations, may be a nursery for madmen and idiots, but not for useful members of society.

Another idea which has suggested itself with regard to the relegation of offenders from the community they have injured, is that of reducing them to a state of slavery or hard labour. The true refutation of this system is anticipated in what has been already said. To the safety of the community it is unnecessary. As a means to the reformation of the offender it is inexpressibly ill conceived. Man is an intellectual being. There is no way to make him virtuous, but in calling out his intellectual powers. There is no way to make him virtuous, but by making him independent. He must study the laws of nature and the necessary consequence of actions, not the arbitrary caprice of his superior. Do you desire that I should work? Do not drive me to it with the whip; for, if before I thought it better to be idle, this will but increase my alienation. Persuade my understanding, and render it the subject of my choice. It can only be by the most deplorable perversion of reason, that we can be induced to believe any species of slavery, from the slavery of the school boy to that of the most unfortunate negro in our West India plantations, favourable to virtue.

A scheme greatly preferable to any of these, and which has been tried under various forms, is that of transportation, or banishment. This scheme under the most judicious modifications is liable to objection. It would be strange if any scheme of coercion or violence were not so. But it has been made appear still more exceptionable than it will be found in its intrinsic nature, by the crude and incoherent circumstances with which it has usually been executed.

Banishment in its simple form is evidently unjust. The citizen whose residence we deem injurious in our own country, we have no right to impose upon another.

Banishment has sometimes been joined with slavery. Such was the practice of Great Britain previously to the defection of her American colonies. This cannot stand in need of a separate refutation.

The true species of banishment is removal to a country yet unsettled. The labour by which the untutored mind is best weaned from the vicious habits of a corrupt society, is the labour, not which is prescribed by the mandate of a superior, but which is imposed by the necessity of subsistence. The first settlement of Rome by Romulus and his vagabonds* is a happy image of this, whether we consider it as a real history, or as the ingenious fiction of a man well acquainted with the principles of mind. Men who are freed from the injurious institutions of European government, and obliged to begin the world for themselves, are in the direct road to be virtuous.

Two circumstances have hitherto rendered abortive this reasonable project. First, that the mother country pursues this species of colony with her hatred. Our chief anxiety is in reality to render its residence odious and uncomfortable, with the vain idea of deterring offenders. Our chief anxiety ought to be to smooth their difficulties, and contribute to their happiness. We should recollect that the colonists are men for whom we ought to feel no sentiments but those of love and compassion. If we were reasonable, we should regret the cruel exigence that obliges us to treat them in a manner unsuitable to the nature of mind; and having complied with the demand of that exigence, we should next be anxious to confer upon them every benefit in our power. But we are unreasonable. We harbour a thousand savage feelings of resentment and vengeance. We thrust them out to the remotest corner of the world. We subject them to perish by multitudes with hardship and hunger. Perhaps to the result of mature reflection banishment to the Hebrides, would appear as effectual as banishment to the Antipodes.

Secondly, it is absolutely necessary upon the principles here explained that these colonists, after having been sufficiently provided in the outset, should be left to themselves. We do worse than nothing, if we pursue them into their obscure retreat with the inauspicious influence of our European institutions. It is a mark of the profoundest ignorance of the nature of man, to suppose that, if left to themselves, they would universally destroy each other. On the contrary, new situations make new minds. The worst criminals when turned adrift in a body, and reduced to feel the churlish fang of necessity, conduct themselves upon reasonable principles, and often proceed with a sagacity and public spirit that might put the proudest monarchies to the blush.

Meanwhile let us not forget the inherent vices of coercion, which present themselves from whatever point the subject is viewed. Colonization seems to be the most eligible of those expedients which have been stated, but it is attended with considerable difficulties. The community judges of a certain individual that his residence cannot be tolerated among them consistently with the general safety. In denying him his choice among other communities do they not exceed their commission? What treatment shall be awarded him, if he return from the banishment to which he was sentenced?—These difficulties are calculated to bring back the mind to the absolute injustice of coercion, and to render us inexpressibly anxious for the advent of that policy by which it shall be abolished.

To conclude. The observations of this chapter are relative to a theory, which affirmed that it might be the duty of individuals, but never of communities, to exert a certain species of political coercion; and which founded this duty upon a consideration of the benefits of public security. Under these circumstances then every individual is bound to judge for himself, and to yield his countenance to no other coercion than that which is indispensibly necessary. He will no doubt endeavour to meliorate those institutions with which he cannot persuade his countrymen to part. He will decline all concern in the execution of such, as abuse the plea of public security to the most atrocious purposes. Laws may easily be found in almost every code, which, on account of the iniquity of their provisions, are suffered to fall into disuse by general consent. Every lover of justice will uniformly in this way contribute to the repeal of all laws, that wantonly usurp upon the independence of mankind, either by the multiplicity of their restrictions, or severity of their sanctions.

CHAPTER VII

OF EVIDENCE

Difficulties to which this subject is liable—exemplified in the distinction between overt actions and intentions.—Reasons against this distinction.—Principle in which it is founded.

HAVING sufficiently ascertained the decision in which questions of offence against the general safety ought to terminate, it only remains under this head of enquiry to consider the principles according to which the trial should be conducted. These principles may for the most part be referred to two points, the evidence that is to be required, and the method to be pursued by us in classing offences.

The difficulties to which the subject of evidence is liable, have been repeatedly stated in the earlier divisions of this work.[1] It may be worth while in this place to recollect the difficulties which attend upon one particular class of evidence, it being scarcely possible that the imagination of every reader should not suffice him to apply this text, and to perceive how easily the same kind of enumeration might be extended to any other class.

It has been asked, 'Why intentions are not subjected to the animadversion of criminal justice, in the same manner as direct acts of offence?'

---

[1] Book II, Chap. VI. Book VII, Chap. IV.

The arguments in favour of their being thus subjected are obvious. 'The proper object of political superintendence is not the past, but the future. Society cannot justly employ coercion against any individual, however atrocious may have been his misdemeanours, from any other than a prospective consideration, that is, a consideration of the danger with which his habits may be pregnant to the general safety. Past conduct cannot properly fall under the animadversion of government, except so far as it is an indication of the future. But past conduct appears at first sight to afford a slighter presumption as to what the delinquent will do hereafter, than declared intention. The man who professes his determination to commit murder, seems to be scarcely a less dangerous member of society, than he who, having already committed murder, has no apparent intention to repeat his offence.' And yet all governments have agreed either to pass over the menace in silence, or to subject the offender to a much less degree of coercion, than they employ against him, by whom the crime has been perpetrated. It may be right perhaps to yield them some attention when they thus agree in forbearance, though little undoubtedly is due to their agreement in inhumanity.

This distinction, so far as it is founded in reason, has relation principally to the uncertainty of evidence. Before the intention of any man can be ascertained in a court of justice from the consideration of the words he has employed, a variety of circumstances must be taken into the account. The witness heard the words which were employed: does he repeat them accurately, or has not his want of memory caused him to substitute in the room of some of them words of his own? Before it is possible to decide upon the confident expectation I may entertain that these words will be followed with correspondent actions, it is necessary I should know the exact tone with which they were delivered, and gesture with which they were accompanied. It is necessary I should be acquainted with the context, and the occasion that produced them. Their construction will depend upon the quantity of momentary heat or rooted malice with which they were delivered; and words, which appear at first sight of tremendous import, will sometimes be found upon accurate investigation to have had a meaning purely ironical in the mind of the speaker. These considerations, together with the odious nature of coercion in general, and the extreme mischief that may attend our restraining the faculty of speech in addition to the restraint we conceive ourselves obliged to put on men's actions, will probably be found to afford a sufficient reason, why words ought seldom or never to be made a topic of political animadversion.

CHAPTER VIII

OF LAW

Arguments by which it is recommended.—Answer.—Law is, 1. endless—
particularly in a free state.—Causes of this disadvantage.—2. Uncertain
—instanced in questions of property.—Mode in which it must be studied.—
3. pretends to foretel future events.—Laws are a species of promises—check the
freedom of opinion—are destructive of the principles of reason.—Dishonesty
of lawyers.—An honest lawyer mischievous.—Abolition of law vindicated
on the score of wisdom—of candour—from the nature of man.—Future
history of political justice.—Errors that might arise in the commencement.—
Its gradual progress.—Its effects on criminal law—on property.

A FARTHER article of great importance in the trial of offences, is that of
the method to be pursued by us in classing them, and the consequent
apportioning the degree of animadversion to the cases that may arise.
This article brings us to the direct consideration of law, which is
without doubt one of the most important topics upon which human
intellect can be employed. It is law which has hitherto been regarded in
countries calling themselves civilised, as the standard, by which to
measure all offences and irregularities that fall under public animadversion. Let us fairly investigate the merits of this choice.

The comparison which has presented itself to those by whom the
topic has been investigated, has hitherto been between law on one side,
and the arbitrary will of a despot on the other. But, if we would fairly
estimate the merits of law, we should first consider it as it is in itself,
and then, if necessary, search for the most eligible principle that may be
substituted in its place.

It has been recommended as 'affording information to the different
members of the community respecting the principles which will be
adopted in deciding upon their actions.' It has been represented as the
highest degree of iniquity, 'to try men by an *ex post facto* law,* or indeed
in any other manner than by the letter of a law, formally made, and sufficiently promulgated.'

How far it will be safe altogether to annihilate this principle we shall
presently have occasion to enquire. It is obvious at first sight to remark,
that it is of most importance in a country where the system of jurisprudence is most capricious and absurd. If it be deemed criminal in any
society to wear clothes of a particular texture, or buttons of a particular
composition, it is natural to exclaim, that it is high time the jurisprudence

of that society should inform its members what are the fantastic rules by which they mean to proceed. But, if a society be contented with the rules of justice, and do not assume to itself the right of distorting or adding to those rules, there law is evidently a less necessary institution. The rules of justice would be more clearly and effectually taught by an actual intercourse with human society unrestrained by the fetters of prepossession, than they can be by catechisms and codes.[1]

One result of the institution of law is, that the institution once begun, can never be brought to a close. Edict is heaped upon edict, and volume upon volume. This will be most the case, where the government is most popular, and its proceedings have most in them of the nature of deliberation. Surely this is no slight indication that the principle is wrong, and that of consequence, the farther we proceed in the path it marks out to us, the more shall we be bewildered. No task can be more hopeless than that of effecting a coalition between a right principle and a wrong. He that seriously and sincerely attempts it, will perhaps expose himself to more palpable ridicule, than he who, instead of professing two opposite systems, should adhere to the worst.

There is no maxim more clear than this, Every case is a rule to itself. No action of any man was ever the same as any other action, had ever the same degree of utility or injury. It should seem to be the business of justice, to distinguish the qualities of men, and not, which has hitherto been the practice, to confound them. But what has been the result of an attempt to do this in relation to law? As new cases occur, the law is perpetually found deficient. How should it be otherwise? Lawgivers have not the faculty of unlimited prescience, and cannot define that which is infinite. The alternative that remains, is either to wrest the law to include a case which was never in the contemplation of the author, or to make a new law to provide for this particular case. Much has been done in the first of these modes. The quibbles of lawyers and the arts by which they refine and distort the sense of the law, are proverbial. But, though much is done, every thing cannot be thus done. The abuse would sometimes be too palpable. Not to say, that the very education that enables the lawyer, when he is employed for the prosecutor, to find out offences the lawgiver never meant, enables him, when he is employed for the defendant, to find out subterfuges that reduce the law to a nullity. It is therefore perpetually necessary to make new laws. These laws, in order to escape evasion, are frequently tedious, minute and circumlocutory. The volume in which justice records her prescriptions is

---

[1] Book VI, Chap. VIII, p. 353.

for ever increasing, and the world would not contain the books that might be written.

The consequence of the infinitude of law is its uncertainty. This strikes directly at the principle upon which law is founded. Laws were made to put an end to ambiguity, and that each man might know what he had to depend upon. How well have they answered this purpose? Let us instance in the article of property. Two men go to law for a certain estate. They would not go to law, if they had not both of them an opinion of their success. But we may suppose them partial in their own case. They would not continue to go to law, if they were not both promised success by their lawyers. Law was made that a plain man might know what he had to depend upon, and yet the most skilful practitioners differ about the event of my suit. It will sometimes happen that the most celebrated pleader in the kingdom, or the first counsel in the service of the crown, shall assure me of infallible success, five minutes before another law officer, styled the keeper of the king's conscience, by some unexpected juggle decides it against me. Would the issue have been equally uncertain, if I had had nothing to trust to but the plain, unperverted sense of a jury of my neighbours, founded in the ideas they entertained of general justice? Lawyers have absurdly maintained, that the expensiveness of law is necessary to prevent the unbounded multiplication of suits; but the true source of this multiplication is uncertainty. Men do not quarrel about that which is evident, but that which is obscure.

He that would study the laws of a country accustomed to legal security, must begin with the volumes of the statutes. He must add a strict enquiry into the common or unwritten law; and he ought to digress into the civil, the ecclesiastical and canon law. To understand the intention of the authors of a law, he must be acquainted with their characters and views, and with the various circumstances, to which it owed its rise, and by which it was modified while under deliberation. To understand the weight and interpretation that will be allowed to it in a court of justice, he must have studied the whole collection of records, decisions and precedents. Law was originally devised that ordinary men might know what they had to depend upon, and there is not at this day a lawyer existing in Great Britain, presumptuous and vain-glorious enough to pretend that he has mastered the code. Nor must it be forgotten that time and industry, even were they infinite, would not suffice. It is a labyrinth without end; it is a mass of contradictions that cannot be extricated. Study will enable the lawyer to find in it plausible, perhaps unanswerable, arguments for any side of almost any question; but it would argue the utmost folly to suppose that the study of law can lead to knowledge and certainty.

A farther consideration that will demonstrate the absurdity of law in its most general acceptation is, that it is of the nature of prophecy. Its task is to describe what will be the actions of mankind, and to dictate decisions respecting them. Its merits in this respect have already been decided under the head of promises.[1] The language of such a procedure is, 'We are so wise, that we can draw no additional knowledge from circumstances as they occur; and we pledge ourselves that, if it be otherwise, the additional knowledge we acquire shall produce no effect upon our conduct.' It is proper to observe, that this subject of law may be considered in some respects as more properly belonging to the topic of the preceding book. Law tends no less than creeds, catechisms and tests, to fix the human mind in a stagnant condition, and to substitute a principle of permanence, in the room of that unceasing perfectibility which is the only salubrious element of mind. All the arguments therefore which were employed upon that occasion may be applied to the subject now under consideration.

The fable of Procrustes* presents us with a faint shadow of the perpetual effort of law. In defiance of the great principle of natural philosophy, that there are not so much as two atoms of matter of the same form through the whole universe, it endeavours to reduce the actions of men, which are composed of a thousand evanescent elements, to one standard. We have already seen the tendency of this endeavour in the article of murder.[2] It was in the contemplation of this system of jurisprudence, that the strange maxim was invented, that 'strict justice would often prove the highest injustice.'[3] There is no more real justice in endeavouring to reduce the actions of men into classes, than there was in the scheme to which we have just alluded, of reducing all men to the same stature. If on the contrary justice be a result flowing from the contemplation of all the circumstances of each individual case, if the only criterion of justice be general utility, the inevitable consequence is that, the more we have of justice, the more we shall have of truth, virtue and happiness.

From all these considerations we cannot hesitate to conclude universally that law is an institution of the most pernicious tendency.

The subject will receive some additional elucidation, if we consider the perniciousness of law in its immediate relation to those who practise it.

[1] Book III, Chap. III.
[2] Book II, Chap. VI, p. 78. Book VII, Chap. IV, p. 378.
[3] *Summum jus summa injuria.**

If there ought to be no such thing as law, the profession of a lawyer is no doubt entitled to our disapprobation. A lawyer can scarcely fail to be a dishonest man. This is less a subject for censure than for regret. Men are the creatures of the necessities under which they are placed. He that is habitually goaded by the incentives of vice, will not fail to be vicious. He that is perpetually conversant in quibbles, false colours and sophistry, cannot equally cultivate the generous emotions of the soul and the nice discernment of rectitude. If a single individual can be found who is but superficially tainted with the contagion, how many men on the other hand, in whom we saw the promise of the sublimest virtues, have by this trade been rendered indifferent to consistency or accessible to a bribe? Be it observed, that these remarks apply principally to men eminent or successful in their profession. He that enters into an employment carelessly and by way of amusement, is much less under its influence (though he will not escape), than he that enters into it with ardour and devotion.

Let us however suppose, a circumstance which is perhaps altogether impossible, that a man shall be a perfectly honest lawyer. He is determined to plead no cause that he does not believe to be just, and to employ no argument that he does not apprehend to be solid. He designs, as far as his sphere extends, to strip law of its ambiguities, and to speak the manly language of reason. This man is no doubt highly respectable so far as relates to himself, but it may be questioned whether he be not a more pernicious member of society than the dishonest lawyer. The hopes of mankind in relation to their future progress, depend upon their observing the genuine effects of erroneous institutions. But this man is employed in softening and masking these effects. His conduct has a direct tendency to postpone the reign of sound policy, and to render mankind tranquil in the midst of imperfection and ignorance. It may appear indeed a paradox to affirm that virtue can be more pernicious than vice. But the true solution of this difficulty lies in the remark, that virtue, such as is here described, is impossible. We may amuse ourselves with enquiring in such instances as this whether theory could not afford us a better system of intellectual progress than the mixed system which takes place in the world. But the true answer probably is, that what we call vice is mere error of the understanding, a necessary part of the gradation that leads to good, and in a word that the course of nature and the course of a perfect theory are in all cases the same.

The true principle which ought to be substituted in the room of law, is that of reason exercising an uncontroled jurisdiction upon the circumstances of the case. To this principle no objection can arise on the score of wisdom. It is not to be supposed that there are not men now existing, whose intellectual accomplishments rise to the level of law. Law we sometimes call the wisdom of our ancestors. But this is a strange imposition. It was as frequently the dictate of their passion, of timidity, jealousy, a monopolising spirit, and a lust of power that knew no bounds. Are we not obliged perpetually to revise and remodel this misnamed wisdom of our ancestors? to correct it by a detection of their ignorance and a condemnation of their intolerance? But, if men can be found among us whose wisdom is equal to the wisdom of law, it will scarcely be maintained, that the truths they have to communicate will be the worse for having no authority, but that which they derive from the reasons that support them.

It may however be alledged that, 'if there be little difficulty in securing a current portion of wisdom, there may nevertheless be something to be feared from the passions of men. Law may be supposed to have been constructed in the tranquil serenity of the soul, a suitable monitor to check the inflamed mind with which the recent memory of ills might induce us to proceed to the exercise of coercion.' This is the most considerable argument that can be adduced in favour of the prevailing system, and therefore deserves a mature examination.

The true answer to this objection is that nothing can be improved but in conformity to its nature. If we consult for the welfare of man, we must bear perpetually in mind the structure of man. It must be admitted that we are imperfect, ignorant, the slaves of appearances. These defects can be removed by no indirect method, but only by the introduction of knowledge. A specimen of the indirect method we have in the doctrine of spiritual infallibility. It was observed that men were liable to error, to dispute for ever without coming to a decision, to mistake in their most important interests. What was wanting, was supposed to be a criterion and a judge of controversies. What was attempted, was to endue truth with a visible form, and then repair to the oracle we had erected.

The case respecting law is exactly parallel to this. Men were aware of the deceitfulness of appearances, and they sought a talisman to guard them from imposition. Suppose I were to determine at the commencement of every day upon a certain code of principles to which I would conform the conduct of the day, and at the commencement of every year the conduct of the year. Suppose I were to determine that no circumstances should be allowed by the light they afforded to modify my conduct, lest I should become the dupe of appearance and the slave of passion. This is a just and accurate image of every system of permanence.

Such systems are formed upon the idea of stopping the perpetual motion of the machine, lest it should sometimes fall into disorder.

This consideration must sufficiently persuade an impartial mind that, whatever inconveniences may arise from the passions of men, the introduction of fixed laws cannot be the genuine remedy. Let us consider what would be the operation and progressive state of these passions, provided men were trusted to the guidance of their own discretion. Such is the discipline that a reasonable state of society employs with respect to man in his individual capacity:[1] why should it not be equally valid with respect to men acting in a collective capacity? Inexperience and zeal would prompt me to restrain my neighbour whenever he is acting wrong, and, by penalties and inconveniences designedly interposed, to cure him of his errors. But reason evinces the folly of this proceeding, and teaches me that, if he be not accustomed to depend upon the energies of intellect, he will never rise to the dignity of a rational being. As long as a man is held in the trammels of obedience, and habituated to look to some foreign guidance for the direction of his conduct, his understanding and the vigour of his mind will sleep. Do I desire to raise him to the energy of which he is capable? I must teach him to feel himself, to bow to no authority, to examine the principles he entertains, and render to his mind the reason of his conduct.

The habits which are thus salutary to the individual will be equally salutary in the transactions of communities. Men are weak at present, because they have always been told they are weak, and must not be trusted with themselves. Take them out of their shackles; bid them enquire, reason and judge; and you will soon find them very different beings. Tell them that they have passions, are occasionally hasty, intemperate and injurious, but they must be trusted with themselves. Tell them that the mountains of parchment in which they have been hitherto intrenched, are fit only to impose upon ages of superstition and ignorance; that henceforth we will have no dependence but upon their spontaneous justice; that, if their passions be gigantic, they must rise with gigantic energy to subdue them; that, if their decrees be iniquitous, the iniquity shall be all their own. The effect of this disposition of things will soon be visible; mind will rise to the level of its situation; juries and umpires will be penetrated with the magnitude of the trust reposed in them.

It may be no uninstructive spectacle to survey the progressive establishment of justice in the state of things which is here recommended.

---

[1] Book V, Chap. XX, p. 291.

At first it may be a few decisions will be made uncommonly absurd or atrocious. But the authors of these decisions will be confounded with the unpopularity and disgrace in which they have involved themselves. In reality, whatever were the original source of law, it soon became cherished as a cloke for oppression. Its obscurity was of use to mislead the inquisitive eye of the sufferer. Its antiquity served to divert a considerable part of the odium from the perpetrator of the injustice to the author of the law, and still more to disarm that odium by the influence of superstitious awe. It was well known that unvarnished, barefaced oppression could not fail to be the victim of its own operations.

To this statement it may indeed be objected, 'that bodies of men have often been found callous to censure, and that the disgrace, being amicably divided among them all, is intolerable to none.' In this observation there is considerable force, but it is inapplicable to the present argument. To this species of abuse one of two things is indispensibly necessary, either numbers or secrecy. To this abuse therefore it will be a sufficient remedy, that each jurisdiction be considerably limited, and all transactions conducted in an open and explicit manner.—To proceed.

The juridical decisions that were made immediately after the abolition of law, would differ little from those during its empire. They would be the decisions of prejudice and habit. But habit, having lost the centre about which it revolved, would diminish in the regularity of its operations. Those to whom the arbitration of any question was intrusted, would frequently recollect that the whole case was committed to their deliberation, and they could not fail occasionally to examine themselves respecting the reason of those principles which had hitherto passed uncontroverted. Their understandings would grow enlarged, in proportion as they felt the importance of their trust, and the unbounded freedom of their investigation. Here then would commence an auspicious order of things, of which no understanding of man at present in existence can foretel the result, the dethronement of implicit faith and the inauguration of unclouded justice.

Some of the conclusions of which this state of things would be the harbinger, have been already seen in the judgment that would be made of offences against the community.[1] Offences arguing infinite variety in the depravity from which they sprung, would no longer be confounded under some general name. Juries would grow as perspicacious in distinguishing, as they are now indiscriminate in confounding the merit of actions and characters.

[1] Book II, Chap. VI, p. 78. Book VII, Chap. IV, p. 378.

Let us consider the effects of the abolition of law as it respects the article of property. As soon as the minds of men became somewhat weaned from the unfeeling uniformity of the present system, they would begin to enquire after equity. In this situation let us suppose a litigated succession brought before them, to which there were five heirs, and that the sentence of their old legislation had directed the division of this property into five equal shares. They would begin to enquire into the wants and situation of the claimants. The first we will suppose to have a fair character and be prosperous in the world: he is a respectable member of society, but farther wealth would add little either to his usefulness or his enjoyment. The second is a miserable object, perishing with want, and overwhelmed with calamity. The third, though poor, is yet tranquil; but there is a situation to which his virtue leads him to aspire, and in which he may be of uncommon service, but which he cannot with propriety accept, without a capital equal to two fifths of the whole succession. One of the claimants is an unmarried woman past the age of childbearing. Another is a widow, unprovided, and with a numerous family depending on her succour. The first question that would suggest itself to unprejudiced persons, having the allotment of this succession referred to their unlimited decision, would be, what justice is there in the indiscriminate partition which has hitherto prevailed? This would be one of the early suggestions that would produce a shock in the prevailing system of property. To enquire into the general issue of these suggestions is the principal object of the following book.

An observation which cannot have escaped the reader in the perusal of this chapter, is, that law is merely relative to the exercise of political force, and must perish when the necessity for that force ceases, if the influence of truth do not still sooner extirpate it from the practice of mankind.

CHAPTER IX

OF PARDONS

Their absurdity.—Their origin.—Their abuses.—Their arbitrary character. —Destructive of morality.

THERE is one other topic which belongs to the subject of the present book, but which may be dismissed in a very few words, because, though it has unhappily been in almost all cases neglected in practice, it is a point that seems to admit of uncommonly simple and irresistible evidence: I mean, the subject of pardons.

The very word to a reflecting mind is fraught with absurdity. 'What is the rule that ought in all cases to prescribe to my conduct?' Surely justice; understanding by justice the greatest utility of the whole mass of beings that may be influenced by my conduct. 'What then is clemency?' It can be nothing but the pitiable egotism of him who imagines he can do something better than justice. 'Is it right that I should suffer constraint for a certain offence?' The rectitude of my suffering must be founded in its tendency to promote the general welfare. He therefore that pardons me, iniquitously prefers the imaginary interest of an individual, and utterly neglects what he owes to the whole. He bestows that which I ought not to receive, and which he has no right to give. 'Is it right on the contrary that I should not undergo the suffering in question? Will he by rescuing me from suffering, do a benefit to me and no injury to others?' He will then be a notorious delinquent, if he allow me to suffer. There is indeed a considerable defect in this last supposition. If, while he benefits me, he do no injury to others, he is infallibly performing a public service. If I suffered in the arbitrary manner which the supposition includes, the whole would sustain an unquestionable injury in the injustice that was perpetrated. And yet the man who prevents this odious injustice, has been accustomed to arrogate to himself the attribute of clement, and the apparently sublime, but in reality tyrannical, name of forgiveness. For, if he do more than has been here described, instead of glory, he ought to take shame to himself, as an enemy to the interest of human kind. If every action, and especially every action in which the happiness of a rational being is concerned, be susceptible of a certain rule, then caprice must be in all cases excluded: there can be no action, which, if I neglect, I shall have discharged my duty; and, if I perform, I shall be entitled to applause.

The pernicious effects of the system of pardons is peculiarly glaring. It was first invented as the miserable supplement to a sanguinary code, the atrociousness of which was so conspicuous, that its ministers either dreaded the resistance of the people if it were indiscriminately executed, or themselves shrunk with spontaneous repugnance from the devastation it commanded. The system of pardons naturally associates with the system of law; for, though you may call every instance in which one man occasions the death of another by the name of murder, yet the injustice would be too great, to apply to all instances the same treatment. Define murder as accurately as you please, the same consequence, the same disparity of cases will obtrude itself. It is necessary therefore to have a court of reason, to which the decisions of a court of law shall be brought for revisal.

But how is this court, inexpressibly more important than the other, to be constituted? Here lies the essence of the matter; the rest is form. A jury is impanelled, to tell you the generical name of the action; a judge presides, to read out of the vocabulary of law the sentence annexed to that name; last of all, comes the court of enquiry which is to decide whether the remedy of the dispensatory be suitable to the circumstances of this particular case. This authority has usually been lodged in the first instance with the judge, and in the last resort with the king in council. Now, laying aside the propriety or impropriety of this particular selection, there is one grievous abuse which ought to strike the most superficial observer. These persons, with whom the principal trust is reposed, consider their functions in this respect as a matter purely incidental, exercise them with supineness, and in many instances with the most scanty materials to guide their judgment. This grows in a considerable degree out of the very name of pardon, which implies a work of supererogatory benevolence.

From the manner in which pardons are dispensed inevitably flows the uncertainty of punishment. It is too evident that punishment is inflicted by no certain rules, and of consequence the lives of a thousand victims are immolated in vain. Not more than one half or one third of the offenders whom the law condemns to death in this metropolis, are made to suffer the sentence that is pronounced. Is it possible that each offender should not flatter himself that he shall be among the number that escapes? Such a system, to speak it truly, is a lottery of death, in which each man draws his ticket for reprieve or execution, as undefinable accidents shall decide.

It may be asked whether the abolition of law would not produce equal uncertainty? By no means. The principles of king and council in such cases are very little understood, either by themselves or others. The principles of a jury of his neighbours commissioned to pronounce upon the whole of the case, the criminal easily guesses. He has only to appeal to his own sentiments and experience. Reason is a thousand times more explicit and intelligible than law; and when we were accustomed to consult her, the certainty of her decisions would be such as men practised in our present courts are totally unable to conceive.

Another very important consequence grows out of the system of pardons. A system of pardons is a system of unmitigated slavery. I am taught to expect a certain desirable event, from what? From the clemency, the uncontroled, unmerited kindness of a fellow mortal. Can any lesson be more degrading? The pusillanimous servility of the man who devotes himself with everlasting obsequiousness to another, because that other, having begun to be unjust, relents in his career; the ardour with which he confesses the rectitude of his sentence and the enormity of his deserts, will constitute a tale that future ages will find it difficult to understand.

What are the sentiments in this respect that are alone worthy of a rational being? Give me that and that only, which without injustice you cannot refuse. More than justice it would be disgraceful for me to ask, and for you to bestow. I stand upon the foundation of right. This is a title, which brute force may refuse to acknowledge, but which all the force in the world cannot annihilate. By resisting this plea you may prove yourself unjust, but in yielding to it you grant me but my due. If, all things considered, I be the fit subject of a benefit, the benefit is merited: merit in any other sense is contradictory and absurd. If you bestow upon me unmerited advantage, you are a recreant from the general good. I may be base enough to thank you; but, if I were virtuous, I should condemn you.

These sentiments alone are consistent with true independence of mind. He that is accustomed to regard virtue as an affair of favour and grace, cannot be eminently virtuous. If he occasionally perform an action of apparent kindness, he will applaud the generosity of his sentiments; and, if he abstain, he will acquit himself with the question, 'May I not do what I will with my own?' In the same manner, when he is treated benevolently by another, he will in the first place be unwilling to examine strictly into the reasonableness of this treatment, because benevolence, as he imagines, is not subject to any inflexibility of rule; and, in the second place, he will not regard his benefactor with that erect and unembarrassed mien, that complete sense of equality, which is the only immoveable basis of virtue and happiness.

BOOK VIII
OF PROPERTY

CHAPTER I
GENUINE SYSTEM OF PROPERTY DELINEATED

Importance of this topic.—Abuses to which it has been exposed.—Criterion of property: justice.—Entitles each man to the supply of his animal wants as far as the general stock will afford it—to the means of wellbeing— estimate of luxury.—Its pernicious effects on the individual who partakes of it.—Idea of labour as the foundation of property considered.—Its unreasonableness.—System of popular morality on this subject.—Defects of that system.

THE subject of property is the key stone that completes the fabric of political justice. According as our ideas respecting it are crude or correct, they will enlighten us as to the consequences of a *simple form of society without government*, and remove the prejudices that attach us to complexity. There is nothing that more powerfully tends to distort our *judgment* and *opinions*, than erroneous notions concerning the goods of fortune. Finally, the period that shall put an end to the system of *coercion* and *punishment*, is intimately connected with the circumstance of property's being placed upon an equitable basis.

Various abuses of the most incontrovertible nature have insinuated themselves into the administration of property. Each of these abuses might usefully be made the subject of a separate investigation. We might enquire into the vexations of this sort that are produced by the dreams of national greatness or magistratical vanity. This would lead us to a just estimate of the different kinds of taxation, landed or mercantile, having the necessaries or the luxuries of life for their subject of operation. We might examine into the abuses which have adhered to the commercial system; monopolies, charters, patents, protecting duties, prohibitions and bounties. We might remark upon the consequences that flow from the feudal system and the system of ranks; seignorial duties, fines, conveyances, entails, estates freehold, copyhold and manorial, vassalage and primogeniture. We might consider the rights of the church; first fruits and tithes: and we might enquire into the propriety of the regulation by which a man, after having possessed as sovereign a considerable property during his life, is permitted to dispose of it at his pleasure, at the period which the laws of nature seem to have fixed as the termination of his authority. All these enquiries would tend to show the incalculable importance of this subject. But, excluding them all from the present enquiry, it shall be the business of what remains of this work to consider, not any particular abuses which have incidentally risen out of the administration of property, but those general principles by which it has in almost all cases been directed, and which, if erroneous, must not only be regarded as the source of the abuses above enumerated, but of others of innumerable kinds, too multifarious and subtle to enter into so brief a catalogue.

What is the criterion that must determine whether this or that substance, capable of contributing to the benefit of a human being, ought to be considered as your property or mine? To this question there can be but one answer—Justice. Let us then recur to the principles of justice.[1]

To whom does any article of property, suppose a loaf of bread, justly belong? To him who most wants it, or to whom the possession of it will be most beneficial. Here are six men famished with hunger, and the loaf is, absolutely considered, capable of satisfying the cravings of them all. Who is it that has a reasonable claim to benefit by the qualities with which this loaf is endowed? They are all brothers perhaps, and the law of primogeniture bestows it exclusively on the eldest. But does justice confirm this award? The laws of different countries dispose of property in a thousand different ways; but there can be but one way which is most conformable to reason.

It would have been easy to put a case much stronger than that which has just been stated. I have an hundred loaves in my possession, and in the next street there is a poor man expiring with hunger, to whom one of these loaves would be the means of preserving his life. If I withhold this loaf from him, am I not unjust? If I impart it, am I not complying with what justice demands? To whom does the loaf justly belong?

I suppose myself in other respects to be in easy circumstances, and that I do not want this bread as an object of barter or sale, to procure me any of the other necessaries of a human being. Our animal wants have long since been defined, and are stated to consist of food, clothing and shelter. If justice have any meaning, nothing can be more iniquitous, than for one man to possess superfluities, while there is a human being in existence that is not adequately supplied with these.

Justice does not stop here. Every man is entitled, so far as the general

---

[1] Book II, Chap. II.

stock will suffice, not only to the means of being, but of well being. It is unjust, if one man labour to the destruction of his health or his life, that another man may abound in luxuries. It is unjust, if one man be deprived of leisure to cultivate his rational powers, while another man contributes not a single effort to add to the common stock. The faculties of one man are like the faculties of another man. Justice directs that each man, unless perhaps he be employed more beneficially to the public, should contribute to the cultivation of the common harvest, of which each man consumes a share. This reciprocity indeed, as was observed when that subject was the matter of separate consideration, is of the very essence of justice. How the latter branch of it, the necessary labour, is to be secured, while each man is admitted to claim his share of the produce, we shall presently have occasion to enquire.

This subject will be placed in a still more striking light, if we reflect for a moment on the nature of luxuries. The wealth of any state may intelligibly enough be considered as the aggregate of all the incomes, which are annually consumed within that state, without destroying the materials of an equal consumption in the ensuing year. Considering this income as being, what in almost all cases it will be found to be, the produce of the industry of the inhabitants, it will follow that in civilised countries the peasant often does not consume more than the twentieth part of the produce of his labour, while his rich neighbour consumes perhaps the produce of the labour of twenty peasants. The benefit that arises to this favoured mortal ought surely to be very extraordinary.

But nothing is more evident than that the condition of this man is the reverse of beneficial. The man of an hundred pounds *per annum,* if he understand his own happiness, is a thousand times more favourably circumstanced. What shall the rich man do with his enormous wealth? Shall he eat of innumerable dishes of the most expensive viands, or pour down hogsheads of the most highly flavoured wines? A frugal diet will contribute infinitely more to health, to a clear understanding, to chearful spirits, and even to the gratification of the appetites. Almost every other expence is an expence of ostentation. No man, but the most sordid epicure, would long continue to maintain even a plentiful table, if he had no spectators, visitors or servants, to behold his establishment. For whom are our sumptuous palaces and costly furniture, our equipages, and even our very clothes? The nobleman, who should for the first time let his imagination loose to conceive the style in which he would live, if he had nobody to observe, and no eye to please but his own, would no doubt be surprised to find that vanity had been the first mover in all his actions.

The object of this vanity is to procure the admiration and applause of beholders.* We need not here enter into the intrinsic value of applause. Taking it for granted that it is as estimable an acquisition as any man can suppose it, how contemptible is the source of applause to which the rich man has recourse? 'Applaud me, because my ancestor has left me a great estate.' What merit is there in that? The first effect then of riches is to deprive their possessor of the genuine powers of understanding, and render him incapable of discerning absolute truth. They lead him to fix his affections on objects not accommodated to the wants and the structure of the human mind, and of consequence entail upon him disappointment and unhappiness. The greatest of all personal advantages are, independence of mind, which makes us feel that our satisfactions are not at the mercy either of men or of fortune; and activity of mind, the chearfulness that arises from industry perpetually employed about objects, of which our judgment acknowledges the intrinsic value.

In this case we have compared the happiness of the man of extreme opulence with that of the man of one hundred pounds *per annum*. But the latter side of this alternative was assumed merely in compliance with existing prejudices. Even in the present state of human society we perceive, that a man, who should be perpetually earning the necessary competence by a very moderate industry, and with his pursuits uncrossed by the peevishness or caprice of his neighbours, would not be less happy than if he were born to that competence. In the state of society we are here contemplating, where, as will presently appear, the requisite industry will be of the lightest kind, it will be the reverse of a misfortune to any man, to find himself necessarily stimulated to a gentle activity, and in consequence to feel that no reverse of fortune could deprive him of the means of subsistence and contentment.

But it has been alledged, 'that we find among different men very different degrees of labour and industry, and that it is not just they should receive an equal reward.' It cannot indeed be denied that the attainments of men in virtue and usefulness ought by no means to be confounded. How far the present system of property contributes to their being equitably treated it is very easy to determine. The present system of property confers on one man immense wealth in consideration of the accident of his birth. He that from beggary ascends to opulence, is usually known not to have effected this transition by methods very creditable to his honesty or his usefulness. The most industrious and active member of society is frequently with great difficulty able to keep his family from starving.

But, to pass over these iniquitous effects of the unequal distribution of property, let us consider the nature of the reward which is thus proposed to industry. If you be industrious, you shall have an hundred times more food than you can eat, and an hundred times more clothes than you can wear. Where is the justice of this? If I be the greatest benefactor the human species ever knew, is that a reason for bestowing on me what I do not want, especially when there are thousands to whom my superfluity would be of the greatest advantage? With this superfluity I can purchase nothing but gaudy ostentation and envy, nothing but the pitiful pleasure of returning to the poor under the name of generosity that to which reason gives them an irresistible claim, nothing but prejudice, error and vice.

The doctrine of the injustice of accumulated property has been the foundation of all religious morality. The object of this morality has been, to excite men by individual virtue to repair this injustice. The most energetic teachers of religion have been irresistibly led to assert the precise truth upon this interesting subject. They have taught the rich, that they hold their wealth only as a trust, that they are strictly accountable for every atom of their expenditure, that they are merely administrators, and by no means proprietors in chief.[1] The defect of this system is, that they rather excite us to palliate our injustice than to forsake it.

No truth can be more simple than that which they inculcate. There is no action of any human being, and certainly no action that respects the disposition of property, that is not capable of better and worse, and concerning which reason and morality do not prescribe a specific conduct. He that sets out with acknowledging that other men are of the same nature as himself, and is capable of perceiving the precise place he would hold in the eye of an impartial spectator, must be fully sensible, that the money he employs in procuring an object of trifling or no advantage to himself, and which might have been employed in purchasing substantial and indispensible benefit to another, is unjustly employed. He that looks at his property with the eye of truth, will find that every shilling of it has received its destination from the dictates of justice. He will at the same time however be exposed to considerable pain, in consequence of his own ignorance as to the precise disposition that justice and public utility require.

Does any man doubt of the truth of these assertions? Does any man doubt that, when I employ a sum of money small or great in the

---

[1] See Swift's Sermon on Mutual Subjection* quoted Book II, Chap. II.

purchase of an absolute luxury for myself, I am guilty of vice? It is high time that this subject should be adequately understood. It is high time that we should lay aside the very names of justice and virtue, or that we should acknowledge that they do not authorise us to accumulate luxuries upon ourselves, while we see others in want of the indispensible means of improvement and happiness.

But, while religion inculcated on mankind the impartial nature of justice, its teachers have been too apt to treat the practice of justice, not as a debt, which it ought to be considered, but as an affair of spontaneous generosity and bounty. They have called upon the rich to be clement and merciful to the poor. The consequence of this has been that the rich, when they bestowed the most slender pittance of their enormous wealth in acts of charity, as they were called, took merit to themselves for what they gave, instead of considering themselves as delinquents for what they withheld.

Religion is in reality in all its parts an accommodation to the prejudices and weaknesses of mankind. Its authors communicated to the world as much truth, as they calculated that the world would be willing to receive. But it is time that we should lay aside the instruction intended only for children in understanding,[1] and contemplate the nature and principles of things. If religion had spoken out, and told us it was just that all men should receive the supply of their wants, we should presently have been led to suspect that a gratuitous distribution to be made by the rich, was a very indirect and ineffectual way of arriving at this object. The experience of all ages has taught us, that this system is productive only of a very precarious supply. The principal object which it seems to propose, is to place this supply in the disposal of a few, enabling them to make a show of generosity with what is not truly their own, and to purchase the gratitude of the poor by the payment of a debt. It is a system of clemency and charity, instead of a system of justice. It fills the rich with unreasonable pride by the spurious denominations with which it decorates their acts, and the poor with servility, by leading them to regard the slender comforts they obtain, not as their incontrovertible due, but as the good pleasure and the grace of their opulent neighbours.

---

[1] I Cor. Chap. III. Ver I, 2.*

CHAPTER II

BENEFITS ARISING FROM THE GENUINE
SYSTEM OF PROPERTY

Contrasted with the mischiefs of the present system, as consisting—1. In a sense of dependence. 2. In the perpetual spectacle of injustice, leading men astray in their desires—and perverting the integrity of their judgments—the rich are the true pensioners.—3. In the discouragement of intellectual attainments.—4. In the multiplication of vice—generating the crimes of the poor—the passions of the rich—and the misfortunes of war.—5. In depopulation.

HAVING seen the justice of an equal distribution of property, let us next consider the benefits with which it would be attended. And here with grief it must be confessed, that, however great and extensive are the evils that are produced by monarchies and courts, by the imposture of priests and the iniquity of criminal laws, all these are imbecil and impotent compared with the evils that arise out of the established system of property.

Its first effect is that which we have already mentioned, a sense of dependence. It is true that courts are mean spirited, intriguing and servile, and that this disposition is transferred by contagion from them to all ranks of society. But property brings home a servile and truckling spirit by no circuitous method to every house in the nation. Observe the pauper fawning with abject vileness upon his rich benefactor, and speechless with sensations of gratitude for having received that, which he ought to have claimed with an erect mien, and with a consciousness that his claim was irresistible. Observe the servants that follow in a rich man's train, watchful of his looks, anticipating his commands, not daring to reply to his insolence, all their time and their efforts under the direction of his caprice. Observe the tradesman, how he studies the passions of his customers, not to correct, but to pamper them, the vileness of his flattery and the systematical constancy with which he exaggerates the merit of his commodities. Observe the practices of a popular election, where the great mass are purchased by obsequiousness, by intemperance and bribery, or driven by unmanly threats of poverty and persecution. Indeed 'the age of chivalry is' not 'gone!'[1] The feudal spirit still survives, that reduced the great mass of mankind to the rank of slaves and cattle for the service of a few.

---

[1] Burke's Reflections.*

We have heard much of visionary and theoretical improvements. It would indeed be visionary and theoretical to expect virtue from mankind, while they are thus subjected to hourly corruption, and bred from father to son to sell their independence and their conscience for the vile rewards that oppression has to bestow. No man can be either useful to others or happy to himself who is a stranger to the grace of firmness, and who is not habituated to prefer the dictates of his own sense of rectitude to all the tyranny of command, and allurements of temptation. Here again, as upon a former occasion, religion comes in to illustrate our thesis. Religion was the generous ebullition of men, who let their imagination loose on the grandest subjects, and wandered without restraint in the unbounded field of enquiry. It is not to be wondered at therefore if they brought home imperfect ideas of the sublimest views that intellect can furnish. In this instance religion teaches that the true perfection of man is to divest himself of the influence of passions; that he must have no artificial wants, no sensuality, and no fear. But to divest the human species under the present system of the influence of passions is an extravagant speculation. The enquirer after truth and the benefactor of mankind will be desirous of removing from them those external impressions by which their evil propensities are cherished. The true object that should be kept in view, is to extirpate all ideas of condescension and superiority, to oblige every man to feel, that the kindness he exerts is what he is bound to perform, and the assistance he asks what he has a right to claim.

A second evil that arises out of the established system of property is the perpetual spectacle of injustice it exhibits. This consists partly in luxury and partly in caprice. There is nothing more pernicious to the human mind than luxury. Mind, being in its own nature essentially active, necessarily fixes on some object public or personal, and in the latter case on the attainment of some excellence, or something which shall command the esteem and deference of others. No propensity, absolutely considered, can be more valuable than this. But the established system of property directs it into the channel of the acquisition of wealth. The ostentation of the rich perpetually goads the spectator to the desire of opulence. Wealth, by the sentiments of servility and dependence it produces, makes the rich man stand forward as the only object of general esteem and deference. In vain are sobriety, integrity and industry, in vain the sublimest powers of mind and the most ardent benevolence, if their possessor be narrowed in his circumstances. To acquire wealth and to display it, is therefore the universal passion. The whole structure of human society is made a system of the narrowest selfishness. If self love and benevolence were apparently reconciled as to their object, a man might set out with the desire of eminence, and yet every day become more generous and philanthropical in his views. But the passion we are here describing is accustomed to be gratified at every step, by inhumanly trampling upon the interest of others. Wealth is acquired by overreaching our neighbours, and is spent in insulting them.

The spectacle of injustice which the established system of property exhibits, consists partly in caprice. If you would cherish in any man the love of rectitude, you must take care that its principles be impressed on him, not only by words, but actions. It sometimes happens during the period of education, that maxims of integrity and consistency are repeatedly inforced, and that the preceptor gives no quarter to the base suggestions of selfishness and cunning. But how is the lesson that has been read to the pupil confounded and reversed, when he enters upon the scene of the world? If he ask, 'Why is this man honoured?' the ready answer is, 'Because he is rich.' If he enquire farther, 'Why is he rich?' the answer in most cases is, 'From the accident of birth, or from a minute and sordid attention to the cares of gain.' The system of accumulated property is the offspring of civil policy; and civil policy, as we are taught to believe, is the production of accumulated wisdom. Thus the wisdom of legislators and senates has been employed, to secure a distribution of property the most profligate and unprincipled, that bids defiance to the maxims of justice and the nature of man. Humanity weeps over the distresses of the peasantry of all civilised nations; and, when she turns from this spectacle to behold the luxury of their lords, gross, imperious and prodigal, her sensations certainly are not less acute. This spectacle is the school in which mankind have been educated. They have been accustomed to the sight of injustice, oppression and iniquity, till their feelings are made callous, and their understandings incapable of apprehending the nature of true virtue.

In beginning to point out the evils of accumulated property, we compared the extent of those evils with the correspondent evils of monarchies and courts. No circumstances under the latter have excited a more pointed disapprobation than pensions and pecuniary corruption, by means of which hundreds of individuals are rewarded, not for serving, but betraying the public, and the hard earnings of industry are employed to fatten the servile adherents of despotism. But the rent roll of the lands of England is a much more formidable pension list, than that which is supposed to be employed in the purchase of ministerial majorities. All riches, and especially all hereditary riches, are to be considered as the salary of a sinecure office, where the labourer and the manufacturer

VIII. II   *Of Property*   423

perform the duties, and the principal spends the income in luxury
and idleness.[1] Hereditary wealth is in reality a premium paid to idleness, an immense annuity expended to retain mankind in brutality
and ignorance. The poor are kept in ignorance by the want of leisure.
The rich are furnished indeed with the means of cultivation and literature, but they are paid for being dissipated and indolent. The most
powerful means that malignity could have invented, are employed to
prevent them from improving their talents, and becoming useful to the
public.

This leads us to observe, thirdly, that the established system of property, is the true levelling system with respect to the human species,
by as much as the cultivation of intellect and truth, is more valuable
and more characteristic of man, than the gratifications of vanity or
appetite. Accumulated property treads the powers of thought in the
dust, extinguishes the sparks of genius, and reduces the great mass of
mankind to be immersed in sordid cares; beside depriving the rich, as
we have already said, of the most salubrious and effectual motives to
activity. If superfluity were banished, the necessity for the greater part
of the manual industry of mankind would be superseded; and the rest,
being amicably shared among all the active and vigorous members
of the community, would be burthensome to none. Every man would
have a frugal, yet wholsome diet; every man would go forth to that

---

[1] This idea is to be found in Ogilvie's Essay on the Right of Property in Land,
published about two years ago, Part I, Sect iii, par 38, 39. The reasonings of this author
have sometimes considerable merit, though he has by no means gone to the source of
the evil.

It might be amusing to some readers to recollect the authorities, if the citation of
authorities were a proper mode of reasoning, by which the system of accumulated property is openly attacked. The best known is Plato in his treatise of a Republic. His steps
have been followed by Sir Thomas More in his Utopia. Specimens of very powerful
reasoning on the same side may be found in Gulliver's Travels, particularly, Part IV,
Chap. VI. Mably, in his book *De la Législation*, has displayed at large the advantages of
equality, and then quits the subject in despair from an opinion of the incorrigibleness
of human depravity. Wallace, the contemporary and antagonist of Hume, in a treatise
entitled, Various Prospects of Mankind, Nature and Providence,* is copious in his eulogium of the same system, and deserts it only from fear of the earth becoming too populous: see below, Chap. VII. The great practical authorities are Crete, Sparta, Peru and
Paraguay. It would be easy to swell this list, if we added examples where an approach
only to these principles was attempted, and authors who have incidentally confirmed a
doctrine, so interesting and clear, as never to have been wholly eradicated from any
human understanding.

It would be trifling to object that the systems of Plato and others are full of imperfections. This indeed rather strengthens their authority; since the evidence of the truth they
maintained was so great, as still to preserve its hold on their understandings, though they
knew not how to remove the difficulties that attended it.

moderate exercise of his corporal functions that would give hilarity to the spirits; none would be made torpid with fatigue, but all would have leisure to cultivate the kindly and philanthropical affections of the soul, and to let loose his faculties in the search of intellectual improvement. What a contrast does this scene present us with the present state of human society, where the peasant and the labourer work, till their understandings are benumbed with toil, their sinews contracted and made callous by being for ever on the stretch, and their bodies invaded with infirmities and surrendered to an untimely grave? What is the fruit of this disproportioned and unceasing toil? At evening they return to a family, famished with hunger, exposed half naked to the inclemencies of the sky, hardly sheltered, and denied the slenderest instruction, unless in a few instances, where it is dispensed by the hands of ostentatious charity, and the first lesson communicated is unprincipled servility. All this while their rich neighbour—but we visited him before.

How rapid and sublime would be the advances of intellect, if all men were admitted into the field of knowledge? At present ninety-nine persons in an hundred are no more excited to any regular exertions of general and curious thought, than the brutes themselves. What would be the state of public mind in a nation, where all were wise, all had laid aside the shackles of prejudice and implicit faith, all adopted with fearless confidence the suggestions of truth, and the lethargy of the soul was dismissed for ever? It is to be presumed that the inequality of mind would in a certain degree be permanent; but it is reasonable to believe that the geniuses of such an age would far surpass the grandest exertions of intellect that are at present known. Genius would not be depressed with false wants and niggardly patronage. It would not exert itself with a sense of neglect and oppression rankling in its bosom. It would be freed from those apprehensions that perpetually recal us to the thought of personal emolument, and of consequence would expatiate freely among sentiments of generosity and public good.

From ideas of intellectual let us turn to moral improvement. And here it is obvious that all the occasions of crime would be cut off for ever. All men love justice. All men are conscious that man is a being of one common nature, and feel the propriety of the treatment they receive from one another being measured by a common standard. Every man is desirous of assisting another; whether we should choose to ascribe this to an instinct implanted in his nature which renders this conduct a source of personal gratification, or to his perception of the reasonableness of such assistance. So necessary a part is this of the constitution of mind, that no man perpetrates any action however criminal, without having first invented some sophistry, some palliation, by which he proves to himself that it is best to be done.[1] Hence it appears, that offence, the invasion of one man upon the security of another, is a thought alien to mind, and which nothing could have reconciled to us but the sharp sting of necessity. To consider merely the present order of human society, it is evident that the first offence must have been his who began a monopoly, and took advantage of the weakness of his neighbours to secure certain exclusive privileges to himself. The man on the other hand who determined to put an end to this monopoly, and who peremptorily demanded what was superfluous to the possessor and would be of extreme benefit to himself, appeared to his own mind to be merely avenging the violated laws of justice. Were it not for the plausibleness of this apology, it is to be presumed that there would be no such thing as crime in the world.

The fruitful source of crimes consists in this circumstance, one man's possessing in abundance that of which another man is destitute. We must change the nature of mind, before we can prevent it from being powerfully influenced by this circumstance, when brought strongly home to its perceptions by the nature of its situation. Man must cease to have senses, the pleasures of appetite and vanity must cease to gratify, before he can look on tamely at the monopoly of these pleasures. He must cease to have a sense of justice, before he can clearly and fully approve this mixed scene of superfluity and distress. It is true that the proper method of curing this inequality is by reason and not by violence. But the immediate tendency of the established system is to persuade men that reason is impotent. The injustice of which they complain is upheld by force, and they are too easily induced, by force to attempt its correction. All they endeavour is the partial correction of an injustice, which education tells them is necessary, but more powerful reason affirms to be tyrannical.

Force grew out of monopoly. It might accidentally have occurred among savages whose appetites exceeded their supply, or whose passions were inflamed by the presence of the object of their desire; but it would gradually have died away, as reason and civilisation advanced. Accumulated property has fixed its empire; and henceforth all is an open contention of the strength and cunning of one party against the strength and cunning of the other. In this case the violent and premature struggles of the necessitous are undoubtedly an evil. They tend to

---

[1] Book II, Chap. III, p. 66.

defeat the very cause in the success of which they are most deeply interested; they tend to procrastinate the triumph of truth. But the true
crime is in the malevolent and partial propensities of men, thinking
only of themselves, and despising the emolument of others; and of
these the rich have their share.

The spirit of oppression, the spirit of servility, and the spirit of fraud,
these are the immediate growth of the established system of property.
These are alike hostile to intellectual and moral improvement. The
other vices of envy, malice and revenge are their inseparable companions. In a state of society where men lived in the midst of plenty, and
where all shared alike the bounties of nature, these sentiments would
inevitably expire. The narrow principle of selfishness would vanish. No
man being obliged to guard his little store, or provide with anxiety and
pain for his restless wants, each would lose his own individual existence
in the thought of the general good. No man would be an enemy to his
neighbour, for they would have nothing for which to contend; and of
consequence philanthropy would resume the empire which reason
assigns her. Mind would be delivered from her perpetual anxiety about
corporal support, and free to expatiate in the field of thought which is
congenial to her. Each man would assist the enquiries of all.

Let us fix our attention for a moment upon the revolution of principles and habits that immediately grow out of an unequal distribution
of property. Till it was thus distributed men felt what their wants
required, and sought the supply of those wants. All that was more than
this, was regarded as indifferent. But no sooner is accumulation introduced, than they begin to study a variety of methods, for disposing of
their superfluity with least emolument to their neighbour, or in other
words by which it shall appear to be most their own. They do not long
continue to buy commodities, before they begin to buy men. He that
possesses or is the spectator of superfluity soon discovers the hold
which it affords us on the minds of others. Hence the passions of vanity
and ostentation. Hence the despotic manners of them who recollect
with complacence the rank they occupy, and the restless ambition of
those whose attention is engrossed by the possible future.

Ambition is of all the passions of the human mind the most extensive
in its ravages. It adds district to district, and kingdom to kingdom. It
spreads bloodshed and calamity and conquest over the face of the earth.
But the passion itself, as well as the means of gratifying it, is the
produce of the prevailing system of property.[1] It is only by means of

[1] Book V, Chap. XVI.

accumulation that one man obtains an unresisted sway over multitudes of others. It is by means of a certain distribution of income that the present governments of the world are retained in existence. Nothing more easy than to plunge nations so organised into war. But, if Europe were at present covered with inhabitants, all of them possessing competence, and none of them superfluity, what could induce its different countries to engage in hostility? If you would lead men to war, you must exhibit certain allurements. If you be not enabled by a system, already prevailing and which derives force from prescription, to hire them to your purposes, you must bring over each individual by dint of persuasion. How hopeless a task by such means to excite mankind to murder each other? It is clear then that war in every horrid form is the growth of unequal property. As long as this source of jealousy and corruption shall remain, it is visionary to talk of universal peace. As soon as the source shall be dried up, it will be impossible to exclude the consequence. It is property that forms men into one common mass, and makes them fit to be played upon like a brute machine. Were this stumbling block removed, each man would be united to his neighbour in love and mutual kindness a thousand times more than now: but each man would think and judge for himself. Let then the advocates for the prevailing system, at least consider what it is for which they plead, and be well assured that they have arguments in its favour which will weigh against these disadvantages.

There is one other circumstance which, though inferior to those above enumerated, deserves to be mentioned. This is population. It has been calculated that the average cultivation of Europe might be improved, so as to maintain five times her present number of inhabitants.[1] There is a principle in human society by which population is perpetually kept down to the level of the means of subsistence. Thus among the wandering tribes of America and Asia, we never find through the lapse of ages, that population has so increased, as to render necessary the cultivation of the earth. Thus, among the civilised nations of Europe, by means of territorial monopoly the sources of subsistence are kept within a certain limit, and, if the population became overstocked, the lower ranks of the inhabitants would be still more incapable of procuring for themselves the necessaries of life. There are no doubt extraordinary concurrences of circumstances, by means of which changes are occasionally introduced in this respect; but in ordinary cases the standard of population is held in a manner stationary for centuries. Thus the

---

[1] Ogilvie, Part I, Sect iii, par 35.

established system of property may be considered as strangling a considerable portion of our children in their cradle. Whatever may be the value of the life of man, or rather whatever would be his capability of happiness in a free and equal state of society, the system we are here opposing may be considered as arresting upon the threshold of existence four fifths of that value and that happiness.

CHAPTER III

OF THE OBJECTION TO THIS SYSTEM FROM THE ADMIRABLE EFFECTS OF LUXURY

Nature of the objection.—Luxury not necessary—either to population—or to the improvement of the mind.—Its true character.

THESE ideas of justice and improvement are as old as literature and reflexion themselves. They have suggested themselves in detached parts to the inquisitive in all ages, though they have perhaps never been brought together so as sufficiently to strike the mind with their consistency and beauty. But, after having furnished an agreeable dream, they have perpetually been laid aside as impracticable. We will proceed to examine the objections upon which this supposed impracticability has been founded; and the answer to these objections will gradually lead us to such a development of the proposed system, as by its completeness and the regular adjustment of its parts will be calculated to carry conviction to the most prejudiced mind.

There is one objection that has chiefly been cultivated on English ground, and to which we will give the priority of examination. It has been affirmed 'that private vices are public benefits.' But this principle, thus coarsely stated by one of its original advocates,[1] was remodelled by his more elegant successors.[2] They observed, 'that the true measure of virtue and vice was utility, and consequently that it was an unreasonable calumny to state luxury as a vice. Luxury,' they said, 'whatever might be the prejudices that cynics and ascetics had excited against it, was the rich and generous soil that brought to perfection the true prosperity of mankind. Without luxury men must always have remained solitary savages. It is luxury by which palaces are built and cities peopled. How could there have been high population in any country, without the

---

[1] Mandeville; Fable of the Bees.*
[2] Coventry, in a treatise entitled, Philemon to Hydaspes: Hume; Essays, Part II, Essay II.*

various arts in which the swarms of its inhabitants are busied? The true benefactor of mankind is not the scrupulous devotee who by his charities encourages insensibility and sloth; is not the surly philosopher who reads them lectures of barren morality; but the elegant voluptuary who employs thousands in sober and healthful industry to procure dainties for his table, who unites distant nations in commerce to supply him with furniture, and who encourages the fine arts and all the sublimities of invention to furnish decorations for his residence.'

I have brought forward this objection, rather that nothing material might appear to be omitted, than because it requires a separate answer. The true answer has been anticipated. It has been seen that the population of any country is measured by its cultivation. If therefore sufficient motives can be furnished to excite men to agriculture, there is no doubt, that population may be carried on to any extent that the land can be made to maintain. But agriculture, when once begun, is never found to stop in its career, but from positive discountenance. It is territorial monopoly that obliges men unwillingly to see vast tracts of land lying waste, or negligently and imperfectly cultivated, while they are subjected to the miseries of want. If land were perpetually open to him who was willing to cultivate it, it is not to be believed but that it would be cultivated in proportion to the wants of the community, nor by the same reason would there be any effectual check to the increase of population.

Undoubtedly the quantity of manual labour would be greatly inferior to that which is now performed by the inhabitants of any civilised country, since at present perhaps one twentieth part of the inhabitants performs the agriculture which supports the whole. But it is by no means to be admitted that this leisure would be found a real calamity.

As to what sort of a benefactor the voluptuary is to mankind, this was sufficiently seen when we treated of the effects of dependence and injustice. To this species of benefit all the crimes and moral evils of mankind are indebted for their perpetuity. If mind be to be preferred to mere animal existence, if it ought to be the wish of every reasonable enquirer, not merely that man, but that happiness should be propagated, then is the voluptuary the bane of the human species.

CHAPTER IV

OF THE OBJECTION TO THIS SYSTEM FROM THE
ALLUREMENTS OF SLOTH

The objection stated.—Such a state of society must have been preceded by great intellectual improvement.—The manual labour required in this state will be extremely small.—Universality of the love of distinction.—Operation of this his motive under the system in question—will finally be superseded by a better motive.

ANOTHER objection which has been urged against the system which counteracts the accumulation of property, is, 'that it would put an end to industry. We behold in commercial countries the miracles that are operated by the love of gain. Their inhabitants cover the sea with their fleets, astonish mankind by the refinement of their ingenuity, hold vast continents in subjection in distant parts of the world by their arms, are able to defy the most powerful confederacies, and, oppressed with taxes and debts, seem to acquire fresh prosperity under their accumulated burthens. Shall we lightly part with a system that seems pregnant with such inexhaustible motives? Shall we believe that men will cultivate assiduously what they have no assurance they shall be permitted to apply to their personal emolument? It will perhaps be found with agriculture as it is with commerce, which then flourishes best when subjected to no control, but, when placed under rigid restraints, languishes and expires. Once establish it as a principle in society that no man is to apply to his personal use more than his necessities require, and you will find every man become indifferent to those exertions which now call forth the energy of his faculties. Man is the creature of sensations; and, when we endeavour to strain his intellect, and govern him by reason alone, we do but show our ignorance of his nature. Self love is the genuine source of our actions,[1] and, if this should be found to bring vice and partiality along with it, yet the system that should endeavour to supersede it, would be at best no more than a beautiful romance. If each man found that, without being compelled to exert his own industry, he might lay claim to the superfluity of his neighbour, indolence would perpetually usurp his faculties, and such a society must either starve, or be obliged in its own defence to return to that system of injustice and sordid interest, which theoretical reasoners will for ever arraign to no purpose.'

---

[1] For an examination of this principle see Book IV, Chap. VIII.

This is the principal objection that prevents men from yielding without resistance to the accumulated evidence that has already been adduced. In reply, it may be observed in the first place, that the equality for which we are pleading is an equality that would succeed to a state of great intellectual improvement. So bold a revolution cannot take place in human affairs, till the general mind has been highly cultivated. The present age of mankind is greatly enlightened; but it is to be feared is not yet enlightened enough. Hasty and undigested tumults may take place under the idea of an equalisation of property; but it is only a calm and clear conviction of justice, of justice mutually to be rendered and received, of happiness to be produced by the desertion of our most rooted habits, that can introduce an invariable system of this sort. Attempts without this preparation will be productive only of confusion. Their effect will be momentary, and a new and more barbarous inequality will succeed. Each man with unaltered appetite will watch his opportunity to gratify his love of power or his love of distinction, by usurping on his inattentive neighbours.

Is it to be believed then that a state of so great intellectual improvement can be the forerunner of barbarism? Savages, it is true, are subject to the weakness of indolence. But civilised and refined states are the scene of peculiar activity. It is thought, acuteness of disquisition, and ardour of pursuit, that set the corporeal faculties at work. Thought begets thought. Nothing can put a stop to the progressive advances of mind, but oppression. But here, so far from being oppressed, every man is equal, every man independent and at his ease. It has been observed that the establishment of a republic is always attended with public enthusiasm and irresistible enterprise. Is it to be believed that equality, the true republicanism, will be less effectual? It is true that in republics this spirit sooner or later is found to languish. Republicanism is not a remedy that strikes at the root of the evil. Injustice, oppression and misery can find an abode in those seeming happy seats. But what shall stop the progress of ardour and improvement, where the monopoly of property is unknown?

This argument will be strengthened, if we reflect on the amount of labour that a state of equal property will require. What is this quantity of exertion from which we are supposing many members of the community to shrink? It is so light a burthen as rather to assume the appearance of agreeable relaxation and gentle exercise, than of labour. In this community scarcely any can be expected in consequence of their situation or avocations to consider themselves as exempted from manual industry. There will be no rich men to recline in indolence and fatten upon the labour of their fellows. The mathematician, the poet and the philosopher will derive a new stock of chearfulness and energy from the recurring labour that makes them feel they are men. There will be no persons employed in the manufacture of trinkets and luxuries; and none in directing the wheels of the complicated machine of government, tax-gatherers, beadles, excisemen, tide-waiters, clerks and secretaries.* There will be neither fleets nor armies, neither courtiers nor footmen. It is the unnecessary employments that at present occupy the great mass of the inhabitants of every civilised nation, while the peasant labours incessantly to maintain them in a state more pernicious than idleness.

It has been computed that not more than one twentieth of the inhabitants of England are employed seriously and substantially in the labours of agriculture. Add to this, that the nature of agriculture is such, as necessarily to give full occupation in some parts of the year, and to leave others comparatively unemployed. We may consider these latter periods as equivalent to a labour which, under the direction of sufficient skill, might suffice in a simple state of society for the fabrication of tools, for weaving, and the occupation of taylors, bakers and butchers. The object in the present state of society is to multiply labour, in another state it will be to simplify it. A vast disproportion of the wealth of the community has been thrown into the hands of a few, and ingenuity has been continually upon the stretch to find out ways in which it may be expended. In the feudal times the great lord invited the poor to come and eat of the produce of his estate upon condition of their wearing his livery, and forming themselves in rank and file to do honour to his well born guests. Now that exchanges are more facilitated, we have quitted this inartificial mode, and oblige the men we maintain out of our incomes to exert their ingenuity and industry in return. Thus in the instance just mentioned, we pay the taylor to cut our clothes to pieces, that he may sew them together again, and to decorate them with stitching and various ornaments, without which experience would speedily show that they were in no respect less useful. We are imagining in the present case a state of the most rigid simplicity.

From the sketch which has been here given it seems by no means impossible, that the labour of every twentieth man in the community would be sufficient to maintain the rest in all the absolute necessaries of human life. If then this labour, instead of being performed by so small a number, were amicably divided among them all, it would occupy the twentieth part of every man's time. Let us compute that the industry of a labouring man engrosses ten hours in every day, which, when we have deducted his hours of rest, recreation and meals, seems an ample allowance. It follows that half an hour a day, seriously employed in manual labour by every member of the community, would sufficiently supply the whole with necessaries. Who is there that would shrink from this degree of industry? Who is there that sees the incessant industry exerted in this city and this island, and would believe that, with half an hour's industry *per diem,* we should be every way happier and better than we are at present? Is it possible to contemplate this fair and generous picture of independence and virtue, where every man would have ample leisure for the noblest energies of mind, without feeling our very souls refreshed with admiration and hope?

When we talk of men's sinking into idleness if they be not excited by the stimulus of gain, we have certainly very little considered the motives that at present govern the human mind. We are deceived by the apparent mercenariness of mankind, and imagine that the accumulation of wealth is their great object. But the case is far otherwise. The present ruling passion of the human mind is the love of distinction. There is no doubt a class in society that are perpetually urged by hunger and need, and have no leisure for motives less gross and material. But is the class next above them less industrious than they? I exert a certain species of industry to supply my immediate wants; but these wants are soon supplied. The rest is exerted that I may wear a better coat, that I may clothe my wife with gay attire, that I may not merely have a shelter but a handsome habitation, not merely bread or flesh to eat, but that I may set it out with a suitable decorum. How many of these things would engage my attention, if I lived in a desert island, and had no spectators of my economy? If I survey the appendages of my person, is there one article that is not an appeal to the respect of my neighbours, or a refuge against their contempt? It is for this that the merchant braves the dangers of the ocean, and the mechanical inventor brings forth the treasures of his meditation. The soldier advances even to the cannon's mouth, the statesman exposes himself to the rage of an indignant people, because they cannot bear to pass through life without distinction and esteem. Exclusively of certain higher motives that will presently be mentioned, this is the purpose of all the great exertions of mankind. The man who has nothing to provide for but his animal wants, scarcely ever shakes off the lethargy of his mind; but the love of praise hurries us on to the most incredible achievements. Nothing is more common than to find persons who surpass the rest of their species in activity, inexcusably remiss in the melioration of their pecuniary affairs.

In reality those by whom this reasoning has been urged, have mistaken the nature of their own objection. They did not sincerely believe that men could be roused into action only by the love of gain; but they imagined that in a state of equal property men would have nothing to occupy their attention. What degree of truth there is in this idea we shall presently have occasion to estimate.

Meanwhile it is sufficiently obvious, that the motives which arise from the love of distinction are by no means cut off, by a state of society incompatible with the accumulation of property. Men, no longer able to acquire the esteem or avoid the contempt of their neighbours by circumstances of dress and furniture, will divert the passion for distinction into another channel. They will avoid the reproach of indolence, as carefully as they now avoid the reproach of poverty. The only persons who at present neglect the effect which their appearance and manners may produce, are those whose faces are ground with famine and distress. But in a state of equal society no man will be oppressed, and of consequence the more delicate affections of the soul will have time to expand themselves. The general mind having, as we have already shown, arrived at a high pitch of improvement, the impulse that carries it out into action will be stronger than ever. The fervour of public spirit will be great. Leisure will be multiplied, and the leisure of a cultivated understanding is the precise period in which great designs, designs the tendency of which is to secure applause and esteem, are conceived. In tranquil leisure it is impossible for any but the sublimest mind to exist without the passion for distinction. This passion, no longer permitted to lose itself in indirect channels and useless wanderings, will seek the noblest course, and perpetually fructify the seeds of public good. Mind, though it will perhaps at no time arrive at the termination of its possible discoveries and improvements, will nevertheless advance with a rapidity and firmness of progression of which we are at present unable to conceive the idea.

The love of fame is no doubt a delusion. This like every other delusion will take its turn to be detected and abjured. It is an airy phantom, which will indeed afford us an imperfect pleasure so long as we worship it, but will always in a considerable degree disappoint us, and will not stand the test of examination. We ought to love nothing but good, a pure and immutable felicity, the good of the majority, the good of the general. If there be any thing more substantial than all the rest, it is justice, a principle that rests upon this single postulatum, that man and man are beings of the same nature, and susceptible, under certain limitations, of the same advantages. Whether the benefit proceed from you or me, so it be but conferred, is a pitiful distinction. Justice has the farther advantage, which serves us as a countercheck to prove the goodness of this species of arithmetic, of producing the only solid happiness to the man by whom it is practised, as well as the good of all. But fame cannot benefit me, any more than serve the best purposes to others. The man who acts from the love of it, may produce public good; but, if he do, it is from indirect and spurious views. Fame is an unsubstantial and delusive pursuit. If it signify an opinion entertained of me greater than I deserve, to pursue it is vicious. If it be the precise mirror of my character, it is desirable only as a means, in as much as I may perhaps be able to do most good to the persons who best know the extent of my capacity and the rectitude of my intentions.

The love of fame, when it perishes in minds formed under the present system, often gives place to a greater degeneracy. Selfishness is the habit that grows out of monopoly. When therefore this selfishness ceases to seek its gratification in public exertion, it too often narrows itself into some frigid conception of personal pleasure, perhaps sensual, perhaps intellectual. But this cannot be the process where monopoly is banished. Selfishness has there no kindly circumstances to foster it. Truth, the over-powering truth of general good, then seizes us irresistibly. It is impossible we should want motives, so long as we see clearly how multitudes and ages may be benefited by our exertions, how causes and effects are connected in an endless chain, so that no honest effort can be lost, but will operate to good, centuries after its author is consigned to the grave. This will be the general passion, and all will be animated by the example of all.

CHAPTER V

OF THE OBJECTION TO THIS SYSTEM FROM THE IMPOSSIBILITY OF ITS BEING RENDERED PERMANENT

Grounds of the objection.—Its serious import.—Answer.—The introduction of such a system must be owing, 1. to a deep sense of justice—2. to a clear insight into the nature of happiness—as being properly intellectual—; not consisting in sensual pleasure—or the pleasures of delusion.—Influence of the passions considered.—Men will not accumulate either from individual foresight—or from vanity.

LET us proceed to another objection. It has sometimes been said by those who oppose the doctrine here maintained, 'that equality might perhaps contribute to the improvement and happiness of mankind, if it were consistent with the nature of man that such a principle should be rendered permanent; but that every expectation of that kind must prove abortive. Confusion would be introduced under the idea of equality to-day, but the old vices and monopolies would return to-morrow. All that the rich would have purchased by the most generous sacrifice, would be a period of barbarism, from which the ideas and regulations of civil society must commence as from a new infancy. The nature of man cannot be changed. There would at least be some vicious and designing members of society, who would endeavour to secure to themselves indulgencies beyond the rest. Mind would not be reduced to that exact uniformity which a state of equal property demands; and the variety of sentiments which must always in some degree prevail, would inevitably subvert the refined systems of speculative perfection.'

No objection can be more essential than that which is here adduced. It highly becomes us in so momentous a subject to resist all extravagant speculations: it would be truly to be lamented, if, while we parted with that state of society through which mind has been thus far advanced, we were replunged into barbarism by the pursuit of specious appearances. But what is worst of all, is that, if this objection be true, it is to be feared there is no remedy. Mind must go forward. What it sees and admires, it will some time or other seek to attain. Such is the inevitable law of our nature. But it is impossible not to see the beauty of equality, and to be charmed with the benefits it seems to promise. The consequence is sure. Man, according to the system of these reasoners, is prompted to advance for some time with success; but after that time, in the very act of pursuing farther improvement, he necessarily plunges beyond the compass of his powers, and has then his petty career to begin afresh. The objection represents him as a foul abortion, with just understanding enough to see what is good, but with too little to retain him in the practice of it.—Let us consider whether equality, once established, would be so precarious as it is here represented.

In answer to this objection it must first be remembered, that the state of equalisation we are here supposing is not the result of accident, of the authority of a chief magistrate, or the over earnest persuasion of a few enlightened thinkers, but is produced by the serious and deliberate conviction of the community at large. We will suppose for the present that it is possible for such a conviction to take place among a given number of persons living in society with each other: and, if it be possible in a small community, there seems to be no sufficient reason to prove that it is impossible in one of larger and larger dimensions. The question we have here to examine is concerning the probability, when the conviction has once been introduced, of its becoming permanent.

The conviction rests upon two intellectual impressions, one of justice, and the other of happiness. Equalisation of property cannot begin to assume a fixed appearance in human society, till the sentiment becomes deeply wrought into the mind, that the genuine wants of any man constitute his only just claim to the appropriating any species of commodity. If the general sense of mankind were once so far enlightened, as to produce a perpetual impression of this truth, of so forcible a sort as to be exempt from all objections and doubt, we should look with equal horror and contempt at the idea of any man's accumulating a property he did not want. All the evils that a state of monopoly never fails to engender would stand forward in our minds, together with all the existing happiness that attended upon a state of freedom. We should feel as much alienation of thought from the consuming uselessly upon ourselves what would be beneficial to another, or from the accumulating property for the purpose of obtaining some kind of ascendancy over the mind of our neighbours, as we now feel from the commission of murder. No man will dispute, that a state of equal property once established, would greatly diminish the evil propensities of man. But the crime we are now supposing is more atrocious than any that is to be found in the present state of society. Man perhaps is incapable under any circumstance of perpetrating an action of which he has a clear and undoubted perception that it is contrary to the general good. But be this as it will, it is hardly to be believed that any man for the sake of some imaginary gratification to himself would wantonly injure the whole, if his mind were not first ulcerated with the impression of the injury that society by its ordinances is committing against him. The case we are here considering is that of a man, who does not even imagine himself injured, and yet wilfully subverts a state of happiness to which no description can do justice, to make room for the return of all those calamities and vices with which mankind have been infested from the earliest page of history.

The equalisation we are describing is farther indebted for its empire in the mind to the ideas with which it is attended of personal happiness. It grows out of a simple, clear and unanswerable theory of the human mind, that we first stand in need of a certain animal subsistence and shelter, and after that, that our only true felicity consists in the expansion of our intellectual powers, the knowledge of truth, and the practice of virtue. It might seem at first sight as if this theory omitted a part of the experimental history of mind, the pleasures of sense and the pleasures of delusion. But this omission is apparent, not real. However many are the kinds of pleasure of which we are susceptible, the truly prudent man will sacrifice the inferior to the more exquisite. Now no man who has ever produced or contemplated the happiness of others with a liberal mind, will deny that this exercise is infinitely the most pleasurable of all sensations. But he that is guilty of the smallest excess of sensual pleasures, by so much diminishes his capacity of obtaining this highest pleasure. Not to add, if that be of any importance, that rigid temperance is the reasonable means of tasting sensual pleasures with the highest relish. This was the system of Epicurus,* and must be the system of every man who ever speculated deeply on the nature of human happiness. For the pleasures of delusion, they are absolutely incompatible with our highest pleasure. If we would either promote or enjoy the happiness of others, we must seek to know in what it consists. But knowledge is the irreconcileable foe of delusion. In proportion as mind rises to its true element, and shakes off those prejudices which are the authors of our misery, it becomes incapable of deriving pleasure from flattery, fame or power, or indeed from any source that is not compatible with, or in other words does not make a part of the common good. The most palpable of all classes of knowledge is that I am, personally considered, but an atom in the ocean of mind.—The first rudiment therefore of that science of personal happiness which is inseparable from a state of equalisation, is, that I shall derive infinitely more pleasure from simplicity, frugality and truth, than from luxury, empire and fame. What temptation has a man, entertaining this opinion, and living in a state of equal property, to accumulate?

This question has been perpetually darkened by the doctrine, so familiar to writers of morality, of the independent operations of reason and passion. Such distinctions must always darken. Of how many parts does mind consist? Of none. It consists merely of a series of thought succeeding thought from the first moment of our existence to its termination.[1] This word passion, which has produced such extensive mischief in the philosophy of mind, and has no real archetype, is perpetually shifting its meaning. Sometimes it is applied universally to all those thoughts, which, being peculiarly vivid, and attended with great force of argument real or imaginary, carry us out into action with uncommon energy. Thus we speak of the passion of benevolence, public spirit or courage. Sometimes it signifies those vivid thoughts only, which upon accurate examination appear to be founded in error. In the first sense the word might have been unexceptionable. Vehement desire is the result of a certain operation of the understanding, and must always be in a joint

---

[1] Book IV, Chap. VII, p. 181.

ratio of the supposed clearness of the proposition and importance of the practical effects. In the second sense, the doctrine of the passions would have been exceedingly harmless, if we had been accustomed to put the definition instead of the thing defined. It would then have been found that it merely affirmed that the human mind must always be liable to precisely the same mistakes as we observe in it at present, or in other words affirmed the necessary permanence in opposition to the necessary perfectibility of intellect. Who is there indeed that sees not, in the case above stated, the absurdity of supposing a man, so long as he has a clear view of justice and interest lying on one side of a given question, to be subject to errors that irresistibly compel him to the other? The mind is no doubt liable to fluctuation. But there is a degree of conviction that would render it impossible for us any longer to derive pleasure from intemperance, dominion or fame, and this degree in the incessant progress of thought must one day arrive.

This proposition of the permanence of a system of equal property, after it has once been brought into action by the energies of reason and conviction, will be placed out of the reach of all equitable doubt, if we proceed to form to ourselves an accurate picture of the action of this system. Let us suppose that we are introduced to a community of men, who are accustomed to an industry proportioned to the wants of the whole, and to communicate instantly and unconditionally, each man to his neighbour, that for which the former has not and the latter has immediate occasion. Here the first and simplest motive to personal accumulation is instantly cut off. I need not accumulate to protect myself against accidents, sickness or infirmity, for these are claims the validity of which is not regarded as a subject of doubt, and with which every man is accustomed to comply. I can accumulate in a considerable degree nothing but what is perishable, for exchange being unknown, that which I cannot personally consume adds nothing to the sum of my wealth.—Meanwhile it should be observed, that, though accumulation for private purposes under such a system would be in the highest degree irrational and absurd, this by no means precludes such accumulation, as may be necessary to provide against public contingencies. If there be any truth in the preceding reasonings, this kind of accumulation will be unattended with danger. Add to this, that the perpetual tendency of wisdom is to preclude contingency. It is well known that dearths are principally owing to the false precautions and false timidity of mankind; and it is reasonable to suppose that a degree of skill will hereafter be produced, which will gradually annihilate the failure of crops and other similar accidents.

It has already appeared, that the principal and unintermitting motive to private accumulation, is the love of distinction and esteem. This motive is also withdrawn. As accumulation can have no rational object, it would be viewed as a mark of insanity, not a title to admiration. Men would be accustomed to the simple principles of justice, and know that nothing was entitled to esteem but talents and virtue. Habituated to employ their superfluity to supply the wants of their neighbour, and to dedicate the time which was not necessary for manual labour to the cultivation of intellect, with what sentiments would they behold the man, who was foolish enough to sew a bit of lace upon his coat, or affix any other ornament to his person? In such a community property would perpetually tend to find its level. It would be interesting to all to be informed of the person in whose hands a certain quantity of any commodity was lodged, and every man would apply with confidence to him for the supply of his wants in that commodity. Putting therefore out of the question every kind of compulsion, the feeling of depravity and absurdity, that would be excited with relation to the man who refused to part with that for which he had no real need, would operate in all cases as a sufficient discouragement to so odious an innovation. Every man would conceive that he had a just and complete title to make use of my superfluity. If I refused to listen to reason and expostulation on this head, he would not stay to adjust with me a thing so vicious as exchange, but would leave me in order to seek the supply from some rational being. Accumulation, instead, as now, of calling forth every mark of respect, would tend to cut off the individual who attempted it from all the bonds of society, and sink him in neglect and oblivion. The influence of accumulation at present is derived from the idea of eventual benefit in the mind of the observer; but the accumulator then would be in a case still worse than that of the miser now, who, while he adds thousands to his heap, cannot be prevailed upon to part with a superfluous farthing, and is therefore the object of general desertion.

CHAPTER VI

OF THE OBJECTION TO THIS SYSTEM FROM THE INFLEXIBILITY OF ITS RESTRICTIONS

Nature of the objection.—Natural and moral independence distinguished—the first beneficial—the second injurious.—Tendency of restriction properly so called.—The genuine system of property not a system of restrictions—;does not require common labour, meals or magazines.—Such restrictions absurd—and unnecessary.—Evils of cooperation.—Its province may perpetually be diminished.—Manual labour may be extinguished.—Consequent activity of intellect.—Ideas of the future state of cooperation.—Its limits.—Its legitimate province.—Evils of cohabitation—and marriage.—They oppose the development of our faculties—are inimical to our happiness—and deprave our understandings.—Marriage a branch of the prevailing system of property.—Consequences of its abolition.—Education need not in that state of society be a subject of positive institution.—These principles do not lead to a sullen individuality.—Partial attachments considered.—Benefits accruing from a just affection—materially promoted by these principles.—The genuine system of property does not prohibit accumulation—implies a certain degree of appropriation—and division of labour.

AN objection that has often been urged against a system of equal property, is 'that it is inconsistent with personal independence. Every man according to this scheme is a passive instrument in the hands of the community. He must eat and drink, and play and sleep at the bidding of others. He has no habitation, no period at which he can retreat into himself, and not ask another's leave. He has nothing that he can call his own, not even his time or his person. Under the appearance of a perfect freedom from oppression and tyranny, he is in reality subjected to the most unlimited slavery.'

To understand the force of this objection it is necessary that we should distinguish two sorts of independence, one of which may be denominated natural, and the other moral. Natural independence, a freedom from all constraint except that of reason and argument presented to the understanding, is of the utmost importance the second injurious to the welfare and improvement of mind. Moral independence on the contrary is always injurious. The dependence which is essential in this respect to the wholsome temperament of society, includes in it articles that are no doubt unpalatable to a multitude of the present race of mankind, but that owe their unpopularity only to weakness and vice.

It includes a censure to be exercised by every individual over the actions of another, a promptness to enquire into them, and to judge them. Why should I shrink from this? What could be more beneficial than for each man to derive every possible assistance for correcting and moulding his conduct from the perspicacity of his neighbours? The reason why this species of censure is at present exercised with illiberality, is because it is exercised clandestinely and we submit to its operation with impatience and aversion. Moral independence is always injurious: for, as has abundantly appeared in the course of the present enquiry, there is no situation in which I can be placed, where it is not incumbent upon me to adopt a certain species of conduct in preference to all others, and of consequence where I shall not prove an ill member of society, if I act in any other than a particular manner. The attachment that is felt by the present race of mankind to independence in this respect, the desire to act as they please without being accountable to the principles of reason, is highly detrimental to the general welfare.

But, if we ought never to act independently of the principles of reason, and in no instance to shrink from the candid examination of another, it is nevertheless essential that we should at all times be free to cultivate the individuality and follow the dictates of our own judgment. If there be any thing in the scheme of equal property that infringes this principle, the objection is conclusive. If the scheme be, as it has often been represented, a scheme of government, constraint and regulation, it is no doubt in direct hostility with the principles of this work.

But the truth is, that a system of equal property requires no restrictions or superintendence whatever. There is no need of common labour, common meals or common magazines.* These are feeble and mistaken instruments for restraining the conduct without making conquest of the judgment. If you cannot bring over the hearts of the community to your party, expect no success from brute regulations. If you can, regulation is unnecessary. Such a system was well enough adapted to the military constitution of Sparta; but it is wholly unworthy of men who are enlisted in no cause but that of reason and justice. Beware of reducing men to the state of machines. Govern them through no medium but that of inclination and conviction.

Why should we have common meals? Am I obliged to be hungry at the same time that you are? Ought I to come at a certain hour, from the museum where I am working, the recess where I meditate, or the observatory where I remark the phenomena of nature, to a certain hall appropriated to the office of eating; instead of eating, as reason bids me, at the time and place most suited to my avocations? Why have common magazines? For the purpose of carrying our provisions a certain distance, that we may afterwards bring them back again? Or is this precaution really necessary, after all that has been said in praise of equal society and the omnipotence of reason, to guard us against the knavery and covetousness of our associates? If it be, for God's sake let us discard the parade of political justice, and go over to the standard of those reasoners who say, that man and the practice of justice are incompatible with each other.

Once more let us be upon our guard against reducing men to the condition of brute machines. The objectors of the last chapter were partly in the right when they spoke of the endless variety of mind. It would be absurd to say that we are not capable of truth, of evidence and agreement. In these respects, so far as mind is in a state of progressive improvement, we are perpetually coming nearer to each other. But there are subjects about which we shall continually differ, and ought to differ. The ideas, the associations and the circumstances of each man are properly his own; and it is a pernicious system that would lead us to require all men, however different their circumstances, to act in many of the common affairs of life by a precise general rule. Add to this, that, by the doctrine of progressive improvement, we shall always be erroneous, though we shall every day become less erroneous. The proper method for hastening the decay of error, is not, by brute force, or by regulation which is one of the classes of force, to endeavour to reduce men to intellectual uniformity; but on the contrary by teaching every man to think for himself.

From these principles it appears that every thing that is usually understood by the term cooperation, is in some degree an evil. A man in solitude, is obliged to sacrifice or postpone the execution of his best thoughts to his own convenience. How many admirable designs have perished in the conception by means of this circumstance? The true remedy is for men to reduce their wants to the fewest possible, and as much as possible to simplify the mode of supplying them. It is still worse when a man is also obliged to consult the convenience of others. If I be expected to eat or to work in conjunction with my neighbour, it must either be at a time most convenient to me, or to him, or to neither of us. We cannot be reduced to a clock-work uniformity.

Hence it follows that all supererogatory cooperation is carefully to be avoided, common labour and common meals. 'But what shall we say to cooperation that seems to be dictated by the nature of the work to be performed?' It ought to be diminished. At present it is unreasonable to doubt, that the consideration of the evil of cooperation is in certain urgent cases to be postponed to that urgency. Whether by the nature of things cooperation of some sort will always be necessary, is a question that we are scarcely competent to decide. At present, to pull down a tree, to cut a canal, to navigate a vessel, requires the labour of many. Will it always require the labour of many? When we look at the complicated machines of human contrivance, various sorts of mills, of weaving engines, of steam engines,* are we not astonished at the compendium of labour they produce? Who shall say where this species of improvement must stop? At present such inventions alarm the labouring part of the community; and they may be productive of temporary distress, though they conduce in the sequel to the most important interests of the multitude. But in a state of equal labour their utility will be liable to no dispute. Hereafter it is by no means clear that the most extensive operations will not be within the reach of one man; or, to make use of a familiar instance, that a plough may not be turned into a field, and perform its office without the need of superintendence. It was in this sense that the celebrated Franklin conjectured, that 'mind would one day become omnipotent over matter.'*

The conclusion of the progress which has here been sketched, is something like a final close to the necessity of manual labour. It is highly instructive in such cases to observe how the sublime geniuses of former times anticipated what seems likely to be the future improvement of mankind. It was one of the laws of Lycurgus, that no Spartan should be employed in manual labour.* For this purpose under his system it was necessary that they should be plentifully supplied with slaves devoted to drudgery. Matter, or, to speak more accurately, the certain and unintermitting laws of the universe, will be the Helots of the period we are contemplating. We shall end in this respect, oh immortal legislator! at the point from which you began.

To these prospects perhaps the objection will once again be repeated, 'that men, delivered from the necessity of manual labour, will sink into supineness.' What narrow views of the nature and capacities of mind do such objections imply? The only thing necessary to put intellect into action is motive. Are there no motives equally cogent with the prospect of hunger? Whose thoughts are most active, most rapid and unwearied, those of Newton or the ploughman? When the mind is stored with prospects of intellectual greatness and utility, can it sink into torpor?

To return to the subject of cooperation. It may be a curious speculation to attend to the progressive steps by which this feature of human society may be expected to decline. For example: shall we have concerts of music? The miserable state of mechanism of the majority of the

performers is so conspicuous, as to be even at this day a topic of morti-
fication and ridicule. Will it not be practicable hereafter for one man to
perform the whole? Shall we have theatrical exhibitions? This seems to
include an absurd and vicious cooperation. It may be doubted whether
men will hereafter come forward in any mode gravely to repeat words
and ideas not their own? It may be doubted whether any musical per-
former will habitually execute the compositions of others? We yield
supinely to the superior merit of our predecessors, because we are
accustomed to indulge the inactivity of our own faculties. All formal
repetition of other men's ideas seems to be a scheme for imprisoning
for so long a time the operations of our own mind. It borders perhaps
in this respect upon a breach of sincerity, which requires that we should
give immediate utterance to every useful and valuable idea that occurs
to our thoughts.

Having ventured to state these hints and conjectures, let us endeavour to mark the limits of individuality. Every man that receives an
impression from any external object, has the current of his own thoughts
modified by force; and yet without external impressions we should be
nothing. We ought not, except under certain limitations, to endeavour to
free ourselves from their approach. Every man that reads the composition of another, suffers the succession of his ideas to be in a considerable degree under the direction of his author. But it does not seem as if
this would ever form a sufficient objection against reading. One man will
always have stored up reflections and facts that another wants; and
mature and digested discourse will perhaps always, in equal circumstances, be superior to that which is extempore. Conversation is a species of cooperation, one or the other party always yielding to have his
ideas guided by the other: and yet conversation and the intercourse of
mind with mind seem to be the most fertile sources of improvement. It
is here as it is with punishment. He that in the gentlest manner undertakes to reason another out of his vices, will probably occasion pain; but
this species of punishment ought upon no account to be superseded.

Another article which belongs to the subject of cooperation is
cohabitation. A very simple process will lead us to a right decision in
this instance. Science is most effectually cultivated, when the greatest
number of minds are employed in the pursuit of it. If an hundred men
spontaneously engage the whole energy of their faculties upon the
solution of a given question, the chance of success will be greater, than
if only ten men were so employed. By the same reason the chance will
be also increased, in proportion as the intellectual operations of these
men are individual, in proportion as their conclusions are directed by

the reason of the thing, uninfluenced by the force either of compulsion or sympathy. All attachments to individuals, except in proportion to their merits, are plainly unjust. It is therefore desirable, that we should be the friends of man rather than of particular men, and that we should pursue the chain of our own reflexions, with no other interruption than information or philanthropy requires.

This subject of cohabitation is particularly interesting, as it includes in it the subject of marriage. It will therefore be proper to extend our enquiries somewhat further upon this head. Cohabitation is not only an evil as it checks the independent progress of mind; it is also inconsistent with the imperfections and propensities of man. It is absurd to expect that the inclinations and wishes of two human beings should coincide through any long period of time. To oblige them to act and to live together, is to subject them to some inevitable portion of thwarting, bickering and unhappiness. This cannot be otherwise, so long as man has failed to reach the standard of absolute perfection. The supposition that I must have a companion for life, is the result of a complication of vices. It is the dictate of cowardice, and not of fortitude. It flows from the desire of being loved and esteemed for something that is not desert.

But the evil of marriage as it is practised in European countries lies deeper than this. The habit is, for a thoughtless and romantic youth of each sex to come together, to see each other for a few times and under circumstances full of delusion, and then to vow to each other eternal attachment. What is the consequence of this? In almost every instance they find themselves deceived. They are reduced to make the best of an irretrievable mistake. They are presented with the strongest imaginable temptation to become the dupes of falshood. They are led to conceive it their wisest policy to shut their eyes upon realities, happy if by any perversion of intellect they can persuade themselves that they were right in their first crude opinion of their companion. The institution of marriage is a system of fraud; and men who carefully mislead their judgments in the daily affair of their life, must always have a crippled judgment in every other concern. We ought to dismiss our mistake as soon as it is detected; but we are taught to cherish it. We ought to be incessant in our search after virtue and worth; but we are taught to check our enquiry, and shut our eyes upon the most attractive and admirable objects. Marriage is law, and the worst of all laws. Whatever our understandings may tell us of the person from whose connexion we should derive the greatest improvement, of the worth of one woman and the demerits of another, we are obliged to consider what is law, and not what is justice.

Add to this, that marriage is an affair of property, and the worst of all properties. So long as two human beings are forbidden by positive institution to follow the dictates of their own mind, prejudice is alive and vigorous. So long as I seek to engross one woman to myself, and to prohibit my neighbour from proving his superior desert and reaping the fruits of it, I am guilty of the most odious of all monopolies. Over this imaginary prize men watch with perpetual jealousy, and one man will find his desires and his capacity to circumvent as much excited, as the other is excited to traverse his projects and frustrate his hopes. As long as this state of society continues, philanthropy will be crossed and checked in a thousand ways, and the still augmenting stream of abuse will continue to flow.

The abolition of marriage will be attended with no evils. We are apt to represent it to ourselves as the harbinger of brutal lust and depravity. But it really happens in this as in other cases, that the positive laws which are made to restrain our vices, irritate and multiply them. Not to say, that the same sentiments of justice and happiness which in a state of equal property would destroy the relish for luxury, would decrease our inordinate appetites of every kind, and lead us universally to prefer the pleasures of intellect to the pleasures of sense.

The intercourse of the sexes will in such a state fall under the same system as any other species of friendship. Exclusively of all groundless and obstinate attachments, it will be impossible for me to live in the world without finding one man of a worth superior to that of any other whom I have an opportunity of observing. To this man I shall feel a kindness in exact proportion to my apprehension of his worth. The case will be precisely the same with respect to the female sex. I shall assiduously cultivate the intercourse of that woman whose accomplishments shall strike me in the most powerful manner. 'But it may happen that other men will feel for her the same preference that I do.' This will create no difficulty. We may all enjoy her conversation; and we shall all be wise enough to consider the sensual intercourse as a very trivial object. This, like every other affair in which two persons are concerned, must be regulated in each successive instance by the unforced consent of either party. It is a mark of the extreme depravity of our present habits, that we are inclined to suppose the sensual intercourse any wise material to the advantages arising from the purest affection. Reasonable men now eat and drink, not from the love of pleasure, but because eating and drinking are essential to our healthful existence. Reasonable men then will propagate their species, not because a certain sensible pleasure is annexed to this action, but because it is right the species should be propagated; and the manner in which they exercise this function will be regulated by the dictates of reason and duty.

Such are some of the considerations that will probably regulate the commerce of the sexes. It cannot be definitively affirmed whether it will be known in such a state of society who is the father of each individual child. But it may be affirmed that such knowledge will be of no importance. It is aristocracy, self love and family pride that teach us to set a value upon it at present. I ought to prefer no human being to another, because that being is my father, my wife or my son, but because, for reasons which equally appeal to all understandings, that being is entitled to preference. One among the measures which will successively be dictated by the spirit of democracy, and that probably at no great distance, is the abolition of surnames.

Let us consider the way in which this state of society will modify education. It may be imagined that the abolition of marriage would make it in a certain sense the affair of the public; though, if there be any truth in the reasonings of this work, to provide for it by the positive institutions of a community, would be extremely inconsistent with the true principles of the intellectual system.[1] Education may be regarded as consisting of various branches. First, the personal cares which the helpless state of an infant requires. These will probably devolve upon the mother; unless, by frequent parturition or by the very nature of these cares, that were found to render her share of the burthen unequal; and then it would be amicably and willingly participated by others. Secondly, food and other necessary supplies. These, as we have already seen, would easily find their true level, and spontaneously flow from the quarter in which they abounded to the quarter that was deficient.[2] Lastly, the term education may be used to signify instruction. The task of instruction, under such a form of society as that we are contemplating, will be greatly simplified and altered from what it is at present. It will then be thought no more legitimate to make boys slaves, than to make men so. The business will not then be to bring forward so many adepts in the egg-shell, that the vanity of parents may be flattered by hearing their praises. No man will then think of vexing with premature learning the feeble and inexperienced, for fear that, when they came to years of discretion, they should refuse to be learned. Mind will be suffered to expand itself in proportion as occasion and impression shall excite it, and not tortured and enervated by being cast in a particular mould. No creature in human form will be expected to learn any thing, but

---

[1] Book VI, Chap. VIII.		[2] Chap. V, p. 440.

because he desires it and has some conception of its utility and value; and every man, in proportion to his capacity, will be ready to furnish such general hints and comprehensive views, as will suffice for the guidance and encouragement of him who studies from a principle of desire.

Before we quit this part of the subject it will be necessary to obviate an objection that will suggest itself to some readers. They will say 'that man was formed for society and reciprocal kindness; and therefore is by his nature little adapted to the system of individuality which is here delineated. The true perfection of man is to blend and unite his own existence with that of another, and therefore a system which forbids him all partialities and attachments, tends to degeneracy and not to improvement.'

No doubt man is formed for society. But there is a way in which for a man to lose his own existence in that of others, that is eminently vicious and detrimental. Every man ought to rest upon his own centre, and consult his own understanding. Every man ought to feel his independence, that he can assert the principles of justice and truth, without being obliged treacherously to adapt them to the peculiarities of his situation, and the errors of others.

No doubt man is formed for society. But he is formed for, or in other words his faculties enable him to serve, the whole and not a part. Justice obliges us to sympathise with a man of merit more fully than with an insignificant and corrupt member of society. But all partialities strictly so called, tend to the injury of him who feels them, of mankind in general, and even of him who is their object. The spirit of partiality is well expressed in the memorable saying of Themistocles, 'God forbid that I should sit upon a bench of justice, where my friends found no more favour than strangers!'* In fact, as has been repeatedly seen in the course of this work, we sit in every action of our lives upon a bench of justice; and play in humble imitation the part of the unjust judge, whenever we indulge the smallest atom of partiality.

Such are the limitations of the social principle. These limitations in reality tend to improve it and render its operations beneficial. It would be a miserable mistake to suppose that the principle is not of the utmost importance to mankind. All that in which the human mind differs from the intellectual principle in animals is the growth of society. All that is excellent in man is the fruit of progressive improvement, of the circumstance of one age taking advantage of the discoveries of a preceding age, and setting out from the point at which they had arrived.

Without society we should be wretchedly deficient in motives to improvement. But what is most of all, without society our improvements would be nearly useless. Mind without benevolence is a barren and a cold existence. It is in seeking the good of others, in embracing a great and expansive sphere of action, in forgetting our own individual interests, that we find our true element. The tendency of the whole system delineated in this Book is to lead us to that element. The individuality it recommends tends to the good of the whole, and is valuable only as a means to that end. Can that be termed a selfish system, where no man desires luxury, no man dares to be guilty of injustice, and every one devotes himself to supply the wants, animal or intellectual, of others?—To proceed.

As a genuine state of society is incompatible with all laws and restrictions, so it cannot have even this restriction, that no man shall amass property. The security against accumulation, as has already been said, lies in the perceived absurdity and inutility of accumulation. The practice, if it can be conceived in a state of society where the principles of justice were adequately understood, would not even be dangerous. The idea would not create alarm, as it is apt to do in prospect among the present advocates of political justice. Men would feel nothing but their laughter or their pity excited at so strange a perversity of human intellect.

What would denominate any thing my property? The fact, that it was necessary to my welfare. My right would be coeval with the existence of that necessity. The word property would probably remain; its signification only would be modified. The mistake does not so properly lie in the idea itself, as in the source from which it is traced. What I have, if it be necessary for my use, is truly mine; what I have, though the fruit of my own industry, if unnecessary, it is an usurpation for me to retain.

Force in such a state of society would be unknown; I should part with nothing without a full consent. Caprice would be unknown; no man would covet that which I used, unless he distinctly apprehended, that it would be more beneficial in his possession than it was in mine. My apartment would be as sacred to a certain extent, as it is at present. No man would obtrude himself upon me to interrupt the course of my studies and meditations. No man would feel the whim of occupying my apartment, while he could provide himself another as good of his own. That which was my apartment yesterday would probably be my apartment to-day. We have few pursuits that do not require a certain degree of apparatus; and it would be for the general good that I should find in ordinary cases the apparatus ready for my use to-day that I left yesterday. But, though the idea of property thus modified would remain, the jealousy and selfishness of property would be gone. Bolts and locks would be unknown. Every man would be welcome to make every use of my accommodations, that did not interfere with my own use of them.

Novices as we are, we may figure to ourselves a thousand disputes, where property was held by so slight a tenure. But disputes would in reality be impossible. They are the offspring of a mishapen and disproportioned love of ourselves. Do you want my table? Make one for yourself; or, if I be more skilful in that respect than you, I will make one for you. Do you want it immediately? Let us compare the urgency of your wants and mine, and let justice decide.

These observations lead us to the consideration of one additional difficulty, which relates to the division of labour. Shall each man make all his tools, his furniture and accommodations? This would perhaps be a tedious operation. Every man performs the task to which he is accustomed more skilfully and in a shorter time than another. It is reasonable that you should make for me, that which perhaps I should be three or four times as long making, and should make imperfectly at last. Shall we then introduce barter and exchange? By no means. The abstract spirit of exchange will perhaps govern; every man will employ an equal portion of his time in manual labour. But the individual application of exchange is of all practices the most pernicious. The moment I require any other reason for supplying you than the cogency of your claim, the moment, in addition to the dictates of benevolence, I demand a prospect of advantage to myself, there is an end of that political justice and pure society of which we treat. No man will have a trade. It cannot be supposed that a man will construct any species of commodity, but in proportion as it is wanted. The profession paramount to all others and in which every man will bear his part, will be that of man, and in addition perhaps that of cultivator.

The division of labour, as it has been treated by commercial writers, is for the most part the offspring of avarice. It has been found that ten persons can make two hundred and forty times as many pins in a day as one person.[1] This refinement is the growth of luxury. The object is to see into how vast a surface the industry of the lower classes may be beaten, the more completely to gild over the indolent and the proud. The ingenuity of the merchant is whetted, by new improvements of this sort to transport more of the wealth of the powerful into his own coffers. The possibility of effecting a compendium of labour by this means will be greatly diminished, when men shall learn to deny themselves superfluities. The utility of such a saving of labour, where labour is so little, will scarcely balance against the evils of so extensive a cooperation. From what has been said under this head it appears, that there will be a

---

[1] Smith's Wealth of Nations,* Book I, Chap. I.

division of labour, if we compare the society in question with the state of the solitaire and the savage. But it will produce an extensive composition of labour, if we compare it with that to which we are at present accustomed in civilised Europe.

CHAPTER VII

OF THE OBJECTION TO THIS SYSTEM FROM THE PRINCIPLE OF POPULATION

The objection stated.—Remoteness of its operation.—Conjectural ideas respecting the antidote.—Omnipotence of mind.—Illustrations.—Causes of decrepitude.—Youth is prolonged by chearfulness—by clearness of apprehension—and a benevolent character.—The powers we possess are essentially progressive.—Effects of attention.—The phenomenon of sleep explained.—Present utility of these reasonings.—Application to the future state of society.

AN author who has speculated widely upon subjects of government,[1] has recommended equal, or, which was rather his idea, common property, as a complete remedy, to the usurpation and distress which are at present the most powerful enemies of human kind, to the vices which infect education in some instances, and the neglect it encounters in more, to all the turbulence of passion, and all the injustice of selfishness. But, after having exhibited this picture, not less true than delightful, he finds an argument that demolishes the whole, and restores him to indifference and despair, in the excessive population that would ensue.

One of the most obvious answers to this objection is, that to reason thus is to foresee difficulties at a great distance. Three fourths of the habitable globe is now uncultivated. The parts already cultivated are capable of immeasurable improvement. Myriads of centuries of still increasing population may probably pass away, and the earth still be found sufficient for the subsistence of its inhabitants. Who can say how long the earth itself will survive the casualties of the planetary system? Who can say what remedies shall suggest themselves for so distant an inconvenience, time enough for practical application, and of which we may yet at this time have not the smallest idea? It would be truly absurd for us to shrink from a scheme of essential benefit to mankind, lest they

---

[1] Wallace: Various Prospects of Mankind, Nature and Providence, 1761.*

should be too happy, and by necessary consequence at some distant period too populous.

But, though these remarks may be deemed a sufficient answer to the objection, it may not be amiss to indulge in some speculations to which such an objection obviously leads. The earth may, to speak in the style of one of the writers of the Christian Scriptures, 'abide for ever.'[1] It may be in danger of becoming too populous. A remedy may then be necessary. If it may, why should we sit down in supine indifference and conclude that we can discover no glimpse of it? The discovery, if made, would add to the firmness and consistency of our prospects; nor is it improbable to conjecture that that which would form the regulating spring of our conduct then, might be the medium of a salutary modification now. What follows must be considered in some degree as a deviation into the land of conjecture. If it be false, it leaves the great system to which it is appended in all sound reason as impregnable as ever. If this do not lead us to the true remedy, it does not follow that there is no remedy. The great object of enquiry will still remain open, however defective may be the suggestions that are now to be offered.

Let us here return to the sublime conjecture of Franklin, that 'mind will one day become omnipotent over matter.'[2] If over all other matter, why not over the matter of our own bodies? If over matter at ever so great a distance, why not over matter which, however ignorant we may be of the tie that connects it with the thinking principle, we always carry about with us, and which is in all cases the medium of communication between that principle and the external universe? In a word, why may not man be one day immortal?

The different cases in which thought modifies the external universe are obvious to all. It is modified by our voluntary thoughts or design. We desire to stretch out our hand, and it is stretched out. We perform a thousand operations of the same species every day, and their familiarity annihilates the wonder. They are not in themselves less wonderful than any of those modifications which we are least accustomed to conceive.—Mind modifies body involuntarily. Emotion excited by some unexpected word, by a letter that is delivered to us, occasions the most extraordinary revolutions in our frame, accelerates the circulation, causes the heart to palpitate, the tongue to refuse its office, and has

---

[1] Ecclesiastes, Chap. I, ver 4.

[2] I have no other authority to quote for this expression than the conversation of Dr Price. Upon enquiry I am happy to find it confirmed to me by Mr William Morgan,* the nephew of Dr Price, who recollects to have heard it repeatedly mentioned by his uncle.

been known to occasion death by extreme anguish or extreme joy. These symptoms we may either encourage or check. By encouraging them habits are produced of fainting or of rage. To discourage them is one of the principal offices of fortitude. The effort of mind in resisting pain in the stories of Cranmer and Mucius Scævola* is of the same kind. It is reasonable to believe that that effort with a different direction might have cured certain diseases of the system. There is nothing indeed of which physicians themselves are more frequently aware, than of the power of the mind in assisting or retarding convalescence.

Why is it that a mature man soon loses that elasticity of limb, which characterises the heedless gaiety of youth? Because he desists from youthful habits. He assumes an air of dignity incompatible with the lightness of childish sallies. He is visited and vexed with all the cares that rise out of our mistaken institutions, and his heart is no longer satisfied and gay. Hence his limbs become stiff and unwieldy. This is the forerunner of old age and death.

The first habit favourable to corporeal vigour is chearfulness. Every time that our mind becomes morbid, vacant and melancholy, a certain period is cut off from the length of our lives. Listlessness of thought is the brother of death. But chearfulness gives new life to our frame and circulation to our juices. Nothing can long be stagnant in the frame of him, whose heart is tranquil, and his imagination active.

A second requisite in the case of which we treat is a clear and distinct conception. If I know precisely what I wish, it is easy for me to calm the throbs of pain, and to assist the sluggish operations of the system. It is not a knowledge of anatomy, but a quiet and steady attention to my symptoms, that will best enable me to correct the distemper from which they spring. Fainting is nothing else but a confusion of mind, in which the ideas appear to mix in painful disorder, and nothing is distinguished.

The true source of chearfulness is benevolence. To a youthful mind, while every thing strikes with its novelty, the individual situation must be peculiarly unfortunate, if gaiety of thought be not produced, or, when interrupted, do not speedily return with its healing oblivion. But novelty is a fading charm, and perpetually decreases. Hence the approach of inanity and listlessness. After we have made a certain round, life delights no more. A deathlike apathy invades us. Thus the aged are generally cold and indifferent; nothing interests their attention, or rouses the sluggishness of their soul. How should it be otherwise? The pursuits of mankind are commonly frigid and contemptible, and the mistake comes at last to be detected. But virtue is a charm that never fades. The soul that perpetually overflows with kindness and sympathy, will always be chearful. The man who is perpetually busied in contemplations of public good, will always be active.

The application of these reasonings is simple and irresistible. If mind be now in a great degree the ruler of the system, why should it be incapable of extending its empire? If our involuntary thoughts can derange or restore the animal economy, why should we not in process of time, in this as in other instances, subject the thoughts which are at present involuntary to the government of design? If volition can now do something, why should it not go on to do still more and more? There is no principle of reason less liable to question than this, that, if we have in any respect a little power now, and if mind be essentially progressive, that power may, and, barring any extraordinary concussions of nature, infallibly will, extend beyond any bounds we are able to prescribe to it.

Nothing can be more irrational and presumptuous than to conclude, because a certain species of supposed power is entirely out of the line of our present observations, that it is therefore altogether beyond the limits of the human mind. We talk familiarly indeed of the limits of our faculties, but nothing is more difficult than to point them out. Mind, in a progressive view at least, is infinite. If it could have been told to the savage inhabitants of Europe in the times of Theseus and Achilles,* that man was capable of predicting eclipses and weighing the air, of explaining the phenomena of nature so that no prodigies should remain, of measuring the distance and the size of the heavenly bodies, this would not have appeared to them less wonderful, than if we had told them of the possible discovery of the means of maintaining the human body in perpetual youth and vigour. But we have not only this analogy, showing that the discovery in question forms as it were a regular branch of the acquisitions that belong to an intellectual nature; but in addition to this we seem to have a glimpse of the specific manner in which the acquisition will be secured. Let us remark a little more distinctly the simplicity of the process.

We have called the principle of immortality in man chearfulness, clearness of conception and benevolence. Perhaps we shall in some respects have a more accurate view of its potency, if we consider it as of the nature of attention. It is a very old maxim of practical conduct, that whatever is done with attention, is done well. It is because this was a principal requisite, that many persons endowed in an eminent degree with chearfulness, perspicacity and benevolence, have perhaps not been longer lived than their neighbours. We are not capable at present of attending to every thing. A man who is engaged in the sublimest and most delightful exertions of mind, will perhaps be less attentive to his animal functions than his most ordinary neighbour, though he will frequently in a partial degree repair that neglect, by a more chearful and animated observation, when those exertions are suspended. But, though the faculty of attention may at present have a very small share of ductility, it is probable that it may be improved in that respect to an inconceivable degree. The picture that was exhibited of the subtlety of mind in an earlier stage of this work,[1] gives to this supposition a certain degree of moral evidence. If we can have three hundred and twenty successive ideas in a second of time, why should it be supposed that we shall not hereafter arrive at the skill of carrying on a great number of contemporaneous processes without disorder?

Having thus given a view of what may be the future improvement of mind, it is proper that we should qualify this picture to the sanguine temper of some readers and the incredulity of others, by observing that this improvement, if capable of being realised, is however at a great distance. A very obvious remark will render this eminently palpable. If an unintermitted attention to the animal economy be necessary, then, before death can be banished, we must banish sleep, death's image. Sleep is one of the most conspicuous infirmities of the human frame. It is not, as has often been supposed, a suspension of thought, but an irregular and distempered state of the faculty.[2] Our tired attention resigns the helm, ideas swim before us in wild confusion, and are attended with less and less distinctness, till at length they leave no traces in the memory. Whatever attention and volition are then imposed upon us, as it were at unawares, are but faint resemblances of our operations in the same kind when awake. Generally speaking, we contemplate sights of horror with little pain, and commit the most atrocious crimes with little sense of their true nature. The horror we sometimes attribute to our dreams, will frequently be found upon accurate observation to belong to our review of them when we wake.

One other remark may be proper in this place. If the remedies here prescribed tend to a total extirpation of the infirmities of our nature, then, though we cannot promise to them an early and complete success, we may probably find them of some utility now. They may contribute to prolong our vigour, though not to immortalise it, and, which is of more consequence, to make us live while we live. Every time the mind is invaded with anguish and gloom, the frame becomes disordered. Every time that languor and indifference creep upon us, our functions

---

[1] Book IV, Chap. VII, p. 178.   [2] Book IV, Chap. VII, p. 181.

fall into decay. In proportion as we cultivate fortitude and equanimity, our circulations will be chearful. In proportion as we cultivate a kind and benevolent propensity, we may be secure of finding something for ever to interest and engage us.

Medicine may reasonably be stated to consist of two branches, the animal and intellectual. The latter of these has been infinitely too much neglected. It cannot be employed to the purposes of a profession; or, where it has been incidentally so employed, it has been artificially and indirectly, not in an open and avowed manner. 'Herein the patient must minister to himself.'[1] How often do we find a sudden piece of good news dissipating a distemper? How common is the remark, that those accidents, which are to the indolent a source of disease, are forgotten and extirpated in the busy and active? It would no doubt be of extreme moment to us, to be thoroughly acquainted with the power of motives, habit, and what is called resolution, in this respect. I walk twenty miles in an indolent and half determined temper, and am extremely fatigued. I walk twenty miles full of ardour and with a motive that engrosses my soul, and I come in as fresh and alert as when I began my journey. We are sick and we die, generally speaking, because we consent to suffer these accidents. This consent in the present state of mankind is in some degree unavoidable. We must have stronger motives and clearer views, before we can uniformly refuse it. But, though we cannot always, we may frequently refuse. This is a truth of which all mankind are to a certain degree aware. Nothing more common than for the most ignorant man to call upon his sick neighbour, to rouse himself, not to suffer himself to be conquered; and this exhortation is always accompanied with some consciousness of the efficacy of resolution. The wise and the good man therefore should carry with him the recollection of what chearfulness and a determined spirit are able to do, of the capacity with which he is endowed of expelling the seeds and first slight appearances of indisposition.

The principal part of the preceding paragraph is nothing more than a particular application of what was elsewhere delivered respecting moral and physical causes.[2] It would have been easy to have cast the present chapter in a different form, and to have made it a chapter upon health, showing that one of the advantages of a better state of society would be a very high improvement of the vigour and animal constitution of man. In that case the conjecture of immortality would only have

---

[1] Macbeth, Act V.*   [2] Book I, Chap. VII, Part I.

come in as an incidental remark, and the whole would have assumed less the air of conjecture than of close and argumentative deduction. But it was perhaps better to give the subject the most explicit form, at the risk of exciting a certain degree of prejudice.

To apply these remarks to the subject of population. The tendency of a cultivated and virtuous mind is to render us indifferent to the gratifications of sense. They please at present by their novelty, that is, because we know not how to estimate them. They decay in the decline of life indirectly because the system refuses them, but directly and principally because they no longer excite the ardour and passion of mind. It is well known that an inflamed imagination is capable of doubling and tripling the seminal secretions. The gratifications of sense please at present by their imposture. We soon learn to despise the mere animal function, which, apart from the delusions of intellect, would be nearly the same in all cases; and to value it, only as it happens to be relieved by personal charms or mental excellence. We absurdly imagine that no better road can be found to the sympathy and intercourse of minds. But a very slight degree of attention might convince us that this is a false road, full of danger and deception. Why should I esteem another, or by another be esteemed? For this reason only, because esteem is due, and only so far as it is due.

The men therefore who exist when the earth shall refuse itself to a more extended population, will cease to propagate, for they will no longer have any motive, either of error or duty, to induce them. In addition to this they will perhaps be immortal. The whole will be a people of men, and not of children. Generation will not succeed generation, nor truth have in a certain degree to recommence her career at the end of every thirty years. There will be no war, no crimes, no administration of justice as it is called, and no government. These latter articles are at no great distance; and it is not impossible that some of the present race of men may live to see them in part accomplished. But beside this, there will be no disease, no anguish, no melancholy and no resentment. Every man will seek with ineffable ardour the good of all. Mind will be active and eager, yet never disappointed. Men will see the progressive advancement of virtue and good, and feel that, if things occasionally happen contrary to their hopes, the miscarriage itself was a necessary part of that progress. They will know, that they are members of the chain, that each has his several utility, and they will not feel indifferent to that utility. They will be eager to enquire into the good that already exists, the means by which it was produced, and the greater good that is yet in store. They will never want motives for exertion; for that benefit which a man thoroughly understands and earnestly loves, he cannot refrain from endeavouring to promote.

Before we dismiss this subject it is proper once again to remind the reader, that the leading doctrine of this chapter is given only as matter of probable conjecture, and that the grand argument of this division of the work is altogether independent of its truth or falshood.

CHAPTER VIII

OF THE MEANS OF INTRODUCING THE GENUINE SYSTEM OF PROPERTY

Apprehensions that are entertained on this subject.—Idea of massacre. —Inference we ought to make upon supposition of the reality of these apprehensions.—Mischief by no means the necessary attendant on improvement.—Duties under this circumstance, 1. of those who are qualified for public instructors—temper—sincerity.—Pernicious effects of dissimulation in this case.—2. Of the rich and great.—Many of them may be expected to be advocates of equality.—Conduct which their interest as a body prescribes.—3. Of the friends of equality in general.—Omnipotence of truth.— Importance of a mild and benevolent proceeding.—Connexion between liberty and equality.—Cause of equality will perpetually advance.—Symptoms of its progress.—Idea of its future success.—Conclusion.

HAVING thus stated explicitly and without reserve the great branches of this illustrious picture, there is but one subject that remains. In what manner shall this interesting improvement of human society be carried into execution? Are there not certain steps that are desirable for this purpose? Are there not certain steps that are inevitable? Will not the period that must first elapse, necessarily be stained with a certain infusion of evil?

No idea has excited greater horror in the minds of a multitude of persons, than that of the mischiefs that are to ensue from the dissemination of what they call levelling principles. They believe 'that these principles will inevitably ferment in the minds of the vulgar, and that the attempt to carry them into execution will be attended with every species of calamity.' They represent to themselves 'the uninformed and uncivilised part of mankind, as let loose from all restraint, and hurried into every kind of excess. Knowledge and taste, the improvements of intellect, the discoveries of sages, the beauties of poetry and art, are trampled under foot and extinguished by barbarians. It is another inundation of Goths and Vandals, with this bitter aggravation, that the viper that stings us to death was warmed in our own bosoms.'

They conceive of the scene as 'beginning in massacre.' They suppose 'all that is great, preeminent and illustrious as ranking among the first victims. Such as are distinguished by peculiar elegance of manners or energy of diction and composition, will be the inevitable objects of envy and jealousy. Such as intrepidly exert themselves to succour the persecuted, or to declare to the public those truths which they are least inclined, but which are most necessary for them to hear, will be marked out for assassination.'

Let us not, from any partiality to the system of equality delineated in this book, shrink from the picture here exhibited. Massacre is the too possible attendant upon revolution, and massacre is perhaps the most hateful scene, allowing for its momentary duration, that any imagination can suggest. The fearful, hopeless expectation of the defeated, and the blood-hound fury of their conquerors, is a complication of mischief that all which has been told of infernal regions cannot surpass. The cold-blooded massacres that are perpetrated under the name of criminal justice fall short of these in their most frightful aggravations. The ministers and instruments of law have by custom reconciled their minds to the dreadful task they perform, and bear their respective parts in the most shocking enormities, without being sensible to the passions allied to those enormities. But the instruments of massacre are actuated with all the sentiments of fiends. Their eyes emit flashes of cruelty and rage. They pursue their victims from street to street and from house to house. They tear them from the arms of their fathers and their wives. They glut themselves with barbarity and insult, and utter shouts of horrid joy at the spectacle of their tortures.

We have now contemplated the tremendous picture; what is the conclusion it behoves us to draw? Must we shrink from reason, from justice, from virtue and happiness? Suppose that the inevitable consequence of communicating truth were the temporary introduction of such a scene as has just been described, must we on that account refuse to communicate it? The crimes that were perpetrated would in no just estimate appear to be the result of truth, but of the error which had previously been infused. The impartial enquirer would behold them as the last struggles of expiring despotism, which, if it had survived, would have produced mischiefs, scarcely less atrocious in the hour of their commission, and infinitely more calamitous by the length of their duration. If we would judge truly, even admitting the unfavourable supposition above stated, we must contrast a moment of horror and distress with ages of felicity. No imagination can sufficiently conceive the mental improvement and the tranquil virtue that would succeed, were property once permitted to rest upon its genuine basis.

And by what means suppress truth, and keep alive the salutary intoxication, the tranquillising insanity of mind which some men desire? Such has been too generally the policy of government through every age of the world. Have we slaves? We must assiduously retain them in ignorance. Have we colonies and dependencies? The great effort of our care is to keep them from being too populous and prosperous. Have we subjects? It is 'by impotence and misery that we endeavour to render them supple: plenty is fit for nothing but to make them unmanageable, disobedient and mutinous.'[1] If this were the true philosophy of social institutions, well might we shrink from it with horror. How tremendous an abortion would the human species be found, if all that tended to make them wise, tended to make them unprincipled and profligate? But this it is impossible for any one to believe, who will lend the subject a moment's impartial consideration. Can truth, the perception of justice and a desire to execute it, be the source of irretrievable ruin to mankind? It may be conceived that the first opening and illumination of mind will be attended with disorder. But every just reasoner must confess that regularity and happiness will succeed to this confusion. To refuse the remedy, were this picture of its operation ever so true, would be as if a man who had dislocated a limb, should refuse to undergo the pain of having it replaced. If mankind have hitherto lost the road of virtue and happiness, that can be no just reason why they should be suffered to go wrong for ever. We must not refuse a conviction of error, or even the treading over again some of the steps that were the result of it.

Another question suggests itself under this head. Can we suppress truth? Can we arrest the progress of the enquiring mind? If we can, it will only be done by the most unmitigated despotism. Mind has a perpetual tendency to rise. It cannot be held down but by a power that counteracts its genuine tendency through every moment of its existence. Tyrannical and sanguinary must be the measures employed for this purpose. Miserable and disgustful must be the scene they produce. Their result will be thick darkness of the mind, timidity, servility, hypocrisy. This is the alternative, so far as there is any alternative in their power, between the opposite measures of which the princes and governments of the earth have now to choose: they must either suppress enquiry by the most arbitrary stretches of power, or preserve a

---

[1] Book V, Chap. III, p. 217.

clear and tranquil field in which every man shall be at liberty to discover and vindicate his opinion.

No doubt it is the duty of governments to maintain the most unalterable neutrality in this important transaction. No doubt it is the duty of
individuals to publish truth without diffidence or reserve, to publish it
in its genuine form without seeking aid from the meretricious arts of
publication. The more it is told, the more it is known in its true dimensions, and not in parts, the less is it possible that it should coalesce with
or leave room for the pernicious effects of error. The true philanthropist will be eager, instead of suppressing discussion, to take an active
share in the scene, to exert the full strength of his faculties in discovery,
and to contribute by his exertions to render the operations of thought
at once perspicuous and profound.

It being then sufficiently evident that truth must be told at whatever
expence, let us proceed to consider the precise amount of that expence,
to enquire how much of confusion and violence is inseparable from the
transit which mind has to accomplish. And here it plainly appears that
mischief is by no means inseparable from the progress. In the mere
circumstance of our acquiring knowledge and accumulating one truth
after another there is no direct tendency to disorder. Evil can only
spring from the clash of mind with mind, from one body of men in the
community outstripping another in their ideas of improvement, and
becoming impatient of the opposition they have to encounter.

In this interesting period, in which mind shall arrive as it were at the
true crisis of its story, there are high duties incumbent upon every
branch of the community. First, upon those cultivated and powerful
minds, that are fitted to be precursors to the rest in the discovery of
truth. They are bound to be active, indefatigable and disinterested. It is
incumbent upon them to abstain from inflammatory language, from all
expressions of acrimony and resentment. It is absurd in any government
to erect itself into a court of criticism in this respect, and to establish a
criterion of liberality and decorum; but for that very reason it is doubly
incumbent on those who communicate their thoughts to the public, to
exercise a rigid censure over themselves. The tidings of liberty and
equality are tidings of good will to all orders of men. They free the
peasant from the iniquity that depresses his mind, and the privileged
from the luxury and despotism by which he is corrupted. Let those
who bear these tidings not stain their benignity, by showing that that
benignity has not yet become the inmate of their hearts.

Nor is it less necessary that they should be urged to tell the whole
truth without disguise. No maxim can be more pernicious than that

which would teach us to consult the temper of the times, and to tell only so much as we imagine our contemporaries will be able to bear. This practice is at present almost universal, and it is the mark of a very painful degree of depravity. We retail and mangle truth. We impart it to our fellows, not with the liberal measure with which we have received it, but with such parsimony as our own miserable prudence may chance to prescribe. We pretend that truths fit to be practised in one country, nay, truths which we confess to be eternally right, are not fit to be practised in another. That we may deceive others with a tranquil conscience, we begin with deceiving ourselves. We put shackles upon our minds, and dare not trust ourselves at large in the pursuit of truth. This practice took its commencement from the machinations of party, and the desire of one wise and adventurous leader to carry a troop of weak, timid and selfish supporters in his train. There is no reason why I should not declare in any assembly upon the face of the earth that I am a republican. There is no more reason why, being a republican under a monarchical government, I should enter into a desperate faction to invade the public tranquillity, than if I were monarchical under a republic. Every community of men, as well as every individual, must govern itself according to its ideas of justice. What I should desire is, not by violence to change its institutions, but by reason to change its ideas. I have no business with factions or intrigue; but simply to promulgate the truth, and to wait the tranquil progress of conviction. If there be any assembly that cannot bear this, of such an assembly I ought to be no member. It happens much oftener than we are willing to imagine, that 'the post of honour,' or, which is better, the post of utility, 'is a private station.'[1]

The dissimulation here censured, beside its ill effects upon him who practises it, and by degrading and unnerving his character upon society at large, has a particular ill consequence with respect to the point we are considering. It lays a mine, and prepares an explosion. This is the tendency of all unnatural restraint. Meanwhile the unfettered progress of truth is always salutary. Its advances are gradual, and each step prepares the general mind for that which is to follow. They are sudden and unprepared emanations of truth, that have the greatest tendency to deprive men of their sobriety and self command. Reserve in this respect is calculated at once, to give a rugged and angry tone to the multitude whenever they shall happen to discover what is thus concealed, and to mislead the depositaries of political power. It sooths them into false security, and prompts them to maintain an inauspicious obstinacy.

---

[1] Addison's Cato, Act IV.*

Having considered what it is that belongs in such a crisis to the enlightened and wise, let us next turn our attention to a very different class of society, the rich and great. And here in the first place it may be remarked, that it is a very false calculation that leads us universally to despair of having these for the advocates of equality. Mankind are not so miserably selfish, as satirists and courtiers have supposed. We never engage in any action without enquiring what is the decision of justice respecting it. We are at all times anxious to satisfy ourselves that what our inclinations lead us to do, is innocent and right to be done.[1] Since therefore justice occupies so large a share in the contemplations of the human mind, it cannot reasonably be doubted that a strong and commanding view of justice would prove a powerful motive to influence our choice. But that virtue which for whatever reason we have chosen, soon becomes recommended to us by a thousand other reasons. We find in it reputation, eminence, self complacence and the divine pleasures of an approving mind.

The rich and great are far from callous to views of general felicity, when such views are brought before them with that evidence and attraction of which they are susceptible. From one dreadful disadvantage their minds are free. They have not been soured with unrelenting tyranny, or narrowed by the perpetual pressure of distress. They are peculiarly qualified to judge of the emptiness of that pomp and those gratifications, which are always most admired when they are seen from a distance. They will frequently be found considerably indifferent to these things, unless confirmed by habit and rendered inveterate by age. If you show them the attractions of gallantry and magnanimity in resigning them, they will often be resigned without reluctance. Wherever accident of any sort has introduced an active mind, there enterprise is a necessary consequence; and there are few persons so inactive, as to sit down for ever in the supine enjoyment of the indulgences to which they were born. The same spirit that has led forth the young nobility of successive ages to encounter the hardships of a camp, might easily be employed to render them champions of the cause of equality: nor is it to be believed, that the circumstance of superior virtue and truth in this latter exertion, will be without its effect.

But let us suppose a considerable party of the rich and great to be actuated by no view but to their emolument and ease. It is not difficult to show them, that their interest in this sense will admit of no more than a temperate and yielding resistance. Much no doubt of the future

[1] Book II, Chap. III, p. 66.

tranquillity or confusion of mankind depends upon the conduct of this party. To them I would say: 'It is in vain for you to fight against truth. It is like endeavouring with the human hand to stop the inroad of the ocean. Retire betimes. Seek your safety in concession. If you will not go over to the standard of political justice, temporise at least with an enemy whom you cannot overcome. Much, inexpressibly much depends upon you. If you be wise, if you be prudent, if you would secure at least your lives and your personal ease amidst the general shipwreck of monopoly and folly, you will be unwilling to irritate and defy. Unless by your rashness, there will be no confusion, no murder, not a drop of blood will be spilt, and you will yourselves be made happy. If you brave the storm and call down every species of odium on your heads, still it is possible, still it is to be hoped that the general tranquillity may be maintained. But, should it prove otherwise, you will have principally to answer for all the consequences that shall ensue.

'Above all, do not be lulled into a rash and headlong security. We have already seen how much the hypocrisy and instability of the wise and enlightened of the present day, those who confess much, and have a confused view of still more, but dare not examine the whole with a steady and unshrinking eye, are calculated to increase this security. But there is a danger still more palpable. Do not be misled by the unthinking and seeming general cry of those who have no fixed principles. Addresses have been found in every age a very uncertain criterion of the future conduct of a people. Do not count upon the numerous train of your adherents, retainers and servants. They afford a very feeble dependence. They are men, and cannot be dead to the interests and claims of mankind. Some of them will adhere to you as long as a sordid interest seems to draw them in that direction. But the moment yours shall appear to be the losing cause, the same interest will carry them over to the enemy's standard. They will disappear like the morning dew.

'May I not hope that you are capable of receiving impression from another argument? Will you feel no compunction at the thought of resisting the greatest of all benefits? Are you content to be regarded by the most enlightened of your contemporaries, and to be handed down to the remotest posterity, as the obstinate adversaries of philanthropy and justice? Can you reconcile it to your own minds, that, for a sordid interest, for the cause of general corruption and abuse, you should be found active in stifling truth, and strangling the new born happiness of mankind?' Would to God it were possible to carry home this argument to the enlightened and accomplished advocates of aristocracy! Would to

God they could be persuaded to consult neither passion, nor prejudice, nor the flights of imagination, in deciding upon so momentous a question! 'We know that truth does not stand in need of your alliance to secure her triumph. We do not fear your enmity. But our hearts bleed to see such gallantry such talents and such virtue enslaved to prejudice, and enlisted in error. It is for your sakes that we expostulate, and for the honour of human nature.'

To the general mass of the adherents of the cause of justice it may be proper to say a few words. 'If there be any force in the arguments of this work, thus much at least we are authorised to deduce from them, that truth is irresistible. If man be endowed with a rational nature, then whatever is clearly demonstrated to his understanding to have the most powerful recommendations, so long as that clearness is present to his mind, will inevitably engage his choice. It is to no purpose to say that mind is fluctuating and fickle; for it is so only in proportion as evidence is imperfect. Let the evidence be increased, and the persuasion will be made firmer, and the choice more uniform. It is the nature of individual mind to be perpetually adding to the stock of its ideas and knowledge. Similar to this is the nature of general mind, exclusively of casualties which, arising from a more comprehensive order of things, appear to disturb the order of limited systems. This is confirmed to us, if a truth of this universal nature can derive confirmation from partial experiments, by the regular advances of the human mind from century to century, since the invention of printing.

'Let then this axiom of the omnipotence of truth be the rudder of our undertakings. Let us not precipitately endeavour to accomplish that to-day, which the dissemination of truth will make unavoidable to-morrow. Let us not anxiously watch for occasions and events: the ascendancy of truth is independent of events. Let us anxiously refrain from violence: force is not conviction, and is extremely unworthy of the cause of justice. Let us admit into our bosoms neither contempt, animosity, resentment nor revenge. The cause of justice is the cause of humanity. Its advocates should overflow with universal good will. We should love this cause, for it conduces to the general happiness of mankind. We should love it, for there is not a man that lives, who in the natural and tranquil progress of things will not be made happier by its approach. The most powerful cause by which it has been retarded, is the mistake of its adherents, the air of ruggedness, brutishness and inflexibility which they have given to that which in itself is all benignity. Nothing less than this could have prevented the great mass of enquirers from bestowing upon it a patient examination. Be it the care of the now increasing advocates of equality to remove this obstacle to the success of their cause. We have but two plain duties, which, if we set out right, it is not easy to mistake. The first is an unwearied attention to the great instrument of justice, reason. We must divulge our sentiments with the utmost frankness. We must endeavour to impress them upon the minds of others. In this attempt we must give way to no discouragement. We must sharpen our intellectual weapons; add to the stock of our knowledge; be pervaded with a sense of the magnitude of our cause; and perpetually increase that calm presence of mind and self posses- sion which must enable us to do justice to our principles. Our second duty is tranquillity.'

It will not be right to pass over a question that will inevitably suggest itself to the mind of the reader. 'If an equalisation of property be to take place, not by law, regulation or public institution, but only through the private conviction of individuals, in what manner shall it begin?' In answering this question it is not necessary to prove so simple a propos- ition, as that all republicanism, all equalisation of ranks and immunities, strongly tends towards an equalisation of property. Thus, in Sparta this last principle was completely admitted. In Athens the public largesses were so great as almost to exempt the citizens from manual labour; and the rich and eminent only purchased a toleration for their advantages, by the liberal manner in which they opened their stores to the public. In Rome, agrarian laws, a wretched and ill chosen substitute for equality, but which grew out of the same spirit, were perpetually agitated. If men go on to increase in discernment, and this they certainly will with pecu- liar rapidity, when the ill-constructed governments which now retard their progress are removed, the same arguments which showed them the injustice of ranks, will show them the injustice of one man's wanting that, which while it is in the possession of another, conduces in no respect to his well being.

It is a common error to imagine, that this injustice will be felt only by the lower orders who suffer from it; and hence it would appear that it can only be corrected by violence. But in answer to this it may in the first place be observed that all suffer from it, the rich who engross, as well as the poor who want. Secondly, it has been clearly shown in the course of the present work, that men are not so entirely governed by self interest as has frequently been supposed. It has been shown, if possible, still more clearly, that the selfish are not governed solely by sensual gratification or the love of gain, but that the desire of eminence and distinction is in different degrees an universal passion. Thirdly and principally, the progress of truth is the most powerful of all causes.

Nothing can be more absurd than to imagine that theory, in the best sense of the word, is not essentially connected with practice. That which we can be persuaded clearly and distinctly to approve, will inevitably modify our conduct. Mind is not an aggregate of various faculties contending with each other for the mastery, but on the contrary the will is in all cases correspondent to the last judgment of the understanding. When men shall distinctly and habitually perceive the folly of luxury, and when their neighbours are impressed with a similar disdain, it will be impossible that they should pursue the means of it with the same avidity as before.

It will not be difficult perhaps to trace, in the progress of modern Europe from barbarism to refinement, a tendency towards the equalisation of property. In the feudal times, as now in India and other parts of the world, men were born to a certain station, and it was nearly impossible for a peasant to rise to the rank of a noble. Except the nobles there were no men that were rich; for commerce, either external or internal, had scarcely an existence. Commerce was one engine for throwing down this seemingly impregnable barrier, and shocking the prejudices of nobles, who were sufficiently willing to believe that their retainers were a different species of beings from themselves. Learning was another, and more powerful engine. In all ages of the church we see men of the basest origin rising to the highest eminence. Commerce proved that others could rise to wealth beside those who were cased in mail; but learning proved that the low-born were capable of surpassing their lords. The progressive effect of these ideas may easily be traced by the attentive observer. Long after learning began to unfold its powers, its votaries still submitted to those obsequious manners and servile dedications, which no man reviews at the present day without astonishment. It is but lately that men have known that intellectual excellence can accomplish its purposes without a patron. At present, among the civilised and well informed a man of slender wealth, but of great intellectual powers and a firm and virtuous mind, is constantly received with attention and deference; and his purse-proud neighbour who should attempt to treat him superciliously, is sure to be discountenanced in his usurpation. The inhabitants of distant villages, where long established prejudices are slowly destroyed, would be astonished to see how comparatively small a share wealth has in determining the degree of attention with which men are treated in enlightened circles.

These no doubt are but slight indications. It is with morality in this respect as it is with politics. The progress is at first so slow as for the most part to elude the observation of mankind; nor can it indeed be adequately perceived but by the contemplation and comparison of events during a considerable portion of time. After a certain interval, the scene is more fully unfolded, and the advances appear more rapid and decisive. While wealth was every thing, it was to be expected that men would acquire it, though at the expence of character and integrity. Absolute and universal truth had not yet shown itself so decidedly, as to be able to enter the lists with what dazzled the eye or gratified the sense. In proportion as the monopolies of ranks and companies are abolished, the value of superfluities will not fail to decline. In proportion as republicanism gains ground, men will come to be estimated for what they are, not for what force has given, and force may take away.

Let us reflect for a moment on the gradual consequences of this revolution of opinion. Liberality of dealing will be among its earliest results, and of consequence accumulation will become less frequent and less enormous. Men will not be disposed, as now, to take advantage of each other's distresses, and to demand a price for their aid, not measured by a general standard, but by the wants of an individual. They will not consider how much they can extort, but how much it is reasonable to require. The master tradesman who employs labourers under him, will be disposed to give a more ample reward to their industry; which he is at present enabled to tax chiefly by the neutral circumstance of having provided a capital. Liberality on the part of his employer will complete in the mind of the artisan, what ideas of political justice will probably have begun. He will no longer spend the little surplus of his earnings in that dissipation, which is at present one of the principal causes that subject him to the arbitrary pleasure of a superior. He will escape from the irresolution of slavery and the fetters of despair, and perceive that independence and ease are scarcely less within his reach than that of any other member of the community. This is a natural step towards the still farther progression, in which the labourer will receive entire whatever the consumer may be required to pay, without having a middle man, an idle and useless monopoliser, as he will then be found, to fatten upon his spoils.

The same sentiments that lead to liberality of dealing, will also lead to liberality of distribution. The trader, who is unwilling to grow rich by extorting from his employer or his workmen, will also refuse to become rich by the not inferior injustice of withholding from his poor neighbour the supply he wants. The habit which was created in the former case of being contented with moderate gains, is closely connected with the habit of being contented with slender accumulation. He that is not anxious to add to his heap, will not be reluctant by a benevolent distribution to prevent its increase. Wealth was once almost the single object of pursuit that presented itself to the gross and uncultivated mind. Various objects will hereafter divide men's attention, the love of liberty, the love of equality, the pursuits of art and the desire of knowledge. These objects will not, as now, be confined to a few, but will gradually be laid open to all. The love of liberty obviously leads to the love of man: the sentiment of benevolence will be increased, and the narrowness of the selfish affections will decline. The general diffusion of truth will be productive of general improvement; and men will daily approximate towards those views according to which every object will be appreciated at its true value. Add to which, that the improvement of which we speak is general, not individual. The progress is the progress of all. Each man will find his sentiments of justice and rectitude echoed, encouraged and strengthened by the sentiments of his neighbours. Apostacy will be made eminently improbable, because the apostate will incur, not only his own censure, but the censure of every beholder.

One remark will suggest itself upon these considerations. 'If the inevitable progress of improvement insensibly lead towards an equalisation of property, what need was there of proposing it as a specific object to men's consideration?' The answer to this objection is easy. The improvement in question consists in a knowledge of truth. But our knowledge will be very imperfect so long as this great branch of universal justice fails to constitute a part of it. All truth is useful; can this truth, which is perhaps more fundamental than any, be without its benefits? Whatever be the object towards which mind spontaneously advances, it is of no mean importance to us to have a distinct view of that object. Our advances will thus become accelerated. It is a well known principle of morality, that he who proposes perfection to himself, though he will inevitably fall short of what he pursues, will make a more rapid progress, than he who is contented to aim only at what is imperfect. The benefits to be derived in the interval from a view of equalisation, as one of the great objects towards which we are tending, are exceedingly conspicuous. Such a view will strongly conduce to make us disinterested now. It will teach us to look with contempt upon mercantile speculations, commercial prosperity, and the cares of gain. It will impress us with a just apprehension of what it is of which man is capable and in which his perfection consists; and will fix our ambition and activity upon the worthiest objects. Mind cannot arrive at any great and illustrious attainment, however much the nature of mind may carry us towards it, without feeling some presages of its approach; and it is reasonable to believe that, the earlier these presages are introduced, and the more distinct they are made, the more auspicious will be the event.

FINIS

EXPLANATORY NOTES

4 *Swift and . . . the Latin historians*: Jonathan Swift (1667–1745), author of *Gulliver's Travels* (1726) and a range of satirical works, first from a Whig perspective but subsequently as a Tory. Godwin read widely, but his principal Latin sources are Livy's history of Rome, *Ab urbe condita*, Suetonius' *Twelve Caesars*, and Tacitus' *Annals of Imperial Rome*. He also drew extensively on the Greek historian Plutarch and his *Lives*.

Système de la Nature, Rousseau and Helvetius: three of the principal Encyclopédists of the French Enlightenment, baron d'Holbach (1723–89), Jean-Jacques Rousseau (1712–78), and Claude-Adrien Helvétius (1715–71). In addition to Holbach's *Système* (1770), Godwin read widely in Rousseau's works, especially the *Discourses* (1755), and his *Social Contract* and *Émile* (1762), and in Helvétius' *De l'homme, de ses facultés intellectuelles et de son éducation* (1773).

the composition was begun . . . unremitted ardour: Godwin recorded the key events in his diary, and from the commencement of *Political Justice* kept a meticulous record of his reading, writing, and meetings. See *The Diary of William Godwin*, ed. Victoria Myers, David O'Shaughnessy, and Mark Philp (Oxford, 2010), <http://godwindiary.bodleian.ox.ac.uk>.

5 *the Shibboleth of the constitution*: Godwin refers to the rise of loyalist associations designed to support the government and combat what was perceived as a rising tide of popular demands for reform of the political system following the influence of the opening events of the French Revolution and the spread of 'French principles'. In May 1792 a royal proclamation against seditious writing was issued, Thomas Paine (1737–1809) was prosecuted for his *Rights of Man* (1791, 1792), and a number of cases were brought against ordinary people for expressions of anti-monarchical sentiments.

12 *from Sydney . . . Helvetius*: Algernon Sidney (1623–83), author of *Discourses Concerning Government* (published posthumously in 1698); John Locke (1632–1704), author of *Two Treatises of Government* (1698); Thomas Paine's *Rights of Man* (1791, 1792). On Rousseau and Helvétius, see second note to p. 4.

13 *Bacchus . . . Cyrus*: Bacchus, the Latin name for Dionysus, son of Zeus, who reputedly conquered far into Asia; Sesostris is a mythical Egyptian king, reported by Herodotus; Semiramis, according to legend, ruled Assyria and built Babylon; Cyrus (559–522 BCE) founded the Persian empire.

The expeditions of Cambyses . . . and of Xerxes against the Greeks: Cambyses, king of Persia (530–522 BCE), son of Cyrus, conquered Egypt in 525 BCE. He was succeeded by Darius I (521–486), who attempted to conquer

Greece and was defeated at Marathon. His son Xerxes invaded again in
480 and was defeated at the battle of Salamis.

13 *The conquests of Alexander . . . one million two hundred thousand men*:
Alexander the Great (356–323 BCE), king of Macedon, was arguably the
greatest military leader in antiquity. Gaius Julius Caesar (100–44 BCE)
conquered Gaul and made inroads into Germany and Britain, as well as
winning the civil war generated by his refusal to surrender his military
commands in 48 BCE.

Their wars in Italy . . . the Carthaginians two hundred: the wars between
the Romans and the Etruscans lasted from the early fifth century BCE
until the defeat of Pyrrhus in 275. The conflict with Carthage is referred
to as the three Punic Wars, 264–241, 218–201, and 149–146 BCE.

The Mithridatic war: the Mithridatic Wars against Asia took place in
89–85, 83–81, and 74–63 BCE.

Sylla . . . and Marius: Lucius Sulla (138–78 BCE) used the troops from
his command against Mithridates, king of Pontus, in 86 to start a civil war
in Italy, in which he eventually triumphed in 82. Gaius Marius (157–86
BCE) vied with Sulla for command in the first Mithridatic War. Sulla
had the support of the senate and the elite; Marius' support came from
the *plebs*. Sulla seized Rome, forcing Marius to flee. In 87 BCE, when
Sulla was in the East fighting Mithridites, Marius led an army against
Rome and then had himself declared consul. He inaugurated a savage
revenge on his enemies before dying suddenly. When Sulla recaptured
Rome in 83 BCE, he followed Marius' example in exacting revenge on
those who had supported his rival.

14 *Mahomet . . . Charlemagne*: Muhammad (*c.*570–632), the Prophet.
Charlemagne (747–814), king of the Franks and Holy Roman emperor.

the exploits of Aurungzebe . . . Spaniards in the new world: Aurangzeb
(1618–1707), Mughal emperor of India; Genghis Khan (1162–1227),
Mongol conqueror; Tamerlane (1336–1405), Turkic conqueror of Persia
and northern India. The reference to Spanish conquerors is to Hernán
Cortez (1485–1547), who destroyed the Aztecs in Mexico (1519), and
Francisco Pizarro (*c.*1475–1541), who destroyed the Incas in Peru (1532).

France was wasted . . . Louis the fourteenth: the Hundred Years War between
England and France began in 1337 over the exclusion by Salic law of
daughters from succession to the French throne and from English
Plantagenet claims to the French throne. The French wars of religion
(1562–98) included the unsuccessful siege of La Rochelle from December
1572 to June 1573 by the future Henri III. His mother, Catherine de'
Medici, had instigated the massacres of French Protestants on 24 August
1572, known as the St Bartholomew's Day massacre. Religious tolerance
was established by Henri IV under the Edict of Nantes in 1598. The
Thirty Years War (1618–48) involved most of Europe in a struggle that
evolved from religion to dynastic control. Louis XIV (1638–1715) was at
war for all but fourteen of his seventy-two-year reign.

Cressy and Agincourt . . . Charles the first and his parliament: Crécy (1346) and Agincourt (1415) were two major English victories in the Hundred Years War. The Wars of the Roses over rival claims by the houses of York and Lancaster lasted from 1455 to 1485. Charles I's reign ended with a war against parliamentary forces, which deposed and executed him in 1648.

No sooner was the constitution settled . . . the king of Prussia: the restoration of the monarchy in the person of Charles II in 1660, and the subsequent succession of the Catholic James II to the throne in 1685, resulted in the revolution of 1688, which deposed James and accepted William and Mary to the throne. This brought Britain into the Nine Years War (1688–97) and the War of Spanish Succession (1701–14). Conflict over the Habsburg monarchy produced the War of Austrian Succession (1741–8), and the Anglo-French (Hanover–Bourbon) conflict also produced the global Seven Years War (1756–63). Godwin also refers to John Churchill, first duke of Marlborough (1650–1722), politician and military leader, who played a major role in the War of Spanish Succession; Maria Theresa (1717–80), queen consort of the Holy Roman emperor and last ruler of the Habsburg empire, whose accession led Prussia to invade Silesia, prompting the War of Austrian Succession, and who sought to regain it in the Seven Years War; and Frederick the Great (1712–86), king of Prussia, who invaded Silesia on Maria Theresa's accession to the throne.

choosing whether Henry the sixth or Edward the fourth . . . haughty Maria Theresa: an issue in the Wars of the Roses, a dynastic civil war between Lancastrians and Plantagenets between 1455 and 1485. The reference to Maria Theresa (see the preceding explanatory note) is to the War of Austrian Succession (1741–8) and the Seven Years War (1756–63).

the free-booter: a reference to Frederick of Prussia (1712–86).

15 *Gulliver's Travels, Part IV. Ch. v*: Jonathan Swift, *Gulliver's Travels* (1726), Part IV, 'A Voyage to the Country of the Houyhnhnms', ch. v, in which Gulliver tries to explain the resort to war by European states.

Locke on Government . . . Burke's Vindication of Natural Society: John Locke, *Two Treatises of Government* (1694), I. i. 1, p. 1; II. vii. 91, pp. 233–4; Edmund Burke, *A Vindication of Natural Society* (1756).

20 *Locke . . . J. J. Rousseau*: John Locke, *An Essay Concerning Humane Understanding* (1690); David Hartley, *Observations on Man, his Frame, his Duty, and his Expectations* (1749); Jean-Jacques Rousseau, *Émile; ou, De l'éducation* (1762).

21 *as Newton has done respecting matter*: Isaac Newton (1642–1727), philosopher and scientist.

Mainwarings, the Sibthorpes, and the Filmers: Godwin's three references are to defenders of the divine right of kings: Roger Maynwaring [Manwaring] (1589/90?–1653); Robert Sibthorpe (d. 1662); and Robert Filmer (1588?–1653), now the best known (thanks to Locke's attack on him in the first of his *Two Treatises of Government*), who defended absolute monarchy in his *Patriarcha; or, The Natural Power of Kings* (1680).

24 *Lord Kaimes*: Henry Home, Lord Kames, *Loose Hints upon Education, chiefly concerning the Culture of the Heart* (Edinburgh, 1781).

Archdeacon Paley: William Paley, *The Principles of Moral and Political Philosophy* (1785); Godwin refers to the seventh edition (1790).

25 *excommunication and interdict*: excommunication is an ecclesiastical punishment wholly excluding a person from the Church; an interdict restricted their participation to certain sacraments only. The medieval Church used both to pressure monarchs to accept their authority. Most dramatically, the emperor Henry IV had to stand for three days barefoot in the palace courtyard at Canossa dressed as a penitent before being accepted back into the Church by Pope Gregory VII.

the Bramin widows of Indostan: referring to the Hindu practice, for those from the high caste of the Brahmin, of suttee, in which the widow was burnt upon the funeral pyre of her husband. 'Indostan' was a common eighteenth-century term for the Indian subcontinent.

26 *The doctrine of transubstantiation*: the Catholic belief that in Holy Communion the bread and wine are in substance transformed into the body and blood of Christ.

27 *Logan . . . p. 69*: John Logan, *Elements of the Philosophy of History* (Edinburgh, 1781). Godwin misquotes Logan's account of Sparta under Lycurgus: 'The people were arrested in the first stage of improvement. A bold hand was put forth to that spring which is in society, and stopt its motion' (pp. 69–70).

31 *the character of the game laws*: game laws restricted rights to take certain fish and animals, generating the activity of poaching and the draconian punishments exacted for the offence. These laws, and the Black Act of 1723, feature in Godwin's novel *Things As They Are; or, The Adventures of Caleb Williams* (1794).

the late revenue laws of France: under France's Ancien Régime, prior to the legislation of 4 August 1789, feudal privileges exempted the nobility from most tax.

32 *the proud satrap*: a satrap was a provincial governor in ancient Persia, a byword for despotism in the eighteenth century, thanks in part to Montesquieu's *De l'esprit des lois* (1748) and *Lettres persanes* (1721).

35 *induced Hartley*: David Hartley, *Observations on Man, his Frame, his Duty, and his Expectations* (1749), i. 308, suggests that picture writing was 'perhaps communicated originally to Adam by God'.

38 *Was the language of Anaxarchus . . . himself*: Anaxarchus of Abdera (fourth century BCE). Diogenes Laertius, *Lives and Opinions of Eminent Philosophers in Ten Books* 9. 59, reports that Nicocreon, tyrant of Salamis, had Anaxarchus pounded to death in a mortar, which he suffered with composure.

39 *Mutius Scævola and archbishop Cranmer ... flames*: Gaius Mucius Scaevola was a legendary Roman hero who, having tried to kill Lars Porsena, king of Clusium, in 508 BCE, thrust his left hand into a fire to demonstrate his indifference to pain. Archbishop Thomas Cranmer (1481–1556) was burnt at the stake for treason but thrust the hand with which he had signed his recantation into the flames first as if to purge it.

43 *'impossible to establish ... climates'*: the thought, although more equivocally expressed, is from Montesquieu's *De l'esprit des lois* (1748), book 14.

Indostan: 'Indostan' was a common eighteenth-century term for the Indian subcontinent.

45 *Diodorus Siculus describes ... and Aristotle*: Diodorus Siculus, author of *Bibliothēkē historikē* (Library of History), in forty books, written between 60 and 30 BCE; see 5. 27–32. Aristotle (384–322 BCE), Greek philosopher; see his *Politics* 2. 1269^{b}25–7, where the reference is to the Celts and homosexuality.

46 *Hume's Essay on National Characters*: David Hume, *Essays, Moral, Political and Literary* (1772).

51 *'he, that will not give just occasion ... political power'*: Godwin truncates the quotation and eliminates punctuation and Locke's use of capitals, but is faithful to Locke's claim.

52 *'Society and government ... a necessary evil'*: the claim opens the second paragraph of Thomas Paine's *Common Sense* (1776), his clarion call for American independence from Britain.

53 *the illustrious archbishop of Cambray*: François de Salignac de La Mothe Fénelon, archbishop of Cambray (1651–1715), author of *Les Aventures de Télémaque, fils d'Ulysse* (1699). The book describes the education of Telemachus by his tutor Mentor (who is Athena in disguise). It was immensely influential in French political thought throughout the eighteenth century. Godwin's 'case' of choosing between Fénelon and his mother has entered philosophical discourse as 'the famous fire cause'. See, for example, Brian Barry, *Justice as Impartiality* (Oxford, 1995), sect. 37.

54 *the Rev. Jonathan Edwards*: Jonathan Edwards, *Essay on the Nature of True Virtue* (1778). Edwards was an American preacher and a major contributor to the mid-century evangelical revival in America.

57 *Swift's Sermon on Mutual Subjection*: Jonathan Swift, *Three Sermons: I. On Mutual Subjection. II. On Conscience. III. On the Trinity* (1744).

59 *Lycurgus ... to render his death a source of additional benefit*: Lycurgus (c.390–c.325 BCE), Spartan statesman, who determined on starving himself to death having served the state to his fullest possible extent. Godwin draws on Plutarch's *Lives*, 'Lycurgus' 29.

Codrus, Leonidas and Decius: Codrus, the legendary king of Athens who stole into the enemy Dorian camp in disguise in order to provoke a quarrel that would lead to his death because he had learned that an oracle had declared that the Dorians would defeat the Athenians if they spared their king. King Leonidas led the Spartan three hundred at Thermopylae in 480 BCE, which sought to delay the advance of a massive Persian force. Decius was a Roman consul who fought to the death in battle with the Latins in 340 BCE.

59 *the much admired suicide of Cato*: Marcus Porcius Cato (Cato the Younger, 95–46 BCE) was a Roman senator and epitome of republican virtue, who committed suicide during the civil war to avoid surrendering to the victorious Julius Caesar. His death is the centrepiece of Joseph Addison's play *Cato: A Tragedy* (1713), which Godwin cites on several occasions.

'*that the blood of the martyrs is the seed of the church*': Tertullian (*c.*160–225), *Apologia* 17. 1.

Junius Brutus did right in putting his sons to death: Lucius Junius Brutus, according to tradition Roman consul in 509 BCE, whose sons sought the restoration of the Tarquins, whom the republic had expelled following the rape of Lucretia. Brutus saw through the responsibilities of his office by overseeing the execution of his sons. The French revolutionary artist Jacques-Louis David captures the republican spirit of the scene in his painting *The Lictors Bring to Brutus the Bodies of his Sons* (1789), of which Godwin may well have been made aware by his friend the artist James Barry (1741–1806).

62 *Clement, Ravaillac, Damiens and Gerard*: Jacques Clement (1567–89) assassinated Henri III of France in 1589; François Ravaillac (1578–1610) assassinated Henri IV of France in 1610; Robert-François Damiens (*c.*1715–1757) attempted the assassination of Louis XV of France in 1757; Gerard may refer either to Balthazar Gérard (1558–84), who assassinated William of Nassau, prince of Orange, or to John Gerard (1632–54), who was executed for plotting the death of Oliver Cromwell.

the fires of Smithfield . . . the daggers of Saint Bartholomew: Smithfield refers to the execution by burning of Protestant clergy at Smithfield under Mary I (1553–8). Godwin treats these as effectively the English analogue to the St Bartholomew's Day massacre of French Protestants in Paris, instigated by Catherine de' Medici on 24 August 1572.

The inventors of the Gunpowder Treason: the Gunpowder Plot was a plan by Catholic conspirators to blow up the House of Lords while King James I was addressing it on 5 November 1605 so as to facilitate the restoration of a Catholic monarchy. Those primarily responsible were Guy Fawkes (1570–1606), Robert Catesby (*c.*1573–1605), Sir Everard Digby (*c.*1578–1606), Thomas Percy (1560–1605), Ambrose Rookwood (*c.*1578–1606), Francis Tresham (1567?–1605), Robert Winter (d. 1606), and John (1568?–1605) and Christopher Wright (1570?–1605).

63 *Calvin . . . Servetus*: Jean Calvin (1509–64), French theologian and Protestant reformer in Geneva, had Michael Servetus (1511–53), a Spanish physician and theologian, burnt at the stake in Geneva for denying the Trinity and the divinity of Jesus Christ.

65 *All government is founded in opinion*: David Hume, 'Of the First Principles of Government', in *Essays, Moral and Political* (1772): 'It is therefore, on opinion only that government is founded.'

'*On a dit . . . sanction.*' *Raynal, Revolution d'Amerique*: the abbé Guillaume-Thomas-François Raynal, *Révolution de l'Amérique, par M. l'abbé Raynal, auteur de l'histoire philosophique et politique des établissemens, et du commerce des européens dans les deux Indes* (London, 1781), 34.

70 *Rights of Man, page 1*: Thomas Paine, *Rights of Man: Being an Answer to Mr Burke's Attack on the French Revolution* (London: J. S. Jordan, 1791), 5.

71 *religious rights of Confucius, of Mahomet*: Confucius, Master Kongfuze (551–479 BCE), Chinese philosopher; Muhammad (*c.*570–632), the Prophet.

74 *Euclid*: (*c.*300 BCE), Greek mathematician and founder of geometry through his *Stoicheia* (Elements).

76 *scandalum magnatum*: the slander of great men. This was a particular form of defamation involving words spoken defaming a peer spiritual or temporal, a judge, or other dignitary of the realm defined under the statutes 3 Edward I, c. 34; 2 Richard II, c. 5; and 12 Richard II, c. 11. The offence was not formally abolished until 1887.

78 *positive law with its Procrustes's bed*: Procrustes was a legendary brigand who required any traveller on the road from Athens to Eleusis who accepted his hospitality to sleep on his bed. Those too short were stretched, those too tall were trimmed. Theseus is credited with laying Procrustes on his own bed and shortening him by cutting off his head.

84 *the usurpation of Cromwel . . . Caligula*: Oliver Cromwell (1599–1658), who played a central role in the defeat of Charles I and the suppression of Ireland in the English civil war, becoming president of the Council of State in 1649 and lord protector from 1655. Caligula (Gaius Julius Caesar Augustus Germanicus, 12–41) was notorious for his erratic despotism; he was eventually assassinated.

Hume's Essays. Part II. Essay xii: David Hume, *Essays, Moral and Political* (1772), 'Of the Original Contract'.

86 *Du Contract Social*: Jean-Jacques Rousseau, *Du Contract social; ou, Principes du droit politique* (1762). The original reads: 'Les deputés du peuple ne sont donc ni ne peuvant, être ses réprésentans . . .'.

90 *Westminster . . . the Royal Exchange*: Westminster is on the west side of the city of London. Blackwall is on the east side of the city of London and was a common place for ships to dock. The Royal Exchange is at the heart of the City.

93 *In the case of ship money under king Charles the first*: ship money was levied on coastal towns for the upkeep of the Navy. In 1635 Charles I sought to impose it upon inland towns, which led to great opposition. The tax was ended by Parliament in 1641.

95 *Esprit des Loix*: Charles-Louis de Secondat, baron de Montesquieu, *De l'esprit des lois* (1748).

an Asiatic cadi: a cadi was a local judge under the Ottoman empire.

Sterne's Sermons: Laurence Sterne, *The Sermons of Mr Yorick* (1759), iv, Sermon XII, 'The Abuses of Conscience Considered'.

96 *A quaker refuses to pay tithes*: tithes were a payment to support the Established (Anglican) Church. Many associated with religious dissent resented their payment, which was enforced by 'tithe proctors'.

100 *Vie de M. Turgot*: Marie-Jean-Antoine-Nicolas Caritat, marquis de Condorcet, *Vie de Monsieur Turgot* (1786), 217.

101 *'Nay my good lord . . . and umpire of itself'*: John Home, *Douglas: A Tragedy* (1757), IV. i. 54. Godwin adapts the quotation, or draws on another unidentified source.

the grand monarque: Louis XIV, king of France (1643–1715).

102 *Quixote plan*: a visionary and impractical plan, based on Cervantes' novel *Don Quixote* (1605–15).

103 *Solon, the Athenian lawgiver*: Plutarch, *Lives*, 'Solon' 15. 2. In the eighteenth century Solon was consistently cited, alongside Lycurgus, as one of the great legislators of the ancient world.

104 *Hume's Essays. Part II. Essay xii*: see second note to p. 84.

109 *the single instance of lord Strafford*: Thomas Wentworth, first earl of Strafford (1593–1641), was executed on Parliament's insistence and with Charles I's extremely reluctant acquiescence.

112 *listed field*: a field prepared for a tilting or jousting tournament.

113 *Sydney and Locke and Montesquieu and Rousseau*: Godwin has referred to these writers before (see first notes to pp. 12 and 95). Both John Locke (1632–1704) and Algernon Sidney (1623–83) were more practically engaged in resistance to James II's succession in 1685. Locke spent time abroad and Sidney was executed for treason.

116 *like the first Brutus*: Lucius Junius Brutus, traditionally recognized as the founder of the Roman republic, and celebrated as such by Livy, *Ab urbe condita* 2. 10. Godwin has already mentioned his supervision, as consul, of the execution of his two sons for conspiring to return the Tarquin monarchy to power.

124 *De l'Homme, Préface*: Claude-Adrien Helvétius, *De l'homme, de ses facultés intellectuelles et de son éducation* (1773), pp. vi–vii.

126 *the conspirators, kneeling at the feet of Cæsar*: Godwin doubtless read Plutarch and Suetonius' lives of Julius Caesar, but he was also well acquainted with Shakespeare's play, III. i. 32–76; in 1812 he attended the play on three occasions in as many months. The principal assassin was Marcus Junius Brutus (*c.*85–42 BCE).

127 *See the Parmenides*: Plato's *Parmenides* is a complex dialogue in which Plato's voice is, unusually, expressed through Parmenides rather than

through Socrates. The dialogue involves a critical examination and refor-
mulation of the doctrine of the Forms, articulated by Socrates in Plato's
Republic.

128 *Apologia, Cap. xlvi*: Quintus Septimius Florens Tertullianus (194–216),
Apology 46. 8–9.

wise enough like Epicurus: Epicurus (341–271 BCE), Greek philosopher
and founder of the Epicurean school, which was committed to achieving
happiness through the proper understanding of nature and the pursuit of
pleasure. Mental pleasures were deemed to be far greater than physical.

129 *Vie de Voltaire*: Théophile Imarigeon Duvernet, *La Vie de Voltaire*
(1786), 46.

130 *A Calvin will burn . . . a Digby generate the gunpowder treason*: on Calvin,
see note to p. 63; on the Gunpowder Plot, see third note to p. 62.

131 *Tully*: a common shorthand for Marcus Tullius Cicero (106–43 BCE),
Roman orator and statesman.

134 *the Pretender in the year 1745*: the Pretender was Bonnie Prince Charlie,
Charles Edward Stuart (1720–88), the son of James II of England (James
VII of Scotland), who sought to return to the throne in a rebellion in 1745
led from Scotland, known as the 'Forty-Five. Following its failure, Charles
returned to exile in France. The source of Godwin's story is unclear.

137 *Vie de Voltaire, Par M***, throughout*: Marie-Jean-Antoine-Nicolas
Caritat, marquis de Condorcet, *Vie de Voltaire* (1791).

140 *Did Themistocles . . . the battle of Marathon*: Themistocles (*c.* 524–459 BCE),
the Athenian statesman who oversaw the resistance to Persian invasion
and commanded the Athenian fleet at the successful battle of Salamis.
Plutarch's life of Themistocles reports that, when asked about his change
of behaviour during the war that culminated in the battle of Marathon,
with the Greeks led by Miltiades, he replied that he could not sleep
at night for thinking of Miltiades' triumph. The place of 'love of fame' as
a motive in virtuous conduct was returned to serially by Godwin, both in
his philosophical writing and in his analysis of himself.

143 *Milton's devil to be a being of considerable virtue*: John Milton's *Paradise Lost*
(1667) famously sustains the reader's appreciation of Satan's cause.

Epictetus or a Cato: Epictetus (*c.* 50–120), a Stoic philosopher, born a slave,
who was later freed. He emphasized the independence of mind and the
power of the human will to conquer circumstance. Cato the Younger
(95–46 BCE) was similarly a model Stoic.

Cæsar and Alexander: Julius Caesar (100–44 BCE) and Alexander III of
Macedon, known as Alexander the Great (356–323 BCE).

144 *doctor Johnson*: Samuel Johnson (1709–84), literary critic and wit. His cutting comment on Gilbert West (1703–56) and his translation of Pindar
(published in 1749) is criticized by Godwin as an instance of someone
attacking others to inflate their own sense of eminence.

144 *Swift has thrown upon Dryden . . . Rousseau and Voltaire*: Jonathan Swift
     (1667–1745) was the cousin of John Dryden (1631–1700), but he ridicules
     him in his *Battle of the Books* (1704). Both were poets and satirists.
     François-Marie Arouet de Voltaire (1694–1778) had been a friend and
     supporter of Rousseau until the latter's attacks on the theatre, which pre-
     vented Voltaire from establishing a theatre in Geneva.

147 *a Cynic*: the passage is not entirely clear but Godwin does not mean by
     a Cynic someone who pours scorn on pretensions of selflessness. Rather,
     he identifies the Cynic (and its associated school of morality that derives
     from Diogenes, 412/404–323 BCE) with the critique of social conven-
     tion and a reliance on the teachings of nature that has much in common
     with the Stoics and is not that distant from aspects of Godwin's own
     position.

148 *the kingdom of Portugal*: Portugal's monarchy had been remodelled, after
     the Lisbon earthquake of 1755, under the guidance of the marquess of
     Pombal (1699–1782), who combined autocratic methods with Enlighten-
     ment concerns to reduce the power of the aristocracy and Church and
     to stimulate commercial life. Pombal fell from grace after the death of
     Joseph I in 1777, leading to a strengthening of aristocracy and Church and
     a resistance to pressures to establish a parliament.

161 *in Hume's Enquiry concerning Human Understanding*: David Hume, *An
     Enquiry Concerning Human Understanding* (1772), later published in 1777
     with his *Dissertation on the Passions*, *An Enquiry Concerning the Principles of
     Morals*, and *The Natural History of Religion*.

162 *Xerxes . . . waves of the Hellespont*: Herodotus reports in his *Histories* 7. 35
     that Xerxes, commanding the Persian forces invading Greece, ordered his
     men to give the Hellespont three hundred lashes and to sink a pair of
     shackles into the sea—even to brand it—for a storm in which the Persian
     bridges were destroyed.

164 *Jonathan Edwards's Enquiry into the Freedom of the Will*: Jonathan Edwards,
     *A Careful and Strict Enquiry into the Modern Prevailing Notions of that
     Freedom of the Will, which is supposed to be Essential to Moral Agency*
     (Boston, 1754), II. x. 99. See also note to p. 54.

166 *sensorium*: the sensorium refers to the seat of sensation in the brain,
     although it is also sometimes used to mean the brain itself.

173 *the celebrated Hartley*: David Hartley, *Observations on Man, his Frame, his
     Duty, and his Expectations* (1749).

178 *Speech upon Oeconomical Reform*: Edmund Burke, *Speech of Edmund
     Burke, Esq., Member of Parliament for the City of Bristol, on presenting to the
     House of Commons (on the 11 of February, 1780) a plan for the better security
     of the independence of Parliament, and the oeconomical reformation of the civil
     and other establishments* (1780). Lasting three and a half hours and judged
     by many to be one of Burke's best speeches, it drew a packed House of
     Commons.

179 *See Watson on Time*: William Watson, *A Treatise on Time* (1785).

Explanatory Notes

193 *Emile, Liv. II*: Jean-Jacques Rousseau, *Émile; ou, De l'éducation* (1762), book II, vol. i, p. 121. Godwin adapts the passage.

194 *Like Pedaretus in ancient story*: Plutarch, *Lives*, 'Lycurgus' 25.

196 *Regulus's interest . . . a tormenting death*: Marcus Atilius Regulus, Roman consul, was captured by Carthaginians in the First Punic War. He was sent back to Rome to negotiate a peace, having promised to return if he failed. He advised the Romans to continue the war but returned to Carthage to die from torture in captivity. Horace, *Odes* 3. 5.

Cato in the play: Joseph Addison, *Cato: A Tragedy* (1713), II. i. 99–100.

206 *peculium*: private property, commonly used to refer to property passed from father to son.

207 *Henry the fourth . . . to a throne*: Henri IV (1553–1610), as Henri III of Navarre, was spared in the St Bartholomew's Day massacre of 1572 on condition that he become a Catholic. For three years he was held a virtual prisoner in the French court before escaping, after which he renounced his false confession. However, he renounced Protestantism and accepted the Catholic faith in 1593. He was crowned king of France in 1594. Elizabeth I (1533–1603), daughter of Henry VIII and Anne Boleyn, was declared illegitimate in 1536; she was reinstated as a potential heir to the throne in 1544. She was imprisoned under the rule of her half-sister Mary I, but succeeded her in 1558.

Alfred: Alfred the Great (849–99) was the Anglo-Saxon king of Wessex, but was forced by the Danish invasion of 878 to hide in the marshes of Athelney.

Frederic and Alexander: Frederick I Barbarossa (c.1123–1190), Holy Roman emperor; Alexander the Great (356–323 BCE), king of Macedon.

208 *Diogenes*: Diogenes of Sinope (412/404–323 BCE), Greek philosopher and Cynic, who embraced poverty and was acutely critical of prevailing social institutions and norms. The main source for his life and beliefs is Diogenes Laertius, *Lives and Opinions of Eminent Philosophers* 6. 20–81.

209 *vitriolised inhabitants of the planet Mercury . . . sun*: references to mythical beings that could survive the intense heat of Mercury or of fire.

210 *Pyrrho*: Pyrrhon (c.365/360–c.275/270 BCE), Greek philosopher and founder of Scepticism. Diogenes Laertius describes him as holding that 'there is nothing really existent, but custom and convention govern human action . . . He led a life consistent with this doctrine, going out of his way for nothing, taking no precaution, but facing all risks as they came, whether carts, precipices, dogs or what not, and, generally, leaving nothing to the arbitrament of the senses': *Lives and Opinions of Eminent Philosophers* 9. 61–2.

212 *madame de Genlis . . . duke d'Orleans*: Stéphanie Félicité, comtesse de Brulart [formerly comtesse de Genlis], *Lessons of a Governess to her Pupils; or, Journal of the Method Adopted by Madame de Sillery-Brulart in the Education of the Children of m. d'Orleans* (1792), ii. 6–7, 3–4 respectively.

Sancho Panza is the earthy, literate companion of *Don Quixote* in Cervantes's novel.

214 *jure divino*: divine right. Daniel Defoe satirized the tradition of the divine right of kings in his *Jure divino: A Satyr* (1706), a twelve-book poem in heroic couplets.

218 *Tragedy of Jane Shore, Act III*: Nicholas Rowe, *The Tragedy of Jane Shore* (1714), III. i. 139–40.

219 *Shakespeare: Henry the Eighth, Act III*: III. ii. 384.

221 *Dudley earl of Leicester*: Robert Dudley, earl of Leicester (*c.*1532–1588). David Hume describes Dudley as being able to conceal from Elizabeth his 'odious vices': *The History of England, from the Invasion of Julius Caesar to the Revolution in 1688* (1767), v. 84.

222 *Cecil earl of Salisbury*: Robert Cecil, first earl of Salisbury (*c.*1563–1612).

Howard earl of Nottingham: Charles Howard, second Baron Howard of Effingham and first earl of Nottingham (1536–1624). David Hume describes how Nottingham and Cecil encouraged Essex in grandiose claims so as to lead to his downfall: *History of England, from the Invasion of Julius Caesar to the Revolution in 1688* (1767), v. 420–1.

229 *Leçons d'une Gouvernante, Tome I*: Godwin cites Mme de Sillery-Brulart, *Lessons of a Governess to her Pupils* (1792), i. 208, 50, 217.

230 *In the riots in the year 1780*: a reference to the anti-Catholic riots of June 1780, known as the Gordon Riots, the most violent disruption of public order in London during Godwin's lifetime.

231 *self love to be the first mover of all our actions*: Godwin refers to François, duc de La Rochefoucauld (1613–80), author of *Réflections ou sentences et maxims morales* (1665).

Cato: Marcus Porcius Cato (95–46 BCE).

Plutarch's Lives: Cicero wrote a pamphlet, *Cato*, to which Caesar replied with *Anticatones*, which is no longer extant. The episode is discussed by Plutarch, *Lives*, 'Caesar' 54, and in Cicero's letter to Atticus, Astura, 9 and 11 May 45 BCE, 12. 40–1.

233 *congé à élire*: leave to elect, as in the royal writ given to a chapter to elect a named priest to a vacant seat.

234 *Considérations sur le Gouvernement de Pologne, Chap. VIII*: Jean-Jacques Rousseau, *Considérations sur le gouvernement de Pologne* (1755), ch. viii, para. 8.

235 *the parliament effected . . . Hanover*: a reference to the revolution of 1688, when James II was overthrown for his Catholicism and William and Mary of Orange were established on the throne. The house of Hanover came to the throne in the person of George I in 1714 after the death of Queen Anne, the last of the Stuart monarchs, in virtue of the Act of Settlement 1701. The interpretation of this is a major element in the 'revolution

controversy of 1790–1793' and in particular in Burke and Paine's disagreements: Edmund Burke, *Reflections on the Revolution in France* (1790), 26–7, 32–4, and Thomas Paine's critical account in his *Rights of Man* (1791, 1792), 7–14.

236 *to bind themselves . . . to this settlement*: Edmund Burke, *Reflections on the Revolution in France* (1790), 33.

238 *Pharaoh's frogs . . . kneading troughs*: Exod. 8: 3: 'And the river shall bring forth frogs abundantly, which shall go up and come into thine house, and into thy bedchamber, and upon thy bed, and into the house of thy servants, and upon thy people, and into thine ovens, and into thy kneading troughs.'

242 *'bow the head . . . Rimmon'*: 2 Kgs. 5: 18.

245 *honourable appellation of tyrant*: the word *tyrannos* was used to describe illegally usurped monarchies, with the seventh and sixth centuries BCE being known as the age of the tyrants. It was not, however, understood as an especially poor or violent form of government. That negative connotation becomes attached in the age of democracy in the fourth century BCE.

246 *'The eaglet . . . his fire'*: John Home, *Douglas: A Tragedy* (1757), scene iii, pp. 28 and 32 (adapted).

247 *Regulus or a Cato*: these examples are used earlier in the text, for example in Book II, Chapter II, Appendix I, and Book IV, Chapter IX.

the writings of Cicero . . . 'optimates': Marcus Tullius Cicero (106–43 BCE), Roman orator and statesman, who rose from relatively humble origins and was known as a 'new man' in contrast to the *optimates*, that is, members of the traditional Roman ruling class who dominated all high offices of state.

249 *Rights of Man*: Thomas Paine, *Rights of Man* (1791), 71: 'the idea of hereditary legislators is as inconsistent as hereditary judges, or hereditary juries; and as absurd as an hereditary mathematician, or an hereditary wise man; and as ridiculous as an hereditary poet-laureat'.

251 *Tragedy of Douglas*: see first note to p. 101.

252 *ignis fatuus*: will-o'-the-wisp, a phosphorescent light on swampy ground at night, an illusion.

253 *the elector of Hanover . . . king of France*: Georgian monarchs in Britain, 1714–1837, were also electors of Hanover and arch-treasurers of the Holy Roman Empire and maintained a claim on the French throne that dated back to 1328 but was relinquished under the Peace of Amiens in 1802.

254 *Bolingbroke*: Henry St John (1678–1751), a Tory leader, negotiated the Peace of Utrecht in 1712 and was made Viscount Bolingbroke. He became a supporter of the Jacobite cause and went into exile to join the Pretender, Bonnie Prince Charlie.

254 *lord Kimbolton . . . duke of Buckinghamshire*: Godwin's cases relate to real ones of men ascending to higher titles and abandoning former nomenclature. Lord Kimbolton was Edward Montagu (1602–71), second earl of Manchester, who was elevated to the peerage as Lord Kimbolton by Charles I in 1626, became Viscount Mandeville when his father was created earl of Manchester, and subsequently inherited his father's title. He went on to become a parliamentarian army officer. Godwin's second case is that of John Sheffield (1647–1721), third earl of Mulgrave from 1658, first marquess of Normanby from 1694, and first duke of Buckingham and Normanby from 1703.

Mr St. John: a further reference to Bolingbroke, who is treated dismissively in Burke's *Reflections on the Revolution in France*, prompting one of his critics to say, 'This spurning of Bolingbroke in his grave, reminds me of the fable of the ass kicking a dead lion, at whose voice, says the writer, when living he would have been panic stricken': *The Writings and Speeches of Edmund Burke*, viii, *The French Revolution 1790–1794*, ed. L. G. Mitchell (Oxford, 1989), 175.

255 *Omar . . . the Alcoran*: Omar, or Umar (d. 644), second Muslim caliph and a supporter of Muhammad. By 'Alcoran' Godwin means to indicate the Qur'ān, or Koran.

256 *government was instituted . . . an usurpation*: Godwin's source is obscure. The thought can be found in Renaissance texts such as Guicciardini's *Dialogo e discorsi del reggimento di Firenze* (1527), but also formed part of the doctrine of the monarchomachs such as François Hotman (1524–90) and George Buchanan (1506–82).

as in Holland: a reference to the appointment in the Netherlands of the stadholder (or chief executive officer) by the ruling council (an aristocratic body) rather than by popular election.

Aristocracy may . . . as in ancient Rome: the Polish diet drew on deputies of the nobility; Venice's ruling body, the senate, was chosen from the nobility, all of whom were members of the Great Council. Godwin wrote a *History of the Internal Affairs of the United Provinces from the Year 1780, to the Commencement of Hostilities in June 1787* (1787), which followed the principle of internal election. See Godwin's comments on Rome in the subsequent paragraph.

257 *except the two Gracchi*: Tiberius Gracchus (d. 133 BCE) and Gaius Gracchus (d. 121 BCE) were tribunes of the people who sought to secure reform but were killed for their pains.

the patricians told of Brutus . . . Cicero: a far from exhaustive list of Roman nobility who committed themselves to the public good. Those not previously cited by Godwin include: Marcus Valerius Corvus (c. 360–300 BCE); Gnaeus Marcius Coriolanus (d. 491 BCE); Lucius Quinctius Cincinnatus (*fl.* 458 BCE); Marcus Furius Camillus (*fl.* 386 BCE); Gaius Fabricius Luscinus (*fl.* 280–270 BCE); Marcus Atilius Regulus (*fl.* 265–256 BCE). The families he mentions are the Gens Fabii (*fl.* 479 BCE); Gens Decii (*fl.* 340–270 BCE); Publius Cornelius Scipio Africanus Maior (236–183) and his son Publius Cornelius Scipio Emilianus Africanus Minor (*c.*185–129 BCE). Lucius Licinius Lucullus (*c.*114–57 BCE) was a supporter of Sulla, and Marcus Claudius Marcellus defeated the Gauls in the third century BCE.

Appius Claudius: a patrician leader appointed in 451 BCE to draw up a legal code who was renowned for his aristocratic arrogance.

262 *Aristides constantly called the Just*: Aristides 'the Just' (d. *c.*468 BCE). Plutarch, *Lives*, 'Aristides' 7, recounts the tale of Aristides being asked by a man to write 'Aristides' on the ostraca used to vote for ostracizing. When he asked why, the man replied that he knew nothing about Aristides but was fed up with hearing him constantly referred to as 'the Just'.

Pisistratus and Pericles: Peisistratus (*c.*600–527 BCE), tyrant (technically, sole absolute ruler) of Athens but remembered as a moderate ruler; Pericles (*c.*495–429), leader of Athens during the Peloponnesian Wars.

the imprisonment of Miltiades . . . Phocion: Miltiades (*c.*550–489 BCE), the victor of Marathon, was the subject of several legal actions; Aristides was ostracized in 482 BCE; Phocion was a fourth-century BCE general under whose rule Athens lost Piraeus and who was condemned to death when democracy was restored in 318 BCE.

266 *fire and brimstone*: Rev. 19: 20, 20: 10, 21: 8. See also Gen. 19: 24 and Deut. 29: 23.

'the smoke . . . ever and ever': Rev. 14: 11.

268 *second letter to Malesherbes*: Rousseau's *Lettres originales . . . à M. de Malesherbes* were written in 1762 and published in 1779, appearing in English in 1799. Malesherbes was the French censor who had helped Rousseau with the publication of *Émile* in Paris (under the name of a Dutch publisher). Malesherbes took a considerable risk in helping Rousseau and the two men remained friends, with Rousseau's letters to him being major exercises in self-analysis that would culminate in Rousseau's *Les Confessions*, completed in 1776 and published in 1782.

Lycurgus, as he observes . . . regulations: Godwin's source is Plutarch, *Lives*, 'Lycurgus' 29. 2–4.

270 *several successive productions of Mr Necker*: Jacques Necker (1732–1804), French finance minister 1788–9, author of *A Treatise on the Administration of the Finances of France* (1784), *An Essay on the True Principles of Executive Power in Great States* (1792), and several other works.

Burke's Reflections: Burke's exact phrase is 'In the groves of *their* [the revolutionaries'] academy, at the end of every visto, you see nothing but the gallows': *Reflections on the Revolution in France* (1790), 115.

275 *wantonness with which . . . extremities*: Godwin's critical comments on the French were balanced with equally critical comments on the English on the eve of war in 1793 in his 'Essay Against Re-opening the War with France', in *Political and Philosophical Writings* (London, 1993), vol. ii.

284 *making every man . . . a soldier*: conscription was introduced in France partially in July 1792, and then in the *levée en masse* of 23 August 1793.

286 *Fabius*: Quintus Fabius Verrucosus, Cunctator (*c.*275–203 BCE), Roman consul who fought a defensive campaign against Hannibal in Italy by avoiding direct engagement.

287 *Ciceronis . . . Secundus, init.*: Cicero, *Academica* 2, a set of imaginary dialogues in which Lucullus (*c.*110–57 BCE) defends Antiochus by attacking scepticism regarding military skills, and Cicero defends it.

290 *Galileo*: Galileo Galilei (1564–1642), mathematician, astronomer, and philosopher.

293 *assembly of notables in 1787*: with the aim of raising additional finance to avoid state bankruptcy, the king's chief minister, Charles-Alexandre de Calonne (1734–1802), called an Assembly of Notables, but the assembly proved incapable of agreement. A second assembly was called the following year, but was no more successful. Their dismissal led to the convoking of the Estates General and the beginning of the French Revolution.

English house of commons: Godwin is praising the multiple readings of legislation in Parliament, which he frequently attended to observe.

304 *the dictator of the ancient Romans*: a Roman magistrate appointed with extraordinary military and judicial powers for a limited period to avert or meet a crisis. The office changed character as Rome expanded its empire, and it was abused under Sulla and Marius, and again under Caesar.

305 *Amphictyonic council of Greece*: a religious association of ancient Greek communities which met twice a year and managed the temples at Delphi and conducted the Pythian games. It had political importance because it could declare sacred wars on those who violated its laws, including laws of war.

311 *a Cato and a Brutus*: see first and third notes to p. 59.

that in reality: this sentence remains unfinished in all three editions of the *Enquiry*.

312 *Gulliver's Travels, Part II, Chap. VI*: Jonathan Swift, *Gulliver's Travels* (1726), Part II, 'A Voyage to Brobdingnag', ch. vi, pp. 111–12, in which Gulliver fails to persuade the king of the excellences of government in England: 'He [the king] said, he knew no reason why those, who entertain opinions prejudicial to the public, should be obliged to change, or should not be obliged to conceal them. And as it was tyranny in any government to require the first, so it was weakness not to enforce the second: for a man may be allowed to keep poisons in his closet, but not to vend them about for cordials.'

Mably: Gabriel Bonnot de Mably (1709–85), *De la législation; ou, Principes des lois* (1776); *Observations sur le gouvernement et les lois des États-Unis d'Amérique* (1784).

318 *the thirty-nine articles*: these are contained in the Book of Common Prayer and set out the Church of England's position on matters of dogma. Candidates for holy orders were required to subscribe to the Articles

until 1865. The Test and Corporation Acts (initially passed in 1672) made membership of the Church of England (and subscription to her dogmas) a prerequisite for holding public office until 1828.

319 *Arminian tenets*: those derived from the anti-Calvinist Jacobus Arminius (1560–1609), who rejected predestination and affirmed the role of the will in salvation.

predestinarian sentiments: sentiments held by those who believed that salvation was predetermined by God and could not be influenced by the individual's will or works.

320 *the victims of Circe*: the goddess Circe turned Odysseus' men into swine in *Odyssey* 10. 239–40 but left their minds unchanged.

323 *the elder Cato*: Marcus Porcius Cato, the Censor (234–149 BCE), who criticized Carneades and Diogenes, Athenian ambassadors in 155 BCE and renowned Sceptics, for their influence on Roman youth: Plutarch, *Lives*, 'Cato' 22–3.

the genius of Shakespeare: William Shakespeare (1564–1616), playwright and poet. Godwin discusses Shakespeare in his *Enquirer* (1797), Essay XII, sect. ii, and was a devotee of his plays, especially the tragedies and the histories. For example, according to his diary he saw *Macbeth* on thirty occasions, *Hamlet* on thirty-three.

the dreams of Ptolemy: Claudius Ptolemaeus (*c.*100–*c.*178), Greek astronomer and mathematician; the most prominent astronomer before Copernicus and Kepler in the sixteenth and seventeenth centuries.

325 *the dogmas of the Athanasian creed*: a Christian statement of belief used from the sixth century in which the equal status of the three persons in the Trinity is affirmed. The creed is so named because it was believed to derive from the beliefs of Athanasius (298–373).

Swift says: see first note to p. 312.

326 *Zoroaster and Confucius:* Zoroaster, also referred to as Zarathustra or Zardusht (*c.*630–*c.*533 BCE), Persian prophet and religious leader; Confucius, Master Kongfuze (551–479 BCE), Chinese philosopher.

330 *everlasting abjuration of monarchy?*: the Constitution of 1791 was completed on 3 September 1791; the king accepted it and swore an oath of allegiance to it in the National Assembly on 14 September: 'to maintain with all their power the Constitution of the kingdom decreed by the National Constituent Assembly in the years 1789, 1790 and 1791, to propose and to consent to nothing during the course of the legislature which might be injurious thereto, and in all matters to be faithful to the nation, to the law, and to the King'. All citizens were required to swear a similar oath. On 10 August 1792 the king was suspended, and the monarchy was abolished on 21–2 September 1792; a National Convention was summoned to draw up a new constitution.

When the law was repealed . . . a very arbitrary manner: the Act for the Further Relief of Protestant Dissenting Ministers and Schoolmasters

1779 (19 George III, c. 44) relieved Dissenters of the requirement to subscribe to some of the Thirty-Nine Articles (see note to p. 318). The 'amatory eclogues of Solomon' refers to Song of Songs (or the Song of Solomon), a book of the Old Testament.

330 *the Alcoran . . . sacred books of the Hindoos*: the Qur'ān, or Koran, the sacred book of Islam; the Talmud, a collection of law and doctrine of the Jewish people; the Hindu texts are the Rig Veda, the Sama Veda, the Yajur Veda, and the Atharva Veda.

the federal oath . . . 'to be faithful . . . the king': see first note to p. 330.

332 *Jesuitism and hypocrisy*: Jesuitism is a reference to the Society of Jesus, formally suppressed by Pope Clement XIV in 1773, and to their reputation as scheming, deceitful, or dissembling.

333 *church-wardens in particular*: churchwardens were required to promise, according to the best of their skill, to present 'such things and persons as to your knowledge are presentable by the laws ecclesiastical of this realm': Richard Burn, *The Justice of the Peace, and Parish Officer*, i (1772), 328.

337 *St. George's Fields to-morrow in arms*: St George's Fields in Southwark was the site of rioting by supporters of John Wilkes following his imprisonment (for an article in the *North Briton* criticizing King George III), leading to the death of six or seven protesters. It was also the place of assembly for the Gordon rioters in 1780, and in October 1795 it was used as a place of assembly to drum up popular support for reform and the end of the war with France, an occasion that Godwin refers to in his *Considerations on Lord Grenville's and Mr Pitt's Bills* (1795), the bills being prompted in part by disturbances following the meeting in which the king's coach was attacked.

343 *fundamental and adscititious*: a distinction between basic and not inherent or essential.

two successive national assemblies of the ordinary kind: see the French Constitution of 1791, Title VII, 'Of the Revision of Constitutional Decrees', Art. 2: 'When three successive legislatures have expressed a uniform wish for the amendment of some constitutional article, there shall be occasion for the requested revision' ('Lorsque trois législatures consécutives auront émis un vœu uniforme pour le changement de quelque article constitutionnel, il y aura lieu à la révision demandée'). Further articles specify requirements or additional representatives and the constitution of an Assembly of Revision.

345 *Rights of Man*: in *Rights of Man* Thomas Paine writes, 'I readily perceive the reason why Mr Burke declined going into the comparison between the English and French constitutions, because he could not but perceive, when he sat down to the task, that no such thing as a constitution existed on his side of the question': *Rights of Man* (1791), 54.

346 *the national convention . . . considered as law*: the Estates General of 1789 adopted for themselves the title National Assembly in June 1789, and

then, in July, the title National Constituent Assembly. The Constituent Assembly presented the Constitution of 3 September 1791, and, following the elections to the Legislative Assembly between 29 August and 5 September, the Legislative Assembly formally replaced the Constituent Assembly.

347 *a very small number of articles*: in fact, the Constitution was some forty pages long.

348 *Amphictyonic council*: see note to p. 305.

351 *We study Aristotle or Thomas Aquinas . . . impregnated with their absurdities*: Aristotle (384–322 BCE), Greek philosopher; St Thomas Aquinas (1225–74), theologian; St Robert Francis Bellarmine (1542–1621), theologian; Sir Edward Coke (1552–1634), jurist and judge. Godwin may be making a general point about a lack of critical engagement with authors, but he may also be pointing to a set of writers associated with Scholasticism and the Counter-Reformation, save in Coke's case.

353 *sending a sack of wool . . . in Spain*: from 1367 to 1824 it was illegal to export wool to France, as a way of protecting the English woollen industry. The practice of smuggling wool was known as owling. In Spain censorship was extensive until the fall of the Spanish monarchy in 1812.

355 *Oeconomical Reform*: adapted from *Speech of Edmund Burke . . . on the 11 of February, 1780* (1780), 66–7. See note to p. 178.

357 *what Eudamidas did . . . his mother by another*: Eudamidas of Corinth. Godwin's source is likely to be Lucian's *Toxaris*, an account of friendship in which the case of Eudamidas is celebrated. The account formed the basis for Nicolas Poussin's depiction of the scene in *Testament d'Eudamidas* (1644–8), of which the British Museum has a print by Jean-Jacques Lagrenée from the 1760s. Both Diderot and Napoleon commented on the painting and its praise of friendship.

358 *the burghers of the Netherlands . . . Austrian yoke*: a revolt against Austrian rule in the Netherlands began in 1787. See Godwin's *History of the Internal Affairs of the United Provinces* (1787).

359 *sortition, by ballot or by vote*: Godwin distinguishes lot, the secret expression of preferences, and the open statement of preferences.

365 *Xerxes . . . the waves of the sea*: see note to p. 162.

370 *Thus in England . . . is the judge*: the attorney-general, a crown appointment, is the chief law officer who is responsible for the prosecution of offences on behalf of the Crown; but judges also held their appointment under the Crown, casting doubt on the independence of the judicial process.

the posse comitatus: sheriffs and magistrates could call on the assistance of any number of adult males to pursue offenders, constituting a *posse comitatus*, or 'power of the county'.

371 *the temerity to kill Marius!*: Plutarch, *Gaius Marius* 39. 2. The scene is depicted by Germain-Jean Drouais in *Marius à Minturnae* (1786).

374 *Beccaria, Dei Delitti e delle Pene*: Cesare Beccaria Bonesana, *Dei delitte e della pene* (On Crimes and Punishments; 1764), ch. 27, 'Dolcezza delle pene' (Of the Mildness of Punishment). Godwin seems to have worked directly with the Italian text. A number of English translations were of a French edition that had changed the text dramatically.

377 *'Questa . . . d'ogni secolo.' Dei Delitti e delle Pene*: Cesare Beccaria Bonesana, *Dei delitti e delle pene* (1767), ch. 8, 'Divisione dei delitti' (Divisions of Crimes), para. 1.

 malice prepense: malice aforethought—an intentionally wrong act. For example, the crime of murder (which assumes an intention wrongfully to kill) is distinguished from both accidental death and an action that intended harm (or was negligent with respect to harm caused) but that did not intend the consequent death (which is termed manslaughter). Manslaughter can be an intentional act, and a wrong act, but the wrong for which the defendant is tried (the killing) was not the wrong that the defendant intended.

379 *'Questa . . . ogni delitto'*: Cesare Beccaria Bonesana, *Dei delitti e delle pene* (1767), ch. 7, 'Errori nella misura delle pene' (Errors in the Measurement of Punishments), para. 1.

380 *Old Bailey*: the City of London Sessions House was at the Old Bailey near the Fleet Prison. The current Central Criminal Court at the Old Bailey was built nearby on the site of Newgate Prison in 1902.

382 *Sir Walter Raleigh . . . the vanity of history*: Sir Walter Ralegh (1552–1618), imprisoned in the Tower of London 1603–16 and executed in 1618. Godwin's source is obscure.

386 *like quakers . . . obey them*: a tenet of the Quakers was pacifism and passive resistance. See also note to p. 96.

389 *The people of England . . . the Restoration*: Richard Cromwell (1626–1712), elected lord protector following the death of his father, Oliver, dissolved Parliament and abdicated. The following year General George Monck (1608–70) entered London with a Scottish army and dissolved Parliament. A convention was elected which offered the crown to Charles II.

 The Roman people . . . the Sacred Mountain: a reference to the secession of the *plebs* from Rome in 495 BCE and their establishment of a separate assembly and magistracy in a fortified camp on the Sacred Mount across the Anio three miles from Rome: Livy, *Ab urbe condita* 2. 32.

395 *'Thou shalt not inflict . . . a Roman'*: Acts 22: 25: 'Paul said unto the centurion that stood by, Is it lawful for you to scourge a man that is a Roman and uncondemned?'

396 *Mr Howard*: John Howard (1726–90), prison reformer and philanthropist.

398 *The first settlement of Rome . . . vagabonds*: Livy, *Ab urbe condita* 1. 8, describes Romulus as opening his settlement as an asylum for fugitives, 'all of them wanting nothing but a fresh start'.

402 *ex post facto law*: a law criminalizing an act after the fact.

405 *The fable of Procrustes*: see note to p. 78.

Summum jus summa injuria: Cicero, *De officiis* 1. 10. 33.

417 *The object of this vanity . . . applause of beholders*: Godwin here seems powerfully influenced by Rousseau, *Discourse on the Origin and Foundations of Inequality among Men* (1755).

418 *Swift's Sermon on Mutual Subjection*: Jonathan Swift, *Three Sermons: On Mutual Subjection; On Conscience; On the Trinity* (1744).

419 *I Cor. Chap. III. Ver I, 2*: 'And I, brethren, could not speak unto you as unto spiritual, but as unto carnal, *even* as unto babes in Christ. I have fed you with milk, and not with meat: for hitherto ye were not able *to bear* it, neither yet now are ye able.'

420 *Burke's Reflections*: Burke's *Reflections on the Revolution in France* (1790), 113, where he proclaims that the age of chivalry is indeed gone.

423 *Ogilvie's Essay . . . Nature and Providence*: Godwin's footnote cites William Ogilvie (1736–1819), *An Essay on the Right of Property in Land* (1781); Plato, *Republic*; Thomas More, *Utopia* (1516); Jonathan Swift, *Gulliver's Travels* (1726); Gabriel Bonnot de Mably, *De la législation; ou, Principes des loix* (1776); Robert Wallace, *Various Prospects of Mankind, Nature, and Providence* (1761).

428 *Mandeville; Fable of the Bees*: Bernard Mandeville, *The Fable of the Bees; or, Private Vices, Publick Benefits* (1714).

Coventry . . . Essay II: Henry Coventry, *Philemon to Hydaspes . . . in four parts* (3rd edn, 1753), Part II, p. 96; no reference to *The Fable of the Bees* is made in the first two editions. David Hume, *Essays, Moral, Political and Literary* (1772), II. ii, 'Of Refinement in the Arts'.

432 *tax-gatherers . . . secretaries*: all minor officials with reputations for officiousness and petty tyranny.

438 *the system of Epicurus*: Epicurus (341–270 BCE), Greek philosopher who combined hedonism with asceticism.

442 *magazines*: storehouses.

444 *of weaving engines, of steam engines*: Edmund Cartwright (1743–1823) developed the power loom in 1784–6 and a spinning machine in 1789–90; James Watt (1736–1819) developed steam engines in partnership with Matthew Boulton (1728–1809) from 1775.

Franklin conjectured, that 'mind . . . matter': Benjamin Franklin (1706–90). Godwin's note 2 on page 453 refers to his authority for the quotation.

no Spartan . . . manual labour: Spartans survived by exploiting the Helots, original inhabitants of Lacedaemonia: Plutarch, *Lives*, 'Lycurgus' 24. 2–3.

449 *memorable saying of Themistocles, 'God . . . favour than strangers!'*: Plutarch, *Lives*, 'Themistocles' 5. 4.

451 *Smith's Wealth of Nations*: Adam Smith, *An Inquiry into the Nature and Causes of the Wealth of Nations* (1776), i. 6–7.

452 *Wallace . . . and Providence, 1761*: Robert Wallace, *Various Prospects of Mankind, Nature and Providence* (1761), 46, Prospect II, 'The Model of a Perfect Government, not for a Single Nation Only, but for the Whole Earth'.

453 *Dr Price . . . William Morgan*: Godwin gives as his source Dr Richard Price (1723–91), dissenting theologian and moral philosopher, whose sermon 'Discourse on the Love of our Country' (1789) was a principal focus of Burke's *Reflections on the Revolution in France* (1790). His nephew William Morgan (1750–1833) was an actuary and pioneer of life insurance, whom Godwin met on the occasion of Price's sermon and two years later while writing his *Enquiry*. See first explanatory note to page 000 (page 000 above).

454 *Cranmer and Mucius Scævola*: see note to p. 39.

455 *Theseus and Achilles*: according to Greek myth, Theseus was a friend of Heracles and a king of Athens before the Trojan War, in which Achilles was the main Greek hero. The war is dated to *c*.1250 BCE.

457 *Macbeth, Act V*: v. iii. 40–7, to which Macbeth replies, 'Throw physic to the dogs. I'll have none of it.'

463 *Addison's Cato, Act IV*: Joseph Addison, *Cato: A Tragedy* (1713), IV. iv. 142.

INDEX

ability 200–3, 240, 249; *see also* talents
abstraction 34, 157
Achilles 455
action, voluntary and involuntary 161–2, 174–5, 183–94, 207, 455; tendency of 73–4, 163–4, 185–6, 191, 373
Addison, Joseph, *Cato: A Tragedy* xix, 463
adversity 207–10, 373–4
ageing 454
Agincourt 14
agriculture 429, 430, 432
Alderson, Amelia xxvii
Alexander the Great (Alexander III of Macedon) 13, 143, 178, 207
Alfred the Great (Alfred) 207
ambition 144, 194, 240, 276, 298, 426
America xxx
Amphictyonic Council 305, 348
anarchism x
anarchy 11, 15, 291, 313, 386–90
Anaxarchus of Abdera 38
Annual Register xiv
Anti-Jacobins xxix
appetite xxxi, 122, 128, 185, 215, 217, 227, 383, 416, 425, 447
Aquinas, Thomas 351
Aristides 262
aristocracy xx, 46, 246–8, 255–60, 263, 273, 448
Aristotle 45, 351
Arminianism 319
assassination 126, 136, 460
association of ideas 17, 39, 157, 159, 164, 175–80, 242, 443
associations xviii, 114–17, 283
Association for the Preservation of Liberty and the Property Against Republicans and Levellers xxiii, 86
Athanasian creed 325
Athena xi
Aurungzebe 14
Austria and Austrian 14, 278, 358
Australia xxv
authority xviii, xx, 75, 85–6, 90–7, 105, 205, 263, 292–3

automatism 173, 175
avarice 200, 232, 309, 394, 451

Bacchus 13
balance of power 278
ballot 359–61
banishment 398–9
Beccaria Cesare Bonesana 377; *Dei delitte e delle pene* 374, 377, 379
benevolence xxxii, 62, 129, 188, 190, 194, 198, 282, 341, 394, 438, 450–1, 454–5, 470; *see also* disinterestedness
Bentham, Jeremy x
Bible, the 330
Blackwall 90
Botany Bay xxiv
Braxfield, Judge xxiv, xxv
Britain ix, x, xix, xxii
British Convention xxiv
British Critic and Quarterly Theological Review xxii
Brunswick coalition (1792) 275
Brutus, Lucius Junius 59, 116, 126, 257, 311
Burke, Edmund xii, xix, xx, xxii, 15, 70, 102; *Reflections on the Revolution in France* ix, x, xv, xxii, 236, 270, 420; *Speech on Oeconomical Reform* 178, 355

Caesar, Gaius Julius 13, 126, 143, 178, 231
Calvin, Jean xiv, 63, 130
Calvinism xiv, xxvi, 319
Caligula 84
Cambyses 13
Camillus, Marcus Furius 257
capacity 63–4, 140; corporate and individual 256–7, 295, 308–11; intellectual 137, 167
Carthage 13, 196
Cato, Marcus Porcius xix, 59, 139, 143, 231, 247, 257, 311, 323; Addison's *Cato* 196, 197, 463
causation 157; *see also* conjunction, necessity
Cecil, Robert (earl of Salisbury) 222
censorship 310

education 22–5, 201, 214, 248–51, 448;
national education 350–4; of the
Prince 206–12
Edward the fourth 14
Edwards, Rev. Jonathan 54, 164
Egypt and the Egyptians 13, 266
elections 92, 233–6, 243, 256, 304–6,
348, 359–60, 420; and papacy 26
Elizabeth I 207, 221, 374
Engels, Friedrich xxxii
England 14, 28, 31, 32, 70, 109, 117, 153,
207, 236, 370, 422; the English 5, 45,
112, 290, 389, 432; English
constitution 70, 85, 101–2, 111, 235,
293, 333; Church of England 330, 351
Enlightenment, the xvi, xix, xx
entail 259, 414
Epictetus 143
Epicurus 128, 438
equality xii, 12, 64–6, 84, 207, 261, 431;
as precondition for virtue 284, 296,
413; system of 460–4
Eudamidas of Corinth 357
error 12, 22–7, 50, 121–2, 264–5, 299,
311–12, 384, 406
Euclid 74
Europe 14, 25, 28, 259, 278–9, 345, 388,
398, 399, 427, 446
evidence 43, 61–3, 71, 78–9, 244, 312,
380–1, 400–1; intrinsic 74, 154, 293
evil, choice of 50
excommunication 25
executive power 95, 205, 294–6, 346
experience 18–19, 38, 155–77,
188, 209
Eyre, Lord Chief Justice xxv

Fabii, Gens 257
falsehood, 21–6, 50, 55, 97, 102–5, 134,
145–52, 210–12, 224, 236–8, 255, 281,
312, 332–6, 367–71, 390
fame, love of 194, 434, 435; *see also*
distinction
famous fire cause, *see* Fénelon
Fawcett, Joseph xxxi
fear 18, 73, 119, 226, 230
Fénelon, François de Salignac La Mothe,
archbishop of Cambray xi, 53, 54,
135, 217; *Les Aventures de Télémaque*
xi, 53, 153
Filmer, Robert 21, 51
Fitzpatrick, Richard ix

force 65, 82, 92–9, 107–10, 299, 303,
336, 342, 362, 390, 425, 443, 466
foresight 18, 38, 157–62, 175, 185–9
fortification 280
fortitude 133–5, 208, 252, 341–2, 354, 357
Fox, Charles James ix
France 3, 14, 31, 44, 102, 123, 124, 226,
254; the French/Frenchmen 4, 13, 24,
45, 70, 101, 275, 293, 329–31, 343, 348,
353; French Enlightenment xiv, xxii;
French revolution ix–x, xv, xviii, 4,
113, 124, 236, 270, 288, 346; National
Assembly 300
Franklin, Benjamin 444, 453
fraud 27, 426, 446
Frederick I Barbarossa, Holy Roman
Emperor 207
Frederick, the Great, king of Prussia
14, 374
freedom 21; of communication 118, 337,
462; conditions for 125, 210, 317; of
enquiry 302, 340, 409; as
independence 66, 441; of
thought 136, 310; of the will 161–5

Galilei, Galileo 290
game laws 31
generation 48, 84, 458
Genghis Khan 14
genius 234–5, 423–4
Genlis, madame de (Félicité Stéphanie,
comtesse de Brulart) 212; *Lessons of a
Governess to her Pupils* 213, 229
Gérard, Balthazar 62
Germany 14
Gerrald, Joseph xxv
Godwin, William ix–xlv; reputation
xxii; *Political Justice* ix–xxiv, xliii, xlv,
revisions xxvi, xxxv–xxxix;
Autobiographical Fragments xv, xxv;
Cloudesley xlv; *Considerations on Lord
Grenville and Mr Pitt's Bills* xxvii;
*Cursory Strictures on the Charge
Delivered . . . to the Grand Jury* xxv;
Diary xv, xxiii, xxxi; *Deloraine* xx;
Memoirs of the Author of a Vindication
xxix; *Of Population* xxi; *St Leon* xxix,
xxx; *The Enquirer* xxix, xxx; *Things As
They Are; or, The Adventures of Caleb
Williams* xx, xxiv, xxv; *Thoughts
Occasioned by the Perusal of Dr. Parr's
Spital Sermon* xxi, xxix

American Literature

British and Irish Literature

Children's Literature

Classics and Ancient Literature

Colonial Literature

Eastern Literature

European Literature

Gothic Literature

History

Medieval Literature

Oxford English Drama

Philosophy

Poetry

Politics

Religion

The Oxford Shakespeare

A complete list of Oxford World's Classics, including Authors in Context, Oxford English Drama, and the Oxford Shakespeare, is available in the UK from the Marketing Services Department, Oxford University Press, Great Clarendon Street, Oxford OX2 6DP, or visit the website at www.oup.com/uk/worldsclassics.

In the USA, visit www.oup.com/us/owc for a complete title list.

Oxford World's Classics are available from all good bookshops. In case of difficulty, customers in the UK should contact Oxford University Press Bookshop, 116 High Street, Oxford OX1 4BR.

HORACE	The Complete Odes and Epodes
JUVENAL	The Satires
LIVY	The Dawn of the Roman Empire
	Hannibal's War
	The Rise of Rome
MARCUS AURELIUS	The Meditations
OVID	The Love Poems
	Metamorphoses
PETRONIUS	The Satyricon
PLATO	Defence of Socrates, Euthyphro, and Crito
	Gorgias
	Meno and Other Dialogues
	Phaedo
	Republic
	Selected Myths
	Symposium
PLAUTUS	Four Comedies
PLUTARCH	Greek Lives
	Roman Lives
	Selected Essays and Dialogues
PROPERTIUS	The Poems
SOPHOCLES	Antigone, Oedipus the King, and Electra
STATIUS	Thebaid
SUETONIUS	Lives of the Caesars
TACITUS	Agricola and Germany
	The Histories
VIRGIL	The Aeneid
	The Eclogues and Georgics
XENOPHON	The Expedition of Cyrus

THOMAS PAINE   **Rights of Man, Common Sense, and Other
                       Political Writings**

JEAN-JACQUES ROUSSEAU **The Social Contract
                       Discourse on the Origin of Inequality**

ADAM SMITH   **An Inquiry into the Nature and Causes of
                       the Wealth of Nations**

MARY WOLLSTONECRAFT   **A Vindication of the Rights of Woman**

Bhagavad Gita

The Bible Authorized King James Version
With Apocrypha

Dhammapada

Dharmasūtras

The Koran

The Pañcatantra

The Sauptikaparvan (from the Mahabharata)

The Tale of Sinuhe and Other Ancient Egyptian Poems

The Qur'an

Upaniṣads

ANSELM OF CANTERBURY	**The Major Works**
THOMAS AQUINAS	**Selected Philosophical Writings**
AUGUSTINE	**The Confessions** **On Christian Teaching**
BEDE	**The Ecclesiastical History**
HEMACANDRA	**The Lives of the Jain Elders**
KĀLIDĀSA	**The Recognition of Śakuntalā**
MANJHAN	**Madhumalati**
ŚĀNTIDEVA	**The Bodhicaryàvatàra**

The Anglo-Saxon World

Beowulf

Lancelot of the Lake

The Paston Letters

Sir Gawain and the Green Knight

Tales of the Elders of Ireland

York Mystery Plays

GEOFFREY CHAUCER — The Canterbury Tales
Troilus and Criseyde

HENRY OF HUNTINGDON — The History of the English People
1000–1154

JOCELIN OF BRAKELOND — Chronicle of the Abbey of Bury
St Edmunds

GUILLAUME DE LORRIS — The Romance of the Rose
and JEAN DE MEUN

WILLIAM LANGLAND — Piers Plowman

SIR THOMAS MALORY — Le Morte Darthur

An Anthology of Elizabethan Prose Fiction

An Anthology of Seventeenth-Century
Fiction

Early Modern Women's Writing

Three Early Modern Utopias (Utopia; New
Atlantis; The Isle of Pines)

FRANCIS BACON **Essays**
The Major Works

APHRA BEHN **Oroonoko and Other Writings**
The Rover and Other Plays

JOHN BUNYAN **Grace Abounding**
The Pilgrim's Progress

JOHN DONNE **The Major Works**
Selected Poetry

BEN JONSON **The Alchemist and Other Plays**
The Devil is an Ass and Other Plays
Five Plays

JOHN MILTON **The Major Works**
Paradise Lost
Selected Poetry

SIR PHILIP SIDNEY **The Old Arcadia**
The Major Works

IZAAK WALTON **The Compleat Angler**

	Travel Writing 1700–1830
	Women's Writing 1778–1838
JAMES BOSWELL	Life of Johnson
FRANCES BURNEY	Cecilia
	Evelina
JOHN CLELAND	Memoirs of a Woman of Pleasure
DANIEL DEFOE	A Journal of the Plague Year
	Moll Flanders
	Robinson Crusoe
HENRY FIELDING	Jonathan Wild
	Joseph Andrews and Shamela
	Tom Jones
WILLIAM GODWIN	Caleb Williams
OLIVER GOLDSMITH	The Vicar of Wakefield
ELIZABETH INCHBALD	A Simple Story
SAMUEL JOHNSON	The History of Rasselas
ANN RADCLIFFE	The Italian
	The Mysteries of Udolpho
SAMUEL RICHARDSON	Pamela
TOBIAS SMOLLETT	The Adventures of Roderick Random
	The Expedition of Humphry Clinker
LAURENCE STERNE	The Life and Opinions of Tristram Shandy, Gentleman
	A Sentimental Journey
JONATHAN SWIFT	Gulliver's Travels
	A Tale of a Tub and Other Works
HORACE WALPOLE	The Castle of Otranto
MARY WOLLSTONECRAFT	Mary and The Wrongs of Woman
	A Vindication of the Rights of Woman